WHEN HE'S RUTHLESS

The Olympus Pride Series, Book 4

SUZANNE WRIGHT

The characters and events portrayed in this book are fictitious. Any similarity to real persons, living or dead, is coincidental and not intended by the author.

Cover design: J Wright

ISBN: 9798809787543

Imprint: Independently Published

For Johnny,

You were a legend, we miss you.

CHAPTER ONE

Blair, age twelve

Snatching the black leather wallet from the floor of the fast food restaurant, Blair Kendrick turned toward the guy who was heading for the door. "Excuse me," she called out, "you dropped your wallet."

Halting, he half-turned. Slate-blue eyes fixed on her, hard and piercing. Eyes that were familiar to her. Yet not. Curiosity reared up inside her, as did her inner animal.

He squinted slightly, his shoulders stiffening. For a long moment, he simply stared at her, looking like he'd been poleaxed.

Finally, the tension seemed to seep from his body. He slowly came toward her, a brown paper bag held against his chest with one arm. *Damn*, he was huge. Even taller than her brother. He was also seriously good-looking. Like a movie star or something. And *definitely* a shifter—he didn't walk, he flowed and glided, light-footed as a cat.

Maybe she should have felt a little nervous having this big, strange dude come toward her like this, but she didn't. And she couldn't explain why.

Stopping in front of Blair, he drew in a breath through his nose, taking in her scent. His own whispered over her. *Cat shifter.* He smelled like spicy clove and lime wood. That scent … it *called* to her. Made her feel safe and relaxed, like someone had just wrapped a soft, fleecy blanket around her.

Her inner animal rose with a happy whine. Usually, she didn't like other breeds of shifter. But the little female wanted to bite the cat and snuggle up to him.

His head tipped to the side in curiosity, and warmth bled into his eyes. They weren't hard now, but they were still piercing. He was totally focused on her. That was okay. She was just as focused on him.

This close to him, she could sense that he was a born alpha. A real powerful one. Dangerous, too. She wasn't nervous, though. This man would never harm her; she knew that down to her bones. Because a *knowing* had hit her mere seconds ago—it came from nowhere, and there was no doubting the truth of it.

"Thank you," he said, carefully taking the wallet from her, which he then stuffed into the back pocket of his jeans without moving his gaze from hers.

She liked his voice. It was soothing. Smooth and low and deep. "You're welcome."

"What's your name?"

"Blair."

"Blair," he echoed, as if trying the name on for size or something. "I'm Luke." He offered his hand.

She easily placed her palm in his. *Obviously* she didn't usually talk to, let alone touch, complete strangers—she wasn't stupid. But he wasn't a stranger.

His hand enfolded hers, gentle and protective. "You know who I am to you, don't you?" he asked, his tone calm and easy, but she sensed just how important her answer would be to him.

She nodded. He felt like, *smelt* like, hers. "We're mates."

The set of his shoulders lost more tension. "That's right."

Her animal yipped, delighted that he knew; delighted that he acknowledged both Blair and her inner female as his. "You're a cat."

"A pallas cat." He released her hand. "And you're a bush dog."

She nodded again. "I heard pallas cats are crazy." That was an understatement, really. In her mom's words: "*they're demonic bantamweight minions of Satan.*"

"But you don't fear me, do you?"

She shook her head. "You wouldn't hurt me. And if you tried, I'd bite your face off."

Surprise flashed in his eyes, and then he chuckled. "You know something? I believe you."

Just then, her brother sidled up to her, his chest all puffed up. "What's going on over—" Mitch cut himself off as he got a good look at Luke. "Devereaux," he greeted, the bluster leeching out of him. He curled his fingers around Blair's upper arm and gently drew her to him. "What're you doing with my sister?"

"Sister? Hmm." Luke rubbed at his jaw. "Are your parents with you?"

"No," he replied, his brow puckering. "Why?"

"Because I'd like to introduce myself to my mate's parents and get a few things straight."

"Your mate's ..." Mitch trailed off, doing a slow blink. He looked at her and then swore. "Are you sure?" he asked Luke.

"Never been more certain of anything."

Mitch scrubbed a hand down his face. "Mom's gonna *freak*."

Yes, Noelle would. Bush dogs generally didn't much like other breeds of shifter, let alone choose to mate with them. Also, ever since Blair's older sister Marianna died a year ago, Noelle had been hyper-protective of Blair and tried holding her *too* close. Her mother wouldn't like the idea of Blair ever leaving the pack; ever leaving *her*.

"Seriously, Luke, she won't handle this well," Mitch warned him.

"Dad won't like it much either," Blair added.

His gaze dropping to her, Luke closed the distance between them in one, fluid step. "You let me worry about that. Everything will be fine. Your parents will accept my place in your life."

He said it as if he'd allow nothing less. Which was good, because neither would Blair. The pull she felt toward him—one that seemed to promise safety and security—would plague her if she fought it. But Blair wasn't confident that he'd find it simple to win her parents' acceptance. He didn't know them. He didn't know how obstinate and controlling Noelle could be.

Blair couldn't help but feel a little anxious that they'd manage to chase Luke away. Which was why she shamelessly lingered outside her Alpha's office later on to eavesdrop while Luke, her parents, and her Alpha—who was also her uncle—closed themselves inside.

"No," Noelle bit out. "No, you're wrong."

A sigh. "I'm not going to argue this with you," said Luke.

"She's twelve-years-old!"

"I'm aware of that. But what I feel toward her right now is purely platonic—you'd sense it if it wasn't, so don't try painting me as someone who'd ever mean to abuse her. You'd know it wasn't true. Just as you know that this situation won't change simply because you'd like it to."

There was a thud, like someone had slammed a palm on a hard surface. "You're not taking her away from us," Noelle all but hissed. "She belongs here."

"For the time being she does, yes. But when she's older—"

"But nothing. Sylvan territory will always be her home. That will not change. Now leave. And do not *ever* come back."

"Do you really think you can dictate whether or not I am part of her life?" asked Luke, eerily calm. "Blair is my mate, Noelle. You need to accept that for her sake."

Blair's inner female let out a low growl, backing him up on that.

"And you're positive that she's your predestined mate?" asked her father, Les, sounding hopeful that just maybe Luke's answer would be a no.

"I wouldn't be standing here now having this conversation with you if I wasn't." A pause. "Let me be abundantly clear. Protest all you want, complain all you want, yell all you want … but I will not be run off. Nor will I stay away until Blair's an adult. It would hurt her if I did, and I'm not prepared to do that. I want access to her in the meantime."

"Of course we'll facilitate contact between you and Blair, Luke," the Alpha, Embry, cut in. "She'd be unhappy if we didn't, and I think we're all in accordance on one thing: we do not want Blair unhappy. Isn't that right, sister?"

Seconds of silence ticked by, rubbing Blair's nerves raw.

"Fine," Noelle eventually said. "You can visit her now and then."

Blair bit back a snort. Her mother would consider "now and then" to be once every few years, if that.

A rumbly growl. "Do not think you can limit my contact with her," said Luke, his voice low and hard. "That isn't going to happen. I'll never allow it. I'll never permit anything that I know would cause her distress, and that would for certain."

"She's just a baby," snapped Noelle.

"I have no nefarious intentions, and you know it," clipped Luke, affronted. "We've been over that already. Nothing you say or do will alter the situation, so why not just make your peace with it? I want us all to get along for Blair's sake. There's no reason why we can't. Do not make this difficult. It doesn't need to be. And she wouldn't thank you for it—not in the short-term, and not in the long-run."

No, Blair definitely wouldn't. Maybe if Noelle placed any real importance in finding a person's true mate, she would instead be happy for Blair. But imprinting was more common among bush dogs, since they often stuck to mating their own breed—true mates weren't always the same kind of shifter. Blair's parents were one of many imprinted couples in the pack.

"What is it exactly that you want, Luke?" asked Les.

"What any shifter would want in this instance—to play a fundamental part in being sure that my mate is happy and safe," Luke replied.

The notes of protectiveness in his voice made Blair's mouth kick up.

Noelle scoffed. "Like she'd be safe with pallas cats. You're all the same. Insane. Vicious. Cruel—"

"Bush dogs don't have the greatest reputation either, so you might not want to throw stones," said Luke. "In any case, Blair will never be anything but completely safe with me. My pride mates will protect her just the same."

Silence again fell.

There was a long, male, heavy sigh of resignation and then … "If you are going to have frequent contact with her, there are certain things we would ask of you," said Les. "Mate or not, you are presently a relative stranger to Blair. Take things slowly. Give her time to get to know you. At first, stick to visiting her here, on her own territory. Once she's comfortable with you, we would not be opposed to you taking her on daytrips—"

"*Daytrips*?" Noelle burst out.

"Sweetheart," began Les, sounding tired, "it is only fair that we support their contact. Other parents do it in our situation—many shifters find their mates when one is young and then choose to watch over them in such a way. It happened to your own cousin. Luke's not asking for anything unreasonable here. All he wants—"

"I don't care what he wants," she clipped.

Yeah, we've noticed, thought Blair, rolling her eyes.

"And what about what is fair to our daughter?" asked Les. "What about what she'll want?"

"Just to be clear," said Luke, "I will never attempt to force Blair to go anywhere with me. I would never do anything that would cause her any upset. I simply want easy access to her. It's my right, Noelle, whether you like it or not. She'd be angry at both of us if I agreed to stay away. Maybe you'd be fine with that, but I wouldn't be. I won't neglect her to placate you or anyone else."

"We wouldn't ask that you neglect her," said Embry. "This news has been something of a shock, that is all."

"It doesn't bother you that your mate is presently a child?" asked Noelle.

"Nothing about Blair could bother me," Luke told her. "She won't remain a child forever. When she's eighteen, I will claim her."

"Eighteen? No," snarled Noelle. "No way. That's much too young."

A heavy exhale. "Many females that age enter into a mating," said Luke.

"You will wait until she turns twenty-one."

"No, I won't."

"You do not get to decide this. I am her *mother*."

"And I'm sure you love her. So you'll want what's best for her. Asking Blair to fight claiming her own mate for longer than necessary isn't what's best for her."

"At eighteen, she'll be barely an adult. You're an alpha, which naturally makes you difficult for anyone to contend with. Give her a few years to discover who she is and develop her own identity before you take over her life."

Blair held her breath as silence again fell.

"I'll wait until she's nineteen," Luke reluctantly conceded.

"Twenty-one," Noelle repeated.

"If she declares she wants more time I'll of course give it to her," said Luke. "If she doesn't, I will claim her when she's nineteen—I'm not budging on that, so don't bother pushing me any more than you already have."

Blair felt her nose wrinkle. She wasn't pleased that he'd agreed to wait an extra year, but she did appreciate that he'd suggested a compromise to keep the peace for her sake.

"Your word, cat," said Noelle. "I want your word that you will wait until then."

"You have my word that I will wait until she turns nineteen before I claim her—"

"*And* that you'll give her additional time if she wants it."

"I will wait however long she needs."

"Fine," Noelle threw out.

Blair narrowed her eyes at her mother's easy agreement. The woman was undoubtedly thinking that she could convince Blair to hold off on mating him until she was twenty-one, or maybe even older.

"However," began Luke, "you must keep to your word. You will agree here and now not to limit my contact with Blair or ever attempt to come between us."

Blair couldn't contain her smile. Oh, her mate was sneaky. He hadn't simply made his concession to be fair, he'd done it to box her mother into a corner. Noelle would know that if she didn't concede to make this vow he would then retract his own promise—and that would be the last thing she'd want.

A long pause. "I will not put restrictions on your contact with her or try to come between you," Noelle grudgingly pledged.

"If at any point you go back on your word, my own vow to you will become null and void," Luke told her. "Are we clear on that?"

"Crystal."

Hearing footfalls head for the door, Blair quickly backed up. It swung open, and then Luke peered down at her.

His face softening, he closed the door behind him. "Hey, there. Eavesdropping, were you?" It wasn't really a question.

She bit her lip. "You're leaving now?"

He nodded. "But I'll be back. And I'll never be far. Whenever you need me, all you'll have to do is call. You have a cell phone, I'm guessing."

She gave a heavy nod.

"Do you have it on you?"

"Yes." She pulled it out of her pocket.

He reeled off a phone number, which she added to her list of contacts. "There," he said. "Now you can text or call me anytime. Even if only to say hi."

"You're *definitely* going to come back?"

He gave her a serious look. "Nothing could stop me."

"My mom probably won't break the vow she just made, but she'll be … difficult sometimes. Maybe even mean to you."

He let out a soft snort of amusement, clearly unbothered. "I don't doubt it. But like I told your parents, I won't be run off, no matter how much or how often she tries to cause problems—I promise you that."

Blair believed him. Or believed that he *meant* what he said. She just wasn't entirely sure he wouldn't one day get so sick of Noelle's crap that he'd nonetheless break his promise. "You'd better keep your word. It would suck to have to stab you."

He grinned. "Yeah, that really would suck. But it won't come to that; I never go back on my word." He gently tugged a lock of her hair. "I'll be seeing you soon, Blair. You need me for anything in the meantime, just pick up the phone. I'll always come for you when you need me. Got it?"

She gave a hard nod. "Got it."

CHAPTER TWO

Six years later

It really wasn't every day that you found a dead body on your porch.

Sitting on her sofa with a cup of untouched tea in hand, Blair only half-listened as several of her pack mates stood around her cabin discussing the messed-up situation. All were varying degrees of unsettled.

Not that anyone here hadn't seen a corpse before. There was a lot of violence in the shifter world. One-on-one duels. Group attacks. Full-on battles. But *this* here, well, this was different. The female on the porch hadn't been killed in a battle for dominance. She hadn't died in the defense of her pack mates. She'd been shot in the head and ... well, *hell.*

If the victim had been part of the pack, everyone would be raging and swearing vengeance instead of calmly deliberating on the matter. But the fox shifter had been no friend to anyone here. Far from it. Despite that she'd only met Blair once, she'd made an enemy of her for life.

The first words the then-smirking fox had spoken to her were, "*Hi, I'm Macy—the woman your mate has been sleeping with for the past six months.*"

Blair had wanted to light the woman on fire. Not that she'd believed Macy. Nope. Not even for a second. Luke was loyal to a fault. He'd never betray Blair that way.

But the fox's bullshit claim had been impossible to simply shrug off—it had sent all sorts of explicit images sailing through Blair's mind. Images that she hadn't been able to declare "imaginary," since he'd bedded Macy long before Blair came into the picture. Blair had learned that little titbit years ago.

Many shifters would have beaten Macy bloody for falsely making such a claim and, essentially, trying to come between mates. But bush dogs much preferred annihilating people's pride. So Blair had instead cleaned her clock, scrawled "I am a liar" on her forehead, cut huge chunks out of her hair, and dragged her to the bush dogs outside who'd then promptly cocked their legs and peed on her.

Macy had started to come round at that point, so Blair had sucker-punched her again and tossed her into the trunk of the fox's sleek convertible. She'd driven straight to a popular shifter club, opened the trunk, and stood back with a smile as a once-more conscious Macy had leapt out of the vehicle … only to see that the people lined up outside the club's entrance were gawking at her. Many had also snapped pictures, and several of those photos were then posted online. One was even made into a meme.

That "incident" took place a month ago directly after Macy slung her false claim at Blair. The redhead hadn't returned, retaliated, or tried to contact Blair. Unsurprising. Generally, people didn't strike back after such incidences, because everyone knew that bush dogs mostly played with you the first time. If there was a next time, what was left of your pride would be shredded. Because if there was one thing that bush dogs were experts at, it was the lost art of crushing people's will to live.

Blair glanced out of the open front door just in time to see two of her pack mates cover the fox shifter with an old sheet. As they then transferred the body to a stretcher and began to carry it away, Blair took a shaky breath. She was far from queasy or easily daunted. But the sight of a corpse holding its own severed tongue while wearing nothing but the shiny red bow that was tied around its neck would turn anyone's stomach.

The cut to her tongue had been too clean for it to have happened prior to her death, but that didn't make it any less nauseating. There were no signs of assault or any marks to suggest that the female had been held captive. By all appearances, it seemed that Macy's death had been a quick, simple execution. As if she hadn't emotionally mattered to whoever took her life.

Kiesha sat beside Blair and crossed one dark-skinned leg over the other. "I know the fox did a seriously cruel thing to you, but she didn't deserve that fate."

Blair turned to the female who was both her close friend and the mate of her brother, Mitch. "No, she didn't. And I think it's safe to say that her pack's gonna lose it."

"It's also safe to say that Luke's gonna freak when he hears that someone left a corpse on your porch." Pulling her gorgeous riot of black curls into a ponytail, Kiesha amended, "Well, maybe not freak *outwardly*. Your guy is good at containing his emotions. It drives your mother nuts, because she never succeeds at drawing him into an argument or making him snap."

A fond smile tugged at Blair's mouth. He did indeed hold back, knowing it grated on Noelle more than any comeback ever would.

Despite having had six years to make her peace with the situation, Noelle simply would not accept Luke's place in Blair's life. She was still utterly determined to keep Blair close and so viewed his claim to her as a threat.

Oh, Noelle hadn't tried to limit their contact—she'd kept her word on that. But she'd never treated him as anything other than an imposition. Yet, he hadn't broken his promise to Blair; he hadn't allowed her mother to chase him away, which Blair adored him for.

Noelle's behavior had increasingly ate at and tainted their mother-daughter relationship. They'd come to blows over it countless times, especially during the period when Noelle had paraded unmated male bush dogs in front of Blair as if there was *any* chance she'd forsake Luke.

Sometimes, it was hard to believe that the same woman who doted on Blair in so many ways—crocheting her pretty blankets, baking her lemon cake every Sunday, treating her with trips to spas, gifting her special editions of her favorite books—would also be so set against Blair claiming her own mate. Noelle simply had a blind spot when it came to him. Or, more specifically, to what he represented—that she'd one day no longer have Blair so close.

Noelle likely would have changed her tune toward Luke if she could have convinced him to join the pack rather than take Blair to his pride. He had actually offered to make the transfer. But when Blair had vetoed it—feeling he'd be unhappy here and that they, as a couple, needed space from Noelle's controlling ways—he'd supported her decision. Then he'd become 'the bad guy' in Noelle's mind once again.

Sweeping her gaze over her pack mates, Blair said, "Someone needs to notify Macy's pack of her death."

"I will contact her Alpha at some point tonight," said Embry, standing near the fireplace.

Noelle crossed to him, pinning him with eyes the same hazel shade as his own. The siblings also shared the same burnished-gold hair and tall build, though his was heavily muscled. "The fox's pack had better not blame Blair for this. She might have had an … altercation with the fox not so long ago, but if my daughter had wanted to kill her she'd have done it that night."

Blair felt her back teeth lock. Her inner animal unsheathed the tips of her claws in annoyance. There wouldn't have been an "altercation" if Noelle hadn't felt it necessary to play games. She glanced at Mitch, who'd propped one hip against the wall; the look on his face said he was having that exact same thought.

"I doubt anyone will consider Blair a suspect," said Les, scraping a hand over his lightly bearded jaw as he moved to stand behind Noelle. "It would make no sense for her to kill Macy and then stage the body on her own porch."

"Whoever did it also did a good job of sneaking onto our territory undetected," said Antoine, the Head Enforcer, one tanned arm braced on the fire mantel. "There's no evidence that she was killed anywhere on our land, so the question is … *why* did they bring the body here?"

"It's not obvious by the bow that Macy's corpse was meant to be some kind of sick gift to Blair?" asked Kiesha. "I can't be the only person who noticed that the bow was identical to those attached to the *other* things that have been recently left on her porch."

Blair had received a few gifts from an anonymous sender over the past couple of months. The previous presents were normal, albeit *entirely* inappropriate. And, like Kiesha, she had the feeling that the sender of said gifts had also killed Macy; that he'd removed the fox's tongue to punish her for the hurtful things she'd said. Macy hadn't only lied that she'd been sleeping with Luke; she'd also tossed all sorts of insults at Blair.

Noelle flapped a hand. "This is not at all connected to the gifts that Blair received. They were obviously from an admirer who wanted to court her but, fearing Devereaux's reaction, didn't feel comfortable openly doing so."

Antoine nodded, making the short, brown waves atop his head ruffle. "No doubt about it, the bow is a red herring," he added, an arrogant surety in his deep-set eyes. "Something to throw us off the scent."

Beside him, Donal said, "That would be my guess. As for why the body was brought here … It's possible that someone just means to scare Blair." The Beta shrugged, scratching at dark stubble that was peppered with the same silver as his equally dark hair. "This seems like psychological warfare to me."

Mitch pushed away from the wall. "But *why* would anyone want to scare her?" he asked, lifting his compact shoulders, clearly unconvinced. "It's not like she has any enemies. Macy's pack mates might well be furious with her for what she did to the fox a month ago, but they'd hardly kill one of their own to frighten her."

Noelle gave a delicate shrug. "It could have been a member of the Olympus Pride. I would imagine that some aren't too happy about Luke's plan to mate a bush dog."

Blair felt her eyelid twitch, and her female peeled back her upper lip. "You are *not* pinning this on his pride." She wished she could say it shocked her that Noelle would try to use this situation to further her own agenda, but it honestly didn't.

"Don't be willfully blind, Blair," said Noelle, her voice fairly vibrating with impatience. "You naïvely persist in believing that his pride will want you to join. Like it or not, being the true mate of one of their own won't be enough to make them welcome you."

"They've never made me feel anything *but* welcome." Particularly his family. Throughout the past six years, they'd made an effort to build a relationship with her, especially his sister Elle and his aunt Valentina. Even when Blair was young, the two women had often took her shopping or on girly outings. Noelle was too intimidated by Valentina—a take-no-shit wolverine shifter—to veto the trips.

"Just because they've never been rude to your face doesn't mean that they want a bush dog for a Beta female."

"Even if you're right, it doesn't mean they'd do something to scare me. I can't even see why they'd bother. They'd gain nothing from it."

"Luke's kind don't need a rational reason to do any of the things they do."

Okay, Blair couldn't really dispute that.

"People say *our* inner animals are unstable. Pallas cats take that to a whole other level."

Blair couldn't argue with that either. They might not be much bigger than domestic housecats when in their animal form, but the precious, snuggly-looking creatures were infeasibly strong and alarmingly vicious. Pallas cats didn't pick fights, but they were always sure to make the first move—attacking with an unparalleled ferocity that was nothing short of hellishly disturbing. In sum, they were batshit.

Of course, Noelle used that to give credence to her "Luke's not good for Blair" claims. And while Les had come to accept that the pallas cat was Blair's mate, he remained stiff and informal toward him. Luke didn't deserve that. All he'd ever done was try to make her life easier.

Luke might not have entered her world until she was twelve, but it didn't feel that way, because he'd been such a huge part of it. He called every day, visited regularly, took her places, bought her gifts—determined that she'd never feel anything but safe, protected, and cared for.

Essentially he'd been, in a word, her guardian. A person she'd trusted above all others. A person she went to when she needed advice or simply someone to *listen*. He'd also been her one and only crush, not to mention her first kiss. The latter, to her frustration, hadn't come until she was seventeen.

She almost smiled at the memory of how she and Kiesha—who'd only ever had eyes for Mitch—had back then made plans to each take their chosen male off-guard with a kiss. Blair had surprised Luke all right. Initially, he'd started to pull away from her, but then she'd sucked on his tongue … and he'd ravished her mouth, stealing her breath and sending her hormones into a tailspin as their—for lack of a better word—attraction finally found an outlet.

He'd also bitten her neck hard enough to permanently mark her that night. So she'd marked him right back. It had only seemed fair.

There had been no more make-out sessions until Blair turned eighteen. He'd also then treated her to a fair few orgasms, but he'd refused to take it further despite her best—and unrepentantly shameless—efforts to seduce him. He was set on taking her virginity on the very same night he officially claimed her.

Blair loathed having to wait. How could she not, when he was one giant magnet to her? It wasn't merely about their predestined connection, it was because he was *Luke*. A fiercely loyal, unrelenting male who might have a darkly calculative streak but never let down the people who mattered to him.

In short, she adored him. He'd made it impossible for her not to. He focused so much energy on her. Made her feel like the center of everything. It was kind of dizzying at times.

She couldn't imagine what it would have been like to *not* have him around all these years. She wasn't sure she'd otherwise be the person she was today. Wasn't sure she'd be as strong and confident and capable.

"You have to at least consider that I could be right," said Noelle, snapping Blair out of her thoughts.

"I won't believe that anyone from the Olympus Pride pulled any of the recent bullshit, let alone killed Macy," Blair firmly stated.

"I can understand why you wouldn't want to believe it, but your mother could be onto something here, Blair," said Antoine. "You know Luke well. You know his family well. But you don't know every pride member that well. I'm sure they've all been nice to you, but that doesn't mean they're *thinking* nice things about you. Let's face it, they'll be leery of offending their Beta male by slighting you.

"It doesn't necessarily follow that they'd rather you weren't part of the pride, true, but there could be some people that don't. And just maybe one of them decided to do something about it. Just maybe they thought they'd scare you into sticking close to home, and they attached the bow to Macy so we'd finger your admirer. It's a theory we should at least explore. It would do no good to dismiss people as possible suspects just because the idea of them being responsible is ... is ... I mean ..." Antoine trailed off as she simply stared at him. Shifting slightly, he averted his gaze.

It really was amazing just how uncomfortable people could get when you merely stared at them without saying a word. It wasn't simply that, in Mitch's words, she had a "death stare." For some, it was that they hated not knowing what you were thinking. For others, it was that receiving no feedback made them feel dismissed. Then there were those whose nerves just couldn't handle dead silence.

"It wasn't anyone from the Olympus Pride," Blair insisted after a moment. "Even if someone there did think to scare me like this, they wouldn't know to use the bow as a 'red herring' when they have no clue I've been receiving gifts with red bows attached. Embry asked me not to tell them." Which wasn't the true reason she'd kept quiet, but still. "He promised he'd get to the bottom of who was sending the gifts, despite that he felt I should be flattered that someone is so interested in me they'd risk Luke's wrath by trying to 'court' me."

Her parents had been equally dismissive of the situation. Neither Antoine nor Donal had thought there was any need for concern either, but they did feel that if a woman didn't want to be pursued then she should damn well not be pursued. So they'd accompanied her as she questioned their pack mates and searched for answers. Mitch and Kiesha—both of whom were *not* happy about the gifts—had also been at her side. But the investigations had come to nothing.

Embry notched up his chin. "I *did* look into the matter."

"But you didn't take it seriously," Blair pointed out. "Yeah, I get why you dismissed the first gift I received as someone's idea of a weird-ass joke. And yeah, I understand why you also initially dubbed the strange phone calls silly pranks. But the longer it all went on, the more uneasy I got. You, however, carried on dismissing everything—including my concerns.

"You can't ignore the obvious any longer, Embry. None of you can. The person doing all this isn't merely a shy admirer or an idiotic prankster. They *killed* someone. And if the bow is anything to go by, they did it because they thought I'd be thankful. That screams 'messed up in the head.'"

"She's right," said Mitch, thrusting his fingers through short hair the exact shade of blond that both he and Blair had inherited from their father. "This is some sociopathic shit right here."

Les held up his hand. "We don't know for sure that the same person is responsible for *all* those things."

Kiesha folded her arms. "It would be a hell of a coincidence if she had a prankster, an oddball admirer, *and* a person willing to kill for her all focused on her at the same time."

Noelle cleared her throat. "If you're right and we're sticking with Blair's theory that this is unrelated to the Olympus Pride … well, the perpetrator can only be Gabriel."

A short silence hit the room. Blair swallowed. She hadn't seen her childhood friend since he left the pack at the age of ten. He'd never been far away, though. And he'd found ways to let her know he was close.

Antoine's dark eyes widened, and his arm slipped away from the fire mantel as he straightened. "You can't be serious."

Noelle sighed. "I know he's your cousin, but you can't pretend he isn't capable of this. Of *worse*."

Antoine took an aggressive step toward her, his face hard. "There was never any proof that he did the things he was accused of."

"Just because Embry wasn't able to prove it doesn't mean that Gabriel was innocent."

"It doesn't mean he was guilty either. And it definitely doesn't mean he's now practically stalking Blair."

Noelle's lips thinned. "Look at the facts. He knows where she lives. He regularly sneaks onto our territory. And he leaves her little gifts—he's been doing it for years."

Antoine sighed. "He wedges *playing cards* between the wooden slats of her porch. He's left similar things on my doorstep. They're not gifts. It's his way of saying hi while also taunting the pack that he can slip past our defenses so effortlessly."

"Whoever left Macy's body on the porch slipped on and off our territory without being sensed. They're also evidently at ease with killing. The same can be said for Gabriel—he made his first kill when he was *ten*."

Antoine's eyes blazed. "You don't know that for sure."

"I know that he used to strip Blair's dolls naked and then yank off body parts. Sounds a little similar to what was done to Macy, doesn't it?"

Shaking his head, Antoine shifted his gaze to Blair. "He wouldn't do any of this. You were his only real friend, Blair. He'd never do anything to scare you."

"But he might try his hand at romancing her," said Les. "And, given he's not quite normal, his efforts at romancing someone wouldn't be quite normal."

Blair placed her cup on the coffee table. "I really don't think he'd be interested in trying to 'romance' me. I don't see why *anyone* would. It's well known that I'll soon bond with Luke. I wear his damn mark, for Christ's sake."

Fiddling with the sleeve of her blouse, Noelle cleared her throat. "Speaking of Luke … I see no need for him to be notified of what happened here tonight."

Blair blinked, and her inner animal bristled. "Say what now?"

Mitch gaped, setting his hands on his tapered hips. "Mom, you can't seriously expect her to keep something this huge from her own mate."

"Why not?" asked Noelle. "You know how ridiculously overprotective he is of her."

Blair felt her brows fly up. *Pot. Kettle. Black.* While Luke was indeed exceedingly overprotective, there was nothing toxic about it. He didn't try to make Blair feel as though she couldn't take care of herself or be trusted to make wise choices. He'd always made a point of building her up, supporting her, ensuring she knew her own worth, and encouraging her to be self-reliant.

The latter was no small thing, since most alpha males who found their mate while she was at a suggestible age would have instead tried conditioning her to rely solely on *them*. But Luke had only ever tried to lift her up, not contain her in a little box where she'd be nice and safe and under his spell.

"He'll completely overreact," Noelle continued. "No offense"—she looked at Embry—"but alphas aren't always rational when it comes to the women in their lives. Luke is no exception."

"She has a point," said Antoine. "Besides, this is pack business. He's not pack."

Les nodded, the traitor.

Donal rubbed the back of his head. "Maybe we *should* hold off telling Luke until we at least know who did this."

Ouch. Blair had honestly expected better of him. Knowing she'd be a Beta herself one day, he'd given her plenty of training; had been supportive of her future with Luke. Apparently, that only went so far.

"Or maybe we should let *Blair* decide what happens," said Kiesha. "It's her life, her mate, her choice."

"No, I think not," said Noelle dismissively. "She will make the decision she believes Luke would want her to make. Not the choice she *should* make."

Yeah. Right. Because Blair *so* didn't have her own mind or anything. She was about to give her mother a ration of shit, but then Embry turned to her.

"Blair, I understand why it might make you feel uncomfortable to say nothing to Luke about this," said the Alpha, "but the situation needs to be handled by the pack, not him. You will hold off on telling him until we know who killed the fox."

As her parents, Embry, Donal and Antoine all moved on without letting her say her piece, Blair felt her nostrils flare. Not a fan of having her input dismissed, she did what she knew would get their attention. She gently gripped her thumb … and slid it out of the joint. The *pop* made everyone go still.

A master at controlled dislocations, she did it to one finger. Then another. And another, filling the room with *clicks* and *pops* and *snaps*. She then slid one arm out of the shoulder socket and—

"Okay, okay, stop!" Embry held up his hands. "Seriously, no more."

Blair unhurriedly righted her joints, hiding a smile at the shudders that ran through her pack mates.

"I hate it when you do that," said Mitch.

Well she knew that. Shifters were used to hearing bones snap and pop—it happened when they made the transformation from human to animal, but those transformations were so super swift that the moment was over in mere milliseconds. Watching someone bend their body in unnatural ways much like a demonically possessed woman from a horror movie? *That*, shifters tended not to like. Especially Mitch, who she'd chased across a room more than once while doing an imitation of a human crab *Exorcist*-style.

Noelle let out a put upon sigh. "Do you really think that such a display of mutiny will have us all reevaluate our decision?"

"Oh no," replied Blair. "The conversation here tonight went pretty much how I thought it would. But that's okay. I already took measures to ensure that things went *my* way."

Noelle stilled. "What?"

"I called Luke before you guys got here. I gave him a quick rundown of the situation and, yeah, he went apeshit." She tipped her head to the side, hearing the rumbling of an engine in the near distance. "That's probably him right now." Her inner animal jumped to her feet, eager to see him.

Embry sighed, his eyes falling closed.

"*Why*, Blair?" Noelle's nostrils flared. "Why did you have to pull him into this? It's pack business."

"It's *my* business," said Blair. "And, whether you like it or not, I'm *Luke's* business. You wouldn't keep something like this from Dad if you were in my position. You know you wouldn't. You also know that Luke isn't quite the villain you make him out to be, but you're determined to hate him nonetheless. All he's ever done is what's best for me—"

"So starry-eyed when it comes to him," Noelle scoffed. "He's convinced you that he's oh so perfect. That he'll be the perfect partner. The reality is that you have no real clue what kind of mate he'll be."

Blair shook her head in annoyance. "Not true." She was quite aware that being bound to him would be vastly different from simply having him in her life. She knew there'd be challenges to having Luke as a mate—she was under no illusions about that. Hell, the need to *take charge* was essentially encoded in his DNA. There'd likely be some pushing and pulling until they found their balance, but they *would* find it.

"Did you also tell him about the phone calls and the gifts?" asked Embry, his voice laced with dread.

Blair nodded. "Yup." The news hadn't washed down well at all. He was mad as hell at her for keeping it from him until now.

Embry swore, scrubbing his hand down his face. "You have no idea what you've done."

"I gave you the chance to address what was happening," said Blair. "You didn't. It escalated. A woman is now dead."

He shook his head. "It doesn't even make sense that a person trying to court you would dump a corpse on your porch."

"You got any other suspects?"

Embry snapped his mouth shut.

Yeah, that's what she'd thought.

Blair glanced outside in time to see an SUV pull up near the cabin. Luke smoothly slid out of it, and the sight of him made her inner animal wag her tiny tail.

Blair stood and moved to the doorway to greet him. It had to be said that he was a treat for the eyes. So sexy it bordered on indecent. And decidedly masculine with his distinct jawline, sharp nose, strong arms, and powerful build. Sometimes, Blair couldn't quite believe he was hers.

He had a great butt, too. Terrific abs. A little stubble that made him look stylish and well-groomed rather than scruffy. His short hair was a deep brown that made her think of burnt umber.

A half-smile often graced his mouth. Not today, though. It was set in a grim line.

His gaze locked on her. So blue. So focused. So openly possessive.

The need that always simmered in her blood ramped up—hot, thick, primitive. The mating urge struck them a few months back, which had come as a surprise. Bush dogs didn't usually experience it, and it was thought that if one person couldn't feel it than their mate wouldn't either. Maybe that was correct, or maybe it differed from couple to couple. It was hard to be certain when bush dogs so rarely mated outside their own kind.

Whatever the case, she and Luke hadn't been spared it. Kiesha had speculated that maybe nature itself had stepped in when he and Blair hadn't immediately claimed each other after she turned eighteen; that it had struck them both with the mating urge to speed things along. It was possible, Blair supposed.

Thankfully, its effects had levelled off after a few days. The mating urge was no longer a raging fire inside her that clouded her thoughts, but it was constant and relentless and gave her no quarter; tiring her mentally and physically, making it hard for her to relax or sleep.

She always felt achy and edgy and over-sensitized—sensations that worsened when they were apart. No amount of orgasms dimmed the need, because it wasn't a mere craving for sexual satisfaction. No, it was a craving to be *claimed.*

Her pulse jumped as he began prowling toward her cabin. He had a *smolderingly* sexy walk. Moved with a menacing grace and a relaxed, purposeful stride.

He always looked like he belonged. Even smack bam in the middle of other shifter territory, he was all ease and self-assurance. A predator who didn't even consider, let alone fear, it would be challenged because it felt that no one nearby was its equal.

Luke ascended her porch and crossed straight to her. His scent settled over her, soothing her ragged nerves even as it fired her arousal. Her nerve-endings felt so raw that the simple feel of his palm settling over her nape was enough to make her shiver just a little.

Luke didn't merely meet her eyes, he *dived* into them, looking deeper than anyone else ever had. "You all right?" he asked.

"I will be when I find out who put a dead body on my porch," she replied, splaying a hand on his chest. She could sense his cat pushing against Luke's skin, making his presence known. Her own animal rose to meet the feline, wanting his attention.

"How long was the body there?"

"I don't know exactly." Lowering her arm, Blair backed up and moved aside to let him pass. He stalked into the cabin … and quite simply filled the space just like that. The others tensed. Of course they did. The alpha vibes he exuded were usually subtle. Right now? Not so much.

She wasn't entirely sure why, but a whole lot of anger lived within her mate. In keeping it on a tight leash, he also kept much of himself contained. But whenever anything prodded his temper, the leash eased up, and then the full force of his personality poured right out. The sheer *power* of him was honestly a little overwhelming.

It would be so easy to let someone like that take over. Take *you* over. Especially when they brimmed with a raw alpha energy that was hardwired into them. So it was really a good thing that Blair had had plenty of practice at bearing the weight of it.

"The body wasn't there when I came home at six pm," Blair told him. "I had dinner, took a shower, pulled on some fresh clothes. I decided to go sit on the front porch for a while. But when I opened the front door …"

"We searched our territory," Mitch cut in. "We found no tracks. Whoever did this managed to leave no trace of themselves behind. It was like they were never here."

"I checked the body," Blair told Luke. "There are no signs of assault. No defensive wounds. No bruising around her wrists or ankles to suggest she was bound at any point. Seems like she was shot in the head before she had the chance to fight and then subsequently had her tongue removed."

"Is it one of your pack mates?" Luke asked her.

Blair bit her lip. She hadn't fully briefed him on the details over the phone, not wanting him to be *too* pissed as he drove. "Her name is Macy Corbitt." She paused as recognition flashed in his eyes. "She came here a few weeks back."

He went unnaturally still. "Came here to your territory?"

Blair nodded. "She wanted to speak to me."

"*Speak* to you? About what?"

Blair slid her gaze to Noelle. "Do you want to tell him or should I?"

Her mother's eyes briefly widened.

He slowly turned to face Noelle, his gaze hard. "What did you do?"

Noelle gave a little sniff. "Nothing any mother wouldn't have done. Macy approached me at the mall one day. She said that she'd been your lover for half a year now. She thought it only right that Blair learn about it, so I brought her here."

A low growl reverberated inside Luke's chest. "You're kidding me," he clipped.

Embry stood a little straighter. "I think we should—"

"You *know* I would never betray Blair," Luke said to Noelle. "You might wish I was that much of a bastard, but you know I'm not. You didn't believe Macy—it's written all over your face."

Noelle licked her lips. "I didn't believe her, no. But it didn't seem right to keep it from Blair. She had the right to hear the fox out and decide the truth for herself."

"You mean you hoped she'd believe that bullshit because you want Blair to renounce me." Luke's jaw went rock hard. "It didn't bother you that she'd have been wrecked if she *had* believed it. No. As long as you're getting your way, nothing else matters, does it?"

Noelle bristled. "I hope you're not insinuating that I care nothing for Blair's feelings. My children are my world."

"But you're only content when you're controlling *their* world," he snapped back. "Did you do anything to help find out who was sending her gifts? Were you even remotely concerned? Or were you too damn excited at the prospect that someone might intend to lure her away from me?"

Defensive, Noelle lifted her chin. "I initially saw no reason to be concerned."

He growled again. "She was sent a bouquet of rolled up lace panties, a box of sex toys, and a jar of love coupons that had everything from 'breakfast in bed' to 'anal sex.' Tell me how that isn't concerning."

Noelle looked away. "I thought they were merely being bold in an effort to ensure that they had her attention. Now, well, it would seem that perhaps there is more to the situation than that. If that is the case, it will be handled."

"It should have already been handled. It should never have gotten to this point. She's supposed to be safe here. To *feel* safe here. Not have her worries brushed off like they're nothing. More, she should never have been asked to keep this from me." A muscle in Luke's cheek ticking, he turned to Blair. "We're leaving."

Noelle stiffened. "*What*? No."

He flicked up a brow. "You *want* Blair to stay here?"

"There's no reason why she can't," insisted Noelle. "We will tighten security. Whoever has been trespassing so often won't manage it again."

"You believe right down to your gut that an outsider did this? That she's one hundred percent safe here? Because I don't. As Mitch said, there's no trace of a trespasser. It's reasonable to conclude that just maybe one of the pack is responsible. You might be willing to take the risk that it wasn't, but I'm not. Blair comes with me."

"You can't just *take* her."

"The only person who could stop me is Blair. She doesn't want to stay here."

Noelle's upper lip curled. "Oh, you know what she wants, do you?"

"Yes, he does," Blair cut in, moving to grab a large duffel from the floor near the front door. "Because I told him."

Her mother's eyes dropped to the bag as Blair lifted it. "What are you doing?"

"Leaving," Blair told her, taking strength from the hand Luke rested on her back as he came up behind her. She'd packed the bag right after calling him. "I'm joining the Olympus Pride."

Soft male curses floated around the room.

Kiesha nodded in understanding.

Noelle lurched forward, her eyes bulging. "You're not going *anywhere*."

Blair shot her a disdainful glare. "The only reason I didn't storm off this territory when you pulled that stunt with Macy was that Luke's pride had a lot going on at the time." Shootings, break-ins, bombings, the lot. "The last thing they needed was to have to take the time to welcome a new member and adjust to having a Beta female. I didn't want them having any kind of distractions, so I waited." And going by the little growl Luke let out, he wasn't pleased that she had.

"Beta female?" Noelle echoed, paling. She slammed her gaze on Luke. "No. No, you can't claim her yet. You *can't*."

"Sure I can," he said. "And I will."

Noelle's eyes blazed. "You swore you'd wait until she turned nineteen!"

"And you promised you wouldn't try to come between me and Blair. But you used Macy to try to do exactly that. You went back on your word, freeing me to go back on mine."

Noelle turned to Blair. "How do you know he didn't arrange Macy's death so that you'd be scared enough to leave our territory?"

Blair's animal bared her teeth at the insane notion. "Because I know *him*. You're very fond of telling me that I don't. But the truth is that the person who doesn't know him is *you*. You never tried to get to know him. You built him up to be a huge asshole in your head for your own selfish reasons, never caring how that makes him feel; never caring how it makes *me* feel."

Les took a step toward her. "Blair, let's talk about this. I realize you're upset, but making a rash decision such as this isn't the answer."

"I made this decision when my mother—*my own mother*—brought a woman here to tell me lies in the hope that afterwards I'd turn away from my mate." The thought of it still made Blair's chest squeeze. She cut her gaze back to Noelle. "Luke was right in what he said. It meant nothing to you that my heart would be broken if I believed those lies. Well, my heart did fracture a little. But not because of anything Macy said; it was because of what *you* did."

"I don't want you to hurt but, dammit, Blair, you have it in your head that him being your true mate means he *has* to be your future," clipped Noelle. "Your father isn't my predestined mate. A lot of the people in our pack imprinted on others. We're all happy."

"That's great, but I don't want to imprint on someone. I want Luke. He is my choice. He is my animal's choice. You just won't respect that, though, will you? It's why you recently tried to convince him to wait longer to claim me. Yes, I heard all about it from one of your many friends—they don't all agree that you have the right to dictate when I claim my own mate."

Noelle's hands balled up. "You're too young to bind yourself to someone."

Blair snorted. "If it was one of the pack who wanted to claim me so soon, you'd have no problem with it."

"I only want what's best for you."

"You love me. I know that. But your definition of what's best for me is, in fact, what's best for *you*."

Noelle's mouth opened and closed. "That's not true."

"Of course it is. But it doesn't surprise me that you'd deny it. It doesn't surprise me that, even now, when I'm about to walk out that door and join Luke's pride, you'd refuse to admit you're in the wrong." Blair slid her gaze to Embry. "I'll come back for the rest of my stuff in a day or so."

"Mitch and I will pack it up for you," Kiesha offered, and Mitch nodded.

Blair gave them a grateful smile and then glanced over her shoulder at Luke. "Let's go." She opened the door and walked out.

"Blair!" Noelle shouted. "Blair, you get back here right now!"

Instead, Blair ignored her and headed right for Luke's SUV.

"You can't leave, you can't—let me go, Mitch!"

"We can't stop her from leaving, Mom," said Mitch. "She's not a child anymore."

Les called out her name, but Blair ignored him as well, waiting as Luke held open the front passenger door for her. He then placed a protective hand on the top of her head as she slid into the vehicle.

"Embry, do something," Noelle pled as the group piled out onto the porch. "Stop him."

Luke pinned the Alpha with a hard glare. "I strongly advise you not to try it. You've pissed me off enough already by not only letting Blair down but telling her to withhold things from me. You really want to make that worse?"

After a long moment, Embry sighed and then shrugged at his sister. "He's her mate. I can't come between mates."

"Right decision." Luke closed Blair's door and then tossed her duffel in his trunk.

Noelle tried dashing down the porch steps, but Mitch cuffed her arm and said, "Mom, just … stop."

Blair turned away from the scene to instead watch as Luke settled on the driver's seat and clicked on his seatbelt. Saying nothing, he switched on the engine and drove off, his muscles bunched, his jaw hard.

"Be sure you want to come home with me, Blair," he said. "If you're not, I can take you to Elle's apartment; you can stay there for however long you need. But if you come home with me, that'll be it; there'll be no going back. I won't claim you tonight—you've had far too shitty an evening, and neither of us are in a good frame of mind. But if you sleep in my bed even just once, you'll never leave it. I won't be able to let you go. So be sure."

She frowned. "Do you want me to hurt you? Is that what this is? You know better than to think that I'd say I was ready to be claimed if I wasn't damn sure. I'd never mess with your head that way. But punch you in the throat for thinking differently *for even a second*? Yeah, that's an appealing thought right now. Asshole."

His lips quirked in amusement. "All right, then."

CHAPTER THREE

Luke fought a smile at his mate's *humph.* It was always best to stay on Blair's good side. He'd learned that early.

Had it not been for the fact that she'd just confirmed she was ready to be claimed, he wouldn't have it in him to smile right now. God, he was pissed. Exponentially pissed. Someone had been sending his mate gifts. Wooing her? Taunting her? He didn't know. He knew next to nothing, because she'd kept it all from him.

More, someone had left a corpse on her goddamn doorstep. The corpse of a woman he used to fuck. A woman who'd lied to his mate that he'd betrayed her.

The entire situation was messed up.

He subtly drew in a breath, pulling Blair's gentle feminine scent into his lungs, letting it settle him and his pacing cat. *Peonies and pink pepper.*

The first time he'd met her, her scent had filled him with a haunting, primal protectiveness that had been his constant companion for years. When the spice of a fully grown shifter female laced her scent, his possessiveness developed a sexual undertone—one that was exacerbated by the mating urge when it crashed into his consciousness three months ago, driving him to take her, bite her, and make her indelibly his.

Although the urge had lessened in its intensity since then, the need to claim her was still an ache in his soul. Resisting was no easier for his cat. The feline had been restless and antsy for months. Now, however, he was calm and smug as hell. This wasn't an occasion where they were collecting their mate to spend a little time with her. No, they would be taking her to their lair, where she belonged … and she wouldn't be leaving this time.

As he finally drove through the gates of Sylvan territory, Luke spared her a sideways glance. If she was regretting her decision to leave, it didn't show on her face. A face so beautiful it made his chest tighten.

Someone shouldn't be able to look both sweet and edgy at the same time, but she did. With her large ivy-green eyes, delicately pointed chin, cute little dimples, and pale blonde hair, she looked like she belonged in a choir of angels. But, even when calm, she had a steely, daring, unnerving stare that said, "fuck with me and no one will ever find your body."

She always drank everything in with that gaze, like a lion surveying its surroundings from a distance. And when she opened her mouth, the sexiest voice came out … and you could never quite be sure what she'd say.

Tall, she was only a few inches shorter than him. Though she was slender, she had round full breasts and gently curved hips. Her ass was a thing of beauty, and those shapely legs went on for days.

The anger that right then vibrated in his bones did nothing to dim his ever-present need for her. He guessed she was having the same issue, because sexual tension bounced from him to her and back again, making the air in the vehicle thick and electric.

Said tension had hounded them for long enough. The drive to claim pulsed incessantly between them like a heartbeat. It was maddening and exhausting and drove his libido insane. He was done fighting it.

Her phone rang, but she didn't bother to pluck it out of her pocket. She probably suspected that the caller was her mother. The woman was no doubt flipping her lid right now.

Highly controlling though Noelle might be, she wasn't unfeeling or cruel. Her whole "I want what's best for you" wasn't bullshit. Luke had seen the love in her eyes as she looked at her daughter. He'd also seen the fear that was twined around that emotion. A fear of loss, of pain, of history repeating itself. A fear that drove her to make selfish decisions and not actually *see* that they were selfish. She truly had convinced herself that she was acting in Blair's best interests.

Noelle had tried driving Luke away over the years. Not in obvious ways—that would have meant breaking her word. But she'd done small, subtle things to grate on his nerves, goad him into picking fights, and make things so hard that he'd decide Blair was more trouble than she was worth. Like he would *ever* have walked away from his mate or allowed any of that to poison his connection with her. Like he could ever have abandoned her even if he'd wanted to—she was too essential to him.

Before Blair, his mind had been a dark place. A place of roiling black clouds, bitterly cold rain, distant claps of thunder, and howling winds that uprooted his thoughts and left mental chaos in their wake. There was no shelter from the storm. Only an endless blackness. A blackness birthed from the grief, shame, and anger that had merged into a raging force inside him. A force that was dark and destructive.

Even surrounded by people, he'd been lonely; never sad, never happy—

just numb. Numb and alone, lost in a fog with no way out. And God, he'd been tired. So goddamn tired—physically, emotionally, mentally. Sleep had been his only escape.

While existing in that shadowy fog that simply wouldn't shift, he'd watched as everyone else had gone about their lives. He'd felt utterly disconnected from everything and everyone. Like he'd been sleepwalking. He hadn't felt like a person. Hadn't felt real.

Not many people had noticed. He'd smiled. Laughed. Bantered. But it had been a performance, nothing more. He'd found no true joy or pleasure in anything.

A constant weight had sat on his chest. There had been times when every breath had felt like a strain on his lungs. But then, six years ago, he'd looked into Blair's eyes … and he'd taken his first real breath in what felt like too long. The fog around him had shifted, the blackness had dimmed, and the sheet of glass through which he viewed the world had cracked.

Intellectually, he'd known that living without the other half of his soul meant he wasn't complete. But he hadn't truly *grasped* that until he'd found her.

She'd changed everything. Changed him. From then on, he no longer felt like he operated on autopilot. She'd given him purpose. A reason for being. A reason to *live* rather than merely exist. More, she'd brought him back to himself.

There were times since meeting her when the mental tempest started up again. Times when clouds began to gather and a thick fog tried to surround him. But he could call Blair, hear her voice, and then the storm would ease off. Because she restored his balance. She soothed him, filled him up, quenched that craving to *feel* something.

Watching her grow, mature, and develop into the person she was today—someone strong enough to go toe-to-toe with him when necessary, despite being twelve years his junior and not a born alpha like him—had been magical. He loved that he'd been able to guide, support, and watch over her all these years. He loved that she'd always known she was valued and that her true mate waited for her; known that she'd never be alone and he'd always be there when she needed him.

She'd sensed the anger he carried, she'd asked about it, but she'd let him get away with only telling her dribs and drabs. That would change when they mated. Blair would *never* stand for anything less than all of him. But that was okay, because he'd expect the same from her. And he'd get it.

There would be nothing easy for her about having him as a mate. He felt for her. He did. Because he was a stubborn motherfucker who wasn't always rational when it came to the subject of her safety. Not *controlling* in his efforts to shelter her, though, which he suspected was the only reason she'd never clawed him for it.

Luke didn't like that he was going to his mate saddled with so much emotional baggage. He didn't want her to see all that he hid inside, but he had no way to spare her that other than to walk away. That he could *never* do. He needed her more than she needed him—he'd always known that.

He had no balance without her. She was the only thing that brought him peace; that quieted the storm inside him. Like his cat, he adored her. Was so totally gone for her it was almost embarrassing.

He didn't worry that she'd struggle to take on the position of Beta female. She might only be eighteen, but there was nothing immature about her. Never had been, really. Mitch once told him she was born forty and had pinned people with that steely stare even when in the cradle. Luke could believe it.

Also, she was highly dominant. And so damn fierce. Cunning as hell, too.

Nonetheless, some of his pride mates doubted that someone so young could truly make a good Beta. They might go as far as to test her. Which would be a massive mistake. She knew how to handle herself—he'd made sure of it. Plus, she was used to dealing with difficult characters. *How* she handled them, well, that was always interesting.

Card-carrying members of the "Ramifications Don't Interest Me" party, bush dogs weren't quite the same brand of crazy as pallas cats. Luke's kind didn't give one solitary fuck. Bush dogs? They gave a fuck. They just didn't give a fuck about you. In fact, they were happy to pretend that everyone outside their pack didn't exist. If you *made* them notice you by screwing them over, they would in turn make it their mission to scar you for life.

They liked to play. With your ego. Mostly by crushing it. If there was a color-coded scale for Self-Esteem Assassins, Blair's kind would be at Level Red.

As for their inner animals … they were like miniature bears. Courtesy of their inborn Napoleon complexes that no one talked about aloud, they could be overly aggressive. Unlike pallas cats, they wouldn't strike hard, fast, and first. They'd feign submission; whine and simper and give you big doggy eyes, doing a perfect imitation of man's best friend to melt your heart.

Then they'd snack on you like raging cannibals.

And if you were up against a group of them, you were quite simply fucked. Because a bunch of bush dogs could overpower *anything.*

Another way they differed from pallas cats was that, unless the situation warranted it, they didn't fight until someone was dead. No, they'd let you live so that you'd forever suffer the shame of being brought down by Corgi-sized balls of lunacy.

To bush dogs, the meaning of fair fight meant "we will blindside you, maul you, humiliate you, and leave scars on your soul."

So, yeah, Luke wasn't worried that Blair would struggle to handle anyone from his pride who dared test her strength. Still, he'd be pissed to all hell about it.

Finally, he pulled into the parking lot outside his apartment building. Much like the neighboring complex and the nearby cul-de-sac, it homed his pride mates and belonged to the pride itself. Unlike most breeds of shifter, pallas cats rarely claimed territories. However, they often grouped together for protection.

There was an additional apartment building that was strictly for lone shifters. His brother's mate, Havana, and her tiny unofficial pack that consisted of various breeds of shifter had resided there before joining the pride.

Luke whipped the SUV into his usual parking space and switched off the engine. Once he'd grabbed Blair's duffel from the trunk, he took her hand and led her into the complex. After an upward elevator ride, they reached his floor.

Inside his apartment, Luke closed the door … and slammed her up against it. He took her mouth in a hot, wet kiss, growling when she fisted his shirt and dragged him closer. He thrust his tongue deeper, feeding on her taste, so hungry for her it all but slayed him.

His Blair was no passive participant. She kissed him back just as urgently, hooking her leg over his hip. She arched into him, grinding against his throbbing cock.

Inwardly cursing, he tore his mouth free, planted his hands on the door either side of her head, and inched his body away from hers. "Don't," he said when she would have yanked him to her. "My control is not at its best."

"I've noticed. I'm trying to take advantage of it. Hush. Don't interfere."

"Blair …"

"Shh, it's all good, it won't hurt, I promise."

He bit her lip. "We're not doing this tonight."

"Why not? You're hard. I'm wet. It makes sense to do something about it. I could make myself come but, well, I'm *far* more acquainted with my fingers than I care to be at this point."

His eyes briefly drifted shut. She liked to tease him with little comments like that, and they never failed to make his cock twitch. "Demure" she was not. His girl was bold as brass and went after what she wanted—something that made him proud. But … "You know I'd never manage to fuck you without also claiming you, and I'm not claiming you tonight."

She pouted. "You always make me feel like a villain trying to divest an innocent of their virtue."

One side of his mouth kicked up. "I'll be doing the divesting. But not tonight." He nuzzled her, dragging that scent into his lungs that called specifically to him, rousing every possessive instinct in his system, awakening his need to protect and shield and claim. When the scent of her filled and surrounded him, he felt like he was home; like all was right in his world.

"Now come on. We need to talk."

Sobering in an instant, Blair sighed as she let him pull her further into his apartment. It wasn't a regular bachelor pad. How could it be, when she'd played a part in selecting the décor? He'd roped her into helping him choose the warm, earthy paint colors and the stylish pine furnishings when she was younger, feeling it was her right; knowing she'd want to leave her touch on his personal slice of territory. He'd also wanted her to view it as her home.

He sank onto the sofa and pulled her onto his lap. She easily settled there, planting her hands on his chest. She'd straddled him like this countless times as they made out for what felt like hours. Shame they wouldn't be doing that now.

He gave her hips a squeeze. "You should have told me that Macy went to see you."

"And pull your attention away from all that was happening around you back then? No. Your focus needed to be on ridding your pride of the danger that hovered over it." When he went to argue, she added, "I'm not saying you don't have a right to be angry that I kept it from you. In your position, I wouldn't like it either. But I'd be lying if I said that I was sorry, so I'm not going to."

His jaw hardened. "The danger to the pride passed three weeks ago. I told you that."

"You did, but I didn't trust that you weren't merely trying to keep me from worrying. You've never once had a problem with me visiting your dad on his birthday. Every year, you take me to see him and then a bunch of us go to a restaurant. But this year, you were opposed to it." Luke had instead brought Vinnie and a bunch of others to Sylvan territory, and they'd had a celebratory meal in her damn cabin. No one had given her a straight answer as to why.

"It wasn't that all the problems weren't truly resolved. We simply have a new, though much more minor, issue."

Her inner animal snapped up her head. "Which is?"

"You'll remember I told you about one of our new pride mates, Camden. When he shifted into his tiger form outside this complex to fight with his uncle, it didn't go unnoticed by humans. Since then, a human male has been hanging around asking the people who work in the pride-owned shops about the 'lone tiger shifter' who lives nearby."

At least they'd assumed that Camden was a loner rather than part of a pride. Pallas cats had no intention of coming out of the shifter closet and posed as humans. "Why?" she asked.

"I don't know. I discreetly took a photo of the human and passed it onto River," he added, referring to a member of the pride who worked for the police. "He ran a background check on him that came up clean. We'd figured he might be a journalist or something, but he works at a pawn shop and by all appearances has nothing to do with shifters or anti-shifter extremists. It could just be that he was simply curious. Still, I don't like it. I didn't want to put you in his sights in case there was something shady going on."

"You didn't have Camden question him? It would have looked weird if *you* or any of your other pride-mates-posing-as-humans did, but not the tiger."

"We thought about having Camden nab the guy, but then he stopped coming around. We haven't seen anything of the human over the last four days."

"You could have just told me. Why didn't you?"

He stroked her hip. "You know why."

"I do. But I want you to say it, because then you can't give me grief when I say the same to you after you fire all kinds of questions at me about my own situation."

He sighed. "I didn't want to worry you when there was every chance that there was no real need for anyone to worry," he admitted. "I intended to tell you once I had all the facts."

"Yeah, I know what that's like."

He narrowed his eyes. "Now it's my turn to ask questions. What exactly did Macy say to you?"

Feeling her claws pricking the inside of her fingertips, Blair replied, "That you were sleeping with her. That it had been going on for six months, and that you'd bedded other females before her while waiting for me to grow up."

A growl rattled in his chest. "You didn't believe her," he sensed.

"Of course I didn't."

"What else did she say?"

"Quite a few things. She said you weren't sure if you wanted to claim me; that you were having doubts because of the age gap. She called me naïve and gullible for assuming that I had what it took to be Beta female. She then went on to criticize my figure, proclaiming that I wasn't curvy enough for your tastes.

"Believe it or not, she also bashed my breed *while on bush dog territory*, declaring that we'd put off any male just by being what we are. She then said she didn't believe you'd claim me because, in her opinion, you needed a *real* woman—not a young girl who wouldn't have a clue how to satisfy the needs of a man like you. That was the point at which I knocked her clean out, so I'm not sure if she had anything else to say."

His mouth tightening, he curled her hair behind her ear. "You know everything she said was utter bullshit, right?"

"I wouldn't be here if I didn't. And you'd be lacking a spleen."

One corner of his mouth kicked up. "That's my girl. What did you do after knocking her clean out?"

"Had some fun, of course," Blair expanded, relaying all she'd done.

His smile widened. "You went right for the ego, huh."

"It was only fair. She went for mine, trying to play on whatever insecurities she thought I might have. It didn't work, though, because I don't worry that my age bothers you or that I'm not perfectly capable of acting as Beta female. Nor do I ponder over whether I have enough curves to rev your engines. Coming at me like that was a waste of her time."

He rubbed the back of his head. "I can't understand why she did it."

"It could have been a jealousy thing. I mean, you *did* used to sleep with her. It was before I came along, I know, but still."

He squinted. "And how is it you know about that?"

"I saw her once when I was sixteen. I was with Elle at the time—she was taking me to see a movie. We bumped into Macy, who asked Elle how you were and made a few comments that suggested you used to shake the sheets with her." Blair's animal had wanted to bite her ear clean off. "Elle confirmed it for me but made it clear that you hadn't touched *any* woman since finding me. I believed her."

"Elle never mentioned it to me. Neither did you."

"At that point, I was used to crossing paths with women from your past. I mean, some are even part of the pride. None ever bitched at me, came to my territory, or actively sought me out. Honestly … I think my mother might have put Macy up to it. I don't want that to be the case. But as much as I like to tell myself that Macy probably did it out of jealousy, I really didn't get the sense that she was holding a candle for you or anything."

"I'd like to say that your mother wouldn't go that far to come between us."

"So would I. But we both know it would be a lie. If she *did* put Macy up to it, she also unknowingly put Macy in the sights of someone who saw total sense in killing her either for me or because of me—I don't know."

Something dark moved behind his eyes. "Tell me about the calls you've been getting and the gifts you received. You didn't give me many details when we spoke earlier."

"The calls started first. The first one came a couple of months ago. It usually happens twice a week. The caller never says anything. I hear light breathing, but that's all. They hang up after five seconds or so."

"You said you thought it was being done via a spoofing site. Why?"

"The caller comes up on my screen as someone I know, like my mother or friend or brother or another pack mate."

Luke swore. "For them to know the numbers of the people close to you, this person either knows *them* or has ways of obtaining such information."

"And might very well be from the pack, I know. Don't think that hasn't played on my mind. Anyway, I got the weird-ass underwear bouquet about a week after the very first call. The box of sex toys came two weeks later—there was all sorts of kinky shit in there. The jar of coupons came about three weeks after that."

His mouth set into a hard line. "You should have contacted me the minute you received that damn bouquet. No, you should have contacted me after you got the first strange call."

"I thought it was the juveniles in the beginning. They were doing all kinds of dares back then and pulling pranks on people—including making dirty calls to some of the females. I only dismissed the theory when the juveniles quieted down and yet my calls and gifts kept coming. Then I suspected it was Noelle; that she'd asked a male to pretend to court me simply to piss you off. It's the sort of thing she'd do."

"If you believed she was playing games, why didn't you say anything to me? You know I'd have wanted to be made aware of it."

Blair folded her arms. "You didn't tell me that she was trying to convince you to postpone claiming me. I can guess why you kept it from me. You were set on keeping the peace. Am I right?" His expression confirmed that she'd guessed correctly. "That was what *I* was trying to do."

He grunted. "What made you think it might not be Noelle?"

"We had a huge row after she brought Macy to see me. I told her I would *never* forgive her for actively trying to come between you and me like that. I even accused her of being behind the gifts, which she flatly denied. I refused to speak to her for days. The last thing she would have done while on paper-thin ice was have someone send me *another* gift. And yet, the jar of coupons came. There were no other gifts, unless you count Macy."

He rubbed his jaw. "I don't like that you kept all this from me. I'm your mate, Blair. It's my right to help you ease even the smallest of burdens."

"I know. But I've already explained why I never mentioned it."

As much as Luke wished that she'd told him everything sooner, he *could* understand why she hadn't. He was just too pissed to make the concession out loud.

"Yesterday, I made the official decision to tell you about everything, but I knew your pride was throwing a mating ceremony today—I wanted to wait until after it was over before I dragged all my shit into your pride's world."

He ground his teeth, *again* understanding her choice but not liking it. "So what made you decide to finally tell me? Something else happened, didn't it?"

She bit down on her lip. "I received an email yesterday. It wasn't signed and it came through a spoofing site, so I don't know who sent it."

His entire body went rigid. "Show me."

She pulled her cell out of her pocket, brought up the email, and then handed him the phone. It read: *I wish I could say all this openly, but I know your mother would try to keep us apart. You know she would, too. That's why you've never told me how you feel—yes, I understand. I've always understood, I'm not mad.*

The only thing I don't get is why you're going around asking people who sent the gifts I gave you. You know it was me. I hope you liked them. I know they were a little 'out there,' but you would have rolled your eyes at typical romantic gestures like flowers or chocolates.

I didn't think it would be necessary to romance you, if I'm honest. I really thought you'd come to me when you turned eighteen. I waited and I waited … and then I realized that you needed me to make the first move. It should have occurred to me sooner that being a virgin would make you too nervous to come to me.

I love that you've kept yourself pure for me, I really do. I'll always treasure that, and I'll prove that to you very soon.

Luke's hand clenched tight around the phone as red-hot rage coursed through his blood. *Motherfucker.* His cat let out a furious hiss, his hackles rising in a rush. "You showed this to anyone else?" he asked, a guttural edge to his voice.

She shook her head. "I wanted to show it to you first. My original plan was to invite you to my cabin tomorrow, spill everything to you, and for us both to then report the email to Embry. That plan got derailed tonight."

Staring at her cell, he ground his teeth again, his nostrils flaring. "Whoever sent you this … they're clearly obsessed with you. They talk like you belong to them; like it was always a given that you'd be theirs. And, going by what they said and the way they said it, I think they're from the pack."

"So do I," she said, her eyes dulling.

He soothingly rubbed her thigh, knowing how much the theory had to hurt her.

"I also think it's highly possible that they killed Macy," she added.

"I'd have to agree. They said they wanted to prove to you just how much they treasured you staying 'pure.' Maybe, to them, ending the life of a woman who so thoroughly insulted you was proof."

"Sick freak," Blair muttered before blowing out a shaky breath. "I don't know who it could be, Luke. I can't think of a single person in the pack who ever gave me the creeps."

"People like that often wear masks. You wouldn't know they were fucked up unless they wanted you to." He tugged her closer and slid a hand up her back. "Did anyone in the pack ever come onto you?"

"No. I would have told you if they had."

"Have any tried to get close to you in what might have seemed like a platonic way?"

She shook her head.

"No guys ever do things to get your attention?"

"Nope. Ever since I read that email, I've done nothing but ask myself who could have sent it. But I just don't know." She licked her lips. "My mother has a theory as to who might be leaving me gifts, but I don't know if I agree with it."

"What theory?"

She shifted slightly. "I don't think I ever told you about Gabriel, did I?"

Luke felt his brows knit. "Gabriel? No."

"He was my friend when I was a kid. He was … well, he was different. Super serious and a little morbid. Obsessed with death. If he found a dead animal, he'd cut it open and dissect it as easily as you'd carve into a watermelon. So when his parents were shot by an intruder when he was ten, a lot of people—my mother included—thought he'd had something to do with it. He was ostracized by Embry. Some thought it right, some didn't."

"What about you? What do you think?"

"I think it was unfair that they pointed fingers at him. He wasn't exactly close to his parents, but he did love them. He had no motivation to kill them. But his uncle—who's human and took him in after his parents' death—is an avid gun collector and taught him how to shoot. That went against Gabriel, even though he didn't own a gun and none were found in his home. It didn't help his cause that he didn't appear to grieve his parents. But I don't doubt that he was in pain. He just wasn't the type to show emotion in front of others."

"Okay." Luke paused. "Even though he was 'different,' as you call it, I don't see why Noelle would think that he might be the one harassing you."

She pulled a face. "He used to strip and disfigure my dolls. He also sneaks onto pack territory sometimes. He leaves playing cards on my porch."

The little hairs on Luke's nape stirred. "Because you liked to build houses of cards when you were a kid?"

She nodded. "He never left me what you'd consider real gifts, though."

"No, but you're eighteen now. Old enough to be claimed, if that's what's on his mind. This would be the right time for him to make a move."

She sighed. "Yeah, I guess. But I don't feel comfortable laying the blame on him without any real reason to do so. I don't even know him. I knew him when we were kids; that's different."

"He's a potential suspect, though. You have to concede that much."

She slightly inclined her head. "Okay. Yes. But I'm not sold on this theory."

"Noted. I'm not leaving any stone unturned, though. Do you know where he lives?"

"No. But his uncle probably does."

"The human who took him in?"

"Yes. His name is Quincy Rendell. He lives somewhere near the outlet mall not far from Sylvan territory. That's all I know."

"It's enough for now." He'd have River dig up the rest of the information. Tossing her phone aside, Luke caught her face in his hands, forcing himself to be gentle when all he wanted was to hunt down whoever sent that email and eviscerate them. "You won't be going anywhere alone for a while."

"I think—"

"Don't argue, hear me out. This email … it doesn't scare you, I see that.

But if the sender *did* kill Macy, he's already shown what he's capable of. And here's the thing, his fantasy world where you'll be his forever is about to fall apart around him. You left the pack. You came home with me. You'll very soon be claimed by me. In his head, you've betrayed him. He may choose to 'punish' you. That can't happen. *No one* can fucking touch you."

She gently cuffed his wrists with her hands. "I'm not planning to make things easy for this bastard."

"Then you'll agree to take precautions and not go anywhere alone."

"I wasn't going to argue with you about it. You just assumed I would. I might not like the idea of being guarded—dominant females generally don't. But I'm not too proud to accept protection when it's needed."

A relieved sigh slipped out of him. "Good. Now here's what we're going to do. We're going to forward this email to Embry. I can't envision him not taking it seriously. Whatever the case, *we* will."

"Embry won't permit you to question everyone in the pack. It would be seen as him submitting to you; seen as a sign of weakness."

"I know," he grumbled. "In the reverse situation, Tate wouldn't allow it for the same reasons. But we don't need to worry that our boy will lay low and remain out of our reach. He's going to show himself because he won't be able to cope with you being away from him. Then we'll snatch the prick, and I'll question him all I damn want—and more. In the meantime, it's imperative that you be careful, Blair."

"I know. And I will be. I promise."

Exhaling heavily, he pressed his forehead to hers. "I'll hold you to that."

"I'd expect nothing less."

Luke kissed her, licking into her mouth. That easily, his system calmed. Her taste, her smell, her size, her weight, the feel of her—soft, warm, toned, curvy—all filled him with a sense of *rightness.*

He gorged himself on her, letting her chase away the rage that purred beneath his skin. His cat pressed against her, needing the contact.

Long minutes went by before Luke pulled back. His gut clenched at the glazed look she wore. He sank his fingers into her hair, flitting his gaze all over her face. "You're finally here. Where you belong."

"And yet, you're not inside me. Lame."

"I'm not going to claim you while anger is riding me." Even though his instincts to possess and take her were on fucking fire on hearing that another man thought he had rights to her. "You deserve better than that. And I do *not* want thoughts of that sick bastard in your head when I claim you anyway."

She stroked his chest. "I don't like that anger's riding you. That's my job."

He groaned. "Witch."

Her lips curled. "I can get another kiss, though, right?"

"One more. Then bed." For the first time, his mate would be in his bed, sleeping beside him. And there would never again be a time when she didn't.

CHAPTER FOUR

The feel of a hot mouth dragging kisses down her neck woke Blair. It took a few moments for her brain to register the situation. She was in Luke's bed. He was spooning her, one hand under her tee stroking the pads of his fingers along her stomach, his cock hard and thick and digging into her butt through his sweatpants.

Well.

She let her eyelids flutter shut, sinking into the sensations as sparks of hot need licked at her flesh. His kisses were soft and almost lazy, just like the fingertips teasingly tracing patterns on her skin. But she could feel the tension in his large frame. She could sense how difficult it was for him to hold himself in check.

The graze of teeth made her gasp. Anticipation beat at her, making her body tighten and her nerve-endings prickle. She was *seriously* wishing that they were both naked, but he'd last night declared that his good intentions would fly out the window if they lay together without clothes—hence her long tee and his sweatpants.

"Morning," he rumbled as the sleek, muscled arm she was seemingly using as a neck-pillow curved around her and rested on her shoulder, pinning her against him.

Like she had any plans to go anywhere.

She'd been craving this, craving *him*, for too damn long. She needed him inside her. Needed him to finally claim her as his. Her inner animal yearned for it just as much.

"Morning." She rocked back, grinding against his cock. He growled low into her ear, stirring the tiny hairs there. She shuddered, her nipples tightening.

Luke softly snaked his warm, calloused hand up her stomach and closed it over her breast. She clenched her thighs. He always touched her that way—with a bold, entitled possessiveness, reminding her that it was his *right*. Branding her in ways she could only feel. It pushed all kinds of delicious buttons for both her and her female.

Blair moaned as he squeezed her breast just right. It made her lower stomach tighten and her clit pulse. Since she turned eighteen, he'd made it his mission to learn what she liked and exactly how she liked it. He clearly meant to exploit that knowledge.

He plumped her breast again and again, fueling the fiery need that coursed through her. Blair arched into his hold, pushing out her ass to rock back against his dick once more.

Hot breath washed over her neck as he growled. "Stop that."

"Why?"

"Because I said so."

She licked her lips. "That's not a real answer." But it was a very *Luke* answer. A reminder that she was in bed with a born alpha.

He suckled on her neck, and damn if her inner walls didn't ripple. She gripped the arm he'd curled around her, digging her fingers into hard muscle as he played with her breasts. Squeezing. Stroking. Kneading.

Her nipples were lavished with just as much attention. He repeatedly pinched and plucked and twisted them until they were tight, throbbing buds. At this point, she was damp and hot and felt ready to crawl out of her skin. Or maybe tackle the teasing bastard so that he was flat on his back and she could impale herself on his dick.

Was she nervous about losing her virginity? Not at all. She'd never quite considered it a big deal anyway. And after months of Luke's brand of torturous foreplay and being in a constant state of arousal, she was more than ready to be taken; more than ready to *take* in return.

His fingertip circled an aching nipple. "Such soft, pretty breasts."

"They've been well and truly pleasured. Your hand needs to head further south."

"You know, I just had the same thought." He slipped his finger into her mouth. "Suck."

She did as he asked, swirling her tongue around the digit. She barely hid a smile when she felt his cock throb against her butt. It didn't take a genius to work out what he'd been imagining right then.

He punishingly bit her earlobe as he withdrew his finger. "It's not nice to tease."

"No, it's not." She almost bucked as a wet fingertip rolled her clit. "And yet you tease me all the time. Why?"

"Because I can." He slipped his finger through her folds and then gently thrust it inside her. He groaned. "So tight." He nipped her earlobe again. "So mine."

Feeling close to intoxicated on the scent of his mate's need, Luke set up a slow, steady rhythm as he fucked her with his finger, going a little deeper each time. Her gasps, her moans, her responsiveness, the hot liquid coating his finger—all of it made the possessive streak inside him unfurl and stretch out like a wild, waking animal.

She appealed to every one of his senses. Stirred them up. Inflamed them. Demanded their attention.

He groaned when he touched the barrier inside her. "You don't know what it does to me," he began, swirling his finger, "to know that no one else has ever touched you this way. That no other man has ever made you come."

Luke kept his pace slow as he continued to pump his finger into her pussy. He'd used his hands on her many times before, so he knew she could handle more, harder, faster. But he wanted to drive her so insane with need that she barely felt any pain when he first slid inside her.

His body wasn't down with the "slow and teasing" plan. It fairly vibrated with the primitive, animalistic need to take his mate hard and fast; to rut on her until she felt owned, mastered, conquered.

He couldn't do that. Wouldn't. Not right now. It would hurt her. But his cock didn't give a single hot shit. It was raging hard, demanding he give into the urge to fuck her raw.

Luke added another finger, gritting his teeth as her tight muscles contracted around them. "Exists solely for me." His cat rumbled his agreement, pressing against Luke's skin in an effort to be closer to her.

"Dammit, can't you pick up the pace a little?"

He felt his mouth curve at her snippy tone. "I could." But he wouldn't.

Luke lazily sank his fingers inside her over and over and over … until she was arching and bucking and snarling at him to move faster. Yeah, snarling. He bit her neck, and her pussy began to blaze and spasm. "Let go, come all over my hand."

She did exactly that seconds later, her thighs clenching and trembling as her inner muscles clamped bitingly around his fingers.

"That's my baby." He withdrew his hand and sucked his fingers clean. "Hmm, I need more of your taste. But first …" He rolled her onto her back, draped his body over hers, and then fit his mouth against her own. He kissed her slow and deep and greedily, until she had to tear her lips free to catch her breath.

"Get inside me," she demanded, her face flushed, her eyes dark with need.

"I'm busy." He almost jumped when warm, soft hands delved into his sweatpants and curled around his cock. "Sneaky little witch."

He'd had his fair share of great sex before Blair came into his life, but the simple feel of her fingers curled around his dick super-charged his nerve-endings and inflamed him far more than any fuck he'd ever had. As if his body recognized hers; reacted to it on a level it could never respond to with anyone else.

Luke grunted as she began to pump. "Tighter." She squeezed his shaft, and he thrust into her hands once, twice. But then he gently removed them. "As much as I enjoy covering those wicked little hands in my come, that will have to wait until another—"

A knock came at the front door. Unexpected. Jarring. Unwelcome.

He completely ignored it and kissed his way down her neck, loving how her scent was so much warmer and sweeter when she was—

The knock came again. He ignored it once more, raking his teeth over her pulse. But then a hand banged on the front door once more.

He swore, snapping up his head.

A little growl rattled in her throat. "Answer it, tell whoever it is to *go away*."

He bit into the swell of her breast. "I don't want to. I told you, I'm busy."

"It could be important."

Luke felt his jaw tighten. "Don't move." Adjusting his cock in his pants, he stalked through the apartment and yanked open the front door. There stood one of the female enforcers, Finley, with a thermal takeout cup in each hand.

Her eyes drifted down his bare chest but quickly snapped back to his face. She cleared her throat. "Good morning. I wanted to talk to you about a few pack-related matters. I meant to do it last night at the party, but you disappeared."

He stared at her. Seriously? He'd walked away from his mate—who was *finally* in his goddamn bed—for this? Luke shut the door in the enforcer's face and returned to Blair.

She was now sat upright, her eyes narrowed. "Was that Finley I heard?"

His step faltered. He knew Blair wasn't a fan of the other female. They'd crossed paths a few times over the years. Finley had never been bitchy or unwelcoming toward her—he wouldn't have stood for that—but she'd been somewhat dismissive of his mate. Not in a cruel way, but as if Blair's age meant that Finley didn't seem to *see* her. "Yes."

Blair's brow inched up. "Does she usually turn up at your apartment first thing in the morning?"

"It's not typical for her, no." He knelt on the bed and gripped her calves. "She only seeks me out when she wants to discuss pride issues."

"Does she still take it upon herself to do Beta female duties?"

He blinked. "I'm guessing it was Elle who mentioned that to you."

Blair only shrugged her shoulder.

"If Finley crosses lines like that, I never fail to point it out."

"I know, I heard all about it." It nonetheless ruffled Blair's fur. She might not have claimed the position yet but it was *hers*. Everyone in the pride knew that. Each time Finley overstepped, she was essentially challenging Blair's claim to the role. More, the enforcer was acting as if she and Luke could be some kind of team.

Her inner female bared her teeth at the thought. "Has she ever come on to you?" The bitch would get reamed with a red hot poker if she had.

"Never. She's not interested in me, Blair."

"But she *is* interested in the position of Beta."

He sighed. "Yes. But she never tried to use me—or Tate when he was Beta, for that matter—to get the role. She wants to be assigned it, not get it by default due to who she mated. That's why Finley applied for the position when Tate became Alpha, suggesting I could remain Head Enforcer. Can we forget about her now?"

Not likely. "Be honest, has she tried crossing lines *more* than usual since it neared the time you were due to claim me, or has it been less?"

He hesitated. "More."

In that case, Finley hadn't resigned herself to the fact that the role belonged to Blair. "So she'll be a problem, then. For you *and* me, really. If she can establish herself as more dominant than me and better suited to the position, she can argue that I need to step down … which would mean that, as my mate, you'd have to step down right along with me."

He nodded. "She's bold enough to try it. She'll test you. She might even encourage others to test you. As much as I'd love to warn everyone to back the hell off, it wouldn't help. It would weaken you in their eyes. But I'm not worried that you'll struggle to handle them. Now can we please get back to—"

A rhythmic knock came at the door.

"*Mother of Christ*."

"You might as well answer it," said Blair. "The mood is somewhat spoilt."

Yeah, Luke had noticed. Silently cursing, he again prowled through his apartment and opened the door. This time, his sister stood on the other side of it. "What?" he bit out.

Elle's brows lifted. "Oh, well, that's very nice, isn't it?" She stepped into the apartment. "I bumped into Finley. She said you slammed the door in her face without speaking a word. She's worried that something's … Wait, do I smell Blair?"

Luke sighed as his sister hurried through the apartment, following the scent of his mate. This was absolutely not how he'd expected the morning to go.

In the bedroom, he found them standing near the bed hugging as they excitedly babbled greetings. It warmed his heart that they got along so well.

Elle pulled back slightly, beaming. "I had no idea you were here, I—*oh*." She winced and then turned to Luke. "Now I get why you didn't want visitors. I'll go. But first, I gotta ask …" She looked at Blair. "Does this mean you're part of the pride now?"

His mate sat on the bed. "It does."

Elle clapped, but then her smile faltered. "On the one hand, I'm delighted. On the other hand, I know Luke wouldn't have broken his promise to your parents unless things went tits up. What happened?"

Blair pulled a face. "It's a long story."

"At least give me the short version before my imagination starts running riot."

Resigning himself to the fact that he wasn't going to be able to rekindle the mood, Luke sank onto the corner armchair and brought his sister up to speed.

Elle did a slow blink when he was done. "Wow, that's so completely wacked I'm struggling to process it." Sitting beside Blair, she looked at her. "You have absolutely no idea who could be stalking you?"

Blair cocked her head. "Would we call them a stalker?"

"They sent you weird-ass gifts, plied you with strange phone calls, wrote a massively creepy email, possibly killed someone to prove their devotion to you, and also seem to believe not only that you're theirs but that you know it. I'd call that stalker behavior. You know, you should speak to River about this. As a cop, he'll be able to educate you on stalker stuff."

"Which is why I asked for him to be present at the meeting," said Luke.

"What meeting?" asked Blair.

"I texted Tate last night to let him know you're here and that there are things he should be made aware of. He wants us to show up at his place in"—Luke glanced at the wall clock—"half an hour. A few others will be there."

Elle stood. "Why don't I make coffee while you two dress?"

"Sounds good," said Luke.

Blair inwardly snorted. He didn't *look* like he thought it would be good. Well, it wasn't. She'd expected to be claimed before she left the apartment this morning. But the appearance of Finley followed by talk of Blair's recent problems in addition to Macy's death … the last thing Blair was feeling was in the mood for sex.

Once they were alone again, Luke fluidly rose from the chair and crossed to her, making her pulse jump. He bent over and fisted her hair. "Tonight, Blair," he told her, his eyes glittering with promise. "Tonight, you'll get claimed."

"So will you."

His gaze heated, and his grip on her hair tightened. He kissed her hard, licking into her mouth, delving his tongue deep. He ended the kiss with a sharp bite to her lip and then straightened. "Goddamn cockblockers," he muttered as he stalked into the bathroom.

Once Blair was washed and dressed, she crossed to the nightstand and snatched the phone she'd placed on silent mode last night. She quickly skimmed through her notifications. Damn, she had dozens upon dozens of text messages, missed calls, and voicemails.

Just as she was reading the last of her messages, Luke appeared in front of her. "Exactly how many texts has Noelle sent you?" he asked.

"Surprisingly, none. She hasn't tried calling either. She's either sulking, or someone has convinced her to temporarily back off. To break it all down ... My father and Donal are asking me to return to the pack. Embry is apologizing for trivializing my concerns. Antoine is saying I should question if I've truly made the right decision for me. Mitch is demanding I let him know if anyone from the pride is mean to me so he can come drop kick the fucker. Kiesha says she'll miss me being part of the pack but also wishes me well. And several of the pack are wondering if it's true that I've left for good—oh, and if you've claimed me yet."

Luke hummed. "Forward the creepy email to Embry. Let's see if it lights a fire under his ass. Just maybe he'll redeem himself and properly act on it."

Nodding, she sent the email to her uncle and then followed Luke into the kitchen. After they'd eaten breakfast and downed their coffees, Elle headed home while he and Blair began the short walk along the street toward the cul-de-sac where Tate and Havana, the Olympus Pride's Alpha pair, resided.

Blair had met Havana once before. The devil shifter, who was relatively new to the pride, had been part of the group who came to Blair's old territory to celebrate Vinnie's birthday not so long ago.

A light breeze whispered over Blair's skin and lightly ruffled her hair as she and Luke strode along the street, passing slim alleyways, cart vendors, a crowded bus stop, and the pride-owned businesses. Various scents filtered out of the open shop windows or doors—coffee beans, herbal soaps, fresh flowers, and newly baked bread.

Peeking through the windows of the stores, she saw that most were quite busy. She recognized a lot of the workers as being members of the pride. Some noticed her and waved, no doubt assuming she'd merely come to visit Luke.

Reaching the cul-de-sac, they headed to one of the cute little houses. It was Luke's father who answered the front door. Smiling, Vinnie pulled Blair into a tight hug. "Well, if it isn't my favorite bush dog."

She felt her lips curve. "You really have to stop saying it like I'm a pet." Drawing back from the hug, she eyed him. "You're looking good, old man."

He gave her a mock frown. "I don't look a day over thirty."

Behind her, Luke snorted. "You keep telling yourself that."

"I will." Vinnie glanced from her to his son as they stepped into the hallway. "You two still holding out on claiming each other?"

Luke's lips thinned. "Not on purpose. We were ... distracted."

Allowing her mate to lead her forward with one hand splayed on her back, Blair entered the living room, where a bunch of people waited.

Tate came straight to her and rested a hand on her shoulder as he kissed her cheek. "Glad to finally have you in our pride. You remember my mate, Havana."

"I do." Blair smiled at the female. "How are you?"

"Absolutely fine." Havana gave her hand a comforting squeeze. "But from the little Luke told Tate, I'm guessing you can't say the same."

"Some bad shit has gone down," Blair confirmed. "But all is not awful—I'm now living with Luke, which is where I want to be."

Havana's face softened. "Whatever's happening, we'll be *all over* it, I promise. We'll also be throwing you a welcome party, too—no, don't argue, it's pointless." She gestured at the two females who stood off to the side. "I told you about my honorary sisters, right?" She pointed at a pretty Asian female. "This is Bailey." Havana then pointed at the tall, curvy female beside her. "And that's Aspen."

Bailey tilted her head. "Havana's right," she said to Blair. "You really do look like you should have freaking angel wings or something."

Aspen nodded. "And you really do have a piercing stare. I want one."

Blair felt one corner of her mouth lift. "My father swears I was born with it."

"Hey, Blair," greeted a familiar male voice.

She turned, her smile widening as she spotted the Head Enforcer. "Farrell, hi." She accepted his quick hug. "I heard you're a dad now."

"You heard right." A proud smile lit his eyes. "You should pop into the bakery at some point. My mate will be glad to see you, and she usually has our boy with her so she'll let you have a hold."

River stepped forward and shook Blair's hand. "Good to see you again."

"Likewise," she said.

An arm looped around Blair's neck. "All right, stop monopolizing my mate's time and space," grumbled Luke.

Tate snickered. "Clingy bastard."

Luke merely flipped him the finger and then led Blair to the sofa, where they both sat.

Blair looked at Vinnie. "How's Damian?" she asked, referring to Luke's younger brother.

Standing in front of the fireplace, Vinnie replied, "Oh, fine. We would have invited him so he could say his hellos, but Tate didn't want many people present for the meeting."

"So," began the Alpha, perched on the arm of the chair that his mate had taken, "tell us what's been happening."

Both Blair and Luke began relaying the details of recent events, starting with the phone calls, the gifts, and Macy's visit. They only got as far as their theory of how Noelle likely brought Macy to the pack's territory before they were interrupted.

"I can't believe your mom would do that," said Havana.

Tate rubbed at his jaw. "I'm personally not surprised that Noelle broke her promise. It seemed inevitable that she would, since she didn't succeed in chasing Luke away, and it was coming closer to the time when she'd have to step aside for him to claim and bring you here."

"As for this Macy person," began Bailey, sitting cross-legged on the floor beside Aspen, "wow, that was harsh. Even if she only did it because your mom put her up to it, it's no excuse for how utterly shitty that was."

Blair nodded. "She didn't deserve to die for it, though."

A silence fell around the room.

"She died?" asked Tate.

"Yes." Luke picked up the story from there, not stopping until he'd revealed every last detail.

Aspen puffed out a breath. "Embry had better do what he can to ID Macy's killer, or her pack will likely go to war with his."

"I think the email I forwarded him earlier might make him up his game," said Blair.

"Would you mind reading it out?" asked Tate. "Luke only gave us a quick summary of it."

"Sure," said Blair.

Once she was done reading it aloud, Farrell let out a low whistle from where he leaned against the wall. "That's some whacked shit. This person obviously believes himself to be in love with you."

"That doesn't mean he is, though," River cut in. "Stalkers are often looked upon as pathetic, weak, socially inept people who have a tendency to develop silly infatuations and can get a little carried away. They're often pitied and not thought of as particularly dangerous. But that isn't always true."

"Did you ever get the feeling that anyone had been inside your cabin while you were gone, Blair?" asked Aspen. "Did any of your things get taken or moved around?"

She shook her head.

"That probably would have been his next step," Aspen hedged.

"Possibly. Not all stalkers exhibit the exact same patterns," said River. "They're not all cut from the same cloth. And the motivations for their actions can differ from person to person. Stalkers all have one thing in common—anger. They have a *lot* of repressed anger, and it's not always directed at whoever they're harassing. Sometimes the rage stems from a past event or the hurt they felt after being slighted by an ex."

Pausing, River refocused his gaze on Blair. "This guy, the way he talks … he's delusional for sure. And that's bad. It means he lives in his own self-created reality. You can't reason with people like that. They twist what they see or hear to fit the narrative in their mind and feed their own fantasy."

"Why oh why do stalkers send weird gifts and stuff?" asked Bailey. "I never understood that. They can't seriously think they're going to successfully seduce someone by doing that, can they?"

"They're not out to please or impress or seduce," River explained. "They want to be on that person's mind. They want their attention, and they'll go as far as they have to in order to get it."

Farrell looked at Blair. "He never speaks to you when he calls?"

"No," she replied. "I don't speak either. I hang up as soon as I realize it's him. That's if he doesn't hang up first."

"Good," said River. "Don't change that. Don't talk to him—not even to tell him to go jump up his own ass. The worst thing you can do in a situation like that is attempt to fix it by speaking with him. You can't give him feedback, positive or negative. Otherwise, it'll feed into his belief that he matters to you. He'll love that he's getting to you; that he's on your mind just as you're on his. It would be better to change your cell number and be careful who you share the new one with. Change your email address, too. And if you're on social media, temporarily close your accounts—give him no way to contact you."

Blair dipped her chin. "I can do that. He's never reached out to me through social media platforms before, but he might resort to it when he no longer has my cell number."

Luke gently squeezed her thigh. "You're safe in our building. The security measures are tighter than ever. He won't get to you there."

"Stay away from any places you frequent, like certain restaurants or whatever," River recommended. "And if you have any routines, now is the time to change them. At least for a little while."

"The only routines I had were based around my position of pack enforcer," said Blair. "I'm no longer part of the pack, so …"

"You have to bear something in mind," said River. "He's not going to react well to being stonewalled. He's going to hate that he has no access to you. He might become aggressive toward you."

"I'd say that's already a probability," said Aspen, glancing from Luke to Blair. "You two will be mated soon. He'll hate that. His fantasy is that she's *his* mate."

River scratched his jaw. "It's not really as simple as that. What you have to understand about people like this is that they're not truly in love. They're not filled with soft, fuzzy feelings. What they feel is more like a black mania. They want to *control* the person they're obsessed with. They want to take over every aspect of their victim's life. He wants Blair, yes. He has deluded himself into believing that she wants him as he does her. He may view her as his perfect mate. But in truth, she's more like a trophy to him."

How lovely.

He turned back to Blair. "Stalking is essentially mental assault. A cat and mouse game. He'll try to confuse you. Terrorize you. Isolate you. The end goal is to own you. To have the ultimate power over you. And if he can't get that, he'll instead seek to destroy you. That's why you have to be very careful, Blair. Do not mistake him for some lonely, lovesick loser who's more of a danger to himself than others. In this instance, the one person in the most danger from him is you—never forget that. Not even for a second."

CHAPTER FIVE

Waiting in the front yard while Vinnie said his goodbyes to the Alpha pair, Luke curled an arm around Blair's shoulders and pulled her close. Restlessness buzzed beneath his skin, making his muscles tight. Talking of the danger that lingered around her had left him as edgy as his pacing cat.

Luke scanned the entire cul-de-sac. One of the pride whistled as he washed his car. Another tended to her flowerbeds while chatting with her neighbor, who was drinking coffee. Although there was nothing out of the ordinary to note, Luke's unease remained. It probably wouldn't leave his system until the threat to Blair was gone.

"Well, that was intense," she said, her voice low.

He glanced down at her. "The things River said spooked you?"

"I wouldn't say they spooked me. But I guess I was guilty of branding my harasser a sick and pathetic—albeit dangerous—loser. I didn't see that there was so much more to the gift sending and prank calling than simply getting my attention. I didn't consider all the angles of the situation."

"And so you'll be sure to follow River's advice?"

"Yes, I will. Starting with changing my number."

Luke pressed a kiss to her forehead. "Good girl."

"Well, it's common sense to—" She cut off as her cell began to chime. Blair whipped her phone out of her pocket. "It's Embry," she told Luke before answering, "Hello."

"*I wish you'd told me about the email sooner*," said the Alpha, the cell's volume setting loud enough for Luke's enhanced hearing to pick up the words.

"I only received it the night before last," said Blair. "And I genuinely did mean to come to you about it once I'd brought Luke up to speed on everything. Though I was worried you'd have insisted someone was either pranking me or merely trying to poke at Luke."

"*I would not have ignored or attempted to downplay this, Blair. Be very assured that I will look into it. I don't believe that the email was written by one of the pack, but I'll question everyone in any case.*"

She narrowed her eyes, no doubt annoyed that he wasn't open to the idea of his pack mates having some involvement. "You think they'd admit to it?" she asked.

"*No. But I'm good at making people slip up.*"

Blair didn't dispute that, so Luke figured it had to be true.

"*I hope you'll call your mother at some point.*"

"We're not doing this, Embry," Blair firmly stated. "Let it alone."

A loud sigh. "*All right, fine. Just let me say one last thing—she might have a funny way of showing it at times, but she loves you more than life, Blair. That's one thing I can say with complete certainty.*" With that, he hung up.

Blair returned her cell to her pocket as she looked up at Luke. "I take it you heard all that."

He nodded. "Embry sounded edgy and tense. Maybe the email whipped off his blinders, or maybe …"

"My mother's pressuring him to insist I return, and he knows that he has to first sort out the present situation and prove it's safe for me to go back there," Blair finished. "Yeah, I had the same thought."

"But you're not going anywhere, are you?" It came out sounding like more of a statement than a question.

"No, I'm not. Lucky you."

His lips canted up. "Oh, I'm definitely lucky." He dropped a soft kiss on her mouth.

"On a darker note, you need to be careful. Like you said, whoever's harassing me will feel like I betrayed them. They'll be angry with you for claiming me. They might target you. And yes, I know you'd prefer that than for them to focus on me. But I need you to be safe. Don't make yourself a target to protect me. You'd ask the same of me."

He sighed, unable to claim that she'd gotten it all wrong and he'd never intended to somehow goad the son of a bitch. His mate would know it for the lie that it was. "I'll be careful."

Just then, his father approached and announced he was ready to leave. Luke kept Blair's hand in his as the three of them exited the cul-de-sac. As they walked along the street of stores, he kept a close eye on their surroundings; noted every pedestrian, checked every rooftop, glanced at the drivers of each car that passed.

He noticed that Blair was doing the same. She didn't seem worried or nervous. There was a determined set to her jaw that told him she was resolute on identifying her stalker as opposed to allowing him to terrorize her.

Vinnie split off at one point, heading to the antique shop above which he lived. Luke and all three of his siblings had once lived there with him, but only Damian hadn't yet moved out.

As Luke and Blair strolled through the parking lot outside their complex, he remained on high alert, taking in everything. Other than Camden and Luke's cousin Alex, who were stood outside the main doors talking, no one was in sight.

"I don't recognize the dude with Alex," said Blair. "Is he a new member?"

"That's Camden, the tiger shifter I mentioned," Luke replied. "He's also Aspen's mate."

"Really? I sensed she was mated, but I didn't know …"

Blair's words were lost on Luke as a dark-blue van caught his eye. The unfamiliar vehicle was slowing as it neared the parking lot. Instinct made his scalp prickle in unease.

Luke sensed his mate tense. He knew she'd either picked up on his discomfort or that something about the situation must have put her on high alert.

The van slowed a little more. The front passenger window lowered. Metal glinted as something poked out of it.

Luke was on the move even before tranquilizer darts zipped through the air. Camden quickly dived to the side, dodging many of the darts, but two buried themselves in his arm. He managed to get back on his feet, but it was clear that his equilibrium was shot to shit.

Two men jumped out of the van's side door and made a grab for the staggering tiger shifter, but Luke's yell had them freezing. One male swore and dragged the other back into the van before it sped away with a screech of tires.

Alex pursued the vehicle just as Camden fell to his knees, his eyes glazed. Luke caught the guy just before he landed face first on the ground.

"Let's get him inside," said Blair, all business even as a sense of urgency laced her voice, and keyed the code into the entrance's security pad. She shoved open the door and indicated for Luke to enter first.

He tossed the tiger over his shoulder and retreated into the building.

One of the pride members in the lobby came rushing toward them. "What happened?"

Luke felt his jaw harden. "Some shitheads tried to kidnap Camden. *That's* what happened." Striding toward the elevator with Blair at his side, he noticed she was texting someone.

"I gave Tate a heads-up," she said.

Luke went to nod in satisfaction, but then she thrust her hand into Camden's pocket. "What are you doing?"

Dangling a set of keys, she replied, "It'll be best to take him straight to his apartment so he'll wake in his own bed. There's a chance his tiger could push for supremacy while Camden's beginning to come round. If the pissed-off-cat isn't entirely sure where he is, he could go AWOL."

She was right. Luke should have thought of that himself. Proud of her for remaining so clear-headed, he would have smiled if he wasn't grinding his teeth at what had been done to his pride mate.

Inside the apartment that Camden shared with Aspen, Luke placed the unconscious tiger on the bed. He was just exiting the bedroom when Aspen came charging into the apartment like a damn Valkyrie in a fury. Without a word, she disappeared into the bedroom.

The Alphas, Bailey, Farrell, and one of the pride's healers Sam walked through the open front door, closing it behind them.

"What in the motherfucking hell happened?" demanded Havana.

While Sam checked on Camden, Luke gave the others a detailed account of what went down. He kept a surreptitious eye on a silent Blair, alert for signs of delayed shock. She was generally cool under pressure—it was one of the things that would make her a good Beta female—but he nonetheless needed to feel sure she was okay.

"I don't believe this shit," said Bailey. "Did you get a good look at the assholes?" Her eyes danced from Luke to Blair.

"They wore masks," he told her.

"I got a text from Alex," announced Tate, his phone in hand. "He wasn't able to track the van for long, it eventually left him in the dust. He did memorize the number plate, though. He called River to pass it on"—Tate looked at Blair—"but River said you'd already texted it to him."

Luke blinked at her. "You did?"

She nodded. "He gave me his cell number in case my harasser strikes again, remember? I asked him to run the plates. He'll hopefully get back to us soon."

Just then, Sam exited the bedroom and confirmed what they'd suspected—the darts weren't poisonous, they simply aimed to sedate. It was a relief, but it didn't lessen anyone's anger. Tate thanked the healer for coming, and Sam then left.

"Personally," began Havana, "I don't think it's a coincidence that a human was asking questions about Camden a few days before he was almost taken."

"Neither do I," said Tate. "We need to speak with the human."

Blair tensed at the deadly note in the Alpha male's voice. It was clear that by *speak*, he meant torture. And each person in the room nodded in bloodthirsty approval. "You'll have to be careful how you go about it."

"In what sense?" asked Tate.

"You can't approach him as a pride unless you're comfortable exposing what you are," said Blair. "Sure, it may be that he's connected to the attempted kidnapping—if that's the case, you can kill him, and then he can't pass on that you're not human. But you don't yet know for certain that you'll have a reason to kill him. He might not be involved."

Havana licked her front teeth. "She's right. I suppose we can have Camden do the questioning. We'll act as if we're simply there to have his back. If it turns out that the human is guilty of anything—"

"I can let out my snake so she can bite him, yes?" asked Bailey, her hands joined as if in prayer.

It was Tate who answered. "I don't see why not."

The black mamba shifter pumped her fist.

"We still have the human's address, right?" asked Tate.

"I have the info that River sent us in my phone," Luke told him.

"Then as soon as Camden is ready to leave, we'll go have a nice, long talk with the human," said Tate. "His name is Davis Regent, if I remember correctly."

Luke nodded. "That's him."

Hearing her phone beep, Blair slipped it out of her pocket and peeked at the screen. A message from her brother read: *If you don't take my next call I'm gonna haul ass to Luke's building and hunt you down.*

Blair silently swore. He'd tried calling her several times in the past fifteen minutes but—considering the severity of the current pride situation—she'd ignored each call with the intention of contacting him later. Knowing he'd live up to his promise, she looked at Luke. "I need to speak with Mitch or he's going to come find me. My guess is he's heard about the email." She gave Luke's arm a brief squeeze and then headed to the kitchen. She called her brother, who answered after two rings.

"I can't believe you didn't tell me about that goddamn email," Mitch complained without so much as a hello.

"I take it Embry debriefed you," she said.

"He told a few of us just now. Kiesha's gonna lose her mind. Why didn't you say anything to me about it?"

She rubbed at her forehead. "Mitch—"

"Hey, I get why you didn't bother taking the matter to Embry. He's been a condescending ass toward you lately, treating you like you're being dramatic. But *I* would have taken the email seriously. You know that."

"I do know that."

"So why didn't you tell me?"

"Two reasons." She leaned back against the counter. "One, I wanted to tell Luke first—God knows I kept him in the dark long enough. Two … Let me ask you a question. Who would you say is responsible for all of this?"

"Probably some stranger who saw you in the street, developed all sorts of messed-up fantasies in his head, and is now acting as if you belong to him."

"And that's why I said nothing to you about it. You're determined to believe it's an outsider. I understand why. But I'm not quite as trusting as you. Way too many things point at the probability that my so-called admirer is from the pack. You would have argued against that. You would have hated that I felt unsafe in the pack, so you'd have gone above my head to Embry, wanting him to back you up on it in the hope that I'd then feel better."

Moments of silence ticked by. "Okay, so *maybe* I would have told him but—"

"You'd have meant well, I know. You'd have thought you were looking out for me. And I couldn't have been mad at you for it, especially when I knew you would have been uncomfortable with keeping a secret from your Alpha. But I still would have hated that you'd told him."

Mitch muttered something beneath his breath. "I can see why you might suspect that it's someone from our pack, and I'm not saying you shouldn't—I want you to be careful who you trust right now. It's just that … we've grown up around these people. I feel like we'd know if one of them was so damn twisted inside."

"I thought that at first but, as Luke pointed out, people like that wear masks. They're often very good at blending. We can't say for sure that that isn't the case here."

He sighed. "I guess I can't deny that." He paused. "Mom and Dad will find out about it soon, so expect a phone call from them."

"I haven't heard from Mom at all since I left."

"She isn't talking much to anyone. She seems … stunned. Like it never occurred to her that you'd truly ever leave."

"She'd convinced herself that her plan to stop me from one day joining the Olympus Pride would pay off. She wouldn't have allowed herself to consider that it might fail."

Mitch puffed out a breath. "I've tried talking to her about it, but she shuts me down every time I bring it up. She's taking the admirer situation seriously now, though. She told Embry that he'd better ID him fast. She's convinced that it can only be Gabriel. Embry's next move is to find and question him. She could be right, you know."

"Yes, she could. She'd just better not pin it all on him so she can say 'case closed' and pressure me to return to the pack."

"You keep saying *the* pack, not *our* pack. You're really not coming back, are you?" The question held no judgement.

"No. I'm where I need to be." Where she wanted to be.

"Has Luke claimed you yet?"

Memories of this morning flashed to the forefront of her mind. "Not yet, but he will."

"Why the delay?"

"Involuntary cockblockers."

Mitch made a weird sound. "I don't want to hear my sister say 'cock.' As far as I'm concerned, you don't know what one is, you'll forever remain a virgin, and any children you may bear will be immaculate conceptions.

Misogynistic, yeah, but whatever."

She snickered. "You're an idiot." Her pulse skittered as Luke stalked into the kitchen, stirring up her hormones with all that natural smolder. "I gotta go."

"Keep me posted, Blair. Don't hold anything else back from me. I want to be kept in the loop—you're my sister, I sort of love you."

A snort popped out of her. "*Sort* of love me?"

"Well, I can't be certain."

She rolled her eyes. "Like I said, you're an idiot." She promised to keep him updated and then ended the call. Studying Luke's grim expression, she asked, "What's wrong?"

He moved to stand between her legs. "I just heard from River. The plates on the van were false."

She sighed. "Of course they were. It can never be that easy, can it?"

"A group of us are going to grab Davis Regent from his house later on this evening so that Camden can question him."

"Question him where?"

"We usually hold interrogations at my dad's apartment. But we don't want to take the human there, so we're going to use the pack's small motorhome. We can haul him inside, question him, and then … well, what happens next will depend on what he has to say."

"Sounds like a plan. You know I'm coming with you, right?" Blair narrowed her eyes when she sensed he'd object. "Don't. This particular plan is not fraught with peril. There'll be a bunch of us. I will be fine. And if you try to dispute that, you'll just be lying your ass off." And yet, he *still* seemed about to argue. "Pick your battles wisely. You won't win many of them and you know it."

His jaw went tight. "It could get ugly."

"I know all about 'ugly.' Bush dogs take it to the extreme, and I've been present for plenty of interrogations. It was all part of my enforcer training. You know that. So quit being difficult, we have things to do. Regent ain't gonna question himself."

Luke drew in a long breath through his nose. "All right, we'll both go."

She pursed her lips. "Not sure why you thought I needed your consent, but okay."

Humor briefly flickered in his eyes. "Brat." Luke skimmed a hand over her hair. "Before we leave, how did your conversation with Mitch go?"

Shoving her phone back in her pocket, she replied, "He isn't happy that he learned about the email from Embry, and he struggles with the idea that someone from the pack could have sent it. But he's not dismissing the idea out of turn. He's going to be open-minded."

"Good. Because it might be that he's the only person in the pack who will be."

CHAPTER SIX

Sitting on the motorhome's sofa, Blair watched as Camden dragged Davis Regent into the vehicle. They'd reached the human's house only to find it empty, so Luke had parked the motorhome out of sight while they waited for Davis to make an appearance. It had been no more than half an hour later that the human had pulled up in his driveway.

He hadn't been hard to grab. Blair had observed from the window as Camden crept up behind Davis, slapped a hand over his mouth, and then dragged him away. Even now, the human struggled and yelled against Camden's palm, but the tiger wasn't whatsoever fazed.

Given that Davis's closest neighbors were half a mile away, there'd been no great need to muffle his shouts. Blair suspected that Camden had done it merely to ramp up the fear factor.

Right then, the tiger unceremoniously dumped Davis on the floor, who quickly scrambled backwards until his back met a wall. The human's eyes bounced from person to person. The Alphas, Aspen, Bailey, Alex, and Blair steadily stared back at him—all casually sprawled around the space, looking right at home.

The engine came to life, and then Luke drove away, muttering something to Farrell, who was riding shotgun. The plan was for her mate to drive around aimlessly. If the human was innocent, they'd let him live and ditch him somewhere. If he wasn't innocent, well, his fate would not be a painless one.

The smell of fear permeated the vehicle as Davis gaped up at Camden, his face ashen, his breathing heavy.

The tiger glared down at him, looking so unnaturally calm it was eerie. "You know who I am."

Swallowing, Davis wildly shook his head.

"Yes, you do," said Camden, his voice flat. "You've been asking questions about me. I heard all about it. And, of course, I have to wonder just why you would have any interest in me."

Davis's panicked gaze again darted around the motorhome, examining every face, probably searching for a possible ally.

"If you're wondering why they're here, well, to be frank ... they don't trust that I won't kill you. Don't think that means you're completely safe from me. They have no issue with me hurting you in order to get the info I want." Camden took a lurching step toward the human, who promptly flinched. "Now, why don't you tell me why you went around asking questions about me."

Davis's lips trembled. "I-I was just curious."

"About?"

"Tiger shifters."

"And why would that be?"

"I've always liked wild cats. Especially tigers. There's so much that humans don't really understand about them, though. I thought a tiger shifter might know things about full-blooded tigers that would help fill the gaps in our knowledge. So when I heard a local person was one of your kind, well, I thought maybe I could talk to you. I meant to, but then I was worried you might take offense or something."

"You were just curious?"

Davis nodded twice, his eyes wide.

Blair saw Aspen grind her teeth, as if biting back words. It was clearly killing her to stay out of this.

Camden pursed his lips. "I suppose I can educate you on a thing or two. Do you know that, out of all the big cats, a tiger's claws are the sharpest?" Lifting his hand, he squatted in front of Davis. "They can grow up to four inches long." He sliced out his own claws, causing Davis to jerk in horror. "Mine are sharper. Longer. And I will drag them down your fucking face if you don't tell me the truth."

"I wasn't lying, I—" Davis cried out as Camden lashed out wicked fast, leaving diagonal claw marks along his face.

The scent of blood laced the air, making Blair's inner animal growl in approval. Her legs quivered with the urge to join in and sink her teeth into the human.

"Next time, I'll slice deeper," Camden warned him. "No more lies."

Davis began to sob. "I told you, I didn't lie."

Camden sliced his claws down the other side of his face. "Yes, you did. I want the truth."

"I gave you the truth!"

Camden struck again, clawing his chest this time, ripping cloth and mercilessly shredding skin. "The. Truth."

"What I told you was true, I swear!" He choked on a pained breath as Camden buried his claws in Davis's thigh. The human's fists clenched as he stared down at the sight in disbelief.

"You can spout denials as many times as you want," said Camden, still cool and composed. "But you're mistaken if you think I'll buy your bullshit." Keeping his claws buried in the human's thigh, Camden sharply twisted his hand.

Davis jerked with an agonizing cry. "Stop, stop, stop, *please*!"

Instead, Camden wiggled his claws. "If you want the pain to end, all you have to do is tell me what I want to know."

"I did it for my friend!" the human burst out.

Camden withdrew his claws but kept his hand elevated over Davis's thigh. "What friend?"

"A guy I know," replied Davis, his breaths sawing in and out of him. "He wanted to be sure you were really the tiger shifter that recently fought with another tiger shifter. He wanted to know ..."

"What?"

"Your habits, your address, if you were a loner."

"Why? Why would he want to know?"

Davis squeezed his eyes shut. "He's a poacher."

Blair's spine snapped straight, and her inner animal went very still.

"Poacher?" Camden ever so quietly echoed.

"He snatches shifters," said Davis, shaking. "Sells fur or tusks or teeth or whatever. Sometimes even heads or full bodies."

"Go on."

"He wants your head and fur. He said there's someone who'll pay good money for them, but he didn't say who. I-I think he works for some kind of company."

The shifters in the vehicle all exchanged grim looks, and Blair knew they were about to drop the human act. Because this waste of skin here wasn't going to live through this night.

Tate leaned forward, pinning Davis with a fierce glare. "And you, what, find information for him on any shifter he might like to capture?"

Davis licked his lips. "Yes, but that's all. I never do anything but report information."

"That makes it okay, does it?" Aspen clipped, rising from her seat. "His name." It was a demand.

"Chester Wilkins." The confession spilled out of him.

Havana hummed. "Where will we find dear old Chester?"

His shoulders hunched up, Davis reluctantly reeled off an address. "You won't find him there for at least a week. His wife doesn't know that he does poaching on the side. So when he needs a few days to capture a shifter and deliver body parts to a client, he tells her he's going on a business trip."

"What about his buddies?" asked Alex.

Davis's brow creased. "Buddies?"

"Fellow poachers," the wolverine elaborated.

"I don't know anything about them," said Davis. "I only know he sometimes works with a group of three other guys, depending on how big the game is."

Aspen flexed her fingers. "The *game*, huh?"

Bailey cricked her neck. "Can I hurt him now?"

"Oh, we can all hurt him," said Havana, standing. "But let's be careful not to let him die *too* quickly."

Davis's eyes went wide and bright with panic as everyone began to gather around him. His gaze slammed back on Camden. "Y-you, you said—"

"That they were here to ensure I didn't kill you." Camden shrugged. "I lied."

Just then, the vehicle slowed to a halt.

Davis once more scanned the faces around him and then settled his attention on Blair. "You can't let him kill me!"

What, he thought her "sweet" appearance meant she was his hope of getting out of here? Wrong. "Why not? It should be fun."

"So, Davis, you're some kind of animal lover." Bailey twisted her mouth. "How do you feel about snakes?" And then she shifted into her mamba form.

Davis whimpered, huddling against the wall in fright.

Tate scratched his cheek. "What you failed to realize, Davis, is that you're the only person here who's actually human."

Blair glanced around. "Anyone have a problem with me lighting him on fire at some point?"

Luke's mouth twitched. "What is it with you and fire?"

"It's so pretty," she said.

"People will notice I'm missing!" Davis yelled, a shake in his voice. "The police will look for me; they'll find out you did this!"

Alex snorted. "How will they find you when there'll be nothing of you left to find?"

Blair wouldn't have thought it was possible for the human's face to go any paler, but she'd been wrong.

He threw up his hands, as if to fend off the shifters glaring down at him. "I only reported information!"

"There's no 'only' about it," snapped Aspen. "The fact that you see yourself as innocent just makes me want to hurt you more."

"Let's take him into the woods outside," said Luke. "There's no need to make a mess in here."

A short time later, once the human was well and truly dead, Alex raised a brow at Tate. "Want me to have my uncles get rid of the body?"

Tate's brow wrinkled. "They're visiting? When did they get here?"

"Last night," replied Alex. "Well, should I call them or not?"

Blair almost snorted at his gruff tone. No one ever took it personally—the surly wolverine possessed few people skills. The only person he made any real effort for was his mate, Bree, who also happened to be the pride's Primary omega.

"Yes, call them," Tate told Alex. "But it disturbs me to know that they'll probably *eat* the body."

Alex shrugged. "Wolverines don't like to waste their food, you know that."

Tate turned to Farrell. "Go scope out Chester's address. I know Davis claimed that Chester won't be there, but I want to be certain. Don't enter the residence; just check out the situation. Call me when you get there and let me know what you find."

"Sure thing." Farrell shifted into his avian form, gripped his cell phone with his talons, and then took to the sky.

Bailey set her hands on her hips. "How absolutely messed up is it that there are actually poachers who go after *shifters*? Animal poaching is bad enough. For people to look upon *us* as animals to the extent that they want our body parts as trophies or whatever … it's sick."

"Don't worry, the bastards will pay," said Tate. It wasn't a statement of assurance, it was a menacing promise. "Once we have Chester, we can find out who his friends are and just who exactly hired him. In the meantime, let's get a little more information on him."

"I'll get River right on it," said Luke before then turning to Blair. "You all right?" he asked, his voice so low it wouldn't carry to the others.

She couldn't resist rolling her eyes. "I'm not shocked or disgusted by anything that went on here tonight, if that's your worry. But it's ever so cute, albeit confusing, that you'd mistake me for queasy."

"Not sure I like that condescending tone, but fine." Luke pulled out his phone. "I need to make this call to River, and then we'll head home." His eyes glinted with promise, reminding her of his earlier vow to claim her tonight.

Blair smiled and lowered her voice as she said, "I hope you don't mind biting and scratching, because me and my animal want you all marked up."

His eyes blazed. "Right back at you, baby."

Having had years to plan how the day of their claiming would go, Luke had had it all planned out in his head—beginning with driving to Sylvan territory on Blair's nineteenth birthday, handing over her birthday gifts, helping her move her things to his place, and then cooking her a romantic meal before he finally took her to bed.

Of course, that plan had been upended by the mere fact that he brought her here early.

Enter the new plan. Which he hadn't properly laid out in his mind. What he'd most wanted was to ensure that the day was special. As such, spending time interrogating a human on the very evening that he finally claimed his mate had been nowhere on Luke's wish list.

He thought about delaying the claiming until tomorrow, but his cat would never stand for it. He doubted Blair or her inner female would either. And with so much currently happening around them, there was no guarantee that tomorrow would be any calmer.

At the very least, he wanted her to be able to wash the day away. So Luke didn't pounce on her the moment they returned to what was now *their* apartment. Ignoring his cat's protests, Luke resisted the urge to take and dominate. He gently herded her into the bathroom, slowly stripped each item of clothing from her body, shed his own clothes, and then ushered her into the shower stall.

Squinting slightly in what appeared to be confusion, she went along with it. But there wasn't a doubt in his mind that she'd attempt to take over if things didn't eventually move fast enough for her liking. His girl had little patience.

As they stood under the hot spray, Luke stroked and soaped her down, every touch reverent with a sensual undertone. He wanted to kindle small flames of arousal inside her; wanted a slow burn to steadily wind her tight until her body was primed for what would come next.

His own body was ready to roll—his blood hot, his skin tight, his dick aggressively hard. The drive to claim her beat at him with a fierce intensity, fueled by the knowledge that he'd very soon answer that drive, rendering his hold on his control a brittle thing.

He'd dreamed of this, of making her officially his, for months. Craved it. Burned for it. Obsessed over it. Until it felt like it was all he lived for.

He massaged her scalp as he shampooed and then conditioned her hair. He spent most of that time gritting his teeth, because her soft hands slid over his body as she washed him down. Each caress was lazy yet still undeniably erotic.

She teasingly skimmed her palm over his cock and then ever so gently whispered her fingers over his balls. He nearly lost it right then. Something he couldn't afford to do. He'd hurt her if he wasn't mindful of her inexperience. Her first time, *their* first time together, wasn't going to be a quick fuck against the shower wall.

Out of the stall, he looped a thick, soft towel around his hips before then holding up a towel for her. Once her feet met the floor mat, he dried her off, gently batting away her hand when she attempted to take over.

She stared up at him, a slight glaze in her eyes, a flush of arousal staining her cheeks, and the scent of her need lacing the air. He couldn't resist dropping his head to swipe his tongue over her lower lip. She slyly captured his tongue and suckled, the teasing little witch.

Luke fisted his hand against the urge to snap it around her throat. "Behave." He kissed her slow and deep, wrestling back the need to ravish her mouth. She palmed the back of his head as she met him kiss for kiss, her free hand yanking the towel from his hips. Her soft fingers curled around his cock and squeezed tight.

He growled. "I said, *behave.*" He tugged her hand away. "You can play with my dick all you want another time. But not here and now." It would eat at what control he had left, and he couldn't afford to lose it.

Once they'd dried off, he lifted her, carried her into the bedroom, and sat her on the edge of the mattress. "Lay back."

Instead, she ran the tip of her finger down his shaft.

He cuffed her wrist, fighting a snarl. "*Blair.*"

"Yup?"

Yup? "Do not fucking test me right now."

"Whyever not?" She leaned forward, as if to lap at his dick.

Hissing, Luke fisted her hair and yanked back her head.

She winced, but her lips curled. "Ah, there you are."

He frowned. "What?"

"Here's the thing. I don't want to get claimed by a diluted version of you. I don't want you to only show me the parts you think I can handle. You don't get to hold back from me—it's the one thing I won't ever tolerate. You wouldn't let me pull that crap either. Take this slow if that's what you want, but don't go all omega on me. Give me *you.*"

Blair metaphorically held her breath, meeting his gaze steadily, unwilling to back down. This was too important. What would be the point in him claiming her if a part of him was locked away the whole time?

Yes, she understood why he'd wish to tone down his natural intensity. An alpha's need for control often became more pronounced in the bedroom—especially when it came to their mates. Given her inexperience, it was natural that he'd worry she'd find it too much.

It was a dumb worry, though.

Blair had been prepared for how he'd be in bed. She knew what she was getting herself into. She was fine with letting him lead so long as he understood she'd never be a passive or full-on submissive participant.

Her inner animal was no less inclined to allow him to hold back. The female wanted to bite him hard and lightly claw him—goad him, poke at him, remind him she wasn't fragile.

Blair raised a brow, daring him to rise to her challenge, knowing it would prick at his dominant instincts.

His eyes momentarily flashed cat. "I'm going to need to take the edge off," said Luke, his voice different now. Not soft and soothing as if she were a skittish animal. It was now low and deep and oozed authority. "I want to be looking at your beautiful ass while I do. I want to mark it with my come. Lie on your stomach."

Not an order she'd expected. Or one she had a problem with. Blair did as he asked, her skin breaking out in goosebumps as he rumbled a low guttural growl.

A hand stroked first one globe of her ass and then the other. She could *hear* him jacking off. Hear his low grunts. Smell his pre-come.

Her pulse quickened. Her mouth went dry. Her inner animal rolled amorously.

Fingertips skimmed along Blair's slit. She moaned, scraping her nails over the bedsheet, as one thick finger slid inside her. He played with her pussy just as expertly as he had that morning, sure and possessive. She was soon damp and aching, bucking back to meet his touch.

Another finger entered her. *Oh, God.* She began pushing back harder, all but fucking herself on his fingers. Her tight nipples repeatedly rubbed against the mattress, sending little streaks of pleasure to her clit. He added a third finger, her pussy spasmed—

A rough groan wrenched out of him as ropes of hot come spurted over her back and ass. "Damn, that's a pretty sight."

She panted, resisting the urge to curse him for not getting her off. He rubbed his come into her skin, writing … something. She wasn't sure what.

"Now I want you flat on your back with your legs spread. Make it happen."

Again with the dominant tone. She couldn't lie, she kind of liked it. "In case you didn't notice, I'm kind of sticky right now. If I roll over, I'll make a mess of the bed."

"Not gonna tell you again."

She bit back a smile and, her nerve-endings raw with anticipation, rolled onto her back. Her breath caught at the look on his face. So cold and carnal and hungry.

He knelt between her spread legs, slid his hands under her thighs, and pulled her closer. "I've been wanting to do this all day." Snaking his rough palms down her inner thighs, he nuzzled her slick folds and then zigzagged his tongue from her clit to her entrance. "This pussy is going to look so good on my cock."

Blair closed her eyes as his tongue swiped through her folds. A tongue that went on to lick and delve and lap like a master—branding her as surely as his teeth had once done. She arched and moaned, scratching at his scalp. Her thighs trembled as her release crept toward her. Then he sank his tongue inside her once more, and Blair imploded right there.

Luke licked his lips. "Move further up the bed." The order vibrated with an urgency that warned her not to mess around. It made her bristle, but she'd asked for this, so she couldn't even complain.

Still a little jittery from her orgasm, Blair blinked hard and did as he asked. He draped himself over her, his eyes dark and ravenous. The feel of every inch of his skin aligned to hers electrified her nerve-endings.

His mouth unexpectedly latched onto her nipple just as his hand palmed her breast. No, she couldn't handle anymore foreplay. She couldn't.

Blair was about to snippily demand he *get moving*, but then he settled his hips more snugly between her own. *Better.* She slid her hands up the sleek, defined muscles of his chest and gripped his broad shoulders. "In me."

"But that's the thing." Gritting his teeth against the urge to slam deep, Luke lodged the head of his dick in her pussy—so slick and scalding hot. "I don't just want to be *in* you." He breezed his mouth along the side of her face to her ear. "I want to fucking consume you. Take you over. Use you all up. Make you feel so possessed you'll never forget who you belong to."

"Then what are you waiting for?"

Luke returned his gaze to hers. "For you to convince me that you want it." He bit her lower lip hard. "Make me believe it."

She swallowed, pricking his shoulders with the tips of her claws. "I want you to fuck me. Claim me. Mark me *inside*, where no one else has ever been."

The latter words shot straight to his cock. His territorialism at an all-time high, he slowly sank into her. A groan got snagged in his throat. Christ, she was tight. If she hadn't been so goddamn wet, he'd have struggled to push any deeper.

His pulse racing, Luke paused when he met the barrier inside her. "Look at me."

Her eyelids lifted, revealing a gaze filled with need and frustration. There was a twinge of discomfort, but he trusted she'd tell him if it was too much.

"Keep your eyes on mine." He reared back slightly and then thrust hard, driving his cock deep, a fierce satisfaction filling him from head to toe. She flinched beneath him with a hiss. He nuzzled her and pressed a kiss to her throat. "Shh, you're good."

It killed him, but he didn't move other than to use his lips, tongue, and teeth on her highly sensitive neck. Little by little, the tension left her body as she adjusted to his size. His cat nudged him, wanting him to move, bite, claim.

She arched, making Luke slide a little deeper inside her. They both groaned. "Well, you gonna make me yours or what?" she challenged.

He snarled. "You're already mine."

Blair gripped his shoulders tighter as he began to move. Jesus, she'd *seriously* underestimated just how big he'd feel when inside her. She felt stuffed full, her pussy *over*stretched. Pain and pleasure blended as his throbbing cock rasped along her supersensitive inner walls. He repeatedly nibbled on her neck, leaving her to wonder when he'd finally bite down.

Each plunge of his dick was slow and sensuous. But not sweet. The thrusts held the bold, dominant, dangerous edge of a warrior staking his claim.

Curling her legs tight around him, she lifted her hips to meet each punch of his own. And, as he gripped her breast while sucking on her pulse, Blair felt her orgasm approaching fast.

She lurched up and sank her teeth into his neck, branding him, *claiming* him.

He swore, going rigid above her. Then he lost it. Every forward roll of his hips was fast, hard, and heavy as he pounded into her like an animal.

She clawed at his shoulders. "Luke …" His teeth clamped around a fleshy spot on her neck and sank deep. Her release slammed into her, stealing her breath. Blair dug her heels into the base of his spine and raked her nails over his back as she came hard, barely feeling the brief flash of pain in her head.

A pain that preceded the mating bond snapping into place.

She sucked in a breath as her world tilted, altering forever. The link was fierce in its strength and intensity. The ball of emotions on the other end of it made her eyes sting. Pride, protectiveness, unconditional adoration, and a possessiveness so deep and wild it was a force all on its own.

Opening her eyes, she found Luke braced on his elbows as he looked down at her. Still panting, she smiled. She was sore and all hollowed out, but … "I want to do that again. Soon. We need to make that happen."

His lips hitched up. "Oh, we will." He dabbed a soft kiss on her mouth. "Our scents have mixed already," he added, his voice velvety with pure male satisfaction.

The combining of scents didn't always happen immediately. It often took certain "steps" for the bond to form.

It didn't surprise her that their bond wasn't yet *fully* formed. They might have known each other a long time and developed a deep emotional connection, but Luke hadn't been completely open with her on certain matters—always seeking to protect her from the ugliness of the world. Of *his* world, in particular … as if he'd feared that sharing them would make Blair feel inclined to take Noelle's advice and choose another mate. *Idiot.* Until those secrets were gone, the frequency of the bond would be jammed.

She wasn't going to hound him about it tonight, though. She wasn't going to ruin the mood by asking him to rip open old wounds. That could wait. For now, she was just going to marvel in the bond, in the joy of what he felt for her, in the fact that she was *finally* irrevocably bound to Luke. And she had the fleeting thought that if anyone tried to part them, the fucker wouldn't live to tell the tale.

CHAPTER SEVEN

The next morning, Luke woke to the feel of warm air feathering over his claiming mark. He quickly became aware that a very naked Blair was half sprawled over him, her face tucked into the crook of his neck. His still-sensitive brand tingled at the feel of her hot breath.

His brand, he thought with a curl of his lips.

They were mated now. Irreversibly bound to each other. Something he'd occasionally worried her mother would find a way to prevent, despite the fact that—even in the beginning, when Luke had been a relative stranger to Blair—his mate hadn't experienced torn loyalties where Noelle was concerned. Blair had always been steadfastly in his corner, her loyalty to him absolute.

It was almost a little surreal to be finally bound to her. For years she had felt *just* out of his reach. So close yet so far.

Not anymore.

She lived inside him now, exactly where she was supposed to be. The knowledge planted itself deep in his system, anchoring him, flowing into his blood, slithering around his bones, smoothing over each and every jagged edge inside him.

The sensation of her soul knitted to his didn't feel whatsoever strange. He'd always had that sense of her being a basic part of him … as if she was engraved into his very being and imprinted on every cell of his body. Blair belonged to him on a level that nothing else ever could or would.

Their bond burned bright, stronger than any steel. He'd psychically touched the knot of emotions that resided at the other end of it. What she felt for him wasn't sweet and tender. It was as fiery and fierce as her personality. She loved him with a ferocity that humbled him—one he returned tenfold.

His sleepy cat did a languid stretch. For the first time in what felt like too long, the feline wasn't restless and moody. He was relaxed. Content. Secure in his hold on Blair.

As memories of their mating flitted through Luke's mind, his cock twitched. She'd so easily rolled with his demands, accepting it was part of who he was; pleasing his cat that she didn't resent that forceful streak both man and animal shared. The way she'd pointblank refused to let Luke get away with holding anything back, trusting he wouldn't take that too far and hurt her … that had touched him.

In general, there'd be very little that she'd let him get away with. Not that she'd fight him on petty shit or put up a protest for the mere sake of it—Blair was too mature for that. But she wouldn't pander to his overprotective nature, fail to call him on his crap, or ever struggle to tangle with him. That thought made him smile.

She stirred, shifting position slightly.

Sensing through their bond that she'd woken, he danced his fingers along the arm that she'd tossed over him. "Morning, baby."

She mumbled a non-intelligible sound.

He felt one corner of his mouth cant up. "Sleep well?"

"Trying to sleep now," she said, a slight slur to her voice. "Woke up 'cause pulses of male smugness are drifting down our bond."

"It'd be impossible for me to not be smug right now." Luke swept his hand down her back and possessively palmed her ass. "I finally have you here, all marked and claimed. Not to mention naked."

"And tired."

"Fucking beautiful, too."

Unable to maintain "cranky" when he said stuff like that and she could *feel* his total sincerity through their bond, Blair smiled against his neck. "And my tits are awesome. Admit it."

He chuckled. "Absolutely awesome. Much like this ass." He gave it a gentle squeeze.

Blair snuggled into him a little more, breathing in their combined scent. He now wore her on his skin just as plainly as he wore the imprint of her teeth. It pleased the possessive heart of her.

That same territorialism had risen inside her like a tidal wave when he took her last night. She understood now why he'd been so sure he'd never manage to have sex with her without also claiming her. The urge to mate that had taunted them for months had intensified by a *thousand* when he had finally slid inside her. She could no more have stopped herself from branding him than she could have stopped herself from breathing. It had been too necessary, too instinctual, too primal.

She wasn't sure how it was for other women after their virginal status altered, but Blair personally felt neither here nor there about no longer having a hymen. Then again, it hadn't been an awkward or incredibly painful experience for her. If so, she might have otherwise felt differently.

"On another note, how is your female this morning?" he asked.

In a word … "Hyper."

"Hyper?"

"She finally has what she wants, so it's put her in a rather excitable mood." Which was massively annoying Blair at the moment, since the little female felt it necessary to yip and bark and butt her head at Blair in an effort to make her wake and go "play." It was like having a small child harass you until you got out of bed in resignation. "How's your cat?"

"More content than he's ever been. And crowing like a rooster."

Her snicker got caught in her throat as a yawn cracked her jaw.

"He's also desperate for some time with both you and your female. We need to let our animals run together at some point today."

"I'm up for it, so long as your cat doesn't try eating my hair again."

"He doesn't try to eat it. Per se. He likes to play with it—"

"Well, it ain't a ball of yarn."

"—and then he gets carried away and ends up nibbling on the strands." Luke doodled circles on her butt with his fingertip. "At least he doesn't nibble on your pinkie."

"Once. My female did that to you *once*."

"It hurt like a mother. Her teeth are like goddamn miniature scalpels."

Dominant males could be such whiners at times. "She only did it because you tried rubbing her belly—she doesn't like that."

"She *showed* me her belly. She rolled right onto her back, her tongue lolling out, looking all playful."

"Well, it's not her fault you fell for the puppy dog act. Some alpha you are." She flinched as the tips of his claws pricked the flesh of her ass. "Ow! That hurts." She bit his neck.

Luke let out a low chuckle, withdrawing his claws. "That bite wasn't much of a punishment, baby." He loved it when his mate marked him—even needed it. "Just to be clear, I'll be doing a lot of things to your ass so it better get used to a little discomfort. I'll be using and ruling every part of you." He had all sorts of fantasies boxed up in his mind. Now that they were mated, he could open that box. "But right now, I have a question."

"Hit me with it."

He rolled onto his side and gently cupped her pussy. "You sore?"

Her pupils dilated. "A little bit."

Luke hummed, urging her to lie flat on her back. "I guess I should kiss it better, then." He did exactly that, not stopping until she came all over his mouth. He then pumped his aching cock and exploded all over her pussy. "I like seeing your skin covered in my come." It was yet another way to mark her as his.

Her face all languid and flushed, she blew out a breath. "I'm kind of sensing that, since this is the second time you've blown your load all over me."

"It won't be the last." He gently tapped her hip. "Shower."

Just as they had last night, they showered together. Luke again washed her hair for her, loving that she let him minister to and pamper her that way. It wasn't always easy for dominant females to shove aside their inborn self-reliance in even the smallest of ways. But Blair didn't bristle or object; she gave him this without hesitation.

Had she not been sore, he would have taken her right then. Later. He'd have her again later.

Washed and dressed, he checked his phone. One particular text made him frown.

"What's wrong?" asked Blair, retrieving her own cell from the nightstand.

"I got a message from Tate. It seems that Chester still hasn't returned home." Once Farrell had scoped the place out the previous night and ascertained that only a woman and two teenagers were inside, he'd called Tate, who'd sent a couple of enforcers to watch the place.

Blair's lips pursed. "It's looking like Davis was telling the truth about Chester feigning that he's on a business trip, then. Do you think it's possible that he and his friends will try to get to Camden again?"

"I do. And I think they'll do it soon. They've only given themselves a week to get the job done, if what Davis said is true."

"Hopefully we'll manage to get our hands on at least one of the poachers when they next strike. If not, we can nab Chester when he returns home. Which he will. He has no reason to go into hiding. It's unlikely that he'd think we'd question Davis or learn Chester's ID some other—*Ugh*."

He felt his brows snap together. "What?"

Glaring at the screen of her cell, she said, "My mother has decided to break her silence."

"And?"

"And I wish she hadn't. The text message is one long-ass lecture. In sum, she's mad that I didn't mention the email to her, she can't understand why I'd suspect one of the pack was behind it, she's hurt that I'd ever think she doesn't want what's best for me, and she maintains that I'll regret mating you so soon and she wants me to know that I can return to pack territory for a 'break' any time I want."

"A break from me?"

Blair shrugged. "You. Mated life. The pride. Who knows? I don't always understand where my mother's trains of thought lead her."

A knock came at the front door.

"I'll get it." Luke wasn't surprised to find that their visitors were his aunt and grandmother. He'd known it was only a matter of time before they turned up to see Blair. Both women had a fondness for her. Ingrid had always been the grandmother that his mate never had. His aunt Valentina had taken Blair under her wing long ago and treated her as a surrogate daughter.

Ingrid smiled. "Morning, darlin'. We thought we'd drop in and see how you and Blair are doing."

Moving aside to let them pass, he said, "She'll be happy to see you."

Valentina's gaze immediately landed on Luke's brand. "Ah, you have mated," she said in her thick Russian accent. "Good. It should have been done months ago," she added with a haughty huff. "You dragged your heels like immature boy who fears commitment."

He frowned, affronted. "It wasn't like that at all. I made a deal with Blair's parents, which you're well aware of."

Valentina flicked her hand. "Bah. There are always loopholes. This you know. Do not give me boring speech about honor. There is no room for integrity in some situations."

That was just the kind of comment he'd expect to hear from a wolverine. They weren't big on ethics. Like *at all.* Particularly Ivanov wolverines. Valentina might have taken her mate's surname of Devereaux, but she was an Ivanov down to the bone.

"Now, where is my Blair?" demanded Valentina.

"I think you'll find she's *my* Blair," he said, but his aunt had already walked off in search of his mate.

Ingrid gave him a tight hug. "Congratulations on your mating, darlin'. Your scent has mixed with Blair's already. That's good. I sense the bond. It's strong. Not yet complete, though."

Something that didn't please his cat. "It soon will be."

"Well, of course it will. You'd stand for nothing else." Ingrid lightly patted his cheek. "I love seeing my favorite grandson so settled and happy."

He snorted. "You call us all your favorite."

"But I'm only truthful when I say it to you."

"Yeah, sure." He followed the sounds of voices into the kitchen, where his mate and aunt were chatting while Valentina switched the kettle on to boil. Watching as Blair embraced Ingrid with a huge smile, Luke felt his chest go warm and tight.

He loved that Blair was so comfortable with his family; that she thought of them as *her* family. That was exactly what they were, but not all people got along well with the relatives of their mate.

He was a perfect example of that.

Luke had tried hard to build some sort of rapport with her family. Only Mitch had been receptive. Les hadn't been rude or difficult like Noelle, but he'd also been nothing more than icily civil.

In general, Luke wasn't a person who needed the acceptance of others. It didn't bother him if someone disapproved of him. It didn't even particularly bother him that his mate's parents had no time for him. But, for her sake, he wished things were different.

Watching her putter around the kitchen—grabbing this, repositioning that—satisfaction filled him. She didn't move around the place like a guest; she moved with the ease of someone who was home. Which she was.

Blair was already stamped all over the apartment. She'd long ago marked it with her scent, her style, her touch, and the brands her animal left here and there.

"You must come for dinner one evening," Valentina announced, her gaze dancing from him to Blair. "I insist. My brothers will come also. It will be nice family meal."

Luke ran his tongue along the inside of his lower lip. "Nice? Really?"

His aunt's eyes widened. "Why would it not be?"

"Because your brothers like to torment and argue with your mate, and they have not one problem with doing it at a dinner table." It made for an uncomfortable situation.

"There is love behind their words."

Luke's brows shot together. "Love?"

"They are not type to say such things. But they do care for my James."

"They've tried to kill him. Several times."

"Well, I do not talk about that."

Luke shook his head with a sigh. "I don't want Blair exposed to their dysfunctional bullshit."

"It's too late for that," his mate cut in, her mouth curved, "I've met them on a number of occasions."

"Yeah, and those occasions were one too many," Luke told her.

Valentina sniffed. "They will seek her out if you keep her from them. They *adore* Blair."

"We'd be happy to come for dinner, Valentina," Blair interjected. "Thank you for the invitation."

"You are most welcome." Valentina cut her gaze to him. "See how easy that was? Always drama with Devereaux males. Even my James. It is in blood, I am sure of it."

Luke snorted. "Ivanov wolverines are the dramatic ones. Jesus, your mother has knocked your father out with chloroform more times than I can count—"

"She had her reasons," Valentina insisted.

"But were they sane reasons?"

Another sniff. "It is not our place to judge what goes on between mates."

Well, Luke *totally* judged them.

"Moving swiftly on," began Ingrid, turning to Blair, "I heard that your mom isn't so pleased that you left with Luke. I don't suppose she's given you two her blessing yet, has she?"

Blair's nose wrinkled. "Noelle thinks I'm too young to mate," she prevaricated.

Valentina sniffed. "Bah. Such foolishness."

Blair felt her mouth quirk. The whole "bah" thing never failed to tickle her. Valentina was regally imperious and blunt as a knife—qualities Blair admired.

"It is never too early for adult shifters to find their mate." Valentina began handing out cups of tea. "Most spend years searching for them. They worry they will not find them. You have been spared those headaches. She should be glad of it. But no. She is selfish woman, wants only to keep you close."

Ingrid sighed. "Maybe things would be different if Noelle hadn't latched onto you to get her through the pain of losing your sister."

Her heart heavy, Blair sipped her tea. "Maybe." Her mother *had* been different before Marianna's death. Softer. More patient. Less strict. Not full of an overprotectiveness that held a panicked edge and birthed an uber controlling streak. "I doubt she'd have ever been okay with me leaving the pack, but she probably wouldn't have been so set against it or created so many issues."

Blair leaned into Luke as he curled a comforting arm around her shoulders. Sometimes, she felt that it would be easier if Noelle was a self-centered bitch who cared nothing for her—Blair could then easily cut her mother out of her life. But there was so much more to Noelle. She might not be cuddly and warm, but she didn't hide that she loved her children. She spoiled both Blair and Mitch. Babied them when they were down or tired. Took care of them in what ways she could without encroaching on their independence.

Although Noelle would rather Luke wasn't in the picture, she'd still invited him to any parties she threw for Blair over the years. She'd never complained about, or tried to make Blair feel guilty for, spending time with him. And when the mating urge kicked in and Blair had been a sexual wreck, it was Noelle who'd been at her side—not cursing Luke, not making snarky comments, just comforting her.

"On a whole other note, my Vinnie told me about your stalker," said Ingrid, pulling Blair out of her ruminations. "The entire pride has been made aware of it. They'll be on alert for anyone acting suspicious. You're officially our Beta female now. We'll all watch out for you, just as you'll watch out for us. That's how it goes."

Blair blinked. It hadn't occurred to her until that moment that she now shared Luke's status. She wasn't nervous about it. She'd prepared herself for it on every level.

She'd tailed Donal for years, learning what it meant to be a Beta. Settling disputes, reporting pride issues to the Alphas, being an ear for those who had problems, breaking up brawls where necessary, and even dealing with indiscretions on behalf of the Alphas would be part and parcel of the position. She was ready to pick up the mantel. She just wasn't sure how hard her pride mates would make it for her to fulfil the role.

"You will get chance to properly meet everyone at your welcome party," said Valentina.

Ingrid nodded. "Bree and the other omegas set the date. It will be in two days' time. Feel free to invite your brother and his mate. Mitch will likely be worrying over whether or not you're happy here. It may put his mind at ease to see that you've been welcomed by the pride with open arms."

Blair's brows flitted upward. "I might just do that. It would go a long way to easing his concerns." As much as she doubted that they'd all *emotionally* welcome her, none were likely to voice or show their displeasure at the party for fear of the repercussions. And if they did ... well, playing with them would be fun. "Now can we have something to eat? I'm starving."

All four of them ate breakfast together. Valentina and Ingrid left shortly after that. Once Luke and Blair had taken care of the dirty dishware, he suggested that they go let their animals run together. They made their way down to the complex's outdoor communal backyard.

There, she was immediately assaulted by the smells of wildflowers, damp earth, stagnant water, and tree bark. Sweeping her gaze over the overgrown grass, thick shrubs, mossy trees, ill-maintained pond, and nonsensical rockeries, she couldn't deny that the large yard looked as neglected as it did chaotic. In reality, though, the small-scale jungle was perfect for pallas cats to play in.

Her female pushed against Blair's skin with an excited yip. The animal had spent lots of time here over the past six years, running and wrestling with Luke's feline. She liked the space a lot and, knowing it was now her territory, she wanted to mark it as hers.

"Don't shift yet," said Luke.

Blair felt her brows dip. "Why not?"

"My cat wants to rub himself all over you—he's not going to settle until he does," said Luke, whipping off his tee. "I want a little time with your female, so I'm going to shift back once you let her out. Then I'll give my cat supremacy and they can play together after that."

More interested in the sleek skin and hard muscle he was revealing than what he was saying, Blair only nodded, drinking in the sight of him as he continued to strip. He was just so damn gorgeous and sexy and lickable. And all hers.

He shifted shape, morphing into a furry creature that, like all his kind, was downright adorable even with his splash of weird. The pupils of his large amber eyes were round rather than vertical. Taller than full-blooded pallas cats—more commonly called Pallas' cats by humans—his body looked less stocky regardless of all that excessively long, thick gray fur. Nonetheless, there was no escaping that he resembled an overfilled plush toy.

She sat back on her haunches. "I've missed you."

He came toward her, looking as fluid and graceful as any feline despite his generous coat. Having a somewhat cranky disposition, he wasn't always in the mood to be petted. That clearly wasn't the case today, because he leapt onto her lap.

"Well, hello." She sank her fingers into his rich, soft fur, admiring the dark snow-leopard-like spots on his forehead and the little black lines across his cheeks that made her think of war paint stripes. "Such a pretty kitty."

He bared a fang even as he rubbed against her chest to mark her with his scent. He might not understand the words, but he wouldn't like the tone in which she'd delivered them.

"Sorry." Knowing his weak spot, she scratched at the creamy white patch of fur on his chin that could also be seen on his throat and inner ears.

His eyes falling half-closed, he purred, all but melting against her.

Blair's female yipped impatiently, wanting to surface and tussle with her mate. *Soon,* Blair promised as she continued to pet and scratch. His small tufty ears pricked up as she whispered compliments to him that Luke no doubt translated.

Finally, the cat climbed off her lap and stretched, gently batting her with his bushy black-tipped tail that was marked by dark rings. Bones then once more snapped and popped, and soon a very naked Luke was squatted in front of her.

He pressed a kiss to her mouth. "If my cat wasn't so determined to have time with your animal, he'd have fallen asleep right there on your lap."

"He was in a very snuggly mood."

"Only because you were the one petting him. He takes a swipe at everyone else." Luke's cock stirred as she began to strip. There was nothing seductive about how she quickly and efficiently took off her clothes, but there was no way for him to remain unaffected by the vision of his mate naked.

She shifted impressively fast, and her female shook her reddish-brown fur as if to settle it. Eerily black eyes studied him for a long moment. She let out a low-pitched bark that was *all* demand.

"All right, all right," he said, stroking a hand over her short fur.

She leaned against his thigh, going pliant with pleasure as he petted her. Unlike his cat, the female liked being stroked. She simply didn't tolerate it from many people.

She was a cute little thing. Like Blair herself, she looked the opposite of fierce and dangerous. Everything about the bush dog was small—her ears, her legs, her tail, her webbed feet. Even her teeth and claws were short, though they were also razor sharp. A small nip or shallow scratch could bring tears to your eyes.

She flopped onto her back, hinting for a belly rub.

He snorted. "Do I look slow to you?"

She wrinkled her little black nose and barked.

"No, I'm not doing it. I like my fingers where they are."

She let out another bark.

"No, I'm not falling for your little trick again." The female was honestly a handful. In terms of behavior, bush dogs were like toddlers. They were mischievous, defiant, curious, playful, failed to think before they acted, and tried to eat anything they could put in their mouths—including poisonous snakes—yet they somehow lived to tell the tale.

Weirdly, they often did handstands and could even run backwards. Normal they were not. And there was really no "managing" them. But they were happy for you to try, because then they could play with your sanity by being a pain in your ass.

She finally jumped to her feet, apparently admitting defeat, and then butted his thigh with her head.

"Yeah, I'm ready." He gave supremacy to his inner animal.

Not much taller than the bush dog, the cat butted his nose against that of the female. She licked at his face in greeting and yipped, wanting to play. But the cat was not done marking her yet.

He rubbed his body along the side of hers, flinching when she bit at his tail. He bared a fang. She gave him a doggy grin. Then she ran.

They spent hours digging, burrowing, wrestling, and chasing each other. When his human began pushing for control, the cat tried nudging the bush dog toward the piles of clothes. She barked and then jumped in the pond.

The cat tapped his tail hard on the ground, growling. She ignored him. He growled louder. She continued to ignore him. He let out a bark-like hiss. She swam further away.

The cat circled the pond, growling and hissing until his mate eventually climbed out. She shook her body hard, soaking his fur with water. He bared his teeth, unimpressed. *Another* doggy grin.

He herded her over to the pile of clothes and then withdrew, giving his human supremacy.

Smiling down at the bush dog, Luke shook his head. "You are just pure trouble." He pulled on his jeans, watching as she did a handstand while scent marking a tree.

Hinges creaked as the door to the complex swung open. Finley stepped out into the yard. *Hell.*

The bush dog instantly went down to all fours, her ears pricking up. Her mood didn't sour, though. No. She started wagging that little tail, and he knew then that she planned to toy with the enforcer if this conversation didn't go well. Which it might not, given the woman's general habit of being somewhat dismissive toward his mate.

His protective instincts rose, urging him to warn the female enforcer to watch her step. But he wouldn't be doing his mate any favors if he did. In fact, Blair would be pissed at him for acting on her behalf.

Whenever Finley had dismissed her in the past, Blair had rolled her eyes. Or snorted. Or snickered. Or otherwise dismissed the woman right back. But being Beta female now, she wouldn't do that any longer. She'd want to establish where she stood in the hierarchy.

Finley strolled toward them, all assertiveness. "Hey, you two." She smiled at the bush dog the way you would a harmless bunny rabbit. It was an insult, pure and simple. Because everybody knew bush dogs were far from harmless.

Knowing the condescending edge to that smile would rankle on his mate, Luke expected the little female to growl or peel back her upper lip. She didn't. She cocked her head, lolling out her tongue, and kept on wagging her small tail.

Finley let out a low snicker, though her features softened in the face of all that puppy-like adorableness. It truly was impossible not to respond to it.

Finley turned to Luke. "I'm sorry about yesterday morning. If I'd known your mate was with you, I wouldn't have disturbed you."

He inclined his head, accepting her apology.

"We really do need to talk. I want to run a few things by you."

He frowned. "You didn't take the matter to Farrell yesterday, since I was occupied?" It would have been the obvious thing to do, given the guy was Head Enforcer.

She blinked. "Well, no."

And he could see that it hadn't even occurred to her to do so. Luke could sense that, for her, it would have felt no different from consulting someone of equal rank. Because Finley's problem was that, in her attempts to act as far more than an enforcer, she tended to forget that she *was* an enforcer.

"You should have," Luke told her. "It is not necessary for you to report specifically to me. Farrell should be more of a go-to person for you than I am. But it often slips your mind that his authority exceeds yours, doesn't it?"

Finley's face flushed, and her mouth firmed.

Eager to return to having quality time with his mate, he asked, "Are any of your concerns urgent?"

"No," she replied, her voice a little brittle.

"Then either take them to Farrell or, if you really feel that the situation warrants the involvement of a Beta, find Blair at some point tomorrow."

Finley's lips parted in surprise. "But she's only …"

"She's only, what?" he prodded, a dangerous note in his tone.

The enforcer peeked down at the bush dog, whose black gaze was pinned on her with such intensity that Finley averted her eyes. "New to her position."

"I don't see what that has to do with anything," he said, his tone cool. "And I don't think it's what you intended to say. Be very careful, Finley. You'd be a fool to underestimate her."

The enforcer glanced down at the bush dog, who was still firmly in the role of man's best friend, and then raised a "I'm seriously supposed to feel threatened?" brow at Luke.

That was when his mate lurched forward.

Finley sucked in a breath, her mouth falling open, her face creasing in pain as the bush dog clamped her jaws around the woman's ankle. "*Ow,* fuck, *get her off, get her off!*"

Try to come between a bush dog and their prey? Not likely. And he felt no need to intervene on Finley's behalf anyway. His mate needed to make her point.

Cursing like crazy, Finley shook her foot, trying to dislodge the little female. Yeah, it wouldn't be that easy. But the enforcer kept trying, still swearing like a sailor.

Her eyes welled up, but she'd get no judgment from him. It was never a case of a "mere ankle bite" when it came to Blair's kind. They went for the most sensitive spot, they dug their teeth deep, and they didn't simply bite down. Nope. They chomped and chewed, making it feel like you were being attacked by a living, breathing meat grinder. And it hurt. Like. Hell.

Now babbling curses in a whiny voice, Finley reached down as if to whack his mate.

"I wouldn't do that," warned Luke. "For one thing, you'd then have to deal with me—which you really don't want. For another, she'll just transfer her teeth to your hand and mangle the fuck out of it."

"She's mauling my ankle!"

"So she is. And you know why. What you don't seem to know is that bush dog shifters have lockjaw. Like a pit bull. If she doesn't want to let you go, she isn't going to let you go. Shaking your foot won't dislodge her."

Finley clenched her fists. "Then order her to let me go!"

"I don't think anyone could *make* Blair or her female do anything. In any case, I'd never bark orders at her—she's my mate, my equal. But you're well aware of that, just as you're well aware of what you have to do if you want her to release your ankle. So do it. Or don't. Your choice."

Annoyance flared in Finley's gaze.

The bush dog started chomping on her foot with renewed vigor.

Finley's eyes bugged, and a high-pitched cry burst out of her. "*Ow, ow, ow!* Shit, okay, okay!" She took a deep breath, relaxed her shoulders, and bowed her head in begrudging submission.

The bush dog released her with a low growl. Then, after an alarmingly quick shift, Blair was up in the enforcer's face, her expression hard and cold. "You're lucky my female is in a good mood, or she wouldn't have stopped at just mauling your foot. And I can promise you right now that if you dismiss me or her ever again, we'll *both* fuck you up in the worst way. And we'll enjoy it. So take that on board, Finley. This will be your only warning."

Blair hadn't yelled, she'd pitched her voice low. But it rang with so much rancor and dominance that it made even Luke's blood run cold.

It also made his dick thicken.

Finley backed away, her eyes on the ground. She then turned and hobbled into the building with as much dignity as she could muster.

Luke drank up his mate's personal space. There were many things he wanted to say to her, including that he was proud of her for not losing her cool, but what came out was … "I am going to fuck the holy hell out of you when we get upstairs."

Blair's eyes blazed, and one corner of her mouth kicked up. "I look forward to it."

Once they were both fully dressed, they returned to the building, sexual tension turning the air between them static. It was as they waited for the elevator that her cell rang.

Still feeling a little worked up after her mini confrontation with Finley, Blair none too gently fished her phone out of her pocket. *Kiesha.* She swiped her thumb over the screen and answered, "Hello?"

"You weren't supposed to leave."

Blair went utterly still as that deep, rough, almost mechanical voice slithered down her spine.

"You're not supposed to be with *him*."

The fuck? She stared up at Luke, who was glaring at the phone so could presumably hear the words.

"This isn't acceptable, Blair," the deep voice went on. "I know you won't sleep with him, but it isn't the point. You're not where you belong."

She broke out in goosebumps. There was something so goddamn creepy about not only how intimately he spoke to her but how confident he was that Luke was no threat to *his* hold on her.

"I know you only wanted to piss off your mother, but … just come home, okay? You're only leading the cat on by staying. He might have convinced himself that you're his mate, but you and me … we know the truth. We know that you're mine. We—"

She hung up fast, sensing how close Luke was to snatching the cell from her hand and roaring at her caller.

His nostrils flared. "That son of a bitch. His? You're not fucking his, you're—shit, give me a minute." He took a calming breath, one hand flying to the back of his head.

She half-expected the phone to ring again, but it didn't. "That voice wasn't natural. He had to have used a voice changer of some kind." Which made her stomach roll, because … "He would only have done that if he knew I'd otherwise recognize his voice. That means I *know* him. And going by his 'just come home' comment, he really is a part of the pack."

Luke drew her to him, curled his arms tight around her, and nuzzled the top of her head. "Don't let him taint what the pack means to you. He's just a piece of shit whose life has reached its expiry date—something he'll soon learn."

"I thought he'd be *crazy* mad at me for being with you; that he'd assume you and I would finally claim each other. But he apparently has it in his head that you're not really anyone of consequence."

Luke nodded. "In his mind, only he matters to you."

When the bastard realized just how wrong he was about that, she suspected he truly would go *crazy* mad. She couldn't say she was looking forward to it.

CHAPTER EIGHT

As Luke entered the kitchen the next morning with a glint of anticipation in his eyes, Blair's inner alarms did a little jangle. She turned away from the coffee machine. "What is it?"

He held up his cell phone. "Just received a message from River. He came through for us. Gabriel has a condo not far from his uncle's house. I have the address here."

Her female got to her feet, her ears pricking up. "Which means we can go question him." Awesome. Because while she still wasn't convinced he—

"It means *I* can go question him," Luke corrected.

Both she and her female stilled. "You can't truly expect me to stay behind." He wasn't serious. He wasn't.

"It's the right decision, Blair."

Okay, so he was serious. And at risk of her punching his throat. She was used to him being all bossy and pushy. It was annoying, but it also challenged her. It had long ago forced her to find and own her strength.

Generally, he was demanding without trying to steamroll her, so she didn't hold it against him. But she also didn't let him get away with it—that wasn't a pattern she intended to change. As such, she asked, "Right for me? Or right for you, since your instinct will always be to cover me in layers of bubble wrap?"

He stuffed his phone in his pocket. "This isn't merely me being an overprotective ass—though, yeah, I'm exactly that when it comes to you. This is me heeding River's advice. He made it clear that it would be a bad idea for you to have direct contact with your stalker, remember?"

"We don't know that Gabriel is that person."

"But it could well be him. And, if it is, a visit from you would be a bad idea. He'll twist that in his head to feed his sick fantasies; he'll tell himself you came to him because it's him you want."

Ugh, did he really have to be rational?

Luke crossed to her and palmed one side of her neck. "I know it will be hard for you to stay behind. I know it will grate on every dominant instinct you have. I know it will grate on your female. But we have to play this smart."

"Don't think I don't know that you like having a reason to insist I stay here."

He sighed, inclining his head. "I'll always rather you were out of harm's way. The mere thought of anything happening to you steals my goddamn breath." He moved closer, soaking up every inch of her personal space. "Knowing there's someone out there who believes you belong to them, who wants to *take* you from me … yeah, I'm not handling that well. It plays on my mind day and night. As you know, newly mated shifters struggle more with their protective instincts, especially if the bond is only partially formed—that makes this situation harder. Not gonna lie to you, I'm going to be unreasonable at times, but that's not what this is."

Blair sighed, unable to dispute that. He had every right and reason to ask that she didn't interact with Gabriel. She'd ask it of Luke if the situation was reversed.

"I'll wait in the car while you speak to him." She lifted a hand when Luke went to object. "It's the best deal you're getting, so don't waste your breath arguing. There's no danger in me coming along for the ride. You'd be lying if you said otherwise."

Luke felt his jaw harden … because she was right. And he didn't like it.

Even the mere thought of parting from her made him antsy—he wanted to be with her, protect her, strengthen their bond—but he needed her to stay home, where he knew she'd be safe. He didn't want her in even the general vicinity of a male who could possibly be stalking her, even if that male had no clue she was close by. His cat was just as opposed to it—he clawed at Luke's insides, insisting he refuse to make any such concession.

"I give you my word that I'll stay in the vehicle," she vowed.

"Then what would be the difference in you waiting here? In both cases, you wouldn't see or speak with Gabriel."

"This isn't about him. It isn't about my wish to question him. It's about *you*. I want to be close in case you need me. You probably won't. But I want to be there as a precaution."

Feeling an ache begin to build in his temples, he exhaled heavily. "Blair—"

"It goes against your every protective instinct to go along with this, I know."

"Then why push me on it?"

She flicked up a brow, visibly bristling. "What about *my* protective instincts, Luke? Don't they count?"

"Of course they do, but—"

"But, what, you don't feel you need me to have your back so I should just suck it up and let this go?" she asked, her tone *daring* him to agree.

"I never said that."

"I'm right, though, aren't I?" She gently poked his chest. "You listen here, Luke Skywhisker—"

"I thought we agreed you'd stop calling me that." Their "agreement" had lasted all of a month.

"You're not the only person in this relationship who gets to invoke their protection rights," she said, ignoring him. "That's not how this works, so don't even entertain the idea that things will play out differently between us. Though it doesn't surprise me that you'd think you'd get away with that shit."

He slid his hand around to her nape and smoothed his free hand up her arm. "Baby—"

"Oh no, don't bother changing tactics and trying to sweetly coax me into giving you your way. That ain't gonna work either."

He felt his lips thin. Well, it had been worth a shot.

"Bottom line? I can't sit here twiddling my thumbs while you're heading off to essentially confront a person who could be dangerous to us—and yes, you *will* be in danger if he's our boy, since he's going to sense you're partially bonded to someone; he'll realize our scents have twined, so he'll know it's *me* you've claimed. More, he'll know it means *I've* claimed *you*. Who knows how he'll react?"

"He might not react at all. He might hide his rage and come at us later."

"Or he might take the opportunity to get rid of you there and then."

The bastard could certainly try, but he wouldn't succeed. Still ... "If it will put your mind at ease, I'll take Deke to Gabriel's condo with me."

"You having an enforcer with you will put my mind at ease, thanks."

Relieved she'd stay behind, Luke held back a smile, figuring she wouldn't appreciate it.

"I'll feel a whole lot better waiting in the car outside Gabriel's building when I know you have someone at your side."

Luke's urge to smile died a fast death. "His condo could overlook the parking lot, in which case he could potentially spot you if he glanced out of his window."

"So take a vehicle that has tinted windows. I know the pride owns a few. No, don't even try to conjure up another pretty excuse as to why I shouldn't go with you. I told you before, this is the best deal you're getting. So can we be done with this now?"

Luke let out a resigned sigh. "Fine," he muttered, knowing he wouldn't convince her to change her mind. His cat rumbled a put-out sound, now annoyed with both her and Luke. "But we'll also take Isaiah with us. He'll remain in the vehicle with you."

Her eyes flared. "You don't trust that I'd stay put?"

Luke felt his brows snap together. "There's no doubt in my mind that you'd keep your word unless there was an emergency that called for you to break it." He trusted her utterly and completely. "I'll simply feel better if you're not alone and have an enforcer with you, much as you'll feel better if I have Deke with me."

She licked her front teeth. "All right."

Luke grunted. "Good." He dropped his forehead to hers. "You're as stubborn as any alpha. You know that?"

In Blair's opinion, that was a good thing. He'd otherwise walk all over her. They'd never have a balanced relationship if that were the case. She was happy to let him lead in certain situations—such as in the bedroom, since that *totally* worked out for her. But she'd never be a partner who failed to speak up or demand to be counted, especially if the matter at hand was important to her. "I do know that. Noelle complains about it often."

"Yeah, well, fuck her."

Blair snickered, melting against him as he curled his arms around her. "Now that we've established I'll be coming along, I need to ask something of you. When you speak to Gabriel, don't outright accuse him of harassing me. He's had enough of people fingering him for crimes they have no proof he committed."

"You aren't at all open to the theory that he killed his parents? Or is it that you just don't want to believe it?"

She felt her nose wrinkle. "It's not that I've closed myself off to the possibility of it, which is why I asked that you don't speak to him alone—I know there's every chance he could be as callous as some believe. It's just ..."

"What?"

"He was ten years old, Luke. *Ten.* And yeah, I know kids are capable of such cruelty, but it's not common. Gabriel was strange for sure, but not cruel. Plus, I simply don't see why he would have done it. His parents weren't abusive, from what I saw. He didn't hate them, unless that was something he hid *really* well. It makes no sense to me that he'd have killed them."

"Sometimes, it's not about cruelty or hate. It could be that he felt nothing for them. That he wanted a certain something and they were some sort of obstacle it seemed logical to him to get rid of."

Blair gave a weak shrug, unconvinced. "Maybe."

"As for your request ... I won't outright accuse him of stalking you, but I also won't deny he's a suspect if he asks," said Luke.

She briefly curled her arms tighter around him. "Thank you."

Luke kissed her hair and then pulled back slightly. "Before we head to his building or do anything else, we need to get your cell number changed. The sooner that's done, the better."

She nodded. "I've changed my email address and closed down my social media accounts."

"Good. We want to make things as difficult for the prick stalking you as possible."

"Just be braced for him to react badly or do something drastic to reach me."

Luke caught her face in his hands, his gaze serious. "He won't get to you. And if he tries, I'll butcher him."

"Not before I slit his throat."

"Hmm, we'll discuss that another time."

"You mean you intend to talk me into agreeing for *you* to make the killing blow." Blair shook her head. "I don't think so."

"We'll see. I can be very convincing," he added, his voice dropping to bedroom territory.

She smiled. "So can I."

His eyes heated. "I don't doubt it."

Standing in the elevator of Gabriel's apartment building, Luke slid a brief look at Deke. The enforcer was a tough bastard armed with a mean right hook that could take a man down with a single punch. Little rattled Deke or garnered an emotional reaction from him. In fact, he seemed to mostly operate on only three settings—chill, tense, or surly. Recently, the latter was the most prevalent. And the guy was being very tight-lipped as to why.

"Are you going to finally tell me what's been bugging you lately?" Luke asked.

Deke cast him an unreadable glance. "No."

"Then maybe you could tell me why your animal is constantly in a foul mood and picking fights with any cats who get too close."

The guy's jaw hardened.

"Is it something to do with Bailey? I've noticed your surliness hits whole new levels when she's near." The way Luke saw it, she was either at the source of the enforcer's frustration or she was merely exacerbating it by … well, by being Bailey—someone who delighted in driving people nuts.

A muscle in Deke's cheek ticked. "Just leave it."

At that moment, the elevator doors opened. Stepping out, Luke said, "The pride will only give you so much space to work through what's wrong."

Deke gave a single nod of acknowledgment.

They both strode along the hallway, stopping when they finally reached Gabriel's front door. On high alert, Luke wrapped his knuckles on the door. It was a few moments before it opened, revealing a lean, blond, smartly dressed male.

"Gabriel Sanders?" Luke asked.

The male glanced from him to Deke, his face blank. "Yes."

Luke eyed him closely, not willing to miss a single micro-expression, as he added, "My name is Luke Devereaux. I'm the Beta of the Olympus Pride."

Recognition flashed in the cool-blue eyes that gazed at him. "What can I do for you?" he asked, his voice so flat it rubbed Luke's cat the wrong way.

"There's currently some … activity going on around my mate," Luke replied. "I believe you know her."

"If the whispers I heard that you are the predestined mate of Blair Kendrick are true, yes, I know her." Gabriel leaned forward slightly, his nostrils flaring. "Ah, yes, her scent is blended with yours. The whispers held truth, then. I haven't spoken to her in years. How is she?"

"Fine. If you don't count that she's presently being stalked."

Something rippled across Gabriel's face so fast that Luke couldn't put a name to it. "Stalked?"

"Yes. Someone repeatedly left gifts on her porch. She's also received strange calls and an email from someone who is clearly obsessed with her. I've been made aware that you often sneak onto her territory. I wondered if maybe you'd noticed others do the same, or perhaps you saw anyone lingering near her cabin?"

"And you also wonder if maybe it could be me," Gabriel sensed, no sign of offense in his expression or that unnaturally dead voice.

"It's not an idea I'm prepared to rule out, though she doesn't believe you're to blame. I'd be a fool to take chances with her safety."

"I suppose you would, but I can assure you that she's correct in this instance." Pausing, Gabriel pursed his lips. "I do trespass on Sylvan territory now and then. It is how I heard that Blair found her predestined mate years ago. But I've never seen anyone hanging around her cabin or picked up any scents of strangers there."

"Why go there at all? Why sneak onto Sylvan territory?"

Gabriel swiped his tongue along his front teeth. "I assume Blair told you why I went to live with my uncle."

"Your parents were killed."

"Losing them at such a young age, in the way I did, was hard enough. Being branded their murderer hurt almost as much. Having all eyes on me while I grieved—having people say I was either faking my grief or didn't seem upset enough for their liking—made the whole thing so much more difficult. Embry insisted that my uncle take me away, and I was told to never return; forbidden from having contact with anyone in the pack, including my relatives."

"That's harsh," said Deke.

"That's spite," said Gabriel. "My mother was Embry's first girlfriend. He took her death hard. He wanted someone to blame. I was a convenient scapegoat. Am I bitter about it? Sure."

Huh. He didn't sound particularly bitter. He didn't sound *anything*.

"Do I hate that, to this day, I have no clue who killed my parents? Yes—which is why I began sneaking onto Sylvan territory. I wanted to do a little spying. I hoped I might hear or see something that would solve the mystery. I never did. But I do find some amusement in just how much my trespassing unnerves the pack." Gabriel shrugged. "Small pleasures and all that. Really, I only go there nowadays when I need a good, long run. I don't see why I shouldn't be able to do it on what is technically my own territory. I should never have been ostracized the way I was."

Luke had to agree with the latter, considering there was no evidence that Gabriel murdered his parents. Pups should be protected, not tossed away.

Deke folded his arms. "Why did you never knock on Blair's door to say hi rather than just leave cards for her to find?"

"She was one of the few people who stood by me," Gabriel explained. "I wasn't going to repay that by putting her in a difficult position. Expecting her to keep secret that a banished member had been in contact with her would have caused her problems. No one could blame her for finding a few cards, though, could they?"

"I guess not," said Deke.

Gabriel cut his gaze back to Luke, studying him. "A bush dog and a pallas cat. An unlikely pairing for sure." He almost sounded amused. Almost. "I'll bet Noelle isn't happy that you have claimed Blair."

"No, she isn't," Luke confirmed.

"She had hoped Blair would one day mate with Antoine, you know. Or so my mother told me when I was younger. He was more interested in Marianna, as I recall."

"Blair's sister?"

Gabriel nodded. "Unsurprising, since Marianna was sixteen and therefore closer to his age. But Noelle felt that Marianna was far too submissive to handle a male as dominant as my cousin, so she thought he'd be better suited to Blair." He paused as a phone rang from somewhere inside the apartment. "I'm sad to say I have no idea who could be harassing Blair. If I happen to see or hear anything of interest next time I step on Sylvan territory, I'll be sure to let you know."

"I appreciate it," said Luke.

"Should I expect a visit from the Sylvan bush dogs?"

"Probably. Noelle has laid the blame at your feet."

"Of course she has." Gabriel took a step back, readying himself to shut the door. "Say hello to Blair for me. I truly hope you resolve this situation soon."

"Oh, I will," Luke assured him, a note of menace in his tone that warned Gabriel he wouldn't get away with this shit if he was in fact the culprit.

Gabriel didn't react other than to close the door.

Outside the building, Luke and Deke crossed straight to the SUV. Luke hopped into the driver's seat while the enforcer headed for the front passenger seat.

Sitting in the back row with Isaiah, Blair leaned forward. "I can sense your frustration and uncertainty, so I'm guessing he didn't plead guilty to harassing me."

"No, he didn't." Luke switched on the engine. "Nor did he claim to have any idea who might be the culprit." As he drove, he repeated the conversation he'd had with Gabriel.

"He seemed unmoved by the fact that you're now mated," Deke told her. "He didn't reek of envy or bitterness."

"But you're not so certain he didn't put on an act," she detected.

"Maybe it's just that something about him ruffles my cat's fur," said Deke. "I can't explain it. His voice is so monotone."

"My cat didn't like that either," said Luke.

Isaiah hummed. "So you're not ready to rule Gabriel out as a suspect, then?"

Luke slowed to a stop as he reached a red light. "No, not yet."

"I hadn't imagined that he was trespassing with the purpose of spying," said Blair. "I guess I can understand it. I'd want answers too, in his shoes."

"Don't be so certain that was his true purpose," Luke told her. "He could have simply wanted to keep a close watch over you. Did you know that your mother intended for you to one day mate with Antoine?"

Blair rolled her eyes. "I wouldn't say she *intended* it; she just thought he'd be a good fit for me. Don't forget that it isn't unusual for my kind to choose as juveniles who they'll later take as a mate. It's a little like calling dibs, I guess. Adults sometimes conspire with friends to push their children toward each other. Noelle was no different in that respect, though maybe a little pushier about it later on. But that was just because she needed to establish control over me and my world so she'd feel in better control of her own."

"Did it stop once you found Luke?" Isaiah asked.

Blair pulled a face. "She introduced me to as many male bush dogs as possible, but she didn't urge me to consider taking any as a mate. I think she hoped that nature would take its course; that I'd simply 'fall' for one. One dared to flirt with me, despite knowing about Luke, but none of the others were brave enough."

Isaiah's lips twitched. "They were terrified of what Luke would do to them, huh?"

"No, they were terrified of what *I'd* do. I made an example out of the first flirt. I knocked him out with a rock, gave him a Joker smile using the blood from his scalp wound, stuffed poison ivy into his boxer shorts, set fire to his shoes just as he was waking up, and then chased him out of the woods

Exorcist-style."

"*Exorcist*-style?"

"I'm double-jointed, so I can bend into all sorts of positions and even dislocate my joints without causing myself pain."

Isaiah's lips parted. "Seriously?"

Stopping at another red light, Luke glanced at him. "You ever seen horror movies where demonically possessed women move all weird and stiff, their joints popping and clicking and cracking? She can do that. And *will* do it when she's being ignored or not getting her own way and doesn't much like it."

Blair offered, "I can show you—"

"No, I'm good," Isaiah quickly said, throwing up his hands.

Deke snorted, twisting to look at her. "It's not much different from shifting, right, so why—*Jesus Christ, what in the fuck?*"

Luke just laughed as she righted her neck.

CHAPTER NINE

Standing before the vanity mirror as she slipped on her earring, Blair caught sight of Luke in the reflection as he entered the bedroom the next evening. In gray slacks and a blue shirt that matched the color of his eyes, he was so utterly edible her stomach did a little flip.

"You look beautiful," he said, his gaze scanning her from head to toe, taking in the red dress and high-heeled strappy shoes that Elle had let her borrow since Blair hadn't yet picked up the rest of her clothes. "But then, you always do."

She smiled. "Thank you. You're looking very handsome. My hormones are all in a tizzy right now."

A low, wicked chuckle rumbled out of him as he curled his arms around her from behind, plastering his front to her back. "You ready to leave? The party will start soon, and we need to arrive before the guests."

"I just have to slip on this other earring and then I'll be ready."

Nuzzling her neck, he lapped at her brand. "You don't need to be nervous."

"I'm not nervous, I'm …" She trailed off, not wanting to raise a subject that could spoil his mood.

His gaze darted back to hers. "You're uneasy about something. I can sense it through our bond. What is it? Tell me."

Both earrings now on, Blair turned in his arms. "There's a chance my mother will turn up with every intention of ruining the party. She'll know about it from Mitch. She won't want it to go smoothly. And she'll resent that it's being thrown when she's spent years trying to convince me that I'd never be fully welcomed by your pride."

A hardness slid into his eyes. "You didn't tell me that."

"You always did your best not to let her antics succeed in causing drama.

Did you really think that I wouldn't do the same?"

He grunted, seeming disappointed that he couldn't argue. "I know it's possible that she'll show, which is why I assigned two enforcers to guard the Tavern's entrance. She won't get past them, I can promise you that."

Blair's chest warmed. Really, she should have guessed he already had this covered. He always set out to ensure every ride went as smoothly as possible for her. "Thank you. I'm sorry she can be such a pain in the ass."

"You're not the one who needs to apologize."

"No," Blair agreed. "But she'll never do it."

"I don't want or need an apology from her. I have what I want and need. *You*. That's all that matters to me."

Damn her chest warmed even more. He was going to turn her into *such* a girl.

"But I do regret that you don't have the support of your parents. I had thought they'd eventually come round. Maybe one day they will."

"I'm not holding my breath," she muttered.

He gave her hips a gentle squeeze. "Come on, let's get our asses to the Tavern. The sooner the party's over with, the better."

"Why?"

"Because seeing you in this dress only makes me want to strip it off your body so I can feast on every inch of you."

Her lower stomach clenched, but she only said, "Interesting."

"Interesting?" he echoed, his brow creasing.

"Kind of."

He snapped his teeth at her cheek. "We'll see if you still merely find it 'interesting' later."

They walked hand in hand to the Tavern. Most of the pride's celebrations took place there. It was also their local hangout and—being a bar, pool hall, and restaurant rolled into one—it had a little something for everyone.

Entering the Tavern, Blair was hit by the scents of leather and oiled wood. She glanced around. It hadn't changed since she last came. Sports paraphernalia and widescreen TVs still hung on the brick walls. Bulky armchairs the same burgundy as the leather cushioned booths still dotted the space. There were also heavy tables, a small arcade area, a stage, and a row of pool tables.

The bartender, Gerard, stood behind the bar wiping glasses. The only other people present were the omegas—all of whom had organized the event. They were currently fussing over some of the decorations.

There were *lots* of decorations. Balloons, lanterns, garlands, votive candles, and cascading lights. The color scheme seemed to be silver, black, and champagne gold. A tinsel curtain had been attached to the wall behind the buffet table, and a balloon arch surrounded it while tissue pompoms and spiral swirls dangled from the ceiling above it.

Touched, Blair swallowed. They'd really gone all out. Maybe for her sake, maybe for Luke's—it didn't really matter either way to Blair. She was still grateful.

Spotting them, Bree smiled. "Hey." She crossed to them and pulled Blair into a hug. "*Love* that dress."

"Thanks," said Blair. "Love the shoes."

"They're fabulous, aren't they?" Bree gave Luke a quick once over, her nose wrinkling. "You'll do."

His brows flew up. "I'll do?"

The omega snickered. "I'm kidding, you scrub up well." Bree looked from him to Blair. "Right, everything's in place. The DJ is ready, the karaoke machine has been dragged out—Elle insisted on it, so don't blame me—and there's enough food that there'll be plenty even though we'll have four wolverines in attendance. You two will position yourselves by the door so you can greet each person who enters."

Blair nodded. To date, she'd met every member of the Olympus Pride at one point or another. But tonight, it would be different. She'd be meeting them as their *Beta*, not merely Luke's mate.

If any were dubious about having her as Beta female, she hoped they hid it well. Not that she needed to feel she had anyone's approval, let alone everyone's—Blair didn't seek validation from others. Also, she understood it would only be natural for some to have their doubts, given her age. But it would offend Luke, and she didn't want that.

"Thank you for the effort and time you put into this," Blair said to Bree.

The feline smiled, flapping her hand. "No thanks necessary. It's only right that we welcome you to the pride in style. Let me formally introduce you to the other omegas before everyone else arrives."

Luke watched as Bree called the small group over to them. His insides relaxed when the omegas were nothing but sweet and friendly toward his mate. He *felt* her restlessness begin to ease.

Blair might claim she wasn't particularly nervous about the party itself, but he wasn't convinced. He wondered if, on a subconscious level, Noelle's dark whispers were now playing on Blair's mind, making her expect negativity where there'd hopefully be none. After all, if someone told you something often enough, the concept could start to slip into your thoughts and muddle them.

Honestly, there were times he longed to throttle Noelle even as he understood her motivations. He knew about loss and grief. He knew that the death of someone close to you could make you overprotective of your other loved ones; could make you desperate to keep them close. Much of his need to cosset Blair admittedly stemmed from that. But whereas he worked to ensure that he didn't subsequently smother Blair, Noelle quite simply didn't allow herself to acknowledge that that was exactly what she was doing.

"Let's go order some drinks," said Luke, curling his hand around Blair's arm.

Gerard gave her a small salute as they approached the bar. "Well if it isn't our new Beta female," he said, approval and acceptance radiating from him. He eyed Luke. "Man, you seem tense. It's that dress she's wearing, ain't it? It's giving you all sorts of ideas—none of which you can currently do anything about."

Luke narrowed his eyes at the male's teasing tone. "Don't make me hurt you, Gerard."

The guy chuckled and set his fists on the bar. "Well, what are you drinking? Lucky for you, Blair, you're not subject to human laws so I can serve you alcohol even though you're not yet twenty-one."

"I'll have a beer," said Luke.

"Shot of whiskey, please," she said.

Hearing the creak of hinges, Luke turned to see the Alphas stride into the Tavern with Bailey, Aspen, and Camden close behind. All five crossed to the bar. Hellos were quickly exchanged, and then the group ordered drinks of their own.

Tate's gaze darted from Luke to Blair. "You both ready for this?"

She nodded. "I can't lie, I'll be glad when the greeting part is over. There's only so many ways you can say 'hi, nice to see you again' before you simply sound repetitive."

Gerard slid Luke's beer and Blair's whiskey across the scarred surface of the bar.

Luke handed her the glass. "Here."

She knocked the contents back, downing it all in one gulp. "Much obliged."

Havana's brows inched up. "You can handle your whiskey."

Blair shrugged. "My mother had a way of driving me to drink."

Tate snickered. "I can imagine."

Luke had no sooner finished his beer than the guests began to arrive. He and Blair took up a position near the door as planned. There were nods, handshakes, hugs, and cheek-kisses. Aside from a stiff and awkward Finley, they were all friendly toward his mate. Some were a touch reserved, though. He made a mental note of who they were, intending to keep an eye on the situation.

If it wouldn't undermine her strength, he'd do more than monitor things. He'd fight every battle for her. Then again … she'd likely throat punch him for that, so maybe not.

The evening quickly turned rowdy as drinks flowed and the DJ took things up a notch. People danced, laughed, mingled, and descended on the buffet.

He and Blair ended up gathering near the long bar with the Alphas, Aspen,

Bailey, Camden, Deke, and Elle.

At one point, Blair leaned into Luke and said, "Damian's girlfriend is so cute. They look good together. And very loved up."

Luke settled his hand in the crook of her neck. "I think it's more serious than they let on," he said, swiping his thumb over the petal soft skin of her nape.

"Which is a problem," Elle commented with a sigh.

Blair frowned. "Why?"

"Mating him would only lead to her doom." Elle scratched her temple. "I don't know how to break it to her that she's dating the Antichrist."

Luke shook his head. "You've got to drop that sometime and learn to get along with him."

Elle did a slow blink. "I'm supposed to get along with the bringer of the apocalypse? The instrument of our destruction? The creature who feeds on my pain and anguish?"

"Well, yeah," said Tate. "Luke fed on mine, but I made my peace with him."

Luke's brow knitted. "Are you shitting me?"

Tate cocked his head. "Did you not repeatedly injure, scar, and attempt to kill me when we were kids?"

"It was a two-way street," Luke insisted. "You were *far* more of a bastard to me than I was to you. Remember the time you tried to make me drink turpentine?"

"You shoved me in front of a bus."

"It was idling at the curb. And I only did that because—"

"Hey, isn't that Mitch and his mate?" asked Elle.

Blair tracked the redhead's gaze, and she felt a smile split her lips. "It is." She hadn't been so sure they'd come, suspecting that Noelle might make them feel guilty for doing so. "You're here," she said as the two bush dogs approached.

Mitch's brow creased. "Of course we're here. We told you we would be."

Delighted, she hugged them both. They said their hellos to Luke, who then introduced them to the others. Greetings were exchanged, and drinks for the newcomers were ordered.

"Wow," said Kiesha, scanning the space. "The pride's bigger than I thought."

"It's predominantly made up of pallas cats," said Blair. "But there's a small bunch of other breeds."

Mitch put his hand on Blair's shoulder. "They're being good to you, right?" His scowl made it clear that he'd cut a bitch up if the answer was no.

"They are," Blair assured him, deciding that Finley simply didn't count. "Luke would tolerate nothing else."

"Pool," Bailey suddenly declared. "We should play pool. Who's up for it?"

Several were, including Luke, so they all migrated to one of the pool tables. Blair was happily ogling her mate's ass as he bent over to aim his cue when Kiesha leaned into her.

"Have you had anymore contact from … you know who?" the female bush dog asked, her voice too low to carry to the others.

"Nope, I haven't heard a peep from him," replied Blair. "I told Mitch that over the phone yesterday. Didn't he mention it?"

"Yeah, but I wondered if there'd been any activity between the phone call and now."

"No, none at all."

"Good. Then we'll drop the subject so you can enjoy your party. Plus, I gotta ask … Who is that woman over there staring at you?"

Blair followed Kiesha's gaze, almost snorting when Finley quickly looked away. "Ah, that would be the enforcer I told you about who thinks she should be Beta female."

"Oh," said Kiesha, drawing out the word, a dark note to her tone. "Can we play with her a little?"

"It's on my schedule. Because it doesn't seem like she intends to heed the warning I gave her." Finley had been civil on arriving at the party, but not deferential—silently communicating that she hadn't accepted Blair as Beta.

"She'll soon regret testing you," said Kiesha before taking a sip of her Cosmo. "You know, she's not the only one who keeps firing looks your way."

Yeah, Blair had noticed. "Don't tell Mitch, but not everyone is sold on me."

Kiesha's brows snapped together. "Why not? Is it just because you're a bush dog?"

"Is what because she's a bush dog?" asked Bailey, appearing at Blair's other side with Havana and Aspen in tow. "Something wrong?"

"Blair keeps getting weird looks," explained Kiesha. "Not *bad* looks, just … well, I don't like it."

Blair sighed. "They're not convinced that an eighteen year old can handle the role of Beta female." Personally, she was just glad that the only enforcer with that attitude was Finley.

Bailey scoffed. "What does age even matter? In truth, you could be ninety-five."

Blair felt a frown tug at her brow. "No, I really couldn't be."

Bailey placed one hand on her hip. "Who says our age should be truly decided by how many times we've orbited a glowing, spinning, hot sphere of gas?"

"Scientists," replied Deke, coming up behind the mamba.

Bailey spared him the briefest glance. "They say all kinds of shit. Like, hey, we have nine planets. And then later they take it away like, no, there's actually eight." She sniffed. "I find science unreliable. And boring."

"Probably because you don't care for logic," said Deke.

"You could be right, Eye Candy."

"My name is Deke."

"So?"

He ground his teeth, his nostrils flaring.

Tilting her head, Aspen looked from Blair to Kiesha. "Is it true that bush dog shifters eat snakes?"

"Yup," replied Kiesha.

"Even venomous ones?" asked Havana.

Blair nodded. "Uh-huh."

Aspen's brow pinched. "But … your bodies can't neutralize snake venom, right?"

"Right," Blair confirmed. "I think that's only a bearcat thing."

Bailey's nose wrinkled. "So, how do you not, like, die?"

"We tend to sweat out the toxins," said Blair. "Usually get a fever, too. We sometimes blackout for a few minutes as well, though that's rare. But we're fine after an hour or so."

Luke sidled up to Blair, a beer bottle in hand. "What are we talking about over here?" He guzzled back some of his drink.

"Butt plugs," replied Blair.

He choked on his beer and coughed. "That was mean."

She grinned. "Totally."

Camden materialized and passed a fruity cocktail to Aspen, who thanked him with a sweet smile.

Bailey frowned at him. "You didn't get any of us drinks?"

Camden's brow furrowed. "Why would I?"

The mamba folded her arms. "Oh, I don't know, to be *polite*."

"He's a tiger," said Havana. "He doesn't do 'polite.' Neither do you. And what does it matter? You have a drink on the table over there."

"It's the principle of the thing," said Bailey.

Aspen's brow creased. "You don't *care* about principles. You have none."

"Not seeing what that has to do with anything," said Bailey.

Camden grunted at her. "Be grateful for what I do give you."

The mamba blinked. "Which is what?"

"The honor of breathing my mate's air," he replied.

Bailey snickered. "It's cute how much you hate sharing her."

"How is it cute?" he asked.

She shrugged. "I don't know. I don't question these things."

Blair shook her head, her mouth quirking.

More time passed as they drank, ate, played pool, and even danced.

Later on, as she and Kiesha were heading to the restrooms, Blair silently swore at the scene they came upon. Two females were up in each other's space, pointing and cursing and engaging in a plentiful amount of colorful smack talk. Words like "whore," "slut," and "skank" were being thrown around.

From what Blair could gather, they were each competing for the same dude and neither liked that the other wouldn't back off. This wasn't the first time she'd caught them arguing over the years. Rhonda and Lucille simply didn't get along.

"This ain't gonna end well," Kiesha predicted as the two women went nose to nose.

Blair's inner female stiffened as Finley came into view, walking toward the arguing women with a mask of determination etched into her face.

Catching sight of Blair, Finley slowed. A calculating glint entered her gaze as she said, "I was going to step in but as you're here, well, I'm assuming you want to handle it." She folded her arms, clearly fighting a smirk.

"Ooh, she thinks she's setting you up to fail," said Kiesha, her face hard. "We need to *definitely* play with her at some point."

"We will. But first ..." Blair stalked toward the arguing cats, who now looked mere seconds away from unsheathing their claws and taking swipes at each other. "All right, enough, break it up."

They spared her the briefest of glances before going back to yelling at each other.

Her eyelid twitching, Blair licked her front teeth. "I can't tell you how much I dislike repeating myself. Break. It. Up."

They didn't. In fact, they completely ignored her this time. Blair's inner female snapped her teeth, slicing out her claws.

"What the hell's going on?" asked a male voice from somewhere behind her. *Isaiah.*

Blair sighed. She'd hoped to take care of this without an audience—having Kiesha and Finley present was quite enough—but she suspected she'd soon have one. "Last warning," she sang.

Lucille tossed her a sneer.

"Mind your own business, bitch," snarled Rhonda, who then promptly went back to shouting at Lucille.

Blair coughed, annoyance clogging her throat. She really *loathed* being dismissed. Her equally affronted inner female demanded retribution. Oh, she could have it.

Blair flexed her fingers. And then dislocated the tip of one. Then another. And another.

The arguing began to ease off, but she continued. There were pops and clicks, followed by a loud crack as she dislocated her shoulder.

Lucille cringed away from her. "Oh my God, please stop!"

One hand covering her mouth, Rhonda gagged as she took in all the unnaturally angled bones. "I think I'm gonna be sick."

It wasn't the first time Blair had garnered that reaction. "Now, if you're quite finished letting down not only yourselves but our entire pride by disrespectfully engaging in a confrontation at a celebratory event, maybe we can have a little chat." She began sliding joints back into place, enjoying the women's winces and shudders. "Had you just stopped arguing when I told you to, you could have escaped this situation with a verbal slap on the wrist. But you didn't do that, did you? In fact, Rhonda, you called me … What was it again?"

"A bitch," Kiesha helpfully supplied, her voice cheery.

"Thank you, Kiesha, yes, that was it."

Rhonda grimaced. "I was pissed at Lucille, and you just wouldn't butt out."

Blair took a slow step toward her. "I don't *have* to butt out. In fact, what with my being the pride's Beta, it's the very last thing I should do. If you'd wanted to keep things private, perhaps you shouldn't have caused a *public* scene. Just a thought." Blair ate up her personal space. "And you really, *really* shouldn't have called me a bitch."

She snapped out her fist, catching Rhonda on the temple. The cat's head whipped to the side, her eyes glazed over, and she hit the floor with a thud. Knowing she needed to make a statement, Blair delved into her purse, fished out a few items she kept for such occasions, and then got to work.

She wrote "dumb but pretty" on Rhonda's forehead with a sharpie, wedged a tampon in each of the cat's nostrils, and dipped a third tampon in a pot of stale crusty moisturizer, which she then stuck it into the side of Rhonda's open mouth cigar-like.

Blair looked at Kiesha. "Gonna need some water."

Her friend nodded and then hurried off.

Blair lifted her hand, unsheathed her claws, and then coated them with sanitizer gel. She didn't look at the murmuring crowd, aware courtesy of her peripheral vision that some were snapping photos. Not one person addressed or approached her. Not even Luke. She knew he was there; sensed him watching; *felt* his amusement through their bond and … something else—a low buzz of arousal.

Kiesha reappeared. "Here ya go. I unscrewed the cap."

Blair took the offered bottle. "Thank you." She tipped water over Rhonda's crotch, leaving a nice big stain in her jeans, and more photos were quickly taken by the crowd.

As expected, the pallas cat began to stir, her eyes fluttering open.

Blair squatted in front of her and smiled. "Hi, welcome back." She shoved her sanitizer-coated claws into the cat's thigh.

Rhonda arched with a loud cry, lines of pain streaking across her face.

"Stings like a mother, doesn't it? Well, hearing you call me a bitch stung. Okay, not really. It's not actually that easy to offend me. But it did piss me off nonetheless, and I can't let your behavior go unaddressed. No Beta would."

Tears welling in her eyes, Rhonda spat out the tampon, grimacing at the taste of the moisturizer. "I-I'm sorry," she said, yanking the other tampons out of her nose.

Blair withdrew her claws. "I do hope that's true, because it means we won't have to go through this again. And Rhonda … round two would go much worse for you, just to be clear." Blair slowly stood and turned to Lucille, who was gaping down at Rhonda, her face pale.

Lucille's gaze flew back to Blair. "I didn't call you names, I—"

"Sneered at me," finished Blair. "I didn't like that. I also don't take kindly to being ignored. It's a pet peeve of mine."

"I'm sorry." The apology bubbled out of Lucille as she lowered her eyes. "It won't happen again."

Blair tilted her head. "You know something? I believe you. I think you truly are sorry. So your punishment will be a little different. You'll take Rhonda into the restroom and help her clean up. Yes, I know you would prefer to eat your own vomit than assist her with anything at all, but you're gonna do exactly that. *Or* I make my point a whole other way."

Lucille licked her lips. "I'll help her."

Valentina sauntered forward. "So you have some common sense, then. Perhaps there is hope for you." She glared down at a sobbing Rhonda, who was putting pressure on her puncture marks. Valentina rolled her eyes. "Oh, get up, foolish woman. It is just little wound. You still live."

"It's the gel," said Rhonda, her voice breaking. "It *hurts* so—"

"No more blubbering," ordered Valentina. She closed her eyes. "Lord, I *despise* weakness. Someone get her up."

Deke helped Rhonda stand and then passed her off to Lucille.

Bailey tossed an arm over Blair's shoulders. "I think you and me are gonna get along *amazingly* well. I mean, we have so much in common. We like to mess with people. We like whiskey. We like vengeance … The list is endless."

"Then why did it stop at three things?" asked Deke.

Bailey didn't even glance at him. "You still here, Eye Candy?"

His eyelid twitched. "Must you keep calling me that?"

"Not really. But I will."

Feeling the weight of Luke's gaze, Blair looked his way. She sucked in a breath. His eyes were hot, hungry, and filled with promise, leaving her in no doubt of what was going to happen the moment they were alone.

Excitement burst to life in her stomach, and she shot him a little smile. The party couldn't end soon enough.

CHAPTER TEN

Blair clung to Luke's shoulders as he mule-kicked the front door closed. He was feasting on her mouth, licking and nibbling. He kept her plastered against him, as if he couldn't bear the thought of there being even an inch of space between them. That was fine with her.

It couldn't have been more than half an hour after *the incident* that he unapologetically ushered her out of the Tavern. It had come as no surprise to her. Not when she'd been able to feel pure male need humming along their bond. It had built in intensity with every minute that passed and caused sexual tension to wind her tighter and tighter.

The moment his mouth had taken hers, the sexual tension had all but exploded. Now a maddeningly feverish need was rampant in her system. Her inner walls pulsed like a heartbeat, damp and achy.

He broke the kiss with a growl, his eyes twin pools of glittering heat. "I'm going to fuck you so hard. And you're going to take it." He sank his teeth into her neck, wrenching a gasp from her. Then his mouth was on hers again.

Angling his head, he drove his tongue deeper, kissed her harder. Wilder. Hungrier. The nips to her lips became rougher. Her female totally got off on how he couldn't seem to get enough.

Blair thrust her hand into his hair and scratched at his scalp, tugging on the soft strands in feminine demand. He poured a growl down her throat, making her nipples pebble and her lower stomach clench. His hands roamed over her skin, the pads of his fingers pressing deep; screaming *mine.*

At this point, her body … it was a mess. Hot and restless and over-sensitized. Anticipation clawed at her insides and fed her desperation to assuage the throbbing ache in her core.

She had to tear her mouth free, so starved for breath she was surprised little white dots weren't obscuring her vision. Snarling, he claimed her mouth again, fisting her hair tight to hold her head in place so she couldn't escape him.

The dark edge to his touch fired her need. He never held back from her in bed dominance-wise—he was always every inch the alpha. But, physically, he'd so far been careful with her, ensuring he was never too rough. That he clearly wasn't taking such care with her tonight ... yeah, she dug it.

He backed her through the apartment, stripping her along the way, tossing clothes everywhere. Naked, she whipped off his shirt—

He spun her so that she faced the sofa. "Kneel," he ordered, his voice deep and jagged and vibrating with an authority she felt in her bones.

Licking her lips, she knelt on the plush cushion and rested her hands on the back of the sofa. Her female's legs quivered, her anticipation as electric as Blair's.

"So much soft, pretty skin to brand." He traced the bumps of her spine. "I want you fucking *covered* in my marks."

Yeah, she got that. He bit her *a lot*. Clawed her often, too. And he wasn't gentle about it. Her female loved the sheer savagery of each territorial act.

He dipped his fingers inside her and groaned. "Soaked. You know what I most want right now?"

"What?" she rasped.

He replaced his fingers with the thick head of his cock. "I want to plant my cock so deep inside my baby I never find my way out." He *slammed* home, burying every inch in her pussy, causing fire to streak up her inner walls at how abruptly he stretched them.

Her head shot up, and her breath snagged in her throat. "Jesus."

He growled. "Yeah, feel me."

A furious need battering at him, Luke pounded into his mate. There was not one thing better than being inside her. It was like being surrounded by a slick, spasming, scorching hot fist.

He kept a harsh grip on her hips as he jacked his own forward again and again. Physically, he'd gone easy on her in bed up until now, conscious of her inexperience; not wanting to scare or hurt her. But after watching her ruthless display of dominance earlier, the drive to reclaim and own and possess became a haunting beat in his blood.

His cat had urged him to answer that drive, sure she could handle it. Luke didn't need to monitor her through their bond to be certain she wanted this. Arching and moaning, she pushed back to meet every thrust, practically bouncing on his cock.

He loved taking her from behind, loved that he could plunge so much deeper. He wanted to go impossibly deep. Wanted to tunnel so far inside her she'd feel him everywhere—her pussy, her womb, her fucking throat.

Maybe once their bond was complete and he felt more secure in their mating, this taunting need to consumingly possess every part of her would ease off. Or maybe he'd always be so savagely territorial when it came to Blair. He didn't know.

He also couldn't find it in him to care right then.

He was swept away by the moment, drowning in the sensual overload. Her scent, her taste, the feel of her skin, the viselike grip of her pussy—she assaulted and delighted his every sense.

Draping himself over her, Luke planted one palm on the back of the sofa and slid the other beneath her to fill his hand with her breast. The soft globe bounced in his grip with every slam of his cock, her hard little nipple grazing his palm. "You're close," he gritted out. "Get there. I want you to come all over my cock, I want you to drench it."

She moaned, her pussy fluttering around him. "Luke …"

"Get there," he repeated, sliding his hand down her body. He rolled her clit once, twice, and she came with a broken scream. Growling, he pounded into her harder and faster. "That's my fucking girl, keep coming, let … *fuck*." White light flashed behind his eyes as his release slammed into him. Biting into her nape, he rammed his hips forward, locking his cock deep inside her, pumping hot streams of come into her body.

Jesus Christ.

For long moments, they stayed there just like that, struggling to catch their breath. Once their orgasms finally subsided, Luke pressed a kiss to the fresh bite on her nape. His cat curled up in a ball, satisfied now that she'd been claimed all over again. "You all right?"

"If what you're really asking is did I mind that you were rough, no."

"Oh, I don't need to ask that, baby. Your pussy squeezed my cock so tight when you came that I'll be surprised if it ain't bruised."

She only snorted.

He carried her to the bathroom, where he cleaned them both up. He waited for her to slip on a long tee and then led her to bed. He settled her down beside him, keeping her front plastered to his.

Luke palmed the side of her face as he drank in every bewitchingly exquisite feature. People often did a double-take when they first met her, struck by just how utterly stunning she was. He could look at her for hours, soaking in the sight of her, submerged in bone-deep satisfaction at how this magnificent creature belonged to him.

He swept his thumb along the apple of her cheek. "Beautiful. Perfect. Mine."

"You use that word a lot."

"What?"

She coasted the tips of her fingers over his chest. "'Mine.'"

"Yeah, because that's what you are. Mine."

"Which you've had, like, six years to get used to. Doesn't seem like something you need to keep marveling over. But you say it as if you can't quite believe it."

He twisted his lips, sliding his hand from her cheek to her hair. "I hadn't expected to find you that day at the restaurant. It caught me off-guard—something that doesn't happen often. My priorities reshuffled in a millisecond. You became the focal point of my life. My own personal sun. I orbited around you for years, waiting for the moment when I could finally close that distance between us. After so long of having you *right there* yet never feeling close enough to you, it's sometimes hard to believe that I've finally solidified my claim to you."

"Never feeling close enough to me? What do you mean by that?"

"I ensured I was a huge part of your life, but I would have been far more up in your business if Noelle hadn't been so difficult. In never welcoming me into your life and your family, she was a constant bump in the road that made the entire ride feel like it could take a wrong turn if I wasn't careful. I wanted it to be a smooth ride for you, but I could never quite manage it. I guess there were times when it felt like we'd never get here; that she'd succeed in pressuring you to drag things out."

Biting her lip, Blair smoothed her hand over his solid shoulder, skimming over a fading bite mark she'd need to renew sometime soon. "I get it. The foundations for what we have now began to form years ago. But until we mated, I didn't feel as secure in our connection as I should have, because even though I knew down to my soul how important I was to you, Noelle was like a threat that hovered around our unborn mating bond." It had made her female constantly antsy.

He nodded. "She would never have succeeded in making me walk away from you. She was a fool to have tried. Before I found you, I was … lost. Then I heard your voice tell me I'd dropped my wallet, and everything changed." He leaned his forehead against hers, gently combing his fingers through her hair. "Thank God I dropped it."

Her chest squeezed at the mere thought of how they might not have realized who they were to each other that day if it hadn't been for the wallet incident. But the twinge of discomfort she felt at that was nothing compared to the ache she felt in her heart at how much anguish had coated the word "lost."

She played with the short strands of hair at the back of his head. "You'll have to tell me about that at some point, you know."

"What?"

"Why you were lost."

He drew in a sharp breath through his nose. "I know. And I will. Not tonight, though, yeah? Tonight is a night for celebrations only. A night I want you to remember for *good* reasons. I don't want anything marring it. Hence why I want to rip Rhonda and Lucille new assholes."

"Don't bother; I rather enjoyed myself." So had her female.

His lips twitched. "I noticed."

"*You* enjoyed it as well."

"I enjoyed watching you own your strength and slap them with the weight of your dominance, yeah. It made my cock hard."

"I noticed." She stroked his chest, smiling when he purred. "You're such a cat. *My* cat."

"Yours." He caught her face between his hands, raking his gaze over every feature. "I love you, Blair. You can feel it through our bond, I know, so this isn't fresh news. But I'm giving you the words because it's selfish of me to leave our connection to say it for me."

Her chest tightening, she swallowed. "I love you, too. I honestly don't remember a time when I didn't."

His mouth hitched up. "Then kiss me."

She did.

Sitting at the table across from his mate the next morning, Luke flexed his grip on his coffee mug, irritation a buzz in his blood. Blair was a smart woman. Wiser than her years. She would often see elements to a situation that no one else had considered. But there was really nothing smart about the request she made half an hour ago. A request that, in truth, was a declaration of intent. And he'd so far had no success in talking her out of it.

"Surely you can hold off for another day or so." Or even ten. A few weeks would be better.

Her brow pinching, Blair sipped her vanilla latte. "I could, but why would I?"

"Oh, I don't know, *maybe* because the person stalking you may well live in the very place you want to go." Something he should not have to point out.

"They don't live in my old cabin."

"But unless the stalker is Gabriel, they probably live on Sylvan territory. It isn't the safest place for you to go." His pacing cat growled, backing him up on that.

"It's not like I'm suggesting that I go alone. I already said I'd like you and a few others to accompany me, just to be on the safe side. Though I don't envision being attacked. Our boy operates from the shadows. He wouldn't launch a full-on attack on a cluster of people in broad daylight. Tell me I'm wrong. You'd be lying if you did. Be honest, you're simply being your usual overprotective self," she accused, though there was no judgement in her tone.

"It's not *simply* that—"

"Sure it is." Her chin inched up. "I need to pick up the rest of my stuff, Luke. I don't trust that someone—whether it be my mother or whoever's harassing me—won't spitefully wreck it all. The longer all my things are at the cabin, the more of a chance that could happen to them."

True enough, but … "The key word is 'stuff.' That's all it is. Things can be replaced. *You* can't be."

"A lot of those things are important to me, including all the gifts you gave me over the years."

He snapped his mouth shut. His stomach churned at the ideas of said gifts being destroyed. He'd given her so many over the years—spoiling her, taking care of her in whatever ways he could, cheering her up when her mother made things difficult. "I don't want them to be trashed either, but I'm more concerned about you."

"Naturally. But I won't be there long. Kiesha and Mitch have already packed up everything. It's just a case of me collecting it all."

"They could drop the boxes here for you."

"I would have asked them to do exactly that, but …" She leaned forward, bracing her elbows on the table, careful not to spill her drink. "I think it would be a good thing for you and me to go Sylvan territory."

He frowned, and his equally frustrated cat stilled in surprise. "I'm not understanding how." At all.

"Because you're not bothering to think past your overprotective instincts. It can't have escaped your notice that our boy has been *real* quiet. Now, granted, we've made it impossible for him to contact me. But he knows where I am, he knows that I now live with you. Yet, there've been no more gifts or anything. Maybe he's decided to lay low. Maybe he's waiting for me to lower my guard. Whatever the case, his silence doesn't work for me. I want him identified. I want him *gone*."

Luke's eyes narrowed as he sensed, "You want to provoke him."

"If he's part of the pack and we go there, he'll see you and me together, happy and claimed. It will do him the *world* of good to be reminded that I don't belong to him at all. It will also piss him off. And yes, I'm aware he could react seriously badly, but at least he'll have done *something*. While he's lying low, we can't catch him at anything."

No, they couldn't. And taunting the asshole wasn't a bad idea. But it would be Blair who said asshole would punish, and Luke was *not* whatsoever good with that.

"Another reason we need to go to the cabin is that we might just find something there that will help us ID him." She placed down her cup. "Aspen asked me if it ever seemed like anyone had broken into my cabin. It hadn't. But that didn't mean they *didn't*. And you know exactly what a shifter would do to the home of a person they believed belonged to them."

Luke nodded as realization settled in. "Mark it."

"Mark it," she agreed. "You marked mine in various ways—clawed doorways, left items of clothing behind, touched my things to scent them.

Just maybe he did the same. And just maybe we'd be able to tell who exactly did it."

Blair watched him digest that. A surge of agitation rippled down their bond. An agitation she sensed stemmed from the fact that he knew she was right but wished she wasn't because to argue would be to lie.

She wasn't mad at him for so badly wanting to shield her from all harm, sensing it wasn't that he didn't believe she couldn't protect herself. It was that it went against everything in him to place her in a situation that carried even a *modicum* of danger. "It's worth checking, Luke. My female is *all* for being proactive in getting rid of this son of a bitch. Surely you and your cat are, too."

Glaring down at his mug, Luke ground his teeth.

"We can take some people with us. They can act as an extra set of eyes while we search the cabin, and they'll be back up should we need it. Come on, Luke, you know I'm talking sense."

He scraped a hand over his jaw. "I don't like it. And not just because to go there could potentially place you in the sights of a sick ass motherfucker who has the insane idea that not only do you belong to him but that you'd consider a corpse a *gift*."

"Why else don't you like it?"

"It's highly likely that Noelle will take the opportunity to come at us. I don't care if she spouts shit at me, but I won't have her do it to you."

There was indeed a possibility that Noelle would give them grief, but it wouldn't be anything that they hadn't handled before. "Did she try to gatecrash last night's party?"

"No. But according to the enforcer who texted me earlier, she parked her car fairly close to the Tavern and sat there a while. She never once exited it. It wouldn't have spoiled our night if she had tried causing a scene outside, though, as we'd left by then. The party continued without us." He chugged back the last of his coffee and placed the mug on the table. "I think the only reason she hasn't sent you shitty texts is that she wants to offload all she's feeling in person."

He was probably right, but … "I have to face her sometime. I'm not afraid to. Much as it pains her, she doesn't intimidate me."

"That isn't the point."

"Then what is?"

"Look, I know she's not some mega villain. She's your mom, she loves you, she wants you to be happy. But she *hurts* you, Blair. She doesn't set out to do it. She just doesn't mind her words or allow herself to *see* that she doesn't put your wants before her own. In being the way she is, in saying the things she does about me, she hurts you."

"Luke—"

"I couldn't fully protect you from her bullshit all these years. It gutted me.

I'm your mate, it's my job—one I treasure—to act as a shield between you and anything that would cause you harm. But I couldn't afford to get into full-blown arguments with her because that only made things worse for you."

Melting inside at not only his words but the sheer torment echoing down their bond, Blair swallowed hard.

"I swore to myself that things would be different when I claimed you. I swore I wouldn't let her hurt you again. I'm not saying I intend to stop you from seeing her. I want you to have her in your life. But right now, she is pissed. She'll be looking to vent. So I'm not comfortable with you being near her at this time."

Blair pushed out of her chair, rounded the table, and perched herself on his lap. She expected him to be stiff and aloof in silent protest, but he curled his arms around her with a deep sigh.

"I get it," she said. "I do. And I adore you for it. But she doesn't get to control my actions, Luke. That's what I'll be letting her do if I tip toe around her mood. I'd say you and I have done enough of that over the years to keep the peace."

He muttered something beneath his breath.

She looped her arms around his neck. "I want to bring my stuff here. I want to *fully* move in. It will help my female settle—switching territories is a major adjustment even when you're happy to make the transfer."

"Blair …"

"You'll be there to protect me. From our boy, from Noelle, from anything. We'll take backup, and we'll call for more if necessary. Also, there'll be people in the pack who'll come if we need them—Mitch, Kiesha, even Embry." She paused. "Be honest with yourself, you don't truly believe there'll be an attack. Noelle might get vocal, but that'll be the most drama we can expect."

Seconds ticked by as he said nothing, his eyes unfocused. Finally, he exhaled long and loud and met her gaze. "All right. We'll go pick up your stuff. But I won't stay silent if your mother appears and starts mouthing off. I won't leave you to deal with it alone even though I know you can."

Blair lifted her shoulders. "Hey, you want to give her a piece of your mind, I'm not going to stop you. It won't be anything she doesn't need or deserve to hear. But with any luck, she'll keep on sulking and leave us be."

He snorted. "There is no such luck."

Hell if she could argue that.

CHAPTER ELEVEN

Entering the cabin's living area later on, Blair felt her brows lift. Kiesha and Mitch hadn't done a half-assed job at packing. There were no open boxes lying around with things tossed haphazardly inside. All were taped shut, tidily stacked, and labelled with a red sharpie. The TV had been neatly swathed in bubble wrap, just like her large framed pictures and canvases.

None of the other furnishings had been gathered near the boxes, since she'd made it clear that she didn't wish to take any. They didn't hold any sentimental value to her, and the apartment she shared with Luke didn't lack furniture so none were needed.

"Nice place," said Isaiah. "Cozy."

It really was. Even with the shelves, walls, and fire mantel now bare, the cabin still had a homey feel.

Nostalgia filled her as she glanced around. She had a lot of good memories of this place. Memories of movie nights with Kiesha, make-out sessions with Luke on the sofa, and the various mini gatherings she'd thrown.

She'd lived with her parents up until she turned eighteen, so she hadn't resided at the cabin long enough for her or her inner female to develop a true attachment to it. Nonetheless, they'd both miss the place. Though not enough to ever regret having to leave it. For them, it had only ever been a temporary home.

"I say we transfer Blair's things to the van before searching the cabin for marks," suggested Deke. "It will make it easier for us to spot any—they'll be hidden well."

"If they are any here, we'll find them." Luke grabbed a box. "Let's get started."

Between the four of them, it didn't take long to transfer her possessions to the vehicle parked outside. A few of her old pack mates observed from a distance, nosy as they were. They gave her either a too-quick smile or weak wave, likely annoyed that she suspected one of the pack was harassing her.

Whatever.

When she and the three male pallas cats were once more gathered in the living area, Blair said, "It's best if we split up, we can search the place faster that way." It wouldn't take long to check out the entire cabin, since it was relatively small and only had one bedroom.

Luke dipped his chin. "Examine every nook and cranny. We need to be thorough." At that, they headed off in various directions.

Blair did a slow, walk-through of the living area. She checked the walls, floorboards, furnishings, and doorways. The only claw marks she found were those left by Luke.

She raked a hand through her hair, frowning. She'd been sure she'd find at least *one* mark. It wouldn't have been sensible for their boy to leave any, no, but he'd done a lot of unsensible things recently.

Deciding to give the room another once-over before moving to another, she moved even slower this time as she began to examine every inch of the living area, wanting to—

"Bedroom," Luke called out.

Blair stalked through the cabin and into the aforementioned room, quickly followed by Deke and Isaiah. "What have you found?" she asked, eyeing the bed that was now tipped on its side.

His jaw hard, her mate pointed to a wooden slat. "Fucker marked the underneath of your bed."

Crouching in front of the slat, she felt anger course through her at the sight of the five grooves there. They were so small and subtle they'd likely have gone unnoticed if someone hadn't actually been searching for them. "Son of a bitch." Her inner female snarled, equally furious.

"There's no scent," Luke told her, a slight growl to his voice. "Whoever did this clawed the wood, but they didn't use their scent glands to solidify the claim they were making. Probably because they knew there was a chance—however slim—that you'd see the marks."

She stood, balling up her hands, shoving aside her rage before it could cloud her thoughts. "This was definitely done by one of my kind. I can say that for certain." She'd seen enough marks made by bush dogs to be sure.

"Let's keep looking," said Deke. "There might be more."

It turned out that there was. The inside of a kitchen cupboard had also been clawed, as had the top of the tall bathroom cabinet. And during yet another examination of the living area, she discovered similar grooves behind the bookcase.

"Essentially, the bastard marked every room," said Isaiah. "In his mind, she's meant to be his and she knows it … so why not leave his scent behind?"

Luke folded his arms. "Most likely for the same reason he's hiding in the shadows and doing things anonymously. Deep down somewhere inside, he knows that what he's doing is wrong. More, he knows that no one would approve. Still, he will have rationalized his behavior by feeding himself an excuse."

One hand on her hip, Blair dipped her chin. "I remember the stuff he wrote in the email. He chooses to believe that the reason I didn't go to him is that I worry my mom would get in the way."

"Yes," said Luke. "He could have told himself that he didn't leave his scent here because she would have come between the two of you if she heard of it."

Blair couldn't help but be impressed at just how calm Luke appeared right then. If she hadn't been able to feel his fury through their bond, she might not have detected just how worked up he was. "Seeing all these marks, I have to wonder how many times he snuck in here. He probably did other messed-up crap too, didn't he? Like rifle through my underwear or some such shit."

Crossing to her, Luke gave her a pointed look. "Don't." He palmed her nape. "Don't let him get in your head. It's what he wants, remember?"

She sighed. "I know, I just … well, I'd like to rip out his spinal cord and shove it down his throat."

Isaiah pursed his lips, his eyes lit with humor. "It won't be easy, but we could give it a try."

"We got company headed our way," Deke announced, glancing out of the window.

Luke tensed. "Noelle?"

Deke shook his head. "Three males. They don't seem pissed or anything. They're strolling over here like they have all the time in the world."

Soon Embry, Donal, and Antoine entered the cabin. Greetings and a few distrustful glances were exchanged. Well, bush dogs didn't much trust pallas cats, and these particular pallas cats didn't whatsoever trust the Sylvan bush dogs right now, so …

Embry gave Blair a shaky smile. "I heard you'd arrived and guessed you'd come to collect your things. I thought I'd come see how you're doing. You look well. Albeit highly annoyed. Is everything all right?"

"No," she said. "Not even a little."

His protective instincts on fire, Luke used his hold on her nape to pull her closer. "Some asshole left territorial markings around the cabin."

A shocked silence fell.

His inner cat wasn't so quiet. No, the feline was a hissing, snarling, pacing mass of anger. Well, of course he was. Not only had some son of a bitch *marked* their mate's previous home, they'd been *inside her bedroom.* And now she was not only pissed but freaked—something Luke sensed through their bond. He hated it, wished they hadn't come.

"Jesus." Embry scrubbed a hand down his face. "We should have taken the situation more seriously before now. I'm sorry, Blair."

Luke felt his mouth flatten. That apology had come a little too late, in his opinion. His mate might hold the same view, because she didn't seem mollified.

Squatting near the wall behind the bookcase, Donal studied the rake marks there. "They were definitely done by a bush dog."

"I spoke with Gabriel," Embry announced, his eyes on Luke. "He said he'd already had a conversation with you and one of your cats."

"He did," Luke confirmed, sliding his hand away from Blair's nape as he slipped his arm around her shoulders. "He claimed to not be responsible for the recent goings-on concerning Blair."

Embry planted his feet. "Yes, he made the same claim to us." It was evident that the Alpha didn't have much faith in that claim.

"I believe him," Antoine piped up. "Not because he's my cousin and I *want* him to be innocent, but because Blair's important to him."

"That's *why* he's an obvious suspect, considering whoever is doing these things is obsessed with her," Donal pointed out, standing. "Look, Antoine, I'm not saying I one hundred percent believe that he's guilty. But I find it difficult to accept that it could be one of our pack. Gabriel knows our land. Knows our people. Knows how to move around undetected."

Antoine's jaw tightened. "I still maintain that someone's using him as a scapegoat."

"That could well be the case," Embry said to the Head Enforcer in an appeasing voice. "We're having him watched," the Alpha then told Luke. "I'd imagine you are also."

"Of course I am." Luke had assigned two enforcers to tail Gabriel wherever the guy went. So far, they'd reported nothing of concern.

"Be warned: he's as slippery as a cat," said Donal. "It won't be easy to monitor his movements."

"I got that impression from how effortlessly he trespasses on your territory," said Luke.

Embry rubbed at his nape. "I've questioned every member of my pack. None stood out to me as potential suspects. But I'm not ruling out the possibility that one of them is in fact our culprit," he hurried to add.

Antoine took a step toward Blair. "How're you holding up?"

"Fine," she replied. "I just want all this to end."

"We all do." Donal glanced from her to Luke. "Your bond is only partially formed. Surprising. I would have thought, given how long you've been in each other's lives, that there'd be no emotional steps left for you to take in order for the bond to fully form."

Both Luke and his cat bristled at the implication that he and Blair weren't solid. But he felt absolutely no need to defend his own mating to this male or anyone else. Evidently, never did Blair, since she merely stared hard at the Beta until he looked away with a sigh.

Embry cleared his throat. "Mitch tells me that you seem to be settling in well with Luke's pride, Blair."

"It's my pride now, too," she pointed out, making Luke's cat rumble a sound of approval.

A wan smile shaped Embry's lips. "So it is. I'm still adjusting to that."

"We have yet *more* company," said Deke.

Luke stilled at the sound of muffled voices coming from outside. He recognized both. And they garnered a snarl out of his cat.

Silently cursing, Luke placed his mouth to Blair's ear. "Need you to stay close, baby. My cat is seriously on edge right now. He still perceives your mother as a threat to our bond. You're the only thing that will keep him calm."

"Don't think my female is much calmer," Blair told him. "She's not."

Noelle regally strode inside with Les close behind her. She gave Blair a long look, her eyes briefly flashing with what might have been longing. She cleared her throat. "Came to collect the rest of your possessions, I see."

"I said I would," Blair reminded her, her tone even.

His eyes sad, Les offered his daughter a smile. "It's good to see you, sweetheart."

"You too," was all Blair said.

Les gave Luke a stiff nod, who returned the greeting with an incline of his head.

Noelle sniffed at Luke. "I suppose you're very pleased with yourself. You got what you always wanted." A bitter smile curved her mouth. "Blair turned on me and left the pack behind."

Luke didn't bother pointing out that the situation wasn't quite that dramatic. But there was one thing he'd like to highlight. "In truth, that's what you *feared* she'd do. You projected that onto me; maintained it was my goal. It never was. All I wanted was to one day claim Blair. So, yes, I now have what I always wanted."

Noelle's eyes flared and then cut to Blair. "There'll come a day when you realize you should have listened to me. A day when you regret mating so early in life. I want you to know that I'll be there for you when that time comes. There will be no 'I told you so's.' Only the support you'll need to power through a difficult time."

Luke tilted his head. "Do you truly believe that will one day happen, or do you just hope that if you plant the idea in her head it will eventually come to pass?"

Les put a hand on his mate's arm. "Honey, can't we just—"

"You should have given her more time," Noelle told Luke. "You didn't because you believed that the younger she was at the time she was claimed the easier she'd be for you to bring to heel."

Confusion puckered his brow. "Bring to heel?" What in the hell?

"You want her under your control," Noelle accused.

"You're projecting again."

"I never sought to dominate her life. Only to ensure that she knew she had *choices*; that she wouldn't believe finding you so early meant that her future was already mapped out."

"You communicated that well," Blair cut in, her voice cold. "I heard you loud and clear. I simply didn't wish to fight the future I saw coming."

The corners of Noelle's eyes tightened. "You were too blinded by him and all his pretty promises. Too overwhelmed by his level of dominance to develop a sense of self that wasn't twined around his."

Blair felt her body stiffen and her lips part. "You honestly tell yourself that I'm co-dependent on him? That I can't think for myself and am firmly under his boot heel?" She shook her head. "Unreal." It was stupid that Blair had hoped her mother would back down now that the claiming was done, wasn't it? The woman was far too obstinate to wave a white flag so soon.

"It's not what I tell myself, it's what I *know*," Noelle clipped. "You don't see the reality of the situation because you're too damn close to it."

"What I see is that the only person who's blind to the truth is *you*." Blair sharply turned to Luke. "I'm ready to go home."

He nodded. "Then we go home."

Normally, it would have bothered her that Luke, Deke, and Isaiah protectively gathered around her to ensure the others didn't get close as she headed for the door. Blair didn't need to be shielded in such a way. But right then, she was so damn pissed she felt like she'd explode if someone so much as touched her. Which Luke must have sensed, because he didn't take her hand or eat up her space.

Les caught her eye as she neared the door. "Sweetheart, I'll … I'll call you, okay?" He grabbed Noelle when she would have stepped forward. "No, just let them go. You've said enough."

Blair kept her gaze firmly on the van as she exited the cabin, descended the porch steps, and headed to the vehicle. Settling on the front passenger seat, she clicked on her seatbelt, grinding her teeth as she wrestled back a snarl.

A wrestle she lost.

God, she was *livid*. So close to letting her anger fly that her skin felt raw. Still, she said not one word, knowing a hell of a rant would *stream* out of her if she opened her mouth.

Neither Luke nor the enforcers said anything as he drove away. She could sense his worry through their bond, but he did no more than occasionally give her thigh a brief rub or squeeze, giving her the space she needed.

Back in their complex, Luke had the two enforcers help cart her possessions up to the apartment. Again, the males gave her a wide berth and didn't push her to talk. It wasn't until she and Luke were alone, when she was halfway through unpacking, that he apparently decided he was done giving her space.

Hugging her tightly from behind, he nuzzled her neck. "Your mother doesn't truly see you as weak, baby."

Blair sniffed, opening yet another box. "But she does feel the need to keep implying it, and *that* hurts."

"She sees your strength. It frightens her. Because it means you don't need her and that she can't hold you to her."

Blair snatched a book out of the box and plonked it on the dining table. "I don't know about that. She's convinced herself that you have me under your thumb."

"She *needs* to believe that, Blair. The alternative? She faces that she messed up and drove you away. So she tells herself that I'm making your decisions for you."

There was some truth in that, yes, but … "It's more than that. She feels that I chose you over her, she can't accept that I'd do that, and so she has to believe that I'm not thinking clearly. Or, more accurately, that I simply can't think for myself. Dammit, Luke, she wasn't the only one whose world exploded when Marianna died."

Luke began to gently rock her from side to side. "But you know yourself that we can be very self-focused in our grief. She might not still be in mourning, but she allows the pain of loss to rule her. Some do. As if to let it go would be to also let the person they lost go. I'm not excusing how Noelle acts—I'm the last person who'd ever defend her. I'm only ensuring you understand that your mother doesn't *want* to hurt you. She just doesn't know how to be close to you without also controlling you."

Blair lifted another book out of the box. "Yeah, well, she can fuck right off with …" She trailed off on noticing a slip of paper tucked between two paperbacks. Blair pulled it out and unfolded it. Her stomach dropped and hardened. *Oh, hell.*

Sensing the change in his mate, Luke glanced at the sheet of paper she held. And his entire body went still. "The fuck?"

A letter. It was a letter. All neatly typed and printed, much like her email.

His cat growling, Luke skimmed through the letter, his blood boiling.

It read: *This thing you're doing with Devereaux—pretending to be his mate, pretending he's who you want—needs to end* now. *There are other ways to get back at your mother. Ways that don't involve you staying with another man.*

Are you hoping to make me jealous? Is that it? If so, mission accomplished. But I thought you were more mature than that.

I'm trying so hard to be patient with you, I really am, but it isn't easy. And don't think I'm not upset that you hung up on me. That was uncalled for. I didn't deserve that.

I don't want to be angry with you. I hate that I am. Everything will be better once you're home, I know it.

I miss you. I'm not used to being without you. I get why you left—you needed to make your point to Noelle. Well, you've done it. Now you can come back. I know you hate her, but it isn't a reason to stay away. And it's not like you can keep up this act with Devereaux forever anyway.

You don't need to worry about Noelle; I'll protect you from her. I'll make sure you never forget that, unlike what she seems to believe, you deserve to be loved. You are *loved. So come home.*

Blair dropped the piece of paper, letting it flutter back into the box. "God, he's insane. He is. I mean, *what in the goddamn hell goes through his head*?"

Breathing through his rage, Luke gave her shoulders a squeeze. "He must have broken into the cabin and stuffed the letter into the box." The words were low. Flat. Guttural. "And since he printed it off a computer, we don't even know what the shithead's handwriting looks like."

Pivoting, Blair rubbed at her arms. "He still firmly believes that I'm his. Not even you and me being mated has shaken that belief."

Luke had thought it would, but maybe that had been naïve of him, considering … "If someone tried making me believe that you aren't my mate, they'd never succeed. He evidently carries that same surety."

"Because he's a nutjob." She blew out a hard breath. "God, I'm gonna ream his ass."

Just then, Luke's phone began to ring. Seeing his brother's name flashing on the screen, Luke told her, "It's Tate, I have to take this."

"You do that. I'm just going to keep internally freaking out, if it's all the same to you."

Massaging her nape, Luke answered the phone, "Yeah?"

"I just got a call from PJ," said Tate, referring to one of the enforcers. "Chester returned home."

Luke felt his brows lift. "Do we think he's given up on trying to snag Camden?"

"I don't believe so," replied Tate. "According to PJ, Chester didn't return with luggage. He seemed intent on making a quick trip in and out of the house. PJ foiled that plan by nabbing him for us. He dumped the human in his trunk and is driving him to an isolated spot so we can have a chat with him."

"What spot?" asked Luke.

"The abandoned theme park near Mercury Pack territory," replied Tate. "I don't want to take him to the spare room at Dad's place because there's a chance Chester's friends are hanging around our street in the hope of grabbing Camden. I don't want them to realize we have Chester. They could flee. Possibly even warn whoever hired them."

"Blair and I will meet you at the theme park," said Luke before ringing off. He turned to her. "I take it you heard all that. You can stay here if—"

"Not a chance. I want to see this situation through, and I need to get out of here and focus on something else anyway. That way, I'm less likely to start throwing shit." She stalked to the door, and it took her a moment to notice he hadn't followed. She planted her hands on her hips. "You coming or what?"

It was on the tip of his tongue to suggest that she remain behind and relax, but he knew she wouldn't. He also knew that she'd not at all appreciate him fussing over her. And, well, he'd rather not suffer a kick to the balls so he simply replied, "Yeah, I'm coming."

CHAPTER TWELVE

Walking through the open rusted gates, Blair looked at her mate, who held her hand in his. "Tate said we'd find them near the Ferris wheel, right?"

"Yes." Luke tipped his chin toward the ride in question, which towered over most of the others. "It's just a short walk away."

Deke and Isaiah flanked them as they headed for the wheel. There was something seriously eerie about strolling through an abandoned amusement park. There was no laughter, no squeals of delight, no smells of vendor food, no *life*.

Veins of rust spiderwebbed along the many rides. Graffiti decorated the benches, ticket boxes, and gloomy haunted house. A lone bumper boat sat in the middle of the pedestrian path, weeds sprouting out of the small boat like it was a planter.

Blair's female sniffed and flexed her claws, still wound tight. Blair herself was no less tense. It wasn't bad enough that Noelle had dished out more crap, was it? Oh no. She'd also had to learn that she'd unknowingly slept in a cabin that had been *branded* by a male other than her mate.

And then there was the totally wacked letter that … Shit, she needed to calm the hell down. Her attention needed to be on the current situation with Chester. But it was hard to stay focused when she wasn't just furious at who invaded her old cabin but also at herself for not sensing that it had been not only broken into but *marked*.

Blair didn't need to ask Luke if he was okay. His own fury was a drumbeat along their bond. If they were alone, she would have made some attempt to soothe him. Right now sadly wasn't the time for that. It would have to wait.

Turning a corner, they found Tate, Havana, Bailey, Alex, Farrell, and PJ gathered around a Ferris wheel car. An unfamiliar male sat in the car, a gag in his mouth, his grip tight on the metal safety bar. This had to be good ole Chester Wilkins. Her female disdainfully peeled back her upper lip.

He wasn't struggling or fighting to talk around his gag. He was still. Watchful. Controlled. But the eyes darting from person to person flickered with fear. The emotion also laced his scent, along with sweat and panic.

Studying Luke's expression, Tate frowned. "Who put that look on your face?"

"I'll fill you in later," Luke replied.

The Alpha's eyes narrowed. "Something happened?" He cut his gaze to Blair. "Your stalker made another move?"

"Like I said, we'll fill you in later," Luke told him before casting the human a glance. "Did he say anything before being gagged?"

Tate stared at his brother, no doubt tempted to push out of concern, but he finally said, "According to PJ, there was a lot of cursing and demands to be released at first. But he hasn't tried communicating since being dragged out of PJ's trunk." Tate paused as a single crow zipped past them with a distinctive *caw*. "We haven't questioned him yet. We're waiting for Camden and Aspen to arrive. They were working when I called."

It wasn't long before the couple showed up. Both looked ready to tear Chester's limbs right off his body—especially Aspen. Well, if it had been *Luke* who'd been targeted by poachers Blair would be just as eager for blood.

A nod from Tate had Alex ripping away the gag. Chester flexed his jaw, his gaze still restless and glimmering with apprehension.

Stood in front of him, Tate folded his arms. "I'd imagine you've spent some time thinking up pretty lies in your own defense. You probably mean to convince us that we have the wrong person, but here's the thing, Chester—we know that isn't the case. We know that you're the man we're looking for. And we have no problem torturing answers out of you, so it's in your best interests to answer our questions honestly."

Camden sidled up to the Alpha, his eyes cold as they pinned the human in place. "I'm pretty sure I don't need to introduce myself, given you recently shot me with tranqs before then attempting to kidnap me with the help of your friends."

"I didn't …" Chester trailed off at a warning growl from the tiger. "It wasn't personal."

"No, it was poaching." Camden nodded as surprise flickered across the human's face. "Yes, we know about that."

Chester's Adam's apple bobbed hard.

Aspen cocked her head. "So how does it work?" she asked, her voice clipped. "You snatch the shifter, force them to change into their animal form somehow, and then kill them before stripping them of parts like they're a stolen car? Or do you do it while they're alive?"

Chester trained his gaze on the metal bar. "We use a drug to force the shift," he reluctantly admitted. "Then we inject them with another drug to … put them down."

Blair stilled. "Put them down? Like they're ill animals?"

"It's humane," Chester weakly insisted.

Luke gave a snort of derision. Like this piece of shit cared what was humane. "Be honest, you kill them with drugs because you want to cause minimal physical damage to their bodies. Damaged parts don't sell well, I'd imagine."

Chester's eyes again bounced from person to person. "You're all shifters, aren't you?" It was a shakily spoken realization.

"Your buddy Davis didn't pick up on that straight away," Camden told him. "He didn't want to give us your name at first but, well, it turned out that he didn't have a high tolerance for pain, so …"

Chester grimaced. "Is he dead?"

"Of course," said Havana. "In making his little reports to you, he condemned shifters to death. That's not something we'd ever overlook."

Bailey leaned over the back of the Ferris wheel car and put her mouth to the human's ear, making him jump. "I'm awful interested to know who hired you to take Camden's head and fur," she said. "Perhaps you could help us with that."

Chester stiffened, his gaze darting to the side.

"Before you think to lie, remember Tate's warning," said Alex.

The human sighed. "I don't have their name. The deal was done through a broker."

Luke felt a muscle in his cheek tick. "Well I'm sure you at least have the broker's name."

"Myra York," said Chester.

"And where will we find Myra?" asked Luke.

"She runs a broker firm. Selfridge House Ltd. I don't know where she lives."

Blair tipped her head to the side. "And your fellow poachers? Where are they?"

Good question. But the human clamped his lips shut.

Camden took a step closer to him. "I'll bet you don't think highly of shifters, do you? There's no way you could otherwise do the things you do. I know one thing that most humans don't like about us. It's that we don't answer to your laws; that we have our own system of justice. And they *really* don't like that that system can be somewhat brutal.

"Here's just how brutal I can be. I have no problem whatsoever with returning to your home and lying in wait for your wife and child. I have no problem slaughtering them in lieu of the friends you seem intent on protecting."

Chester's nostrils flared. "Bastard," he spat.

"Indeed," said Camden. "Now choose. Your family, or your friends."

Luke didn't for one second believe that the tiger would go after Chester's wife and child. Camden wasn't the most ethical of people, but he wouldn't target innocents. Still, Chester thankfully didn't seem inclined to call his bluff, because he squeezed his eyes shut and rattled off an address that wasn't far from the theme park.

"It's the duplex me and my co-workers use when we're on jobs," Chester added. "You'll find them there."

"That had better be the truth, Chester," said Tate. "I'm about to send my Head Enforcer to check the place out. If it turns out you lied, your family will pay for that with their lives."

Again, it was a false threat. Again, Chester didn't sense it.

"No lie, you'll find the other three poachers I work with at the duplex," he told Tate.

The Alpha turned to Farrell. "Confirm that for me."

Once the Head Enforcer had disappeared in his avian form, Blair pulled out her cell phone. "I'll call River and ask him to find out as much as he can about Myra York and Selfridge House."

Tate dipped his chin in thanks. "Appreciated."

As she walked away to make the call, he crossed to Luke. "While we wait for Farrell to get in touch," Tate began, his voice low, "you can tell me why you look ready to burn shit down."

Luke rolled back his shoulders. He thought about once more blowing his brother off, but Tate wasn't so easy to sidetrack. And just maybe spitting the words out would help Luke calm the hell down. "We made a trip to her old territory to grab her stuff. We discovered a little something. Whoever's obsessed with her left claw marks in every room of her old cabin."

Tate's jaw hardened, and a growl vibrated in his chest. A growl that Luke's cat echoed.

"He hid them well, but they're there," Luke added. "No scent, though. He clearly wasn't taking any chances."

"Can you tell what type of shifter caused the marks?"

"Definitely a bush dog." Luke flexed his fingers. "More, while Blair was unpacking, she found a letter from him." He gave his brother a brief summary of it. "The prick truly has convinced himself that she wants *him* and that my claim to her means nothing. Then again, Noelle holds the latter opinion as well. She felt the need to make it clear that Blair made a mistake in letting me claim her so early."

Tate frowned. "When?"

"Earlier. And now my cat is pitching an unholy fit—not only because her old cabin was marked and she received that damn letter, but because she's hurting due to the things Noelle said. He's showing no signs of calming, and

I know that's because my own anger is fueling his, but I can't shake it off."

"No one could simply *shake off* that their mate is hurting and in danger." Tate rested his hand on Luke's shoulder. "He won't get to Blair. As for Noelle … she'll back down eventually."

"That's what I always thought. I held that belief for six long years. I'm beginning to wonder if it was merely wishful thinking." He quieted as he noticed his mate heading back to him.

Tucking her phone in her pocket, she looked at Tate, "River said he'll get straight on it first thing in the morning when he starts his shift."

Luke gave the back of her neck a squeeze, proud of her for owning her role without hesitation. She no doubt felt that pride through their bond, because her mouth curved slightly. The shadows didn't clear from her eyes, though.

Feeling driven to comfort and soothe, Luke barely resisted the urge to haul her against him and rain soft kisses all over her face. He wanted to take her home. Feed her. Coddle her. Pet her pain out of her. Wanted to put her to bed and hold her close; remind her that she was loved and cherished. He hated that his attention couldn't be fully on her right now.

While Bailey and Aspen taunted and poked at Chester merely for something to do, the others waited in silence for Farrell's call. It eventually came, after which Tate said to Chester, "You were telling the truth. Good. Killing an innocent woman and a child wouldn't have sat well with us."

Bailey fisted the human's hair and wrenched back his head. "What happens next is for all the shifters you've killed and butchered over the years so you could sell them to sick fucks who'd likely use them as trophies."

Havana gave him a pitying smile. "Sadly for you, we don't have any lethal drugs lying around. We're not really into 'humane' methods of death when it comes to people like you who've earned a much worse fate. As such, yeah, this is gonna hurt."

It turned out that Chester's tolerance for pain wasn't much stronger than Davis's. The poacher mentally checked out at one point, so Luke then swiftly executed him.

"What do we do with what's left of the body?" asked JP.

"My uncles will be happy to take him off our hands," said Alex.

Isaiah grunted. "Figured as much."

Tate twisted his mouth. "We'll pay Myra York a visit some time tomorrow. I want a little info on her from River first. As for Chester's friends … they need dealing with now or they'll get spooked when they realize he's MIA."

"I can handle that," Camden volunteered, evidently wanting vengeance.

"*We'll* handle that," Aspen corrected.

Tate nodded and assigned a few people to go with them. Everyone then began making their way out of the park. Other than Bailey, who was staring into space.

Luke was about to get her attention, but then Deke nudged her and said, "Unless you want to wait for Alex's uncles and watch them devour the body, get moving."

Bailey looked up at the enforcer. "You ever think how crazy it is that the T-Rex's closest non-extinct relative is the chicken?"

Deke blinked. "No. No, I never think about it at all."

"You don't? Well that's weird."

He frowned. "No, it ain't. I doubt many people think about it."

"That's their problem." The mamba walked off.

Trailing after her, Deke said, "I don't see *how* it's an actual problem."

"*Also* not my problem, Eye Candy."

A low growl. "You know my name. Use it."

"Why?"

Her lips twitching, Blair cast a concerned glance at Luke. "You're a little calmer, but your cat isn't. What can I do?"

Warmth flooding his chest, he gave her hand a soft squeeze. "You're doing it just by existing. He'll settle down once we're away from here and he and I have you to ourselves."

"Good," she said. "I want to go home, unpack the rest of my things, and then fuck you stupid."

His body tightened. "Is that so?"

"It very much is. Don't worry, you'll like it."

He felt his lips quirk. "Oh, I don't doubt that I will."

Finished dabbing on a light layer of makeup the next morning, Blair carefully returned her cosmetics to her pallas cat-themed case—a novelty gift from Elle. It turned out that Blair had been right to assume that her inner animal would lose some of her edginess once Blair unpacked all her possessions. Shifters were innately territorial. It was important for them to have their own territory, even if that was merely an apartment. It anchored them. And although the place already felt like home to both Blair and her inner female, this made it more official.

Blair's gaze flew to the mirror as she noticed Luke entering the en suite bathroom. Pressing his front to her back, he snaked his arms around her and nuzzled her neck, his eyes gleaming with satisfaction.

"What has you feeling so smug?" she asked, though she could guess.

"I like seeing all your things mingled with mine. Some were already here, I know. But this is different. It's not about you leaving little touches here and there. You're *all* moved in, you've made the space fully ours. I like it. Like how easily our lives clicked together."

She felt her brow crease slightly at the latter comment. "You worried that they wouldn't?"

"I thought it might take some time before they did. You've had a lot to adjust to. You had to leave your home, your territory, and your pack. You had to take on not only me but the role of Beta female—I can't even say for sure which of the two is the trickiest. More, it all happened fast, and you've barely had time to settle into mated life thanks to how much is going on."

It hadn't occurred to her that he'd worry she was a little overwhelmed. Turning in his arms, she curved her own around his neck. "I always knew those changes would come. I knew they'd happen in quick succession. I guess, for you, it all came out of nowhere—you expected us to bond later down the line. You had no idea that my mother had invited your ex bed-buddy to Sylvan territory, spurring me into speeding things along, until only a few nights ago."

He squinted. "Something I'm still pissed about."

Ignoring that, she continued, "But it wasn't sudden for me. I was ready. I'd been ready for weeks. Not simply for change, but to embrace it. And I have. It hasn't been a hardship. I don't have any regrets."

His expression went all warm and lazy. "No?"

"No. So don't let my mother get in your head."

"It isn't about her, baby. It just sometimes hits me how much you've given up for me and our bond."

"I don't see it as making sacrifices. You long ago offered to join the pack rather than transfer me here. I vetoed that, because I knew that—as much as I hated it—the pack would never make you feel fully welcome. They wouldn't have given you the rank you deserve either." They were too distrustful of other breeds of shifter, and Luke was far too dominant to have been content with being a mere member of the pack.

"Their attitudes might have altered over time."

"But not enough for Embry to have made you Beta or even Head Enforcer. You wouldn't have been happy there. Here in the pride, you're happy. I knew I could be happy here, too. I like how the pride is run. I like its members—well, most of them. And I outright adore your family. It was really a no-brainer that you and I would be better off here than in my old pack. Plus, I need distance from Noelle if I'm to have any chance of living a life that doesn't involve her attempting to control it."

"On that, we agree." Luke knew that if he *had* joined the Sylvan Pack, there would have been constant drama. Because while he understood why Noelle felt driven to hold Blair so tight, he would never excuse it. If they had lived in close proximity to Noelle, he would have found himself arguing with the woman every time she tried imposing her will on Blair.

"When I say that it's been no hardship to make the changes I've made, I mean it. You have never simply been a mere part of my life, Luke. You're the most important thing in it. You have been since the moment you found me—

or I found you. Whatever. Having you in my life has always been as easy as breathing. Always will be. Okay?"

His chest squeezed, and he felt his face soften. "Okay, baby." His cat pressed against his skin, straining to be closer to her. Thinking that wasn't such a bad idea, Luke drew her closer and fit his lips to hers. He sipped from her mouth, slow and shallow and sensual.

Sometimes, the knowledge that she was *finally* officially his hit him like a slap. It hadn't fully sunk in yet. As she'd said, the whole thing was pretty sudden for him. Not that he had a single complaint.

She nipped at his bottom lip. "We should let our animals run together later. It would do them good."

His cat perked up at that. "We'll make it happen."

Just then, her phone began to chime. His gut hardened. She'd changed her cell number, but he was still uneasy each time her phone rang; still wondered if just maybe her harasser had obtained that number somehow.

She glanced at the screen of her cell. "It's River." She slid her thumb over the screen and answered, "Hello."

"*I have news,*" declared River with no preamble.

Hearing his pride mate's voice, Luke relaxed.

"*Selfridge House is located on Elmhurst Avenue.*"

Blair hummed. "So not too far away, then."

"*Get this: Myra Rogers has shifter blood.*"

Both Luke and Blair stilled. Damn, he hadn't seen that coming.

"Shifter blood?" she asked.

"*Yes,*" said River. "*Her mother is half wolf.*"

"And yet Myra has no issue brokering deals that lead to shifters being poached?" Blair snorted and shook her head.

"*I trust you'll pass on the news to our Alphas.*"

"I will. Thanks, River." She hung up. "I take it you heard all that."

Luke nodded. "I wasn't expecting the latter piece of news."

"Me neither. Maybe she has beef with her mom or something—I don't know." Her nose wrinkling, Blair tilted her head. "Why is it that you look close to smiling?"

Luke settled his hands on her hips. "It pleases me that River called you with the information."

She frowned. "Well, it was me who asked him to look into Myra and her firm."

"Sure, but he wouldn't have reported directly to you unless he and his animal acknowledged you as their Beta female. It's one thing for people to accept you. It's another for them to recognize your authority."

"Huh, I guess so." She shrugged. "Well, they all need to get with the program, because I don't want to go through one dramatic scene after another just to make my point like I did at the Tavern." She paused. "Now we need to call Tate and bring him up to speed."

"Then get to it." It was *her* news to relay, after all.

Her brows inched up. "All right."

Not long after she'd updated Tate, a bunch of the pride were gathering at the Alpha pair's house at his request. It didn't take long for them to agree on a plan of action. But it wasn't until later that day, when Selfridge House would soon be due to close, that they acted on that plan.

Parked not far away from the firm, Luke watched as yet another person left. When Farrell had minutes ago taken a good look through the windows while in his avian form, there were only six people in the building.

At this point, only three remained.

Their hope was that Myra would be the last to leave, given it was her firm. If so, she would soon be alone in the building, and then they could sneak inside before she had the chance to vacate it. But if not, they'd simply follow her home and deal with her there.

Riding shotgun, Blair once more glanced at her cell screen, studying the photo of Myra that River sent her. "She looks so sweet. Like a kindergarten teacher or something. You'd never think she brokers shifter poaching deals. I don't know how people can do that and still sleep at night."

Luke lightly squeezed her thigh. "Me neither. I've come to believe that there are some people in this world who somehow don't have a soul. Or, if such a thing is possible, that their soul is quite simply dead."

"You know, I don't find any of that hard to agree—Hold up, someone else is leaving. A woman. Not Myra, though."

Soon, another person left.

"And then there was one," said Luke. He peeked through the gap between the headrests, sweeping his gaze over the group in the rear of the SUV. "She's officially alone. We need to move now."

As they'd earlier agreed on, Alex led the way since—as a wolverine—there was no lock or security system that could keep him out. He easily tackled the lock on the building's rear door, and then they all filed inside.

Tate nodded at Bailey, who then headed to the front entrance to secure it closed from the inside. With that done, they all followed the sound of a woman's voice up the stairs and onto the second floor. Guessing Myra was on the phone, they waited outside her office for her to finish the call before they entered.

In the process of slipping papers into the drawers of her mahogany desk, it took Myra a few moments to sense that she wasn't alone. When she did, her entire body went still. For all of five seconds. She then jumped to her feet, her eyes wide with outrage. "What the hell? You can't just walk on up here. Who are you people?"

As they all fanned out in front of the desk, Tate replied, "The kind who don't like it when humans help people get their hands on shifter fur and body parts."

Myra tensed, her indignation quickly replaced by uneasiness.

"Not a safe occupation by any means," said Luke, his inner cat snarling at her. "You had to have known someone would come for you sooner or later."

Her lips trembling slightly, Myra gave an aloof shrug and sank back into her chair, going for cool and uncaring. "I had hoped it would be a case of 'later.'"

Blair cocked her head. "You got mommy issues or something?"

Myra blinked. "W-what?"

"Well she's half shifter," said Blair. "That should surely make you supremely opposed to shifter poaching. But it would seem not. Why?" Because Blair just didn't get it. Then again, she didn't get how *anyone* could involve themselves in such a thing.

Myra swiped her tongue along her lower lip. "It's just business."

Aspen wagged a finger at her and tutted. "That right there was a lie," she said, voicing Blair's thought.

Her face hardening, Myra jutted out her chin. "Having shifter DNA isn't necessarily something to be proud of. You all like to think that you're better than humans, but you're not."

Havana pursed her lips. "We don't think we're better than *all* humans. But people like you, yeah, we're sure as shit better than you."

"Shifters are just as prejudiced against humans as humans are of them. My mother was kicked out of her pack at the age of nineteen simply for imprinting on a human—my father. And they sent her away when she returned after he died. It didn't matter that she had a six-year-old daughter at her side. Not to them. They didn't give a shit. Nor did they come to her funeral after she died a few days later—the snapping of her imprint bond was too much for her, you see."

Bailey frowned. "So just because one pack of asshole wolves fucked over you and your mom, every other shifter in the world is also a supreme twat who deserves to die?"

"I didn't say they all deserve to die." Myra rested her clasped hands on her lap, her knuckles white. "I simply don't care if they do die. You shifters have no real sense of humanity in you. You're more animal than anything else. You just hide it well from most of the population."

Camden hummed. "It's good that you recognize how ruthless we are, because you'll know I'm not bluffing when I tell you that if you don't answer our questions honestly, we'll subject you to a truck load of agony the likes of which you can't imagine exists."

Myra huffed. "Don't expect cooperation. I have no incentive to tell you anything—there's no way you'll allow me to live. Even if you offered me some sort of deal I'd never believe you'd honor it, so I guess that leaves us at a stalemate."

"No. No, it really doesn't," said Havana. "Bailey."

The mamba didn't bother stripping. She shifted instantly, and her snake then slithered out of the clothes that puddled on the floor.

Myra froze, her face losing some of its color, but she continued with the cool and indifferent act.

Deciding this bitch needed shaking up a little, Blair crossed to the desk. Bending over, she braced her elbow on the surface of the desk, and leaned her face into her palm. "It must be hard."

Myra flicked her the smallest glance, loathed to remove her gaze from the mamba. "Excuse me?"

"To be you, I mean. I personally would hate it if, too insecure and afraid to face who I truly am, I lived in a false reality." Blair exhaled a sigh of mock sympathy. "You sit in that big ole fancy chair, the queen of your kingdom, wielding power over shifters—condemning at least one to death per day. You believe it makes you strong. That it proves you're superior to your mother's old pack mates, all of whom are clueless to the power you hold over their kind." Blair gave her a pitying look, knowing it would cut her to the quick. "Really, though, you're just a lost little girl who feels weak and lonely and abandoned."

Red stained the human's cheekbones. "Shut up."

Blair noted the white mark on Myra's third finger. "Divorced, huh? I suppose you couldn't have been an easy wife. Controlling, I'd wager. Definitely needy. Overly critical, too, I suspect. I'll bet you were always finding faults in your ex. And most likely unable to celebrate his successes because it made you feel threatened in comparison."

"Shut up," Myra snarled.

"He probably felt like he was constantly walking on eggshells around you. I'm sure all that bitterness you carry didn't help matters." Blair narrowed her eyes. "Was it before or after the divorce that you decided to go so heavy on the Botox and plastic surgery? That nose, wow, it's so narrow I don't even know how you can breathe through it. It's got to be a medical marvel."

"*Shut up.*"

Blair offered her a sad smile. "You probably thought your face lift, reconstructed nose, and boob job would make you feel better about yourself. They didn't, though, did they? Of course they didn't. Because in truth, it isn't your surface that you find so ugly, it's what's *inside*. Though, to be real, you're not much of a looker, are you?"

Snarling again, Myra jerked toward Blair. Maybe she'd have done more, maybe she wouldn't have. They'd never know, because Bailey's mamba—who'd climbed onto the desk while the human was distracted—let out an unholy hiss and lurched toward Myra. The bitch jumped in her seat, and Blair could *hear* the woman's heartbeat gallop like crazy in her chest.

Blair hummed. "I don't think she likes you, Myra. But then … does anyone? Really?"

The human's nostrils flared, but she kept her eyes on the mamba. "Fuck you."

"Hoping to cling to your dignity," Blair sensed. "Admirable. Also impossible because, well, Bailey's venom is gonna put you through the ringer. We're talking stomach cramps, diarrhea, vomiting galore. You'll soon be sitting in a puddle of your own piss, puke, and shit. Are you much of a sobber? I hope so. It'll make the photos look even better. Because yes, I'll be taking pictures. Lots and lots of 'em. Maybe even a video. Yeah, that would work."

"Or you could just answer our questions and suffer a swift execution," Luke cut in, his voice holding no trace of the amusement that skipped down their bond. "We want the name of the person who tried hiring poachers to get themselves some white tiger fur, and we want the records of other poach-hiring clients. More, we'll do absolutely anything to get those things. *Anything.* To you, that is. If you want to suffer for a while, we can make that happen. But I promise you'll regret not being straight with us right from the outset. I know Chester Wilkins sure was. He and his friends died hard, if you're interested. So, what'll it be?"

CHAPTER THIRTEEN

Gathered around the Alpha pair's dining table a short while later, they all stared down at the pile of records they'd swiped from a hidden safe in Myra's office. She'd given up its location fairly quickly, in addition to the many answers they'd wanted. That hadn't surprised Luke—he'd sensed that her bravado was as paper-thin as the self-confidence that had shriveled the more his mate toyed with it to rattle her. A spectacle his cat had rather enjoyed.

Rubbing at his nape, Luke once more read the name of the asshole who'd recently contacted Myra wanting to get his hands on the head and fur of a white tiger shifter. "If I couldn't see the proof for myself, I'd wonder if the bitch fed us a bunch of bullshit."

Zayne Whiteford wasn't a regular human. The child actor was now a pop singer with a boyish face and a lily-white image that appealed to teenage girls everywhere. Clearly, he wasn't quite as innocent as he seemed. Only twenty-four years old, Zayne had hired poachers through Myra on several occasions, an apparent collector of shifter fur and heads.

"I wonder what all his fans would think if they knew about this sick shit," mused Blair, her eyes flashing. "Celebrity or not, he needs to be dealt with. I know it's not easy to make someone so famous quite simply disappear, but . . ."

"He'll be dealt with," Tate vowed.

"It's going to be practically impossible for us to get to him right now," said Bailey, looking down at the screen of her cell. "He's on tour, which means he's hopping from hotel to hotel when he's not sleeping on his tour bus. He has a massive security detail."

Behind the mamba, Deke peered over her shoulder to glance at her phone. "He's also currently in New York, which isn't exactly a short drive away."

Tate began to pace. "When does his tour end?"

"Not for another two months," replied Bailey, pocketing her cell.

Aspen swore, sinking her hands into her hair and leaning back against Camden. "We can't wait that long to deal with Zayne. He won't be worried on hearing that Selfridge House burned down with Myra still in it, because he won't think it has anything to do with him; won't worry that his dirty secret is no longer so secret. Therein lies the problem. He'll simply go to another broker, and so Camden will still be at risk of being taken. We need to nip this in the bud."

Idly snaking his hand up his mate's back, Luke said, "We could anonymously make these records public, but then it will be obvious that shifters were responsible for Myra and her firm burning down. That wouldn't be good."

"No, it wouldn't," agreed Deke. "The human authorities won't take kindly to the idea of our kind seeking justice in such a supreme way, and anti-shifter extremists will pounce on it to make us out to be dangerous vigilantes."

Isaiah nodded. "We personally wouldn't suffer blowback, since humans believe us to be human ourselves, but shifters in general would suffer."

Tate stopped pacing and rolled his shoulders. "Then we need to instead privately and anonymously make a statement to Zayne. We need to do something to alert him to the fact that we know what he's been up to; something that will make him inclined to pull back. We can then deal with him up close and personal at a later date, when he's least expecting it."

"If we alert him that we're onto him, it'll put him on guard," Farrell pointed out. "He'll be paranoid—and rightly so—that we won't stop at a simple warning, so he'll be more careful."

"It's that or take the chance that Camden could get shot at again in the meantime," said Aspen. "And I'm not good with that."

"Neither am I," declared Havana, folding her arms. "So, like Tate said, we make a statement."

Alex licked his front teeth. "Give me a copy of that document stating the history of Zayne's transactions with Myra. I'll break into his LA home, pin it to a wall, and claw said wall—it'll be obvious that shifters have left some form of warning. He'd be a damn fool not to heed it."

Camden's brows inched up. "That would work. He might suspect it was me, given I'm the latest transaction and he put Myra onto me in the first place, but I doubt he'd act on it. And if he tries, well, he'll die for his stupidity."

Indeed he would. According to Myra, Zayne hadn't asked that the poachers specifically target Camden, but the singer *had* put the male's name forward as a possibility after reading the online article about Camden and another tiger dueling—until then, Zayne hadn't known there were white tiger shifters.

Blair lifted the list of poachers who Myra kept a file on. "What about these fuckheads?"

"Their lives need ending for sure." Havana looked at Alex. "Do you think your uncles will be interested in taking care of them?"

"Oh, they'll be happy to," replied the wolverine. "They'll also be happy to take care of Zayne at some point. They're good at making deaths look accidental."

"Really? Interesting," said Havana. "If they offer, we might take them up on that. As for Myra's clients, they need to be taken care of just the same. But it's not our justice to mete out. It doesn't seem right for us to do it ourselves."

In agreement with that, Blair twisted her mouth as she contemplated how best to handle the situation. An idea came to her. "These records clearly state the identities of each shifter who was killed. It wouldn't be hard for us to ID and locate their nearest and dearest. We could contact them, pass on the identity of whatever client owns pieces of the deceased, and allow them to mete out their own justice and retrieve the shifters' remains."

Tate slowly dipped his chin. "I like that idea. Alex, contact your uncles about the list of poachers. The rest of us will work on locating and unearthing contact details for the families of the deceased shifters. I'll gather others here to help. We're going to need as much aid as possible if we're to get through that list by tonight."

As it was, even with so many assisting, they only managed to get three quarters of the way through the list. There were just *so many* victims of poaching. It had been going on for years.

Tate eventually sent everyone home, probably sensing that they needed a break. Blair was glad of it. There had been nothing easy about repeatedly breaking the news of a shifter's death to their families. Many had sobbed, utterly devastated.

She could relate to their anger and pain and disbelief—she'd felt it all herself when she lost her sister. And by the way Luke pulled inward, she knew he was thinking of his mother. So when they later lay in bed, their minds still a place of unrest, she pressed a kiss to his shoulder and said, "It's been a messed up day, huh?"

"Yeah," he replied simply, coasting his fingers up her bare back as she lay flat on her stomach.

Tired of one-word answers, she inwardly sighed. She'd spoken to him several times since they returned home, but he hadn't done much talking in return. He'd withdrawn too far—not emotionally or physically, but mentally. So even as he kept her close and touched her with utter reverence, he was a million miles away. And she felt so very alone right then.

But there was no way for her to be truly irritated with him. Not when she could feel his turmoil through their bond. Dealing with others' grief had pulled his own to the surface, and he was struggling to wrestle it back.

Her female whined, distressed that her mate was in pain. She wanted to alleviate it but didn't know how. She kept butting Blair, urging her to do something. Blair had tried. And tried and tried. She'd done everything from giving him space to pushing him to talk, but she couldn't reach him.

No quitter, Blair whispered, "Come back to me."

His brow ever so slightly furrowed, he looked at her. "I'm right here."

"No, you're not," she said, keeping her voice gentle. "You're mentally someplace else. Somewhere I can't go. And I need you to come back."

He returned his gaze to the ceiling, sighing.

"Look, I'm going to guess that your thoughts are centering around not only your mom but the things you haven't yet shared with me. We need to talk about all that sooner or later. Why not now?"

He scrubbed a hand down his face.

"*Talk* to me. You're hurting, and I hate it. Let me help. Offload it."

Returning his gaze to hers, he stroked her hair. "Not tonight. You're hurting too—"

"There'll never really be a 'good time' for you to dredge up what you've been holding back from me for so long. It's always going to be hard on you. Do it now, when your grief is already near the surface, so you won't have to dig it up all over again."

He didn't speak. Only stared at her, unblinking. And she thought he might deny her this, but then he let out a resigned sigh and said, "Only if you'll talk about Marianna. I can feel your own grief and pain like it's my own."

Her stomach twisted, and her inner animal pulled in on herself. "You already know about her."

"I know how she died, but I don't know much about her. Whenever I brought her up, all you ever really said was that you loved and missed her." He gave Blair's shoulder a small squeeze. "Tell me about her."

Knowing it was only fair that she pick at the scabs on her own wounds when she expected him to soon do the same to his, Blair swallowed and said, "She was such a gentle soul. Full of compassion. Didn't have a judgmental bone in her body. No one ever had a negative word to say about her. There was nothing negative *to* say. She was an amazing person … and so I can't help hating the part of myself that's still angry with her."

"Baby." It was a soft murmur.

"All she had to do was stay down and not move. The gunman would have scampered once the gas station clerk handed over the cash. But no. Not Marianna. She was apparently sure she could talk him into lowering the damn gun. Knowing her, she probably felt sorry for him when she realized he was a hopped-up addict. She was all about helping people. And he killed her. Shot her right in the head."

Luke's chest tightened as his mate's eyes welled up. Sweeping a hand up her back, he edged closer and kissed her temple. His cat rubbed up against her, feeling powerless to help.

"Why didn't she just stay down, Luke? Why put her life at risk, knowing what her death would do to those she loved, purely to help someone who'd long ago stopped helping themselves?"

He squeezed her nape, wishing he could erase her anguish. "It doesn't make you cruel that you're still angry with her."

Blair averted her gaze, but not before he saw the lick of shame there. An emotion that slicked its way along their bond.

"It doesn't make you cruel," he repeated.

"I miss her," said Blair. "Anytime something big happens—good or bad—I wonder what she would have thought about it. Wonder what she would have said. She had *so much* to give. Her death was a total waste of life. She died for nothing. The gas station *still* got robbed. The addict *still* later got arrested. The bastard killed himself in prison, leaving a note to say he couldn't handle the guilt. Well then he shouldn't have shot her."

Luke swiped his thumb over her cheek to wipe away a tear. He'd known the shooter died in prison, but he hadn't known it had been suicide.

"Realizing I'd have to live a life that didn't include my big sister ... it scared me. She'd always been there, always looked out for me. She was my role model. And then I didn't have her anymore. All of a sudden. Just like that."

Luke tucked her hair behind her ear. "It's a shock to lose someone. You might have moments throughout your life when you think of how horrible it would be to lose them, but you don't think you truly will. Then they're gone, and there's nothing you wouldn't do to turn back the clock."

"Nothing," she agreed, her voice breaking. "What was your mom like?"

Luke drew in a breath, almost wincing at the pang in his chest. "Funny as fuck. Quick to laugh. The life and soul of every party." He swallowed, his throat thickening. "We argued the day she died. It wasn't a big fight or anything. She was just riding my ass about the chores I hadn't done, and I gave her a load of classic juvenile back-talk. I asked her why she couldn't be more like my friend's mom, who didn't assign her kids more than one chore each," he admitted, a crushing sense of shame settling on his shoulders. "She just rolled her eyes, told me not to be a brat, and then left. An hour later, she was dead."

"I can see that you feel like a sorry sack of shit for saying that stuff to her, but you didn't do it to be cruel. And it sounds to me like she wasn't hurt by it. Not if she rolled her eyes. I very much doubt she walked out of the apartment thinking you didn't love her or something."

"I know all that intellectually, but the shame is there anyway. And I'll always hate that those were the last words I spoke to her." Luke took a long breath. "It's ironic that she was killed by anti-shifter extremists when they didn't even know she was a shifter."

Blair doodled soft circles on his shoulder with her finger. "Their target was the family who owned and worked at the hardware store they bombed, right?"

He nodded. "To the extremists, any humans inside were simply collateral damage." He paused as Blair pressed a kiss to his collarbone. "I didn't think my dad would survive her loss. She was his other half in every way a person can be. He was a shell of a man without her. He weakened a little more every day. Faded and faded, until it was like he was only half-here; like his soul had partially moved on. And there was nothing I could do. I've never felt so fucking helpless." So fucking *terrified.* "I don't know how he fought his way back to us, but he did."

"I adore him for it," she said.

"So do I." Luke again stroked a hand over her head, letting the silky strands of her hair sift through his fingers, grounding himself in the feel of his mate. "I struggled to process her death. No, that's not right. I didn't *want* to process it. I didn't want to accept that she was gone for good. So I was already a mess when me and Toby were taken."

Blair stilled, her brows snapping together. "Taken? Wait, who's Toby?"

"My childhood friend. Best friend, really." Luke very rarely spoke of him or what happened. Just thinking about it made the bottom fall out of his stomach.

"You said you were both taken. What did you mean?"

Luke hesitated, his fingers flexing. It was instinctive to shut the conversation down and pull back. But he didn't, because the mating bond would never progress if he didn't share his secrets with Blair. "A few years prior, a handful of our pride left to begin their own. They weren't the first to do so, and they won't be the last. It happens. What doesn't happen is that they return, insisting on reconnecting the prides but having a change of leadership."

"The Alpha of the mini pride wanted Vinnie to step down so he could take over?"

"Yes. My dad laughed in Franco's face. The guy was no match for Vinnie. Their animals battled for dominance. My dad's cat won. Franco and his little group scurried off, but not for good."

She splayed a warm hand on his chest. "They took you and Toby."

"Their intention was to punish Vinnie. But they were also blackmailing him. They wanted cash so they could disappear. And they promised not to hurt me so long as he cooperated. But they didn't promise not to hurt Toby." Luke buried a hand in her hair as the memories battered at him. "I could hear him screaming. Begging them to stop. I couldn't help—I was strapped to a chair and locked in another room. They'd injected us with something to be sure we couldn't shift and to keep us physically weak. The drug worked well."

Blair shuffled closer and burrowed into his body.

Luke rubbed his cheek against hers, letting her attempt to soothe him although he knew nothing truly would. Not when it came to Toby. "My dad wired over the cash. Franco and his people headed out in a hurry, leaving me and Toby behind, and texted our location to my dad. We were rescued pretty fast, and the bastards were caught and killed. Toby … he didn't talk afterwards. Didn't even look at me. Not that day, not any other day. He and his parents left the pride shortly after that."

"It was another loss for you," said Blair, an ache in her voice that matched the one in his chest.

"Another moment of sheer helplessness. Another time in which someone important to me was suffering and I could do nothing to help. And not having my mom there afterward to hug me and tell me everything would be fine forced me to accept that she was gone." Luke paused as pure feminine despair zipped up their bond. "We can stop here. I can tell you the rest another time."

She shook her head. "No, get it all out."

Half-wishing she'd asked him to stop, he nonetheless went on, "I didn't really grieve the way I should have. I was conscious of how hard it was for my dad to cope without her that I thought it best if he didn't need to deal with my pain on top of his own. And I think part of me felt that, after what I'd said to her before she died, I didn't feel I had the right to grieve anyway."

"So everything just built up inside you—anger, hurt, guilt, shame—and never found a way out," she understood.

"I ventured into an emotional dark place I didn't know existed. There was this sheet of ice between me and the world. An emptiness. A thick fog. An ever-present mental storm that dragged me under."

"Sounds a little like depression."

"Whatever it was, it reached a point when I even felt a sense of detachment from my cat. Everyone thought that I was fine, because I made sure I seemed fine. Only a few people sensed I was having issues—Tate, Deke, Elle, and later my dad. For a while, he was caught up in his own pain so he didn't sense mine.

"They tried to help, but they couldn't. No one could. I was lost. Until you." Luke palmed her face, sweeping his thumb over her cheekbone. "I saw you, and everything changed in an instant. The ice fractured. The fog around me lifted. The emptiness faded. The mental storm calmed. You were a light that pierced the endless blackness—a light I followed like a beacon that showed me the way out."

At that point, he'd had to confront the anger, guilt, and shame he'd buried deep. It had been hard, but he'd done it, determined to never emotionally check out on his mate. Those dark emotions still lived inside him, but they were no longer a hum in his blood. Instead, they were small, weak, flickering flames in his belly.

Sometimes those flames flared up, which was why … "The mental storm I mentioned occasionally begins to build. But you always quash it in time. You're what stands between me and that dark, empty place. It's a hell of a weight for you to carry—I know that. I wish it wasn't so."

She frowned and jabbed his chest with her finger—the last thing he'd expected. "It's not a weight, it's a privilege," she said. "You've been my shield all these years. It was never a burden, right? You were glad to be whatever I needed. Well, same goes."

His heart squeezed. Shit, she got to him. Like nothing and no one else ever had.

He dropped his forehead to hers, dragging a breath into his lungs, drowning in her scent. Needing her taste, he closed his mouth over hers, swallowing her little gasp.

Arousal thickened his blood, but he didn't roughly dominate her mouth. He sipped. Savored. Gently feasted. Poured everything of himself into it.

They touched, stroked, teased, explored. Then he was inside her. Each thrust was soft and lazy and exquisitely sensuous. They tumbled over the edge together, her pussy spasming as harsh blasts of come erupted out of his cock. Peace once more stole over him.

Shuddering from aftershocks, he buried his face in her neck, enjoying the feel of her fingers ghosting over his back.

"Thank you for sharing all that with me," she said.

He pressed a kiss to her throat and then lifted his gaze to hers. "Thank you for telling me about your sister."

"And thank you for making me come really, really hard."

He felt his lips quirk. "I aim to please."

"Hmm, well, I'll do the pleasing in the morning. Right now, I need sleep."

"You'll do the pleasing?" he asked, intrigued. "What does that mean?"

She gave him a mysterious smile. "You'll find out when you wake up, won't you?"

CHAPTER FOURTEEN

A handful of her hair bunched in his fist, Luke watched as his mate swallowed his cock over and over. He'd woken to the feel of her tongue lapping and swiping along his shaft. Once she'd been sure he was fully awake, she'd taken him in her mouth.

He'd spent the past ten or so minutes battling back the orgasm that was hot on his heels. He was losing that battle. The heat of her breath, the tight suction of her mouth, the little hums she let out, the rasp of her tongue against each ridge and vein … There was only so much he could take.

He remembered the first time she'd blown him. It had been shortly after her eighteenth birthday, when they'd been making out on his sofa. She'd surprised him by slipping off his lap and, without a word, unbuttoning his fly to wrap her fingers around his cock. There'd been no awkward fumbling. No, she'd shot him a confident smile, told him he might be interested to know she'd read a lot of magazines filled with tips about oral sex, and then she'd promptly sucked him deep.

That was Blair. A damn minx through and through. One who shamelessly took and gave—something he loved about her.

He growled as her tongue flicked the sensitive spot beneath the head of his dick. "I'm going to fill your mouth with come," he told her as she went back to swallowing his length. "I want it in your belly while I fuck you. Because I *will* fuck you. But not until I've eaten that pussy I own."

A moan vibrated around his shaft. Inwardly cursing, he dragged in a breath, fighting for control. It didn't help, because he got another lungful of her heady scent. It infused the air, laced with arousal. It was more intoxicating than any drug or aphrodisiac. It called to him and his cat on a primal level.

"Make me come, baby."

She tightened her lips. Upped her pace. Sucked harder. Took him deeper.

His balls drew up tight, and the base of his spine tingled. Luke began pumping his hips, fucking her mouth with short, shallow digs of his cock. "Swallow it, Blair. Don't miss a drop." An electric pleasure coursed through him and seemed to zip up the length of his dick as he exploded.

Her jaw aching just a little, Blair pushed up onto her hands and knees and licked her lips. His breathing a little choppy, her mate stared at her through sex-drunk eyes that made her stomach clench.

"We need to frame those articles you read," he said.

Blair felt her mouth curve. She and Kiesha had pored over several back when they were eighteen, each determined to blow their male's mind despite their inexperience.

Luke grabbed her arms, dragged her to him, and kissed her hard. His tongue swept into her mouth, bold and sure, as he rolled her onto her back. "Now it's my turn to play." He slid down her body and settled himself between her thighs. His warm breath washed over her slick folds as he used his thumbs to part them. And then his mouth was on her.

Sweet Jesus, he knew how to use that tongue. It circled and rubbed at the sides of her clit, pausing now and then to lick and lap at her slit. His fingertips bit into her thighs as he held them in place while he tasted and touched and *took* the responses he wanted from her.

She burned. She moaned. She writhed. She wound tighter and tighter.

And then her release swept over her—dazing, consuming, devastating.

Her orgasm had no sooner subsided than Luke was bringing his body over hers, giving her his weight. She splayed her hands on the twin columns of his back, her lips parting as the blunt tip of his cock stretched her entrance, causing the most delicious burn.

Then he slammed home, savagely forcing her pussy to take every inch.

She almost choked on the ragged breath that got trapped in her throat. "Christ, Luke." Wanting to ride him, she tried flipping him onto his back. It didn't work.

His eyes dark and fevered, he pinned her hip down, the pads of his fingers digging into her skin. "No," he rumbled, *all* alpha. "You'll stay where I put you." His pace fast, he began roughly pounding his hips forward, taking her in viciously hard thrusts.

She scored her nails down his back, moaning at *how damn deep* he sank. The sex last night had been sweet and tender. This was savage and explosive. He all but rutted on her, and her animal reveled in it. Reveled in being so elementally *taken*.

"You were born for this," he snarled. "Born to be fucked by me."

His sharp teeth repeatedly scraped and bit as he plowed into her body, leaving little marks on her lip, her jaw, her neck, and her breasts. Each sting fed the orgasm building inside her. It was a hot, spasming, bubbling force in her lower stomach that kept stretching and stretching like an elastic band destined to snap.

Still hammering hard and deep, he delivered a soft bite to the side of her face. "My baby needs to come, don't you?"

"So do you." She could feel his cock swelling and pulsing.

Teeth raked over her claiming brand. "You first." He bit down hard, ramming his cock faster and deeper ... and the elastic force in her belly finally snapped.

She scratched at his scalp, a silent scream snagging her breath, her pussy clutching and rippling and milking. He locked his cock deep, filled her with hot bursts of his come, her name a growl in his throat.

Aspen chuckled at the TV screen. "God, I love this movie. So much blood and gore. Sadly, no matter how often I try, I can't get Camden to watch it. And I've tried *really* hard."

Sitting on the Alpha pair's sofa beside the bearcat, Blair dived her hand into her bag of popcorn. "He's not into zombie movies, I take it?"

"No, not even a little. Which I just don't get. They're not only ace, they double as training videos."

Blair blinked. "Training videos?"

"Yeah. For Z-Day. It'll arrive at some point. I intend to be ready."

At a loss for words, Blair looked from Havana to Bailey, who both smiled.

"To answer the question that's got to be floating through your head, yes, she's totally serious," said Havana, curled up at the other corner of the sofa.

Huh. Well okay.

Blair chucked popcorn in her mouth, returning her gaze to the TV. The girls had invited her to a "movie afternoon." Not a movie night, because the Alphas would apparently be busy later.

Wanting to know the girls better, Blair had easily accepted the invite. She would have done so even if she hadn't gotten the sense that she could *really* like these women, because it was important for the pride's inner circle to know each other well and hopefully get along.

As nosy as he was overprotective, Luke had accompanied her but headed onto the back deck, where Tate, Deke, Camden, and Isaiah were then sat drinking beers. Not that Luke had *stayed* out there. He'd popped his head into the room every fifteen minutes or so, or even crossed to her to drop a kiss on her head and ask if she was fine—like he couldn't sense for himself through their bond that she was indeed perfectly fine.

As much as she adored him, the constant *are you all rights* got old fast. So she'd been glad when Tate earlier asked both him and Isaiah to accompany the Alpha while he handled a pride issue that required his personal attention.

Comfortable with the other pride members, Blair had no problem remaining behind. She suspected that Tate had taken Luke because he'd wanted Blair to have uninterrupted quality time with the other females. Or maybe he'd noticed how close she'd been to throwing her popcorn in Luke's face.

Sinking deeper into the armchair, Bailey said, "If there ever is a zombie apocalypse—"

"If?" echoed Aspen.

"—we'll hardly need to kill any. They don't eat animals, right? So we can shift into our animal forms whenever they're around. *Boom*."

Aspen held up a finger. "Okay, first of all, there *will* be an apocalypse. Let's not pretend otherwise. Secondly, there's actually no clear-cut answer as to whether or not animals will be at risk. Different instruction videos show different scenarios."

"Movies, Aspen," Havana corrected with a sigh. "They're movies. Fiction. Forms of entertainment."

"*Educational* forms of entertainment," Aspen insisted.

The Alpha female rolled her eyes.

Blair's phone chimed. Digging it out of her pocket, she snickered at the funny meme Kiesha sent her by text.

"Is that Luke checking up on you?" asked Havana.

Blair shook her head. "It's Kiesha. But I don't doubt that I'll receive a message from him soon to make sure I'm good, despite that he knows I'm safe here. Just the very idea of me being out of his sight makes him a little edgy."

"Ordinarily, I'd tease him about it," said Havana. "But with the way things are right now, I can't blame him. Tate told me about the latest note you received. The person obsessed with you really isn't in touch with reality. The stuff he says, the way he says it … It's more chilling than any threat. And to know the sicko isn't simply a from-afar-admirer but someone who *knows* you only makes it worse."

Aspen nodded. "Your animal must have lost her mind when she realized he'd marked her old territory."

"Oh, she did," confirmed Blair. "She still snarls whenever she thinks about it. Like right now."

"I heard she tore into Finley's ankle," said Bailey, a twinkle in her eye.

The memory made Blair's inner female bare her teeth in a feral grin. "The bitch dismissed her like she was no more than a gerbil. Not sure why Finley thought that would be advisable. The woman really needs to make better life choices. Such as dropping the idea that she can take my status from me."

"She will drop the fantasy eventually," began Havana, "she just won't do it easily."

"Yeah, I sensed that. It doesn't help that some of the pride seek out her rather than me regarding matters that should be taken to the Beta female. It reinforces the idea in her head that the position should be hers." Blair tossed more popcorn into her mouth and chewed a little harder than necessary.

"What you did at the Tavern went a long way to convincing people that you'll be the Beta female they need," said Havana. "But some are so loyal to Finley—either because they're her friends, family, or people who feel indebted to her—that they go to her for assistance rather than you. That won't last long, though, if for no other reason than that their inner animals will push them to go to you, recognizing you as stronger and more dominant."

"Which will leave Finley with two options—back down, or challenge me to establish herself as the stronger female."

"She'll probably do the latter," said Aspen, taking the words right from Blair's mouth, "but I don't doubt that you can handle her. Luke said you're quite the scrapper."

"I've had to be," Blair told her. "Bush dogs begin fighting for dominance among their peers at the age of eight."

Aspen's brow puckered. "Eight?"

"It's instinctive for us," said Blair with a shrug. "There are no fights to the death when we're that young, though."

"Well at least there's that," said Aspen.

"We generally don't try to kill each other during duels until we're eleven or so."

Havana's mouth opened and closed. "I really don't know what to say to that."

Blair snickered. "Luke said those exact same words when I told him about it years ago. He also plainly and publicly stated that he'd murder the shit out of anyone who even entertained the thought of ending my life. I don't think he ever realized that the other female bush dogs only found it cute."

Bailey angled her head. "What was it like finding your true mate so early and having him around all this time watching over you?"

Blair felt her face soften. "Like the most natural thing in the world. He was always there when I needed him. Always had my back and built me up. I never felt alone. Never felt unsafe. Never doubted myself. He wouldn't have accepted anything else."

A slow, warm smile curved Havana's mouth. "I think that's beautiful."

"I've had Camden in my life since we were kids," said Aspen. "We grew up together. We had a tight bond even before we mated. We didn't actually realize we were predestined mates until recently, but having him at my side through all my highs and lows and all that jazz … I loved it. It's a special thing to have your true mate with you as you grow and mature and establish your sense of self."

"I'll bet having Luke around as you aged wasn't always easy, though," hedged Havana with a teasing smile. "He must have been an interfering pain in the ass at times. Such is the life of an alpha."

"For the most part, he was careful not to be too pushy," said Blair. "But that changed when I reached my mid-teens. He got more intense with each year that passed. My hormones kind of loved it, though. Even when he went all growly and caveman on me one night."

"Growly and caveman?" echoed Havana. "Ooh, I wanna hear about the growly and caveman incident."

Bailey leaned forward. "Yeah, *do* tell."

Blair smiled. "He came to a party on Sylvan territory when I was seventeen. I was talking to a bunch of people, including a few unmated males, when I sensed that Luke was nearby. Just before I turned toward him, one of the guys put his hand on my arm. The same guy Luke once caught trying to stroke my hair."

Aspen sucked in a short breath. "Oh, how unbelievably stupid."

"Yup." Blair crossed one leg over the other. "As you can imagine, Luke stalked right over like a Viking warrior. The male who'd touched me, Ryker, noticed him coming and backed away. But Luke got right in his face, threatened to snap each of his fingers if they ever touched me again, and then hauled me off to a dark corner where he backed me up against the wall."

Bailey fanned her face. "Stop, I might swoon."

Blair chuckled, her mind replaying the incident …

Luke shoved his way into her personal space, growling. "You smell of that fucker. I don't like it. My cat doesn't like it. He shouldn't be touching you."

She frowned. "It's not like he tried feeling me up or anything."

"Not the point. Has he made a move on you?"

"Of course not. No one would dare."

Luke planted a hand on the wall either side of her head. "Would you tell me if they did?"

"No, I'd probably just settle for breaking their will to live. Maybe also their nose. Stop growling. There's no way women don't come on to you sometimes. You never tell me about it."

"That's different, because they don't know I'm taken until I make it clear—which I do. The males here know *not to touch you. They know you belong to me."*

"You're still growling." She playfully snapped her teeth at him. "Bad kitty."

"You will not *make me smile."*

"He says while smiling."

"What did you do?" asked Aspen, pulling Blair back to the present.

Blair delved a hand into her popcorn again. "I planted a kiss on him. It was the last thing he expected. He almost pulled back. Almost. I ended up having the breath kissed out of my lungs, and then he marked me right there."

Bailey fanned herself again. "Well damn. It's not often the dude loses his composure like that."

"He's very self-contained a lot of the time," Blair agreed before chucking popcorn into her mouth.

"He's different with you, though," Bailey added. "He doesn't hold back from you. And he's a lot less restless now that he's mated to you. At peace, even, despite all that's happening."

Just then, Deke prowled into the room, fluid and smooth—no doubt coming to check on Blair on Luke's behalf.

Growing up, she hadn't *seen* other males. Luke took up all her mental space, he was the only man she'd ever wanted. But she could certainly objectively acknowledge that another guy was attractive. And there was no denying that Deke was supremely hot.

He glanced from one female to another. "What are you four talking about?"

Bailey sighed. "They don't believe me that bees can actually detect bombs."

He pinned her with a blank stare. "*I* don't believe you."

Her eyes widened. "It's true. Look it up. They can detect them with their tongues. Though how someone discovered that, I don't know. I didn't even know bees had tongues."

Shaking his head, Deke slid his gaze to Blair. "I'm surprised that Luke left you alone with the unholy trinity."

"Unholy trinity," Bailey echoed, her lips curling. "I like that."

Deke snorted. "You would." He muttered something beneath his breath and then returned to the backyard.

Blair looked at Bailey. "There's some kind of weird tension between you two." One that carried a sexual undertone. "Is he an ex bed-buddy?"

"What? Oh no," said Bailey with a chuckle. "He just doesn't like me. As such, he *really* doesn't like that I've gone on the occasional date with one of his BFFs. In Deke's opinion, Shay can do better."

Blair's brow furrowed. "He actually said that?"

"No," replied the mamba. "It's just plain obvious."

Aspen's nose wrinkled. "I'm not so sure that's the case at all, though I agree he doesn't like that you're dating Shay. I know you disagree, but I still think there's some jealousy involved."

Bailey snorted. "Deke wouldn't touch me with someone else's cock, let alone his. I annoy the hell out of him."

"You annoy the hell out of most people," Aspen pointed out. "And you do it on purpose."

"Life is for living," said Bailey.

Aspen frowned. "How does deliberately irritating people count as 'living?'"

"Why you gotta ask me rhetorical questions? You know I don't like them."

"It wasn't rhetorical. I genuinely don't understand."

"Well that's a *you* issue. Don't drag me into your problems."

Aspen ground her teeth. "You know, sometimes, I *really* want to hurt you."

"Yeah?" Bailey raised a daring brow. "Bring it, Montgomery."

"No," Havana cut in, slashing her arm through the air, "there'll be no *bringing*."

Feeling her mouth curve, Blair put her bag of popcorn on the table. "Is it okay if I use your bathroom, Havana?"

"I'd be bothered if you didn't," replied the Alpha. "I don't condone people peeing on my floor." She shot Aspen a hard look.

Aspen sighed. "I apologized for that."

Blair reared back. "You took a piss on her floor?"

"No, but my bearcat did while she was fighting with Bailey's mamba."

"Dirty bitch," Bailey muttered.

Aspen bristled. "Don't start throwing stones at my bearcat. Your damn snake is *no* innocent."

As the two females proceeded to argue once more, Blair left the room and headed to the half-bath that branched off the hallway. It was as she finished washing her hands that she heard loud hisses and yowls.

Racing into the living room, she skidded to a halt. Aspen and Bailey had shifted into their animal forms and, well, things weren't going well. The bearcat was slamming the snake's head on the coffee table, wheezing from the pressure of the mamba's body constricting around her body.

Havana charged into the room with Deke trailing behind her. "Both of you stop!" she ordered. "*Now*."

Thankfully, they did stop. Though not before the tip of the snake's tail bitch slapped the bearcat. Aspen's animal then bared her teeth and gripped said tail, her claws unsheathed. The mamba lunged at her with a hiss.

"I said, *stop*!"

Again, they did.

Havana looked at Blair. "I stepped out onto the deck to speak to Deke for *mere seconds*—I repeat, seconds—and in that short time the situation somehow managed to devolve to the point that they were brawling. Unreal."

At her side, Deke grunted. "I can guess who started it." He fired a harsh look at the black mamba, who then hissed at him—it was a long, drawn-out, chilling sound. To his credit, he didn't flinch or back away. Instead, he flicked up a brow. "You got a problem, Hissy Elliot?"

The snake launched herself at him.

Swearing under his breath, he snapped his hand closed around her neck before her fangs could get near him.

Havana growled. "*Enough with the lunging*!"

As Luke strolled along the street toward the cul-de-sac with Tate and Isaiah, he kept a close eye on his surroundings. He noted that his enforcers—most of whom currently posed as pedestrians to fool humans, since they couldn't afford to *look* like they were on patrol—were just as vigilant.

Finally done dealing with the pride issue that pulled him away from his mate … Okay, to be fair, *Tate* had pulled him away from Blair—rightly pointing out that Luke needed to give her the space to get to better know the other females rather than constantly invading said space.

His cat urged him to walk faster, eager to return to their mate. She was fine—they could feel it through the bond. Nonetheless, the feline wanted to be with her. Whether or not she'd be pleased that Luke had returned he didn't yet know.

Had he sensed that his hovering had quickly begun to grate on her nerves? Yes. It was a wonder she hadn't clawed him, really. In truth, though, Luke hadn't really been hovering so much as reminding Havana, Aspen, and Bailey that he was close in case they got the stupid idea to mess with Blair.

He didn't believe they'd give his mate any shit—so far, they hadn't been anything but friendly toward her. And the fact that they were attempting to pull her into their circle said good things. But his level of protectiveness had hit an all-time high the moment his bond with Blair partially formed. Pretty much *everything* felt like a potential threat to it.

That would settle once their bond fully snapped into place—something he believed should have happened by now. He had thought that their sharing of secrets and grief would have been enough to ensure it. However, it seemed that something else was blocking the bond's frequency, because it remained incomplete. It bugged Luke's cat just as much as it did him.

He'd ruminated on it for most of the day, trying to understand what the problem could be. Generally, fears, secrets, and barriers were responsible for jamming mating bond frequencies. But he had no more secrets from Blair. His barriers were down for certain, and he *felt* through their bond that she was not emotionally holding back from him.

All he could figure was that either she had a secret or two that she hadn't yet shared with him, or one of them harbored fears about mating—perhaps consciously, perhaps subconsciously.

Luke had searched within himself; found no fears. It was possible that Blair worried that mating with him would mean losing her mother for good. Luke was inclined to believe that Noelle would eventually get her act together rather than lose her daughter forever. But if Blair didn't hold that same belief, it could be interfering with their bond's development.

"Yo, Luke!" Damian called out.

Tracking his brother's voice, Luke spotted him standing across the street.

"You got a minute?" Damian asked.

Luke nodded and then turned to Tate and Isaiah. "You two head back. I won't be long." After a quick check of the road, Luke began to cross it.

A mechanical roar filled the air, and a screech of tires quickly followed.

Luke's head whipped to the right just in time to see a car gunning his way. His pulse leaping, he rushed toward the sidewalk.

A hard impact slammed into his leg, making his body roughly spin before he hit the pavement. Pain barreling through his limb, Luke ground his teeth and watched the vehicle speed away.

Damian, Tate, and Isaiah quickly materialized, their faces lined with both rage and shock.

"Jesus," said Damian, his eyes wide.

Tate squatted beside Luke. "You all right?" he asked, his voice almost a growl.

No, Luke wasn't *all right.* It was like a scorching hot force had *exploded* in his leg. And now it throbbed like a goddamn bitch even as it began to feel numb. He gently prodded it and hissed out a breath through his teeth. Definitely broken. "Could be worse." Which placated neither him nor his currently raging cat.

Tate flicked the grocery store a quick look. "Get Helena," he told Isaiah, referring to one of their healers. "She should still be at work."

Isaiah gave a curt nod and ran off just as several of their other pride mates gathered around Luke to check on him.

Luke's phone rang in his pocket. Since he could feel Blair's anxiety and panic spiking along their bond, the sight of her name flashing on the screen of his cell was of no surprise.

"I'm okay, baby," he assured her on answering.

"No, you're not," she gritted out. "I can *feel* that you're in pain. What happened? Where are you?"

His heart jumped at the thought of her leaving the Alpha pair's house. Which was exactly what she would do once she knew where to find him. He didn't want her out in public right now, fearing that whoever pulled the hit and run would return.

"I'm going to be fine," Luke told her. "The healer is on her way. I'll be at your side in a matter of minutes. I'll tell you everything then."

"*What happened, and where the hell are you*?"

Odd as it might sound, hearing her voice soothed him and his cat even though it rang with fury. "I know I'm not being fair right now, but I'm asking you to stay where you are. I'm not lying when I tell you I'll be fine, I promise."

At that moment, Helena appeared and crouched before him.

"I *swear*," began Blair, "if you don't tell me what happened I am gonna fuck your shit up, Skywhisker."

He winced. "My leg got clipped by a speeding car. Helena is healing the break right now." The healing energy crackled through his limb.

A long pause. "A speeding car?" asked Blair, a shake to her voice.

"Yes. I would imagine you're thinking exactly what I'm thinking; that our boy is done sticking to the shadows. He could have done this to not only draw you out but to weaken me enough that I can't do *shit* when he nabs you. So please, stay where you are."

He never begged anyone for anything. Ever. Didn't need to anyway. He dished out an order, and people obeyed. But he could never do that to his mate—they were equals. And if he had to beg to be sure she was safe, he'd do it.

"Okay." The word was a whisper.

Luke closed his eyes, relief blowing through him. "Thank you." He knew it was killing her to give him this; that it went against her every instinct to not come to him. "I'll be with you soon, baby, I swear." He rang off.

"You're healed," said Helena, standing.

Luke thanked her as he rose to his feet. "Did anyone get the license plate of the car that hit me?"

"I did," said Tate, his thumbs tapping his cell phone. "I'm currently texting it to River."

"It had to have been whoever's locked on Blair," said Damian. "They hit you on purpose, Luke. They sped up as they neared you."

"I know." If he'd been a second or two slower, the vehicle wouldn't only have clipped his leg. "The son of a bitch will pay for that."

"Yeah," said Damian. "But you'll be lucky if you get the chance to make him pay. In my opinion, Blair will beat you to it."

CHAPTER FIFTEEN

Finished recounting the hit and run to the people sprawled around the Alpha pair's living room, Luke looked at his mate. She stood near the fireplace, her arms folded, her face blank, her eyes hard.

Blair had come rushing out of the cul-de-sac just as he'd returned. She'd faffed and fussed and hugged him tight, snarling "I'll kill him." Then they'd all come inside, and she hadn't spoken a single word since.

She was also keeping a physical distance from everyone. Even him. Her body language *screamed* "stay back." Her inner female was just as edgy—he could sense it.

There was no tumultuous knot of emotions at the other end of their mating bond. Not since a cold anger had washed over Blair, drowning out everything else. Now she was gloriously pissed, and she showed no signs of calming.

Like everyone else, he was giving Blair and her animal the space they needed. But he didn't like it. He wanted to close the gap between them. Wanted to hold Blair, touch her, thank her again for remaining here. His cat *hated* that they couldn't. But she was too worked up to accept comfort right then.

It gave Luke a small taste of how hard it must have been for her not to go to his side while he was hurting. He didn't believe that was Blair's reason for silently demanding space—she wasn't passive-aggressive, and she wouldn't purposely hurt him. But it gave him a taste of how she'd felt all the same.

"Well I think it's safe to say that Blair's stalker is escalating," said Tate. "That hit and run was no accident, and I can think of no other person who'd specifically target you that way."

"It had to have been him." Luke cut his gaze back to his mate. "He wanted you to 'come home.' You didn't. He likely blames me for that, not you. In his mind, that was bad enough. But then I claimed you—something he would have heard about from your other old pack mates, since they noticed the brand when we went to Sylvan territory. He probably won't believe that the claiming mark is real, but I suspect he wanted to punish me all the same for branding you."

Blair ground her teeth, her eyelid twitching.

Deke rubbed at his nape. "Shame you didn't get a glimpse of the driver."

"The sun was reflecting off the front window," said Luke. "I noticed a blue cap, but that's all." And since River discovered that the license plate not only didn't belong to the car that hit Luke but came from a stolen vehicle, they couldn't trace the culprit that way.

"Were there any symbols or logos or anything on the cap?" asked Tate.

"Not that I noticed," replied Luke. "But it all happened very fast, so I can't be sure."

Havana looked at Blair. "I know the driver probably recently bought the cap to help shield their face, but on the off-chance that it was something they dug out of their wardrobe I figure it's worth asking: Do you know of anyone who owns a blue cap?"

She only shook her head.

"What about the vehicle?" asked Tate. "It was a black Mercedes."

"I can't think of anyone who owns one," replied Blair, her voice somewhat flat.

River leaned forward in his seat, his gaze darting from Tate to Luke. "You may remember that I asked if we could all meet at some point today."

Both Luke and his brother nodded.

"I received some information that I think you should know," River added.

Luke cocked his head. "What is it?"

"As we all agreed that it was highly likely Blair was being targeted by someone from her old pack," began River. "I ran very thorough checks on every single, adult member—male and female, because we can't discount the possibility that it could be a woman. It took me a while to unearth all the information. Shifter groups are very private and exceptionally good at burying anything they don't want outsiders to know."

Havana crossed her arms over her chest. "What did you find out?"

River's eyes slid to Blair. "Did you know that the Head Enforcer, Antoine, is dating a human?"

Her brows dipped. "No, I didn't. But I never paid attention to his love life or anyone else's, and he never volunteered the information—he's kind of private when it comes to that stuff."

"He's dated many human females," River told her. "Two of whom contacted Embry at different times, asking him to insist that Antoine leave them alone."

The hairs on the back of Blair's neck lifted. "Leave them alone?" she echoed. Her inner female went very still, just as uneasy about where the conversation was heading.

"He apparently hadn't taken too kindly to them ending the relationship," River explained. "He bombed them with calls, gifts, and text messages. He often hung outside their homes in his vehicle. One claimed that he turned up at her place of work so often demanding to see her that she got fired."

Felled by shock, Blair gaped, her thoughts grinding to a halt. It took a few moments before she could speak. "Are you sure?"

"Positive," replied River.

Her arms slipped to her sides. "I had no idea." She would *never* have suspected Antoine of something like that. Although she didn't believe that River would lie or claim to be certain unless he absolutely was, she still found it hard to believe it was true. Surely Embry wouldn't have Antoine as Head Enforcer if it were. Then again, her uncle didn't much care for humans. He might not have considered it a big deal merely because the women weren't shifters.

Luke pushed to his feet and began to fluidly pace, tension bunching his muscles. "Given all that, how the hell can Embry claim that he has no reason to believe that anyone in the pack could be the person harassing Blair? Antoine is an obvious suspect."

"We don't know that Embry *doesn't* suspect him," said Tate. "In his position, we wouldn't easily admit to an outsider that we believed one of our own could be stalking someone. We'd want to handle the matter internally."

"At least a few others must know what Antoine did to the humans," said Aspen. "Embry probably swore them to silence."

"My brother can't possibly know or he'd have mentioned it for sure, regardless of if Embry forbid it or not," said Blair.

Even as he continued to pace, Luke fired her a reassuring look. "I would never think otherwise—Mitch adores you too much."

Her gut unknotted. He meant that, she sensed. He hadn't thrown out the words simply to calm her. Which was a huge freaking relief, because she wouldn't have to worry that he would try to secretly interrogate her brother.

River looked at Blair. "Are you aware that the pack's Beta, Donal, almost imprinted on someone when he was your age?"

Nodding, Blair licked her lips. "I heard about it. She's a bush dog from his old pack. He transferred to Sylvan territory shortly after he failed to fully imprint on her. That's all I know."

"Her name is Alayna." River tapped his thumbs on his cell a few times and then held it up to Blair. "This is a photograph of her."

The bottom dropped out of Blair's stomach, and her startled inner animal gave a quick shake of the head.

"I take it you've never seen a picture of her before," said River.

"No," Blair confirmed.

He slowly moved his phone from side to side, giving everyone a look at the photo on the screen … which was right about when Luke stopped pacing and burst out, "*Son of a bitch.*"

Bailey looked from Blair to the phone. "That is one *freaky* resemblance."

Yeah, she'd have to agree. Shit, she needed to sit down. But then Luke turned to her, pinning her in place with his intense gaze.

"No one mentioned that you look so much like her?" he asked.

"No," replied Blair. "But they might not have known. Donal never talked about her." Curious, she had once come close to asking him about the woman and what went wrong between them, but she'd worried it would be too sore a subject.

"If it's him who's stalking you, his obsession with you is likely to be more about her," Aspen said to Blair. "He'd probably see you as his second chance at getting everything he wants."

Blair wiped a hand down her face, unable to even *consider* that the male would think of her in a sexual sense. Not merely because he was twenty-five years her senior, but because … well, because she didn't want to. She'd always thought of him as sweet and uncle-y. "It doesn't make sense that it would be him. He's always been supportive of us being mates," she told Luke.

"Just because he seems supportive doesn't mean he truly is," Aspen gently pointed out.

River pocketed his phone. "I also did some digging on Gabriel. The guy is squeaky clean. No arrests, no fines, not even a single speeding ticket. He has little to no contact with shifters. His friends are human, his ex-girlfriends are human, his lifestyle is that of a human."

"You said *little* to no contact with shifters," Blair noted.

"Ah, yes, I discovered something that surprised me." River paused. "He co-owns Enigma."

Blair felt her brow furrow. "The shifter club?"

"Yes. He's a silent partner." River leaned back in his seat. "I had a long talk with one of the bartenders. Apparently Gabriel goes there occasionally. He selects a female from the crowd—always a leggy, submissive redhead—and fucks her in the club. He never takes a woman home. Never hangs around to talk to her. It's said that he doesn't even ask for names."

"His animal isn't satisfied with humans, so Gabriel occasionally gives him what he needs," mused Isaiah.

"That would be my guess," said River.

Blair rocked forward on the balls of her feet. "He clearly has a type. I'm not submissive. I'm also no redhead."

"That doesn't have to mean anything," Aspen told her. "Camden slept with *guys* before me—some of whom were submissive."

"There was one time that Gabriel deviated from his usual 'fuck them without talking to them' routine," said River. "It was another submissive, leggy redhead. Someone the bartender knew well. A fox shifter." He looked at Blair. "Macy Corbitt. The woman you found dead on your porch."

Everything inside Blair went still, including her female. *Hell to the no.*

Luke swore long and loud. "When did Gabriel sleep with her?"

"Two months before she ventured to Sylvan territory to lie that she'd recently shared your bed," replied River.

"Gabriel could have put her up to it," said Deke. "He might have hoped it would come between Luke and Blair. Did the bartender hear what they talked about?"

River shook his head. "No."

Blair puffed out a breath, utterly stunned. She met Luke's gaze, finding it focused on her.

"We need to speak with Donal, Antoine, and Gabriel," he said.

Tate poked the inside of his cheek with his tongue. "We could interrogate Gabriel without anyone attempting to interfere. But Embry isn't going to consent to you questioning any of his pack mates. Not even if they don't have an alibi for earlier today when you were hit by the car."

"He might be cooperative when he realizes that we know he's been keeping important info from us," clipped Luke.

"True," allowed Tate with an incline of his head. "But if the culprit is either Donal or Antoine, you'll tip their hand by questioning them. Right now, they have no clue that we have all this information about them. It might be better to keep it that way. They're more likely to slip up if they don't think we're focused on them."

Havana raked her teeth over her lower lip. "I'd have to agree with Tate. What do you think, Blair?"

Rubbing the back of her neck, Blair replied, "I think whoever's harassing me isn't going to hold their hands up and admit to it." She cut her gaze to her mate. "Especially not to you, who they seemingly hate enough to want dead. I'm not certain anything productive would come of you questioning them."

"I'm good at making people talk," said Luke, a deadly note to his voice.

"I'm sure you are," said Blair. "And they might well confess under duress. But Embry will *never* permit any of us to full-on interrogate them. Not unless they're caught at something. That could in fact happen at some point, considering the shithead is escalating, but not if they're aware that they're officially suspects."

Luke clenched his jaw tightly shut, likely to bite back a string of objections that he knew wouldn't be founded in logic but instead a *need* for answers.

"When it comes to Gabriel, it's a different situation," said Blair. "You already made it clear to him that you consider him a suspect. As such, unlike with the oblivious Donal and Antoine, he's already on his guard. You have nothing to lose by revealing that you know he slept with Macy. But you can't subject him to an interrogation."

Luke's eyes flared. "I can't?"

"No. We don't have grounds for it. That he slept with Macy doesn't make him a suspect. *You* slept with her."

Luke very slowly angled his head. "You think it's a coincidence that he fucked a woman who was killed and then dumped on the porch of your old cabin?"

"What I think is that it's not enough to implicate him. Did you ask the enforcers who keep watch over him if he left his condo earlier?"

"Yes," said Luke, his voice curt. "They reported that he hadn't left, but that doesn't mean he didn't find a way to sneak out without their knowledge."

True enough. He'd certainly proven that he was good at circumventing guards and security measures. Still … "Personally, I'm leaning more toward Antoine, considering he's exhibited *actual* stalker behavior in the past."

"He is a more obvious suspect, yes, but I'm not ruling either Donal or Gabriel out."

Blair wasn't ready to do that either. "I'm not suggesting that you should. Gabriel should definitely be questioned. I'm only pointing out that we can't justify putting him through the kind of gruesome interrogation you have in mind."

A long, gruff sigh slipped out of Tate. "She's right. We can't. He slept with Macy but, and I don't say this with disrespect, so did a lot of shifter males. It doesn't make him guilty of anything."

"We could do with Gabriel what we did with Davis Regent," said Camden. "We could take him somewhere for a friendly chat but keep our claws sheathed this time."

"It wouldn't work out that way," said Blair. "Gabriel would fight back if you tried nabbing him, so blood would naturally be shed. The absolute last thing he would then do is answer any questions you have. *I* sure as hell wouldn't." She switched her focus to Luke. "You'd have more success with him if you just paid him a visit and asked a few questions the way you did last time."

It was Tate who responded. "A chat with him might not get us the answers we need, but it's worth a try." He slid his gaze to Luke. "I could come with you, but it will seem a much more official visit if your Alpha is present. That might make him less inclined to talk."

"It likely would, and I don't want that," said Luke. "I'll take Deke again. Isaiah, you'll stay in the car with Blair." Once all three had agreed to the plan, he sighed. "Let's get it over with, then."

T*his was what pussy got you*, thought Luke as he crossed to Gabriel's building, his mind's eye still focused on the trusting look Blair had given him as he'd told her he'd be back soon. She believed down to her soul that Luke wouldn't ignore what was "fair" to Gabriel and quite simply interrogate the motherfucking shit out of him. And now Luke felt cornered.

If he did what he wanted to do, he'd disappoint her; violate her trust. It would gut him to do that. It would gut *her* that he'd done it. So what could he do but be "fair" to Gabriel?

Yeah, Luke was boxed in all right.

Deke pushed the front door of the building open, and they both filed inside. They crossed the lobby, stopping in front of the elevator. It *dinged.* The doors opened. And a familiar male stepped out.

"Gabriel," said Luke—more in surprise than in greeting.

The male's shoulders tensed. "You're back."

His cat's hackles rising at that flat tone, Luke said, "We should talk." Preferably somewhere dark and isolated where they could have privacy and no one would hear the guy scream. But that wasn't going to happen, unfortunately.

Gabriel's gaze darted to the door. "Can this wait? I have somewhere I need to be."

"Someone hit me with a car a couple of hours ago."

Gabriel's lips parted in what seemed like genuine surprise.

"They drove off before they could be caught or even identified. It's not a stretch to guess it's the same person who's been harassing Blair. A person who we recently learned marked each room of her old cabin."

Gabriel's eyes flashed with an emotion that Luke couldn't quite define. "Marked?"

Luke nodded, folding his arms. "She also received a letter. It was much like the email that he sent her, only he threw in some rebukes that would suggest he's getting frustrated with her for not dancing to his tune. He's certainly not happy that she hasn't returned to the pack, and he's going to get unhappier because that will *never* happen. I need to know if you've discovered anything since the last time we spoke."

"You'll know from the people you have watching me that I've been nowhere near Sylvan territory."

"We also know you're exceptionally good at moving about unseen," Deke told him. "It would be no shock to learn that you left without detection and went for a wander around your old territory."

Gabriel glanced away, exhaling heavily. He tipped his chin toward the far wall, and the three of them moved away from the elevator. "I didn't see or hear anything of interest while there," he said. "There's a lot of unrest. People are nervous, speculating on which of them could possibly be stalking Blair."

"Is there anyone in particular they're leaning toward?" asked Luke.

"No. If Blair had any admirers within the pack, said admirers kept it quiet."

"Have you spoken with your cousin, Antoine? Does he have any suspects?"

"I haven't spoken with him since the day I was banished. From what I overheard him say to others, he doesn't suspect anyone in particular. Not even me, unlike some of the others."

"You never heard Embry or Donal toss any names about?" Luke narrowed his eyes when the other male hesitated. "What do you know?"

A few seconds of silence ticked by. "Donal said something to Embry about how it was possible that Antoine was up to his old tricks, whatever that means, but the Alpha insisted that Donal was wrong."

Luke's scalp prickled. "You have no clue at all what Embry could have been referring to?"

"The only thing I can think of is that Antoine was a persistent pranker as a juvenile. He often made anonymous, idiotic calls to females within the pack. You said Blair received many strange calls, so …" Gabriel shrugged. "I suppose, in your eyes, I'm still a suspect."

"I wouldn't take it personally. If it makes you feel better, she still doesn't suspect you. She was surprised to learn that you co-own Enigma." He expected the bush dog to tense or otherwise exhibit some show of surprise, but he only smiled.

"You did your homework," said Gabriel. "I thought you might."

"Why be a *silent* partner?"

"Why not?"

Touché.

Gabriel cocked his head. "I have to wonder why you would come to me for information when you're hardly likely to trust a word I say. Do you hope that I will accidentally say something to implicate myself? If so, you are wasting your time—and, unfortunately, mine. I am not the man who stalks Blair." He flicked a quick look at his wristwatch. "I really do have to go. If I find out anything more, I will pass on the information to the enforcers you have watching me."

"You like redheads," Luke tossed out. "You like to fuck them fast and then leave, no chats. But you broke that habit with Macy Corbitt."

Confusion marred Gabriel's brow. "Who?"

"You don't know her?"

"It's possible that I do, but I can't be sure. I don't exchange names with women at Enigma."

That much was true at least. "It was said that you had quite a talk with a particular redheaded fox shifter."

Realization dawned on him. "Ah, yes. I thought she'd been drugged at first."

"Drugged?" echoed Deke.

Gabriel nodded. "She was trembling. Seemed a little out of it. I was worried her drink had been spiked. That was why I wanted to talk to her. The problem wasn't drugs, it was touch-hunger."

"You didn't talk about Blair with her?" asked Luke.

The bush dog again frowned. "Why would I have?"

"That wasn't an answer."

Gabriel sighed, seeming more bored than anything else. "No, I did not. Why the interest in the fox shifter?"

"Because it was her corpse that found its way to Blair's old cabin."

The bush dog went utterly rigid. "You're certain?"

"Absolutely positive."

"And you think I killed her?" asked Gabriel, no inflection in his voice. "Left her on Blair's old doorstep?"

"Maybe," said Luke. "Maybe you also encouraged her to go to Blair with lies that I'd been sleeping with Macy in recent months."

"Well I did not. As I've told you before, I'm not the man you're looking for. Believe me or don't. It won't change that it's true." He skirted around Luke and stalked off. Didn't hurry, didn't march, didn't move with anger. Just casually breezed out of the building.

Exiting the complex at a slower pace, Luke watched as the male headed to a town car. Without even a mere glance in Luke and Deke's direction, Gabriel drove off.

"He doesn't seem in the least bit offended that we'd suspect him," commented Deke. "The only thing he seemed to feel was inconvenienced. The letter and email from Blair's stalker carry a lot of emotion. I can't imagine Gabriel writing stuff like that."

No, neither could Luke.

"I'm not saying we should cross him off our suspect list. It's just something to consider."

Yes, it was. Back inside the SUV, Luke clicked on his seatbelt and started up the engine.

"Well?" prompted Blair, riding shotgun.

"He answered my questions, I just don't know if I believe he answered them truthfully." Luke gave her a rundown of the conversation. "He seemed genuinely shocked when he learned that the fox shifter he spoke with at the club was the same woman you found dead outside your old home."

"But you're not convinced that his shock was real," she sensed.

"No, I'm not. I'll bet he's a very good actor—any shifter who has spent most of their life pretending to be human would have to be extremely good at pretense." Luke knew that from personal experience.

She hummed. "Valid point. I can tell you that that thing he said about

Antoine pulling a lot of pranks as a juvenile was true. But I suspect Donal wasn't talking about that when he spoke about 'old tricks.'"

Luke nodded. "He was referring to Antoine's history of stalking women. Donal probably helped Embry cover it up."

"Speaking of the pack Beta," began Isaiah, "don't be so distracted by Antoine and Gabriel that you dismiss Donal."

Blair's nose wrinkled. "He's a lot older than me. The guy is in his forties."

"And remains single, yes?" asked Isaiah.

She frowned. "I've never known him to date. And though he's had plenty of bed-buddies, none have ever been from the pack."

Deke sank back into his seat. "Maybe he's saving himself for his true mate. Maybe he's too hurt after his failure to imprint on that Alayna person that he has trouble committing to women. Or maybe he's focused on you."

Her shoulders sagged. "I always liked him," she said, her voice low and sad. "I liked them all. It sucks that one of them is likely stalking me; that I never really knew that particular person at all."

Luke splayed a hand on her thigh. "I know, baby. I know."

Finally back in their apartment, Blair roughly shrugged off her jacket and none too gently hung it on a peg near the door. "Today started off fine, but it went progressively downhill." She fisted her hands. "I still can't believe that rat bastard tried mowing you down with his car." She frowned when Luke hauled her close. "What are you doing?"

He nuzzled her neck. She smelled of him, of home, of everything he needed. "Giving you the comfort I wanted to give you earlier but you were too edgy to accept."

He soothingly stroked her hair, scalp, nape, back, and arms … until the tension finally leached out of her muscles. His cat rubbed up against her, kneading Luke's insides with his claws, desperate to ease her hurt and anger.

She melted against Luke. "Do we take the hit and run as a sign that he *finally* sees you as something other than a person I'm pretending to be mated to? I mean, he wouldn't otherwise seek to hurt you, would he?"

"I'd say I'm no longer a background character in his fictional world. I'm, at the very least, a secondary character now."

"One he'll try to kill off," she added, her voice slightly guttural. "I always knew there'd be a few hiccups when we finally mated. I never imagined we'd be dealing with a situation like this."

Luke wrapped her ponytail around his fist and gently tugged so that she'd let her head fall back. "I can feel you starting to get riled up all over again. How about we shove everything other than us out of our heads for a little while? It won't be easy, no, but we need it. And maybe we can spend some time working out why our bond hasn't fully snapped into place yet. I don't get it."

She pulled a face. "Me neither. I really thought it would happen after we offloaded all the crap we've tried protecting each other from all these years."

"No more secrets in your closet?"

"None. What about you?"

"There's nothing I'm keeping from you." He swept his hand down her back. "It could be that …"

"What?"

"Fears can act as blocks. Maybe you fear that you'll lose Noelle for good once you and I are fully mated."

"Actually, I'm more hopeful that it'll force her to accept defeat and maybe she'll then get her shit together."

Huh. Well there went that theory. "In that case, I don't know what could be jamming the frequency of the bond."

She splayed a hand on his chest right above his heart. "We'll work it out eventually. I guess, in the meantime, we just have to be patient."

He bit her chin. "I've waited long enough to be fully bound to you. I don't like that I have to wait longer."

"I'm not fond of the situation either, but there's nothing we can really do about it. Which makes the whole thing suck even more."

"Yeah. Yeah, it does."

CHAPTER SIXTEEN

Looking down at the bush dog playfully attacking the living room rug a few days later, Luke exhaled heavily. She could be as destructive as a bored pup at times. In her view, everything was a potential chew toy. She'd lunge at whatever she could sink her teeth into. Chew it. Claw it. Even eat it.

He didn't know what bothered him more—that she was wrecking yet another object in their home, or that his cat wanted to join in the "fun."

Luke scratched his cheek. "How about we go outside?" he proposed, knowing Blair would communicate his words to the animal. "You can play in the backyard."

The little female didn't even look at him.

"So that's a no, then." Luke would have tried to take the rug from her if he didn't know she'd misinterpret the move as a *let's play a game of tug of war.* That was how it always went if he tried taking away a new "toy" she'd claimed. And he never won such games, or walked away uninjured.

There would be no distracting her with another toy either. Once she'd settled on one, she wouldn't abandon it until she was ready. And by ready, he meant bored.

The phone on the coffee table rang. Blair's phone.

Luke grabbed it, checked the screen, and then held up the cell. "Your brother's calling."

Eerily dark eyes slid his way, but she didn't release the rug. Just kept on growling and snarling and tearing into it.

"You gonna answer the phone or not?"

She attacked the rug with renewed vigor. Which basically meant that Blair wasn't pushing for supremacy, likely enjoying his frustration with her female.

Little witch.

"Don't think you won't pay for this later, Blair." He swiped his thumb over the phone's screen and answered, "Hey, it's Luke. Your sister can't come to the phone right now. Her female is currently in charge, and she's busy tussling with inanimate objects."

Mitch snickered. "If the bush dog's in one of those moods, you'd be wise not to take your eyes off her for long—she'll get into all kinds of shit."

"I know that from prior experience. Want me to pass on a message to Blair?"

"Yeah, if you don't mind. Quick warning, I don't think you're going to like this much. The odds are that her female won't like it much either, so you might want to move away from sensitive canine ears. A pissy bush dog is not fun to deal with."

His scalp prickling, Luke stalked into the kitchen but didn't close the door, enabling him to keep an eye on the little female. "I'm out of earshot. Tell me."

"My parents want to meet with Blair."

Luke froze, and his cat let out a long hiss. "Why?"

"They don't like the growing distance between her and them. It's eating them up. They want to fix it."

He narrowed his eyes. "You're certain that that's truly what they want? That they aren't simply hoping to have the chance to toss more dogshit on her doorstep or to talk her into returning to your territory?"

"My mother swears that she has no intention of making an ugly scene. She says that, like my dad, she wants to make peace."

"Just like that?" asked Luke, his voice oozing disbelief.

"I can see why you'd be skeptical—"

"Of course I'm skeptical." Luke paused as the bush dog darted out of sight. Well at least she'd gotten bored savaging the rug. "As much as I figured that Noelle would back down eventually, I didn't think she'd do it this soon."

"I don't believe she would have if it wasn't for one thing—she's scared for Blair right now. Truly afraid. There's no missing that the stalking is escalating, especially after the hit and run, and my mother is terrified that she'll lose another daughter. Noelle wouldn't survive the loss, Luke. I know she wouldn't."

Luke let out a long breath, rubbing at his nape. Could Noelle's fear for Blair have lit a fire under her ass and led her to back down? Maybe. That kind of terror could certainly shift a person's priorities and remind them of what was truly important. It could make them determined to fix any rifts even if only so that they'd then be around to protect their loved ones. But that didn't mean this was the case with Noelle, did it?

"I'll pass the message onto Blair and see how she feels about it," said Luke.

"I appreciate it."

Luke frowned as the again-growling bush dog dragged a sneaker past the doorway by its laces like she was heaving dead prey to a den, quickly disappearing out of his line of sight. He shook his head at her antics.

"How is Blair?" asked Mitch.

"Fine." Albeit frustrated that her stalker remained unidentified and uncaught.

"She hasn't called in a few days."

"There hasn't been anything new to report." Nothing more had happened since the hit and run.

"Embry mentioned that you spoke to Gabriel again to try to rattle his cage."

Luke wouldn't have told the Alpha at all if Embry hadn't contacted him to ask about it. It seemed that Embry had assigned people to watch Gabriel's complex, and they'd reported that Luke paid Gabriel a second visit.

Initially, Luke had considered telling the Alpha what he'd learned of Gabriel from River. But Luke worried that Embry—so desperate to believe his own pack mates weren't at fault—would then insist on believing that the guilt lay with Gabriel. After all, he'd thrown accusations at Gabriel's door without full proof of guilt once before, hadn't he? As such, Luke had merely claimed that he'd had another chat with Gabriel in the hope of somehow tripping him up.

"He also thinks that maybe there was a little more to it than that you wanted to simply rattle Gabriel's cage," said Mitch. "Embry suspects that you have info you're not passing on."

The Alpha hadn't said as much to Luke. "If that *were* the case, he wouldn't be in a position to judge."

"What does that mean?"

Luke couldn't exactly share what he'd discovered about Donal and Antoine. Not that he believed Mitch would break his confidence. It simply wouldn't be fair to expect Mitch to keep secrets from his own Alpha. So, Luke simply replied, "Surely you haven't forgotten that when Blair was part of your pack he kept from me everything that recently happened to and around her."

A heavy exhale. "He shouldn't have done that, I know. But if he'd thought she was in true danger back then, he would have contacted you."

Frowning at the sight of Blair's female balancing on her front paws as she once more moved past the doorway, Luke said, "I'm not so sure of that. It was made obvious by Macy's death that the person who's obsessed with Blair is dangerous. Nonetheless, Embry asked her not to tell me anything."

"You think Embry's covering up for someone?"

"Not necessarily." Luke doubted that, being her uncle, the Alpha would do such a thing. "I'm just not convinced that he's keeping me fully in the loop. I find it incredibly difficult to believe that he doesn't have at least *one* suspect. He questioned every member of your pack. He investigated the matter thoroughly—or so he claims, just as he claims he's making impartial judgements. If the latter were true, there'd be at least one or two people he'd be keeping his eye on. And if that is the case, it's not something he's bothered to share with me or Blair."

"On the one hand, I agree that he should suspect *someone*. But to be fair, *I* don't have a single suspect. There's no one who's ever come across as obsessed with Blair."

"But they wouldn't, would they? You're expecting this person to stand out somehow as 'creepy.' People like that rarely do, Mitch. On the contrary, they often seem personable, helpful, and even charming. They often also exhibit obsessive tendencies, so watch out for that."

Luke paused as his bush dog once more came into view—this time wrestling frantically with a plastic shopping bag, unable to get away from it since she'd somehow managed to hook one of its handles around her neck. He swore. "I have to go if I'm to save Blair's female from herself."

Mitch snorted. "Well good luck with that. Tell Blair I said hi and to call me when she can."

"Will do." Luke rang off and crossed to the bush dog. "You're worse than any pup, you know that?" Ignoring her little growl, he freed her from the shopping bag. "Blair, I need you to shift back before she starts trying to—"

There was a brisk knock on the front door.

The bush dog yipped and then pounced on the rug yet again.

Great. Really.

Leaving the nutcase to her own devices, Luke crossed to the front door and pulled it open. He raised his brows in greeting at the male cat standing on the other side of it. "Evander. How're you doing?"

"Fine," replied the male who worked in the pride's barbershop with his father and also Luke's cousin, Mila. "My dad wanted me to stop by and give you a brief message. You know how much he hates using a phone."

Luke snickered. "I do."

Partway through delivering said message, Evander paused as a loud feminine laugh floated along the hall.

Luke's eyes darted toward the sound. Two female pallas cats stood near the stairwell, their backs to him.

"I have to go, I'm meeting with Finley," said Posy, who happened to be the female enforcer's younger sister.

"How's she holding up?" asked Posy's friend, Kalia. "It has to be hard for her that she can't be Beta female—it was always her dream. I feel bad for her."

Posy frowned. "Just because she hasn't been appointed Beta female doesn't mean she doesn't hold the position. She's acted as Beta for years, really. It was simply never official."

"Yeah, but Luke's mate is now part of the pride—"

A snort. "Him claiming and bringing her here grants her the position, but it doesn't make her a *true* Beta female. She doesn't have what it takes to fulfil the role or shoulder all the responsibilities. She's just a little kid playing at being an adult."

Luke felt his jaw tighten, his cat swiping at his insides, wanting *out* to deal with the mouthy female.

"I don't know, Posy," said Kalia. "Blair's done okay so far. And she handled Lucille and Rhonda well."

"But she'd never handle my sister if Finley challenged her," Posy insisted. "Hell, *I* could kick the bush dog's ass—and I could do it in my sleep."

His jaw clenching, Luke turned back to Evander. "Can you give me a minute? I need to go deal with—"

His little bush dog sprinted out from between his legs and galloped down the hall.

Shit. Luke swiftly pursued her but, Jesus, she was *fast.* Too fast for him to catch up quickly enough. And then she was biting into Posy's heel like a possessed gremlin.

Posy screeched in both pain and shock. "*The fuck—Get off me, you bitch!*" She shook her leg, but it only made the bush dog sink her teeth deeper and chomp harder. Posy screamed again. "*Someone grab her!*"

But no one did. Kalia gaped, frozen. Evander watched, his lips twitching. Luke ... well, as Beta male, he usually *ended* such fights. But Posy had claimed she could take on Blair, had effectively challenged her dominance, and the little bush dog had every right to point out the wrongness of that. She was being rather savage about it, yes, but this was how bush dogs rolled—they blindsided, attacked, mauled, humiliated.

No one could say the vicious little shits weren't consistent.

Luke folded his arms. "If you don't want to experience the pain of having your foot completely mutilated, you should submit," he said, matter-of-fact.

Posy's pain-filled eyes widened. "Submit? She *attacked* me! She's feral or something, she—"

"Overheard you mouthing off about her," Luke finished. "And now she's making a statement. But you should be able to handle her. You can kick her ass in your sleep, right? Isn't that what you said?"

Posy snapped her mouth shut, shaking her leg again. "*Someone* get her—"

Snarling, the bush dog began chomping *hard.*

Posy stumbled with a loud cry, crashing into Kalia. He wondered if the animal had bitten into her Achilles heel. Probably.

Her eyes watery, Posy looked at him. "Oh God, you have to get her off me!"

"Submit, and she will let you go," said Luke.

Nowhere near as stubborn as her older sister, Posy immediately yielded.

The bush dog released her foot and licked her bloody muzzle. She then turned, braced herself on her front paws ... and peed on Posy, who promptly squealed in horror. His cat bared his teeth in approval.

Evander chuckled as the bush dog casually trotted off.

Hiding his own amusement, Luke aimed a severe glare at Posy. "You don't have to like Blair. You don't have to like that she's Beta female. But you *will* respect her. Talking shit about her in a public hallway is nothing close to respectful."

Posy licked her lips. "I didn't call her any names."

"No, you did worse. You said she doesn't have what it takes to be Beta; that you could easily kick her ass; that she's only a kid playing at being an adult. And you said it where anyone could overhear you. If she hadn't punished you for that show of disrespect, I would have." He slid his gaze to Kalia. "Help her get to her apartment and call a healer if she needs one."

Her eyes wide, Kalia gave a firm nod.

Luke turned and began strolling back to his apartment with Evander at his side.

"She peed on me, Kalia," said Posy behind them, sounding traumatized. "She *peed* on me."

Evander cast him a sideways glance. "Your mate takes bitchy to a whole new level."

Luke smiled. "Doesn't she, though?"

Outside his front door, Luke waited while Evander finished relaying his father's message. The two males then parted, and Luke headed into his living room, where his little bush dog was sprawled on the floor, her tongue lolling out.

Squatting in front of her, Luke tilted his head. "You enjoyed that, didn't you?"

She let out a happy yip.

"Yeah, that's what I thought." Sitting on the floor, his legs bracketing her, he indulged her with strokes and scratches, whispering sweet nothings to her as she all but melted into the half-ruined rug. Bones soon began to pop and snap as she withdrew, and then Blair lay in her place.

Luke pulled his naked mate onto his lap and slid his hand up her sleek back. "Your female is a magnificently vicious little creature."

Blair's mouth curled. "Ooh, she likes that compliment."

"She definitely made her point with Posy."

"God, that woman. How dumb can you be to talk smack about your Beta female *mere feet away* from said Beta's apartment? Didn't she notice you standing at the door?"

He shook his head. "Posy's not the brightest lamp in the street. Or the most aware. But she received your message loud and clear. And gave your female something other than our rug to chew on, which was nice. Did she really have to ruin it?"

Blair snickered. "You're such a whiner. She was only playing with the damn thing."

"She tore into it like it had fucked her mother."

"And you, what, have some deep attachment to this rug?" Blair teased, looping her arms around his neck.

"No. But it would be nice if she didn't chew on everything. I ask her not to, and I'm even polite about it. But she doesn't listen to a word I say."

"Be honest, the latter bothers you most of all. You're used to instant obedience. She doesn't give you that. It galls you." Blair rubbed his nose with hers. "My opinion? Both you and your cat need someone to keep you on your toes. She's good at that."

His mouth kicked up. "She is, I can't lie." He hummed, nuzzling her neck. "I like this fresh bite right here." He licked the mark and then swirled his tongue around it. "Nice and deep and visible."

Feeling his hand glide up her thigh, Blair bit her lip. "Before you start getting me all wet and tingly, tell me what Mitch wanted."

Luke hesitated, his hand pausing its journey. "He asked how you were doing. He wants you to call him when you can. Also … he wanted to pass on a request from your parents."

Blair felt tension begin to creep into her muscles. "And what request would that be?"

"They wish to meet with you." Luke tucked her hair behind her ear. "It seems they hope to mend the breach."

"'Seems?' You don't think it's true?"

He blew out a breath. "I want it to be true for your sake, but I don't know. Mitch believes that you got through to Noelle at the cabin. He also claims that she's afraid for you right now; afraid of losing you to whoever is stalking you. It could be that, now seeing what's truly important, she's decided to throw in the towel."

"Stranger things have happened, I suppose. But backing down so abruptly isn't her style."

"No, it's not. But her intention has never been to push you away. She only ever wanted to push *me* out of the picture. Faced with the prospect of losing you altogether while also terrified something might happen to you, she could have chosen to let things lie just as Les seemingly has. People can often surprise you."

It amazed Blair that he'd think to give them the benefit of the doubt, all things considered. She let her fingers drift through his hair. "You're kinder to them than they deserve."

"Not for their sake. For yours. Look, I'll never be their champion. Not after how emotionally difficult they made it for you to have me in your life.

They could have shoved aside their reservations all these years even if only to make it easier for you. They didn't. I can't forgive it. I don't feel an inclination to try. Their wants and feelings don't matter to me. But *yours* do. And I know that the present situation hurts you. I don't want you hurting."

God, he was the best. Seriously *the best.* She wasn't sure if, in his shoes, she would have been as selfless.

Blair would have found it horrible if his family not only hadn't welcomed her but had tried convincing him to forsake her. More, she would have been devastated on his behalf, because *he* would have found it just as horrible. She definitely wouldn't have forgiven them for such a thing, so she completely understood why he didn't feel open to forgiving her parents.

"You don't have to make up your mind right now. There's no rush." He smoothed his hand up the length of her spine. "I'll back you whatever you decide."

"I know you will. You're awesome that way."

His lips hitched up. "I'm glad that hasn't gone unnoticed."

"Nothing about you goes unnoticed by me. Including that you're currently rock hard."

"You're naked. Of course I'm hard." He drew her closer and bit her lip. "I'm also going to fuck you."

He did. Right there on the floor. Slammed into her so fast and deep it almost hurt. In a word, it was glorious. And she came seriously hard—always a plus.

Once she'd cleaned up and redressed, they made dinner together. Wanting to watch something while they ate, they settled in front of the TV with their plates and chose a docuseries on a streaming service. It was hours later, when they were midway through the third episode, that a knock once more came at the door.

Blair pushed to her feet. "I'll get it this time." She wasn't all that surprised to find Finley on the other side of the door. In fact, Blair had been expecting the visit. "Well hello there."

Her face diamond hard, Finley balled up her hands. "Your female savaged my sister's foot."

Savaged? *Pfft.* "She chomped on it some, but that was pretty much it."

"She also urinated on Posy!"

"Her bladder often plays up when she's annoyed." Blair wandered into the apartment, counting on the enforcer to follow her. They needed to have this out once and for all, and they didn't need an audience while doing it.

Seeing Luke uncurl from his seat, his eyes cold, Blair gave him a look, warning him not to interfere. This was between her and Finley … who marched right up to her, all superiority. Ooh, what a mistake.

The enforcer jabbed a finger at Blair. "You're going to apologize to Posy. Publicly."

Blair almost snorted. "Oh, you're funny."

"Do you think that being Luke's mate gives you a free pass to do whatever the hell you like without facing any consequences?"

Blair arched a brow. "You think there should be consequences to my animal handling how she was so horribly disrespected? Really?"

Finley jutted out her chin. "You just don't like that Posy doesn't believe you're Beta material."

"On the contrary, I don't give a rat's first fuck what she believes. She's fully entitled to her opinion. But she isn't entitled to diss me in public—I won't tolerate that. Nobody would, ranked or unranked."

"Sharing her opinion with her friend *hardly* counts as dissing you in public."

"Oh, so the hall *isn't* a public place where many people wander and could easily overhear her?" Blair slammed up a hand when Finley went to speak again. "She messed up. My animal dealt with it. End of. There's no need to have a *Come to Jesus* over it."

"She's just a kid!"

"She's twenty-one. Older than me."

"And *you're* just a kid whether you like it or not." Finley threw her a condescending look. "I've been an enforcer for as long as you've been alive. I have more life experience than you. I have more experience as an enforcer than you. I am far more suited to the position of Beta than you. *Everyone* knows that. You can't expect them not to comment on it. Personally, I don't know how you can be so happy to have the status of Beta. It's not something you earned like I did and … and you … um …"

Luke wasn't surprised that Finley fumbled and trailed off. Not when she was on the receiving end of one of his mate's death stares. They were genuinely unnerving.

The enforcer looked away for a brief moment, and Luke then watched as Blair's eyes went soft and she gave Finley a pitying smile—the same smile she'd given to Myra while verbally shredding her. Uh-oh.

"Look, I get that this is hard for you, I do," said Blair, her words coming out slowly, her tone gentle and compassionate. "You've spent years trying to fight your way up the ranks, trying to prove you have something unique to offer. And here you are, thirty-six years old, *still* an enforcer."

Finley's lips flattened and her ears turned red.

"Over and over you applied to be promoted, but it just didn't happen, did it?" Blair shook her head sadly. "Not only were you never appointed Beta or even Head Enforcer, you didn't manage to become part of the inner circle of enforcers who are called on regularly, trusted with risky assignments, and who act as bodyguards. No, despite your best efforts, you've simply never succeeded in standing out from the crowd."

Luke inwardly winced, unsurprised by the flush that bloomed up Finley's neck and face.

Blair placed her hand over her chest. "I can understand how that would bite. Some people are happy to blend. They don't need the spotlight. They don't crave acknowledgment or admiration. Usually because they're at ease with who they are—faults and all. And that's their biggest strength, I think. They *see* they're not perfect.

"Others, well, they've convinced themselves that they have little to no weaknesses. And because of that, they never seek to improve themselves. They never evolve on any level. They remain static, never learning new lessons or growing in personal strength. In essence, they hold themselves back but don't even see it. It's heart-wrenchingly sad."

Finley's eyes flickered as she swallowed hard.

"You say you earned the position of Beta," said Blair, her voice still soft. "But what did you really ever do to earn it? Spending years in the role of enforcer doesn't count. Being a highly dominant female doesn't entitle you to hold the position either. Nor does the fact that you've tried taking on Beta female duties for years, particularly when you were *specifically* told not to. You knew all that time that someone else had a claim to the position, but you ignored and disrespected that—which is totally un-Beta-like behavior, by the way."

His mate wasn't wrong there. Finley must have had the same thought, because her shoulders curled forward *ever* so slightly in embarrassment.

"I always knew the position would one day be mine," Blair went on. "But I didn't therefore think I was *entitled* to have it. I didn't feel that I could simply learn on the job. Over the years, I soaked up as much knowledge and training as I could from a whole number of people—Luke, Tate, Vinnie, Valentina, my old pack mates.

"I might not have the same life experience as you, Finley, but that doesn't make me unsuited to my role. Because I was determined to ensure that I was *never* unsuited to it. This pride deserved that much from me. But you ... you don't think about the pride. Not really. If you did, you wouldn't make this situation hard for them. You wouldn't be so content that they're not all on the same page right now. But that actually suits you just fine. Again, not Beta-like behavior."

Finley opened her mouth as if she might object, but Blair spoke again before she had the chance.

"The truth is you've earned *shit.* You set your sights on the role, decided it should be yours, and that's really it. Hey, I'm all for believing in the power of envisioning success and thereby attaining it, but not to the extent that I don't also *work* for that success. And Finley, you didn't.

"Believe it or not, I really do regret that we had to have this conversation. I would have been happy to let you live with your illusions. If someone wants to believe that they're perfect, well, who am I to interfere with that? But you left me no choice. And I get that you probably want to launch yourself at me right now. Understandable. To have to face that you're not quite the big deal that you thought you were … it would cut anyone deep."

Luke squeezed one eye shut because, yeah, *ouch.*

"But you can learn from this, Finley. You can buck up, *shape* up, better yourself so you can hopefully be trusted with more enforcer responsibilities and perhaps even one day become Head Enforcer. Or you can refuse to see your faults and never progress from where you are now. I'll leave that up to you." Blair flapped a hand toward the front door. "Now go, I'm all talked out." She retook her seat on the sofa and grabbed her glass of soda from the coffee table.

Seconds ticked by as Finley stood still, looking lost and disoriented—all superiority gone. Finally, she shook herself out of her daze and stiffly walked out.

Returning to the couch, Luke took the glass from his mate's hand, set it on the table, and then hauled her onto his lap. "Woman, you are brutal at times. I probably shouldn't like it, but I do." He squeezed her hip. "I'm proud of you."

Blair cocked her head. "You are?"

"You didn't just play with Finley's self-esteem for your own entertainment, you also gave her some home truths and very Beta-like advice."

"She wouldn't have listened to any advice from me if I hadn't first broken down all that bravado. Now, whether she'll take anything I said on board is another thing altogether. No one likes having a mirror held up to them like that. What she does next will depend on if she's strong enough to handle her true reflection."

He slid his hand under the curtain of her hair to splay it on her nape. "I know she's come across as a bitch lately, but she's not one. She just feels threatened by you, *loathes* that you make her feel threatened, hates that her opportunity to be made Beta is officially gone, and is handling it all the wrong way. There's a chance that she'll get her shit together. I guess we'll soon see if she will."

Blair sniffed, not really giving much of a damn right then. She just wanted to get back to relaxing with her mate. "Now can we continue watching this episode? Because it was starting to get *really* good."

Using his hold on the back of her neck, he pulled her closer. "I want a kiss first."

Blair fit her mouth to his, sliding her hands up his chest. The kiss was slow and lazy and hungry.

He smoothly thrust his hand up her top and closed it over her breast. He didn't squeeze or stroke, though. No, the move wasn't meant to be foreplay—she knew that. It was a statement. An act of entitled possessiveness. One she and her female kind of liked. A lot. Hence why Blair's hormones got all flustered and her blood began to heat.

"My other boob is feeling neglected."

One corner of his mouth hitched up. "It is?"

"Uh-huh. You should really do something about that."

He hummed. "I suppose I could. But I'll want you naked. And then I'll want your pussy wrapped around my cock again."

"I see no problems with this arrangement."

"Good. Then strip. And be quick about it."

CHAPTER SEVENTEEN

Luke honestly didn't know how his father did it. Didn't know how, year after year, Vinnie got through the anniversary of his mating without losing his mind.

It was clear to see that, despite the smiles he gave Blair and Elle as all four of them sat at Vinnie's kitchen table, the man wasn't completely with them. Not mentally. He often pulled inward during the few days before, during, and after the anniversary, which was why Luke and his siblings always made a point of staying especially close to him during this time.

Damian would avoid venturing out in the daytime unless someone else was with their father. Tate, Luke, and Ingrid would regularly visit him. More, Elle always had a reason why she needed to stay in her old bedroom for several days. This year, it was that she'd redecorated her apartment and couldn't stand the smells of fresh paint and gloss so wanted to give it time for the scents to dissipate.

Vinnie never called Elle on her bullshit or complained that people were keeping a close watch on him. He simply rolled his eyes or gave them knowing smiles. Perhaps because he was well aware that nothing he said would make them back off. Or maybe he understood that they *needed* this; needed to be certain he'd never fade away like he'd almost done once before.

Luke had always admired him for surviving Gaia's death. Now, mated himself, he admired Vinnie all the more. No one could truly appreciate what it felt like to be bound to the other half of their soul unless they'd experienced it for themselves.

Blair was more a part of Luke than his own skin and bones, because her connection to him wasn't simply physical, it ran far deeper. She was *inside* him, rooted deep. He couldn't imagine it was possible for his heart to beat without her.

Hell, she was even a part of his scent. Vinnie's own scent was still mixed with Gaia's. Did that make it worse for Vinnie, being able to smell her every day? Or was it comforting to have at least that part of her?

Luke wasn't sure if he himself could find *anything* comforting in such a devastating situation. Blair might be one half of his soul, but he honestly felt like he'd lose his own half if he ever lost her. She was his everything. Always would be. Not even death could alter that.

His cat would be just as empty without her. He would exist, not live. Luke doubted that the feline would find any joy in anything. She *was* his joy.

Their mating bond felt so much like a metaphysical extension of Luke's mind that he knew he'd acutely feel the absence of it if it broke. He'd become used to *feeling* Blair through their link. Used to the echoes of her emotions taking up a portion of his awareness. For Luke to lose all that … no, he couldn't understand how anyone managed to live through it. Yet, Vinnie had.

Luke wondered if his father felt a constant pull to give up the fight and follow his mate into death. After all, the struggle to survive it couldn't possibly have ended when Vinnie "recuperated" all those years ago. The loss of a mate had to be something that haunted you every day.

Bree's father had powered through the death of his own mate for her sake. But shortly after her eighteenth birthday, his health had begun to deteriorate until he'd eventually died in his sleep. Bree believed he'd only ever intended to hold out until she officially became an adult, too lost to exist without his mate.

Luke and Tate had worried that Vinnie might similarly "let go" once Damian reached adulthood. Fortunately, their father hadn't. Still, they never gave up worrying that he one day would.

Blair stood, pulling him out of his thoughts. "Gotta use the bathroom," she said. "I'll be back in a sec." With that, she left the room.

Elle's gaze flicked to the chair that Deke vacated twenty minutes ago when he headed home. "Deke was pretty quiet." She lifted her can of soda. "We can't give him much longer to brood. Does anyone have any idea what could be playing on his mind?"

Luke rubbed the back of his head. "I think he's been doing some thinking about the promise he made a few years ago, and I think the reason is that Bailey's tempting him to break it."

Vinnie dipped his chin. "I had the same thought."

"I tried getting him to talk, but he blew me off," said Luke.

Elle took a sip of her soda. "Personally, I hope he tosses his vow aside. It isn't fair for him to be held to his word like this for so long. It has to be wearing on him at this point."

"Possibly," began Luke, "but that doesn't mean he'll go back on his promise. Personally, I'm not so sure he will. It would be out of character for him."

Vinnie nodded. "Deke's word is golden. I've never known him to break it."

The sound of footfalls proceeded Blair re-entering the kitchen. She took the seat beside Luke once more and asked, "So, what are we talking about?"

"Promises." Elle placed her can of soda on the table. "Which brings me neatly back to a question I meant to ask you earlier but then forgot … Do you think Noelle will keep hers?"

Luke's cat bared a fang on hearing the woman's name. Blair had called Les this morning and informed him that she'd agree to the meeting if Noelle swore she wouldn't throw around any insults or cause a scene. Noelle had then taken the phone from Les and given her word to Blair that she'd remain civil.

Blair blew out a breath. "Once upon a time, I'd have said yes. She doesn't make promises lightly. *But* she vowed not to try to come between me and Luke, and yet she used Macy to do just that, so …"

Draping his arm over the back of his mate's chair, Luke played with her hair, knowing it relaxed her. "That was before you made it abundantly clear that her attempts would only result in her eventually losing you for good. She won't want that."

"I told her many times that I'd cut her out of my life if she didn't support our mating when the time came."

"But, as you yourself once said, she would never have believed that you'd choose me over her—which is how she perceives the situation. You've proven now that you truly meant it when you threatened to turn your back on her. She has no choice other than to admit defeat if she doesn't want to burn her bridges."

"Your mother is as stubborn as they come, Blair—I learned that early," Vinnie cut in. "But I also learned that her attempts to run your life were fueled by the fear of losing you. I agree with Luke, she's likely to keep her promise so she can mend things between you and her. Of course, there might also be a bit of spite behind her intentions. She wouldn't want to give Luke the satisfaction of having you all to himself, which she seems to have convinced herself is his goal."

"*That* I can definitely agree with," said Blair. "Yeah, there could be some spite at play."

"If that is the case, I doubt she'll cause a scene or anything," said Elle.

Vinnie rose from his seat and crossed to the fridge. He'd no sooner pulled out a beer than the cell phone he'd left on the table began to ring.

Elle peeked at the screen. "It's Grams."

"Put her on speakerphone," said Vinnie before tugging off the bottle cap with his teeth.

Elle swiped her thumb over the cell. "Done."

By way of answering, Vinnie said, "No, I don't want more tea. I've drank enough in the past couple of days to last me a lifetime."

Ingrid scoffed. "Oh, hush you, I'll faff if I want to. Right now, I don't."

He retook his seat. "Then why are you calling?"

"There are three men down here asking to speak to you. *Humans*," she added in a whisper. "Should I send them up?"

Vinnie frowned. "I'm not expecting anyone. Who are they?"

"One introduced himself as Beau," she replied, her voice low, "but I recognize him. It's Zayne Whiteford."

Blair double-blinked, her head almost jerking back in surprise. She might have thought she'd heard Ingrid wrong if disbelief wasn't lined into the faces of the people around her.

"I see," Vinnie finally said. "Did you tell him you know who he is?"

"Of course not," replied Ingrid. "I played the clueless old lady."

"Good. I'm going to need a minute. Pretend you're still on the phone to me—prattle on about an antique or something—and then escort them up." With that, Vinnie ended the call and flicked his gaze around the table. "You three need to head to Elle's room and stay out of sight."

Luke bristled. "Wait, what?"

Vinnie stood. "My guess, since I don't see why else he'd come here? Zayne was sent my way by anti-shifter extremists. I think, hoping for advice or intervention, he went to them after Alex broke into his LA home. Zayne likely thought it was Camden. They'd have been all too willing to assist someone as high profile as Zayne. One quick look at Camden's personal information would have unearthed that he lives in a building my son owns. As I'm an informant for the extremists—or so they believe—they would have recommended that Zayne ask for my assistance."

"He might have the bright idea that you'll tell Tate to keep Camden off his back or something," said Blair.

Vinnie dipped his chin. "Maybe. Whatever the case, the extremists must have tossed my name at him."

"Or he could be an extremist himself," Luke cut in. "Either way, I don't want you alone with him and two other humans who are probably his security detail."

"You'll be able to hear the conversation from Elle's bedroom," Vinnie pointed out. "You'll know if intervention is needed. But I highly doubt it will come to that."

"Dad—"

"We don't have time to dispute this. Zayne will be straight with me because he believes I'm of his ilk. But he's not going to be so talkative in front of three random people who *aren't* informants. He'll want you to leave, and then you won't be able to overhear anything unless I insist that you stay.

And if I do, he'll likely find that suspicious. More, he'll probably just leave rather than trust that you'll keep what you hear private, and then we'll have no clue why he came. So stop arguing and scamper."

Unable to deny that the man made sense, Blair nodded and rose from her seat. Elle did the same, though she looked close to protesting.

Luke swore, pushing out of his own chair. "Fine. But you tell him that your daughter is in the apartment. I don't want him thinking that you're alone here. And if I hear anything happening that I don't like, I won't stay out of sight."

Vinnie accepted that with a dip of his chin.

Luke turned to Blair. "Come on." He took her hand in his and led her out of the kitchen with Elle hot on their heels.

Inside her bedroom, Elle spoke. "You two should hide. Zayne's bodyguards will probably search every room to confirm that Dad isn't lying when he says that I'm the only other person in the apartment. They'll also want to know exactly where I am and be sure that I'm no threat."

"I mean this in the nicest possible way, Elle," began Blair, "nothing about you says *no threat* so you might wanna tone down that predatory air of yours." She always made Blair think of those female assassins you saw in movies.

"I'm not very good at playing harmless." Elle's eyes narrowed. "But *you*, well, you look as pure as an angel."

Seeing where Elle was going with this, Blair said, "In the closet. Both of you. I'll be fine," she hurried to assure Luke when he went to argue. "You'll know if I'm not, you'll hear everything. You can barge out and deal with any problem that arises."

He shot her a put-out look as she backed him toward the closet. "I do *not* like this, Blair. Not one little bit."

"I'll give you a blow job later, if that'll help."

He blinked, his glower easing ever so slightly.

Elle rolled her eyes. "Boys."

Once the siblings were inside the closet, Blair shoved down her jeans, yanked off her tee, and pulled on Elle's slinky robe. Her cell phone in hand, she pressed her ear to the bedroom door and listened.

"Wait a minute, *the* Zayne Whiteford?" she heard Vinnie ask.

"That's right," confirmed a smoky male voice.

"Wow," said Vinnie. "Well wow. I, uh … Sorry, I'm a little starstruck," he added with a self-depreciating laugh.

"It's fine, no need to apologize, I'm happy to meet you," Zayne told him.

"Not that I'm complaining, but why are you here? If it's about an antique—"

"No, I'm here to discuss another matter."

"Okay, well—Wait, where's he going?"

"He's part of my security detail," said Zayne, all assurance. "It's routine for him to scout out whatever place we enter."

"The only person here other than me is my daughter. She's a big fan of yours, actually."

"I'd offer to meet her, but it's imperative that no one realizes I'm here. That's why I gave a false name to the woman downstairs."

Blair moved to the vanity table, put her phone to her ear, and chatted away as if taking a call. It wasn't long before the bedroom door swung open. A bald, bulky male blinked at the sight of her.

She let out a girlish squeal. "What the hell? *Dad!*" she called out, forcing her voice to tremble.

The human held up his hands. "It's fine, no need to be scared, your father knows I'm here."

"It's okay, Elle, he's just looking for the bathroom, he took a wrong turn!" Vinnie shouted from the kitchen.

"It's down the hall," Blair told the human, whose gaze dropped down her body as he swallowed hard. She widened her eyes. "Get out, jeez!"

Flushing, he mumbled an apology and backed fully out of the room, closing the door behind him.

Elle peeked out of the closet and mouthed, "Nice acting." She and Luke then padded out of the closet on silent feet.

He dropped a quick kiss on Blair's hair as all three of them gathered near the bedroom door, straining to tune into the conversation in the kitchen. God bless shifter-enhanced hearing.

"Sit down, please," Vinnie invited. There was the sound of wood scraping tile, and then his voice came again. "So, how can I help you?"

"I have a … situation," said Zayne. "One I believe you could assist me with."

"Oh?" was Vinnie's only response.

"Yes," said Zayne. "I discovered that we have some mutual friends. I believe you … inform them of certain things regarding shifters."

A long pause. "Your information is incorrect," Vinnie told him, his voice tight, his tone wary.

"This isn't some sort of set up to make you incriminate yourself. Search all three of us for wires, if it will make you feel better."

Faint sounds of clothes rustling and hands patting reached Blair. Wood then once more scraped tile.

"What is it you want?" asked Vinnie, sounding guarded.

"I hear your son owns a few nearby buildings," said Zayne. "I suppose it was you who urged him to lease apartments to shifters—it's a fantastic way for you to keep your pulse on what's happening in their world so you can adequately report important information to extremists. What brings me here is that one of those tenants has become a problem for me. His name is Camden Priest. He's a white tiger shifter."

"I know of him," said Vinnie, his voice still holding a note of wariness as if he wasn't quite ready to trust Zayne.

"He has information on me that could blacken my name and ruin my career."

"What sort of information?"

"Have you heard of shifter poaching?"

"I have, yes," Vinnie confirmed, sounding admiringly nonjudgmental. In his position, Blair wasn't sure she'd have been able to keep a growl out of her voice.

"I have purchased the occasional item from poachers via a broker. The same broker attempted to fulfil my most recent order by using body parts from Camden. But it all went wrong. I don't know exactly what happened. Only that the broker is now dead, her firm burned to the ground, and he must be to blame."

"Why him?"

"Because one of my housekeepers called me while I was on tour. They informed me that a document had been attached to my wall—a wall that now also sports shifter claw marks. That document turned out to be a record of the orders I placed with the broker. The claw marks were definitely made by a tiger. I had an expert in shifters confirm it."

Blair silently snorted. Some "expert" he was.

"Sounds to me like he was warning you that he knows of your involvement," Vinnie told him. "He must hope it will be enough to make you leave him be."

"Maybe that was all it was, and maybe he's not interested in taking this further. But then maybe I'm wrong." Zayne paused. "I can't trust that he won't come for me at some point. It could be that he would have killed me if I'd been home. I also can't chance that he won't take any information to the press."

"I still don't understand why you would come to me."

"Shifters have no clue that you're an informant, I'm guessing. The loners of their kind surely wouldn't otherwise be comfortable with having your son for a landlord."

"Shifters are unaware of my extracurricular activities, yes."

In truth, shifters were very aware that Vinnie pretended to be a loyal follower of the extremists so that he could pass on what he learned to the Movement—a group of shifters who retaliated against anti-shifter extremists.

"Do you personally know Camden?" Zayne asked.

"I wouldn't say I *know* him. I've spoken to him on occasion."

"If you asked him to go somewhere with you, do you think he would agree?"

A short pause. "You want me to lure him to you?"

"As I said, I don't trust that he will be content with merely delivering a warning to me. I need to be proactive in dealing with this situation; I need to take him out of the equation before he gets the chance to hurt me. I can't do that by sending more poachers his way—that will spur him into leaking my part in it to the public, and my career would then be over. Besides, after what happened to him recently, it will be next to impossible for anyone to take him off-guard right now. *Except* someone he knows. Someone like you."

Blair exchanged looks with both Luke and Elle. She hadn't suspected that Zayne would concoct such a plan. Although he sounded calm and casual, there was a distinct note of apprehension in his tone. His world could so very easily fall apart, and he was seemingly prepared to do whatever it took to preserve it. Despite the gravity of his situation, she had the sense that he was more desperate to protect his career than his actual life.

"Would he be at all suspicious if you invited him to go somewhere?" pressed Zayne.

Vinnie puffed out a breath. "I've never taken him anywhere before, but I doubt he'd be suspicious. I could probably manage to convince him to head somewhere with me. What's in it for me?"

"The kind of cash you'd never otherwise make in a lifetime." He tossed out a number that made Vinnie whistle low. "I will bring the money with me to the drop-off point."

"And where is it you wish me to drop him off?"

Zayne rattled off a location. "I need a few days to pull in more people and arrange adequate transport for him."

"Transport?"

"Yes. I don't intend to kill the tiger, Mr. Devereaux. I intend to sell him."

Luke felt his back teeth lock. Zayne had spoken like Camden was a damn TV or something. It had become abundantly clear during the past ten minutes that this human was one sorry piece of shit.

"Can you have him to me by Friday?" Zayne asked.

"Three days … That's doable," Vinnie replied.

"Good. Here's a number you can reach me at." Zayne reeled off a phone number, adding, "Our mutual friends assured me that you could be counted on. I'm glad to see that they weren't wrong."

A few more things were said, and the humans left soon after.

Blair looked from Luke to Elle. "*That* I did not see coming."

"Fair play to Dad for not whacking the little prick over the head with a cast iron frying pan," said Elle.

When Blair went to follow his sister out of the room, Luke stayed her with a hand on her arm and tipped his chin toward her pile of clothes.

"Shit, forgot," she muttered.

Luke waited while she redressed, his thumbs flying over the screen of his phone as he brought his brother up to speed. Tate's responding text was one of pure indignation.

"Done," Blair declared, flicking her hair out of her collar.

They returned to the kitchen, where Vinnie and Elle were once more seated at the table.

"Tate and Havana will be here soon," Luke announced as he and Blair reclaimed the chairs they'd vacated earlier. "I texted him just now and told him about your visitor. He ain't a happy bunny. He's even unhappier that you spoke to Zayne alone."

"It needed to go down that way." Vinnie tapped his fingers on the table. "It was ballsy of that sorry excuse for a human to come here like this."

"The extremists know you like face-to-face contact because you're paranoid that the human authorities monitor your phone," Luke reminded him.

"They do monitor it," said Vinnie. "They simply monitor the wrong one."

The Alpha pair soon arrived, their expressions hard, their eyes dark.

"Whiteford is one bold motherfucker," said Tate as he stalked into the kitchen.

"Who just handed us a way to get to him that wouldn't require us to get through mounds of security guards or break into a mansion," Blair pointed out.

Luke nodded. "There'll be no CCTV near the drop-off point. It's a very isolated spot. We could get rid of him once and for all."

Tate narrowed his eyes at him. "I sense a plan brewing in your head. What exactly have you got in mind?"

Keeping a hand splayed on his mate's thigh, Luke relayed his plan.

Blair's brows lifted. "That could work."

"It could," said Tate. "Camden will agree to play his part in it."

"Without a doubt, but"—Havana pulled a face—"the trick will be getting his hyper-protective mate to agree."

Yeah, there was that.

CHAPTER EIGHTEEN

As Luke whipped the SUV into a parking space, Blair let out a shaky breath and studied the nearby coffeehouse. She couldn't see her parents, but she knew they were inside. Their car was parked at the other end of the lot. It was Luke who'd suggested the venue, feeling that it would be better if they were all on neutral ground.

He turned to look at Deke and Isaiah, who were currently in the rear seats. "Do a quick check of the area, make sure there aren't any surprises waiting for us."

As the two enforcers exited the vehicle, Blair turned to Luke. "You don't think my parents have set some kind of trap, do you?"

His brow creased. "No, not at all. I just know that there's a possibility your stalker may have heard about the meet. They could have decided to hang around in the hope of making a grab for you at some point."

Blair supposed it was possible. She hoped it was the case, since either Deke or Isaiah could then nab the little shit. *Fingers crossed.*

Sliding her gaze back to the coffeehouse, she put a hand to her churning stomach. "I don't know why I'm so nervous about the meet."

Luke rubbed her thigh. "You're nervous because you know in your heart that if your parents mess up in there you might lose the will to ever bother with them again. You might be mad as hell at them right now, but you don't want to lose them."

She bit her lip. "Does that make me a sucker for punishment?"

"No, it makes you normal. No one wants to cut their parents out of their life unless they have to or unless said parents are toxic." He flipped over his hand so that the back of it rested on her thigh and, taking the hint, she placed her hand in his. "Noelle and Les have made mistakes. Many mistakes, in her case. But they do love you. They're not all bad."

"No, they're not," she softly conceded. "Mitch truly believes that they're backing down. And maybe he's right. It would be a good thing, yes. But part of me resents that because they're ready to be gracious and wave a white flag *we* should give them a second chance just like that."

"Baby—"

"There's no sense in us clinging to our anger, I know. If they make genuine apologies, I won't throw said apologies back in their face."

"I know you won't, you're too mature for that. But Blair, accepting their apologies doesn't mean that you don't still have a right to be annoyed at all they've done. Forgiving doesn't always mean forgetting."

"Will no part of you be even a little pissed if you have to grant them the opportunity to buck up? It's not as if they've earned the right to ask that of you."

Luke slowly tilted his head. "Are you worried that I'll be upset with you if you choose to give them another shot?"

"No. Maybe. Not quite, it's just … Gah, forget it."

Luke cursed himself for not seeing it before. Of course she'd worry that to give her parents a second chance would be to also anger him. Generally, he could easily predict where Blair's thoughts or emotions would lead her. He knew her, *understood* her, on a deeper level than anyone else could—something he relished. But she nonetheless occasionally managed to surprise him.

He knew right then that if he told her he wouldn't like it, she'd declare that there'd be no second chance. He knew he had that power. But he didn't want to isolate her from her parents, though he'd do it in a split second if he felt that it was warranted.

"Look at me." He swiped his thumb over the back of her hand, not speaking again until she met his gaze. "I know what it's like to not have your mom in your life. It sucks in every way it possibly can suck. I don't want that for you. I miss mine every day. And, though Noelle drives you crazy sometimes and you're not as close to her as you once were, you'd miss her if she was out of the picture. It might not feel that way now, but it's true. So no, I won't be upset if you choose to give them a second chance. Far from it, I promise."

Swallowing, she gave a slow nod. "Are you sure you don't mind coming in there with me?"

"Try to stop me." Luke wouldn't let her face these people alone; not when he couldn't trust that they'd mind their words. "I need you to hear me on something. I'm all for giving them an opportunity to show that they're genuine. But if they say even *one* thing I don't like, we're out of there. I won't let them hurt you anymore. No fucking way."

Smiling, she gave a little shiver. "Dude, it has to be said that you *rock* the whole protective vibe. You can't make my stomach all fluttery when I'm about to talk to my parents."

His lips twitched. "We'll address the flutters later."

"I look forward to it. But it will have to be *later* later—we're having dinner at Valentina and James' place, remember?"

Deke materialized beside the driver's door and mouthed, "All clear." Soon after, Isaiah returned and shook his head to signal that he'd found nothing suspicious.

Satisfied, Luke squeezed Blair's hand and asked, "Ready?"

She pulled in a breath through her nose. "Ready."

"We can leave any time you want to. Just say the word and we'll go. Remember, I'll back you whatever you choose to do." With that, Luke exited the SUV.

As they'd agreed before arriving, the enforcers stationed themselves outside the coffeehouse while Blair and Luke swanned inside. It was like walking into a wall of scents—cinnamon, caramel, vanilla, nutmeg, and freshly brewed coffee but to name a few. His cat's nose wrinkled.

Luke skimmed his gaze along the counter, padded chairs, bistro tables, and—*there*. Noelle and Les sat in a booth opposite Donal and Antoine. The sight of the four bush dogs—not one of whom his cat was comfortable having near Blair—made the feline snarl.

Luke wasn't happy about it either, but he also wasn't surprised that Noelle and Les hadn't come alone. Embry would have insisted that they have backup should it be needed, considering the Olympus Pride members weren't exactly fans of Blair's parents and there was a chance that the conversation would go south.

As the Sylvan bush dogs spotted Luke and Blair, she gave them a single nod of acknowledgment and then glanced up at him. "Let's grab a drink first."

That done, they crossed to the booth just as both Donal and Antoine slid out of it. Greetings were quickly exchanged. Luke studied both males long and hard, searching for any sign that either were upset at seeing her with Luke. They seemed somewhat tense, but that was all.

Donal's eyes flitted from Blair to Noelle to Les. "We'll leave you three to talk in private." He cut his gaze to Luke. "You can sit with me and Antoine, if you'd like."

Leave Blair's side? *Not likely*. Luke looked at him steadily. "I'm staying with Blair. I doubt anyone has a problem with that." It was a dare for someone to protest.

"Of course not," said Les.

"No problem at all," added Noelle.

Luke gestured for Blair to slide into the booth. It wasn't until Donal and

Antoine walked to a corner table that Luke finally seated himself next to her. His cat eyed her parents carefully, not inclined to give them the benefit of the doubt—or a second chance, for that matter. As the feline saw it, these bush dogs had burned their bridges.

Les gave Blair a trembly smile. "You look good, sweetheart."

"He's right, you do," said Noelle. "Thank you both for agreeing to see us."

Blair sipped her coffee, barely tasting it while she was wound so tight. Her inner female was rigid, the fur on her back standing on end. "I'm really hoping that neither of you give us a reason to regret it." As her mate supportively palmed her thigh beneath the table, she rested her hand on his.

"We want only to talk," said Les. "The fact is, well, you were right in what you once said. Me and your mom … we let you down."

"More so me than your father," Noelle admitted.

Les pulled a face. "Your mom might have been more verbal than I, Blair, but we both messed up. We were so sure we knew what was best for you, so convinced you could be as happy with a male you imprinted on as you could be with your true mate, that we didn't place any real importance in Luke's presence in your life."

"There's nothing we can say that will excuse that, but we can explain it," said Noelle.

Their voices rang with enough sincerity that Blair's inner animal lowered her hackles. Blair set down her cup. "I'm listening."

Long seconds ticked by, and then Les said, "Marianna … she was like a butterfly." His lips flickered into a small smile. "Beautiful. Gentle. Light. Delicate. You're just as beautiful inside and out, but far from fragile. You're strong. Self-reliant. Iron-willed. Impossible to pin down. And that's scary for parents who've lost a child."

Noelle nodded. "You were with us, but you didn't need us; you had massive wings to spread, and it was terrifying to think you'd one day fly away; to think that you might be hurt if you did. I wasn't very good at handling that. Wasn't very good at parenting *period*."

Les frowned at his mate. "Sweetheart—"

"It's true," said Noelle, her gaze not moving from Blair. "I know I haven't been the best mother. I was never very maternal—I'm sure you noticed that. Protective to the core, but never really affectionate. I'm not good at expressing love. In that respect, I'm very much my mother's daughter," she added, her tone one of self-depreciation. Noelle glanced down at her hands. "I failed Marianna."

Blair blinked, taken off-guard by the comment.

"I was so determined to not be as strict as my mother that I let it override my good sense at times," Noelle went on. "I gave both Marianna and Mitch too much freedom. With her, I shouldn't have. I knew better. She was never streetwise. I thought that stipulating she never went out alone would be enough, since I knew her pack mates would look out for her. But they weren't able to save her from her far too soft nature. I should have accounted for that. I didn't. And now she's dead."

Les exhaled a sad sigh as he gazed at his mate.

Noelle fired him an annoyed look. "Yes, I know you feel my guilt is senseless, but *I* don't feel that way."

He flattened his mouth, clearly resisting the urge to argue.

She resettled her gaze on Blair. "You're a much stronger personality than Marianna. You fought for more space and freedom than she ever did. It was frightening for your father and me at times. I had it in my head that the only way to keep someone such as you safe was to give you firm boundaries. I didn't allow myself to recognize that it was more of an effort to control and hold you close, just as you accused. I did the same thing to you that my mother did to me, falling back on what I know because my own parenting techniques failed spectacularly."

Until then, Blair had had no idea that her grandmother behaved that way toward Noelle. The woman had died before Blair was born, and Noelle rarely spoke of her.

Noelle licked her lips. "You were right. I wasn't thinking of what was best for you. I was too determined not to lose you. Too afraid of what might happen to you if you were out of my sight. Too unwilling to trust that others would keep you safe because I can't forgive myself for trusting our pack mates to keep Marianna safe," Noelle added, her voice breaking.

Les took his mate's hand in his and gave it a squeeze.

Noelle cleared her throat before continuing. "When I went to your old cabin and saw you collecting your possessions, I wanted to say so many things. I wanted to plead with you not to go. I wanted to tell you that I loved you. I wanted to ask that you let me fix what I'd broken. But I instead blurted out things I should never have said; things I never meant. I don't know if you can forgive me for any of the things I said or did. But for what it might be worth, I am sorry."

Blair heard the ring of truth in her voice; knew her mother's regret was real. The raw honesty in her tone was sometimes painful to hear, especially during the moments she spoke of Marianna.

If Noelle's self-flagellation was merely a bid for sympathy, Blair would have sensed it; could have held onto her mad. But Noelle wasn't raking herself over the coals for manipulative reasons, she was doing it because she was desperate to mend things, and that made it hard for Blair to remain detached.

Really, she should have expected that her mother would be so candid. Blair could count on one hand the number of times that Noelle had issued an apology—she didn't easily admit to being in the wrong. But one thing that could be said for Noelle was that she never did a half-assed job of apologizing.

"Did you ask Macy to lie to Blair?" Luke asked. "Was the whole thing your idea?"

"No," replied Noelle. "I was being truthful when I said that Macy approached me at the mall. She was all attitude as she smugly boasted that she'd been sleeping with my daughter's intended mate. I didn't believe her. My feeling was that she'd been put up to it by her Alpha female, who stood not too far away wearing a little smirk."

Blair frowned. "Why would the Alpha have done that?"

"Hyacinth once had her eye on your father," said Noelle, to which Les flushed. "So did I at the time, but he hadn't yet agreed to take me as a mate. I didn't like her interference, so I … expressed that."

"In other words, you humiliated her," said Luke.

"In a spectacular fashion," Les told him.

"When I invited Macy to come speak to you, I expected her to back down or for Hyacinth to step in," Noelle told Blair. "Both females looked as if they wanted to backtrack, but neither did. So I found myself taking Macy to our territory. While I was quite certain you wouldn't believe her claims, a part of me thought it wouldn't be so awful if you did. Because then you'd remain in the pack, and I could keep you safe. But if you had believed her—and I truly mean this—I wouldn't have been able to keep my mouth shut; I'd have told you not to heed her. As much as I wanted to keep you close, I didn't want to see you in pain."

Again, honesty coated every syllable. A knot in Blair's gut fell away.

"I'm sorry, Blair. Truly." Noelle slid her gaze to Luke. "And I'm sorry for the way I treated you all these years. I couldn't find it in me to welcome you into Blair's life. In my mind, you were an interloper who prevented me from keeping my own daughter safe from the world at large. An interloper who could incidentally force me to once again fail to protect my child. I made you pay for my own fears and shame."

Pausing, Noelle swallowed audibly before adding, "And yes, perhaps I resented how close you were to Blair. I felt her slipping through my fingers, and I couldn't handle it. That's not a justification for the things I did, it's merely the reason why I did them."

Les looked as if he'd place his hand over Blair's but then seemed to think better of it. "Your mom and I had managed to convince ourselves that our motives weren't quite so selfish, which is yet another thing that shames us. The truth of the matter is that what we did, how we acted, was wrong. And we apologize for that. Do you think you can forgive us? Or at least give us a chance to earn that forgiveness?"

Blair's mind was genuinely blown from all they'd told her. There was so much more behind their actions than she had first thought.

She wasn't a mother herself, but she could imagine that the loss of a child would be something that affected a parent's relationship with the rest of their children. She could see that, yes, it would be so easy to fall into letting your fear of losing them drive you to behave in ways that both Noelle and Less had behaved. Their actions still weren't excusable, no, but they were understandable.

"I can give you a chance, yes," said Blair. "But only if you both from now on treat Luke the way you should have done from the start." That was a deal breaker for her.

"You have my solemn promise that things will be different from here on out," said Les, his face sober.

"You have that same promise from me," said Noelle. "What about you, Luke? Can you agree for us to start afresh?"

Luke twisted his mouth, reluctantly impressed. He hadn't expected either Noelle or Les to be so open and fully own their shit. It was never easy for a person to admit to their mistakes, let alone explain their reasoning—especially for dominant shifters, who were naturally proud creatures. It was far easier to just say a short, simple "*I'm sorry, it won't happen again*" and then move on.

But the couple opposite Luke hadn't gone down that road. They'd confessed their fears and shame and guilt. They'd given their daughter the apology she deserved. While his cat—seemingly determined to hold a grudge—was completely unmoved, Luke could respect that.

Not that he suddenly had a newfound respect *for them.* He wasn't quite ready to forgive them for all they'd done, or ready to trust them not to fall back into their old patterns at some point. But ... "I can agree to a fresh start. However, let it be known that if either of you ever cause Blair any more pain, there'll be no more chances. I want Blair to have you both in her life, but not at her detriment."

"You'd cut us out of the picture if we hurt her again?" asked Noelle, her tone even.

Luke met her gaze head-on. "In a fucking heartbeat."

One side of her mouth curved. "Good."

Well, all right then.

A silence tinged with relief settled over the table.

"Thank you both for being willing to give us another shot," said Les.

Noelle dipped her chin. "It won't be something we make you regret." She reached out and touched Blair's hand. "I've missed you." Her voice broke. "I thought about visiting you a million times but could never quite muster the courage. I even almost attended the welcoming party that the Olympus ... that *your* pride threw for you. I was going to apologize then but, again, my courage failed me."

Les cocked his head at Blair. "How is life at the Olympus Pride?"

As the conversation moved onto lighter things, Luke kept his contribution minimal. Not in a gesture of rudeness, but because he was busy observing the bush dogs sitting opposite him. Despite that he believed their apologies were genuine, it was difficult to digest that finally—after all these years—they'd decided to buck the hell up.

It didn't particularly surprise him that they had, though. Not when the alternative would have been something they couldn't handle. Still, after so long of having them treat him like an unwanted guest, it wasn't easy to settle into the new dynamic—one in which they smiled at him, asked him questions, didn't snark at or pointedly ignore him.

No one raised the subject of Blair's stalker, as if determined not to taint the conversation. They kept it light and casual. And when it came time for him and Blair to leave, her parents were sure to not only give her a hug but to shake Luke's hand. Huh. His cat haughtily sniffed at the gesture.

"Perhaps you two could come visit us sometimes soon?" asked Noelle.

Uh, that was a hard no. "I'm not comfortable with Blair being on Sylvan territory right now."

Donal, who'd just approached with Antoine, asked, "You still believe the person harassing her is one of us?" His voice was carefully even.

"I believe it's very possible, yes, and I don't intend to take any chances," replied Luke, unapologetic, before turning back to Blair's parents. "You're welcome to visit us anytime." Well … maybe not necessarily *welcome*, but he'd tolerate it.

Noelle's mouth curved. "That would be nice, thank you."

Look at them being all civil and shit.

The six of them exited the coffeehouse, where they then parted ways. Luke's cat settled slightly once Donal and Antoine were away from Blair, but he'd be nothing close to relaxed until she was back in their domain.

Opening the SUV's front passenger door for her, Luke heard his name being called. He turned to see Antoine jogging toward them, and it wasn't easy to stop his mouth from tightening.

Antoine stopped a few feet away, his gaze on Luke. "Embry said you spoke with Gabriel again. You consider him your main suspect?"

"I consider him *a* suspect," replied Luke, gently ushering his mate into the SUV, grateful she didn't resist. "Then again, the background check that my pride mate did on Gabriel didn't come up with anything alarming."

"Background check?" Antoine echoed.

"It was very thorough." Luke closed the SUV door. "As were the checks that were done on my other suspects." Let the Head Enforcer make what he would of that.

Antoine kept his face blank. "People from my pack, you mean?"

"Yes," Luke replied as he rounded the vehicle.

"And?"

"And I won't have dug up anything that you don't already know. After all, you and Donal and Embry have conducted your own very thorough investigation. If your Alpha wants to compare notes, tell him to call me." Luke slid into the SUV and switched on the engine, not failing to notice that Antoine was making a concerted effort not to look at Blair. In fact, the Head Enforcer didn't even grant her a brief wave before he walked away.

"It wasn't hard to tell that Antoine was probing you for information because he wants to know if he's a suspect," said Deke as they drove away. "Do you think he worries you've managed to unearth that he has a history of stalking human women?"

Luke glanced at the enforcer via the rearview mirror. "He might. But it could simply be that he's aware I'll naturally suspect any unattached male in his pack."

Blair hummed. "Your face gave nothing away, so he'll probably assume that you have no clue what he's done," she said to Luke. "Still, he'll likely fret on it all the same."

"How did the talk with your parents go?" Deke asked her.

"Pretty well," she replied before giving he and Isaiah a bullet point version of the conversation.

"They kept their promise to be civil today," said Isaiah. "Maybe they'll also keep the promises they made you in the coffeehouse."

"Maybe," said Luke.

Back inside their apartment building, he and Blair took the elevator up to the floor on which Valentina and James lived. Walking toward the apartment, Blair said, "So. My parents. They seemed genuine, didn't they?" Even she heard the plea for reassurance in her voice. It was hard to let herself believe that they'd been sincere, even though they were so convincing.

"They did," Luke confirmed. "I suppose time will tell whether they meant all they said."

"Yeah, I guess it will." Blair bit her lip. "My mom shocked me. She's not one to open up." Noelle had rarely spoken of Marianna since her death.

"She knew she'd have to in order for you to understand why she's behaved the way she has," Luke pointed out. "As much as she claimed to know it was no justification, I think she *did* hope that you'd find her pain a reason to excuse everything."

Blair gave a slow nod. "I didn't know she blamed herself for Marianna's death."

"It's normal to take on senseless guilt when you lose someone who matters so much to you. My dad hates himself for not going to the hardware store to save my mom the trip—then she'd be alive, but he'd be dead. I hate myself for not being strong enough to get out of the locked room and help Toby the day we were taken."

Blair worried her lower lip. "I hate that I didn't ask Marianna to stay with me the day she died. I was tired after my sleepover with Kiesha. I wanted to just lie in bed and watch movies. I thought about asking my sister to join me, but I was too tired to drag myself out of bed and go find her. She might have said yes—"

"But she might not have. Just as I might not have been able to help Toby even if I *had* got out of that room. Just as my mom might not have agreed for my dad to go shopping in her place. Yet, we can sometimes feel weighed down with guilt all the same. And that can color our decisions and opinions. So, yeah, I can understand why Noelle felt motivated to do a lot of the shitty stuff she did."

"I think she was telling the truth when she claimed that it wasn't her who instructed Macy to spout those lies," said Blair. "And if it *was* Macy's Alpha who put her up to it, we're wrong in thinking that Gabriel could be behind it."

"Yes, but we can't know for certain that the Alpha female was to blame. There's no point in us asking her—she wouldn't incriminate herself." Reaching Valentina and James's apartment, Luke knocked on the door. It swung open mere moments later.

"Ah, here you are." Valentina stepped aside, urging them to enter. Quick hugs later, she led them into the kitchen. She scowled at her brothers. "Will you three stop rummaging through fridge! We are about to eat!"

Mumbling to themselves, they closed the fridge and turned.

Sergio smiled at Blair. "It is our little bush dog."

"Not so little now, though," Dimitri pointed out.

"She still eyes us like female wolverine protecting young," Isaak said in approval. He sniffed at Luke. "You are lucky to have bush dog for mate. Not like my poor Valentina, who was lumbered with cat."

"*I'm* a cat," Luke patiently told him, but the comment was waved away. He rolled his eyes, used to them disparaging his kind in front of him. It was far too ridiculous to get worked up about.

Isaak turned to his sister. "Speaking of your mate, Valentina … where is useless fool?"

She sighed. "James is behind you. This you know. And he is *not* useless or—"

"It's all right, sweetheart," James cut in. "Don't let him rile you up. It's not his fault he's mentally an infant."

Luke bit back a smile, watching as Isaak's face flushed. The wolverine didn't respond despite his annoyance, clearly still determined to discount the presence of their sister's mate.

James flashed a smile at both Blair and Luke. "Thank you both for coming. I hope you're hungry, my mate's been cooking up a storm all day."

"It was no hardship to come," said Blair. "Especially when I adore Valentina's cooking."

The female wolverine lifted her chin, looking chuffed.

James's gaze swept over the three brothers. "For the sake of present company, maybe you could pretend not to hate me for at least one evening."

Isaak glanced at Sergio, his brow furrowed. "Did you hear that?"

"The squeaking?" asked Sergio.

"Enough," barked Valentina as she slashed her hand through the air. "We *will* have normal meal for once. Now everyone sit. Food is ready."

Soon, they were all settled at the table, digging into their dinner.

"How did meeting with your parents go, Blair?" asked Valentina.

"Good, actually," replied Blair. "They apologized and promised that things would be different from now on. We decided we'd give them the opportunity to back up their words with actions."

Sergio's brow pinched. "Why did they need to apologize?"

Blair drew in a breath. "To sum up, they were never accepting of Luke. They made it hard for us from the beginning; they wanted me to mate with another bush dog and remain in their pack."

Isaak scowled. "But Luke is your predestined mate. How can they not accept him and respect your choice?"

James blinked. "Yes, how can *anyone* not do such things for their own family members?"

Either oblivious to the verbal dig or pointedly ignoring the pallas cat, Isaak asked Blair, "Do you believe apology was sincere?"

"It seemed to be." Blair sighed. "Maybe it makes me a sucker that I chose to give them a chance, but ..."

"If you had not, you might have later wondered if you made mistake," said Sergio. "This way, you will see for yourself if it was right choice to trust their word."

"My brother is right," Isaak told her. "Still, I would find it hard to be so forgiving if anyone failed to accept my mate. She is other half of my soul. No man or woman has right to interfere in something dictated by outside forces like fate."

"I couldn't agree more," said James.

Luke clamped his lips shut to hold back a laugh. Jesus, the brothers were wacked. He didn't know what it said about him that he nonetheless liked them.

Isaak took a swig of his vodka. "I once heard of man who tried to poison his sister's mate to keep them apart."

James's mouth flattened. "That was Dimitri, and he did it to *me*."

Isaak blinked. "Ah, so it was." He shrugged. "You survived."

"Unfortunately," muttered Sergio.

Dimitri sighed. "Mama was so disappointed."

"I *did* tell her to make stronger poison." Isaak sniffed. "She did not listen."

"She was distracted by Papa," Sergio reminded him. "He was wailing loud enough to wake dead."

"Let me guess," said James. "Olga tested the poison on him."

Isaac frowned. "I hear judgment in your voice. What happens between man and woman is their business alone." His gaze then bounced from Blair to Luke. "So, how you find mated life?"

"Despite all the crap happening around us, I'm enjoying every minute," said Blair.

"Ah, yes, Aleksandr told us you have idiot stalker," said Dimitri. "Does he remain unidentified?"

The uncles always called Alex by his given name, Aleksandr.

"Unfortunately, yes," Luke told him. "But not for much longer. He'll slip up eventually." And then Luke would slit the prick's throat.

"Do you have idea of who it could be?" asked Sergio.

Luke lifted his bottle of beer. "We have some suspects, yes."

"You must look at their family situations," said Isaak. "If any grew up without father, they should be prime suspects. Being without father figure is hard for young boys. Just ask Aleksandr."

James sighed. "This again? Honestly?"

Isaak ignored him. "Harsh family dynamics can cause children to become very maladjusted."

"Now *that* I can agree with," said James. "You three are evidence of it. Not that it's your fault your mother's a nut and your father's a man slave."

With that, the chests of all three wolverine males puffed right up.

Dimitri's grip on his cutlery flexed. "Have we not warned you to speak of our mother with respect?"

James's brow creased. "Why would I respect someone who keeps shooting at me?"

"You should be grateful she acknowledges you exist at all," said Isaak. "You are nothing. Psychopathic cat with teeny IQ. You bring shame upon our sister by mating her. Yet, you do not care. And then you whine like babe when sweet old lady points gun at you. If it was not for her hand tremor, your gut would be filled with bullets and your heart would be—"

Valentina slammed her hand on the table. "I cannot *begin* to tell you how much I tire of this. You will be civil toward my mate or *you will leave*."

Isaak inched up his chin. "I owe no civility to dumb cat who sneers when he speaks of Mama. *My* Valentina would not stand for it. She would defend Mama. He has you so cowed you say nothing."

Valentina ground her teeth. "She makes it hard for me to defend her when she continually tries to kill him."

"The last bullet grazed my throat and took away a chunk of skin," said James. "You know that already, Isaak. You were there."

Isaak shrugged. "I was busy."

"You were helping Olga hold the gun steady," said James.

"As any dutiful son would."

Luke exchanged a quick glance with Blair, who was clearly trying to contain a laugh.

Exhaling heavily, James turned to Luke. "I really do hope you have more luck getting along with your mate's family than I do mine."

Luke felt his mouth curve. "Yeah, so do I."

CHAPTER NINETEEN

Having finished her cereal the next morning, Blair washed her bowl and spoon. She and Luke usually ate breakfast together, but he was still in the bedroom talking with Tate, who'd called him mere minutes after she and Luke had gotten out of the shower. Too hungry to wait for him, she'd sought food.

From the kitchen, Blair could vaguely hear Luke, but she couldn't decipher the words. She suspected that the two brothers were finalizing the plans for tomorrow, when the pride would deal with Zayne once and for all.

Havana and Camden had managed to talk Aspen into agreeing to said plans, but it allegedly hadn't been easy. Blair could understand why. She wouldn't like Luke putting himself in the path of danger, no matter what kind of, or how many, precautions were in place.

Her inner female was all revved up, likely affected by the fine ribbon of anticipatory tension that buzzed in Blair's system. Which was why Blair had decided that she'd spend the day relaxing. If she wound down a little, so would her animal. That would be best, because it was never good for her female to be worked up. The animal would push for freedom and then start destroying furniture to burn off her tension.

Blair grabbed her empty coffee cup and moved to the counter, intending to get a refill. The sound of footfalls made her glance over her shoulder. And there was her mate. Unlike her, he was fully dressed and his hair was now dry. She'd done no more than pull on a tee after their shower before seeking food. Well shower sex could make a girl work up an appetite.

His eyes took her in, heating. "I like seeing you in my tees."

"I've noticed." She retrieved a mug from the cupboard and turned to the coffee pot, asking, "Am I right in thinking that you and Tate were finalizing the plans for tomorrow?"

"You are." Pressing his front to her back, Luke snaked his arms around her before relaying his conversation with the Alpha. "We're pretty sure it'll flow smoothly enough, since it isn't likely that Zayne will bring many people with him."

Blair agreed. "As a celebrity with an image to protect, he'll be reluctant to trust his plans with more than a few."

"He'd be a fool otherwise." Luke pressed a kiss to her temple. "Have you eaten yet?"

"I had cereal." She poured coffee into both her cup and his. "Do you want me to make you anything? I'm feeling all magnanimous after the whopping big orgasms you gave me earlier."

He rumbled a laugh. "That's kind of you, but"—keeping her pinned against him with one arm, he lifted his mug and took a swig—"I'll grab a Danish from the bakery on the way to the antique store. I need to go over the plans for tomorrow with my dad. I could do it on the phone, but ..."

"But you want to go check on him in person, and this is the perfect excuse to do it," she understood. Luke and his siblings were still careful to keep an eye on their father.

Luke nuzzled her neck. "Want me to wait for you to get ready so you can come?"

"Nah, you go have some father-son time with him. I'll be fine here." She sipped her drink. "I'm in the mood to have a lazy morning."

"What does that entail?"

She felt her brow furrow. "Being lazy."

He chuckled. "All right." He took another swig of coffee and then set the cup on the counter. "I won't be long."

"There's no rush. I'll be waiting."

The arms around her waist gave her a quick squeeze, and then he slowly began pulling them back, sliding his hands along her belly as he did so. "At some point today," he began, setting his hands on her hips, "we need to let our animals run to—" He stilled, his fingers digging into her hips. "Why don't I feel a waistband beneath this tee? You're not wearing any underwear, are you?"

Feeling a smile tug at her lips, she shrugged. "As I said, I feel like being lazy." Her blood heated as she felt his cock begin to harden against her.

He dropped his forehead to the back of her head and swore. "Now I need to fuck you." He hiked the tee around her waist and smoothed his hands over her ass, humming when she reflexively arched into his touch.

"We had sex, like, half an hour ago," she said. "And don't you have somewhere to be?"

Cupping her pussy, he slipped a finger through her folds. "I can be quick."

He expertly toyed with her clit, rubbing and rolling it, knowing her body well; knowing how to make it instantly sing for him. Need rose inside her, making her stomach twist, her skin feel tight, and her inner walls clench.

Then he plunged two fingers into her pussy hard enough to make her jolt.

"*Jesus*, Luke." She gasped as he began pumping those fingers inside her, making her wetter, hotter, needier. Her tight muscles kept spasming and fluttering around them as an orgasm slowly started to unfurl deep in her core.

He growled against her ear, stirring the little hairs there. "Put your cup down."

"Trying to get between me and caffeine isn't a good idea," she said, the words low and breathy.

"Trying to get between me and this pussy I own isn't a good idea."

Moaning as he swirled the fingers inside her, she set her mug down beside his and gripped the edge of the countertop.

"Do not move." Hard and heavy and aching for his mate, Luke stepped back, snapped open his fly, and shoved his jeans down slightly as he freed his cock. Once more pressed against her sleek back, he kicked her legs further apart. "Stay like that." He positioned his dick at her entrance, gritting his teeth as the scorching heat of her pussy bathed the head. "This is gonna be rough."

"You'll hear no complaints from me."

"As if it would matter if I did." Growling, Luke snatched a fistful of her hair, yanked her head back, and shoved his cock inside her. He groaned as her inner muscles tightened around him. "Like a red-hot vise." He slipped his hand down to again cup her pussy. "Mine." He took her like that—one hand tangled in her hair, the other possessively holding her pussy.

"Oh, God." Arching a little, she tipped her ass toward him, making his cock slide in even deeper.

Luke groaned. That was what he needed. To be as deep as he could possibly go. To touch every part of her, because each part was *his* to touch.

Inside him, his cat paced, urging him on. The feline, uneasy over their incomplete bond and hating that another male thought to steal her away, wanted Luke to stake his claim all over again.

Still pounding his hips hard and fast, relishing the sound of flesh smacking wet flesh, Luke bit her earlobe. "You knew what you were doing when you skipped the underwear, didn't you? You knew it would get you royally fucked."

One corner of her mouth twitched. "I like your royal fucks," she rasped.

The little minx thought she could manipulate him so easily, did she? Oh, she thought wrong. And she'd pay for her deviousness.

Upping his pace, he took her brutally, *feeling* how much she loved it through their bond. Every pulse of pleasure that came down their connection was like a stroke to his balls, adding fuel to his building release—as did every gasp and moan and ripple of her tight muscles.

When he felt her orgasm approaching, he said, "*I* come first. Then you."

"But—"

"You played me to get what you want. This is your punishment."

"Asshole," she grunted.

He hammered into her—savage, merciless, unrestrained. The tension inside him built and built until, finally, his release hit him like a two-by-fucking-four. It swept over him and through him, making his cock goddamn erupt. "Now you," he said the moment the last blast of come spurted out of him. "Fuck yourself on my dick while you come."

She reared her hips back over and over, taking him deep, chasing her orgasm. And then abruptly it hit her, reverberating down their bond as she screamed. When it finally subsided, she slumped forward, bracing her elbows on the counter.

Fighting to catch her breath and gather her wits, Blair let out a satisfied sigh. Utterly sated, she looked over her shoulder at her mate. "You really do have a marvelous cock."

A low chuckle of surprise burst out of him and danced over her nerve-endings. "Why thank you, baby," he said as he withdrew.

"Seriously." She turned to face him, righting her tee. "It deserves a ribbon or something. No wonder so many of your past floozies wanted more from you. I must say, my female wants to pee all over every woman who's ever taken your dick for a ride. I could actually get behind that idea."

Luke frowned even as his eyes glinted with humor. "What is it with your female and peeing on people?"

Blair shrugged. "It's a bush dog thing. Humiliating people makes us feel whole."

He shook his head, his mouth curved. "You're all nuts, in my opinion."

Blair flicked up an imperious brow. "And pallas cats have room to judge?"

"Not even an inch." He kissed her hard. "I won't be long."

Once she'd cleaned herself up, Blair pulled on some panties and sweats before settling on the plush armchair in the living area. She snatched the remote from the table, intending to find a movie on the streaming service.

It was weird having the apartment to herself, but not in a bad way. She was totally at ease there, felt completely at home. It was simply that Luke was such a powerful personality that he could make a place feel almost empty when he left it.

Her inner female didn't like that he was gone. Not that she was clingy or anything. The animal was just so damn nosy and wanted to know what she was missing.

Knuckles rapped on the front door. Opening it, Blair was pleasantly surprised to find Havana, Aspen, and Bailey there. "Oh, hi." She stepped aside for them to enter.

"We heard from Tate that the meeting with your parents went well," said

Havana as Blair closed the door behind them. "But we thought we'd come see how you're doing anyway."

"I'm good, thanks," said Blair as they filed into the living area.

"I had a feeling they'd go big rather than go home," Havana told her as they all claimed a seat. "So I wasn't surprised to hear that no shit went down."

Aspen glanced around. "Where's Luke?"

"He's visiting his dad," replied Blair.

Bailey did a slow blink. "He actually left you on your own? Whoa."

"I think he preferred I stay here where he feels I'm safest, but I don't doubt that he'll text me every now and then to check in." Blair splayed her hands on the armrests of the chair. "I hope you aren't gonna ask me to go anywhere because I'm planning to have a lazy day, starting with binge watching some TV."

Humming, Havana tilted her head. "Feel like having some company?"

"Sure," said Blair, grabbing the remote.

Aspen's eyes widened in delight, and she clasped her hands together. "Ooh, we could watch *Dawn of the Dead*."

Groaning, Bailey lifted a hand. "No. No zombie movies. Not today. I need a break."

Aspen huffed, folding her arms. "Well *I* need a break from *you*. We don't always get what we want in this world."

Bailey smiled. "You love me really. So much it's actually creepy."

Havana snickered. "Stop being idiots. *I* think we should watch a feel-good movie. Like *Where The Devil Hides*."

Bailey pointed at her. "Good choice."

They were ten minutes through the movie when Luke texted Blair to ask how she was doing. A second message came fifteen minutes later. A third came twelve minutes after that.

Blair groaned. "This dude is driving me crazy."

Aspen chuckled. "He and his cat will be fretting. This building has tip-top security, but *every* system can be circumvented—wolverines are proof of that."

"I know." Blair sighed. "I want to be mad about the constant checking in, but I can't. He has every reason to be worried about me right now. It would be different if his overprotectiveness was toxic or oppressive, though."

"Camden's just as hyper-protective but, like with Luke, he's not a tyrannical dick so I mostly let it fly over my head," said Aspen.

"I admit, I chafe a little under Tate's insistence on trying to shield me from the world, but that's the Alpha in me." Havana cut her gaze to Bailey. "I guess we better hope that your mate is nothing like ours, because you will laugh in the face of anyone who tries to coddle you."

"Too true," said Bailey, crossing one leg over the other.

"Do you think that the guy you're dating could be your mate?" Blair asked her.

The mamba's nose wrinkled. "I wouldn't say we're *dating* dating. But to answer your question, no, I'm not getting that feeling."

Blair had suspected as much, since Bailey rarely spoke of him … as if he simply wasn't on her mind. "Do you look forward to finding your mate?"

"Not really."

"Why not?"

"Because if he's anything like me, he'll be incredibly irritating. Regularly. And probably on purpose."

Havana snorted. "No one can ever say that you're not self-aware. You know, sometimes true mates are polar opposites."

Bailey's brow creased. "Oh God, don't say that. If he's nice, he'll annoy me. 'Nice' is for losers."

Since the mamba claimed that lots of stuff was 'for losers,' Blair had to ask, "Do many things annoy you?"

"Oh yeah," Bailey easily admitted. "My mamba is equally intolerant. Even when it comes to those she adores. That's why she often fights with Aspen's pissy bearcat."

Aspen's brows flew up and then snapped together. "Whoa, she's not pissy."

"Puh*lease*," scoffed Bailey. "She's always doing bitchy stuff."

"Yeah, *to your snake*," clipped Aspen. "She's perfectly normal with, and pleasant toward, everyone else. Mostly. Anyway, she'd be perfectly normal with your mamba if the damn serpent didn't constantly pick fights with her."

"How about we stop the conversation before it turns ugly," Havana cut in. "Just watch the movie. Breathe. Relax."

Bailey sniffed. "Fine." She slid Aspen a brief look. "But your bearcat *is* pissy."

Aspen ground her teeth. "Say that again, I *dare* you."

Bailey said it again.

The last thing that Luke expected to find when he walked into his apartment was, as Deke called them, the unholy trinity. Aspen and Bailey were yelling in each other's faces while Havana ordered them to calm their asses down—something they didn't do.

He was about to ask what the hell was going on, but then Blair came walking out of the bedroom. *Like a crab*, a few of her joints displaced. She rushed at the arguing females, who promptly *squealed* and ran into the kitchen. Blair chased them around the dining table, ignoring their pleas for her to stop.

Havana's mouth curved into a Cheshire cat smile. Noticing Luke, she said, "Dude, I *really* like your mate. She is now officially my favorite person *ever*."

He felt his lips quirk. "Mine too."

Apparently done tormenting the other females, his mate stood upright and slid her displaced joints back into place.

Huddled against Aspen, Bailey said, "As much as that freaks me out, it's also morbidly fascinating."

Aspen reluctantly nodded. "But please don't *ever*, ever do it again."

Blair only smiled.

Wanting to be alone with his mate, Luke politely ushered the others out of the apartment—which took longer than he would have liked, since they made plans for a movie night at Havana's place even as they began making their way to the front door.

Finally alone with his mate, he turned to face her. "You know, I would have said that nothing could unnerve either Aspen or Bailey, but they actually squealed just now." He hauled Blair to him and slid a hand up her back. "I'd like to say that you didn't creep me out as much as you did them, but I'd be lying."

Blair chuckled. "Mitch squeals even louder." She curved her arms around his neck. "How's your dad?"

"He seems okay. *Seems*. I'm not buying it. He can't possibly be all right—I certainly wouldn't be in his position."

"I suppose he thinks he's protecting you by hiding how much he's hurting; that he doesn't want to burden you with it."

"It's more than that. He holds it all back because he doesn't want comfort. He wants to feel the pain of my mom's loss, because he feels that he should; that to *not* feel it would be the same as being at peace with her death. That's how I'd feel if I was him."

Blair frowned. "I wouldn't want that for you. It wouldn't be a betrayal if you didn't—"

"No, we're not having this conversation. We don't need to, because I don't intend to lose you. It won't happen."

"Luke—"

"I'd never survive it. I'd venture back into that dark place, and I'd get lost in it. I'd never find my way out. I'd never look for a way out." Palming one side of her face, he swept his thumb over her cheekbone. "You're what holds me here. I need you a little *too* much, really. Need you more than you need me. Sometimes … sometimes it feels like maybe our soul wasn't split into halves; like instead I got a quarter of it and you got the rest."

"That's bullshit. As is the whole 'I need you more than you need me' part. I know what it's like to feel swallowed up by grief. I was like that after Marianna died. I didn't feel anything close to whole. But then I found you. You became my focus, just as I was yours. You made everything okay simply by being there. You're an integral part of me, Luke. If you were gone, I'd be an absolute wreck. There'd be nothing—not one thing—that could make me want to live. I need you as much as you need me. Don't ever think differently."

Luke stared into those ivy-green eyes, swallowing hard. Nothing and no one had ever gotten to him the way she did. She had a direct line to his heart—made it squeeze, melt, race, even hurt with her moments of raw honesty. Just the same, she was a balm to his cat's soul, soothing him, completing him, anchoring him.

She was everything that Luke needed; everything he'd never known he needed. She might not be a born alpha like him, but she was his match on every level. She handled him in her own way—rolling with his dominant behavior, demanding to be counted, compromising when necessary, brooking none of his bullshit.

She challenged him. Fascinated him. Delighted him. In sum, she was an absolute joy to him. And despite all the crap that was currently going on around them, Luke had never been more content in his life … because she was finally part of it on every level.

Living with Blair hadn't required any "getting used to." Mostly because he'd already known her quirks and habits and patterns, just as she had his. But also because it felt easy and natural to have her there, sharing his space and making it *theirs*. They'd quickly developed a rhythm, totally in tune with each other, their lives merging effortlessly.

"You get me?" she pushed.

A smile pulled at his mouth. "I get you."

"Good. You may kiss me now."

He chuckled. "I may?"

"Yes, you may."

A rhythmic knock came at the front door.

Luke gave her nape a squeeze. "Hold that thought." His stomach hardened when he found a solemn-faced James standing at the other side of the door … holding a square, gift-wrapped box that sported a shiny red bow. *Fuck*. Luke's cat jumped to his feet with a rumbly hiss.

"I found this on the bench outside," said James. "Someone left it there. It's addressed to your mate."

Grinding his teeth, Luke took the damn thing from James. "Did anyone see who left it there?"

"I doubt it, or they'd have picked it up to see what it was."

Luke felt a muscle in his cheek tick. "We need to be sure." It would have been helpful if they'd had camera footage to check, but they didn't have CCTV near the building since it was too easy to tap into camera feeds nowadays. They didn't want outsiders seeing things they weren't supposed to see. "Ask around. Get back to me on that."

James gave a quick nod and then left.

Anger bunching every muscle in his body, Luke strode into the living area, hating the way Blair paled. "This was left on the bench outside the building."

She swallowed, padding closer. "It's the same bow that was attached to the other gifts," she said, her voice flat. "Wrapping's different, but that's never the same anyway."

"It doesn't carry anyone's scent other than James', who brought it up here. You good with me opening it for you?"

She gave him a "knock yourself out" shrug. "Be braced for weirdness."

Luke placed the gift on the coffee table. Sensing Blair sidle up to him, he tore off the wrapping, revealing a simple, blue cardboard box. Luke removed the lid. The scents of silk, musk, and ink greeted him. And as he stared into the box, he and his cat snarled.

Grimacing, Blair said, "It's all the underwear from the bouquet thing he sent. I put it in the trash and—oh, Jesus, is that crusty stuff what I think it is?"

"Yes," growled Luke, anger bubbling in his blood. "He jerked off all over what, in his mind, are your panties." *Son of a bitch.*

She put the back of her hand to her mouth. "God, this sick piece of shit needs decapitating."

"I'm leaning more toward chopping off his dick." Luke snatched the pen from the table and used it to move aside the underwear. Beneath the scraps of lace were photos—so many damn photos—of Blair. None were indecent. They were of her talking with Sylvan Pack members, going to and from her old cabin, smiling or waving at people out of view. Others were taken from outside the cabin, showing her cooking, reading, sleeping, or watching TV.

"Bastard," Blair bit out, backing up a few steps. She drew in a deep breath. "He must have a long range camera. There's no way he could have gotten so close to the cabin without my sensing him. No way."

Spotting the edge of a sheet of paper, Luke moved some pictures aside, revealing a drawing of Blair's face. He found two similar ones beneath other photos.

"You're always smiling," Luke observed.

"What?"

"On the photos. Even while doing inane things, you're wearing a ghost of a smile or laughing. The drawings depict you in the same light. This is how he sees you. Sweet. Serene. Wholesome. The classic girl next door."

"Which isn't me at all," she said, moving back to his side.

"He sees only what he wants to see. He's shaped you in his mind to be his perfect match."

"Well I'm not." Blair hooked her hands around her nape. "I don't understand why he boxed this crap up and left it for me. Is he, what, giving me all this as a gesture that he's 'done' with me? Kind of like someone packs up all their ex's stuff and hands it back?"

"I might have thought so if he hadn't jacked off all over it. I think this is supposed to be both proof of his devotion and a reminder that—in his messed-up version of reality—you're his, not mine." Noticing yet more paper, he expected to find another drawing. He quickly realized that, actually, it was a letter. "Shit."

"What? What did—oh."

The letter read: *Why are you doing this, Blair? Why are you dragging things out this way? I don't know exactly what got said between you and your parents, but it seems you all came to an understanding. Yet, you didn't return home with them. You're still staying with Devereaux. Do you not care how much this hurts me?*

At this point, all I can think is that you haven't yet come to me because you need me to be the one who makes all the moves. You want me to take control. Is that it? I can do that. I can prove how much you mean to me. I'm simply sad that it's come to this. I always assumed we wouldn't need to play any such games.

Maybe it's my fault. Maybe I shouldn't have waited until you aged before I secured my claim to you. Are you angry with me for that? Is that why you let the cat near you?

I saw how he touched you at the cabin. As if he owned you. You didn't push him away like you should have and, honestly, it's hard not to doubt that you're still pure. I'd like to think you wouldn't betray me that way, but a lot of things you've done lately have surprised me.

Not that I mean to walk away from you. That I would never do. All I want is to love you. That's all. But we will *be having a long conversation about this once you're home.*

You best be rid of the cat by the time I come for you. I mean it, Blair. I warned him to back off. He didn't. And believe me, I will fucking kill him if you continue to stay with him. His blood will stain my hands, yes, but every single drop of it will be on yours.

A sudden chill in her blood, Blair rubbed at the prickling skin of her arms. "Oh my God. It's official, he's freaking insane. His thought patterns are just *wow*. Every sentence creeps me out."

She licked her lips, her stomach rolling and churning. Her inner female was going berserk, wanting to rip apart this person who thought to threaten her mate. "He said he warned you. He means the hit and run, doesn't he?"

"Yes," Luke replied, his jaw tight as he replaced the lid on the box. "That was never really about causing me harm. It was merely a message. Back then, he saw me as relatively inconsequential."

"That's clearly changed. He threatened to *kill* you." Her chest tightened and her breathing went to hell.

Luke pulled her close and squeezed her shoulders. "It's going to be okay, Blair. It's a threat he won't be able to follow through on. He also won't be taking you, no matter what he might think. I get that this letter is worthy of a major freak out, but remember: He wants to scare you. Don't let him. Don't let him get in your head. Don't give him that control over you."

Easier said than goddamn done.

"I know you hoped he'd at some point get the message that you're mine and then leave you alone. But people like him … that's not how their minds work."

"Yeah, I see that." She let out a long, loud sigh. "What do we do now?"

"Report this to Tate and Havana. There's no point in us asking River if he can do a DNA search using the semen or any fingerprints he might find. No shifter is ever arrested, so their records wouldn't be in a database."

Blair's insides jumped at the knock on the door. Her little female stiffened, her gut in knots, her anger still hot.

"That's probably James," said Luke.

Her mate turned out to be right. James stalked inside wearing a frustrated expression.

"No one saw the gift being left on the bench," Luke guessed.

James gave a slow shake of the head. "Not a soul. Nor does anyone seem to have noticed any strangers lurking." His gaze flicked to the box. "What's inside it?"

Blair plopped her butt onto the armchair. "You don't want to know."

"Have you notified Tate and Havana yet?" asked James.

"No, I'm about to do that now," Luke told him.

The Alphas showed up mere minutes after he reported it. Havana—her temper as precarious as that of any devil shifter—went on an epic rant that Blair might have found entertaining if she wasn't both freaked and *pissed.*

Once Tate had calmed his mate down, he turned to Luke. "I suppose we should have expected that he'd do something like this in response to Blair *still* failing to return to the pack even after making peace with her parents."

"I figured he'd do something," said Luke. "Just not so soon."

"He was apparently feeling motivated to get his point across *fast.*" Havana folded her arms. "It would seem he's done waiting for Blair to fall in line. The limp-dick motherfucker should have known better than to think she would."

"But as that letter illustrates," began Blair, "he doesn't *see* me. Not the real me. And now that you've scanned the contents of the box, I want all that crap out of here." She slid her gaze to Luke. "I don't care what you do with it, I just don't want it here. I don't want any part of *him* in our home."

Luke gave her a reassuring look. "Don't worry, I'll get rid of it. Just like I'll eventually get rid of him."

Not if Blair did it first.

CHAPTER TWENTY

Late the following evening, Luke stood with a fairly large group in a field not far from the drop-off point, watching as Farrell swooped down in his avian form. Dark shadows stretched along the ground, giving them plenty of cover. The only source of light this far out was that of the waning moon.

His cat's ears pricked up as he pressed against Luke's insides, eager to hear what the Head Enforcer had learned. Luke was equally eager and raring to get moving. Adrenaline pulsed through his blood, heightening his senses and flooding his system with anticipation.

Farrell shifted shape and rolled his shoulders. The murmuring crowd went silent and joined Luke in gathering around him.

"What kind of scene are we facing?" asked Tate.

"One you're not gonna like." Farrell puffed out a breath. "It's a good thing we brought extra backup on the off-chance that we'd need it."

"Why?"

"There are four vehicles packed with humans."

Luke felt his brows snap together. "Four?" He'd expected one, maybe two. "Why would Zayne bring such a large entourage?"

"That was my initial question," said Farrell. "The answer? He didn't. From what I was able to gather as I listened to various conversations, Zayne brought seven people along—three seem to be his usual bodyguards; they're sitting with him in the first SUV. The other four are in a second SUV that's towing a metal box which I presume is meant to contain Camden."

Aspen spat a vicious curse.

"Maybe," began Luke, "Zayne brought so many because he isn't prepared to take the chance that Camden might free himself and overpower anyone close by."

"*Or* the people towing the box have purchased Camden from Zayne," suggested Havana. "After all, Zayne might have figured that it was safer for him to not have to store Camden somewhere while he arranged for a buyer to come collect him."

Blair turned to Farrell. "Who are the people in the other two vehicles?"

The Head Enforcer rubbed the back of his head. "Well, it seems that Zayne has unexpected company in the form of anti-shifter extremists."

Luke felt his brows fly up. *The fuck?*

"I recognized a few of them." Farrell cut his gaze to Vinnie, who stood with Camden, Aspen, and Bailey. "They've met with you at the antique store on occasion. One is Hank Wheeler."

Seeing his mate's brow furrow in confusion, Luke told her, "Wheeler is pretty high up in the hierarchy of extremists."

"He and Zayne had a brief conversation," said Farrell. "Wheeler claimed he was just there to make sure everything ran smoothly."

Blair pursed her lips. "In other words, like us, Wheeler doesn't trust that Zayne doesn't intend to kill Vinnie to hide his crime."

That would be Luke's guess. "Dad's been an informant for the extremists for years—or so they believe. They wouldn't want to lose a contact so valuable. Wheeler must figure his presence will be enough to ensure that Zayne sticks to his word."

"I think that Zayne made the same assumption, because he seemed offended by Wheeler's appearance," said Farrell. "Zayne told him that his assistance wasn't necessary, but Wheeler won't budge."

"Which is inconvenient for us, because it increases the number of humans that we'll need to take out," said Tate. "In total, how many will we be dealing with?"

"Twenty-two," replied Farrell. "Wheeler piled quite a few into his van."

"He likes to have a large entourage," said Vinnie. "He may have also brought extra people as a scare tactic. After all, he'd rather discourage Zayne from doing anything stupid than actually have a shoot-out with him and his men."

Havana twisted her mouth. "They only outnumber us by two."

"Yeah, but we're not armed," the Head Enforcer pointed out. "Most of them probably are. The extremists always carry guns. At the very least, Zayne's people will have tranqs in the event that they need to knock Camden out. Plus, Helena won't be fighting; she'll be on hand in case anyone needs healing—that leaves us one person down."

"Not an ideal situation, all things considered," said Havana. "We can still take out twenty-two, though. We'll simply need to be careful how we proceed, because we don't want them driving off. Have any exited the vehicles?"

"Zayne, Wheeler, and their respective bodyguards did, but they returned to their vehicles after ending their little chat," replied Farrell.

Tate turned to Vinnie and Camden. "Lure out as many as you can. It will make it easier for the rest of us to crowd and tip over the vehicles before the humans have a chance to mow us down as they hightail it out of there."

Pausing, Tate scanned the crowd of Olympus Pride members and their three wolverine allies—Valentina's brothers had asked to come along, promising to eat the dead as a thank you. As you do. "You heard Farrell's news, so you know we'll be implementing Plan B. This will be a matter of all hands on deck. It may not be easy to get to the humans inside the vehicles. Zayne's SUVs will no doubt have bulletproof windows and tires, given that he's a celebrity. The extremists are known to occasionally take such measures with their own vehicles. So don't concentrate on smashing car windows. Go for ripping off doors."

Havana turned to their healer. "Helena, obviously you'll stay behind ready to take care of any wounded who are sent your way. Farrell and Isaiah will ride with Vinnie and Camden. Everyone else needs to get moving. We need to arrive at the drop-off point before Vinnie pulls up."

At that, shifters promptly began to strip. Stashing her clothes in one of the pride's vehicles, Blair clashed eyes with Finley's. The female enforcer didn't give her a false smile or any sarcastic shit. In fact, she merely inclined her head before looking away. Hoping that meant that the woman had pulled said head out of her ass, Blair turned to a now naked Luke.

He gave her chin a soft squeeze, his gaze intent. "Be careful."

She nodded. "You, too."

"Always."

They then both shifted.

Her female butted her mate in a silent order for him to stay alert. He bared a fang, insulted that she would feel he needed the reminder. She only sniffed.

The Alpha male's cat let out a low-pitched call, and then he and his mate took off. Recognizing the signal, the herd of shifters followed, moving fast and quietly.

The bush dog ran alongside her mate as they bounded across the field. She approved of the long grass. It would help conceal them, much like the darkness of the night.

When the Alphas slowed, the others did the same. The bush dog pricked her ears, picking up the sound of muffled voices. *Too* muffled. The humans were close, but not out in the open.

Like the other shifters, she lowered to her belly as she crept forward until she was in position. From where she lay, the female could see four vehicles parked on a short strip of road at the other side of the field's fence.

The female wasn't put-off by the sight of the fence. It wouldn't be hard to climb. It was small. Wooden.

She wanted to climb it now.

She didn't like having to stay still. She wanted to hunt. Maul. Punish. Protect her pride. But she remained still and watchful, like her mate.

Her head cocked at the sound of an engine in the distance. Bright lights soon cut through the darkness. The rumbling slowed as a car came into view and parked near the other vehicles.

She felt her mate tense as his father exited the car. The door of a large van then opened, and a man stepped out.

"Vinnie," he greeted, a note of pleasure in his tone.

"Hank," said Vinnie. "I wasn't expecting to see you here."

"Zayne told me you'd scheduled a meet. I thought I'd come by and ensure it went without incident, if you get my meaning."

A whirring sound came from an SUV as a door slid open, and then … "You came through for me after all, Mr. Devereaux. Good man." *Zayne*, the bush dog sensed, recognizing his voice. "It seems Hank was right when he insisted that I could trust your word." He hopped out of the SUV, along with two large males, both of whom held guns.

The female bared her teeth in a silent snarl.

"You're not alone," one human said to Vinnie—the same male who had barged into Elle's bedroom only days ago.

Vinnie frowned. "Of course I'm not alone. Who'd come alone to a meet like this? Now, I don't think I'm the only one here who wants this over and done with, so how about we move things along and someone collects Camden from the car? You'll be fine, he's out cold. I had to drug him or he'd have fled the moment he saw you guys."

Zayne barked out some orders. Men piled out of the second SUV. Two remained near the vehicle, tranquilizer guns raised, while the other two cautiously crossed to Vinnie's car.

Vinnie looked at Zayne. "My payment?"

Zayne tipped his chin toward one of the large males beside him, who took a small case from the vehicle and then carried it over to Vinnie.

"Much obliged," said Vinnie, taking the case from him.

"Thank you for your services, Mr. Devereaux," said Zayne. "I truly appreciate your help in this matter. Perhaps we could do business again in the future."

Vinnie gave a small, noncommittal shrug. "Perhaps."

"Jesus, this guy weighs a ton," exclaimed one human as he and another struggled to carry Camden toward an SUV.

The female tensed in readiness, knowing it would soon be time to move. Beside her, her mate fairly quivered with the urge to pounce.

It all happened fast.

Camden's claws sliced out. His eyes snapped open. His claws stabbed into the chest of the human nearest to him. Before any humans could even think to shoot, the shifters came at them from all sides—some still in their animal forms, some shifting back as they ran.

Vehicles were tipped over. Doors were yanked off. People were dragged out and dumped on the floor. Cries went up, and shots rang out.

Most humans braced to fight, weapons raised or fists up. Other humans attempted to flee, running aimlessly.

Her upper lip peeling back, the bush dog ran for the nearest fleer, latching onto his ankle. He tripped with a curse and awkwardly fell forward, catching his weight on his elbows … right at the feet of a white tiger. The large cat slammed his paw onto the human's head, smashing his skull. *Dead.*

With a sniff of satisfaction, the bush dog turned her attention to another fleeing human. She charged, dodging another human who was staggering backwards with a pallas cat wrapped around his face, and quickly brought her target down. A passing wolverine finished him off by brutally biting a chunk out of his neck.

The bush dog approved.

Again and again, she pursued those who would run. The humans cried out and cursed and screamed. Bullets whizzed and cracked and thudded into metal. But those sounds were barely heard beneath the growls, roars, hisses, yowls, squawks, and bloodcurdling screeches of the shifters.

In the bush dog's opinion, it was mayhem at its finest.

An engine roared to life. She saw that someone was trying to escape in Vinnie's car. They would fail, because snarling animals swiftly leaped into the vehicle. The human jumped out of the other side of it only to be quickly dispatched by a waiting wolverine.

Out of bullets, a human threw his gun at an injured pallas cat and sprinted off. The bush dog galloped after him as he made a beeline for the fence. He saw her coming and cursed, putting on a burst of speed, but he had no chance of outrunning her.

Latching onto his ankle, she used her weight to trip him. He fell hard and—

Fire blazed across her ear. *Bullet.* She released the human, darted aside, and crawled under Vinnie's car. More shots rang out. Bullets peppered the ground near the car, kicking up dirt.

There was a loud cry. The firing stopped.

The female shuffled forward on her belly, ready to peek out from under the car, but then a human fell to the ground in front of her, taken down by a wolverine who savagely clawed at his back.

His face a mask of agony, the human spotted her. He weakly aimed his gun her way, his finger on the trigger. She let out a puppy-like whine and fell limply onto her side. He hesitated. The wolverine pounced on his head, all but bursting it.

With a yip of thanks, the bush dog edged out from under the car. Hearing a feline cry of pain, she looked to see a large male stomping on a pallas cat. The bush dog sprinted toward him and sank her teeth into the ankle of his offending foot. She bit and chomped and growled while he yelled and kicked out and tried batting her away with his hand.

A bearcat whizzed by, slashing the Achilles tendon of his other foot. The human dropped like a stone. And then the bush dog's mate was there, attacking the man's face and scalp with claws and teeth, while a black mamba struck and buried her fangs in the human's leg.

Leaving the others to finish him off, the bush dog backed away and—

Running. Another human was running. Far and Fast.

She burst into motion, snarling when he cleared the fence and ran through the field. The female scooted under one of the wooden slats of the fence and pursued him, rocketing through the long grass. Little by little, she closed the distance between them.

She sprang, burying her teeth and claws into his calf and clinging tight. Her weight unbalanced him, but he didn't fall. He spun, reaching backwards to knock her away, but the angle was too awkward for him.

She clawed at his leg, hooking and shredding skin, delighting in his screams. He shook his leg hard. Rather than dislodging her, he fell. *Finally*.

She shifted.

In mere milliseconds, Blair stood in the place of her female. She didn't give the human a chance to react. She dropped to her knees onto his back, reached down, and snapped his neck.

Done. He was dead.

Breathing hard, she got to her feet. Jesus, this had been one hell of a night. Turning toward the pure chaos commencing nearby, she noticed that the number of standing humans had dropped liked flies. They'd put up one hell of a fight—she'd give them that much.

Shivering slightly at the evening chill, she pulled back and gave her female supremacy once more.

Her sides heaving as she struggled to catch her breath, the bush dog shook her body to settle properly into her fur. She sniffed haughtily at the corpse, disappointed the human had died so quickly. He hadn't deserved such mercy.

With a snort, she turned away from him. Pain blasted down their mating bond. *Shot*. Her mate had been shot. The shock of it tensed her—

A net came down over the female, plunging her into darkness. Panic had no sooner flooded her than something sharp dug into her flank. Her vision went hazy as the world seemed to get further and further away.

She was being lifted. Moved. *Fast*. But any emotions she might have felt were swiftly snuffed out as her awareness faded and faded.

Her human fought to surface and help. She failed. The drug was seeping the strength from them both.

The female's vision turned black as her world tilted. Then she was out.

Luke's cat growled at the human pointing a gun at him. The male frantically pressed the trigger, biting out harsh curses when no bullets fired. He charged the pallas cat, the gun raised like a club. A blur of red and orange crashed into his side like a battering ram, knocking him down.

The cat pitched forward, swiping his claws along the human's throat, severing arteries. The bearcat nodded at him and then ran off, landing on the back of a human who was crawling toward an abandoned gun; burying her claws into both sides of his neck.

Another human rushed past him, stinking of fear. A mamba twined fast around his leg and pulled him to the ground. A devil shifter then leaped at him, her mouth agape. She snapped her powerful jaws closed around his nape.

The cat glanced around, searching for his mate.

A hot impact punched his shoulder. Agony rippled along his foreleg. A warm wetness gathered in his fur.

Instinct made him seek cover. He fled toward—

Panic and dizziness reverberated along the mating bond. He staggered, dazed. A bullet sank into his back leg. Then another, making it crumple beneath him. He hit the ground just as another bullet buried itself in his flank. But he didn't care about the threat or the pain … because he knew his mate was now unconscious.

Dread pumped through him, spurring him to stand. He tried. Fell.

A human stood over him, weapon aimed to fire. *Wheeler.* He sneered. "I should have known you were all shifters. Should have seen it. I didn't think—"

A large avian descended on him, raking at his face and eyes.

Wheeler dropped the gun with a guttural scream, his hands flying up to slap at the bird.

The cat would have again tried to stand, but his human half forced his way to the surface.

Grinding his teeth against the agony drumming through him, Luke snatched the pistol from the ground and turned it on Wheeler. He didn't fire. Didn't need to. Because Vinnie appeared in his human form and sliced the human's throat.

"Always did hate that bastard," said Vinnie, dumping the body on the ground.

Still flooded with panic, Luke dropped the gun as he said, "Blair's unconscious somewhere. One of these shitheads must have hit—"

"Whoa, whoa, whoa, don't try to get up yet," ordered Vinnie, crouching at his side and putting a hand on his uninjured shoulder to pin him down. "Someone get Helena!"

"*I need to find Blair.* She's passed out somewhere." And Luke couldn't see any sign of her anywhere.

"She'll be found. Aspen, Bailey—get Blair. She's out cold. Be quick about it. She might need healing."

The two females nodded and disappeared. It was then that Luke took a moment to study the scene. Bodies littered the ground—necks broken, arteries severed, stomachs sliced open, skin bitten and clawed. There was blood everywhere, slick and shiny.

Only a few humans were still alive, and it was clear that the only reason they weren't yet dead was that shifters were having fun with them. One human had multiple pallas cats crawling over him, biting and hissing. Another was weakly wrestling a wolverine, trying to punch it in the snout even while bloody and broken. A fourth human was sluggishly army crawling along the ground, swollen lumps on his face that looked like snake bites, while a devil shifter savagely bit into his scalp.

It had been a slaughter for sure.

Luke looked around frantically, a stone lodged in his chest as he waited for either Aspen or Bailey to reappear, carrying his still-unconscious mate.

Just then, Helena appeared at his side. "Please tell me the bullets are out," she said, examining his wounds. "Damn, this one's not. Sorry, Luke, but this is gonna hurt."

He grunted. "Not anything I haven't felt be—*mother of fuck*."

Tate crossed to him, his lips twitching, covered in streaks of blood but no wounds, so the Alpha had already been healed, apparently. "Stop whining."

"Whining? Fuck you, asshole. Make yourself useful and *find my mate*. She's unconscious somewhere."

His amusement dimming, Tate nodded. "Got it." With that, he left.

Luke drew in a breath as Helena's healing energy began to crackle through him. His injuries faded before him until they disappeared altogether, and then the pain itself was also gone. "Thank you."

He jumped to his feet … and his heart stopped at the grave looks that both Aspen and Bailey wore as they came toward him. "What is it?"

Aspen licked her lips. "We can't find Blair. But … we found tracks. Tire tracks."

CHAPTER TWENTY-ONE

The breath slammed out of Luke's lungs. His gut hardened. "Where?"

The females led him to the spot in question, passing a dead human that Blair had evidently killed. And sure enough, there were tire tracks on the ground. His chest tight, he took off, following them ... but they disappeared on reaching the road.

The bottom dropped out of Luke's stomach, and bile burned the back of his throat. "Someone took her," he said, the words like crushed stone. His cat went AWOL.

"Maybe there were more extremists hanging around," said Farrell as he and several others came up behind Luke. "Maybe it was one of them," the Head Enforcer added.

Maybe. But Luke didn't think so. "He said he'd come for her soon."

"You think it was her stalker?" asked Bailey.

Luke swallowed hard. "Yeah. Yeah, I fucking do." Fear—so thick, so blinding, so incapacitating—stabbed deep into Luke's chest, making every inhale *hurt.* At that same time, he found himself at the mercy of a rage so hot and consuming he could easily lose himself in it. And he felt his breathing go to shit.

Tate gripped his arm. "Don't lose it. You can't lose it right now."

Luke felt his face go tight. "*He has her, Tate.*"

"But he won't kill her," the Alpha insisted. "Cling to that. She'll still be alive when we get to her. And we *will* get to her. She needs you to stay calm."

How could Luke be anything close to calm, when he didn't even have an inkling of a clue where the hell she could be? He was always cool and rational in the face of danger or opposition; always the voice of reason even in situations where emotions ran intensely high. But none of said situations had ever before involved his mate being *taken*.

Havana took a step toward him, her face soft with sympathy. Luke slammed up a hand, halting her. He couldn't handle anyone touching him right now. Couldn't handle having his personal space invaded. Not when the dark emotions running riot inside him left him so close to exploding into violence.

Luke dragged a hand through his hair. Fuck, this wasn't happening. He'd promised Blair that her stalker would never get to her. It hadn't occurred to him that the bastard would follow them tonight; that he would take advantage of the pride's distraction and make a move. The sly little bastard.

Luke's cat clawed his insides, wanting out; wanting to hunt. He wasn't the only one who longed to go hunting. But he needed a solid plan first.

He drew in a long breath, trying to center himself and quash the dread that ran rampant in his system. But it was hard. So goddamn hard. Dark scenarios kept playing out in his mind's eye, and his cat's blinding fury kept his own alive.

There were so many places she could be. So many plans her captor could have. So many terrible things that could happen to her if Luke failed to find her.

Tate was right, her kidnapper wasn't likely to kill her. But he might well hurt her. He was already angry with her—his last letter had made that clear.

Blair was even angrier. And, far from meek or easily cowed, she wouldn't feel compelled to keep her mouth shut and do as she was told. No, she'd let loose on him. There was no knowing how the bastard would react to that.

She would also be sure to tell the son of a bitch that she wasn't his mate at all; that she'd never want him, never be his. And if he would rather see her dead than mated to another …

A cold shard of fear pierced Luke's chest. If the worst happened, he'd keep his foot in this world, realm, whatever it was long enough to avenge her. Then he'd let go. Because even if he existed, he'd be dead without her anyway.

Hell, he'd been half-dead when he found her six years ago. She'd saved him. It was only her and their bond that gave him peace … though, he suddenly realized, he'd subconsciously worried that the mental tempest would return, mating bond or no. He'd worried that it would sweep him under again, submerging his mind in darkness. Worried that she'd be stuck mated to a man she couldn't emotionally reach; one who saw her but felt disconnected from her; one so numb and lost and shrouded in a thick fog that he might as well not be there.

Luke realized something else, too. He realized that, desperate to ensure she never met that fate, he'd involuntarily and subconsciously held back from fully committing to her—scared he'd otherwise doom her.

Intellectually, he knew that the fear was groundless. He *felt* how their bond stabilized him, and he was certain right down to his bones that it would always be that way. But the matter had nonetheless caused him to shy away from the bond on a level that he hadn't seen until now.

He cursed himself for holding back from his own mate out of some unnecessary fear that he'd—

A sharp, dazing pain knifed through his head and chest. His world tilted, and his vision blurred and grayed around the edges. But then the pain and disorientation subsided … and he realized that the mating bond had fully snapped into place.

His heart began to gallop as sheer joy flowed through him and his cat, smoothing over their ragged nerves. God, Luke could feel her so much more intensely now. Could feel her *inside* him, not merely linked to him.

Maybe it was the stability of knowing that their bond was complete, but his panic receded slightly, allowing him to focus. He *shoved* energy down their link, determined to wake her; to give her the strength to fight.

Eying him closely, Tate narrowed his eyes. "The bond is complete."

Luke gave a curt nod, rolling his shoulders. "My cell. I need my cell." With that, he quickly headed back to the pride's vehicles.

"Why?" asked Tate as he and the others ran after him.

"Because I need to call Mitch. I need to find out where Donal and Antoine are right now. You contact the enforcers who are watching Gabriel; ask them where he is. At least one of them will be off the radar. Maybe if we work out who took her we can work out *where* they took her."

Again, Luke sent more energy rippling down their link, silently willing her to wake up, praying to the universe and every possible celestial force to keep her safe.

Surges of energy pushed down the mating bond, dragging Blair out of sleep. She distantly noted the rumbling of an engine—a rumbling that reverberated against the hard floor beneath her, seeming to vibrate against the side of her body that was all but plastered to it. Her mind was all hazy and cottony. She drifted. Floated. Could barely put her thoughts together.

Sleep once more tried to claim her despite the queasiness in her stomach and the ache in her head, but another rush of energy slinked through her system. Her female butted her hard, slamming her body against Blair's insides. Well that was uncalled for. There was—

The battle. The field. The net. The darkness that swallowed her whole.

Blair's heartbeat stuttered, and then the organ began to pound like crazy. Drugged. She'd been drugged. Which explained why her muscles throbbed and she felt weak as a newborn kitten.

Worse, she'd been taken.

She didn't dare let her eyes snap open. She had no way of knowing how closely she was being watched. She quickly got her breathing under control—the quick rise and fall of her chest would be a dead giveaway that she was no longer unconscious.

Relief abruptly tumbled down the mating bond—a bond now so vivid, so solid, so *complete*. That masculine feeling of relief told her that Luke had sensed she was awake.

When the hell had their bond become complete? Later. Blair would figure that out later.

She sent a "pulse" of reassurance along the bond, even knowing he would sense the anger and anxiety that vied for supremacy inside her and battered at what little mental composure she had.

Blair breathed through her inner struggle, determined to somehow remain calm, much like her female was doing—a female who'd either withdrawn to give Blair control or had been suppressed by whatever drug she'd been given, because she'd evidently shifted back into her human form.

She kept her eyes closed as she stretched out her senses. She was in a vehicle of some sort—that much was for sure. She didn't think she was in a trunk. A trunk was carpeted, and her body was *not* pressed against anything remotely soft right now. Beneath the country music playing low was the sound of steady breathing.

The scents of oil, dirt, and metal surrounded her, but there was another scent. A smell that clung to the material that had been draped over her. A scent that belonged to someone all too familiar. And with that, Blair knew who'd taken her.

Her churning stomach bottomed out, and a sense of betrayal slapped her so hard she almost cursed aloud. Her female growled, equally stung and getting more pissed with each moment that passed. Their combined anger stomped out the flames of fear in their bellies. All they wanted was to *ream* his ass.

Not that Blair was in any condition to do that just yet. Her head still pounded, her muscles still ached, and she still felt ridiculously weak. If Luke hadn't shoved energy down their bond, she probably would have remained out cold for a while longer.

Not wanting to alert her captor to the fact that she was conscious, Blair only opened her eyes a little. Dark, blurry images swam in front of her vision. She double-blinked, struggling to bring everything into focus. *Bars*. Thin, metal bars were only a few inches in front of her.

Using her peripheral vision, she was able to catch a glimpse of the space above her while still lying on her side. More bars. Oh God, she was in a crate. A large crate that was built to hold animals.

Motherfucker.

Although it was dark, her shifter enhanced vision allowed her to see just fine. Her mode of transport seemed to be a small van. With the exception of a crate, some boxes, and a few rucksacks, it was empty.

Her female rubbed against her, sure that Luke would come for them. Oh, he would. *If* he had any way of finding them. But Blair had no plans to wait for him or anyone else to save her. She intended to take care of that part herself.

The problem was … she was so weak she felt both light as a feather and heavy as concrete at the same time. More, the son of a bitch who'd taken her wouldn't have put her in any old crate. He'd have purchased one specifically used to contain shifters. That meant there'd be no sense in trying to kick open the door or have her female chew through the bars. That would achieve one thing only—alert him to the fact that she'd woken.

Damn the bastard for putting her in a crate. He couldn't have simply cuffed her wrists behind her back or something, could he? She could have freed herself by dislocating her thumbs. Which, of course, he knew.

Her pulse spiked at the sound of a low male curse. She felt the van slow until, eventually, it came to a halt. Shit, had she given herself away?

Keys jangled, and then a door creaked open. It shut with a clang, and she heard footfalls. They weren't coming *closer*, though. No, they were fading away.

She froze, listening hard. Seconds of silence ticked by. Her female paced, urging Blair to *move, move, move.*

Deciding it might not be a bad idea to use the moment of privacy to try escaping, Blair kicked at the crate's door. *Ow.* It was like booting a stone wall. Being barefoot made it hurt even more. Still, she gave it another admittedly weak kick, wincing at the ache in her muscles.

A loud curse rang out in the distance, making her heart slam against her ribcage. She tensed once more, hearing thuds and muffled snarls. What the hell?

A muttered oath preceded the snapping of branches, and then a quiet swiftly fell. But the silence was soon broken by the sound of yet more footfalls, and these were heading toward the van. Quickly.

Panic racing through her system, Blair practically *attacked* her crate, hitting and kicking it with everything in her—and she sadly still didn't have much in her at all. The whole time, those footfalls came closer and closer, getting louder and louder … and headed to the rear of the van.

The double doors opened wide. Moonlight beamed into the vehicle, slashing through the shadows. A tall figure stood silhouetted in the doorway. But not the one she'd expected to see.

Blair double-blinked. "Finley?"

The female leaped into the van and crossed to the crate. "We've got to get you out of this *now*. I don't know if I killed him."

"What? What's happening? Shit, you're hurt." The woman sported puncture wounds, rake marks, and a split lip.

"Back at the field, I saw him dragging you off, but I was too far away to do anything," she said, her words coming fast as she struggled to open the crate, pain etched into her face. "I roared out a warning, but no one heard me while there was so much damn noise going on. So I followed the van, managed to climb onto the bike rack, and then held on. He stopped because there's a dead deer in the road and he wanted to move it out of the way."

Pausing, Finley cursed at her failed attempts to open the door, sliced out her claws, and tried using one to pick the lock. "I pounced on the opportunity to take him out, but he's one tough mother. We tussled for a bit, ended up wrestling on the ground, and I hit his head hard with a rock. He rolled off the road and down the steep hill, but I don't know if he's out cold or dead." There was a *snick*, and she smiled. "*Finally*."

Blair's stomach lurched as she rolled onto her front. More, her head spun and the edges of her vision smudged. Cursing inwardly, she nonetheless crawled out of the crate and went to follow the pallas cat out of the van.

"Come on, I'll drive us out of here," said Finley.

Something caught Blair's eye. Crossing to one of the boxes, she pulled out a sweater. "This is mine. All the clothes in here are mine. It's all old stuff that I bagged up last year for my mom to take to a charity store."

Pulling out jogging pants and a tee, she threw them at Finley. "They should fit you." Blair also retrieved a tee and shorts for herself before hopping out of the van, cursing when her knees almost gave out. Dragging on her clothes, she glanced around, seeing nothing but road and woodland. "Do you know where we are?"

"Yes." Finley winced as she shoved an arm through her sleeve while they made their way to the front of the van. "Got a broken rib for sure. We're about twenty minutes away from the drop-off—Dammit, no keys. I don't suppose you know how to hotwire a car, do you?"

"No, but I don't intend to drive off anyway. Not until I know for certain that he's a goner." Blair snatched the cell phone she spotted in the cupholder. "How long will it take the pride to get to us?"

"Ten minutes or less if they floored it."

Blair's lips flattened as she realized that the cell required a password to unlock it. She typed "Blair" on a hunch. That didn't work. Nor did any of the random words she came up with.

Shit.

An idea slipped into her mind. Biting down on her lip, Blair typed in her first name followed by his surname, leaving no space between the two.

The phone unlocked.

Blair grinned. "Yes! We can—"

They both froze as a guttural roar split the air.

Her smile fading, she pushed the phone into Finley's hand. "Hide in the van and call Luke. Now. Then stay out of sight."

The enforcer's eyes went wide. "Are you kidding me?"

"Look, neither of us are up to taking him down right this second. I'm still weak and woozy from the drug. You're injured and in pain. We need to give ourselves a little time to physically recover before we act. That means keeping him distracted. I can manage that, but not if his attention isn't fully on me. As such, I need you to hang back."

Finley huffed. "Fine. But don't get killed, or your mate will *slay* me."

Predictably, Mitch lost his mind on hearing that his sister had been taken. Luke was in no position to judge—hell, his cat still hadn't pulled himself together. Nonetheless, Luke heard himself clip, "I need you to focus, Mitch. It has to have been her stalker who took her. And I have reason to believe that either Donal or Antoine could be that stalker—I don't have time to go into the why of it right now, so I need you to trust me on this. More, I need you to tell me where they are."

Seconds of silence ticked by. "Donal or Antoine?"

"*Mitch.*"

The male cursed. "All right. Fine. Give me five minutes, I'll call you back."

"Good. And Mitch? Say nothing to your pack about this. Any who don't believe that your pack mates are involved might warn Donal and Antoine that they're suspected to have taken her. If one of them is our culprit, they might panic. I don't want our boy running scared—especially since he might kill her so that she won't slow him down."

Luke rang off, stilling as his mate's emotions danced along their bond. Relief gripped his gut, though he knew they weren't out of the woods yet. "She's awake. I feel her. She's shaken, but more than anything she's *pissed*."

"That's better than terrified," said Aspen.

"*Providing* she doesn't aggravate her kidnapper too much," mused Havana.

Luke nodded, afraid his mate would do exactly that.

"According to the enforcers who are watching Gabriel, he's at a bar having drinks with people from work," Tate revealed. "They can't see him from where they're parked outside the building, so they're going to head inside the bar and search for him."

Luke ground his teeth, not much liking that all they could do for the moment was wait for others to return their calls.

"Whoever he is … he'll do one of two things—head off to the hills with her, or stash her somewhere local because he intends to go on about his normal life while also keeping her captive," said Camden. "Right?"

"Right," Tate agreed.

"He'll do the second," Luke stated. "He won't feel the need to go on the run, because he doesn't believe that he's doing anything wrong. He has this neurotic notion that he and Blair are meant to be; that they will start a life together. *But* he's not so crazy that he doesn't know on some level that he's not who she wants." He'd have otherwise handled several things differently.

Vinnie nodded. "Another reason I can't envision him fleeing is that he'll know she'd try to escape; that she wouldn't be a cooperative captive. And that's not an ideal scenario for a man on the run—and he *would* be on the run, because both our pride *and* the Sylvan Pack would hunt him down."

"I don't think that he'll take her to a random location," said Bailey.

"No, he'll have chosen it in advance," Luke agreed. "Possibly even prepared it for her arrival. It'll be isolated, but not too far from his home because he'll want to always be close to her. Plus, he'd be unable to both spend plenty of time with her *and* live his life as normal if he needed to go off on long drives all the time."

Alex twisted his mouth. "Neither Gabriel's address nor Sylvan territory are all that far from here, so his hidey hole shouldn't be too far away either."

Luke's phone chimed. He answered it fast, "Yeah?"

"Neither Donal nor Antoine are on pack territory right now," began Mitch, "and no one has any clue where they are. Now, can you *please* tell me why they're suspects."

Luke quickly brought him up to speed, giving him the bare facts. "Before you claim that none of that makes them guilty, note that I'm aware of that. It's why I haven't beaten the holy hell out of either of them."

Mitch swore. "I had no clue Antoine harassed women in the past. If I had—"

"You'd have said something, I know." Luke's head whipped to the side on hearing his brother's phone ring. "I have to go, Mitch. I'll call you back when I have news to share. You do the same." He hung up and, unable to overhear the other side of Tate's phone conversation, waited until his brother ended it before asking, "Well? I'm guessing one of the enforcers tailing Gabriel called you again."

"They did," confirmed Tate, his face hard. "He's in the wind."

Luke hissed, clenching his fists so tight it was a wonder a tendon or two didn't snap. "So we have nothing. No idea which of them is our guy."

"*For now*," said Havana.

Luke scrubbed a hand down his face. "I need to get out of here. I need to go look for her."

Tate put a hand on his shoulder to stay him. "It's unlikely that you're going to stumble upon her—"

"You think I don't know that?" Luke burst out. "I can't stay here like this and do nothing while she's out there with whoever the fuck believes that she's his. I can't." Every muscle in Luke's body fairly quivered with the urge to do *something*.

"I get it, I do, but—" Tate cut off as the cell in Luke's hand once more began to ring.

Luke frowned at the screen. "I don't recognize the number." He answered, "Hello?"

"Luke, it's Finley. Listen to me. You need to head straight toward the old junkyard near the docks. I saw your mate get taken. I followed her. We're on that road. I managed to get her out of the van, but we're both weak and in no condition to run. Her kidnapper … he's hurt but heading our way, and she's got her heart set on beating his ass to a pulp. *Hurry.*" The line went dead.

For a moment, Luke didn't move, struggling to process her words. Then he leaped into action, jumping into an SUV, saying, "I know where Blair is. We need to move *now.*"

CHAPTER TWENTY-TWO

Blair slashed yet another tire as she waited for *him* to appear at the top of the hill. She could hear him coming closer. Could hear grass rustling and branches snapping.

She'd expected him to come barreling up the hill, but either the climb wasn't so easy or the asshole was a little dazed. Or maybe it was a little of both.

Finley peeked out of the rear of the van. "I called Luke," she said, her voice low. "He'll be on his way as we speak."

"Get back inside," hissed Blair, slashing the fourth tire. "I told you, you need to stay out of sight. I know it goes against your instincts to hide, but I need him to focus on me."

The enforcer's mouth thinned. "I know, but I don't have to like it." She paused as a cry of alarm rang out, followed by thuds and snaps that suggested he'd fallen back down the hill. "Are you *sure* you don't want to just make a run for it? I know we're in bad shape, but he can't follow us by car now."

"He'd give chase on foot. Our scents would lead him straight to us."

"*And* you'd rather face off with him."

"And I'd rather face off with him."

Finley muttered an oath. "Fine. Just know that if he attacks you, I'm not gonna stay in hiding—injured or not." She retreated into the van.

Letting out a long breath, Blair moved to stand in front of the vehicle's hood. She could hear *him* once more trying to make his way up the hill. Ten minutes. Luke would be here in ten minutes—maybe less if he really hit the pedal hard. She could keep her captor distracted for that long.

Blair's inner female planted her feet, more than ready to make this asshole *pay*. Even if it hadn't been for her current state and she thought that she had a shot of outrunning him, Blair wouldn't have fled. She wasn't *anyone's* prey—least of all his. And she wouldn't have wanted to take the chance that instead of tracking Blair he'd quite simply take off and come at her some other time. She wanted all this to end tonight.

Blair prayed that he'd fall again but there was no such luck. Her gut tightened as he finally reached the top of the hill, his expression hard, his fists clenched. Scratches decorated his face and arms. There was some light bruising here and there. Blood dripped from an ugly wound on his hairline.

His mouth tightened. "You're supposed to be in the van."

"I'm *supposed* to be in the very spot from where you grabbed me." As she stared at him, a shard of ice lanced her chest. His betrayal was still too much to process. She hadn't fully trusted him—had never fully trusted anyone but Luke, Mitch, and Kiesha—but she hadn't ever thought she was in danger from him.

She'd been wrong.

Keeping her cool was *not* going to be easy when there was so much she wanted to *scream* right into the delusional asshole's face. Especially when her female longed to rip him to shreds and kept urging Blair to do it. But what she needed was to buy herself some time, and that meant not going apeshit just yet.

He scanned their surroundings. "Where's the damn cat?"

"She ran to get help," Blair told him.

He grunted, unconcerned. Well of course he was. It might be a ten-minute drive back to the drop-off point, but it wouldn't be so quick a run. Especially not for someone as injured as Finley.

Blair tipped her head to the side as she studied him. "You know, I can't say that anything about you ever gave me the creeps."

His gaze snapped back to hers.

"I never had a single moment where I thought, 'This dude is a little weird.' I never once felt uneasy around you. It has to be said, you're very good at hiding your true self."

His brow pinched. "I didn't hide any part of who I am from you."

"Not true. You hid parts. Faked others. Played a role. You fooled everyone, including me. Fooled me into thinking that I was safe with you." It shamed both her and her cat that they hadn't seen through his act. No one had, true, but still.

His face firmed. "You've always been safe with me."

Blair very slowly lifted a disbelieving brow. "Not sure if it has *slipped* from your memory, Donal, but you drugged me. You scooped me up with a net like I was a goddamn fish. You locked me in a *crate* and drove off with me against my will."

For a brief moment, his eyes flickered with what might have been shame.

"I gained no pleasure from any of that. It wasn't what I wanted. But you left me no choice."

He thought he could throw the weight of this on her? "You had plenty of choices." Plenty of *sane* ones.

His gaze went hard. "And you had plenty of chances to come home. You didn't."

"Sylvan territory isn't my home anymore."

He took two steps toward her. "Your home is with me."

She gestured at the van with her thumb. "In that little crate, you mean?"

Swearing beneath his breath, he thrust a hand into his hair. "Things weren't supposed to go this way."

"No? How were they supposed to go? Tell me."

"We should have been mated by now. We *would* have been if you weren't intent on playing immature games and making me prove myself to you. None of that should have been necessary, Blair. We had a silent understanding that I'd claim you once you came of age."

"We did, huh? I never got that memo."

Taking another step toward her, he gave her a pointed look. "You know you're mine. You've always known that."

"How can you honestly tell yourself that when you're perfectly aware that Luke and I discovered we were mates years ago?"

He waved that away. "There was no discovery. It was like your mother used to say, *he* made the claim; you agreed, thinking it was true. Children are often confused about such things. You eventually realized that you'd made a mistake, but you said nothing because the entire situation pissed off Noelle and that suited you fine."

Her lips parted, Blair stared at him for long seconds. "It is truly *amazing* how much you lie to yourself. You could explain away pretty much anything that you don't want to believe, couldn't you? If something doesn't fit your narrative, you rewrite it to suit you."

"There is no narrative, there is only the truth. That being that we are mates. If I'd thought you needed me to make the first move, I would have done it the day you turned eighteen. You've never been shy or hesitant about going after what you want before. I should have been mindful that … certain things would make you nervous."

By "certain things," he no doubt meant her virginity. "If you really believed that I wanted the same things you do, you wouldn't have drugged and kidnapped me. You wouldn't have confined me in a crate. You would have simply *asked* me to come with you."

He snapped his mouth closed.

"You know this is wrong, Donal. Deep down, you know you shouldn't—"

"What I *know* is that we're predestined mates." He paced as he began to rant—going on about how people so often blinded themselves to the truth and how plain fruitless it was to fight fate.

Blair didn't properly take in the words, her focus instead on taking stock of herself. Some of her strength had returned, but not enough for her to overpower him. As Finley had pointed out, he was one tough mother. If Blair pounced, he'd soon subdue her and then she'd be back in the crate.

Finley would help her try to take him down, of course, but Blair knew his style; knew what he'd do—go right for her injuries to further weaken the feline. It seemed more logical and less risky to keep him talking. Which was something he was doing plenty of at that moment.

More than happy to let him waste time, Blair remained still and silent. She took a moment to tune into Luke's emotions via their bond. His panic wasn't quite as electric. Determination and anger were his most dominant emotions. She wasn't sure if it was her imagination, but he *felt* closer than he did before.

Probably her imagination.

Still, he couldn't be too far away now, could he? Five minutes had to have gone by, at the very least. Maybe even more. It was hard to tell.

Donal stopped pacing and turned toward her. "You're not listening to me, are you?"

"Of course I am."

He snorted. "Time to leave. We'll talk more in the van."

Her pulse jumped as he took a step toward her. "I'm not her," Blair blurted out.

He halted, his brows pulled together. "What?"

"Alayna. The woman you once almost imprinted on."

His expression iced over. "Where did you hear that name?"

"I'm not her," Blair repeated.

"Well of course you're not her."

"But I remind you of her."

He scoffed. "You're nothing like her. She was weak. Spineless. You're the opposite. You're my equal. You'll make a perfect Beta female."

And that was when Blair realized … "All these years that you gave me advice and training on being a Beta wasn't really to prepare me for life at the Olympus Pride. No, you did it because you'd convinced yourself that you and I would be the Beta pair of the Sylvan Pack."

"That was always the plan. We both knew that you would never mate with Devereaux. But we also knew that if I'd declared my intentions, Noelle would have lost her mind. She might have paraded all those young male bush dogs in front of you, but she didn't want you to mate any of them early on in life. She only wanted you to date them. She wasn't ready to let you go. She's still not ready, but she'll just have to deal with it."

"You truly think that you can take me to Sylvan Pack territory and that everyone will just *accept* we're now together?" It wouldn't surprise her. He was off his rocker.

Donal hesitated. "You're not ready for that. You and I need some … quality time alone first. I've prepared a home for you. I'll spend as much time with you there as I can. Once you fully accept and admit that you're mine, once the mating bond is complete, I'll take you back to our territory."

Wait, he intended to jail her somewhere and not free her until he'd brainwashed her into thinking that they were mates? Oh, he was *high.* "That's not gonna happen."

"You'll only have to stay there for as long as it takes for you to—you know what? We can talk about this later. Let's move."

Not likely. "Your plan has zero potential, Donal. Even if you did manage to imprison me somewhere, it wouldn't last long. Everyone will be searching for me."

"They'll never find you."

"Sure they will. They already suspect you."

"I have plans to make Gabriel take the fall."

Blair would have pointed out that Finley had seen Donal and would describe him to others, but that might inspire him to go hunt her down before she could "get help." It was better to keep him talking. "Gabriel take the fall?" she echoed.

"Yes. It won't be difficult to make him … disappear. Everyone will then instantly believe that he took you." Donal cleared his throat. "I won't enjoy using him as a scapegoat—the boy's been through enough. Not that he isn't better off without his parents."

Her scalp prickled. There was something about the way he'd said the latter words, something that made her instincts *scream.* "You killed them, didn't you?"

A muscle in Donal's cheek jumped. "I never intended to kill *her,*" he insisted, defensive. "I only meant to shoot Warrick. I wouldn't have hurt Milly, not for the world. But she wouldn't stop trying to protect him. And after I shot him, she lunged at me to grab the gun and … it just went off."

"It just went off?"

"What, you don't believe me?"

"I believe you lie to yourself quite often. What did Warrick ever do to you anyway?" She narrowed her eyes as his words replayed in her mind … "*I wouldn't have hurt Milly, not for the world.*" And then Blair understood. "You developed a little obsession with Milly. You pursued her, even though she was claimed by another male. You thought she'd make a good mate for you—"

"For a time, yes, I did mistakenly think that she was fated to be mine. Even though she proved that my belief was wrong when she risked her life to save his, I still found it hard to accept at first. But it all worked out fine, because as you grew up I learned that *she* wasn't the woman I'd been waiting for at all. It was you."

Blair couldn't help but wonder if there'd been other women over the years he'd become obsessed with. Others he'd convinced himself were meant to be his mate. Hell, even *Alayna* could have been a female he'd developed an unhealthy attachment to as opposed to someone who had wanted to imprint on him.

He rolled his shoulders. "Like I said before, we can talk more in the van."

"I'm not going anywhere with you."

He heaved a sigh. "If you want to sulk about the drug, fine, knock yourself out. But you know in your heart I wouldn't have resorted to that if you hadn't forced my hand."

"How did I force your hand?"

"*You're* the one who wanted me to take control. Well, I did. It isn't my fault if you don't like the reality of it."

"Reality," she drawled. "I have the distinct feeling that you and I live in totally different versions of reality. In mine, we're not mates. Not even close. The claiming bite on my neck only proves it."

His eyes flared. "Don't think that you won't pay for letting Devereaux mark you."

"I didn't simply allow Luke to mark me. You can tell that my scent has mixed with his. You can probably even tell that the mating bond is complete. You're willfully ignoring all of that because it suits you to do so, but that doesn't make any of it untrue. Face it, Donal, I'm not your—"

"Don't say it," he bit out, taking a lurching step forward. "Like I said, we'll talk … what the hell?" he growled, finally noticing the punctures in the tires. "Tell me you didn't do that."

"I could. But I'd be lying. You should have expected it, really. But then, you truly have managed to convince yourself that I want to be with you. Well, like I said, I'm not going anywhere with you."

He clenched and unclenched his fists. "Don't make me hurt you, Blair. I'd hate to have to do it, I really would."

"But you'd do it anyway, which just goes to prove that we're not mates."

Something ugly rippled across his face. "Make no mistake about it, Blair, you belong to me."

"No, she fucking doesn't."

Blair's heart jumped. The male voice came from behind her. A voice that belonged to her mate. *Thank God.*

Luke had to have parked somewhere close by so he could scope out the situation before planting himself in it. She hadn't sensed him arrive or creep up on them. But cats were sneaky that way.

She saw in her peripheral vision that Luke and a bunch of others were rounding both ends of the van to flank her. She longed to drink in the sight of Luke, but she didn't dare look his way, determined to keep Donal in her line of sight. She didn't trust that he wouldn't lunge at her or something, despite that his attention seemed to now fully be on the male cat who sidled up to her. Her female bared her teeth in a smug, feral grin, sure that their mate would make Donal pay.

Donal's face contorted into one of sheer rage. "*You.*"

Luke planted his feet. "Yeah. Me."

"You shouldn't be here."

"You thought I wouldn't come for my mate?"

Donal snarled. "She isn't yours."

"Wrong." And seeing her alive and unharmed untied the knots in Luke's gut, but his fury remained. This sick freak needed to be put down like a rabid dog, and Luke had every intention of making that happen. "Blair was meant for me."

"You are *nothing* to her."

"Wrong again. She's the other half of my soul. I knew it the first time I met her." Luke tilted his head. "You can't say the same, can you? Not from what I just overheard. It sounds as if you jump from one woman to another—you pin your entire focus on them, you convince yourself that they're your mate, you no doubt also stalk them, and when things don't work out the way you hoped, you oh so suddenly realize that *another* female is actually your mate."

"Blair is mine." The words were sure. Hard. Nonnegotiable.

Luke shook his head—not only in objection, but in sheer wonder. The other male didn't seem in any way mentally unbalanced. There was no yelling. No sharp, jerky movements. No signs that he was on the verge of exploding. Yet, he was quite clearly unstable.

"She's only ever been mine, Donal. The evidence of that is right in front of you. But I won't bother trying to force you to acknowledge the mating bond—you're clearly not going to. Besides, I'm more interested in tearing you apart." Luke took two predatory steps forward, a spike of adrenaline pouring into his bloodstream. "You'll die tonight, Donal. Let's face it, it's been a long time coming."

Donal inched up his chin. "It will be you who breathes their last." He cricked his neck, his mouth curled into a smug grin that said he was certain he'd win the duel. "I've been looking forward to this moment."

Keeping his muscles loose, Luke took another fluid step forward. "Not half as much as I have."

They both charged.

Luke went in hard and fast and vicious. Donal retaliated ferally, attacking like a wild animal. The duel was ugly. Dirty. No holds barred.

Flesh thudded into flesh. Blood splattered on the ground. Grunts and growls rang through the air.

It quickly became clear that Donal was well-trained in combat. That was only to be expected, given he was Beta of his pack. Every counterstrike was wicked fast and brutally accurate. The bastard had one hell of a steely punch.

It also became clear that Donal had one major weakness—he allowed his anger to rule him. And so he often failed to block the pitiless blows that came his way, too focused on fighting offensively.

Luke took full advantage of it, repeatedly landing devastating punches on Donal's head wound, making it bleed and bleed. His fury still hot and electric, Luke's cat egged him on. The animal wanted the other male to suffer. *Craved* his fear. Hungered to brutalize him. Luke was quite happy to oblige his cat. He wouldn't stop until the bush dog was bloodied, mauled, and dead.

Luke unsheathed his claws and took a swipe at Donal's belly. Cloth ripped. Skin tore. Blood welled up.

Breathing hard, Donal tightened his fists. "Bastard." He punched out his balled up hand.

Luke caught the fist and twisted sharply, hearing a tendon *snap*. The asshole's pained grunt was music to the cat's ears. "I was thinking the same of you." Luke followed up the move with a vicious blow to the bastard's jaw that made his head whip to the side.

Donal spat a glob of blood and saliva on the ground, and Luke's cat bared his teeth in a grin of cruel satisfaction. Then the Beta came at Luke in a flurry of fists, hitting him with one body shot after another.

The bystanders egged on Luke, but he tuned out their voices, focusing on his opponent. He was torn between incapacitating him fast and dragging out the fight. Luke was eager for this threat to his mate to finally be eradicated, but he was in no mood to end the bush dog's suffering soon—not after what the bastard had put Blair through.

Pain rippled up Luke's body as a rib cracked. Jesus *Christ.* He snapped out his fist, smashing it into the wound on Donal's scalp once again.

The bush dog hissed, his eyes blazing. "It won't matter how hard or many times you hit me. It won't make her yours."

"She already is mine." Luke jerked back, evading the claws that came at his face, and then savagely rammed his fist into the Beta's face, hearing his cheekbone fracture.

Donal jerked back, sucking in air … and Luke sensed the moment that Donal lost his confidence. Gone was the smugness of earlier. In its place was an uncertainty tinged with fear—the smell of it tainted the air.

Relishing the scent, Luke attacked again with his claws—shredding flesh, stabbing into Donal's sides, swiping at his throat. The Beta dodged and weaved, but not fast enough. Soon, he was easing back under the pressure.

Still, Donal didn't wave a white flag. He continued to throw punches—even managed to deliver a solid blow to Luke's jaw that had so much power behind it he was surprised his teeth didn't rattle—but Luke was now dominating the fight and they both knew it.

Grabbing the bush dog firmly by the throat, Luke sent his fist smashing into Donal's ribs again and again and again. Choked breaths *whooshed* out of Donal, who would have doubled over if Luke hadn't had a grip on his throat.

A grip Luke then tightened. "Told you you'd die tonight."

His eyes widening, Donal struck out, wheezing.

Luke's head snapped back as the bastard landed a mean uppercut. *Son of a bitch.* He retaliated fast, landing a punch on the spot behind Donal's ear. The bush dog stumbled backward, double-blinking, his body swaying, his knees buckling.

Luke didn't give him a moment to recover. He attacked like a savage, slamming his fists into the bush dog's temples over and over, dazing him further. Soon, Donal dropped to his knees, his eyes completely glazed over. Luke wasted no time in acting. He unsheathed his claws once more and sliced the fucker's throat, severing arteries.

It was no swift death. Donal gurgled and choked for what seemed like endless minutes. Then, finally, he slumped to the ground, unmoving.

Swiping at the blood dripping from his nose, Luke turned to face his mate. She sucked in a breath. Unsurprising. He knew he was a mess. His knuckles were red and swollen. His utter lip was split. Rake marks scored his face, chest, and sides. A deep gash sliced through his eyebrow, stinging like fuck courtesy of the sheen of sweat on his forehead.

Blair slowly came to him, reaching out to touch him but hesitating.

Knowing she was worried she'd hurt him, Luke curled an arm around her shoulders and tugged her close. She shuddered against him, and he could *feel* how much it pained her to see him so wounded. He put his mouth to her ear, whispering, "It's over, baby. It's all over."

Healed, clean, and thoroughly sated, Blair sprawled over her mate later that night as they lay in bed. She couldn't quite make her mind go quiet. It was currently a hub of activity, replaying the evening's events again and again.

Well it wasn't as if they'd been able to relax the moment Donal's corpse hit the ground. There had been so much to do. Like getting rid of evidence and notifying her old pack about Donal.

Mitch had lost it when she'd returned his call and told him what happened, as had her parents when she'd later called them. They felt guilty for upholding that none of their pack mates could be her stalker, as well as for trusting Donal.

Breaking it to Embry that his Beta was not only her stalker but had killed Gabriel's parents had been hard. Absolutely devastated by Donal's betrayal and by Embry's own mistakes, the Alpha had expressed an intention to visit Gabriel and "make things right." Blair wasn't sure that was doable, but she hadn't said as much.

Donal's body was now nothing but crumbs, according to Isaak—and yeah, *ew*. Dimitri had claimed the Beta's van for himself on learning it wasn't registered to Donal, so that was sorted.

None of the pride were shocked to hear that Finley had come to her rescue. But then, as Vinnie pointed out, the female enforcer might be a pain from time to time but she would always protect her pride mates whether she had a fondness for them or not.

After Blair thanked her for all that she'd done that night, Finley had responded, "*Yeah, well, don't read anything into it. I still don't like you.*" There had been no heat in her words, though. In fact, there'd been a playful glint in her eye.

Blair doubted that they would ever be friends, but she did get the feeling that they'd no longer be foes. Going by how Finley had earlier deferred to her as they cleaned up the evidence, the enforcer had clearly decided it was time to stop pushing for the position of Beta. Maybe it was Blair's advice that made the difference, maybe it was something else. Whatever the case, Blair was glad of it.

As for the standoff between the humans and the shifters … the only casualties had been human, thankfully. Valentina's brothers had tossed the bodies into Hank Wheeler's van, promising that they would "take care" of them. Blair hadn't asked what that meant, but she suspected it involved them using certain body parts as edible delicacies.

The pride members had gotten rid of the other vehicles and cleaned up all evidence of the battle. Unfortunately, that might not be enough to erase every trace of the meeting, since Wheeler or his cronies might have told other anti-shifter extremists about it. If so, their associates would for sure turn their attention to Vinnie when they realized that so many had gone missing.

No one was concerned about that, though. If contacted, Vinnie intended to claim that he'd delivered Camden and then driven away. As the extremists firmly believed that Vinnie was in their corner and trusted him implicitly, he didn't believe they would at all consider that he could be connected to the "disappearance" of Hank and his fellow assholes.

Although Zayne wasn't exactly a person who could go missing without it being noticed by many and then thoroughly investigated, the pride wasn't much concerned that it would be linked to them. After all, it didn't seem likely that the police would learn he'd recently paid Vinnie a visit. But if they did, Vinnie already had a story whipped up that would connect Zayne with extremists and shifter poaching—the police tended to avoid getting involved in such matters. And River would be a big help in ensuring that their attention was diverted anyway if necessary.

No one felt it was likely that the police would find something to link Zayne to Camden either. Zayne would have been a fool to leave a paper trail of his shifter poaching hobby lying around, including the document that Alex pinned to his wall. But if the police *did* somehow uncover such proof, they'd have no evidence to suggest that the tiger had any part in the human's disappearance. Plus, Camden would have plenty of alibis in the form of pride members—all of whom the police thought were human so would be inclined to believe. And again, River would prove helpful in diverting their attention.

"I can practically hear you thinking," said Luke, his voice low. He gave her hair a gentle tug. "What's wrong?"

She propped her chin on his chest, meeting his eyes. "Nothing at all. I just can't switch off. Sorry if I'm keeping you awake." He'd no doubt feel her restlessness through their bond. Speaking of which ... "I wasn't conscious when our bond snapped fully into place earlier. What brought that on?" With all the activity around them, she'd forgotten to ask.

"It was my fault that it was incomplete until now," he admitted. "I was holding back from fully committing to you, worried I'd go back to living in a fog and that you'd then be stuck tied to a man who was sleepwalking through life." He stroked a hand over her hair. "I *knew* that being fully bonded to you would stop that from happening, but the fear was stupidly still there."

"Not stupidly." She traced the eyebrow that was now healed. "I think I'd have harbored that same worry in your shoes. It was probably something you were subconsciously working through all this time. But just so you know, I wouldn't have considered myself being 'stuck tied' to you in a negative way if our bond hadn't been able to prevent the fog from coming along again. You wouldn't have been to blame, and I wouldn't have *looked* to lay any blame anywhere. I'd have only wanted to be there for you. I would still have wanted nothing more than to be mated to you. If the situation was reversed, you'd have felt the same."

His face softened. "You're right, I would have." He searched her eyes. "You're not mad at me for subconsciously holding back, then?"

"Of course not. You'd be bleeding right now if I was." She smiled as a chuckle rumbled out of him. Earlier, he'd been in no mood to even *smile*. It was during their shower that he'd confessed how much it had wrecked him to hear she'd been taken.

Blair had gotten a little growly when she realized that he idiotically blamed himself for not guessing that Donal would choose to act tonight. Luke had eventually agreed that it was dumb of him to feel such guilt, but she wouldn't be surprised to learn that he'd only been placating her. Dominant males had a habit of shouldering blame that didn't truly belong to them.

"I'm guessing your parents will turn up tomorrow," said Luke. "They'll want to see you in person; see with their own eyes that you're fine."

"Probably. It's still hard to believe that it was Donal who did all those things. I'd agreed that he was a possible suspect, yeah, but that was different from being confronted with the knowledge that he *was* actually the culprit we'd been seeking."

"It hit you hard," Luke sensed, hating her pain, wishing he could pound Dolan into the ground all over again.

She nodded. "Just as it would hit you hard if you discovered one of the pride betrayed you. That was what he did. Betrayed my trust in him. Made me grow up believing that I *knew* him. Made me believe that the mask he wore wasn't a mask at all. And not only did all kinds of weird shit but killed a woman who, though bitchy toward me, did not deserve to have her life taken from her. All the time I spent with him, I never felt in danger from him; never sensed he had some dark, creepy obsession with me."

Luke gave her a fierce look. "That does not mean that your judgement can't be trusted. You're not at fault for not seeing through his bullshit. Nobody did."

"I know. I'm pissed at him, not myself."

"Good." Lifting his head, Luke planted a quick kiss on that mouth he loved and then settled down again. Sliding his hand up the smooth skin of her back, he added, "I bet you never thought that you'd be happy to see Finley."

"You'd be right on that. But she came through for me. As did you. I needed you, and there you were. Like always."

He stroked a hand over her hair. "And that's how it'll always be."

"I know. I'm lucky that way."

He felt his lips curve. "Yeah, you are. But then, so am I."

CHAPTER TWENTY-THREE

Two months later

Blair's release crashed into her out of absolutely nowhere, wrenching at her spine and trapping a scream in her throat as sheer bliss flooded her body. The pleasure went on and on and on until, finally, it subsided.

She melted into the mattress, heaving in breaths. Her thigh muscles jumped. Her heart pounded. Her lungs burned.

God bless that tongue, she thought as Luke wiped his face on her inner thigh and then gave it a quick nip.

He rose above her, his blue eyes dark and hot and glittering with something that made her shiver. He'd given her two delicious orgasms, and now her pussy was aching to be filled. Her body felt all jittery and jumpy, like every sense and nerve-ending was heightened.

Luke slowly raked his gaze over her, masculine satisfaction dancing along their bond. "Such a delectable sight." He settled the full weight of his body over hers, making her breath catch.

She totally loved it when he surrounded her this way, becoming all she could feel and see and smell. His body was so big and broad it was like he curved around her. Like she perfectly fit into that groove there.

Blair went to rest her hands on the solid bulk of his shoulders, but his fingers snapped around her wrists. He stretched her arms straight above her head and held her wrists against the mattress. Her hormones lost their mind.

Luke's eyes gleamed. "A shot of excitement just pulsed right down our bond." Curling one hand tight around both her wrists, he used his free hand to lodge the smooth head of his cock inside her. "I'm going to take you like this, so you can barely move."

She flexed her fingers. "But I want to touch you. Scratch you. Mark you all up." Her animal was driving her to do that very thing.

He dipped his face to hers. "Tough."

Tough? A little growl rattled in her throat.

He smiled. "Do that again."

"Fuck off."

"I'd rather just fuck *you*." He brought his mouth down on hers and kissed her with such need and urgency it made her head spin.

She pulled in a breath as he began to sink inside her, stretching her perfectly. The pressure was just … she loved it. Needed it. Craved it.

Halfway inside her, Luke paused, his gaze firmly latched on hers. "Say it."

She swiped her tongue along her lower lip. "I love you."

Satisfaction, adoration, and triumph burst along their connection. "And I love you, baby. Always will. In this life and even after." A mask of intensity slipped over his face as he abruptly jacked his hips forward, driving so deep inside her it hurt in the best way.

He didn't give her a moment to adjust. He aggressively slammed his hips forward again and again. She curled her legs around him, eager to take every savage thrust.

She wasn't going to last long. Neither was he—she could feel through their bond that he was as tightly wound and frantic to come as she was.

Pinned down by his weight with her wrists shackled by his hand, she felt *taken*. Possessed. Claimed. Her little female soaked it all up.

He said something, but Blair didn't take in the words, caught up in sensation—the deep slams of his cock, the heavy weight of his body, the slapping of flesh against wet flesh, the tight grip on her wrists.

He bit her jaw hard. "I said, give me your throat." The sheer power in his voice made her skin prickle.

She might have fought him on it if she wasn't so desperate to come. A building orgasm coiled in her lower stomach, raring to strike. Each brutal drive of his cock made it contract and tauten and thicken.

Blair gave him her throat, almost smiling at his groan. "Harder."

He buried his face into the crook of her neck and licked a line up her throat. "Such a greedy little girl."

Drunk on the taste and feel and scent of his mate, Luke plunged harder and faster. Her body jolted with each heavy punch of his hips, and her breasts chafed against his chest as they bounced. His balls audibly slapped her flesh, blending with the wet sound of her pussy sucking at his dick.

His cat urged him to bite her neck again, to leave yet another mark. The animal felt relaxed and secure in their mating now, but he was no less territorial; no less eager to always ensure she felt owned. Especially at moments like these, while her arousal-spiced scent flooded his lungs and she submissively exposed her throat to him.

Luke switched his angle, pounding deeper, hitting a spot inside her that made her pussy clench and ripple. He felt through their bond as her release surged towards her; watched a hot flush sweep up her chest, neck, and face.

An echo of white-hot pleasure thundered along their bond as she fractured with a scream, her body shaking and tightening, her heels digging into his lower back. Like that, his own blinding release swallowed him whole. He cursed against her neck and then sank his teeth down hard as he fucked his orgasm into her body, his cock pulsing with every harsh blast of come.

Boneless and sated, he fairly collapsed over Blair, struggling to catch his breath. She lay beneath him, her eyes closed, her swollen lips parted, her cheeks flushed.

Releasing her wrists, he pressed soft kisses down one side of her face and then withdrew his softening cock. Curling an arm around her waist, he rolled them both onto their sides. "Good morning."

"Morning," she slurred, burrowing into him.

Nuzzling the fresh bite on her neck, Luke coasted his fingertips down her arm. "By the way, you're forgiven."

She looked at him, her eyes dazed, her brow furrowed. "For what?"

"Slapping me on the head."

"You were taking too long to make me come. And you were doing it on purpose. Besides, I didn't slap you. It was more like a swat. Though you would have deserved worse after the smacks you dished out last night. My poor butt felt like it was on fire."

Chuckling, he stroked a hand down her back to palm her ass. "You liked it." Feeling the lingering indentation of his teeth there, he carefully traced the mark with one fingertip. He'd had a whole lot of fun with that luscious ass the night before—bit it, spanked it, fucked it. "You sore?"

"A little." She gave him a mock glare and poked his chest. "But that doesn't bother you much, does it?"

He tried stifling a smile but failed. "Do I like that every time you sit down today you'll remember that I took your ass last night? Yeah. Yeah, I do like it."

She rolled her eyes. "It's not like you haven't done it before, but whatever."

He'd first claimed her ass the night before their mating ceremony six weeks ago—a ceremony that was a little on the tense side, since the entire Sylvan Pack insisted on being present. After the mess with Donal, his pride hadn't been so comfortable with having them around. And since bush dogs weren't fans of pallas cats, the whole thing had had the potential to go tits up.

It hadn't, though.

Everyone had been on their best behavior. And after the drinks began to flow during the after-party, the guests had started to officially relax and were soon mixing just fine.

Luke still wasn't quite used to her parents being so welcoming toward him—it felt a little odd. His unforgiving cat wasn't inclined to trust the couple and still didn't like them, but he didn't always growl while in their presence anymore. Progress.

Blair shivered a little in his arms as he breezed his fingers over the sensitive spot between her shoulder blades—a spot he often zeroed in on just to get that exact response from her, so he wasn't surprised that she bit his chest in retaliation. He'd mapped every inch of her body in his mind. He knew every line, curve, freckle, scar, and sensitive zone on her body.

She stretched. "Come on, I need coffee, a shower, and food. And not necessarily in that order."

"We still on for spending the day together?" he asked as she sat upright. "We need some alone time."

"I'm up for it, I'm just not so sure it will happen. Whenever we set aside a day for us to have some quality time, it somehow gets hijacked."

"Not today it won't."

"You really think so?"

"I know so."

"I have to tell you, I am *fascinated*," said Bailey, watching as four bush dogs playfully attacked a befuddled grizzly in the complex's communal backyard a few hours later. "They're just so small, and yet they're definitely gonna take him down—something they appear to be dragging out for fun."

"He really shouldn't have dared them," said Blair.

Havana sighed. "He's a little slow that way."

It would appear so. Everyone knew that a group of bush dogs could overpower any animal, but the grizzly hadn't believed it—something he'd expressed to her relatives, who were delighted to have the opportunity to humiliate someone. It always made their day.

Blair didn't know the grizzly very well, but she did know that he was something of a clown—a very likeable, good-looking clown who surprisingly still made a very valuable enforcer. Uber strong or not, his bear was having no luck shaking off the bush dogs.

She looked at Finley, trying to gauge whether or not the female might feel like jumping to her new boyfriend's defense, but the woman seemed entertained. She was far less serious these days. There had been no more silliness from her or the rest of the pride about Blair holding the position of Beta female. Finley had officially backed off, and her followers had taken her lead.

Feeling a rush of amusement tumble along the mating bond, Blair turned her head to see Luke laughing with Tate, Vinnie, and Elle. The joke might have been at Alex's expense, because he was looking pretty surly over there in their little group. Then again, that was kind of his default mode unless he was with Bree.

Other groups were here and there—some in their animal forms, some not. Blair wasn't even sure how it came about that so many gathered out here. She and Luke had meant to let their animals run together in the yard but had hesitated on finding Aspen and Camden near the pond in their animal forms—his tiger was pretty antisocial. She and Luke had been about to return inside, but then her parents, Mitch, and Kiesha were escorted to the backyard by Bailey … and somehow everyone got talking. Little by little, more and more people had begun to trickle outside.

Bye, bye alone time with Luke.

As Blair's family visited every couple of weeks or so, the pride was used to them now. But a few did still hold it against Embry that he'd been so closed to the idea that one of his own was Blair's stalker; they believed he might have otherwise seen that his old Beta was a freaking maniac, despite the fact that no one else had.

It was really no surprise that Embry had promoted Antoine to Beta, or that he'd then given Mitch the position of Head Enforcer. Although both males were happy with their promotions, they claimed that the whole thing felt tainted by what had led to them.

The Donal clusterfuck was still an unhealed wound for the pack, as was the fact that they'd once mistakenly pinned the blame for two deaths on a ten-year-old child who they'd subsequently ostracized. Embry had invited Gabriel to return to the Sylvan Pack but he'd declined. Blair was pretty sure she'd have done the same in Gabriel's shoes.

"*And* the grizzly bites the dust," said Havana just as he toppled over like a dead weight.

The four bush dogs let out satisfied little yips and then jumped into the pond like kids doing cannon ball moves.

Bailey smiled at Blair. "I'm finding that I *really* like bush dogs. Your family's animals are fun. My snake wants to play with them."

Blair felt her brow furrow. "I don't think that would work out so well. Your mamba would try to bite them, and then they'd eat her. And if she didn't try to bite them, well, they'd likely still eat her."

"In which case, you should totally let your mamba go play with them," snarked Aspen, approaching with Camden and Deke.

Bailey gave her a bored look. "You're not still being whiny because she bit your bearcat's nipple, are you?"

Aspen's mouth thinned, and she opened it as if to yell … but then

Camden put a hand on her shoulder and said, "Don't waste your time pointing out that she did anything wrong. It will fly right over her head."

Smiling at him, Bailey put a fist to her heart. "I love how well you get me."

Aspen rolled her eyes and then cut them to Blair. "Your family seems to be enjoying themselves. Are your parents still making an effort to be nice to Luke?"

"Yup," replied Blair. "I wouldn't allow anything else."

"Do you think it'll stay that way?" asked Havana.

"I do." Blair had been doubtful at first, but it was clear to see that her parents had officially changed their stance on her relationship with Luke. As if the moment their own personal bullshit stopped clouding their opinions they'd finally *seen* him.

He told her that Noelle recently said to him, "*You love her, you make her happy. Keep doing that.*"

That the woman acknowledged he made Blair happy said everything.

"It's surprising how well she and Ingrid now get along," said Blair. "I wasn't so sure if Ingrid would give her another chance."

"I think she only did it for your sake," said Havana. "As for Valentina … yeah, I think it's gonna take a few years before she does anything but snarl at your mom."

Blair winced. "Probably. Can't say I blame her, really. Luke is her nephew after all, and Noelle was always rude to Valentina whenever the woman took me on day trips when I was a kid." Wolverines could sure hold a grudge.

"What are you doing?" asked Deke, frowning at Bailey.

The mamba's unfocused eyes cleared, and she stopped dancing her fingers along her inner arm. "Wondering why we can't tickle ourselves. Don't you think it's weird? I mean, we can make ourselves come just fine. There ain't much of a difference."

Blair exchanged an amused look with Havana.

Deke sighed at Bailey. "You'll just blurt out any ole thing, won't you?"

"Tact is for losers," she told him.

He snorted. "You just like making people uncomfortable."

"Well … I prefer to piss them off, but 'uncomfortable' will do in a pinch."

"Why? Why not simply let people be?"

"I don't question your life choices."

"But you *should* question your own."

"Whatever for?"

The enforcer stared at the mamba, as if desperately trying to understand her. Or to intimidate her, maybe. It was hard to tell with him at times. He was difficult to read.

Bailey's lips curved as she met his stare with her own. "All this intense eye contact … I feel like we're bonding right now. Don't you?"

Grunting, he shook his head and walked away.

Watching him go, Bailey blew out a breath. "He *so* doesn't deserve that butt."

Blair frowned. "What?"

"It's a spectacular ass," said Bailey. "Nature should have given it to someone worthy."

Aspen blinked at her. "By 'worthy,' you mean someone who'll take your shit without dishing it back or asking you to be more conscious of your behavior?"

"Yes," said Bailey. "That is exactly what I mean."

Tate exhaled heavily. "Do you have to bring up old shit?"

Luke felt his brows draw together. "When said 'shit' left me with a scar, yeah."

"You can't still be pissed about that. We were kids. I don't even know why you made such a big deal about it back then."

"Oh, you don't?" Unbelievable.

"It's not like it was the first time I stabbed you with scissors."

"But it *was* the first time you did it unprovoked."

Tate's brow creased. "You threw a balloon at me."

"Yeah. *A balloon.*"

"It was filled with paint, you little shit."

"Good God, boys, can you not stop squabbling?" Vinnie broke in. "You're too old for this now. I—" He cut off, his brow pinching as Deke approached. "What's wrong with you?"

"Nothing," the enforcer clipped, his expression dark, his nostrils flaring.

"Well you seem fine," Alex deadpanned.

Deke fired the wolverine a narrow-eyed glare.

Elle sighed. "You're grumpier than Alex these days, and that's saying something. You recently got to kill a bunch of extremists. That should have cheered you up. Especially since we got away with it."

The extremists had contacted Vinnie about Wheeler, but they'd bought his story that all had been fine at the meeting when he left the drop-off point. The police hadn't contacted either Vinnie or Camden regarding Zayne, so they were all currently presuming that there'd been no evidence to link the celebrity to them.

"I'm not grumpy," Deke told Elle.

"Ooh, I beg to differ," she said. "And I'm thinking that Bailey"—she tipped her chin toward the mamba—"has something to … God, I honestly feel sorry for Havana at times."

Tracking his sister's gaze, Luke saw the Alpha female standing between Aspen and Bailey, palming each of their foreheads as they argued about God knew what. Blair was battling a smile, her shoulders shaking.

As if she felt his attention settle on her, Blair looked his way. A smile did curve her mouth, then. It wasn't one of amusement. It was a wan "I told you our quality time would be invaded" smile. Yeah, it was becoming too much of a pattern for his liking.

"Havana told me that those two have been bickering about the most senseless stuff since the day they first met," said Tate.

Deke grunted. "I can believe that. They'll argue over just about anything."

"Like there aren't bigger things going on in the world," said Elle, shaking her head. "They should be more concerned that the Harbinger will soon be born." She glanced over at Damian, who was snuggling on a bench with the girlfriend he'd recently discovered was also his true mate. "When those two reproduce, we are *fucked*."

Vinnie frowned. "Instead of branding their future child the Harbinger of Death, could you not just make peace with Damian and congratulate them on their mating?"

"I offered the girl my condolences," Elle told him. "There's really nothing else to be said on the matter."

Vinnie rolled his eyes. "I worry about you, Elle. I really do."

"Why? *I* didn't mate Beelzebub."

"Your brother is not—forget it, let's just drop the subject."

"As you wish," said Elle, ever so graciously. "I want to return to the topic of why Deke's being so grumpy anyway. Tell us what's wrong."

The enforcer sighed. "Nothing is wrong, I'm perfectly—*what the fuck*?"

Whipping his head to the side, Luke saw his mate running at Aspen and Bailey like a human crab. The two females ceased arguing in an instant, their eyes going wide. They squealed like little girls and took off, but an undeterred Blair chased them around the yard.

Scraping a hand over his jaw, Luke chuckled. Not a lot could spook a pallas cat, but people were quick to move out of his mate's way, all looking varying degrees of freaked out. Damian and his mate actually jumped up onto the bench.

"Please, no more!" Bailey cried out, almost falling into the pond as the bush dogs leapt out of the water. Mitch's animal nearly crashed into the grizzly, who then snapped his jaw at him, grazing the bush dog's ear and eliciting a little yelp from him.

Blair stopped running, her muscles tensing. Uh-oh. She slowly turned toward the bear, who froze. She twisted—*Jesus Christ*—only the front half of her body 360 degrees and planted her palms back on the ground. That was when the grizzly bolted.

Materializing beside Tate, Havana laughed as Blair pursued the freaked out grizzly. "Luke, your mate is an absolute treasure."

He grinned. "Not telling me something I don't already know." When said mate finally righted her body and stood, he crossed straight to her and drew her close. She melted into him, her body aligning perfectly to his—a reminder of how every inch of her was tailor-made to "fit" him. "Are you finished terrorizing people?" he asked.

"For now," replied Blair, linking her fingers at the back of his neck.

Luke brushed his nose against hers. "I'm pretty sure you scarred that grizzly for life, by the way. Never seen one climb a tree before."

Her lips flattened. "He made my brother bleed. *I* can do that to Mitch. No one else is allowed that privilege."

"I'd call you a nut, but I have pretty much the same mindset when it comes to my siblings." Luke dipped his head and fit his lips to hers. He sank into the moment as he sipped from her mouth, savoring her taste, swallowing her breathy little moan, and breathing her in, feeling "home."

Breaking the kiss, he slid his fingers into her hair and began a light massage that made her eyes fall closed.

"I really do love your hands," she said.

His lips curved. "They aim to please." He pressed another kiss to her mouth. "I say we head back to our apartment."

"Abandon my family when they've come all this way to visit us?" she asked, not opening her eyes.

"Is that a problem?"

"No."

Seeing that Aspen and Bailey were trying to creep up on his mate from behind, each holding a long branch, he inwardly sighed. Their gazes locking on his, they both put a finger to their mouths. He gave them a quick shake of the head and mouthed "go away." They paused, their shoulders slumping.

Luke pressed a kiss to the tip of Blair's nose. "Then let's go."

She did a long, languid stretch. "One thing first."

"What?"

A *pop* rang through the air as she pulled down one arm at an awkward angle. He cringed. Turning toward the women behind her, she did the same with the other arm, making them both wince. Then she did something with her neck that made even Luke's gut clench.

Dropping the branch she held, Aspen slapped her hands to her face. "*This is so wrong!*"

A shuddering Bailey backed up. "And too weird even for me."

As the two females ran off, Blair turned back to him and said, "Given that Bailey's capacity for weird is close to bottomless, I'll take that as a compliment."

He couldn't help but smile. His mate was nuts. Utterly and completely. She was also wrapped around his heart so tight it almost hurt. Her name was carved into his soul like a brand, deep and binding, and he wouldn't have it any other way. "I fucking love you, you know."

Warmth bled into her expression. "I do know. And I love you right back."

"Then you'll slide your joints back into place so my stomach stops rolling and curdling."

She sighed. "If I must."

"You really, really must."

There were *pops* and a distinct *snap* as she righted her joints. "There. Happy?"

He felt his face soften. "Of course. There's no way I could be anything else when I have you, is there?"

ACKNOWLEDGEMENTS

I have to thank my family first and foremost -- for your support, your patience, and the fact that you don't laugh at how I mostly live in my head.

Thank you so much to my son for the book cover. You're so freaking talented it astounds me, be super proud of yourself.

I need to say a big thanks to my PA, Melissa -- you are absolutely indispensable to me, I don't know what I'd do without you.

I'd also like to thank my editor, Donna Hillyer. Not only for your invaluable advice and insight but also for working so fast so that I could pull the release day forward.

Finally, a huge thanks to all my readers, you're the most fantastic bunch of people EVER and I adore you for life.

Take care

S :)

ABOUT THE AUTHOR

Suzanne Wright lives in England with her husband, two children, and two Bengal cats. When she's not spending time with her family, she's writing, reading, or doing her version of housework—sweeping the house with a look.

TITLES BY SUZANNE WRIGHT

The Deep in Your Veins Series
Here Be Sexist Vampires
The Bite That Binds
Taste of Torment
Consumed
Fractured
Captivated
Touch of Rapture

The Phoenix Pack Series
Feral Sins
Wicked Cravings
Carnal Secrets
Dark Instincts
Savage Urges
Fierce Obsessions
Wild Hunger
Untamed Delights

The Dark in You Series
Burn
Blaze
Ashes
Embers
Shadows
Omens
Fallen
Reaper

The Mercury Pack Series
Spiral of Need
Force of Temptation
Lure of Oblivion
Echoes of Fire
Shards of Frost

The Olympus Pride Series
When He's Dark
When He's an Alpha
When He's Sinful
When He's Ruthless
When He's Torn (coming 2023)

The Devil's Cradle Series (coming 2023)
The Wicked in Me
The Nightmare in Him
The Monsters We Are

Standalones
From Rags
Shiver
The Favor
Wear Something Red – An Anthology

Zwischen Forschungsfreiheit und Menschenwürde

Sibylle Rolf

Zwischen Forschungsfreiheit und Menschenwürde

Unterschiede beim Umgang mit menschlichen Embryonen in England und Deutschland

Sibylle Rolf, Dr. theol., Jahrgang 1972, ist Privatdozentin an der Universität Heidelberg und war bis zum Sommer 2009 Stipendiatin der Deutschen Forschungsgemeinschaft an der Universität Durham, England. Forschungsschwerpunkte: Theologische Ethik und Anthropologie, Bioethik, sowie die Theologie Martin Luthers. Auszeichnung mit dem Martin-Luther-Preis für den Wissenschaftlichen Nachwuchs 2008

Gedruckt mit Hilfe der Deutschen Forschungsgemeinschaft

Die Deutsche Nationalbibliothek verzeichnet diese Publikation in der Deutschen Nationalbibliografie; detaillierte bibliografische Daten sind im Internet über http://dnb.d-nb.de abrufbar.

Umschlaggestaltung und Entwurf Grundlayout
Hansisches Druck- und Verlagshaus GmbH

Satz
Sibylle Rolf

Druck und Bindung
Hubert & Co GmbH und Co KG

Printed in Germany

ISBN 978-3-86921-007-0

Meinen Patenkindern:

*Sophia Elisabeth (*1996), Cornelius Felix Sebastian (*2001), Lisa Katharina (*2003), Charlotte Elisabeth (*2004)*

Vorwort

Wie jedes andere Buch hätte auch dieses nicht ohne die vielfältige Hilfe und Unterstützung anderer geschrieben werden können. Ich danke zunächst der Deutschen Forschungsgemeinschaft, die meiner Familie und mir durch ein großzügiges Forschungsstipendium einen zweijährigen Aufenthalt an der Universität Durham und durch eine Publikationsbeihilfe den Druck dieses Buches ermöglicht hat. Zu danken habe ich auch dem Hansischen Verlagshaus, vor allem Frau Dr. Annette Weidhas, die mein Buch in die edition chrismon aufgenommen und die Drucklegung in gewohnter Kompetenz und mit großem Wohlwollen begleitet hat.

Die Kollegen und Kolleginnen am Department of Theology and Religion in Durham haben mich herzlich und interessiert in ihre Mitte aufgenommen, mir ein Arbeitszimmer und Arbeitsmittel zur Verfügung gestellt und mir die ganze Zeit hindurch das Gefühl vermittelt, ich sei eine gern gesehene und willkommene Kollegin. Mir hat dieses Willkommen das Einleben in neuer Umgebung und neuer Kultur sehr erleichtert, und ich bin besonders dankbar für viele Anteil nehmende Fragen und kurze Tür-und-Angel-Gespräche, häufig bei einer Tasse Tee (oder Kaffee). Dabei sollen zumindest einige Kollegen genannt werden, mit denen mich besonders viel verbunden hat: Prof. Loren Stuckenbruck hat jedes deutsche Wort verstanden, das ich nicht angemessen ins Englische habe übersetzen können und mir damit über manche linguistische Hürde geholfen. In seiner Funktion als *Head of Department* hat er außerdem unermüdlich dafür gesorgt, dass mein Dienstcomputer tatsächlich zu laufen begann. Dr. Paul Murray ist für mich ein wichtiger katholischer Gesprächspartner in Fragen der Rechtfertigung und des Kirchenverständnisses geworden, und ich verdanke ihm einige neue Einsichten in die katholische Ekklesiologie-Debatte. Dr. Christopher Insole hat mir spannende Einblicke in die Interpretation von Thomas von Aquin durch die evangelische Theologie vermittelt, mit mir über Kant gesprochen und wichtige Fragen zu Luther gestellt. Schließlich aber hat Dr. Robert Song mit seiner bioethischen Expertise dieses Projekt allererst möglich gemacht und vorangebracht. Mit kollegialer Großzügigkeit hat er mir Türen zur britischen Theologie geöffnet und war mir in unzähligen kurzen und längeren Diskussionen ein konstruktiver und gerne konsultierter Gesprächspartner. Dass wir auch inhaltlich eine so große Einigkeit gefunden haben, habe ich in diesem Zusammenhang als besonders beglückend empfunden.

Zu danken habe ich auch unseren Durhamer Freundinnen und Freunden, allen voran Dr. Jennifer Moberly und Dr. Gwendolyn Leysinger-Vieli und ihren Familien. Sie haben auf unterschiedliche Weise dafür gesorgt, dass wir uns in unserer temporären Wahlheimat rundum wohl gefühlt haben und diese mit einem großen Schuss Wehmut verlassen werden.

Aus der Ferne haben Kollegen und Kolleginnen und Freunde und Freundinnen Anteil an unserem Weg genommen, wofür ich dankbar bin. Mein Heidelberger Lehrer und Mentor war in dieser Zeit einer meiner wichtigsten Gesprächspartner, und es gehört zu den wunderbaren Erfahrungen der zwei Jahre im Ausland, dass ein Austausch möglich war und aufgrund von E-Mail-Kommunikation möglich wurde, der vor einigen Jahren noch undenkbar gewesen ist. Herr Professor Wilfried Härle hat wohlwollend und konstruktiv begleitet, was ich erlebt und gedacht habe und mich zu verschiedenen Gelegenheiten bei persönlichen Begegnungen seiner Wertschätzung vergewissert. Aber auch Dr. Judith Becker, Dr. Frank Martin Brunn und Dr. Christian Polke haben den intensiven Gesprächsfaden, den wir schon in Heidelberger Zeiten miteinander hatten, nicht abreißen lassen.

Das, was sich mit der Zeit als meine ethische Position herausgearbeitet hat, verdankt sich vor allem dem gemeinsamen Weg mit den Menschen, die mich begleitet und geprägt haben und mit denen ich immer noch unterwegs bin. Meine Mutter hat den Grundstein zu dem gelegt, was ich als Achtung vor Menschen in ihrer Beziehungsfähigkeit empfinde. Meine drei „Männer“, mein Mann Christian und unsere beiden Kinder Arthur Benedict und Elias Clemens, haben auf unterschiedliche Weise wesentlich dazu beigetragen, dass dieses Buch geschrieben werden konnte: mit meinem Mann verbindet mich ein jahrelanges Gespräch über medizinethische Fragen und ein Suchen nach menschenfreundlichen bioethischen Positionen. Seine medizinische Expertise hat mir in unseren Diskussionen Perspektiven eröffnet, die mir als Geisteswissenschaftlerin verschlossen geblieben wären, und sein stetiges liebevolles Interesse hat mich immer wieder herausgefordert, nach Antworten zu suchen. Unsere Kinder prägen mich allein durch ihr bloßes Dasein, weil mir an ihnen immer wieder deutlich wird, dass unser Menschsein nicht in sich selbst steht, sondern als zutiefst angewiesen auf Andere zu kennzeichnen ist. Wer könnte mir das besser zeigen und zueignen als meine Kinder?

Bevor ich eigene Kinder hatte, bin ich Taufpatin geworden, und auch jetzt noch verbinden uns mit den Familien meiner inzwischen vier Patenkinder enge Freundschaften. Einer der Paten unserer Kinder hat dieses Beziehungsnetz treffend als „extended family“ bezeichnet. In dieser erweiterten Familie lebt eine Ahnung davon, wie Menschen auf Beziehungen angewiesen sind und in ihnen und von ihnen leben, und wie wertvoll jeder einzelne Mensch, jedes einzelne Kind in diesem Gefüge ist. Darum widme ich dieses Buch meinen Patenkindern und ihren Familien: Sophia, Cornelius, Lisa und Charlotte.

Durham, in der Osterzeit 2009

Inhalt

I. Einleitung

Anthropologische Grundentscheidungen haben Folgen. Denn wie in einer Gesellschaft Menschsein verstanden wird, hat Auswirkungen auf den Umgang mit menschlichem Leben. Wann etwa beginnt Menschsein? Und welche Eigenschaften muss ein menschliches Wesen aufweisen, damit es zunächst als Mensch, dann aber auch als schutzwürdig anerkannt wird und darum unter dem Schutz der Rechtsgemeinschaft steht? Wann endet Menschsein? Und wie ist mit menschlichen Wesen umzugehen, die bestimmte Charaktermerkmale noch nicht, nicht mehr oder gar nicht aufweisen? Anthropologische Grundentscheidungen definieren Antworten bei diesen strittigen Fragen und geben Handlungsrichtlinien vor, die Auswirkungen in die gesellschaftliche Meinungsbildung und die Gesetzgebung hinein haben.

Dabei sind diese Grundentscheidungen nicht notwendigerweise explizit, sondern prägen und beeinflussen mindestens ebenso häufig *implizit* den gesellschaftlichen *common sense* oder die geltende Gesetzgebung und Rechtsprechung. Implizite Anthropologumena sind darum allererst offenzulegen; anschließend sind sie – ebenso wie explizite Aussagen zum „Wesen" des Menschen – in ihren Stärken und Schwächen zu analysieren. Dazu sind Positionen zum Umgang mit menschlichem Leben zu untersuchen und daraufhin zu befragen, welches Menschenbild sie transportieren.

Die theologische Ethik besitzt für die Offenlegung von anthropologischen Grundannahmen ein Kommunikations- und Reflexionspotential, um gesellschaftliche Debatten zu befragen und zur ethischen Orientierung in einer Gesellschaft beizutragen. Dabei sieht sie ausgehend von der Selbsterschließung Gottes in Jesus Christus jeden Menschen als Geschöpf Gottes an und beurteilt von der christlichen Wahrheitsgewissheit her auch ethische Grund- und Folgeentscheidungen.[1]

---

[1] Dieser Ansatz, dass theologische Ethik *dogmatische* theologische Grundentscheidungen reflektiert und von ihnen her gesellschaftliches Handeln wahrnimmt und beurteilt, versteht sich keineswegs von selbst. Ich vertrete ihn deswegen, weil ich davon ausgehe, dass unser Denken und Reflektieren denjenigen Gewissheiten folgt, die sich uns als wahr erschlossen haben und die etwa von der theologischen Dogmatik reflektiert werden. Von diesen Gewissheiten her, die als solche ihrerseits zu durchdenken und

Den Zweck einer Analyse und einer Überprüfung von impliziten und expliziten Anthropologumena rechtlicher, politischer und gesellschaftlicher Entscheidungen verfolge ich mit dem vorliegenden Buch, das während eines zweijährigen Forschungsaufenthaltes an der Universität Durham, England, entstanden ist. Das ursprüngliche Ziel meines Forschungsaufenthaltes war es, das Verhältnis von Menschenwürde und Menschenrechten im Ländervergleich von Deutschland und England mit besonderer Berücksichtigung der rechtlichen und ethischen Probleme am menschlichen Lebensbeginn zu untersuchen. Während der Zeit, die ich in England verbrachte, präzisierte sich die Fragestellung zu einer ländervergleichenden Studie über die Forschung an menschlichen *Embryonen* zur Gewinnung von humanen embryonalen Stammzellen und den Gebrauch des Menschenwürde-Begriffs in diesem Zusammenhang.

Diese Fokussierung ergab sich vor allem deswegen, weil während dieser Zeit sowohl die englische Gesetzgebung für die Forschung an menschlichen Embryonen grundlegend dem immens gewachsenen Wissen und den enorm gestiegenen Möglichkeiten dieser Forschung durch eine Gesetzesnovellierung Rechnung zu tragen versuchte, als auch die Verschiebung des Stichtags im deutschen Stammzellgesetz und die vorhergehenden und nachlaufenden öffentlichen Debatten in genau dieser Zeit stattfanden. Die Universität von Durham, mein Arbeits- und Forschungsort, hat aufgrund der Nähe zur und der engen Kooperation mit der Universität Newcastle, an der beispielsweise die Erzeugung der ersten cytoplasmischen Hybriden durch Dr. Lyle Armstrong erfolgte, darüber hinaus einen besonderen Impetus in der Forschung an humanen embryonalen Stammzellen und bot eine große Menge von kompetenten Gesprächspartnern und Gesprächspartnerinnen, die mir dabei halfen, die Entwicklung der britischen Gesetzgebung zu verstehen und auf ihre Anthropologie hin zu beleuchten.

Aus diesem Grund beschäftigt sich das Buch mit der Entwicklung in der Gesetzgebung zur Erzeugung von und der Forschung an humanen embryonalen Stammzellen in England und Deutschland, deren Hintergründen und deren Grundannahmen in ideengeschichtlich prägenden Konzeptionen mit besonderem Bezug zum Konzept der *Menschenwürde*, das offensichtlich in der deutschen und britischen Diskussion unterschiedlich verstanden wird. Das Verhältnis von Menschenrechten und Menschenwürde spielt allerdings insofern noch eine Rolle, als mir während der Forschungsarbeit die zunehmende Relevanz von *Menschenwürde/human dignity* in ihrer rechtsbegründenden Funktion in internationalen Menschenrechtstexten und (vor allem) *bioethischen* und *biopolitischen* Texten seit der Mitte des 20. Jahrhunderts deutlich geworden ist.

---

sich ständig neu anzueignen sind, haben sich meines Erachtens etwa anthropologische Grundentscheidungen innerhalb der ethischen Debatte als konsistent zu erweisen.

Dabei geht es mir neben einer kritischen Analyse von grundlegenden Anthropologumena mit einer Erhellung von deren Wurzeln und ideengeschichtlichen Hintergründen zugleich darum, unterschiedliche Grundentscheidungen in ihrer Entwicklung zu dokumentieren und berichtend darzustellen.[2] Ich konzentriere mich in diesem Zusammenhang auf die bioethische Debatte zum *Beginn* des menschlichen Lebens mit besonderer Berücksichtigung der Forschung an menschlichen Embryonen zur Gewinnung von embryonalen Stammzellen, und zwar aus mehreren Gründen:

- Sowohl die britische Gesetzgebung[3] als auch die ethische Debatte in Großbritannien unterscheiden sich in so starkem Maße von der deutschen Debatte, dass ein Vergleich der Differenzen und ihrer Hintergründe lohnend erscheint.[4]
- Gleichzeitig findet sich in der deutschen Wissenschaftslandschaft kein Buch, das aus theologisch-ethischer Sicht über die unterschiedliche gesetzgebende Entwicklung im deutschen und britischen Recht zur Forschung an Embryonen[5] informiert.
- Der Umgang mit menschlichem Leben sowohl zu Beginn als auch am Ende des Lebens wird auch innerhalb der deutschen bioethischen Diskussion unterschiedlich beurteilt und ist als strittig wahrzunehmen.

---

[2] Ein weiteres Motiv für die Abfassung des Buches ist die Frage nach einer theologischen Bestimmung des Menschseins und seiner Würde, die am Ende des Buches zu leisten sein wird.

[3] Ich nenne an dieser Stelle die jüngste Entscheidung des britischen Parlaments, eine erneuerte *Human Fertilisation and Embryology Act* zu verabschieden, die im November 2008 mit der Unterzeichnung der Queen als Gesetz in Kraft getreten ist, nach der unter anderem eine Kreuzung von menschlichen und tierischen Keimzellen in der Erzeugung von Hybrid- und Chimären-Embryonen erlaubt ist.

[4] In diesem Zusammenhang muss unterschieden werden zwischen der säkularen Ethik in Großbritannien und der theologisch-ethischen Debatte zum Thema. Hier bestehen Unterschiede, die zumindest ansatzweise darzustellen sind.

[5] Gleichwohl ist ein Buch greifbar zum unterschiedlichen Umgang mit PGD/PID (Preimplantation Genetic Diagnosis/Präimplantationsdiagnostik) in England und Deutschland. Vgl. Uta Ziegler, Präimplantationsdiagnostik in England und Deutschland: ethische, rechtliche und praktische Probleme, Frankfurt/Main 2004. Juristische ländervergleichende Bücher sind inzwischen zahlreich erschienen; vgl. etwa M. B. Friele, Rechtsethik der Embryonenforschung. Rechtsharmonisierung in moralisch umstrittenen Bereichen, Paderborn 2008; M. Heyer, Präimplantationsdiagnostik, Embryonenforschung, Klonen. Ein vergleichender Überblick zur Rechtslage in ausgewählten Ländern, Freiburg/München 2007; J. Taupitz, Rechtliche Regelung der Embryonenforschung im internationalen Vergleich, Heidelberg/Berlin 2003; H. Haßmann, Embryonenschutz im Spannungsfeld internationaler Menschenrechte, staatlicher Grundrechte und nationaler Regelungsmodelle zur Embryonenforschung, Heidelberg/Berlin 2003.

Die wesentlichen Argumente sind ausgetauscht,[6] und eine ländervergleichende Studie könnte insofern nochmals zur Klärung beitragen, als sie Positionen in einen größeren Zusammenhang stellt und Begründungsmodelle miteinander vergleicht.

- Bei einer Untersuchung des Umgangs mit dem menschlichen Lebens*beginn* treten strittige Aspekte über das Menschsein im allgemeinen in den Fokus, werden aber an einem konkreten Beispiel untersucht, so dass eine Konzentration auf wesentliche Aspekte ermöglicht wird.

Haben Deutschland und England unterschiedliche Gesetzgebungen im Bereich der Embryonenforschung und also hinsichtlich des Umgangs mit menschlichen Wesen am Lebensbeginn gefunden, so gibt es offenbar unterschiedliche Argumente, die sich in beiden Ländern durchgesetzt haben, die wiederum auf unterschiedlichen philosophischen und ideengeschichtlichen Hintergründen beruhen. Während in der Debatte im deutschen Sprachraum der *Menschenwürde*-Begriff häufig verwendet wird, um Stellungnahmen im Zusammenhang mit der Embryonenforschung zu begründen,[7] spielen in der englischsprachigen Debatte andere Sprachfiguren eine zentrale Rolle. Dabei könnte im Ländervergleich ein hermeneutischer Schlüssel hilfreich sein, mit dem die unterschiedliche Gesetzgebung in ihrer historischen Entwicklung transparenter wird.

Der Begriff der „Menschenwürde" könnte sich dabei deswegen als besonders aufschlussreich erweisen, weil mit ihm eine anthropologische Bestimmung explizit in Verfassungsdokumente sowie internationale Menschenrechtsdokumente und – zumindest in Deutschland – bis in die Gesetz-

---

[6] Vgl. dazu zahlreiche Veröffentlichungen aus den letzten Jahren im deutschsprachigen Bereich, u. a. K. Braun, Menschenwürde und Biomedizin. Zum philosophischen Diskurs der Bioethik, Frankfurt/Main 2000; P. Dabrock/L. Klinnert/S. Schardien, Menschenwürde und Lebensschutz. Herausforderungen theologischer Bioethik, Gütersloh 2004; G. Damschen/D. Schönecker (Hrsg.), Der moralische Status menschlicher Embryonen. Pro und contra Spezies-, Kontinuums-, Identitäts- und Potentialitätsargument, Berlin/New York 2004; N. Knoepffler, Menschenwürde in der Bioethik, Berlin u. a. 2004. Für die theologische Ethik vgl. auch den Sammelband R. Anselm/ U.H.J. Körtner (Hrsg.), Streitfall Biomedizin. Urteilsfindung in christlicher Verantwortung, Göttingen 2003. Allein auf dem gegenwärtigen deutschen Buchmarkt werden mehr als 150 Monographien und Sammelbände verkauft, die sich mit dem Schlagwort „Menschenwürde" beschäftigen. Hinzu kommt eine breite Aufsatzliteratur. Aufgrund dieser Breite der Literatur arbeitet die vorliegende Studie exemplarisch. Sie stellt ausdrücklich keinen *forschungsgeschichtlichen* Beitrag zur Verwendung der Begriffe *Menschenwürde/human dignity* dar, sondern hat einen *systematischen* Fokus.

[7] Vgl. nur U. Eibach, Menschenwürde an den Grenzen des Lebens. Einführung in Fragen der Bioethik aus christlicher Sicht, Neukirchen-Vluyn 2000. Aber auch Bundespräsident Rau hat sich als Staatsoberhaupt in seiner Berliner Rede 2001 unter Rückgriff auf „Menschenwürde" kritisch zu einem unbegrenzten bioethischen Fortschritt geäußert.

gebung zum Embryonenschutz hinein Eingang gefunden hat, auch wenn der Begriff in der gegenwärtigen Diskussion hoch umstritten und nicht klar und zweifelsfrei definiert ist. Wie Menschenwürde verstanden wird und welche ethischen und rechtlichen Folgen sich aus diesem Verständnis ergeben, könnte eine sinnvolle Frage sein, um implizite Anthropologumena innerhalb der bioethischen Diskussion zu entdecken und kritisch zu reflektieren. Dazu müssen allerdings unterschiedliche Verständnisformen von „Menschenwürde" offen gelegt und mit ihren Begründungen dargestellt und untersucht werden. Unter Umständen wird es sich nach einer solchen Untersuchung erweisen, dass der Menschenwürdebegriff als international überzeugender Begriff im postmodernen Pluralismus innerhalb der bioethischen Debatte nicht (mehr) hilfreich ist bzw. einer genauen differenzierenden Bestimmung bedarf.[8]

Der bioethische Rekurs auf *Menschenwürde*, der innerhalb der deutschen Debatte nicht nur mit Zustimmung, sondern auch mit Kritik gesehen wird,[9] fokussiert in der gegenwärtigen Diskussion zum Lebensbeginn vor allem auf die verbrauchende Forschung an menschlichen Embryonen zur Gewinnung von Stammzellen, aber auch auf die Frage der ethischen Legitimation von Gentherapie, Klonierung, Schwangerschaftsabbruch und PID. Dabei wird der Menschenwürde-Begriff vor allem als hermeneutischer Schlüssel für die Frage verwendet, ob ein bestimmtes Vorgehen in biomedizinischer Forschung mit der Menschenwürde vereinbar ist bzw. gegen die Achtung der Menschenwürde verstößt.

Nicht nur innerhalb der deutschen Debatte aber genießt der Menschenwürdebegriff hohes Ansehen, sondern wird als international anerkannte

[8] Diese Schlussfolgerung zieht J. Habermas in seinem Buch Die Zukunft der menschlichen Natur. Auf dem Weg zu einer liberalen Eugenik? Frankfurt/Main 2005. Habermas unterscheidet zwischen der *Unantastbarkeit* der *Menschenwürde* nach Art. 1 I GG und der *Unverfügbarkeit* „vorpersonalen" menschlichen Lebens und wendet auf dieses den Menschenwürdebegriff nicht an. „Ich gebrauche 'Unantastbarkeit' nicht gleichbedeutend mit 'Unverfügbarkeit', weil eine *nachmetaphysische* Antwort auf die Frage, wie wir mit vorpersonalem Leben umgehen sollen, nicht um den Preis einer reduktionistischen Bestimmung von Mensch und Moral erkauft werden darf." (Habermas, a.a.O., 62.)

[9] Vgl. das Votum von E. Schmidt-Jortzig, „Menschenwürde" als Zauberwort der öffentlichen Debatte. Demokratische Meinungsbildung in hoch komplexen Problemfeldern, ZEE 52, 2008, 50-56. Neben Begriffen wie „soziale Gerechtigkeit" sei auch „Menschenwürde" auf dem besten Wege, zu einem „Zauberwort" zu werden: „Schon wer den Begriff in die Debatte einführt und für sich reklamiert, hat gewonnen. Dagegen anzuargumentieren, ist zwecklos. Wer es versucht, grenzt sich nur aus... Das Zauberwort taugt damit regelrecht sogar zum Totschlagargument... Wenn nicht alles täuscht, ist auch der Bezugspunkt 'Menschenwürde' dabei, sich in der öffentlichen Debatte zu einem solchen Zauberwort zu entwickeln. In der biomedizinischen Diskussion ist dieser Vorgang bereits fast vollendet." (A.a.O., 51.)

Kategorie innerhalb von Menschenrechtsdokumenten[10] auch in internationalen bioethischen und biopolitischen Dokumenten als Begründungsfigur verwendet.[11] Dabei ist aber die Argumentation mit *Menschenwürde* bzw. *Human Dignity* keineswegs so eindeutig, wie es den Anschein hat:[12] sie hat zwar den Vorteil, dass sie mit einem in hohem Maße positiv konnotierten Begriff operiert, aber der Begriff ist an sich so weit, dass eine Vielzahl von Interpretationen mit ihm verbunden werden kann. Eine Untersuchung und Offenlegung der Interpretationen von *Menschenwürde*[13] in ihren unterschiedlichen Gebrauchskontexten und mit den unterschiedlichen ideengeschichtlichen Voraussetzungen bezogen auf den deutschsprachigen und englischsprachigen Kontext könnte darum hilfreich sein.

Ich konzentriere mich in den Ausführungen dieses Buches auf die Frage der verbrauchenden Embryonenforschung zur Gewinnung von humanen embryonalen Stammzellen, zu der auch das „therapeutische", nicht aber das reproduktive Klonen, sowie die seit 2008 in Großbritannien[14] rechtlich geregelte Herstellung von Hybrid- und Chimären-Embryonen gehören. Die Unterschiede in der deutschen und britischen Gesetzgebung sind dabei zunächst

---

[10] So etwa in der UN-Deklaration für Menschenrechte (1948), s. unten unter III.5, S. 171ff.

[11] Vor allem in der sog. Bioethik-Konvention der EU. Mit der Menschenwürde wird etwa auch in der UN-Deklaration zum menschlichen Klonen (2005) das Verbot der Klonierung von Menschen begründet.

[12] Das Verhältnis von Menschenwürde und Menschenrechten ist ebenso wenig abschließend geklärt wie eine inhaltliche Bestimmung des Menschenwürde-Begriffs innerhalb der Bioethik. Zur Frage nach Menschenwürde und Menschenrechten vgl. meinen Aufsatz Menschenwürde – Grund oder Spitze der Menschenrechte?, in: F. M. Brunn u.a. (Hrsg.), Menschenbild und Theologie. Beiträge zum interdisziplinären Gespräch, Festgabe für Wilfried Härle zum 65. Geburtstag, MThS 100, Leipzig 2007, 141-160.

[13] Bei der Frage nach einer inhaltlichen Bestimmung von Menschenwürde ist entsprechend auch die Frage strittig, was *menschlich* ist, wann Menschsein beginnt und endet und wie das „Wesen" des Menschen angemessen bestimmt werden kann. Vgl. auch J. F. Kilner, Art. Human Dignity, Encyclopedia of Bioethics, ³2003, 1193-1200, 1197: „Rooting human dignity in being human, like basing it on specific human characteristics, faces at least two important hurdles. First, although it avoids the problematic idea that there could be human beings without human dignity, it begs the question of who is a human being. Does anyone with a human genome qualify, and if so, how much of the human genetic code must be missing or nonfunctional before the status as a human being is lost? Are certain capacities instead or in addition what constitute a human being, and if so, must the exercise of those capacities be actual or may it be potential?"

[14] Teilweise unterscheiden sich innerhalb der britischen Gesetzgebung vor allem englische und schottische Gesetzgebung voneinander. Grundsätzlich untersuche ich die Gesetzgebung und die öffentliche Diskussion von Großbritannien im Ganzen und mache Unterschiede, die sich in der *englischen* Diskussion zur Position von *schottischen* Institutionen und der *schottischen* Kirche ergeben, kenntlich.

berichtend darzustellen[15] und anschließend auf ihre theoretische Begründung und ihre Hintergründe hin zu befragen. Darüber hinaus stellt sich die Frage, ob, mit welchem Verständnis und mit welcher Reichweite innerhalb der unterschiedlichen Rechtsbegründung mit dem Menschenwürde-Begriff operiert wird, dann aber auch, welche anthropologischen Implikationen sich mit den rechtlichen und politischen Entscheidungen im einzelnen verbinden, mit anderen Worten, auf welchen kulturellen und ideengeschichtlichen Hintergründen die Unterschiede bei britischer und deutscher Gesetzgebung in der Forschung an Embryonen beruhen.[16]

Eine vergleichende Analyse zur Gesetzgebung und ihrer Begründung hat aus diesem Grund einen doppelten Nutzen: sie dient zum einen der Information über die Gesetzgebung, die öffentliche Debatte und deren Hintergründe in einem europäischen Nachbarland. Sie verhilft zum anderen zu einem tieferen Verständnis der eigenen Tradition mit deren Hintergründen und Wurzeln und gibt möglicherweise Argumente an die Hand, die innerhalb der gegenwärtigen Diskussion hilfreich sind, und trägt mit der Offenlegung von Grundannahmen, die hinter einer Position stehen, zur Klärung und Versachlichung in einer emotional hoch aufgeladenen gesellschaftlichen Debatte bei.

Das vorliegende Buch hat zwei Hauptteile: nach einem berichtenden Teil, der die Entwicklung sowohl der britischen als auch der deutschen Gesetzgebung darstellt und zuvor knapp die Entwicklung des Embryo in den ersten 14 Tagen nach der Befruchtung referiert, konzentriert sich der zweite Hauptteil auf die Frage danach, welche Begründungsfiguren im Ländervergleich für einen schwachen bzw. starken Embryonenschutz traditionell angeführt werden. Neben der Argumentation in der säkularen Bioethik spielt dabei die Entwicklung der theologischen und kirchlichen Bioethik insofern eine Rolle, als auch für diese anthropologische Grundannahmen zu erheben sind, aus denen sich unterschiedliche Stellungnahmen zur biomedizinischen Forschung ergeben.

Bei einer ersten Annäherung fällt die unterschiedliche Prägung in England und Deutschland auf: Während die kontinentale Philosophie deutlich stärker von einem kantischen deontologischen Ansatz ausgeht, sind in der britischen Ethik-Diskussion mit der von Jeremy Bentham, John Stuart Mill

---

[15] Dabei kann es nicht darum gehen, die derzeitige rasante Entwicklung der embryonalen Stammzellforschung detailgetreu darzustellen. Vielmehr fokussiere ich zum einen auf die unterschiedlichen *rechtlichen* Bestimmungen, die mit dieser Forschung einhergehen, zum anderen – vor allem – auf die theoretischen, ethischen und philosophischen Hintergründe dieser Bestimmungen und versuche eine eigene theologische Position zu finden.

[16] Nicht unterschätzt werden darf in diesem Zusammenhang sicherlich die (auch kontingente) Meinungsbildung im Vorfeld der Gesetzesfindungen und der Einfluss, den pragmatische Überlegungen, Lobbybildungen etc. gehabt haben.

und ihren Nachfolgern geprägten utilitaristischen Konzeption andere Prioritäten bestimmend geworden. Diese Unterscheidung darf aber vor allem deswegen nicht überstrapaziert werden, weil es im deutschsprachigen Bereich inzwischen eine breite Zustimmung zu utilitaristischer Argumentation in der Bioethik gibt, und auf der anderen Seite innerhalb der englischsprachigen Bioethik nach Alternativen sowohl für eine deontologische, als auch für eine utilitaristische Ethik gesucht wird. Insofern bildet die Alternative Kant – Mill nur eine erste orientierende Kartographie, die differenzierend zu präzisieren ist.

Bevor ich mich diesen inhaltlichen Fragen zuwende, stellt das folgende Kapitel die Entwicklung der Gesetzgebung zur Forschung an menschlichen Embryonen in England und Deutschland dar.

II. Differenzen beim Embryonenschutz in England und Deutschland

II. 1 Zum Umgang mit menschlichen Embryonen in Deutschland und England

Der Umgang mit menschlichen Embryonen wird in Großbritannien und Deutschland grundsätzlich unterschiedlich gehandhabt. Nicht nur war Großbritannien weltweit das erste Land, in dem 1978 ein durch In-Vitro-Fertilisation (IVF) gezeugtes Baby zur Welt kam und 1996 mit „Dolly“ das erste Säugetier geklont wurde,[17] hier ist auch das „therapeutische Klonen“[18] rechtlich geregelt worden, und mit der Verabschiedung der erneuerten *Human Fertilisation and Embryology Act*, die im November 2008 von der Queen unterzeichnet wurde, wird international erstmals die Erzeugung von tierisch-menschlichen Mischembryonen (*human-animal admixed embryos,* sowohl als cytoplasmische Hybrid-Embryonen, kurz „Cybrids“, als auch als „true hybrids“) rechtlich geregelt. Während sich demgegenüber schon auf den ersten Blick die deutsche Gesetzgebung mit ihrem Verbot der Herstellung von embryonalen Stammzelllinien als restriktiv darstellt, verfährt die britische Gesetzgebung pragmatisch und forschungsfreundlich.

---

[17] Das Schaf „Dolly“ steht inzwischen ausgestopft im Museum of Scotland in Edinburgh.

[18] Die *Human Reproductive Cloning Act* trat 2001 in Kraft. Alle Gesetzestexte, auch die 1990 erstmals in Kraft getretene *Human Fertilisation and Embryology Act* (HFE Act) oder das Gesetz zum Schwangerschaftsabbruch (*Abortion Act*) von 1967 finden sich im Internet unter http://www.opsi.gov.uk/acts.htm.

Im europäischen Vergleich[19] können England[20] und Deutschland unterschiedlichen Typen für die rechtliche Regelung im Umgang mit dem menschlichen Lebensbeginn zugeordnet werden.[21] Dabei stellen sich schematisch drei Regelungstypen dar:

- Länder, die Embryonenforschung grundsätzlich ausschließen und nur eine Forschung erlauben, die mit dem Leben des Embryo verträglich ist, die also eine „verbrauchende Embryonenforschung" verbieten,[22]
- Länder, in denen Embryonenforschung nur erlaubt ist, wenn sie grundsätzlich zum therapeutischen Schutz von *Embryonen* bzw. zu einem besseren Verständnis von Schwangerschaft und Embryonalentwicklung führt, auch wenn der spezielle Embryo, an dem geforscht hat, unter Umständen keinen Nutzen davon hat,[23] die aber eine Forschung ausschließen, die nicht Embryonen zugute kommt, sondern auf einen therapeutischen Nutzen etwa für degenerativ Erkrankte zielt,

[19] Im außereuropäischen Vergleich ist die Gesetzgebung zur Stammzellforschung schwierig zu klassifizieren. Australien, Israel und die USA vertreten eine liberale Gesetzgebung, nach der an Embryonen grundsätzlich geforscht werden darf, wobei in den USA nach Beginn der Regierung von George W. Bush – unter Rückgriff auf den Menschenwürdebegriff – keine öffentlichen Mittel zur Finanzierung dieser Forschung zur Verfügung gestanden haben. Diese Regelung ist von Präsident Obama im März 2009 rückgängig gemacht worden. In China, Korea und Russland existieren keine rechtlichen Vorgaben hinsichtlich der Embryonenforschung, wobei China und Korea für sich in Anspruch nehmen, dass sie bereits erfolgreich menschliche Embryonen geklont haben.

[20] Die britische Gesetzgebung umfasst in Fragen der Embryonenforschung auch die walisische und die schottische Gesetzgebung, nicht aber die nordirische, die in Fragen des Schwangerschaftsabbruchs und der Forschung an menschlichen Embryonen deutlich strikter urteilt.

[21] Vgl. H. Bedford-Strohm, Sacred body? Stem cell research and human cloning, The Ecumenical Review 54, 2002, 140-150.

[22] Dazu gehören Deutschland, Irland, Luxemburg, Österreich, Norwegen, Litauen, Polen und Italien. Die Schweiz, die zunächst embryonale Stammzellforschung verboten hatte, erlaubt seit dem 2005 in Kraft getretenen Stammzellgesetz eine Forschung an „überzähligen" menschlichen Embryonen. In dieser Gruppe ist nochmals zu unterscheiden zwischen Ländern, die Embryonenforschung kategorisch ausschließen und verbieten (1) und Ländern, die Forschung an importierten Stammzelllinien erlauben, aber selbst keine Stammzelllinien produzieren dürfen (2). Deutschland gehört auch nach der Verschiebung des Stichtags innerhalb des Stammzellgesetzes vom 1.1.2002 auf den 1.5.2007 zur zweiten Gruppe.

[23] Dazu zählten vor einer Lockerung der Gesetzgebung Dänemark, Frankreich und Schweden. Offenbar ist die Differenzierung zwischen einer Forschung, die dem Embryo nützt, und einer Forschung zugunsten von an degenerativen Erkrankungen leidenden Patienten aber nur schwer aufrecht zu erhalten gewesen, so dass in den genannten Ländern eine Lockerung eingetreten ist und diese inzwischen der dritten Gruppe zugehören.

- Länder, in denen – häufig unter strengen Auflagen und genauer Kontrolle – Embryonenforschung bis zum 14. Tag nach der Befruchtung erlaubt ist.[24] Die Forschung muss nicht lediglich Embryonen und einem vertieften Verständnis von Embryonalentwicklung und Schwangerschaft nützen, sondern generell „hochrangigen Forschungszielen" (*necessary or desirable research*[25]) dienen, so dass als Forschungsziel auch Grundlagenforschung in Frage kommt und die potentielle Therapie von degenerativen Erkrankungen vertreten werden kann.

Bei dieser schematischen Typologisierung ist die deutsche Gesetzgebung der ersten, die englische der dritten Gruppe zuzuordnen: Während in Deutschland eine Forschung an menschlichen Embryonen und eine Erzeugung von Embryonen zu Forschungszwecken grundsätzlich nicht erlaubt ist, die Einfuhr von im Ausland erzeugten Stammzelllinien vielmehr nur unter bestimmten, streng regulierten Bedingungen gestattet wird, ist in England sowohl die Erzeugung von Embryonen zu Forschungszwecken auf dem Wege von In-Vitro-Fertilisation (IVF) und somatischem Zellkerntransfer („therapeutisches Klonen" oder Produktion von cytoplasmischen Hybrid-Embryonen), als auch die Forschung an Embryonen bis zum 14. Tag nach der Befruchtung – wenn auch unter strengen Auflagen – erlaubt. Der 14. Tag hat sich dabei nicht nur in England als kritische Grenze, bis zu der hin die Forschung an menschlichen Embryonen gestattet ist, weitgehend durchgesetzt.

Dieser unterschiedliche legislative Umgang mit menschlichen Embryonen in England und Deutschland hat Folgen auf europäischer Ebene: Die 1997 in Oviedo verabschiedete „Convention for the Protection of Human Rights and Dignity of the Human Being with Regard to the Application of Biology and Medicine: Convention on Human Rights and Biomedicine", im Deutschen häufig kurz als „Bioethikkonvention" bezeichnet, nimmt eine mittlere Position in der offenbar höchst umstrittenen Frage der Embryonenforschung ein: in Ländern, in denen Embryonenforschung erlaubt ist, soll der Embryo nach der Konvention in adäquater Weise geschützt werden, wobei aber eine Erzeugung von Embryonen zu Forschungszwecken in jedem Falle verboten

---

[24] So gegenwärtig etwa Dänemark, Frankreich, Finnland, Griechenland, Großbritannien, die Niederlande, Belgien, Schweden und Spanien. In dieser Gruppe ist nochmals zu unterscheiden zwischen Ländern, die ausschließlich Forschung an bei IVF überzähligen Embryonen erlauben, und Ländern, die eine Erzeugung von Embryonen zur Forschungszwecken ebenso gestalten wie eine Erzeugung von Embryonen durch Somatischen Zellkerntransfer, also Klonen und Cybrid-Bildung. Großbritannien gehört dieser zuletzt genannten Gruppe zu. Auch Belgien und Schweden lassen Klonierung zu.

[25] So in der *Human Fertilisation and Embryology Act* (1990/2008).

ist.[26] Dabei zielt die Konvention schon in ihrem Titel auf den Schutz der Menschenrechte und der Menschenwürde und gibt ethische und rechtliche Mindeststandards für den Umgang mit menschlichem Leben an seinen Grenzen vor. Weder Deutschland noch Großbritannien haben die Konvention bislang ratifiziert – sie ist für die deutsche Gesetzgebung zu liberal,[27] während sie der britischen Gesetzgebung nicht weit genug geht.[28]

Wenn aber Deutschland und England zwei einander entgegengesetzte Pole innerhalb der Debatte um die Embryonenforschung besetzen: worin genau liegen die Differenzen, und welche Hintergründe haben sie? Diese Fragen versuche ich in den kommenden Abschnitten zu beantworten, indem ich zuerst die Entwicklung der britischen, sodann die Entwicklung der deutschen Gesetzgebung zum Embryonenschutz berichtend darstelle.

Zunächst aber widme ich mich in aller Kürze der Entwicklung des menschlichen Embryo in den ersten 14 Tagen, um die Fragestellung zu vertiefen, was eigentlich in diesem Zusammenhang der Kernpunkt der politischen, moralischen und rechtlichen Auseinandersetzung ist.[29] Weil sich vor allem in England der 14. Tag innerhalb der embryonalen Entwicklung als eine kritische Grenze durchgesetzt hat, scheint es mir erforderlich zu sein, sich das Geschehen innerhalb dieser ersten 14 Tage in Erinnerung zu rufen. Daran anschließend stelle ich die unterschiedlichen Verfahren zur Gewinnung von Stammzellen dar, auch mittels der schon häufiger genannten Produktion von Hybrid-Embryonen.

---

[26] „Article 18 – Research on embryos in vitro: 1. Where the law allows research on embryos in vitro, it shall ensure adequate protection of the embryo. 2. The creation of human embryos for research purposes is prohibited." Die Konvention findet sich unter http://conventions.coe.int/Treaty/EN/Treaties/Html/164.htm.

[27] Eine einschlägige Protestseite findet sich unter http://www.bioethik-konvention.de.

[28] Die Konvention wurde von zahlreichen europäischen Staaten unterzeichnet. Unterzeichnet haben bis 2008 Bosnien-Herzegowina, Bulgarien, Kroatien, Zypern, Tschechien, Dänemark, Estland, Finnland, Frankreich, Georgien, Griechenland, Ungarn, Island, Italien, Lettland, Litauen, Luxemburg, Moldavien, die Niederlande, Norwegen, Polen, Portugal, Rumänien, San Marino, Serbien, Slowakien, Slowenien, Spanien, Schweden, die Schweiz, Mazedonien, die Türkei, die Ukraine und Montenegro.

[29] Dieses Referat zielt nicht auf einen eigenen Beitrag zur Forschung, wofür ich als Geisteswissenschaftlerin nicht kompetent bin. Es verdankt sich darum wesentlich der Arbeit anderer, die an den entsprechenden Stellen nachgewiesen wird.

II. 2 Die Entwicklung des menschlichen Embryos in den ersten 14 Tagen und die Gewinnung von Stammzellen

II. 2. 1 Zur Entwicklung des Embryos in den ersten 14 Lebenstagen

Der in der gegenwärtigen Debatte strittig beurteilte Zeitraum für die Forschung an menschlichen Embryonen umfasst vor allem die ersten 14 Tage nach der Kernverschmelzung. Spätestens mit dem Abschluss dieser Periode ereignet sich für die allermeisten Forscher eine den moralischen Status des Embryos verändernde Zäsur, jenseits derer eine Forschung an ihm nicht mehr erlaubt werden sollte. Was aber geschieht in diesen ersten 14 Tagen?[30]

Der Vorgang der Befruchtung der Eizelle durch die Samenzelle dauert bis zu seinem Abschluss ca. 24 Stunden, währenddessen sich die beiden einfachen Chromosomensätze von Mutter und Vater mit jeweils 23 Chromosomen zu einem neuen doppelten Chromosomensatz des neuen Individuums mit der Festlegung von dessen Geschlecht und dessen genetischer Identität vereinigen. Während der Zustand vor dem Abschluss der Kernverschmelzung als „Vorkernstadium" bezeichnet wird, ist nach etwa 24 Stunden die Kernverschmelzung abgeschlossen, und die Entwicklung des Embryos mit einer neuen DNA beginnt. Nach dem Abschluss der Kernverschmelzung hat der sich entwickelnde Embryo ein individuelles Genom, das sich nicht mehr ändern wird.

Mit dem Auftreten der Teilungsspindel wird die Teilung des bis dahin einzelligen Embryos eingeleitet, der zunächst seine Größe nicht verändert, sondern die Anzahl seiner Zellen durch Teilung vermehrt. Der sich entwikkelnde Embryo, wegen seiner Kugelform „Morula" (Maulbeere) genannt, besteht nach etwa 40 Stunden aus 4 Zellen. Im 4- oder 8-Zell-Stadium setzt die Bildung von embryoeigenen Proteinen ein, weswegen dieser Zeitpunkt als möglicher Beginn der genetischen Selbststeuerung angesehen wird.

Bis etwa zu diesem Stadium hat jede Zelle in dem sich teilenden Embryo Totipotenz[31] inne, so dass jede Zelle, die ihm entnommen wird, zu einem eigenständigen Embryo heranwachsen, eine Plazenta ausbilden und sich in die

---

[30] Zur Entwicklung des Embryos in den ersten Tagen vgl. den Überblick in dem von G. Damschen und D. Schönecker hrsg. Sammelband Der moralische Status menschlicher Embryonen. Pro und contra Spezies-, Kontinuums-, Identitäts- und Potentialitätsargument, Berlin/New York 2003, 269-277 (C. Viebahn, Eine Skizze der embryonalen Frühentwicklung des Menschen).

[31] Ich gebrauche in diesem Zusammenhang die Begriffe „totipotent" und „pluripotent", bin mir allerdings darüber im klaren, dass eine genaue zeitliche Abgrenzung von Totipotenz und Pluripotenz innerhalb der embryonalen Entwicklung nur schwer möglich ist. Darum wird auch eine genaue begriffliche Abgrenzung häufig nicht vollzogen. Ich folge der Definition im Springer Lexikon Medizin (P. Reuter, Berlin u. a. 2004, S. 2134f.),

Gebärmutterschleimhaut implantieren kann.[32] Jenseits des 8-Zell-Stadiums formiert sich aus der Morula allmählich die Blastozyste, aus der sich Plazenta und Embryo entwickeln werden (Trophoblast und Embryoblast). Die Zellen des sich entwickelnden Embryos verlieren ihre Totipotenz, können also ab diesem Zeitpunkt nicht mehr jede denkbare Differenzierung vollziehen und keine Plazentazellen mehr ausbilden. Zellen, die dem Embryo in diesem Stadium entnommen werden, können nicht als Embryo weiter wachsen; ihnen eignet aber trotzdem noch ein immenses Differenzierungsvermögen, weswegen sie meist als „pluripotent“ bezeichnet werden.

Nach dem fünften oder sechsten Tag beginnt die befruchtete Eizelle sich in der Gebärmutterschleimhaut zu implantieren, wobei die Phase der *Implantation* oder *Nidation* etwa sechs bis acht Tage in Anspruch nimmt und am 14.-16. Tag nach der Kernverschmelzung abgeschlossen ist. Nach dieser Zeit hat sich die mütterliche Gebärmutterschleimhaut über der eingenisteten Blastozyste geschlossen. Während des Prozesses der Implantation beginnt sich die Struktur der Plazenta zu bilden, die den Embryo optimal mit Nährstoffen versorgt. Der Embryoblast hat in dieser Phase die Form einer Scheibe und wird darum auch als Keimscheibe (*embryonic disc*) bezeichnet, woraus er sich allmählich zum embryonalen Körper entwickelt.

Während und nach der Phase der Implantation finden im Embryoblasten weitere Differenzierungsvorgänge statt, im Zusammenhang derer sich der primäre Dottersack und die Amnionhöhle bilden. Vor allem ist diese Phase der *Gastrulation* durch das Auftreten des Primitivstreifens (*primitive streak*) etwa am 14. Tag nach der Befruchtung gekennzeichnet, der sich im Laufe des Wachstumsprozesses zum Neuralrohr weiterentwickeln wird. Das Auftreten des Primitivstreifens bezeichnet den spätesten Punkt, an dem der Embryo sich in zwei Embryonen teilen kann; erscheint nur *ein* Primitivstreifen in der Keimscheibe, ist die Zwillingsbildung ausgeschlossen, erscheinen *zwei* Primitivstreifen und damit zusammenhängende Primitivknoten, entwickelt sich der Embryo als Zwillinge weiter. Dabei kann sich die Duplikation auch schon vorher während verschiedener Phasen der Entwicklung ereignet haben;[33] das Auftreten des Primitivstreifens stellt aber den spätesten Zeitpunkt

---

nach der eine totipotente Zelle über *sämtliche* Entwicklungsmöglichkeiten verfügt, sich also auch als Embryo weiter entwickeln kann.

[32] Aus diesem Grund bestimmt das deutsche Embryonenschutzgesetz (ESchG 1990) in § 8 totipotente Zellen als Embryonen: „(1) Als Embryo im Sinne dieses Gesetzes gilt bereits die befruchtete, entwicklungsfähige menschliche Eizelle vom Zeitpunkt der Kernverschmelzung an, ferner jede einem Embryo entnommene totipotente Zelle, die sich bei Vorliegen der dafür erforderlichen weiteren Voraussetzungen zu teilen und zu einem Individuum zu entwickeln vermag.“

[33] Für die Zwillingsbildung bestehen folgende Möglichkeiten: durch Duplikation während der *Furchung* entstehen zwei Blastozysten und es entwickeln sich zwei Embryonen mit zwei unabhängigen Plazenten (1), durch Duplikation des *Embryoblasten* (in dersel-

dar, an dem sich aus anfänglich einem Embryo zwei Embryonen entwickeln können.

In der weiteren Entwicklung des Embryos kommt es zwischen der 4. und 8. Entwicklungswoche zur Ausbildung der Organsysteme und zur Ausprägung der embryonalen Körperform. Häufig wird der Keim bis zum Abschluss dieser Phase als „Embryo“ bezeichnet, während sich die fetale Phase, also die Entwicklung des „Fötus“ während des 3.–9. Entwicklungsmonats anschließt, die durch Wachstum und Differenzierung der Organe sowie der Körperform gekennzeichnet ist.

Aus der Entwicklung von Embryonen in den ersten 14 Tagen nach der Kernverschmelzung folgt keine normative Vorgabe zum Umgang mit menschlichem Leben an dessen Beginn. In dieser Frage sind von deutscher und britischer Gesetzgebung grundlegend unterschiedliche Urteile gefällt worden. Bevor diese Entscheidungen im Ländervergleich von Deutschland und England eingehender dargestellt werden, stelle ich – dem Fokus der Ausführungen in diesem Buch entsprechend – kurz die Fakten zur Gewinnung von humanen Stammzellen dar.

II. 2. 2 Die Gewinnung humaner Stammzellen

Die Gewinnung von menschlichen embryonalen Stammzellen und die mögliche Entwicklung einer Therapie durch Stammzellen sind Gründe, warum die Forschung an Embryonen von zahlreichen Forschern unterstützt wird.

Stammzellen sind Zellen mit einem hoch entwickelten Ausdifferenzierungspotential. Sie können zum einen sich selbst reproduzieren (weswegen ihnen bis zu einem gewissen Grad „Unsterblichkeit“ eignet), zum anderen aber auch – je nach Differenzierungspotential – unterschiedliche Typen von Zellen hervorbringen. Dabei werden mehrere Formen von Stammzellen unterschieden:

- **Embryonale Stammzellen,** die aus wenige Tage alten Embryonen isoliert werden, die im Verlauf dieses Isolierungsprozesses meist zerstört werden.[34] Embryonale Stammzellen haben das Potential, sich in praktisch alle Zelltypen ausdifferenzieren zu können, können sich allerdings

ben Blastozyste) entwickeln sich selbstständige Zwillinge mit einer gemeinsamen Plazenta (2), nach Duplikation des *Primitivstreifens* und des Primitivknotens innerhalb einer Keimscheibe entstehen mehr oder weniger miteinander verwachsene (siamesische) Zwillinge (3). Vgl. Viebahn, in: Damschen/Schönecker, Moralischer Status, 275f.

[34] Jüngste Versuche in England haben gezeigt, dass es möglich ist, embryonale Stammzellen zu gewinnen, ohne den Embryo zu zerstören. Dabei ist dem Embryo bereits in der Morula-Phase (wenn der Embryo aller Wahrscheinlichkeit nach aus totipotenten Zellen besteht) eine Zelle entnommen worden, aus der sich fast unbegrenzt neue Zellen herstellen ließen. Dieses Verfahren wird in Deutschland aber nicht angewandt, weil die Forschung an (und die Zerstörung von) totipotenten Zellen nach dem Embryonenschutzgesetz und dem Stammzellgesetz verboten ist.

nach Verlust ihrer Totipotenz nicht eigenständig als Embryonen weiterentwickeln und eine Plazenta ausbilden. Je nach den im Experiment verwendeten Wachstumsfaktoren behalten die Zellen ihre ursprüngliche Pluripotenz oder bilden aufgrund ihrer Plastizität Strukturen einer bestimmten Form (z.B. Blutzellen, Nervenzellen etc.) aus. Wegen ihrer immensen Flexibilität und Plastizität haben diese Zellen offenkundig ein großes Potential für die Forschung, aber auch für mögliche Therapien von degenerativen Erkrankungen und werden ihrer Herkunft wegen als embryonale Stammzellen (ES) oder humane embryonale Stammzellen (HES) bezeichnet.

- **Fetale Stammzellen** werden aus Embryonen nach Schwangerschaftsabbruch aus den angelegten Keimzellen der Föten (primordiale Keimzellen), also den Vorläuferzellen von Eizellen und Spermazellen, isoliert. Bei einer Kultivierung verhalten sich diese Zellen wie embryonale pluripotente Stammzellen, sind aber deswegen nicht leicht zu gewinnen, weil es sich bei den Föten nach Schwangerschaftsabbruch um totes Gewebe handelt, aus dem sie isoliert werden. Zu ihrer Gewinnung werden allerdings keine Embryonen „verbraucht".
- **Nabelschnur- und Plazentastammzellen,** die nach der Geburt aus dem Gewebe der Nabelschnur bzw. der Plazenta isoliert werden, haben nicht das Potential von embryonalen Stammzellen, sind aber verhältnismäßig leicht zu gewinnen. Aufgrund ihrer bereits vorliegenden Differenzierung können sie nicht mehr als pluripotent gelten. Darüber hinaus sind Stammzellen auch aus dem Fruchtwasser zu isolieren, wobei aber auch diese nicht als totipotent oder pluripotent, sondern (meist) als „multipotent" bezeichnet werden. Ihr Differenzierungspotential weist sie als adulte Stammzellen aus.
- **Adulte Stammzellen** sind in allen (geborenen) Menschen zu finden. Ihre Gewinnung ist nicht immer unkompliziert, und ihr Differenzierungsvermögen ist nicht in dem Maße ausgeprägt wie bei embryonalen Stammzellen, aber sie werden für Therapien wie Knochenmarktransplantationen bereits seit langem genutzt. Die im Jahr 2002 aus Knochenmarkzellen gewonnenen multipotenten adulten Progenitorzellen weisen ein ähnliches Differenzierungspotential auf, das bisher nur von embryonalen Stammzellen bekannt war. Der Vorteil von adulten gegenüber embryonalen Stammzellen besteht – neben den ethischen Vorteilen – vor allem darin, dass bei der Therapie mit körpereigenen adulten Stammzellen keine Abstoßungsreaktionen zu erwarten sind, die es bei der Verwendung von embryonalen Stammzellen ebenso geben kann wie bei jedem anderen transplantierten Gewebe. Darüber hinaus bergen adulte Stammzellen weniger das Risiko, canzerogen zu wirken als die in dieser Hinsicht deutlich aktiveren embryonalen Stammzellen, die relativ leicht zu Tumorzellen entarten können.

2007 ist es zwei Forschergruppen[35] unabhängig voneinander gelungen, aus adulten Hautzellen Stammzellen zu gewinnen und diese so zu reprogammieren, dass sie ähnliche Eigenschaften besitzen wie embryonale Stammzellen, ohne dass dafür Embryonen zerstört werden mussten. Diese Stammzellen werden als *induzierte pluripotente Stammzellen* bezeichnet und könnten ein Lösungspotential für die technischen, immunologischen und ethischen Probleme beim Gebrauch von embryonalen Stammzellen bieten.[36] Die Erfolge, die in diesem Zusammenhang erzielt werden konnten, wären ohne die Forschung an embryonalen Stammzellen als Vergleichsmaterial allerdings unter Umständen nicht möglich gewesen, wie von Befürwortern der embryonalen Stammzellforschung immer wieder betont wird.

Die Gewinnung, Kultivierung und therapeutische Nutzung von adulten Stammzellen wird im internationalen Vergleich übereinstimmend gestattet. Die weiteren Ausführungen dieses Buches konzentrieren sich demgegenüber auf den ethisch hoch umstrittenen und im Ländervergleich rechtlich unterschiedlich geregelten Umgang mit embryonalen humanen Stammzellen,

---

[35] Die Forschergruppen waren in Wisconsin, USA, und Kyoto, Japan, angesiedelt. Die entsprechenden Veröffentlichungen finden sich in *Science* und *Cell* (beide aus dem Jahr 2007).

[36] Die zunächst von japanischen und amerikanischen Forschern erfolgreich durchgeführte Erzeugung von induzierten Stammzellen ist inzwischen auch deutschen Forschern gelungen, die das Verfahren noch vereinfachen konnten. Vgl. einen Artikel in der *Frankfurter Allgemeinen Zeitung* (FAZ) vom 30. Juni 2008. Die sich ständig selbst überholende und sich in rasantem Tempo verändernde Forschung an embryonalen, adulten und induzierten pluripotenten Stammzellen kann ich in diesem Zusammenhang nicht detailgenau darstellen. Ich verweise dafür auf die medizinische Fachliteratur, etwa im *New England Journal for Medicine*, in dem die Forschung ausführlich dokumentiert wird, aber auch auf die überregionale Tagespresse. Hilfreich ist das *Journal Watch*, in dem Ergebnisse aus in medizinischen Fachzeitschriften publizierten Studien zusammengestellt werden. Im Herbst 2008 ist von Fortschritten in der Erzeugung von induzierten pluripotenten Stammzellen aus Hautzellen von älteren Patientinnen berichtet worden, die in Hirnzellen umprogrammiert werden konnten. Solchen Forschungen an menschlichen Zellen gingen erfolgreiche Forschungen an tierischen Zellen voraus: 2007 berichtete Journal Watch von erfolgreichen Studien an adulten Mäusezellen. Im März 2009 konnte das Verfahren von Forschern in Edinburgh und Toronto nochmals verbessert werden, indem die in die Zelle zur Reprogrammierung eingeschleusten Gene nicht mit Viren, sondern mit der „Piggyback-Technik“ in die Zellen verbracht wurden, was ihre Entfernung ermöglichte und die Gefahr einer Entartung der Zelle zu einer Krebszelle verminderte. Mit diesen viel versprechenden Forschungserfolgen verbinden sich allerdings noch zahlreiche ungeklärte Grundsatzfragen, was die Pluripotenz und das Verhalten der so erzeugten induzierten Stammzellen betrifft. Von diesem Erfolg berichtet auch das Deutsche Ärzteblatt, Jg. 106, Heft 11, vom 13.3.2009, S. C 404.

der in der obigen Darstellung den zuerst genannten Bereich umfasst.[37] Die ethische Umstrittenheit ergibt sich dabei aus der Tatsache, dass embryonale Stammzellen meist unter Zerstörung von Embryonen gewonnen werden.

Für die Gewinnung von embryonalen Stammzellen ist entweder die Spende von *in vitro* erzeugten Embryonen erforderlich, die bei einer IVF-Behandlung übrig geblieben sind und nicht zur Herbeiführung einer Schwangerschaft in den Uterus implantiert worden sind („überzählige Embryonen"), oder die Verwendung von Embryonen, die eigens zu Forschungszwecken erzeugt worden sind. Dieser Unterschied in der Gewinnung von embryonalen Stammzellen, der sich durch die Verwendung von *überzähligen* Embryonen und von *eigens erzeugten* Embryonen ergibt, wird ethisch unterschiedlich beurteilt und im Ländervergleich rechtlich unterschiedlich gehandhabt.

Nach der Bioethik-Konvention von Oviedo (1997) und der Gesetzgebung zahlreicher europäischer Länder ist eine Erzeugung von Embryonen zu Forschungszwecken nicht gestattet, weil dies der Selbstzwecklichkeit von menschlichen Wesen widerspricht. Geforscht werden darf danach lediglich an überzähligen Embryonen nach IVF. Großbritannien erlaubt demgegenüber unter den Auflagen und Regulierungen einer staatlichen Kontrollbehörde (*Human Fertilisation and Embryology Authority*, HFEA) auch die Erzeugung von Embryonen zu Forschungszwecken, wobei sowohl Eizellen als auch Samenzellen gespendet sein müssen, um sicherzustellen, dass keine Kommerzialisierung in diesem Bereich stattfindet.

Ein weiterer Weg zur Gewinnung von humanen embryonalen Stammzellen ist neben der klassischen Erzeugung von Embryonen *in vitro* der Transfer eines (adulten) Zellkerns in eine entkernte Eizelle zum Zweck der Erzeugung eines Embryos und der Gewinnung von embryonalen Stammzellen, ein Vorgang, der auch als somatischer Zellkerntransfer bezeichnet wird: in eine entkernte Eizelle wird keine Samenzelle eingebracht, sondern der Kern einer adulten menschlichen Zelle (meist einer Hautzelle), welcher die genetische Information im zweifachen Chromosomensatz der adulten Zelle transportiert. Der so entstehende Embryo ist mit dem Spender der adulten Zelle genetisch zum allergrößten Teil identisch: die DNA des adulten Zellkerns entspricht der DNA des Zellkerns der sich entwickelnden Zelle. Lediglich die DNA der von der entkernten Eizelle bereitgestellten Mitochondrien unterscheidet sich von der DNA des eingebrachten Zellkerns. Diese Differenz wird als 0,5–1% beziffert.

Aufgrund des strikten Verbots, menschliche Eizellen zu kaufen und zu verkaufen, kommt es aber auch in der britischen Forschung zu einer Knapp-

[37] Die Informationsseiten der Deutschen Forschungsgemeinschaft (DFG) haben Schaubilder ins Internet gestellt, die über die Gewinnung von Stammzellen informieren: http://www.dfg.de/aktuelles_presse/themen_dokumentationen/stammzellen/was_sind_stammzellen.html.

heit an für die Forschung zur Verfügung stehenden Eizellen. Bei dem Verfahren des Zellkerntransfers, das bei der Verwendung von *menschlichen* Eizellen auch als „therapeutisches Klonen“ oder „Forschungsklonen“ bezeichnet wird, können aber nicht nur rein menschliche Embryonen hergestellt werden.[38] Ebenso können *tierische* Eizellen entkernt werden und einen menschlichen Zellkern erhalten, so dass die Mitochondrien der Zelle zwar tierischen Ursprungs sind, der allergrößte Teil der genetischen Information der Zelle aber von dem humanen Zellkern stammt. Dieser Vorgang scheint vor allem deswegen viel versprechend zu sein, weil er der Knappheit von menschlichen Eizellen entgegenwirkt. Mit diesem Verfahren werden Embryonen erzeugt, die zu einem sehr großen Teil menschlich sind;[39] sie werden in der englischsprachigen Debatte als „human-animal admixed embryos“,[40] „cytoplasmic embryos“ oder kurz „Cybrids“ benannt.[41]

Damit unterscheidet sich die Technik sowohl des „therapeutischen“ als auch des „reproduktiven“ Klonens nur insofern von der Technik zur Erzeugung von Cybrid-Embryonen, als erstere eine menschliche, letztere einen tierische entkernte Eizelle verwendet. Die Erzeugung von Hybrid-Embryonen ist in der jüngsten parlamentarischen Debatte von beiden britischen Häusern genehmigt worden, 2008 ist von einem Forscherteam in Newcastle un-

---

[38] Zur Frage nach dem Klonen vgl. die Studie von J. Clausen, Biotechnische Innovationen verantworten: Das Beispiel Klonen, Darmstadt 2006.

[39] Mit der Mischung von tierischem und menschlichem Material fallen diese Embryonen in die Gruppe der „Hybride“ oder „Chimären“. Zur Unterscheidung von Hybrid- und Chimären-Embryonen vgl. P. Reuter, Springer Lexikon Medizin, Berlin u. a. 2004, 348; 958. Danach zeichnen sich Hybride durch die Abstammung von genetisch unterschiedlichen Eltern aus, während Chimären eine DNA aus unterschiedlichen Spezies aufweisen. In der Debatte werden die Begriffe nicht immer sauber getrennt. In der britischen Debatte wird über die oben genannte Unterscheidung noch zwischen „true hybrids“ und „cybrids“ unterschieden. *True hybrids* bezeichnen ein Produkt einer Kreuzung zwischen zwei verschiedenen Arten: eine Eizelle wird mit einer Samenzelle befruchtet, deren Spender einer anderen Art angehört. *Cybrids* hingegen werden mit der Technik des somatischen Zellkerntransfers erzeugt, und ihre DNA besteht zu etwa 99 % aus den genetischen Informationen des in die entkernte Eizelle gebrachten adulten Zellkerns. Die DNA der Mitochondrien wird von der entkernten Eizelle bereit gestellt. Vgl. auch A. Sutton, Christian Bioethics. A Guide for the Perplexed, London 2008, 109ff.

[40] Die „human-animal admixed hybrids“ sind in diesem Zusammenhang der Oberbegriff für *Cybrids*, bei denen nur die Mitochondrien tierischen Ursprungs sind, und *true hybrids*, die aufgrund der Kernverschmelzung einer menschlichen und einer tierischen Keimzelle entstehen.

[41] Ein Schaubild zur Erzeugung von cytoplasmischen Hybriden findet sich in dem Bericht der HFEA (Human Fertilisation and Embryologie Authority) zur Frage nach Hybrid- und Chimären-Embryonen (2007).
Vgl. http://www.hfea.gov.uk/en/1517.html#report.

ter großer Beachtung der Öffentlichkeit der erste „admixed embryo" aus der entkernten Eizelle einer Kuh und dem Zellkern einer menschlichen Hautzelle erzeugt worden.

Im Anschluss an die Darstellung der embryonalen Entwicklung innerhalb der ersten 14 Tage und der Gewinnung von humanen embryonalen Stammzellen referiert der nun folgende berichtende Teil, wie sich die britische und deutsche Gesetzgebung in dieser Frage entwickelt haben und welche gesellschaftlichen, parlamentarischen und politischen Debatten ihnen vorhergegangen sind.

II. 3 Die Entwicklung der Gesetzgebung zur Embryonenforschung in England und Deutschland

Während in der deutschen Gesetzgebung der fast frühest mögliche Zeitpunkt gewählt worden ist, ab dem die Schutzwürdigkeit des Embryo vom Recht gewährt wird,[42] hat die britische Gesetzgebung demgegenüber mit der Grenze des 14. Tages nach der Kernverschmelzung einen späteren Zeitpunkt gesetzt. Im folgenden Abschnitt stelle ich die Entwicklung der englischen und deutschen Gesetzgebung im Ländervergleich dar. Dabei konzentriere ich mich neben der Berichterstattung auf die Frage, welche *Gründe* zu dieser Entscheidung geführt haben.

II. 3. 1 Der Umgang mit menschlichen Embryonen in England. Die gegenwärtige Gesetzgebung und ihre Geschichte

Der 14. Tag nach der Kernverschmelzung spielt für die britische Gesetzgebung eine zentrale Rolle für die Begründung des Lebensschutzes: Bis zu dieser Grenze dürfen nach englischem Recht Embryonen zu Forschungszwecken verwendet und auch eigens erzeugt werden, wobei zum einen diese Forschung der Aufsicht einer Regelungsbehörde, der *Human Fertilisation and Embryology Authority* (HFEA) unterliegt und Embryonen, an denen geforscht worden ist, zum anderen nicht zur Herbeiführung einer Schwangerschaft implantiert werden dürfen.

Das entsprechende Gesetz, die *Human Fertilisation and Embryology Act* (zuerst 1990) rezipiert vor allem den später so genannten 1984 vorgelegten „Warnock-Report", in dem eine Kommission unter dem Vorsitz von Lady Mary Warnock nach der erstmals erfolgreichen Zeugung eines Embryo *in*

---

[42] Ein noch früherer Zeitpunkt wäre das Eindringen des Spermiums in die Eizelle, mit dem ein Eindringen anderer Spermien ausgeschlossen wird. Dieses Stadium noch vor der Verschmelzung der Vorkerne ist aber noch nicht der *Beginn* des genetisch eigenständigen Individuums, sondern dessen *Voraussetzung*, weswegen auch mit diesem Zeitpunkt in der deutschen Diskussion nicht argumentiert wird.

vitro (1978) nach Regelungen gesucht hatte, wie mit extrakorporal erzeugten menschlichen Embryonen zu einem sehr frühen Zeitpunkt kurz nach der Kernverschmelzung umzugehen ist. Die britische Gesetzgebung hat von der Präsentation des Warnock-Reports bis zur Verabschiedung der *Human Fertilisation and Embryology Act* eine weit reichende Wendung genommen. Vor einer Darstellung dieser Entwicklung zeigt die folgende Übersicht zunächst überblicksartig die Chronologie bei der Gesetzgebung[43] zur Forschung an humanen embryonalen Stammzellen in Großbritannien.[44]

Juli 1978 Geburt von Louise Brown, dem weltweit ersten *in vitro* gezeugten Menschen in England. Mit der ersten gelungenen *in vitro*-Befruchtung eröffnet sich allererst die Möglichkeit, an im Labor erzeugten menschlichen Embryonen zu forschen und diese auch zu Forschungszwecken zu erzeugen.
Juli 1984 *Report of the Committee of Inquiry into Human Fertilisation and Embryology* unter dem Vorsitz von Lady Mary Warnock (Warnock-Report) im Auftrag der Regierung zur Erarbeitung einer Gesetzesvorlage.
November 1990 Verabschiedung eines Gesetzes zum Umgang mit menschlichen Embryonen: *Human Fertilisation and Embryology Act*, die sich weitgehend an den Warnock-Report anschließt.
August 1991 Einsetzung der Regelungsbehörde zur Forschung an menschlichen Embryonen: *Human Fertilisation and Embryology Authority* (HFEA).
1998 Weltweit erste Kultivierung von humanen embryonalen Stammzellen aus Embryonen nach IVF in Wisconsin, USA.
Januar 2001 *The Human Fertilisation and Embryology (Research Purposes) Regulations* für den bis dahin gesetzlich nicht geregelten Umgang mit embryonalen Stammzellen als Ergänzung zur *Human Fertilisation and Embryology Act.*
Dezember 2001 Verabschiedung der *Human Reproductive Cloning Act*: ausdrückliches Verbot von reproduktivem Klonen an Menschen, explizite Erlaubnis von „Forschungsklonen".
Februar 2002 Report of the House of Lords Select Committee on Stem Cell Research zur Erarbeitung eines eigenen Stammzellgesetzes.
November 2004 Verabschiedung der *Human Tissue Act.*
August 2005 Veröffentlichung der *Government's Review of the Human Fertilisation and Embryology Act: a public consultation* zur Überarbeitung der *Human Fertilisation and Embryology Act* als Reaktion auf die immensen Forschungsfortschritte in diesem Bereich, vor allem hinsichtlich der embryonalen Stammzellforschung.

---

[43] Die Entwicklung der britischen Gesetzgebung ist im Internet ausgezeichnet dokumentiert. Unter www.opsi.gov.uk finden sich die verabschiedeten und in Kraft getretenen Gesetzestexte; die Gesetzesentwürfe sowie die Debatten sind unter www.parliament.uk verzeichnet.

[44] Wesentliche Erkenntnisse verdanke ich dem Bericht von Michael Mulkay, The embryo research debate. Science and the politics of reproduction, Cambridge 1997.

März 2006 Veröffentlichung einer unabhängigen Zusammenfassung von öffentlichen und nichtstaatlichen Erwiderungen auf die *Review of the Human Fertilisation and Embryology Act: a public consultation.*

März 2006 Verabschiedung der *Human Tissue Act* (Scotland).

Dezember 2006 Veröffentlichung eines Gesetzentwurfs der britischen Regierung für ein erneuertes Embryonengesetz in Reaktion auf den Forschungsfortschritt: *Review of the Human Fertilisation and Embryology Act: proposals for revised legislation (including establishment of the Regulatory Authority for Tissue and Embryos,* RATE), Vorschlag einer gemeinsamen Behörde zum Umgang mit menschlichen Embryonen und mit menschlichem Gewebe.

März 2007 *House of Commons Science and Technology Committee Report*: Vorschläge für den rechtlichen Umgang mit Hybrid- und Chimären-Embryonen.

Juli 2007 Human Fertilisation and Embryology (Quality and Safety) Regulations.

Herbst 2007 Diskussion über ein neues Gesetz zur Forschung an Embryonen; der Plan, *eine* Aufsichtsbehörde für Embryologie und menschliches Gewebe (*Regulatory Authority for Tissue and Embryos,* RATE) zu schaffen, wird wieder fallen gelassen.

Januar 2008 Die britischen Lords beschließen mit einer Zweidrittelmehrheit, dass Embryonen aus menschlichen und tierischen Anteilen (Hybrid- und Chimären-Embryonen) gesetzlich zulässig sein sollen, um dem Engpass von menschlichen Eizellen entgegenzuwirken.

März 2008 Der erste Embryo aus einem menschlichen Zellkern und einer entkernten tierischen Eizelle wird an der Universität Newcastle erzeugt.

April 2008 Das britische Unterhaus diskutiert den Gesetzentwurf des neuen Embryonengesetzes (*Human Fertilisation and Embryology Bill*), das unter anderem die Erzeugung von menschlich-tierischen Mischembryonen erlaubt und zugleich rechtliche Neuregelungen für den Schwangerschaftsabbruch enthält. Dem Gesetzentwurf wird in zweiter Lesung zugestimmt. Eine dritte Lesung folgt im Herbst 2008.

13.11.2008 Die Queen unterzeichnet die HFE Bill mit den Ergänzungen aus den parlamentarischen Debatten; die Bill tritt als neue HFE Act in Kraft.

Das Jahr 1978 stellt in der biotechnologischen Forschung einen immensen Einschnitt dar.[45] Denn mit der weltweit ersten Geburt eines Babys, das in England *in vitro* gezeugt, anschließend in einen Uterus implantiert und ge-

[45] Die Vorgeschichte des Beginns der englischen Forschung an menschlichen Embryonen, die schließlich in der ersten erfolgreichen In-vitro-Fertilisation mündete, ist maßgeblich von einer Liberalisierung der Gesetzgebung zum Schwangerschaftsabbruch geprägt. Mit der Verabschiedung und dem Inkrafttreten der *Abortion Act* 1967 unter der liberaleren Labour-Regierung verbindet sich eine grundsätzliche Liberalisierung der Sexualethik, und auch wenn keine direkte Verbindung zwischen den Forschern, die seit den späten 60er Jahren an einer Möglichkeit der Befruchtung außerhalb des Mutterleibs für kinderlose unfruchtbare Paare und der den Schwangerschaftsabbruch befürwortenden Lobby gezogen werden kann, kam diese Gesetzgebung auch der Entwicklung der IVF zugute.

boren wurde, eröffnete sich für die Embryonenforschung eine Reihe von neuen Möglichkeiten, die zunächst vor allem in zweierlei Hinsicht formuliert wurden:

- die Aussicht, aufgrund der Forschung an Embryonen ungewollt kinderlosen Paaren zu helfen, ein Kind zu bekommen,
- dann auch die Aussicht, mit Hilfe der Embryonenforschung genetische Erkrankungen bei Embryonen zu erkennen und zu vermeiden, sowie die Vorgänge innerhalb der Schwangerschaft besser zu verstehen und Anomalien besser behandeln zu können.

Eine über die Schwangerschaft hinausgehende Forschung ist mit der Möglichkeit der Erzeugung von Embryonen *in vitro* in den auf das Jahr 1978 folgenden Jahren zunächst noch nicht impliziert. Dabei ist angesichts neuer Möglichkeiten der Forschung aber zugleich die ethische Problematik einer Forschung an menschlichen Wesen in einem frühest möglichen Stadium gesehen worden. Die Bedenken, die gegen die IVF und ihre Implikationen für die weitere Forschung geäußert wurden, sahen diese Entwicklung zum einen als zu schnell und zu weitgehend, zum anderen als eine Bedrohung der Menschenwürde an.[46]

Aufgrund größter moralischer Vorbehalte gegenüber der Forschung an menschlichen Embryonen hat die britische konservative Regierung unter Margaret Thatcher[47] darum in den frühen 80er Jahren eine Kommission unter dem Vorsitz der Ethikerin Lady Mary Warnock ins Leben gerufen, die die ethischen Implikationen der Embryonenforschung klären und der Regierung Vorschläge für die Gesetzgebung in dieser Frage machen sollte.[48]

Der 1984 dem Parlament präsentierte Report der Warnock-Kommission beschäftigt sich auf diesem Hintergrund mit dem Umgang mit Unfruchtbarkeit, der zunächst im Fokus der Forschung an außerhalb des Mutterleibs erzeugten Embryonen stand. Darüber hinaus aber ist bereits die Frage nach der ethischen Zulässigkeit von Embryonenforschung als solcher im Blick, weil,

---

[46] So das Votum von Lord Campbell am 9. Juli 1982 im House of Lords: „My Lords, will my noble friend the Minister agree that without safeguards and serious study of safeguards, this new technique [IVF] could imperil the dignity of the human race, threaten the welfare of children, and destroy the sanctity of family life?" (Zitiert nach Mulkay, a.a.O., 16.)

[47] Der Regierungswechsel fand 1979 statt. Der gesellschaftliche Druck der Pro-Life-Allianz auch im Zusammenhang von Embryonenforschung, Schwangerschaftsabbruch und IVF hatte – gewiss als ein Faktor neben weiteren – dazu geführt, dass sich das politische Klima zur konservativen Seite hin neigte. Vgl. dazu den Bericht von Mulkay, a.a.O., 12ff.

[48] Der Report ist 1984 publiziert und damit sowohl dem Parlament als auch der Öffentlichkeit zugänglich gemacht worden: *Report of the Committee of Inquiry into Human Fertilisation and Embryology*, London 1984.

wie der Report schon Anfang der 80er Jahre feststellt, mit der Ermöglichung von IVF zugleich die Möglichkeit eröffnet worden ist, „that human embryos might be brought into existence which might have no chance to implant because they were not transferred to a uterus and hence no chance to be born as human beings. This inevitably led to an examination of the moral rights of the embryo."[49] Die entscheidende Frage, die der Report klären musste, war aus diesem Grund die Frage nach dem *moralischen Status* von menschlichen Embryonen.

Der Warnock-Report konnte sich in dieser Frage nicht zu einer eindeutigen Antwort durchringen: Während der moralische Status von *geborenen* Menschen für die Mitglieder der Warnock-Kommission unstrittig ist, wird für den Umgang mit Embryonen vom Bericht eine Unsicherheit angezeigt, die sich an der Tatsache äußert, dass ungeborene menschliche Wesen vom Recht anders gestellt werden als geborene, und die britische Gesetzgebung *de facto* keine Aussagen über den Umgang mit ungeborenem menschlichen Leben macht. „The human embryo *per se* has no legal status."[50] Er wird, weil er keinen rechtlichen Status hat, darum auch geborenen Menschen – Kindern oder Erwachsenen – nicht gleichgestellt, soll aber nach der Empfehlung der Warnock-Kommission einen besonderen Status und „some protection in law"[51] erhalten. In diesem Zusammenhang vermeidet der Report explizite anthropologische Aussagen und stellt fest, dass es keine sicheren Erkenntnisse darüber gibt, welchen Schutz Embryonen von Rechts wegen genießen sollten: Weil sie sich zu Menschen entwickeln, seien sie aber in ihrem besonderen Status zu respektieren.

Eine Forschung an *in vitro* erzeugten Embryonen sollte nach den Empfehlungen der Warnock-Kommission darum nur unter strengen Auflagen und durch Kontrolle geregelt erlaubt sein. Zwischen einer Position, nach der Embryonen eine *ve* Schutzwürdigkeit haben und aus diesem Grund Embryonenforschung *keinesfalls* erlaubt werden dürfe, und der Gleichsetzung von Embryonen mit anderem menschlichen Gewebe, das unbegrenzt zu Forschungszwecken verwendet werden könne, nimmt der Warnock-Report mit der Aussage, der Embryo habe einen besonderen moralischen Status und verdiene rechtlichen Schutz, eine vermittelnde Position ein. Weil er aber gleichzeitig explizite anthropologische Aussagen zum Wesen und dem Personstatus des Embryo vermeidet, kann er als pragmatische Position gekennzeichnet werden.

Bei ihren Empfehlungen zum Umgang mit Embryonen setzte die Kommission dabei die Grenze, nach der Embryonen keiner Forschung mehr unterzogen werden dürfen, sondern vielmehr zerstört werden sollen, beim 14.

---

[49] Warnock-Report, 60.

[50] Warnock-Report, 62.

[51] Warnock-Report, 63.

Tag nach der Kernverschmelzung. Mit dem Auftreten des Primitivstreifens etwa zu diesem Zeitpunkt sei die Möglichkeit der Mehrlingsbildung ausgeschlossen, so dass sich der Embryo nach diesem Zeitpunkt zweifelsfrei zum Individuum weiterentwickele.[52]

Trotz seiner Zurückhaltung bei expliziten anthropologischen Aussagen versteht der Report als ein einen Rechtsanspruch konstituierendes Kennzeichen des Menschseins darum offenbar die Individuation oder die Entwicklung als menschliches Individuum, die allererst nach dem 14. Tag mit Sicherheit angenommen werden könne. Das Argument der Schmerzvermeidung erhält darüber hinaus bei der Überlegung zur zeitlichen Grenze der Forschung an Embryonen einiges Gewicht. Der Report geht in diesem Zusammenhang davon aus, dass von einem embryonalen Schmerzempfinden vor dem Beginn der Ausprägung des zentralen Nervensystems nach etwa 22 Tagen nicht gesprochen werden könne.[53]

Damit spielen für die Festsetzung der zeitlichen Grenze für die Forschung an menschlichen Embryonen im wesentlichen drei Argumente eine Rolle, auch wenn diese im Report nicht nebeneinander stehen, sondern über die Empfehlungen des Textes verteilt sind:

- das Argument, es handele sich beim frühen Embryo um ein „potential human being",[54] das zwar nicht denselben Lebensschutz genießt wie geborene Menschen, aber doch „some protection in law"[55] erhalten soll,
- das Argument, es solle ein Zeitpunkt gewählt werden, an dem die Neuralentwicklung und damit die Fähigkeit des Embryo zur Schmerzempfindung noch nicht eingesetzt habe,
- das Argument schließlich, dass mit dem Auftreten des Primitivstreifens die Möglichkeit der Zwillingsbildung ausgeschlossen sei und an diesem Zeitpunkt die Individualentwicklung beginne. Dieses zuletzt genannte Argument hat sich als das wichtigste der drei Argumente herauskristallisiert und wird bis in die Gegenwart von der britischen Gesetzgebung vertreten.

Nachdem ein Embryo den Zeitpunkt des 14. Tages erreicht hat, soll er, wie die Kommission empfiehlt, sofern an ihm geforscht wurde, nicht mehr im-

---

[52] „As we have seen, the objection to using human embryos in research is that each one is a potential human being. One reference point in the development of the human individual is the formation of the primitive streak. Most authorities put this at about fifteen days after fertilisation. This marks the beginning of individual development of the embryo." (Warnock-Report, 66.)

[53] Vgl. Warnock-Report, 65.

[54] Warnock-Report, 66.

[55] Warnock-Report, 63.

plantiert, sondern zerstört werden.[56] In diesem Zusammenhang spricht der Warnock-Report eine doppelte Empfehlung aus: Forschung an Embryonen sollte (bis zum 14. Tag) gestattet sein, aber in engen Grenzen unter der Aufsicht einer noch einzusetzenden Kontrollbehörde erfolgen. Dabei sei die Forschung sowohl an überzähligen („spare embryos") als auch an eigens für die Forschung erzeugten Embryonen ethisch akzeptabel.[57]

In den Jahren nach der Veröffentlichung des Warnock-Reports fand in Großbritannien eine breite öffentliche Debatte über die ethische Zulässigkeit der Forschung an menschlichen Embryonen statt. Die parlamentarische Mehrheit hatte in dieser Zeit (seit 1979) die konservative Partei inne, nachdem vorher unter der Mehrheit der Labour Party das mit einigen kleineren Ergänzungen bis 2008 geltende Gesetz zum Schwangerschaftsabbruch (*Abortion Act*, 1967) verabschiedet worden war.[58] Im Zusammenhang mit der konservativen Mehrheit wurden die Empfehlungen des Warnock-Reports zur Forschung an Embryonen fast einhellig als zu liberal und zu weit gehend abgelehnt.[59] Am Ende des Jahres 1984 wurde dem Warnock-Report von einer breiten Mehrheit im Parlament in beiden Häusern und auch von Vertretern der Wissenschaft mit der Begründung widersprochen, dass Experimente an Menschen ethisch nicht zulässig seien. Eine Gesetzgebung konnte in dieser Zeit noch nicht beschlossen werden.

1985 wuchs die Ablehnung einer Forschung an menschlichen Embryonen innerhalb des Parlaments, als auf Initiative eines Abgeordneten, des konservativen Ministers Enoch Powell, mit großer Unterstützung der *Pro-Life-Lob-*

[56] „We accordingly recommend that no live human embryo derived from in vitro fertilisation, whether frozen or unfrozen, may be kept alive, if not transferred to a woman, beyond fourteen days after fertilisation, nor may it be used as a research subject beyond fourteen days after fertilisation. This fourteen day period does not include any time during which the embryo may have been frozen." (Warnock-Report, 66, im Original hervorgehoben.)

[57] Vgl. Warnock-Report, 66: „Second [nach der Möglichkeit einer Verwendung von überzähligen Embryonen], clearly it is also possible to produce embryos in vitro, using donated eggs and semen, with the sole intention of using them for research."

[58] Das Gesetz erlaubt Schwangerschaftsabbruch bis zur 24. Woche bei der Gefahr des physischen und/oder seelischen Schadens der Schwangeren und des ungeborenen Kindes. Auch eine embryopathische Indikation ist im britischen Gesetz explizit vorgesehen. Im Zusammenhang der Debatte zum Embryonen-Gesetz ist auch die Gesetzgebung zum Schwangerschaftsabbruch in die *Human Fertilisation and Embryology Bill* aufgenommen worden und innerhalb der *Human Fertilisation and Embryology Act* 2008 in Kraft getreten.

[59] „In both Houses, the few supporters of licensed research on the early human embryo were swept aside as the great majority of speakers rose to express their passionate indignation at the use of human individuals for experimental purposes and to press for the immediate cessation of these immoral activities." (Mulkay, Embryo Research, 23.)

by[60] und einer Reihe von Parlamentariern dem Parlament ein Gesetzentwurf vorgelegt wurde, der einen weit reichenden pränatalen Lebensschutz vorsah (*Unborn Children Protection Bill*). Die Abstimmung über diesen Gesetzentwurf erfolgte ohne Parteienzwang als Gewissensabstimmung, wobei aber die konservative Regierung unter Margaret Thatcher deutlich vertrat, dass eine zukünftige Gesetzgebung die Empfehlungen des Warnock-Reports nicht gänzlich ablehnen solle.[61] Die *Unborn Children Protection Bill* konnte in der parlamentarischen Debatte keine Mehrheit finden.

Eine allmähliche Öffnung der Debatte gegenüber den Empfehlungen der Warnock-Kommission lässt sich vor allem an begrifflichen Akzentverschiebungen feststellen. 1986 wurde von Seiten der Forschung der Begriff „Prä-Embryo"[62] in Abgrenzung zum von der Pro-Life-Lobby verwendeten Term der „ungeborenen Kinder" eingeführt und stieß zunächst wie der Bericht der Warnock-Kommission auf Ablehnung weiter Teile des Parlaments.[63] *Prä-Embryo* sollte den Embryo vor dem 14. Tag bezeichnen, der noch das Potential in sich trägt, sich zu Zwillingen zu entwickeln und noch keine sichtbaren Strukturen aufweist, die auf die weitere embryonale Entwicklung schließen lassen. *Prä-Embryo* bezeichnete den im Labor erzeugten Embryo, der – anders als in der Darstellung der Gegner der Embryonenforschung – eben noch kein „ungeborenes Kind" und sogar noch nicht einmal ein Embryo, sondern nur dessen Vorstufe sei, der zwar das Potential zum Menschen in sich trage, an dem aber aufgrund seines „Prä-Status" geforscht werden könne.

---

[60] Die Pro-Life-Allianz spielt bis in die Debatte zur HFE-Bill der Gegenwart noch eine Rolle. Vgl. die Seite http://hfebill.org der parteienübergreifenden *Pro-Life-Group* innerhalb des britischen Parlaments.

[61] Diese Position der britischen Regierung wurde deutlich in einem Regierungspapier zum Ausdruck geracht, das die Regierung in die parlamentarische Debatte einbrachte, nachdem die *Unborn Children Protection Bill* zweimalig vom House of Commons abgelehnt worden war. *Gegen* dieses Regierungspapier ist von der Anti-Forschungslobby eine Kampagne unter dem Titel „Upholding Human Dignity: Ethical Alternatives to Embryo Research" begonnen worden. Zu dieser Zeit hatte aber die Forschungslobby ebenfalls eine Kampagne gestartet, die die *Vorteile* und das *Potential* der Embryonenforschung innerhalb der öffentlichen Debatte vertrat.

[62] „Both Progress and the Voluntary Licensing Authority had decided to replace the word 'embryo' with 'pre-embryo' when referring to the human organism during the period of approximately two weeks between fertilization and the emergence of the first structural features. This new terminology was intended to help undermine their opponents' use of the phrase 'unborn children' and to convey to lay people that the potential subjects of laboratory experiment were not even proper human embryos." (Mulkay, a.a.O., 31.)

[63] Vgl. Mulkay, a.a.O., 30. Von einem Parlamentarier ist der Begriff „pre-embryo" danach als „Humpty Dumpty word" bezeichnet worden, das nichts zur Klärung der Debatte um eine neue Gesetzgebung beitragen könne.

Im weiteren Prozess der Gesetzesfindung zur Forschung an Embryonen in der zweiten Hälfte der 80er Jahre veröffentlichte die Thatcher-Regierung einen Gesetzentwurf (*White Paper*), der – reagierend auf die Dissense in der parlamentarischen und öffentlichen Debatte – in der Beschränkung der Forschung an menschlichen Embryonen deutlich weiter ging als der Warnock-Report und sich explizit auf die Befürchtungen bezog, Embryonenforschung könne zu genetischer Züchtung und Aussonderung von Menschen führen, die von der Öffentlichkeit ausdrücklich unerwünscht seien.[64]

Während der parlamentarischen Diskussion in der Folgezeit ist gegenüber der vorsichtigeren Stellungnahme der Regierung eine Liberalisierung der öffentlichen Meinung hinsichtlich der Forschung an Embryonen zu beobachten: Unter den Bedingungen des *White Paper* und der Auflage der strengen Beschränkung der Embryonenforschung durch eine noch einzusetzende Kontrollbehörde, die auch von der Warnock-Kommission empfohlen worden war und die die unerwünschten Folgen einer Forschung an Embryonen retrospektiv einschränken und damit eine Planungssicherheit in der Frage nach der Forschung an Embryonen schaffen sollte, sprachen sich in den Debatten der folgenden Jahre bis 1990 zunehmend mehr Parlamentarier beider Häuser für eine Zulassung der Forschung an Embryonen aus.[65]

Unter dem Titel *Upholding Human Dignity: Ethical Alternatives to Embryo Research*[66] ist in dieser Zeit von Kritikern der Embryonenforschung im Zusammenhang mit der allmählichen Öffnung zugunsten der Forschung an menschlichen Embryonen ein Text *gegen* die Verabschiedung des *White Papers* als verbindliches Gesetz veröffentlicht worden. Der Entscheidungsprozess war in dieser Zeit zwar noch offen; sowohl die vorgesehenen strengen Auflagen im Gesetzentwurf als auch der schon im Warnock-Report gegebene Vorschlag der Einsetzung einer kontrollierenden Behörde motivierten aber eine Reihe von Parlamentariern, schließlich *für* eine rechtliche Zulassung der Embryonenforschung zu votieren, weil sich die Meinung durchsetzte, dass Freiheit der Forschung auf diesem Terrain um der erhofften therapeutischen Folgen willen wünschenswert sei und gleichzeitig unerwünschte Folgen kontrolliert werden könnten.

---

[64] Vgl. den Bericht bei Mulkay, a.a.O., 33ff.

[65] „The formal debates on the White Paper in January and February 1988 turned out to be more favourable to embryo research than the scientific press had expected." (Mulkay, a.a.O., 35.)

[66] Vgl. Mulkay, a.a.O., 36 und s. oben, Anm. 61. Für einen Vergleich von englischer und deutscher Gesetzgebung in dieser Frage s. auch Nicole Richardt, A Comparative Analysis of the Embryological Research Debate in Great Britain and Germany, Social Politics: International Studies in Gender, State and Society 10.1, 2003, 86–128.

Die sich in den Jahren 1989 und 1990 vollziehende Öffnung der parlamentarischen Meinung hin zu einer Zulassung der Forschung an Embryonen[67] hat schließlich zur Verabschiedung der *Human Fertilisation and Embryology Act* im Jahr 1990 geführt, die eine Forschung an menschlichen Embryonen erlaubt, soweit diese von der 1991 eingesetzten *Human Fertilisation and Embryology Authority* (HFEA) ausdrücklich genehmigt worden ist. Diese Erlaubnis impliziert auch, dass Embryonen zu Forschungszwecken erzeugt werden dürfen, wenn die HFEA zustimmt und Forscher keine überzähligen Embryonen zur Verfügung haben. Damit schließt sich die britische Gesetzgebung inhaltlich weitgehend an die Empfehlungen des Warnock-Reports an. Eine *explizite* anthropologische Aussage zum Wesen von Embryonen wird in der *Human Fertilisation and Embryology Act* ebenso vermieden wie im Report der Warnock-Kommission.

Dass sich das Blatt so überraschend eindeutig nach der einhelligen Ablehnung der Embryonenforschung in den späten 70er und bis Mitte der 80er Jahre zugunsten der Embryonenforschung Ende der 80er und Anfang der 90er Jahre gewendet hat, liegt wahrscheinlich[68] vor allem an drei Faktoren:

- Der Durchsetzung des Begriffs „pre-embryo" für Embryonen bis zum 14. Tag nach der Kernverschmelzung, die dazu geführt hat, dass Embryonen *vor* dem 14. Tag ein anderer moralischer Status zugeschrieben werden konnte als älteren Embryonen,[69] so dass sich eine Position, die

[67] Dieser Meinungswandel steht im Zusammenhang damit, dass Parlamentarier eingeladen worden sind, Kliniken zu besuchen und sich selbst von dem Potential zu überzeugen, das die Forschungslobby in der Forschung an Embryonen gesehen hat. Exemplarisch für den Meinungswandel steht folgendes Zitat eines Parlamentariers: „Over three years ago I spoke in the debate on the Warnock Report. I found it much easier then to decide what I believed to be right and wrong than I do now. Since then I have taken steps to inform myself on the exact nature of the so-called embryo research which is being done… If the research now being carried out involved the murder of a child it could not be allowed under the law; but having seen what I have seen and learned what I have learned I do not believe that it does. In fact I am inclined to the view that up until the appearance of the primitive streak the pre-embryo cannot be regarded as a human being. I also believe that abortion is wrong." (Zitiert nach N. Richardt, Comparative Analysis, 95f.)

[68] Ich folge dabei der Analyse von Mulkay, Embryo Research, 132f.

[69] Weder der Warnock-Report noch die *Human Fertilisation and Embryology Act* gebrauchen den Ausdruck explizit. Dieser ist erst nach der Fertigstellung des Warnock-Reports in der Debatte aufgekommen, wird aber vom Gesetzestext nicht rezipiert. Implizit ist er aber an der Stelle vorhanden, an der dem Embryo *nach* dem 14. Tag ein dem jüngeren Embryo gegenüber unterschiedlicher moralischer Status zugeschrieben wird. Wenn im Warnock-Report und in der Gesetzgebung dafür votiert wird, dass die Schutzwürdigkeit des Embryo erst damit beginnt, dass die Mehrlingsbildung ausgeschlossen ist, so wird damit eine implizite anthropologische Aussage gemacht, die mit dem Begriff „pre-embryo" expliziert werden kann.

Embryonenforschung unterstützte, mit einer Position vereinbaren ließ, die sich gegen Schwangerschaftsabbruch aussprach. Der frühe Embryo *in vitro* wird darüber hinaus unterschieden vom Embryo *in vivo.*
- Der gesteigerten Betonung der Möglichkeiten, die sich durch die Methodik der IVF eröffnen, genetische Krankheiten (zunächst bei Embryonen) zu diagnostizieren, zu therapieren und zu vermeiden.
- Der von der Forschungslobby gepflegten Rhetorik der *Hoffnung* auf das *Potential* einer Forschung an Embryonen gegenüber einer Rhetorik der *Furcht* vor den Folgen bei den Forschungsgegnern.

Nach dem Inkrafttreten des Gesetzes hat sich der Schwerpunkt bei der Embryonenforschung langsam, aber signifikant verschoben. Auch wenn diese zunächst mit dem Ziel im Fokus stand, Schwangerschaften besser zu verstehen und pathologische genetische Fehlentwicklungen bei Embryonen besser diagnostizieren oder behandeln zu können, hat sich seit den späten 90er Jahren mit der Entwicklung der embryonalen Stammzellforschung das Forschungsziel insofern verändert, als inzwischen die Hoffnung auf Therapie von degenerativen Erkrankungen wie Morbus Parkinson, Morbus Alzheimer, Diabetes Mellitus und Krebserkrankungen bei bereits geborenen Menschen (Kindern und Erwachsenen) im Vordergrund vor der Therapie an Ungeborenen steht.

Diesem sich in den letzten Jahren verschobenen Forschungsschwerpunkt trägt gegenwärtig (2008/2009) eine erneuerte Gesetzgebung Rechnung, nachdem bereits 2001 einige Präzisierungen zur Erforschung ernsthafter Erkrankungen nicht nur von Embryonen, sondern auch und vor allem von erwachsenen Patienten und zur Erforschung von Therapiemöglichkeiten mit Hilfe von embryonalen Stammzellen in das 1990 in Kraft getretene Gesetz eingefügt worden sind.[70]

Während die HFE Act von 1990 den Umgang mit Embryonen hinsichtlich der Frage der künstlichen Befruchtung regelt und noch keine Aussage zur Embryonenforschung zur Stammzellgewinnung macht, ist diese Erweiterung 2001 damit ausdrücklich vorgenommen worden,[71] als die Gewinnung

[70] Die entsprechende Passage lautet: „(1) The Authority [HFEA] may issue a licence for research under paragraph 3 of Schedule 2 to the Act for any of the purposes specified in the following paragraph. (2) A licence may be issued for the purposes of - (a) increasing knowledge about the development of embryos; (b) *increasing knowledge about serious disease*, or (c) enabling any such knowledge to be applied in *developing treatments for serious disease*." Der Text findet sich unter http://www.opsi.gov.uk/si/si2001/20010188.htm (Hervorhebung S.R.).

[71] „Most significantly, in 2001, regulations were introduced to extend the list of purposes for which such research could be licensed by the HFEA. Under these amendments, the use of human embryos for research was to be licensable not only for the essentially reproductive purposes as set out in the 1990 Act, but also for increasing knowledge

von embryonalen Stammzellen zur Erforschung und späteren Therapie von degenerativen Krankheit rechtlich geregelt worden ist. Eine solche Ergänzung der Gesetzgebung war im Jahr 2000 auch von dem regierungsunabhängigen Nuffield Council on Bioethics vorgeschlagen worden.[72] Der von der HFE Act 1990 intendierte Fokus der Forschung an Embryonen hat sich aufgrund der immensen Forschungsfortschritte in diesem Bereich verschoben und ist nachlaufend, die Empfehlungen der Warnock-Kommission auch nachträglich modifizierend, rechtlich angepasst worden.

Weil mit dem 1990 in Kraft getretenen und 2001 ergänzten Gesetz aber nicht alle Entwicklungen erfasst werden konnten, die mit der Forschung an *in vitro* erzeugten Embryonen zusammenhingen, hat die britische Regierung die Notwendigkeit gesehen, zu einer Revision des Gesetzes zu finden und Ende 2006 eine *Review*[73] über die *Human Fertilisation and Embryology Act* und

about the development of embryos, increasing knowledge about serious disease, and enabling any such knowledge to be applied in developing treatments for serious disease. The 2001 provisions allowed for ‚therapeutic cloning' i.e through cell nuclear replacement (CNR), the creation of an embryo by taking an egg (or oocyte) from which the nucleus had been removed, and replacing it with the nucleus of a donor cell (e.g. a human skin cell). Work such as this is designed to facilitate the production of stem cells from early-stage embryos which could be used to grow perfectly matched brain cells, blood, heart muscle and other tissue for treatment or repair in disease." (House of Commons, Science and Technology Committee, Government proposals for the regulation of hybrid and chimera embryos, 2007, 9.)

72 Nuffield Council on Bioethics, Stem cell therapy: the ethical issues. A discussion paper, Dorset 2000. „We conclude that the removal and cultivation of cells from a donated embryo does not indicate a lack of respect for the embryo. We take the view that there are no grounds for making a moral distinction between research into diagnostic methods or reproduction which is permitted under UK legislation and research into potential therapies which is not permitted. *We therefore recommend that research involving human embryos be permitted for the purpose of developing tissues to treat diseases from derived embryonic stem (ES) cells and that Schedule 2 of the Human Fertilisation and Embryology Act be amended accordingly.*" (AaO, vii.) Forschung an gespendeten Embryonen sei ethisch akzeptabel, auch wenn der Embryo dabei ein Mittel zu einem anderen Zweck werde. („This research involves using the embryo as a means to an end", in dem zitierten Diskussionspapier auf S. 13.)

73 In einer diesem Text vorangehenden zweijährigen Phase der öffentlichen Meinungsbildung fragte die Regierung, ob 1. „there is a case at present for either an extension or a reduction to the 14-day time limit for keeping an embryo; 2. research undertaken on embryos using the cell nuclear replacement technique for the purpose of studying mitochondrial diseases should be permissible in law, subject to licensing."
Darüber hinaus holte die Regierung Meinungen ein, ob folgende Dinge sinnvoll und gesellschaftlich erwünscht seien: 1. „removing the current prohibition on 'replacing a nucleus of a cell of an embryo with a nucleus taken from the cell of any person, another embryo or a subsequent development of an embryo' for research purposes, subject to licensing; 2. whether the law should permit altering the genetic structure of an

Empfehlungen für weitere Gesetzgebungen in dieser Sache veröffentlicht.[74] Grundsätzlich sollte dabei der mit der HFE Act (1990) eingeschlagene Weg weitergegangen werden, weil er sich bewährt habe. Unter die *Act* falle jeder Embryo außerhalb des Uterus, der bis zum 14. Tag nach der Befruchtung zu Forschungszwecken verwendet werden dürfe.

Diese Gesetzesempfehlung von 2006 nimmt die *Human Reproductive Cloning Act* (2001) auf und mündet in die Verabschiedung einer novellierten *Human Fertilisation and Embryology Act*, die – auch mit novellierten Regelungen zum Schwangerschaftsabbruch – 2008 in Kraft getreten ist. In dieser novellierten *Human Fertilisation and Embryology Act* sollten grundlegende Fragen rechtlich geregelt werden: die embryonale Stammzellforschung im Anschluss an die immensen Entwicklungen der Forschung in diesem Bereich inklusive der Erzeugung von cytoplasmischen Hybrid-Embryonen, darüber hinaus die Erlaubnis von mittels IVF gezeugten und mittels PID/PGD ausgewählten „Retter-Geschwistern" (*saviour siblings*), die einem schwer erkrankten Geschwisterkind etwa zur Knochenmarkstransplantation zur Verfügung stehen. Schließlich sollte über 40 Jahre nach Inkrafttreten der ersten *Abortion Act* (1967) der Schwangerschaftsabbruch neu geregelt werden, indem etwa die erlaubten Fristen für einen Schwangerschaftsabbruch dem medizinischen Fortschritt im Umgang mit frühgeborenen Kindern angepasst würden.[75]

---

embryo for research purposes, subject to licensing; 3. whether the law should permit the creation of human-animal hybrid or chimera embryos for research purposes only (subject to the limit of 14 days culture in vitro, after which the embryos would have to be destroyed); 4. whether the current list of legitimate purposes for licensed research involving embryos remains appropriate; 5. whether the purposes for which research using embryos may legitimately be undertaken should, as now, be defined in law and research projects should continue to be approved by a national body in order to ensure compliance with the law, national consistency and appropriate ethical oversight; 6. whether additional regulatory requirements should apply to the procurement and use of gametes for purposes of research; and 7. on the desirability of allowing the creation of embryos for the treatment of serious diseases (as distinct from research into developing treatments for serious diseases which is already allowed)."
(In einer Zusammenfassung durch das Science and Technology Committee des House of Commons, Government proposals for the regulation of hybrid and chimera embryos, Fifth report of session 2006/2007, 12f.)

[74] Review of the Fertilisation and Embryology Act. Proposals for revised legislation (including establishment of the Regulatory Authority for Tissue and Embryos), presented to Parliament by the Secretary of State for Health, by Command of Her Majesty, December 2006.

[75] Neben den erwähnten Aspekten beschäftigt sich die novellierte HFE Act mit dem gesetzlich nicht mehr vorgeschriebenen „need for a father" im Zusammenhang einer IVF und weiteren Detailfragen, die aufgrund der Fokussierung des Buches auf die embryonale Stammzellforschung und ihre Implikationen an dieser Stelle nicht weiter verfolgt werden. Die Frist für den erlaubten Schwangerschaftsabbruch konnte in der erneuerten

Vor allem die Klonierung und die Erzeugung von cytoplasmischen Hybriden sind für unseren Zusammenhang relevant: Um der Knappheit an menschlichen Embryonen[76] entgegenzuwirken, haben britische Forscher seit dem Ende der 90er Jahre mit dem *Cell-Nuclear-Replacement* (CNR) neue Wege gesucht, Embryonen zu erzeugen, was im Falle der Verwendung menschlicher Eizellen als („therapeutisches") Klonen bezeichnet wird, im Falle der Verwendung einer tierischen Eizelle zu cytoplasmischen Hybrid-Embryonen führt.[77] Beide Formen des CNR sind in Großbritannien inzwischen gesetzlich geregelt: die *Human Reproductive Cloning Act* (2001) regelt das therapeutische Klonen und schließt reproduktives Klonen aus, während die 2008 vorgenommenen Ergänzungen zur *Human Fertilisation and Embryology Act* die Erzeugung von tierisch-menschlichen Misch-Embryonen rechtlich regeln[78] und unter der Auflage einer Genehmigung durch die HFEA erlauben.[79]

In der Frage der Klonierung von menschlichen Zellen war England das weltweit erste Land, das Klonen rechtlich geregelt hat, wobei die Auflagen der HFEA nur bestimmte Fälle der Embryonenforschung an Klonen erlau-

HFE Act nicht von 24 auf 20 Wochen verkürzt werden; allerdings wird von zahlreichen Kliniken des britischen NHS (National Health Service) ein Abbruch jenseits der 18.-20. Woche nicht vorgenommen.

[76] Weil die *in vitro* stattfindende Befruchtung von Eizellen nicht wie in Deutschland reglementiert ist, sind in den Jahren zwischen 1995 und 2005 Schätzungen zufolge etwa 1,2 Millionen überzählige Embryonen in Großbritannien entstanden, die tiefgekühlt gelagert werden und von denen ein kleiner Teil zur Adoption und ein weiterer kleiner Teil für die Forschung freigegeben worden sind. Dass an „überzähligen" Embryonen geforscht wird, erfordert das Einverständnis (den „informed consent") der genetischen Eltern. Nach deutscher Gesetzeslage dürfen nur genau so viele Eizellen *in vitro* befruchtet werden, wie auch implantiert werden. Die Regelung findet sich im Embryonenschutzgesetz (1990) in § 1.

[77] Zum Verfahren s. oben unter II.2.2, S. 25 ff.

[78] Im 2007 veröffentlichten fünften Report des Komitees für Wissenschaft und Technologie aus dem Unterhaus empfiehlt die Regierung für die weitere Gesetzgebung die Erlaubnis zur Forschung an Hybrid- und Chimärenembryonen. House of Commons, Science and Technology Committee, Government proposals for the regulation of hybrid and chimera embryos, Fifth Report of Session 2006/2007, 3. Auch in diesem Zusammenhang ist die Grenze für die Forschung der 14. Tag nach der Befruchtung: „We find that the creation of human-animal chimera or hybrid embryos, and specifically cytoplasmic hybrid embryos, is necessary for research. However, we maintain the view of the previous Science and Technology Select Committee that development of human-animal chimera or hybrid-embryos past the 14-day stage should be prohibited and that a prohibition should be put in place on the implantation of human-animal chimera or hybrid embryos in a woman."

[79] http://www.opsi.gov.uk/acts/acts2001/20010023.htm.

ben.[80] Reproduktives Klonen, also die Klonierung von Erwachsenen wird dabei ebenso verboten wie die Implantation eines zu Forschungszwecken erzeugten Klons und schon seine Kultivierung über den 14. Tag hinaus.

Die Forschung an Hybrid-Embryonen[81] hat 2008 mit der ausdrücklichen Billigung des Parlaments einen offiziellen Status bekommen. Im Frühjahr 2008 ist ein solcher Embryo erstmalig am Stammzellforschungszentrum der Universität Newcastle erzeugt worden;[82] die Erzeugung dieser Embryonen ist im Frühjahr 2008 in zweiter Lesung diskutiert worden, und das entsprechende Gesetz ist nach der dritten Lesung im Herbst 2008 am 13. November 2008 von der Queen autorisiert worden. Das novellierte Gesetz erlaubt ausdrücklich die Erzeugung von „human-aninmal admixed embryos", sowohl als „cybrids" als auch als „true hybrids".[83] Verboten ist nach dem Gesetz allerdings ein Wachstum dieser Hybriden über den 14. Tag bzw. das Auftreten des Primitivstreifens hinaus, eine

[80] House of Commons, im angegebenen Report, 2007, 10: „Under the current law, research must relate to one or more of the following purposes:
1. to promote advances in the treatment of infertility;
2. to increase knowledge about the causes of congenital diseases;
3. to increase knowledge about the causes of miscarriage;
4. to enhance knowledge in the development of more effective contraception;
5. detection of genetic or chromosomal abnormalities before implantation;
6. to increase knowledge about the development of embryos;
7. to increase knowledge about serious disease; or
8. to enable any such knowledge to be applied in developing treatment for serious desease."

[81] Schon seit mehreren Jahren erlaubt (und in der deutschen Debatte eher unbekannt) ist neben der Erzeugung von Hybriden der „hamster egg test", bei dem menschliche Spermazellen im Zusammenhang einer IVF in eine Hamstereizelle verbracht werden, um ihre Qualität zu prüfen.

[82] Auch wenn die Lizenzierung der Erzeugung eines „Cybrids" im Januar 2008 erfolgte, werden *admixed embryos* zum jetzigen Zeitpunkt aber vor allem deswegen nicht erzeugt, weil die Finanzierung nicht gesichert ist.

[83] In der entsprechenden Passage der HFE Act (2008) findet sich eine Definition dessen, was ein „admixed embryo" ist: „(6) For the purposes of this Act a human admixed embryo is – (a) an embryo created by replacing the nucleus of an animal egg or of an animal cell, or two animal pronuclei, with – (i) two human pronuclei, (ii) one nucleus of a human gamete or of any other human cell, or (iii) one human gamete or other human cell, (b) any other embryo created by using – (i) human gametes and animal gametes, or (ii) one human pronucleus and one animal pronucleus, (c) a human embryo that has been altered by the introduction of any sequence of nuclear or mitochondrial DNA of an animal into one or more cells of the embryo, (d) a human embryo that has been altered by the introduction of one or more animal cells, or (e) any embryo not falling within paragraphs (a) to (d) which contains both nuclear or mitochondrial DNA of a human and nuclear or mitochondrial DNA of an animal ('animal DNA') but in which the animal DNA is not predominant." Diese Passage ist der Schlüsseltext für die Erzeugung von Hybriden als *Cybrids* und *true hybrids*.

Implantation der Hybriden in einen tierischen oder menschlichen Uterus, sowie die Erzeugung von Hybriden ohne eine Lizenzierung durch die HFEA.[84]

Nach dieser Entwicklung hat sich eine liberale und pragmatische Gesetzgebung in Großbritannien hinsichtlich der Forschung an menschlichen Embryonen weitgehend etabliert. Auch wenn es in den Jahren nach 1990 in der britischen Öffentlichkeit Widerstände gegen die Embryonenforschung vor allem von Seiten der Pro-Life Allianz gab,[85] die eine Zurücknahme der liberalen Gesetzgebung forderte, um menschliche Embryonen von der Befruchtung an rechtlich zu schützen und verbrauchende Embryonenforschung grundsätzlich zu verbieten, hat sich die liberale Position der britischen Gesetzgebung bis in die Gegenwart auch unter der Labour-Regierung fortgesetzt und erlaubt Forschung an Embryonen, die *in vitro* durch Kernverschmelzung oder durch Klonierung bzw. CNR entstanden sind, bis zum 14. Tag nach der Befruchtung bzw. bis zum Auftreten des Primitivstreifens.[86]

Embryonale Stammzellforschung entwickelte sich in den Jahren nach 2001 zu einem hauptsächlichen Forschungsgebiet in Großbritannien mit mehreren Zentren, in denen diese Forschung vorrangig und mit einer weltweiten Führungsrolle betrieben wird. Nach einem Report der *UK Stem Cell Initiative* aus dem Jahr 2005, in dem die britische Vorreiterrolle in der embryonalen Stammzellforschung betont wird, verdoppelte die britische Regierung den Etat, der für diesen Forschungszweig in den Jahren 2006-2008 und in den Folgejahren zur Verfügung gestanden hat und stehen wird.[87]

---

[84] Dass in die Bill überhaupt die Erzeugung von „true hybrids" aufgenommen worden ist, wird weitgehend und übereinstimmend kritisch beurteilt, zumal Zellbiologen zum jetzigen Zeitpunkt die Erzeugung von *true hybrids* gar nicht intendieren. Möglicherweise handelt es sich in diesem Fall um ein vorauslaufendes Entegegenkommen der Regierung an die Forschung.

[85] Heftigen Widerspruch gab es etwa nach der Erlaubnis durch die HFEA, Föten nach Schwangerschaftsabbruch zur Stammzellgewinnung zu verwenden. Vgl. Mulkay, Embryo Research, 143ff.

[86] Dabei hat die Forschung an menschlichen Embryonen im allgemeinen einen breiten gesellschaftlichen Konsens hinter sich, um den auch in der Forschung an Hybriden geworben wird. Vgl. die Empfehlungen der HFEA aus dem April 2007: „Hybrids and Chimeras. A consultation on the ethical and social implications of creating human/animal embryos in research". In diesem Text wird ausdrücklich keine eigene Stellungnahme der HFEA oder eine Empfehlung zum weiteren Vorgehen gegeben, sondern es werden Informationen zusammengestellt und Argumente für und gegen die Erzeugung von tierisch-menschlichen Embryonen referiert. Das einführende Vorwort wirbt aber um das „Vertrauen" und die „Unterstützung" der britischen Bürger in dieser Frage: „We don't want to hold research up unnecessearily. On the contrary, we want research to prosper. But it can only do so in an environment of public support and trust, something which has a long tradition in the UK."

[87] S. http://www.advisorybodies.doh.gov.uk/uksci/. „The UKSCI vision is for the UK to consolidate its current position of strength in stem cell research and mature, over the

Zusammenfassend lässt sich folgendes feststellen: Innerhalb der am Ende eines längeren Prozesses stehenden Gesetzestexte werden explizite anthropologische Aussagen vermieden, auch wenn in den vorhergehenden Debatten etwa mit dem Begriff *pre-embryo* solche Aussagen gemacht worden sind. Dieser Befund ist auffallend, lässt aber die Folgerung zu, dass offenbar eine Mehrheitsentscheidung zur Frage nach dem Status des Embryos gefallen ist, die für die Inkraftsetzung des Gesetzes konsensbildend war. Dabei muss von einer *impliziten* Anthropologie der britischen Gesetzgebung ausgegangen werden.

Denn wenn Embryonenforschung – gleichwohl unter strenger Aufsicht durch die zuständige Behörde HFEA – bis zum 14. Tag nach der Befruchtung grundsätzlich erlaubt ist und lediglich eine Forschung jenseits des 14. Tags sowie die Implantation eines zu Forschungszwecken erzeugten und verwendeten Embryos in die Gebärmutter verboten wird, so scheint sich damit die Ansicht zu verbinden, dass es sich beim Embryo *vor* dem 14. Tag um eine Entität handelt, die zu Forschungszwecken verwendet und anschließend zerstört werden darf, dass also ein früher Embryo kein Wesen ist, dessen Recht auf Leben absolut zu schützen und nicht gegen die Hoffnung einer „hochrangigen Forschung" oder eines größeren gesellschaftlichen Nutzens abzuwägen ist. Vorsichtiger formuliert: die britischen Gesetzestexte legen nahe, dass von einer graduellen Entwicklung des Embryos *zum* Menschen ausgegangen wird, dessen Personstatus allmählich wächst, auch wenn er schon im frühen Stadium einen besonderen Respekt verlangt.

Wenn in diesem Zusammenhang der Embryo vor dem 14. Tag als „Präembryo" bezeichnet wird, so ist dabei das unterschiedliche moralische Ansehen von Embryonen und geborenen Menschen bzw. Embryonen nach dem 14. Tag besonders deutlich. Der 14. Tag mit dem Auftreten des Primitivstreifens ist schon vom Warnock-Report als zeitliche Grenze benannt worden, bis zu der eine Forschung an Embryonen gestattet werden könne, weil zu diesem Zeitpunkt deutlich werde, ob sich ein oder zwei Lebewesen aus der befruchteten Eizelle entwickeln.

Menschsein wird offenbar als sich *individuell* entwickelndes Sein verstanden, wenn der Prozess der Individuation als die kritische Grenze angesehen wird, an dem die Schutzwürdigkeit beginnt. Auf dem Hintergrund der in Abschnitt II.2.1 in Erinnerung gerufenen *kontinuierlichen* Entwicklung des Embryos stellt sich dabei allerdings die Frage, ob diese Grenze des 14. Tags nicht eine willkürliche Setzung ist,[88] in deren Hintergrund politische und

next decade, into one of the global leaders in stem cell therapy and technology." In dem Report auf der oben angegebenen Website S. 5.

[88] Die relative Willkürlichkeit des 14. Tags zeigt sich etwa im Bericht der aus dem House of Lords eingesetzten Kommission zur Stammzellforschung (2002): „If the respect to be accorded to an embryo increases as it develops, this is a gradual process

wirtschaftliche Interessen, die Sorge um nationales Forschungs-Prestige und eine pragmatische Meinungsbildung stehen und die anthropologische Grundaussage der Individuation nach dem 14. Tag erst nachträglich aufgrund des politischen Drucks durch die Forschungslobby eingefügt worden ist.

Innerhalb der Debatte um das britische Embryonengesetz ist zu beobachten, dass

- sich der Status des Embryo für die britische Gesetzgebung mit dem 14. Tag nach der Kernverschmelzung ändert,
- für die Veränderung des moralischen Status das Argument der Individuation geltend gemacht wird,
- die Hoffnung auf Therapie, Linderung oder sogar Heilung von degenerativen Erkrankungen, die für die Grundlagenforschung an embryonalen Stammzellen argumentativ herangezogen wird, den Status des frühen Embryo überwiegt,
- schließlich wirtschaftliche und Forschungsprestige-Fragen wie die internationale Anschlussfähigkeit auf dem Gebiet der Stammzellforschung für die parlamentarischen Debatten und Entscheidungen nicht unerheblich waren.

Neben dem Aspekt der Vermeidung einer anthropologischen Wesensbestimmung durch die Gesetzestexte ist der Prozess der öffentlichen Meinungs- und Gesetzesbildung in der britischen Diskussion auffallend von dem gesetzbildenden Prozess in der deutschen Debatte unterschieden. Parlamentarische Gesetzentwürfe (*Bills*) und Regierungsvorschläge zu Gesetzen (*White Papers*) werden ausführlich sowohl in der Öffentlichkeit als auch im Parlament diskutiert und müssen vor ihrer Verabschiedung einen gesellschaftlichen *common sense* hinter sich haben. Was der Mehrheitsmeinung entspricht, wird nicht rückgebunden an einen Verfassungstext, und es kann vor einem Verfassungsgericht nicht dagegen geklagt werden. Im Fall der Forschung an Embryonen verhilft die Möglichkeit einer Kontrollbehörde dazu, eventuell unerwünschte Folgen der Gesetzgebung zu vermeiden und konsensfähige Entscheidungen

---

and it may be difficult to establish precisely the point of transition from one stage to the next. The 1990 Act established 14 days as the limit for research on early embryos. Fourteen days has an objective justification insofar as it represents the stage at which the primitive streak, the precursor of the development of a nervous system, begins to appear. This limit seems to have been widely accepted, and the research done under the Act under licence from the HFEA has attracted very little criticism from those who accept the case for research on early embryos. We have received no evidence to suggest that, if research on human embryos is to continue, there should be a different limit. In point of fact the stage at which stem cells need to be extracted for research is very much earlier than that – at the blastocyst stage – when the early embryo is still smaller than a pinhead. The Committee considers that 14 days should remain the limit for research on early embryos." Der Report findet sich im Internet unter http://www.parliament.the-stationery-office.co.uk.

bei veränderten Rahmenbedingungen herbeizuführen. Dem steht eine an das Grundgesetz zurückgebundene Gesetzgebung im deutschen Kontext gegenüber.

Bevor ich kirchliche und theologische Stellungnahmen zur britischen Gesetzgebung referiere und auf die Argumentation mit dem *Menschenwürde*-Begriff innerhalb der Diskussion zum Lebensbeginn fokussiere, stelle ich die Entwicklung des deutschen Stammzellgesetzes dar, die von einer der britischen Diskussion durchaus vergleichbaren Ausgangslage ausgeht, aber andere Folgeentscheidungen getroffen hat.

II. 3. 2 Zur Entwicklung des deutschen Stammzellgesetzes

Um einen ersten Überblick zu geben, soll ähnlich wie für die britische Gesetzeslage eine Übersicht die geschichtliche Entwicklung in der deutschen Gesetzgebung darstellen.

1978 Geburt des ersten *in vitro* erzeugten Babys in England.

Beginn der 80er Jahre Einsetzung von Untersuchungsgremien zur Frage der Zulässigkeit einer Forschung an menschlichen Embryonen unter der Regierung von Helmut Kohl (wichtig und einflussreich sind vor allem die „Benda-Kommission" und die Enquete-Kommission des Deutschen Bundestages).

1986/87 Gesetzentwurf zur Frage der Forschung an menschlichen Embryonen, in dem eine streng regulierte Forschung an bei IVF überzähligen Embryonen vorgesehen ist.

1990 Embryonenschutzgesetz (ESchG), das in der Regelung über die Empfehlungen der Kommissionen hinausgeht, indem es keinen Unterschied hinsichtlich des personalen Status von frühen Embryonen und desjenigen von älteren menschlichen Wesen macht. Die Forschung an „überzähligen" Embryonen ist mit dem Gesetz ebenso unvereinbar wie die Präimplantationsdiagnostik (PID) zumindest an totipotenten Zellen, die Klonierung, die Herstellung von Hybriden und Chimären und die Erzeugung von Embryonen zu Forschungszwecken.

1998 Weltweit erstmalige Kultivierung von humanen Stammzellen aus Embryonen nach IVF in Wisconsin, USA.

2002 Inkrafttreten des Stammzellgesetzes (StZG), das eine Erzeugung von embryonalen Stammzellen in Deutschland verbietet und nur unter strengen Auflagen eine Einfuhr von Stammzelllinien gestattet, die im Ausland vor dem 1.1.2002 erzeugt worden sind. Sowohl „therapeutisches" als auch „reproduktives" Klonen bleiben explizit verboten.

November 2006 Stellungnahme der Deutschen Forschungsgemeinschaft (DFG), die aufgrund des eingeschränkten Zugriffs auf embryonale Stammzelllinien in Deutschland und deren Verunreinigung eine Abschaffung des Stichtags empfiehlt.

2007 Das 7. Forschungsrahmenprogramm der Europäischen Union unterstützt die Forschung an embryonalen Stammzellen, auch an solchen Linien, die nach dem 1. 1. 2002 erzeugt worden sind. Deutsche Forscher sind nach geltendem Recht von dieser Forschung ausgeschlossen, die Forschung wird aber aufgrund der EU-Anbindung auch mit deutschen Geldern finanziert.

Ende Dezember 2007 Der EKD-Ratsvorsitzende Wolfgang Huber hält eine einmalige Verschiebung des Stichtags im Stammzellgesetz für ethisch akzeptabel.

April 2008 Nach längerer gesellschaftlicher Debatte beschließt der Deutsche Bundestag eine einmalige Verschiebung des Stichtags im Stammzellgesetz: es dürfen fortan Stammzelllinien nach Deutschland eingeführt werden, die vor dem 1.5.2007 erzeugt worden sind.

21.8.2008 Das Gesetz mit der verschobenen Stichtagsregelung tritt in Kraft.

Ähnlich wie in England hat auch in Deutschland mit der Geburt des ersten extrakorporal gezeugten Babys im Jahr 1978 eine breite Diskussion um den Umgang mit menschlichen Embryonen eingesetzt, die zunächst im Embryonenschutzgesetz (1990) und später im Stammzellgesetz (2002) ihren gesetzlichen Ausdruck fand.[89]

Das Embryonenschutzgesetz impliziert im Unterschied zur britischen *Human Fertilisation and Embryology Act* für den frühen Embryo schon vor dem 14. Tag nach der Befruchtung Personstatus und verbietet alle Handlungen am Embryo, die diesen Personstatus missachten.[90] Erlaubt ist lediglich eine Erzeugung von Embryonen, die dem Herbeiführen einer Schwangerschaft dient;[91] Hybrid- und Chimärenbildungen werden 1990 ebenso verboten wie die Klonierung.[92] Dabei wird im Embryonenschutzgesetz für jede totipotente Zelle definiert,[93] sie sei als Embryo anzusehen, weil sie sich, wenn sie isoliert weiter wächst, unter normalen Bedingungen als Embryo entwickelt.

[89] Die parlamentarischen Debatten, die im Vorfeld der Gesetzgebung stattfanden, suchen sowohl in England als auch in Deutschland einen Kompromiss zwischen Forschungsfreiheit und Lebensschutz. Das von der Kohl-Regierung in Deutschland eingesetzte Untersuchungskomitee unter Ernst Benda empfiehlt in der Frage eine Forschung an überzähligen Embryonen und schließt eine Erzeugung von Embryonen zu Forschungszwecken aus. Auffallend ist, dass die Gesetzesvorschläge beider Regierungen weitgehend in Übereinstimmung mit den nationalen Forschern standen, von denen das *Potential* embryonaler Stammzellen betont worden ist.

[90] Von Personalität des frühen Embryo ist freilich nur implizit insofern die Rede, als dieser schon in den ersten 14 Tagen nach der Kernverschmelzung als schutzwürdig angesehen wird. Eine explizite anthropologische Aussage findet sich erst im Stammzellgesetz.

[91] So in § 1 ESchG: „(1) Mit Freiheitsstrafe bis zu drei Jahren oder mit Geldstrafe wird bestraft, wer 1. auf eine Frau eine fremde unbefruchtete Eizelle überträgt, 2. es unternimmt, eine Eizelle zu einem anderen Zweck künstlich zu befruchten, als eine Schwangerschaft der Frau herbeizuführen, von der die Eizelle stammt".

[92] Vgl. ESchG §§ 6 und 7.

[93] Zentral für dieses Verständnis ist die Begriffsbestimmung ESchG § 8: „(1) Als Embryo im Sinne dieses Gesetzes gilt bereits die befruchtete, entwicklungsfähige menschliche Eizelle vom Zeitpunkt der Kernverschmelzung an, ferner jede einem Embryo

Dieser in Deutschland auch gegenwärtig noch geltenden Gesetzgebung ging – ähnlich wie in Großbritannien – die Berichterstattung von untersuchenden Kommissionen voraus.[94] Vor allem der Bericht unter dem damaligen Bundesverfassungsrichter Ernst Benda sprach sich *gegen* die Erzeugung von Embryonen zu Forschungszwecken aus, öffnete sich aber vorsichtig der Möglichkeit, nach IVF überzählige Embryonen zu Forschungszwecken zu verwenden, da diese ohnehin eine nur sehr geringe Lebenserwartung hätten und vernichtet würden.

Diese Konzession, die Stellungnahmen seitens der Forschungslobby, der Deutschen Forschungsgemeinschaft (DFG) und eines großen Teils von Expertengruppen entsprach,[95] deckte sich in dieser Zeit weitgehend mit der Position der Regierung unter Helmut Kohl, die sich in einem Gesetzentwurf insofern für eine vorsichtige Lockerung des Embryonenschutzes aussprach, als zwar keine Embryonen zu Forschungszwecken erzeugt werden sollten, aber eine Forschung an überzähligen Embryonen zu einem besseren Verständnis von Schwangerschaft und Embryonalentwicklung gestattet werden sollte.

Während in den dem Embryonenschutzgesetz vorlaufenden Debatten die Christdemokraten eher eine Position zugunsten einer *Lockerung* des Embryonenschutzes unter strengen Auflagen vertraten, waren die Sozialdemokraten anders als in Großbritannien, sowie die Grünen und einzelne Gruppen innerhalb der Bevölkerung aber strikt gegen eine solche Lockerung. Der Entwurf zu einem Embryonenschutzgesetz, das in strengen Grenzen die Forschung an überzähligen Embryonen nach IVF erlaubt, wurde nach kontroversen parlamentarischen Debatten vom Bundestag abgelehnt. Das stattdessen 1990 in Kraft getretene Embryonenschutzgesetz (ESchG) verbietet jegliche Form von Forschung an Embryonen und erlaubt eine Befruchtung von Embryonen *in vitro* lediglich zum Zweck der Herbeiführung einer Schwangerschaft. Dabei dürfen nur genau so viele Embryonen befruchtet werden, wie anschließend implantiert werden.

---

entnommene totipotente Zelle, die sich bei Vorliegen der dafür erforderlichen weiteren Voraussetzungen zu teilen und zu einem Individuum zu entwickeln vermag."

[94] Dabei sind unterschiedliche Dokumente zu nennen: neben dem Bericht, der unter dem Vorsitz von Ernst Benda mit dem Titel „In-vitro-Fertilisation, Genomanalyse und Gentherapie" entstand, zwei Berichte des Wissenschaftlichen Beirats der Bundesärztekammer und ein Bericht der Enquete-Kommission des deutschen Bundestages „Chancen und Risiken der Gentechnologie". Vgl. zur Entwicklung der deutschen Gesetzgebung A. Eser, Forschung mit Embryonen in rechtsvergleichender und rechtspolitischer Sicht, in: H.-L. Günther (Hrsg.), Fortpflanzungsmedizin und Humangenetik – strafrechtliche Schranken?, Tübingen 1987, 263-292. Eser nennt neben den Berichten, die ich genannt habe, weitere Stellungnahmen. A.a.O., 274-277.

[95] Vgl. R. Ratzel, Die Präimplantationsdiagnostik und Embryonenforschung, in: H.-D. Lippert/W. Eisenmenger (Hrsg.), Forschung am Menschen – Der Schutz des Menschen, die Freiheit des Forschers, MedR, Heidelberg/Berlin 1999, 81-98.

Mit der Entwicklung der medizinischen Forschung und der erstmalig geglückten Kultivierung von humanen embryonalen Stammzellen in den USA ergab sich Ende der 90er Jahre aber auch für den deutschen Gesetzgeber die Notwendigkeit einer rechtlichen Neuregelung der Forschung an menschlichen Embryonen, weil sich im weiteren Verlauf der 90er Jahre des 20. Jahrhunderts die Frage nach der ethischen Zulässigkeit von verbrauchender Embryonenforschung zur Gewinnung von humanen embryonalen Stammzellen stellte. Diesem rechtlichen Orientierungsbedarf versucht das Stammzellgesetz (StZG, 2002) Rechnung zu tragen, welches anders als das Embryonenschutzgesetz eine explizite anthropologische Wesensbestimmung zur Begründung der rechtlichen Entscheidung enthält.

Mit Verweis auf die staatliche Verpflichtung zur Achtung der Menschenwürde und zur Gewährung des Lebensschutzes regelt es den Umgang mit humanen embryonalen Stammzellen, indem es die Erzeugung und Einfuhr von embryonalen Stammzellen grundsätzlich verbietet.[96] Um dennoch Forschungsfreiheit in Deutschland zu gewährleisten, ist zunächst mit dem 1.1.2002 ein Stichtag bestimmt worden: Stammzelllinien, die *nach* dem 1.1.2002 im Ausland hergestellt wurden, durften weder nach Deutschland eingeführt werden, noch in Deutschland zu Forschungszwecken verwendet werden. *Vor* diesem Stichtag erzeugte Stammzelllinien durften demgegenüber bei Vorliegen eines hochrangigen Forschungsziels, das eine Forschung an embryonalen Stammzellen erforderte, und unter Genehmigung der zuständigen Behörde mit Stellungnahme der Zentralen Ethikkommission für Stammzellenforschung am Robert-Koch-Institut Berlin nach Deutschland importiert werden. Der dahinter stehende Kompromiss sah vor, dass in Deutschland zu Forschungszwecken, auch wenn diese hochrangiger medizinischer Forschung dienten, keine Embryonen getötet oder „verbraucht" werden sollten. Allenfalls zur Zeit der Verabschiedung des Gesetzes schon *bestehende* Stammzelllinien sollten unter strengen Auflagen der Forschung zugänglich gemacht werden, um für deutsche Forscher den Anschluss an die internationale Forschung zu gewährleisten.[97]

[96] „Zweck dieses Gesetzes ist es, im Hinblick auf die staatliche Verpflichtung, die Menschenwürde und das Recht auf Leben zu achten und zu schützen und die Freiheit der Forschung zu gewährleisten, 1. die Einfuhr und die Verwendung embryonaler Stammzellen grundsätzlich zu verbieten, 2. zu vermeiden, dass von Deutschland aus eine Gewinnung embryonaler Stammzellen oder eine Erzeugung von Embryonen zur Gewinnung embryonaler Stammzellen veranlasst wird, und 3. die Voraussetzungen zu bestimmen, unter denen die Einfuhr und die Verwendung embryonaler Stammzellen ausnahmsweise zu Forschungszwecken zugelassen sind." (StZG § 1.) Das Gesetz findet sich unter www.bmbf.de /pub/stammzellgesetz.pdf.

[97] Als Kernpunkt des Kompromisses muss dabei vor allem die Intention angesehen werden, dass in Deutschland zu Forschungszwecken keine Embryonen „verbraucht" werden sollen, weil dies menschliche Wesen für einen Zweck gebraucht (und vernichtet), der nicht in ihnen selbst liegt. Dieser Kompromiss ist aber insofern vor allem im Ausland schwer

Der 2002 erzielte Kompromiss ist nachträglich vermehrt kritisiert worden, weil zum einen die Anzahl der *nach* dem Stichtag erzeugten Stammzelllinien deutlich größer sei als die Anzahl der vor dem Stichtag erzeugten Linien, weil darüber hinaus das nach dem Stichtag erzeugte Material eine deutlich bessere Qualität aufweise als die bis 2002 erzeugten Stammzelllinien, die durch tierische Proteine verunreinigt seien, weil deutsche Forscher, die im Ausland an embryonalen Stammzellen forschten, zum dritten eine Strafverfolgung zu befürchten hätten, die ihre Arbeit unzumutbar erschwere, und weil schließlich mit der Verabschiedung des 7. Forschungsrahmenprogramms der Europäischen Union, das explizit die Forschung an embryonalen Stammzellen vorsehe, eine Forschung auch mit deutschen Geldern gefördert werde, die in Deutschland aber verboten sei.

Stellungnahmen etwa der Deutschen Forschungsgemeinschaft (DFG) plädierten darum für eine vollkommene Aufhebung des Stichtags.[98] Andere Institutionen hielten eine Verschiebung des Stichtags oder eine nachlaufende Stichtagsregelung für denkbar.[99] Während die katholische Kirche in Deutschland eine Liberalisierung des StZG ablehnte, kam von der Evangelischen Kirche in Deutschland Ende Dezember 2007 durch den Ratsvorsitzenden der EKD, Bischof Wolfgang Huber, ein vorsichtiges Signal, dass der Stichtag einmalig verschoben werden dürfe, um deutschen Forschern Anschluss an die internationale Stammzellforschung zu gewährleisten[100] – ein Votum, das auch

---

vermittelbar, als es deutschen Forschern dennoch erlaubt ist, in Grenzen auf im Ausland gewonnene embryonale Stammzelllinien, die durch „verbrauchende" Forschung erzeugt wurden, zurückzugreifen. Vgl. R. Deech/A. Smajdor, From IVF to Immortality. Controversy in the Era of Reproductive Technology, Oxford 2007, 207: „It has been suggested that there is a certain amount of ethical hypocrisy here. German scientists are permitted to work with the – by implication – unethical products of the research of other countries."

[98] Vgl. die Texte der DFG vom November 2006, sie sind abrufbar unter www.dfg.de. Auch die FDP und einige Politiker aus anderen Parteien haben sich einer Abschaffung der Stichtagsregelung gegenüber aufgeschlossen gezeigt. Darüber hinaus ist die öffentliche philosophisch-ethische Debatte in Deutschland (auch) von einer Infragestellung des Menschenwürde-Status von frühen Embryonen gekennzeichnet.

[99] Eine differenzierte Stellungnahme ist 2007 vom Nationalen Ethikrat verabschiedet und veröffentlicht worden (http://www.ethikrat.org). Darin werden unterschiedliche Lösungsansätze zur Novellierung des Stammzellgesetzes diskutiert, die von einer Beibehaltung des Gesetzes aus unterschiedlichen Gründen, einer Verschiebung des Stichtags und einer nachlaufenden Stichtagsregelung bis hin zu einer Abschaffung der Stichtagsregelung reichen und von unterschiedlichen Mitgliedern der Kommission vertreten werden. Darüber hinaus spricht sich der Nationale Ethikrat (inzwischen: Deutscher Ethikrat) dafür aus, die Strafandrohung für deutsche Wissenschaftler, die in Stammzellforschungsprojekte involviert sind, aufzuheben.

[100] Ähnlich argumentierte schon Mitte 2007 der Präsident des Kirchenamtes der EKD, Hermann Barth, in der Stellungnahme des Nationalen Ethikrats zur Novellierung des Stammzellgesetzes.

von der Bundesregierung unter Angela Merkel und der Bundesforschungsministerin Annette Schavan unterstützt wurde.

Im April 2008 ist der Stichtag nach einer offenen Debatte im Bundestag mit der Begründung verschoben worden, dass die vor 2002 erzeugten Stammzelllinien verunreinigt seien und für die Forschung auch an adulten Stammzellen neues embryonales Stammzell-Material benötigt werde. Die neue, am 21. August 2008 in Kraft getretene Stichtagsregelung sieht vor, dass Stammzelllinien, die vor dem 1. Mai 2007 erzeugt worden sind, unter Genehmigung der Aufsichtsbehörde und der Ethik-Kommission am Robert-Koch-Institut nach Deutschland importiert werden dürfen, was die Breite der jetzt in Deutschland verwendbaren Stammzellen um ein Vielfaches erhöht.

Mit diesen Entscheidungen legt die deutsche Gesetzgebung schon im ESchG, dann aber auch im StZG ausdrücklich keinen Zeitpunkt *nach* der Kernverschmelzung der Keimzellen fest, mit dem der Schutz der Menschenwürde beginnt. Vielmehr eignet für den deutschen Gesetzgeber offenbar schon dem frühen Embryo (zumindest potentielle) Personalität und Schutzwürdigkeit, die mit dem aus Art. 1 I GG entlehnten Begriff der Menschenwürde interpretiert wird. Auch wenn sie innerhalb der deutschen Diskussion teilweise heftig diskutiert werden,[101] sind darum folgende Aspekte festzuhalten:

- Der im Stammzellgesetz geregelte Schutz von Embryonen wird ausdrücklich mit einer anthropologischen Wesensbestimmung (*Menschenwürde* in StZG §1) begründet, wobei allerdings ebenso wie im deutschen Grundgesetz keine inhaltliche Bestimmung dieses Begriffs gegeben wird.
- Es wird kein Zeitpunkt *nach* der Befruchtung im Sinne der Kernverschmelzung gesetzt, an dem die Schutzwürdigkeit menschlicher Wesen beginnt. Vielmehr wird jede „totipotente“ menschliche Zelle als Embryo definiert und untersteht dem rechtlichen Schutz.
- Die Erzeugung von Embryonen zu Forschungszwecken wird verboten, ebenso das „therapeutische Klonen“ und die Erzeugung von Hybrid- und Chimären-Embryonen. Auch die Verwendung von nach IVF überzähligen Embryonen wird nicht gestattet. Vielmehr setzen sowohl das ESchG als auch das StZG fest, dass eine Erzeugung von Embryonen durch IVF ausschließlich zur Herbeiführung einer Schwangerschaft erlaubt ist.

Es zeigt sich mit dieser Darstellung, dass die deutsche und britische Gesetzgebung, auch wenn zunächst durchaus ähnliche Vorbehalte gegenüber der

[101] Die Diskussion konzentriert sich dabei auf folgende Aspekte: die stark umstrittene Frage danach, was *Menschenwürde* ist (1), sowie die Frage nach der Notwendigkeit eines absoluten *Lebensschutzes* für frühe Embryonen (2). Beide Aspekte können mit den ebenfalls hochgradig strittigen Aspekten von *Personalität* und *Autonomie* verbunden werden. Alle genannten Aspekte werden im weiteren Verlauf des Buches noch eine Rolle spielen.

Forschung an Embryonen bestanden haben,[102] sich in geradezu entgegengesetzte Richtungen entwickelt haben. Ein zentraler Aspekt dieser Unterschiedlichkeit liegt im Begriff von *Menschenwürde/human dignity*: Während in Großbritannien der Begriff an keiner Stelle innerhalb der Gesetzgebung verwendet wird, und während gleichzeitig innerhalb der Debatten *human dignity* als eine persönlich und individuell zu füllende, für die Gesetzgebung aber letztlich vage Idee verstanden wird,[103] legt die deutsche Gesetzgebung im deutschen Grundgesetz und seiner Auslegung bis ins letzte Drittel des 20. Jahrhunderts[104] eine Unabwägbarkeit der – vorpositiven – Menschenwürde und ihre allgemeine, universale Geltung auch in der bioethischen Diskussion nahe, was sich daran zeigt, dass die Pflicht des Staates, die Menschenwürde zu schützen, im Stammzellgesetz (StZG) ausdrücklich erwähnt ist und gesetzesbegründend wirkt.

Auf diesem Hintergrund scheint im Ländervergleich von Deutschland und England ein unterschiedliches Verständnis von „Menschenwürde" zu bestehen, so dass der Begriff als solcher noch nicht geeignet erscheint, zu einer international befriedigenden Lösung in der Stammzelldebatte zu kommen. Was *Menschenwürde* ist, muss an dieser Stelle noch offen bleiben. Dass sie allerdings in der Debatte um humane embryonale Stammzellen eine Rolle spielt, kann konstatiert werden, sowohl was die Rechtsbegründung in Deutschland, als auch, was die Kritik an der rechtlichen Regelung etwa durch die christlichen Kirchen in England und Deutschland angeht, aber darüber hinaus auch in der internationalen Bioethik-Debatte, was die in Oviedo verabschiedete „Bioethik-Konvention" deutlich macht.

Der nun folgende Abschnitt hat eine Scharnierfunktion zwischen den beiden Teilen des Buches. Bisher war es vor allem darum gegangen, Entwicklun-

---

[102] Konzediert werden muss allerdings, dass die deutsche Diskussion von Anfang an darauf gedrungen hat, dass allenfalls nach IVF *überzählige* Embryonen zu Forschungszwecken gebraucht werden dürften, während schon der Warnock-Report sich dafür ausspricht, dass unter genau geregelten Bedingungen die Erzeugung von Embryonen zu Forschungszwecken ethisch akzeptabel sei.

[103] So etwa das Votum in den *Government proposals for the regulation of hybrid and chimera embryos*, 2006/07, S. 24f., in dem das Konzept von *human dignity* als „vague" bezeichnet wird.

[104] Die Interpretationsoffenheit, die naturrechtliche und vorpositive Geltung des Menschenwürdeartikels, die in der Grundgesetzauslegung von Günter Dürig (1958) noch unhinterfragt angenommen werden, werden in den neueren Kommentierungen des Grundgesetzes von Horst Dreier und Matthias Herdegen eher hinterfragt. Die Kommentierung durch Herdegen (2003) veranlasste den ehemaligen Verfassungsrichter Ernst-Wolfgang Böckenförde zu einem scharfen Widerspruch in der Frankfurter Allgemeinen Zeitung unter dem Titel: „Die Würde des Menschen war unantastbar", woraufhin Herdegen seinen Kommentar zu Art. 1 I GG weitläufig überarbeitete (2005). Die juristische Diskussion an dieser Stelle ist nicht abgeschlossen.

gen nachzuzeichnen. Es geht in den folgenden Überlegungen zum Menschenwürdebegriff innerhalb der Debatte zur Embryonenforschung um eine erste inhaltliche Annäherung.

II. 3. 3 Menschenwürde im Zusammenhang mit dem Schutz von Embryonen?

Die deutsche Gesetzgebung hat den Menschenwürdebegriff aus Art. 1 I GG explizit in das Stammzellgesetz aufgenommen, indem dieses die staatliche Verpflichtung formuliert, die Menschenwürde und das Recht auf Leben zu achten und zu schützen und Forschungsfreiheit zu gewährleisten.[105] Damit rekurriert die deutsche Gesetzgebung explizit auf die auch zur Begründung der Menschenrechte im internationalen Völkerrecht verwendete und in Art. 1 I GG an prominenter Stelle festgeschriebene *Menschenwürde* und appliziert diesen Begriff auf jede Form menschlichen Lebens ab dem Zeitpunkt der Kernverschmelzung. In der britischen Gesetzgebung wird auf eine staatliche Verpflichtung zur Achtung und zum Schutz der Menschenwürde demgegenüber nicht Bezug genommen; allerdings wird der Begriff *human dignity* von einigen Stellungnahmen zur aktuellen Gesetzgebung angeführt. Ich stelle im folgenden den Gebrauch des Begriffs *Menschenwürde* resp. *human dignity* hinsichtlich der Forschung an menschlichen Embryonen zunächst in England, anschließend in Deutschland dar.

Vor allem die in England jüngst gesetzlich geregelte Erzeugung von und Forschung an Hybrid- und Chimären-Embryonen ist trotz einer einhelligen Zustimmung zur embryonalen Stammzellforschung als solcher in der Öffentlichkeit nicht unumstritten. Die ethischen Bedenken gegen eine Forschung an Hybrid- und Chimärenembryonen werden in einer Stellungnahme des *Science and Technology Committee* aus dem *House of Commons*, die schließlich zu der Empfehlung gelangt, die Erzeugung von Hybrid-Embryonen zuzulassen, in drei Kategorien aufgeteilt, von denen die Missachtung der *Menschenwürde* für das Komitee allerdings den am wenigsten greifbaren Einwand darstellt:[106]

- Einwände gegen eine Erzeugung von Hybrid- und Chimären-Embryonen, die diese Forschung als einen Verstoß gegen die *Menschenrechte* beurteilen,
- Einwände, die den Wert dieser *Forschung als solcher* in Frage stellen, sowie

[105] StZG § 1.

[106] House of Commons, Science and Technology Committee, Government proposals for the regulation of hybrid and chimera embryos 2007, 24: „In very broad terms, the main arguments for and against the creation of human and human-animal embryos can be divided into three categories: arguments which take into account potential violation of human rights; arguments which centre on the value of the research; and arguments which consider the impact of such research on human dignity."

· Einwände, die in dieser Forschung eine Missachtung der *Menschenwürde* sehen.

Schon die ersten beiden Einwände werden von dem Untersuchungskomitee als nicht überzeugend beurteilt: Ein Verstoß gegen die *Menschenrechte* aufgrund einer Forschung an Mischwesen wird verneint, weil die entstehenden Embryonen keine „Menschen" würden und ihre Implantation in einen menschlichen Uterus, also ihre weitere Entwicklung als Menschen verboten sei. Vielmehr könne sogar argumentiert werden, dass aufgrund der möglichen Therapien, die aus der Forschung an embryonalen Stammzellen, inklusive der Forschung an cytoplasmischen Hybrid-Embryonen, zu erhoffen sei, eine ausdrückliche *Achtung* der Menschenrechte und sogar ihre Erweiterung eingeschlossen sei.[107] Aufgrund der Knappheit an Eizellen, die für eine Erzeugung von Embryonen zu Forschungszwecken notwendig sind, und der Hochrangigkeit der Forschung zur Entwicklung neuartiger Therapien gegen degenerative Erkrankungen sei die Produktion von Mischembryonen als ethisch angemessen zu vertreten, so dass sich auch das zweite Argument gegen die Forschung als solche erübrige.

Die Argumentation mit der *Menschenwürde* wird deswegen als schwierig beurteilt, weil diese Konzeption eine gewisse Vagheit aufweise und sich aufgrund ihrer Komplexität und Interpretationsoffenheit nicht als Argument in dieser Debatte eigne.[108] *Human dignity* wird zwar als zentral angesehen, wegen der Unklarheit des Konzepts und der Offenheit für zahlreiche unterschiedliche Interpretationen aber letztlich für ungeeignet in der Debatte um die Forschung an Embryonen gehalten.

Diese Beobachtungen legen die Folgerung nahe, dass *Menschenwürde* zwar auch in Großbritannien über positive Konnotationen verfügt, im Bewusstsein vieler an den ethischen Debatten zur Forschung an humanen Embryonen beteiligter Menschen aber so wenig verankert ist, dass der Begriff nicht konsensbildend wirkt, sondern als unklar empfunden wird. Diese Folgerung wird von der Tatsache unterstützt, dass *human dignity* in der Diskussion nur von einigen wenigen Expertengruppen und Einzelpersonen verwendet wird[109] und in der inhaltlichen Bestimmung unpräzise bleibt.

---

[107] Der Text vertritt damit implizit die Ansicht, dass Menschsein sich allmählich entwickelt und seine Entwicklung davon abhängt, in welcher Umgebung es wächst. Damit ist noch keine Aussage darüber gemacht, ob tierisch-menschliche Mischembryonen als solche als Menschen zu beurteilen seien.

[108] House of Commons, a.a.O., 24: „However, what is meant by the phrase human 'dignity' is vague."

[109] Etwa im Memorandum von *Christian Action for Research and Education* (CARE): „Thus respect for human life and human dignity must be an intrinsic aspect of the whole bioethics framework in the UK." (In einem gemeinsamen Text vom *House of Lords*

Vor allem die römisch-katholische Kirche gebraucht in diesem Zusammenhang den Begriff und appliziert ihn auf die Forschung an Embryonen. Das in London ansässige *Linacre Centre for Health Care Ethics*[110] zielt etwa darauf, die römisch-katholische Position zum Lebensschutz für die gegenwärtige Bioethik in Geltung zu bringen. In zahlreichen Veröffentlichungen des Centres[111] sind kritische Äußerungen zur Forschung an menschlichen Embryonen zu finden, die ausdrücklich mit der *dignity*[112] des Embryos argumentieren.[113]

---

und dem *House of Commons, Joint Committee on the Human Tissue and Embryos (Draft) Bill*, 2006/2007, Volume II, Evidence, 309.) Das *Scottish Council of Human Bioethics* stellt fest: „It is because human personhood and dignity are not decided through majority votes that a considerable debate remains concerning the status of the early embryo!" (House of Commons/House of Lords, a.a.O., 452.) In diesem Zusammenhang sind auch Stimmen laut geworden, die eine Revision der gegenwärtigen Gesetzgebung einfordern und dafür votieren, dass der Embryo aufgrund seiner Würde vom Beginn der Kernverschmelzung an geschützt wird. „It is my earnest hope that those charged with voting upon this bill will focus their attention not on the question, 'Can we do x or y?', but rather, 'Is it right? Does this respect the dignity of the human person?' This is a question to be answered from the depths of the human heart, and one which should be undertaken with utmost sincerity and clarity of thought. I would urge you to scrap the current draft Human Tissue and Embryos Bill, and to replace it with legislation which protects the human person from the exact moment when his or her life begins ie at the moment of conception." (In einem Memorandum von Mr Chris Wotherspoon, House of Commons/House of Lords, a.a.O., 487.) Auffallend ist bei allen Äußerungen, dass auch ausdrückliche Referenzen auf *human dignity* den Begriff nicht inhaltlich definieren.

[110] Vgl. den Internet-Auftritt www.linacre.org.

[111] Ähnlich kritisch sind die Äußerungen der katholischen Bischofskonferenz von England und Wales, vgl. http://www.catholicchurch.org.uk/ccb/catholic_church. In einer auf dieser Seite zu findenden Stellungnahme zur HFE Bill argumentiert Erzbischof Peter Smith explizit mit *human dignity*, die mit einer Forschung an menschlichen Embryonen missachtet werde.

[112] So auch in der jüngsten Stellungnahme des Vatikan zu Fragen der Bioethik, die 2008 unter dem Titel „dignitas personae" erschienen ist: „Jedem Menschen ist von der Empfängnis bis zum natürlichen Tod die Würde einer Person zuzuerkennen." (S. 1.) Auch wenn der Text die eindeutige Bezeichnung des Embryo als Person vermeidet, wird festgehalten: „Der menschliche Embryo hat... von Anfang an die Würde, die der Person eigen ist." (S. 5.)

[113] So etwa im Linacre Centre Submission to the Science and Technology Committee Inquiry into Government Proposals for the Regulation of Hybrid and Chimera Embryos, 2007, oder im Submission to Department of Health Review of the Human Fertilisation and Embryology Act, 2007. In beiden Texten wird mit dem Argument der Würde eine extrakorporale Erzeugung von Embryonen grundsätzlich als problematisch angesehen, die Verwendung von Embryonen zu einem ihnen fremden Zweck und die Erzeugung von tierisch-menschlichen Mischembryonen aber als ethisch inakzeptabel beurteilt. Die Texte des Linacre-Centres schließen sich damit inhaltlich eng an die päpstlichen Texte Donum Vitae (1968) und Evangelium Vitae (1995) an.

Die anglikanische Kirche hält gegenüber den Voten der römisch-katholischen Kirche den besonderen moralischen Status des Embryo für entscheidend, nimmt aber in der Frage der Embryonenforschung eine liberalere Position als die katholische Kirche ein. Danach ist es nach Ansicht der *Church of England* aufgrund des Ethos des Heilens und der Hoffnung auf Entwicklung von Therapien für zahlreiche degenerative Erkrankungen möglich, überzählige Embryonen zu verwenden,[114] nicht aber, Embryonen zu Forschungszwekken zu erzeugen.[115] Neben einem Nein zu „true hybrids" steht ein vorsichtiges Ja zur Forschung an cytoplasmischen Hybrid-Embryonen.[116]

Eine ähnliche Position wie die *Church of England* nimmt die in reformierter Tradition stehende *Church of Scotland* ein, wobei sie auf ihre Verpflichtung zu einer heilenden und helfenden Ethik verweist, die auch eine Forschung an Embryonen einschließe, um neue Heilungsmethoden zu gewinnen.[117] Weder

---

[114] „Because of the Christian mandate to seek healing, we believe that there are situations, addressing the serious medical need of others, in which it is permissible to use or select against in vitro embryos. This means we take a similar view to that already stated in UK law that the in vitro embryo has a special status which protects it from being used, selected against or destroyed for trivial purposes. However we do not believe that embryos should be produced by IVF purely for research, where there is no intention of their ever being implanted to fulfil their potential. Only "spare" embryos left over from IVF treatment should be used in research. This means embryos are always created as an end in themselves and helps to safeguard their special status." (In einer Stellungnahme innerhalb der Debatte zur Novellierung der HFE Act, House of Commons/House of Lords, in dem genannten Report, Evidence, 320.)

[115] Gleichwohl gibt es auch innerhalb der anglikanischen Kirche kritische Stimmen gegen eine Forschung an Embryonen, vgl. etwa die Predigt von Bischof Tom Wright von Durham am Ostersonntag 2008, http://www.durhamcathedral.co.uk/schedule/sermons/242. Insgesamt ist die *Church of England* in dieser Frage – ähnlich wie die EKD – nicht vollkommen einig.

[116] So in einer Stellungnahme des Mission and Public Affair Council innerhalb der *Church of England* vom 23. Juli 2007: „ The Mission and Public Affairs Council of the Church of England has opposed the creation of true human hybrids but given a cautious acceptance to the proposal to produce cytoplasmic hybrid embryos for research into the alleviation of serious diseases. Research using human embryos donated by IVF patients, it adds, is acceptable but using human embryos created specifically for research from donated eggs and sperm is not." (s. http://www.cofe. anglican.org/info/socialpublic/science/hfea/).

[117] „As a foundation to discussing stem cell research, we have re-examined the theological and ethical arguments concerning the moral status of the human embryo, and the theological significance that might be attributed at various stages of biological development. We start from the premise that all humans are equally creations of the triune God, uniquely made in God's image, regardless of any functional framing of the human condition, and so are of inestimable value. We understand the human person in the light of the incarnation, life, death and resurrection of Jesus Christ, and as relational and communal, called to relationship with Christ, one another and to the rest of creation."

für die anglikanische noch für schottische Kirche ist der Begriff *human dignity* in großem Maße meinungs- und konsensbildend innerhalb der bioethischen Debatte zur Forschung an menschlichen Embryonen und zur jüngsten Debatte um die Forschung an tierisch-menschlichen Misch-Embryonen.[118]

Am häufigsten wird *human dignity* in dieser Debatte in Stellungnahmen des *Scottish Council on Human Bioethics* verwendet, innerhalb der aufgezählten Gruppen die einzige, die sich nicht ausdrücklich einer bestimmten Kirche zurechnet und darüber hinaus in Schottland, nicht in England ansässig ist. Nach Darstellung des Forschungs-Direktors des Centre kann *human dignity* auf dreierlei Weise verstanden werden:[119]

- nach dem Verständnis von *Kant*, nach dem *dignity* zum einen mit Autonomie assoziiert wird und Wesen, die mit Würde begabt sind, zum anderen nicht als Mittel zu einem Zweck gebraucht werden dürfen, der ihnen fremd ist,
- im Sinne eines Verständnisses des „würdigen Verhaltens", in dem Menschen sich anderen Menschen gegenüber, auch wenn diese keine Würde haben, „würdig" *verhalten*,
- in dem Sinne, in dem das *Scottish Council* selbst sie versteht, als – konsistent mit der UN-Deklaration der *Menschenrechte* (1948) – Fundierung von Grundrechten und in diesem Sinne als intrinsische menschliche Weseneigenschaft, zugleich aber auch als Glaubensgut, das nicht bewiesen werden kann und gleichzeitig individuell gefüllt wird.

Während das *Scottish Council on Human Bioethics* die dritte Möglichkeit eines Verständnisses von Menschenwürde für plausibel hält, wurde im Verlauf der

(So in einem Summary Report from the Church and Society Council to the 2006 Church of Scotland General Assembly: Embryo Research, Human Stem Cells and Cloned Embryos, S. 2.) Der Report versteht Menschwerdung als einen allmählichen Prozess und kommt zum Schluss: „For the majority of the working group, however, a more gradual view of the moral status of the embryo allows some embryo research." (S. 38.)

[118] In der durch die Commons und die Lords gegebenen Dokumentation argumentieren aus den christlichen Kirchen vor allem die Initiative *Christian Action for Research and Education* (CARE), das *Christian Medical Fellowship*, das (römisch-katholische) *Linacre Centre for Health Care Ethics* und das *Brethren Christian Fellowship* mit *human dignity*, gegen die ihrer Ansicht nach eine Forschung an menschlich-tierischen Mischembryonen verstößt. Dabei wird *human dignity* meist im Sinne der *imago Dei* verstanden. Vgl. die Stellungnahme von CARE: „As stated above, humans are qualitatively different from all non-human animals. Unlike these, we alone are made 'in the image of God' and therefore have unique attributes and responsibilities. Humans have an innate dignity absent from the animal kingdom, and there is a rich meaning to being human." (In den Evidences der Lords/Commons, 2007, S. Ev 87.)

[119] In einer Anhörung am 5. Februar 2007 von Callum McKellar, dem derzeitigen Forschungs-Direktor des Centre. In dem angegebenen Bericht S. Ev 22. Siehe die Website des Councils: www.schb.org.uk.

Diskussion mit dem Direktor des *Council* innerhalb einer Expertenanhörung zur Frage nach der rechtlichen Regelung von menschlich-tierischen Misch-Embryonen die erste, an Kant angelehnte Bestimmung von Menschenwürde aufgenommen und als die überzeugendste verstanden.[120] In diesem Zusammenhang und bei einem solchen Verständnis von *dignity* wird ausgehend von einer Begründung von *dignity* mit Autonomie davon ausgegangen, dass die so verstandene Würde mit der Erzeugung von Hybrid-Embryonen nicht verletzt werden kann, da es sich dabei nicht um eine Verletzung von Autonomie handele. Denn Autonomie sei bei Embryonen noch nicht auszumachen. Es stelle vielmehr sogar eine *Steigerung* von Menschenwürde dar, diese Forschung (unter bestimmten regulativen Bestimmungen) durchzuführen, weil sie zahlreichen Patienten nützen und bei erfolgreicher Entwicklung von Therapien gegen degenerative Erkrankungen deren Würde vergrößern könne. Ob Kants Würde-Interpretation damit korrekt wiedergegeben ist, hat das folgende Kapitel des Buches zu untersuchen.

Das kantische Verständnis von Würde ist zur Begründung von *dignity* von den englischen kirchlichen Stellungnahmen nicht herangezogen worden, die ihrerseits zur Würdebegründung von menschlichen Wesen auf die menschliche Gottebenbildlichkeit verweisen. Sowohl die Würde-Konzeption der Aufklärungs-Philosophie bei Kant als auch die Begründung von Menschenwürde mit einem dezidiert theologischen Topos wie der *imago Dei* werden uns im zweiten Hauptteil des Buches noch zu beschäftigen haben.

Der dargestellte Zusammenhang zeigt, dass die Argumentation mit dem *dignity*-Begriff bei der Gesetzesfindung innerhalb der britischen Debatte nur eine Nebenrolle gespielt hat und allenfalls bei einigen wenigen kritischen Stellungnahmen verwendet worden ist, dies dann auffallend häufig (so beim *Scottish Council for Bioethics* und damit für den *schottischen* Kontext), aber ohne eine konsensbildende Funktion für außenstehende Entscheidungsträger, die den Begriff konsequent im weiteren Verlauf der Debatte entweder gar nicht aufgenommen oder ihn so verwendet haben, dass eine intrinsische, unverfügbare menschliche Wesenseigenschaft mit ihm nicht ausgesagt werden und er gegen andere Rechtsgüter (wie das Gemeinwohl, die Forschungsfrei-

[120] In einer Äußerung von Professor Raanan Gillon: „As has already been indicated in the previous panel, the concept of human dignity is a very complex one and people have different accounts of what they mean by it. I think that the first of the three offered by Dr MacKellar is the most plausible one, which is to do with the autonomy of the individual, the Kantian view of dignity. On that basis, it seems to me perfectly clear that this sort of research does not offend anybody's dignity and, on the contrary, may very well enhance dignity, in the sense that medical treatment does enhance dignity, of the people who may benefit from it, and to ensure it is in the public interest and being done in the best possible way and within the tightest regulatory mechanisms possible. It is not without due concern to what is ethically appropriate and right." (Im Bericht der Commons, S. Ev 29.)

heit oder den Nutzen und die Gesundheit vieler) abgewogen werden konnte. Seine Vagheit und Offenheit, die in der deutschen Debatte eher dazu geführt haben, dass er von zahlreichen Stellungnahmen verwendet worden ist, hat es ihm in der britischen Debatte offenbar schwer gemacht. Als menschliche Wesenseigenschaft von Beginn an wird *human dignity* in den wenigsten Fällen verstanden und kommuniziert. Der zweite Hauptteil des Buches hat im Anschluss an diese Beobachtungen darum vor allem folgende Fragen zu klären:

- Warum ist offenbar *human dignity* in der englischen Diskussion nicht in dem starken Maße konsensbildend wie in der deutschen Debatte?
- Wie wird *human dignity*, wenn der Begriff gebraucht wird, verstanden, und inwiefern ist dieses Verständnis mit einem in der deutschsprachigen Diskussion verbreiteten Verständnis vergleichbar oder nicht vergleichbar?
- Ausgehend von welchem Verständnis könnte der Begriff auch für die internationale bioethische Diskussion orientierend wirken?

Bevor ich mich diesen Fragen zuwende, werfe ich einen wesentlich knapperen Blick auf die Verwendung des *Menschenwürde*-Begriffs seitens der deutschen Kirchen, die schon aufgrund der Verankerung des Begriffs sowohl im deutschen Grundgesetz als auch in der gegenwärtigen Gesetzgebung zur Forschung an humanen embryonalen Stammzellen einen deutlich breiteren öffentlichen Konsens hinter sich hat als in Großbritannien, auch wenn der Begriff weder im Grundgesetz noch im Stammzellgesetz inhaltlich bestimmt wird.

Trotz der inhaltlichen Unklarheit von *Menschenwürde* sind in der deutschen bioethischen Debatte zahlreiche Texte erschienen, die den Begriff für die Begründung einer Stellungnahme zur Forschung an humanen embryonalen Stammzellen verwenden.[121] Schon 1989, noch vor dem Inkrafttreten des Embryonenschutzgesetzes, verabschiedeten der Rat der EKD und die deutsche Bischofskonferenz in Zusammenarbeit mit den anderen Kirchen in Deutschland, die der Arbeitsgemeinschaft Christlicher Kirchen angehören, die Schrift „Gott ist ein Freund des Lebens. Herausforderungen und Aufgaben beim Schutz des Lebens",[122] in der für alle Grenzbereiche menschlichen Lebens mit *Menschenwürde* argumentiert wird. Auch wenn sich in diesem

[121] Vgl. nur N. Knoepffler, Menschenwürde in der Bioethik, Berlin 2004. Außerdem verweise ich auf die bereits oben S. 14, Anm. 6 genannten Monographien und Sammelbände, die den Begriff im Titel haben.

[122] Gott ist ein Freund des Lebens. Herausforderungen und Aufgaben beim Schutz des Lebens, gemeinsame Erklärung des Rates der Evangelischen Kirche in Deutschland und der Deutschen Bischofskonferenz in Verbindung mit den übrigen Mitglieds- und Gastkirchen der Arbeitsgemeinschaft christlicher Kirchen in der Bundesrepublik Deutschland und Berlin (West), Gütersloh 1989.

Zusammenhang die Frage nach der ethischen Zulässigkeit der Erzeugung von humanen embryonalen Stammzellen noch nicht stellt, wird schon für den Embryo *in vitro* formuliert: „Der Embryo ist individuelles Leben, das als menschliches Leben immer ein sich entwickelndes ist... Dann aber kann... Forschung am ungeborenen Leben nur insoweit gebilligt werden, wie sie der Erhaltung und der Förderung dieses bestimmten individuellen Lebens dient... Gezielte Eingriffe an Embryonen..., die ihre Schädigung und Vernichtung in Kauf nehmen, sind nicht zu verantworten – und seien die Forschungsziele noch so hochrangig." [123] Dieser gemeinsame Text der Kirchen in Deutschland argumentiert zur Begründung des Lebensschutzes von Anfang an[124] mit drei ethischen Argumentationskonzepten: dem Menschenwürdebegriff, dem Personbegriff und dem Lebensbegriff.

Die Argumentation mit *Menschenwürde* und die strikte Ablehnung einer verbrauchenden Forschung an menschlichen Embryonen, weil diese menschliches Leben zu einem fremden Zweck verbrauche, setzt sich in den Stellungnahmen der katholischen Deutschen Bischofskonferenz fort, ähnlich wie es sich bei der Bischofskonferenz der katholischen Bischöfe von England und Wales und den Veröffentlichungen des Linacre-Centres beobachten ließ.[125]

Auch die Argumentationshilfe der EKD „Im Geist der Liebe mit dem Leben umgehen" (2002)[126] argumentiert mit Menschenwürde. Allerdings wird darin aufgrund von Uneinigkeit innerhalb der Kammer für Öffentliche Verantwortung die Frage nicht entschieden, ob bereits frühen Embryonen Menschenwürde zukommt.[127] Die Frage des moralischen Status des Embryos *vor*

[123] Gott ist ein Freund des Lebens, 64.

[124] Der Lebensschutz am Beginn des Lebens ist gleichwohl nicht der einzige Aspekt, mit dem die Schrift umgeht. Nach einer theologischen Grundsatzklärung werden vielmehr „Bereiche besonderer Verantwortung für den Schutz des Lebens" (S. 53ff.) und „Aktuelle Herausforderungen beim Schutz menschlichen Lebens" (S. 62ff.) benannt, zu denen medizinethische Kontroversfragen zählen.

[125] So in einer Erklärung des Ständigen Rats der Deutschen Bischofskonferenz zum Import von embryonalen Stammzellen am 21.1.2002 (vgl. http://www.dbk.de/aktuell/meldungen/2920/index.html), oder in der Stellungnahme des Sekretärs der Deutschen Bischofskonferenz zur öffentlichen Anhörung des Ausschusses zur Bildung, Forschung und Technikfolgenabschätzung des Deutschen Bundestages zum Thema Stammzellforschung am 9. Mai 2007 (siehe http://www.dbk.de/aktuell/meldungen/01354/index.html). Ähnlich wird auch in der Stellungnahme zu den Vorschlägen des Nationalen Ethikrats zur Novellierung des deutschen Stammzellgesetzes im Juli 2007 argumentiert.

[126] Im Geist der Liebe mit dem Leben umgehen. Argumentationshilfe für aktuelle medizin- und bioethische Fragen. Ein Beitrag der Kammer für Öffentliche Verantwortung der Evangelischen Kirche in Deutschland, Hannover 2002.

[127] „Von daher besteht in der Kammer Einmütigkeit darüber, dass die Menschenwürde und der Lebensschutz, der dem Menschen fraglos zukommt, bis in die allerersten An-

der Nidation wird offen gelassen,[128] für den moralischen Status des Embryos *nach* der Nidation wird allerdings Menschenwürde festgestellt. Dabei vertritt die Schrift einen relationalen Ansatz, nach dem jeder Mensch deswegen zu schützen ist, weil er „sein Sein als Person und seine darin liegende Würde der Anerkennung durch Gott verdankt".[129]

Uneinigkeit besteht darum in der Evangelischen Kirche in Deutschland (EKD) nicht darüber, ob menschliches Leben an sich zu schützen und in seiner *Würde* zu achten ist, sondern darüber, wann menschliches Leben beginnt. Die in Frage stehende Zäsur ist die Nidation, die als Interaktion des Embryos mit seiner Umgebung eine konstitutive Bedingung für seine weitere Entwicklung darstellt. Auch wenn in dieser Frage keine Einigkeit erzielt werden konnte, hat die Evangelische Kirche in Deutschland die im Stammzellgesetz (2002) gefundene rechtliche Regelung als Kompromiss empfunden und auch die von der Synode der EKD im November 2007 ausgesprochene Empfehlung, den Stichtag einmalig zu verschieben, in ihrem Charakter als Kompromiss verteidigt und die Hoffnung bekräftigt, dass embryonale Stammzellforschung sich als Grundlagenforschung aufgrund der gewonnenen Ergebnisse bald zugunsten der Forschung an adulten Stammzellen erübrige.[130] Die kritischen Stellungnahmen der Kirchen in Deutschland verwenden nicht nur signifikant häufiger den Menschenwürdebegriff, sie gehen in ihrer Kritik an der Forschung mit Embryonen damit auch weiter als die *Church of England* und die *Church of Scotland* in ihren offiziellen Äußerungen.

---

fänge des Menschseins reicht und einen ethischen Schutzanspruch begründet. Uneinigkeit besteht jedoch darüber, ob alle menschlichen Embryonen als Menschen zu verstehen sind und ihnen deshalb Würde und Lebensschutz in vollem Umfang zukommt." (A.a.O., 10. Im Internet unter http://www.ekd.de/EKD-Texte/30655.html.)

[128] Die Kammer für Öffentliche Verantwortung stellt in Auseinandersetzung mit mehreren Urteilen durch das Bundesverfassungsgericht in den 90er Jahren fest, dass der Status des Embryo bis zur Nidation vom Bundesverfassungsgericht offenbar offen gelassen worden ist, dass aber die Frage gestellt werden muss, „ob es in einem Gemeinwesen, das die Achtung und den Schutz der Würde des Menschen zum obersten Leitprinzip allen Handelns gemacht hat, erlaubt sein darf, mit menschlichem Leben so wie mit einem anderen Gut zu verfahren." (A.a.O., 12.)

[129] A.a.O., 23.

[130] Nicht nur innerhalb der Evangelischen Kirche in Deutschland, auch in der deutschen evangelischen Theologie ist die Frage nach dem Status des frühen Embryos und dem Beginn des Lebensschutzes umstritten. In einem Diskussionsbeitrag in der Frankfurter Allgemeinen Zeitung vom 23. Januar 2002 ist eine Stellungnahme evangelischer Ethiker unter dem Titel „Starre Fronten überwinden" veröffentlicht worden, in der unter ausdrücklicher Begründung mit *Menschenwürde* dafür votiert wird, eine Forschung an „verwaisten" Embryonen und bereits existierenden Stammzelllinien zu erlauben. Das Votum ist abgedruckt in dem Sammelband R. Anselm/U.H.J. Körtner (Hrsg.), Streitfall Biomedizin. Urteilsfindung in christlicher Verantwortung, Göttingen 2003, 197ff.

Diesen nur angedeuteten Beobachtungen zufolge ist in kirchlichen Verlautbarungen genauso wie in nicht-kirchlichen Texten und Gesetzestexten innerhalb der deutschen Debatte deutlich häufiger von *Menschenwürde* im Zusammenhang mit der Forschung an menschlichen Embryonen die Rede als in der britischen Debatte. Ob der Begriff inhaltlich klarer ist als in Großbritannien, wo er als vage empfunden wird, ist damit noch nicht ausgemacht. Er scheint für zahlreiche Menschen aber positive Konnotationen zu haben und eher in einem allgemeinen sprachlichen Bewusstsein verankert zu sein als in der britischen Debatte. Diese Beobachtung leitet zum nun folgenden zweiten Hauptteil des Buches über. Dieses beschäftigt sich mit unterschiedlichen Interpretationsmodellen von *Menschenwürde* und deren Hintergründen.

III. Menschenwürde gegen Heilungshoffnung? Für und gegen den Schutz von Embryonen

Bei der Darstellung der unterschiedlichen Entwicklung der Embryonenschutzgesetzgebung in Deutschland und Großbritannien sind unterschiedliche Begründungsmuster deutlich geworden. *Für* die Forschung werden vor allem folgende Argumente geltend gemacht, die miteinander zusammenhängen können, aber nicht aufeinander bezogen sein müssen:

- die Erwartung, mit einer *Grundlagenforschung* an menschlichen embryonalen Stammzellen verbessere sich das Verständnis von Embryonalentwicklung und Schwangerschaft, aber auch das Verständnis von adulten Stammzellen, die dann zu Therapieformen verwendet werden könnten,
- die *therapeutische* Hoffnung auf Linderung oder sogar Heilung und Vermeidung von degenerativen Erkrankungen mit Hilfe von humanen embryonalen Stammzellen.
- Darüber hinaus wird mit der internationalen *Anschlussfähigkeit* biomedizinischer *Forschung* argumentiert: im Zusammenhang der Forschung an Embryonen spielt Großbritannien international eine Spitzenreiterrolle, die mit Regierungsgeldern noch ausgebaut werden soll. Forschungsfreiheit ist aber auch im deutschen Grundgesetz verankert (Art. 5 III GG).

Mit diesen Argumenten *pro* Embryonenforschung verbindet sich häufig die anthropologische Grundannahme, der frühe Embryo sei ein Wesen, das sich allererst *zum* Menschen entwickle, aber die volle Seinskriteriologie noch nicht erfülle, die für die Zuerkennung eines absoluten Lebensschutzes notwendig wäre. Ein besonderer Status besteht zwar, aber keine absolute Notwendigkeit eines Lebensschutzes. Zusammenfassend kann diese Konzeption als „gradualistisch" charakterisiert werden, weil sie davon ausgeht, dass Menschsein sich prozessual entwickelt, und darum auch der dem Menschsein zukommende Lebensschutz graduell zunimmt.

Eine Alternative zur gradualistischen Auffassung, nach der sich die Schutzwürdigkeit menschlichen Lebens *allmählich* entwickelt, besteht in der Annahme, bestimmte Merkmale wie Selbstbewusstsein haben zweifelsfrei und konkret nachweisbar vorzuliegen. Während die gradualistische Position von einer *allmählichen* und *kontinuierlichen* Entwicklung ausgeht, ist die Annahme der Notwendigkeit bestimmter Kriterien, die häufig mit der Unterscheidung von nicht-personalem und personalem Leben einhergeht, insofern eine Alles-oder-Nichts-Variante, als sie nicht einen „gewissen Schutz" annimmt, der menschlichem Leben als solchem von Anfang an zukommt und sich allmählich steigert, sondern den Lebensschutz an Kriterien bindet, die sich erst zu einem bestimmten Zeitpunkt einstellen.

Demgegenüber wird von den Vertretern eines strengen Embryonenschutzes und *Kritikern* einer liberalen Gesetzgebung häufig das Argument verwendet, Embryonen seien bereits ab dem Zeitpunkt der Kernverschmelzung schützenswert. Sowohl der gradualistischen als auch der „Alles-oder-Nichts-Position" wird damit eine Position entgegengesetzt, die – mit unterschiedlichen Begründungsmodellen – dem Menschsein *als solchen* eine *absolute* Schutzwürdigkeit zuspricht. Befürworter eines strengen Embryonenschutzes argumentieren meist mit mindestens einem der folgenden Argumente:

· Forschung an Embryonen widerspricht dem
· Prinzip der *Menschenwürde* und ist deswegen ethisch inakzeptabel. Das Menschenwürde-Prinzip kann auf Embryonen angewandt werden, weil diese vom Zeitpunkt der Kernverschmelzung an Menschen sind und darum vollen Lebensschutz genießen.
· Forschung an Embryonen ist deswegen *nicht sinnvoll*, weil die Risiken ihrer Anwendung bisher noch nicht hinreichend erforscht worden sind und darum keine begründete Hoffnung auf therapeutische Anwendung von embryonalen Stammzellen bestehen kann.
· Zumindest aus *Vorsichtsgründen* sollte davon abgesehen werden, menschliche Embryonen zu Forschungszwecken zu „verbrauchen".

Das in diesem Zusammenhang inhaltlich wichtigste *Menschenwürde*-Argument kann seinerseits in unterschiedlichen Formen und mit unterschiedlichen Begründungen verwendet und unterschiedlich stark gewichtet werden. Aufgrund seiner unterschiedlichen Begründungsmodelle ist es in sich mehrdeutig. Der nun folgende Teil des Buches beschäftigt sich mit unterschiedlichen Interpretationsmodellen von *Menschenwürde* und mithin zugleich ideengeschichtlichen Konzeptionen und Voraussetzungen, die mit diesen Interpretationsmodellen und der im Ländervergleich differenten Gesetzgebung zusammenhängen. Diese Darstellung verfolgt vor allem das Ziel, zu einer Klärung bei der Frage nach dem Umgang mit menschlichem Leben beizutragen.

Ich stelle zunächst Verständnismodelle von Menschenwürde dar, die ich im weiteren Verlauf der Ausführungen interpretiere und exemplarisch mit einflussreichen theologisch- und philosophisch-ethischen Konzeptionen aus dem deutschen und englischen Sprachraum verbinde, womit ich eine präzisierende Klärung des in der britischen Diskussion als „vage“[131] bezeichneten Begriffs intendiere, die dann im abschließenden Teil des Buches versucht und mit der Frage nach dem ethischen Umgang mit menschlichen Embryonen verbunden werden soll.

III. 1 Menschenwürde als Fundament des Embryonenschutzes?

Der Begriff „Menschenwürde“ spielt in der deutschen bioethischen Debatte um die ethische Zulässigkeit der Forschung an Embryonen eine zentrale, wenn auch nicht unangefochtene[132] Rolle. Dabei ist aber alles andere als klar, ob Menschenwürde als menschliche Eigenschaft ab der Kernverschmelzung,[133] als sich prozessual entwickelnde Begabung oder als allererst aufgrund bestimmter qualitativer Merkmale zu erwerbender „Status“ verstanden werden muss. Auch wenn „Menschenwürde“ bei vielen Menschen positive Assoziationen weckt,[134] können nur die wenigsten den Begriff definieren, so dass er *als solcher* für die bioethische Debatte noch nicht notwendigerweise konsensbildend wirkt.

Zum rechtsbegründenden und ethisch einflussreichen Begriff ist *Menschenwürde* politisch breit wirksam erst nach 1945 geworden,[135] wobei der

---

[131] S. oben, S. 56, Anm. 108.

[132] Der Jurist Bernhard Schlink etwa hat sich im „Spiegel“ am 15. Dezember 2003 kritisch gegenüber einer Verwendung des Menschenwürde-Begriffs in der aktuellen bioethischen Debatte geäußert: „Die überforderte Menschenwürde. Welche Gewissheit kann Artikel I des Grundgesetzes geben?“ Ähnlich kritisch gegenüber einem inflationären Gebrauch von *Menschenwürde* äußert sich Matthias Herdegen in seinem Grundgesetzkommentar, oder E. Schmidt-Jortzig, „Menschenwürde“ als Zauberwort in der öffentlichen Debatte. Demokratische Meinungsbildung in hochkomplexen Problemfeldern, ZEE 52, 2008, 50-56.

[133] Wird Menschenwürde als menschliche Eigenschaft ab der Kernverschmelzung verstanden, kann nochmals unterschieden werden zwischen der Annahme einer *intrinsischen* Wesenseigenschaft und der Annahme einer *relational zugesprochenen* Wirklichkeit. Diese Differenzierung wird weiter unten (Abschnitt II.2.4, S. 106ff.) eine Rolle spielen. Darüber hinaus kann Menschenwürde als Wesensmerkmal auch ab der *Nidation* angenommen werden.

[134] Vgl. D. Feldman, Human dignity as a legal value, Public Law 1999, 682-702.

[135] Als endes Prinzip in Verfassungstexten findet sich *Menschenwürde* im deutschen Grundgesetz und in den europäischen Verfassungen von Irland, Spanien,

Begriff vor allem im letzten Drittel des 20. Jahrhunderts und zu Beginn des 21. Jahrhunderts eine enorme Wertschätzung in der bioethischen Diskussion im Zusammenhang mit den ethischen und rechtlichen Problemen am menschlichen Lebensbeginn und Lebensende erlebt hat: Der zunächst philosophisch-theologische Begriff in der Tradition von Stoa, Christentum und Aufklärung ist im 20. Jahrhundert zu einem rechtlichen und vor allem im letzten Drittel des 20. Jahrhunderts zu einem bioethischen Konzept mit weit reichenden positiven Konnotationen geworden. Im Zusammenhang mit dem immens gewachsenen Wissen vor allem in der biomedizinischen Forschung bildet er inzwischen häufig einen hermeneutischen Schlüssel für die Frage, welche Forschungs- und Therapiemöglichkeiten (noch) mit der Menschenwürde vereinbar seien und welche Forschung bzw. Therapie als Verstoß gegen die Achtung der Menschenwürde[136] abgelehnt werden müssen. Dabei weist der Menschenwürdebegriff aber eine enorme Bandbreite an Deutungs- und Begründungsmöglichkeiten auf, die zu seiner Charakterisierung als „begründungsoffen" und zu einer Suche nach einer konsensfähigen Minimaldefinition[137] von *Menschenwürde* im

---

Italien, Griechenland, Portugal, Finnland, Schweden und Belgien, außerdem in der Schweiz und in Südafrika. Darüber hinaus steht sie an zentraler Position in der Internationalen Erklärung der Menschenrechte und der Europäischen Verfassungs-Charta. In die irische Verfassung ist der Begriff schon 1937 übernommen worden. In Abschnitt 5 dieses Kapitels (S. 171ff.) wird dieser Zusammenhang nochmals aufgegriffen.

[136] In diesem Zusammenhang wird umgangssprachlich nicht immer sauber zwischen der Gewährung der *Achtung* vor der Menschenwürde und einer Gewährung der *Menschenwürde* unterschieden. Dass es sich hierbei aber um unterschiedliche Dinge handelt, wird etwa daran deutlich, dass die Gewährung der *Menschenwürde* diese in einen Zuständigkeitsbereich von Menschen legt, während die Gewährung der *Achtung* die Menschenwürde als unantastbares und unverfügbares Gut ansieht. Im Zusammenhang mit dieser Unterscheidung kann die Frage gestellt werden, ob die Formulierung in Art. 1 I GG („Die Würde des Menschen ist unantastbar") *präskriptiv* oder *deskriptiv* zu verstehen ist („die Würde des Menschen *soll* unantastbar *sein*" bzw. „die Würde des Menschen *ist* unantastbar"). Diese Differenz hat weit reichende Folgen für das Verständnis von Menschenwürde.

[137] Wolfgang Vögele versteht Menschenwürde als tragfähigen Begriff sowohl für die Ethik als auch für die Gesetzgebung innerhalb des Pluralismus. „Menschenwürde" als offener Minimalbegriff für eine Vielzahl von Interpretation müsste dann aber folgende Merkmale aufweisen:
· Universalität,
· Voraussetzung, nicht Aufgabe des Menschseins,
· intrinsische Werthaftigkeit,
· breit gefasstes Prinzip und
· rechtsbegründendes Prinzip.
(Vgl. Vögele, Menschenwürde und Gottebenbildlichkeit, in: Dierken/Scheliha (Hrsg.), Freiheit und Menschenwürde. Studien zum Beitrag des Protestantismus, Tübingen

Sinne eines politisch, ethisch und rechtsbegründend wirksamen Konzepts geführt haben.[138]

Eine Differenzierung dessen, was Menschenwürde aussagt und bedeutet, ist darum sinnvoll, um die Tragfähigkeit des Begriffs für die internationale bioethische und biopolitische Debatte zu prüfen, zumal *human dignity* in völkerrechtlichen Texten offenbar eine tragende Rolle spielt, in der britischen Debatte aber nur auffallend wenig rezipiert wird. Nach den angedeuteten Verständnisdifferenzierungen, die der Begriff mit sich bringt, können im Anschluss an Horst Dreier[139] mindestens drei Begründungsmodelle für Menschenwürde ausgemacht werden, die ich im folgenden knapp skizziere, auf die Frage nach dem Würdebeginn bei frühen Embryonen beziehe und im Anschluss daran in den folgenden Abschnitten dieses Kapitels anhand von ethischen Konzeptionen exemplarisch interpretiere und illustriere.[140]

· Die *Mitgifttheorie*, nach der Menschenwürde jedem menschlichen Wesen (meist) ab der Kernverschmelzung von Ei- und Samenzelle, zumindest aber ab der Nidation[141] uneingeschränkt und unabwägbar zukommt. Menschenwürde beruht für dieses Begründungsmodell auf Vorausset-

2005, 268-270.) Zumindest die Merkmale eines universalen intrinsischen und rechtsbegründenden Prinzips verstehen sich aber keineswegs von selbst.

[138] Die von Theodor Heuss geprägte Formulierung der „nicht-interpretierten These" (vgl. Härle, Menschenwürde - konkret und grundsätzlich, in: Ders., Menschsein in Beziehungen, Tübingen 2005, 379-410, S. 380f.) hat sich allerdings nicht bis in die Gegenwart fortgesetzt.

[139] Dreier, Grundgesetz-Kommentar, Tübingen 1996, ²2004, Randnummer 54ff. Vgl. auch K. Haucke, Mitgift, Leistung, Anerkennung. Ein philosophischer Vorschlag für ein integrales Verständnis menschlicher Würde, Ethica 14, 2006, 227-254; S. Rolf, Menschenwürde - Grund oder Spitze der Menschenrechte?, in: F.M. Brunn u. a. (Hrsg.), Menschenbild und Theologie, Festgabe für Wilfried Härle zum 65. Geburtstag, MThS 100, Leipzig 2007, 121-140.

[140] Dabei ist nochmals zu unterscheiden zwischen *Menschenwürde* und der Annahme eines notwendigen *Lebensschutzes*, die sich als ethische und rechtliche Folgerung aus dem Verständnis von Menschenwürde ergibt.

[141] Die Mitgifttheorie argumentiert, wenn sie von einer Würdebegabung *ab* der Nidation ausgeht, weniger, wie die Vorschläge der Warnock-Kommission, mit dem Beginn der *Individuation* als dem Beginn der Schutzwürdigkeit, sondern eher mit der *Interaktion* des sich entwickelnden Embryos mit seiner Umwelt, im Falle der Nidation mit dem mütterlichen Leib. So in der Argumentationshilfe der EKD „Im Geist der Liebe mit dem Leben umgehen", 2002, in der die beiden Ansichten einander gegenüberstehen, nach denen Menschenwürde menschlichem Leben von der Kernverschmelzung an und ab der Nidation zukommt. Die zweite Auffassung argumentiert mit der Bedeutung der menschlichen Entwicklungsfähigkeit: „Nach dieser Auffassung kann von einem sich entwickelnden Menschen nur gesprochen werden, wenn die äußeren Umstände für eine Entwicklung gegeben sind." (A.a.O., 22.) In diesem Zusammenhang spielt die häufig vertretene Ansicht der moralischen Relevanz des *Ortes* des Embryos eine Rolle und

zungen wie der Gottebenbildlichkeit oder der menschlichen Vernunftnatur und entzieht sich als unverfügbares Gut dem menschlichen Zugriff.

- Die *Leistungstheorie*, die menschlichen Wesen Menschenwürde aufgrund einer besonderen Leistung zuerkennt, die diese zu erbringen haben, beispielsweise ihr aktueller *Vernunftgebrauch*, die Ausbildung von *Identität*[142] oder ihre Fähigkeit, sich als Wesen innerhalb eines zeitlichen Kontinuums mit bestimmten *Interessen* zu begreifen. Es gibt darum keine absolute, vorgegebene oder intrinsische Schutzwürdigkeit von frühen Embryonen oder anderen menschlichen Wesen, die diese entsprechende Leistung nicht erbringen können.
- Menschenwürde kann nach diesem Begründungsmodell bei fortschreitender Entwicklung auch graduell zunehmen, insofern einem menschlichen Wesen desto mehr Würde zugeschrieben wird, je mehr es in der Lage ist, bestimmte Kriterien zu erfüllen.[143]
- Die *Kommunikationstheorie*,[144] für die der moralische Status eines menschlichen Wesens kontextabhängig zu bewerten ist. Ob einem Embryo Menschenwürde eignet oder nicht, entscheidet sich an der Situation und den mit dem Nasciturus im Verhältnis Stehenden. Eine von *allen* Mitgliedern der menschlichen Gattung geteilte Menschenwürde beginnt mit dem Eintritt in den Kommunikationszusammenhang, das heißt aber häufig erst mit der Geburt.[145]

---

die daraus abgeleitete Unterscheidung von „befruchteten Eizellen" (*in vitro*) und „Embryonen" (*in utero*), die einen unterschiedlichen moralischen Status nach sich zieht.

[142] Vgl. N. Luhmann (Grundrechte als Institution. Ein Beitrag zur politischen Soziologie, Schriften zum Öffentlichen Recht 24, Berlin 1965, 68f.): „Die Würde des Menschen ist keineswegs eine Naturausstattung wie vermutlich gewisse Grundlagen der Intelligenz... Würde muß konstituiert werden. Sie ist das Ergebnis schwieriger, auf generelle Systeminteressen der Persönlichkeit bezogener, teils bewußter, teils unbewußter Darstellungsleistungen und im gleichen Maße Ergebnis ständiger Kooperation, die ebenfalls bewußt, latent oder durchschauend... praktiziert werden kann."

[143] In Frage kommende Zäsuren bei der embryonalen Entwicklung sind etwa die Nidation, die Ausbildung des zentralen Nervensystems, die Geburt, die Fähigkeit zur Schmerzempfindung oder der Bekundung eigener Interessen als zeitliches Wesen.

[144] Würde ist hier ein Relations- und Kommunikationsbegriff, „als deren Schutzgut die mitmenschliche Solidarität firmiert" (Dreier, Grundgesetz-Kommentar, 185).

[145] So Jürgen Habermas, Die Zukunft der menschlichen Natur. Auf dem Weg zu einer liberalen Eugenik?, Frankfurt/Main [4]2002, 62: Menschenwürde sei keine „Eigenschaft, die man von Natur aus 'besitzen' kann", sondern eine Form der „'Unantastbarkeit', die allein in den interpersonalen Beziehungen reziproker Anerkennung, im egalitären Umgang von Personen miteinander eine Bedeutung haben kann." Erst mit der Geburt vollziehe sich „der gesellschaftlich individuierende Akt der Aufnahme in den *öffentlichen* Interaktionszusammenhang einer subjektiv geteilten Lebenswelt" (64f).

Diese drei Interpretationsmodelle von Menschenwürde liefern eine Topographie, um Konzeptionen innerhalb der Debatte zum Embryonenschutz auf ihre Hintergründe zu befragen. Sie geben zugleich für die weiteren Überlegungen einen strukturierenden Rahmen vor.

Darüber hinaus kann Menschen*würde* im Anschluss an völkerrechtliche Texte wie die Menschenrechtsdeklaration der UNO (1948)[146] als *rechtsbegründender Begriff* im Zusammenhang mit den Menschen*rechten* verstanden werden.[147] Dieses vierte Modell ist aber insofern kategorial von den anderen dreien zu unterscheiden, als mit diesem Verständnis einer Zuordnung von Menschenwürde und Menschenrechten *jedes* der drei zuvor genannten Modelle verbunden werden könnte, die Reichweite der Menschen*rechte* sich also nach dem Verständnis von Menschen*würde* richtet.

In der Darstellung des nun folgenden Teils des Buches sind alle vier Deutungsmodelle von Menschenwürde relevant für die Gliederung, wobei die kommenden Abschnitte – der Typologisierung der drei bzw. vier Interpretationsmodelle folgend – zunächst unterschiedlichen Verständnismodellen von Menschenwürde im Rahmen der Mitgifttheorie nachgehen und sich anschließend Konzepten zuwenden, die sich eher der Leistungs- und Kommunikationstheorie zuordnen lassen, um schließlich das Verhältnis von Menschenwürde und Menschenrechten in England und Deutschland und im internationalen Kontext vor allem hinsichtlich der bioethischen Urteilsbildung in den Blick zu nehmen. Dabei steht auch die im vorangegangenen Abschnitt gestellte Frage im Hintergrund, warum innerhalb der britischen Diskussion der Menschenwürde-Begriff als so spröde erscheint und so auffallend selten rezipiert wird.

Diese Darstellung hat den Sinn, unterschiedliche Voraussetzungen in englischer und deutscher Ideengeschichte mit dem Menschenwürde-Begriff an *einem* Beispiel aufzuzeigen, deren Auswirkungen sich in unterschiedlicher Gesetzgebung hinsichtlich des Umgangs mit menschlichen Embryonen mani-

---

[146] Ein Verweis auf die Menschenwürde findet sich im Text in der Präambel und in Artikel 1. Die Erklärung kann in offizieller deutscher Übersetzung eingesehen werden unter http://www.unhchr.ch/udhr/lang/ger.htm.

[147] Die Struktur von Begründung und Durchführung kann auch im Aufbau des deutschen Grundgesetzes im Verhältnis von Art. 1 I, der die Achtung der Menschenwürde vorschreibt, und den übrigen Grundrechtsartikeln festgestellt werden. In seiner Kommentierung des Grundgesetzes versteht Günter Dürig die Menschenwürde als unantastbares Tabu, das rechtsbegründend für die Grundrechte fungiert (in: Maunz/Dürig, Kommentar zum Grundgesetz, München 1958, Randnummer 81ff.). Diese *eindeutige* Zuordnung wird in der Neukommentierung des deutschen Grundgesetzes durch Matthias Herdegen angezweifelt. Eine rechtsbegründende Funktion der Menschenwürde für die Menschenrechte bestreitet Franz-Josef Wetz, Die Würde des Menschen: antastbar? Eine Provokation, 1998.
(S. www.politische-bildung.de/niedersachsen/wuerde_menschen.pdf).

festieren. Die Gliederung der folgenden Abschnitte folgt den eben dargestellten Modellen zum Verständnis von Menschenwürde, wobei sich gleichzeitig ein Gefälle von einem starken zu einem schwachen Embryonenschutz ergibt. Dabei bilden vor allem die Mitgift- und die Leistungstheorie zwei einander entgegengesetzte Pole.

III. 2 Menschenwürde als vorgegebenes und unverfügbares Gut im Rahmen der „Mitgifttheorie"

Gegen die Forschung an menschlichen Embryonen wird sowohl in der deutschen als auch in der englischen Debatte von Vertretern der christlichen Kirchen und von Theologen, aber auch von sich nicht einer Kirche zugehörig fühlenden Institutionen das Argument der *Menschenwürde* herangezogen, gegen deren Achtung eine Forschung an Embryonen, die diesen nicht direkt zugute komme, im allgemeinen, und die jüngst in Großbritannien rechtlich erlaubte Erzeugung von tierisch-menschlichen Misch-Embryonen im besonderen verstoße. Das sich dabei meist kommunizierende Verständnis von Menschenwürde entspricht nach der oben gegebenen Klassifizierung häufig dem Mitgiftmodell, das seinerseits in unterschiedlichen Ausprägungen interpretiert werden kann. Für Kritiker der Forschung an menschlichen Embryonen stellt „Menschenwürde" eine von Beginn an gegebene menschliche Wesenseigenschaft oder eine anzuerkennende Realität dar, gegen deren Achtung die „verbrauchende Forschung" verstößt.

Ich wende mich zunächst der Begründung von Menschenwürde mit der theologischen Annahme der menschlichen Gottebenbildlichkeit zu, um anschließend das ebenfalls klassische Würdeverständnis von Immanuel Kant knapp zu referieren.

III. 2. 1 Menschenwürde als Gottebenbildlichkeit? Theologiegeschichtliche Diskontinuitäten

Eines der traditionellen Begründungsmodelle für „Menschenwürde" ist das theologische Konzept der Gottebenbildlichkeit (*imago Dei*),[148] das sich aufgrund der *Vorgegebenheit* und der *Unverfügbarkeit* der menschlichen Gottebenbildlichkeit der Mitgifttheorie zuordnen lässt. Auch wenn das Theologumenon der *imago Dei* aber bereits in der biblischen Theologie eine Rolle spielt und in den ersten Kapiteln der Genesis (Gen 1,27; auch Gen 5,1; 9,6) die besondere Stellung des Menschen innerhalb der geschöpflichen Welt aus-

[148] Das Verhältnis von Menschenwürde und Gottebenbildlichkeit wird im abschließenden Kapitel noch einmal eine Rolle spielen. S. unten, S. 199ff.

sagt,[149] findet sich die Verknüpfung mit *Menschenwürde* theologiegeschichtlich erst später.[150]

Innerhalb der alttestamentlichen Exegese ist in der zweiten Hälfte des 20. Jahrhunderts festgestellt worden, dass Israel mit dem Topos der menschlichen Gottebenbildlichkeit ein Anthropologumenon aus seiner altorientalischen Umwelt, vor allem aus Ägypten, aufnimmt und transformiert. Während es in ägyptischer Tradition der *Pharao* ist, der als Gottes Ebenbild die Gottheit auf Erden repräsentiert, gilt diese Repräsentations-Relation in alttestamentlicher Theologie für *jeden* Menschen (Mann *und* Frau), so dass in der biblischen Aufnahme der altägyptischen Königstheologie in der Formulierung der menschlichen Gottebenbildlichkeit eine Universalisierung hinsichtlich der Herrschaftsvorstellung des Topos und ein ideologiekritischer Impuls gegen die Deifizierung des herrschenden Königs liegen.[151]

Die sich an dem doppelten Ausdruck צלם und דמות in Gen 1,26f. orientierende klassische Unterscheidung von *imago* und *similitudo* hat theologiegeschichtlich seit der Patristik zu dem Verständnis geführt, dass mit dem Sündenfall die Ähnlichkeit des Menschen mit Gott hinsichtlich des *Verhaltens* verloren worden, die Ebenbildlichkeit hinsichtlich des *Seins* aber erhalten geblieben sei und die besondere Würde des Menschen begründe. Die Gottebenbildlichkeit ist in diesem Zusammenhang meist als geschöpfliche menschliche Ausstattung mit Vernunft und Willen verstanden worden, die auch nach dem Fall bestehen bleibt, während das Gott entsprechende Verhalten im Halten der göttlichen Gebote aufgrund der Sünde als korrumpiert galt.[152] Die als klassisch angesehene Verbindung von Menschenwürde und menschlicher Gottebenbildlichkeit ist dabei theologiegeschichtlich aber auffallend locker. Dabei ist noch einmal zu unterscheiden zwischen einem *theologischen* Begriff von *dignitas humana*, der mit der Gottebenbildlichkeit assoziiert, und einem *ethisch* und *politisch* wirksamen Begriff, der erst nach der Aufklärung entwickelt worden ist und an dem die christliche Theologie zunächst keinen Anteil hat.

---

[149] Auffallend ist in diesem Zusammenhang allerdings, dass nach Gen 9 die menschliche Gottebenbildlichkeit terminologisch nicht wieder aufgenommen wird und erst in der zwischentestamentarischen Weisheitsliteratur und dann im Neuen Testament wieder erscheint.

[150] Noch später werden aus der Verbindung von Menschenwürde und Gottebenbildlichkeit eine Würdebegabung *aller* Menschen (nicht nur von Christen) abgeleitet und politische Konsequenzen gezogen.

[151] Zur alttestamentlichen Theologie der Gottebenbildlichkeit vgl. B. Janowski, Die lebendige Statue Gottes. Zur Anthropologie der priesterlichen Urgeschichte, in: M. Witte (Hrsg.), Gott und Mensch im Dialog, FS für O. Kaiser zum 80. Geburtstag, Berlin/New York 2004, 183-214, vor allem S. 193ff.

[152] Vgl. kurz zusammengefasst bei W. Härle, Dogmatik, Berlin/New York ²2000, 434-437.

Bei *Ambrosius von Mailand* (340-397) findet sich theologiegeschichtlich wahrscheinlich erstmals die Begründung von Menschenwürde (*dignitas humana*) mit der menschlichen Gottebenbildlichkeit. Ambrosius versteht die die Menschenwürde begründende Gottebenbildlichkeit allerdings nicht schöpfungstheologisch als menschliche Vernunftnatur, sondern als Ähnlichkeit mit der Dreieinigkeit Gottes[153] in der Trias des menschlichen Geisteslebens in Seele, Geist und Willen. Damit begründet er Menschenwürde und Gottebenbildlichkeit trinitätstheologisch mit der menschlichen Verfasstheit in der Ähnlichkeit zu Gott dem Vater, dem Sohn und dem Heiligen Geist.[154] Die Würde des Menschen besteht für Ambrosius darin, dass er in seiner konstitutiven, sich auf das Wirken Gottes zurückführenden Verfasstheit auf seinen Schöpfer verwiesen ist, allerdings nicht ausschließlich in seiner vernünftigen Natur, sondern in seiner leib-seelisch-geistigen Einheit.

Die Begründung einer universalen menschlichen Würde durch die Gottebenbildlichkeit kann sich zu dieser Zeit aber noch nicht zu einem orientierenden Referenzpunkt in Kirche, Gesellschaft und Politik entwickeln, weil die Differenz von Christen, Häretikern und Nichtchristen in der mittelalterlichen Theologie vorherrscht und darüber hinaus die menschliche Sündhaftigkeit für eine Formulierung einer allen Menschen zukommenden Würde als Begründung von universalen Menschenrechten hindernd erscheint. Diese Akzentuierung ändert sich in der Zeit von Humanismus, Renaissance und Reformation.[155]

Der italienische Renaissancephilosoph *Pico della Mirandola* (1463-1497) sieht als diejenige Eigenschaft des Menschen, die vor allen anderen seine Gottebenbildlichkeit ausmacht, wiederum nicht die menschliche Vernunftnatur, auch nicht seine leib-seelisch-geistige Verfasstheit, sondern die menschliche Freiheit an, mit der dieser seine Selbstverwirklichung zu wählen habe. Die Würde des Menschen besteht für Pico darin, aus der Fülle der Möglichkeiten

[153] Vgl. Ambrosius, De dignitate conditionis humanae, MPL 17, 1105ff. Horst Dreier vermutet einen anderen Autor als Verfasser der Schrift, die erst in der karolingischen Zeit entstanden sei (Dreier, Menschenwürde aus verfassungsrechtlicher Sicht, in: Härle/Preul (Hrsg.), Menschenwürde, MJTh XVII, MThS 89, Marburg 2005, 167-210, 175.) Dabei bezieht sich Dreier auf die Monographie von J. Marenborn, From the Circle of Alcuin to the School of Auxerre, Cambridge u. a. 1981.

[154] Damit kann für Ambrosius der Mensch nicht nur auf dem theologiegeschichtlich später festgestellten und bedeutsamen Weg der vernünftigen Erwägung aufgrund der *analogia entis* zu Gotteserkenntnis gelangen, sondern findet den Spiegel des dreieinigen Gottes in seiner eigenen Verfasstheit von Seele, Willen und Geist.

[155] Weitere Beispiele für eine Neuakzentuierung des Menschenwürde-Begriffs ab dem 15. Jahrhundert bei W. Huber, Art. Menschenrechte/Menschenwürde, TRE 22, 1992, 577ff.

zu wählen und in Freiheit mit eigener Kraft das höchste Glück zu erreichen,[156] wobei er menschliches Sein in Anlehnung an die aristotelische Seelenlehre so beschreibt, nicht wie die übrigen geschöpflichen Lebewesen (Pflanzen und Tiere) auf einen bestimmten Zustand wie den vegetativen oder physischen festgelegt zu sein, sondern mit Hilfe von Freiheit die eigene Lebensweise als die Lebensweise eines *geistigen* Wesens wählen zu können. Auch bei Pico wird Menschenwürde deskriptiv, nicht präskriptiv gebraucht, insofern Pico keine Folgerungen aus seiner Menschenwürdekonzeption etwa hinsichtlich einer gebotenen Gleichbehandlung aller Menschen ableitet.

In der Reformationszeit wird aufgrund der Neuformulierung der Rechtfertigungslehre die Freiheit des Gewissens des Einzelnen neu akzentuiert und als Begründung individueller Rechte der Gemeinschaft gegenüber ausgelegt.[157] Die klassische patristische Unterscheidung hinsichtlich der Gottebenbildlichkeit zwischen *imago* und *similitudo* wird von der reformatorischen Theologie vor allem deswegen nicht übernommen,[158] weil für die Reformatoren auch die Vernunft, die gleichwohl als die den Menschen gegenüber den Tieren auszeichnende Besonderheit verstanden wird, als korrumpiert gilt.[159] Diese Korruption der Vernunft – und auch des Willens – betrifft die Gottebenbildlichkeit als ganze, so dass *Martin Luther* nicht von einer geschöpflichen, auch nach dem Fall intakten Würde jedes Menschen sprechen kann. Seinem christologischen Fokus entsprechend, versteht er die Gottebenbildlichkeit als in Christus verwirklicht und jedem Menschen im Glauben zugeeignet, darin zugleich aber als menschliche Bestimmung.[160]

---

[156] Oratio de hominis dignitate, Über die Würde des Menschen, übersetzt von Norbert Baumgarten, hrsg. und eingeleitet von A. Buck, Hamburg 1990.

[157] Vgl. etwa Luthers Auslegung des Magnifikat (1521, WA 7, 544-604), in der Luther nicht nur von „groben menschlichen Rechten" ausgeht, sondern auch von den „höchsten Gütern" des Glaubens und des Evangeliums.

[158] Gegenwärtige römisch-katholische Theologie sowohl in der englischen als auch der deutschen Diskussion nimmt von der Unterscheidung zwischen der Ähnlichkeit des Verhaltens (*similitudo*) und der Ähnlichkeit in der Wesensbestimmung (*imago*) inzwischen auch Abstand, tendiert aber zu einem ontologischen Verständnis der menschlichen Gottebenbildlichkeit, nach dem der Mensch nach der *analogia entis* mit Hilfe seiner geschöpflichen Vernunft Einsicht in Gottes Wesen erhalten könne und darum in seiner Vernunftnatur, die als Abbild auf das Urbild der göttlichen *ratio fidei* verweise, besonders ausgezeichnet sei.

[159] So prominent Luther in der Disputatio de Homine (1536), in zweisprachiger Ausgabe greifbar in LDStA 1, 663ff. Neben Luthers theologischem Vorbehalt, auch für den postadamitischen Menschen Gottebenbildlichkeit anzunehmen, spielt das linguistische Argument eine Rolle, nach dem mit den Begriffen צלם und דמות ein Hendyadioin gebraucht wird.

[160] Für Luthers Verständnis der Gottebenbildlichkeit im Zusammenhang mit der christlichen Gerechtigkeit verweise ich auf S. Rolf, Zum Herzen sprechen. Eine Studie zum

Weit reichende politische Folgerungen ergeben sich darum aus dem reformatorischen *Freiheits*- und *Gewissens*begriff, nicht aber aus dem Verständnis der menschlichen Gottebenbildlichkeit und einer damit assoziierten Menschenwürde. Der Menschenwürdebegriff firmiert demgegenüber im Zusammenhang mit dem Menschenrechtsbegriff im *außerkirchlichen* Kontext vor allem innerhalb des Liberalismus zu einer zentralen Konzeption, die von den Kirchen zunächst kritisch beurteilt und nicht rezipiert wird. In den großen Konfessionen besteht eine große Zurückhaltung gegenüber der Idee, die menschliche Gottebenbildlichkeit konstituiere eine für *alle* Menschen geltende Würde, aus der politische, ethische und rechtliche Konsequenzen abgeleitet werden könnten.[161] Auch die Ausweitung einer allen Menschen zukommenden Würde schon auf ungeborene Menschen steht bis ins 20. Jahrhundert hinein nicht im Fokus der Theologie.[162]

Die Vorbehalte der christlichen Kirchen gegenüber einem politisch-rechtlichen universalen Konzept von Menschenwürde haben ihren Grund dabei nicht nur in unterschiedlichen Auffassungen vom Menschen und von der menschlichen Gottebenbildlichkeit, sondern vielmehr darin, dass *Menschenwürde* im Anschluss an die Renaissancephilosophie in der Philosophie der Aufklärung mit der menschlichen *Freiheit* und *Vernunftnatur* begründet wurde und bei stärker einsetzender Säkularisierung von der Konzeption der Gottebenbildlichkeit gelöst worden ist. In der französischen Revolution wird Menschenwürde vollkommen ohne den Rekurs auf die menschliche Gottebenbildlichkeit verstanden, was dazu geführt hat, dass vor allem die katholische Kirche in dieser Zeit dem (säkularen) Konzept der Menschenwürde kritisch gegenüber steht, aber auch die evangelische Theologie aufgrund ihrer Ablehnung einer *natürlichen* Ausstattung des Menschen zum Guten eine nichtchristlich begründete Würde des Menschen nicht vertreten kann. Das eher den englischsprachigen Raum prägende und in starkem Maße vom Liberalis-

---

imputativen Aspekt in Martin Luthers Rechtsfertigungslehre und zu seinen Konsequenzen für die Predigt des Evangeliums, Leipzig 2008.

[161] Auch wenn diese Zurückhaltung im Raum der katholischen Kirche inzwischen international nicht mehr besteht, setzt sie sich im Kontext sowohl der *Church of England* als auch der *Church of Scotland* fort. Es gibt nur wenige Publikationen über *human dignity*, und auf den Websites der Kirchen wird *human dignity* nicht mit der *imago Dei* konnotiert. Vgl. http://www.cofe.anglican.org und http://www.churchofscotland.org.uk.

[162] Vor allem in der katholischen Theologie hat die aristotelische und thomanische Vorstellung lange nachgewirkt, dass die Beseelung des Embryo im Mutterleib erst einige Wochen *nach* der Kernverschmelzung stattfinde, so dass frühe Embryonen noch nicht die Kriteriologie zum Menschsein erfüllen können. Vgl. den Artikel von Heike Schmoll in der Frankfurter Allgemeinen Zeitung vom 31. Mai 2001: Wann wird der Mensch ein Mensch? Über den Zeitpunkt der „Beseelung" eines Embryos streiten die Gelehrten seit der Antike.

mus beeinflusste Konzept der Menschenrechte als Freiheitsrechte ist von den Kirchen aus ähnlichen Gründen ausgesprochen kritisch beurteilt worden.

Menschenwürde entwickelt sich ebenso wie *Menschenrechte* darum vom 18. bis zum 20. Jahrhundert als Konzept außerhalb von Theologie und Kirche zunächst in der Philosophie, aber mit zunehmendem Gewicht auch in der Politik. In den 20er Jahren des 20. Jahrhunderts wird die Rede von der Menschenwürde, die zu der Zeit noch kein rechtsbegründender Begriff in nationalen Verfassungen ist, im deutschen Sprachraum vor allem in attributiven Verbindungen („menschenwürdig") in der sich entwickelnden sozialdemokratischen Politik gebraucht und von Kirchen und zahlreichen Theologen kritisch beurteilt. In Konkurrenz zu der als sozialistisch geprägt empfundenen *Menschenwürde* werden in der deutschen liberalen protestantischen Theologie vor allem die *christliche Freiheit* und der unendliche Wert der *Menschenseele*[163] in der Tradition von Kant und Hegel hervorgehoben.[164] Mit einer theologischen Interpretation des *Werts* der menschlichen Seele treten aber die bei Kant äquivalent gebrauchten Begriffe „Würde" und „Wert" auseinander, während gleichzeitig die Korrelation von Menschenwürde und Gottebenbildlichkeit in der liberalen Theologie nicht (mehr) im Bewusstsein ist. Eine Verbindung von Menschenwürde und Gottebenbildlichkeit mit *politischen* Konsequenzen war in der Theologiegeschichte ohnehin noch nicht gesehen worden.

Erst seit der Mitte des 20. Jahrhunderts können auch die christliche Theologie und die christlichen Kirchen[165] vor allem im deutschen Sprachraum den Menschenwürdebegriff rezipieren und von einer Würde nicht nur der Angehörigen der jeweils eigenen konfessionellen Gemeinschaft, sondern von einer Würde des Menschen an sich ausgehen. Als die Konzeption von Menschen-

[163] Einen Wert hat die Seele in diesem Zusammenhang als Organ der Gottesbeziehung, weil sich in der Seele die Vereinigung von Glaubendem und Gott ereignet. Damit ist etwa für Adolf von Harnack der Begriff der Seele – im Gegensatz zum Menschenwürdebegriff – eine religiöse Kategorie, so dass die Auszeichnung des Menschen mit der Gottesbeziehung nicht mit dem Menschsein an sich gegeben ist und darum nicht als universale Kategorie ausgesagt werden kann. Die von Kant vertretene Würde der menschlichen Vernunftnatur wird von der deutschen Theologie im frühen 20. Jahrhundert nicht rezipiert.

[164] Vgl. A. von Scheliha, „Menschenwürde" – Konkurrent oder Realisator der christlichen Freiheit? Theologiegeschichtliche Perspektiven, in: Ders./J. Dierken (Hrsg.), Freiheit und Menschenwürde. Studien zum Beitrag des Protestantismus, Tübingen 2005, 241-263, 254.

[165] Ein Beispiel für die Aufnahme des Menschenwürdebegriffs in die katholische Soziallehre bildet die Konstitution *Dignitatis Humanae* im 2. Vaticanum (7. 12. 1965) als Erklärung über die menschliche Religionsfreiheit (DH 4240-4245). Aber auch schon in der Enzyklika *Pacem in terris* von Johannes XXIII. (1963) findet sich ausdrücklich ein Bekenntnis zu den menschlichen Freiheitsrechten (DH 3958-3969). Die Enzyklika *Redemptor Hominis* von Papst Johannes Paul II. (1979) stellt sich ausdrücklich auf den Boden der Allgemeinen Erklärung der Menschenrechte.

würde rechtsbegründenden Status sowohl in internationalen Menschenrechtsdokumenten als auch im deutschen Grundgesetz erhalten hat, hat die deutsche evangelische Theologie zunehmend die Idee der Menschenwürde aufnehmen und zentrale Theologumena wie die Gottebenbildlichkeit und die Bezogenheit des Menschen auf Gott mit der Menschenwürdekonzeption verbinden können.[166] In der Demokratie-Denkschrift (1985) fasst die EKD universale Menschenwürde und Gottebenbildlichkeit ausdrücklich als korrelative Begriffe auf. Im britischen Kontext der protestantischen Kirchen (sowohl in der *Church of England* als auch in der *Church of Scotland*) spielt der Begriff demgegenüber bis in die Gegenwart keine zentrale Rolle. Dies gilt auch für die akademische Theologie.[167]

Die katholische Theologie, die bis ins 20. Jahrhundert hinein die universalen Menschenrechte als Irreleitungen des Liberalismus verbannt und demgegenüber an der christlich begründeten Gottebenbildlichkeit des Menschen festgehalten hat, sucht ebenfalls erst mit dem Vaticanum II in den Konstitutionen *Gaudium et Spes* und *Dignitatis Humanae* sowie in der Enzyklika *Redemptor hominis* (1979) von Papst Johannes Paul II. eine vorsichtige Öffnung gegenüber einer universalen Menschenwürde, die Menschenrechte als Freiheitsrechte für alle Menschen begründet. Dabei erstreckt sich die Rezeption des Menschenwürde-Konzepts durch römisch-katholische Theologie und Kirche sowohl auf den deutschen als auch auf den englischen Sprachraum.

Weil Menschenwürde und Gottebenbildlichkeit erst seit wenigen Jahrzehnten in der Theologie konsensual und als universale Konzeption miteinander verbunden werden, kann von einer theologischen „Geschichte der Menschenwürde" nicht begründet gesprochen werden, auch wenn es einige wenige Belege gibt, die Menschenwürde und Gottebenbildlichkeit aufeinander

---

[166] Noch Karl Barth hatte in der Zuerkennung einer Würde des Menschen aufgrund seines *Menschseins* (und nicht seines Erlöstseins durch Christus) die Freiheit Gottes angetastet und die Sünde des Menschen unterboten gesehen. Vgl. KD I/2, 444f.: „Der Mensch als solcher hat nach [der heiligen Schrift] keinen Selbstwert und die Gemeinschaft von Mensch zu Mensch auch nicht." (A.a.O., 445.) Obwohl Barth eine dezidierte christologische Theologie der Gottebenbildlichkeit des Menschen als *Bezogenheit auf Gott* ausarbeitet, verwendet er die Gottebenbildlichkeit nicht als Begründungsmodell für eine *universale* Menschenwürde.

[167] Die neueren im englischen Sprachraum erschienenen Monographien zu *human dignity* sind der römisch-katholischen Theologie zuzuordnen (so der Sammelband Made in God's Image. The Catholic Vision of Human Dignity, hrsg. von R. Duffy und A. Gambatese, Mahwah, New Jersey 1999), kommen aus dem US-amerikanischen Kontext (so der Sammelband God and human dignity, hrsg. von R. Kendall Soulen und L. Woodhead, Grandrapids 2006, der auch Beiträge von deutschen Theologen enthält) oder sind Übersetzungen aus dem Deutschen. Ein wichtiges neueres britisches *rechtsphilosophisches* Buch über *human dignity* wird bei der Rezeption der kantischen Philosophie noch eine Rolle spielen: D. Beyleveld/R. Brownsword, Human Dignity in Bioethics and Biolaw, Oxford 2001.

beziehen. Diese gehen allerdings nicht von dem Begriff der Menschenwürde im Sinne eines rechtlichen und politischen universalen Orientierungsguts aus, der seit Mitte des 20. Jahrhunderts auf der politisch-rechtlichen Ebene in nationalen Verfassungstexten und internationalen Menschenrechtsdokumenten und zunehmend im Kontext der Bioethik geprägt wurde.

Gegenwärtige theologische Rezeptionen des Menschenwürdebegriffs rekurrieren aufgrund dieser geschichtlichen Diskontinuität entweder auf die Aufklärung und den Idealismus und deren Konzeptionen von Menschenwürde oder interpretieren die biblische Tradition von der Gottebenbildlichkeit in Auseinandersetzung mit ihrer Interpretation innerhalb der Theologiegeschichte von neuem, um eine gegenwärtig anschlussfähige Theorie von Menschenwürde und Gottebenbildlichkeit zu erhalten.

Nach diesem knappen theologiegeschichtlichen Abriss zeigt sich, dass das Verständnis von Menschenwürde, selbst wenn sie mit *Gottebenbildlichkeit* (und keinem anderen Modell) begründet wird, in unterschiedlichen Formen immens variiert. Denn diese – und diesem Verständnis folgend auch die Menschenwürde – ist theologiegeschichtlich unterschiedlich verstanden worden als etwa begründet durch die

- geschöpfliche Begabung mit Vernunft und Willen,
- Ähnlichkeit der menschlichen Verfasstheit mit Gottes trinitarischem Wesen,
- menschliche Freiheit,
- geschöpfliche „Gerechtigkeit“ oder auch
- im Sinne eines relationalen Begriffs als menschliche Fähigkeit, auf Gottes Ansprache zu antworten.[168]

Um ein adäquates Verständnis von Menschenwürde wird zumindest in der deutschen Theologie darum gegenwärtig gerungen. Dabei steht ebenfalls ein gegenwärtig adäquates Verständnis der menschlichen Gottebenbildlichkeit in Frage, das sowohl die menschliche Relationalität auf Gott hin, als auch die menschliche Verfasstheit als Geschöpf Gottes, die menschliche Sünde und

[168] Dieser zuletzt genannte Aspekt wird vor allem in der evangelischen Theologie der zweiten Hälfte des 20. Jahrhunderts, Karl Barth folgend, herausgehoben. Der vor allem in der gegenwärtigen evangelischen Theologie gesuchte Anschluss an ein *relationales* Verständnis, nach dem die Gottebenbildlichkeit des Menschen weniger in seiner Begabung zur Vernunft besteht, als vielmehr darin, personal auf Gott bezogen zu sein, hat gegenüber einer *eigenschaftsgestützten* Interpretation den Vorteil, dass eine Bezogenheit des Menschen auf Gott schon ausgesagt werden kann, bevor diese Bezogenheit von seiten des Menschen realisiert wird. Soll an der Vernunftnatur als dem menschlichen Spezifikum festgehalten werden, stellt sich das Problem, wie mit denjenigen menschlichen Wesen umzugehen ist, die noch nicht, nicht mehr oder niemals aktuell vernünftig handeln können. Diese Fragen werden uns im weiterem Verlauf des Buches noch zu beschäftigen haben.

die Rechtfertigung sowie die Hoffnung auf Erlösung ernst nimmt. Mit dem Ringen um ein theologisch angemessenes Verständnis einer (universalen) Menschenwürde kann zugleich der Versuch unternommen werden, den Begriff für die bioethische Debatte der Gegenwart anschlussfähig zu machen, gleichzeitig aber den spezifisch theologischen Beitrag innerhalb dieser Debatte zu bewahren.

Dass innerhalb der deutschsprachigen theologischen Debatte der Menschenwürde-Begriff offenbar ein größeres Integrationspotential besitzt als im englischen Sprachraum, hat auf diesem Hintergrund seinen Grund nicht in einer „klassischen" oder „traditionellen" theologischen Zusammengehörigkeit von Menschenwürde und Gottebenbildlichkeit.

Von den oben herausgearbeiteten Aspekten her deutet sich darüber hinaus eine Unterscheidung an, die im folgenden noch auszuführen ist: neben der Möglichkeit, die menschliche Gottebenbildlichkeit und die mit ihr korrespondierende Menschenwürde als *intrinsische* Wesenseigenschaft des Menschen zu verstehen, die mit der Geschöpflichkeit des Menschen gegeben ist, deutet sich vor allem in der deutschen evangelischen Theologie im 20. Jahrhundert an, Gottebenbildlichkeit als *relationale* Realität zu verstehen, die nicht mit dem Menschsein *an sich* gegeben ist, sondern als Wirklichkeit innerhalb von *Beziehung*, zugesprochen an den Menschen, unverfügbar gilt. Dieses Detail unterscheidet ein evangelisch-theologisches Verständnis von Gottebenbildlichkeit und Menschenwürde etwa vom kantischen, aber auch vom römisch-katholischen Verständnis der Menschenwürde.

Die Begründung der Menschenwürde mit der Gottebenbildlichkeit hat abschließend, auch wenn sie innerhalb der Theologie teilweise eine maßgebliche Rolle spielt, ihre Schwierigkeit in der Unklarheit und Interpretationsoffenheit auch des Begriffs von Gottebenbildlichkeit.[169] Die Offenheit, die der Begriff Menschenwürde schon an sich selbst hat, wiederholt sich beim Begriff der Gottebenbildlichkeit, so dass das Begründungs- und Bestimmungsproblem der Menschenwürde mit dem theologischen Rekurs auf die menschliche Gottebenbildlichkeit nicht gelöst, sondern verschoben ist. Es muss aus diesem Grund in der theologischen Diskussion versucht werden, zu einem adäquaten Verständnis der menschlichen Gottebenbildlichkeit zu finden, die auch eine theologisch angemessene Deutungsmöglichkeit von *Menschenwürde* bereitstellt. Von hier her kann dann ein Anschluss an die bioethische Debatte gesucht werden.

Eine weitere Schwierigkeit der Argumentation innerhalb der Menschenwürdediskussion mit dem Begriff der *Gottebenbildlichkeit* liegt über die Un-

[169] Die Interpretationsoffenheit und die unterschiedlichen Deutungen der Gottebenbildlichkeit referiert auch Ruth Page, The Human Genome and the Image of God, in: C. Deane-Drummond (Hrsg.), Brave new World? Theology, Ethics and the Human Genome, London/New York 2003, 68-85.

eindeutigkeit des Begriffs hinaus darin, dass dieser für die postmoderne Debatte außerhalb des kirchlichen Kontextes eher wenig kommunikabel ist, was zur Suche nach Alternativbegriffen ermutigt hat. Der folgende Abschnitt wendet sich exemplarisch einer solchen Konzeption zu, die (im englischsprachigen Bereich einflussreich) mit der „Heiligkeit" (*sanctity*) auf einen anderen Begriff als den der Gottebenbildlichkeit rekurriert.[170]

III. 2. 2 Heiligkeit des Lebens – ein Analogon zum Würdebegriff?

Von einem liberalen nicht-theologischen Standpunkt aus hat der renommierte amerikanische Rechtsphilosoph Ronald Dworkin (*1931) die Unverfügbarkeit des menschlichen Lebens zu begründen versucht, indem er *Heiligkeit* als einen Wert versteht, den viele Menschen intuitiv erfassen können, der aber nicht auf eine so reiche Voraussetzungsklärung angewiesen ist wie der Begriff der Gottebenbildlichkeit.[171] Weil der Begriff der Heiligkeit zur Begründung der Schutzwürdigkeit (auch) menschlichen Lebens fungiert und damit strukturell eine dem Menschenwürde- und *imago Dei*-Begriff vergleichbare Funktion einnimmt, *Heiligkeit* von Dworkin zum anderen als intuitiv erfassbare *vorgängige* menschliche Wesenseigenschaft verstanden wird, legt es sich nahe, die Konzeption von Dworkin zunächst jedenfalls vorläufig der Mitgifttheorie zuzuordnen.

Für die Begründung, dass Menschen bestimmte Entitäten als *heilig* empfinden, unterscheidet Dworkin unterschiedliche Formen der Wertschätzung, die Menschen Dingen oder anderen Menschen entgegenbringen: „we will discover a crucial distinction between two categories of intrinsically valuable things: those that are *incrementally* valuable – the more of them we have the better – and those that are not but are valuable in a very different way. I shall call the latter *sacred* or *inviolable* values."[172] Der Wert von *menschlichem Leben* wird dabei von Dworkin im Sinne der zweiten Wertschätzung verstanden, weil seine Zerstörung gegen die Empfindung verstößt, dass es aufgrund seiner *Heiligkeit* nicht beschädigt werden darf. „Something is sacred or inviolable when its deliberate destruction would dishonor what ought to be honored."[173]

Im Anschluss an diese Feststellung fragt Dworkin danach, worin die Heiligkeit eines Wesen oder eines Objekts gründet. Er unterscheidet in diesem

---

[170] Der Begriff der Heiligkeit des Lebens (*sanctity of life*) wird von Theologen ebenfalls verwendet, die diese – wiederum als Alternative zum Würdebegriff – in der Schöpfung des Menschen zum Ebenbild Gottes begründen. Vgl. S.B. Rae/P.M. Cox, Bioethics. A Christian Approach in a Pluralistic Age, Grand Rapids/Michigan/ Cambridge 1999, 128-156.

[171] Vgl. Dworkin, What is sacred?, in: J. Harris (Hrsg.), Bioethics, Oxford/New York 2001, 157-204.

[172] Dworkin, a.a.O., 159.

[173] Dworkin, a.a.O., 162.

Zusammenhang zwischen zwei Aspekten: zum einen wird etwas (oder jemand) heilig aufgrund einer *Repräsentations-Relation*: im Alten Ägypten etwa durften keine Katzen getötet werden, weil sie die Gottheit repräsentierten. Der Flagge eines Landes gebührt Respekt, weil der Respekt vor der Flagge den Respekt vor dem Land repräsentiert. Zum anderen wird etwas (oder jemand) aufgrund seiner *Geschichte* heilig. Kunstwerke werden aus diesem Grund geschützt, weil sie besondere menschliche Kulturleistungen darstellen, die als schützenswert angesehen werden. Beide Aspekte können für Dworkin in der Intuition der Heiligkeit einer Entität zusammenfinden – etwa im Wunsch, Tierarten vor dem Aussterben zu retten, weil es als Schande empfunden wird, dass bestimmte Arten durch den Menschen ausgerottet werden. Der Respekt vor der vom Aussterben bedrohten Rasse repräsentiert den Respekt vor der Natur als solcher, und ein respektvoller Umgang mit der Natur nimmt die sich in diesem Zusammenhang geschichtlich-natürlich verstehende Menschheit ernst.

Diese intuitiv empfundene Scham angesichts der Heiligkeit des Lebens als solchen steigert sich für Dworkin, wenn es um den Menschen selbst geht.[174] „It is an inarticulate, unchallenged, almost unnoticed, but nevertheless absolute premise of our political and economic planning that the human race must survive and prosper."[175] In dieser Sorge um die Menschheit kommen nach Ansicht von Dworkin beide Aspekte des Respekts vor der Heiligkeit zusammen, weil wir nicht nur um das biologische, sondern auch um das kulturelle Überleben der Menschheit Sorge tragen, die über die Gegenwart hinausgeht und auch zukünftige Generationen von Menschen umfasst.[176] Die intuitiv begriffene Heiligkeit des menschlichen Lebens beruht darum sowohl auf der Assoziation, dass der Schutz des Einzelnen ein Schutz der Gesamtheit aller Menschen bedeutet, als auch auf der kulturellen und geschichtlichen Bedeutung, die Menschen haben und deretwegen ihr Leben zu schützen ist, weil sie eine bestimmte Geschichte und Kulturleistung repräsentieren, die nach rückwärts und vorwärts deutet.

Dabei bezieht sich die Sorge um zukünftige Generationen aber nicht nur auf *bestimmte* Menschen oder ihre Nachkommen: „in fact our worries about

---

[174] Mit dieser auf Intuition beruhenden Unterscheidung zwischen der Heiligkeit menschlichen Lebens und der Heiligkeit anderen Lebens setzt Dworkin einen anderen Akzent als *Albert Schweitzer*, auch wenn die auch von Dworkin rezipierte *Ehrfurcht* vor dem Leben und der Lebensbegriff als solcher an Schweitzer erinnern. Bei Schweitzer wird aber grundsätzlich eine Ethik der Ehrfurcht vor *allem* Leben begründet, weil sich der Mensch mit seinem Willen zum Leben inmitten von Wesen vorfinde, deren Willen zum Leben er in Ehrfurcht zu achten habe. Vgl. A. Schweitzer, Kultur und Ethik, München 1996.

[175] Dworkin, What is sacred, 165.

[176] Dworkin, ebd.

humanity in centuries to come make sense only if we suppose that it is intrinsically important that the human race continues even though it is not important to the interest of particular people."[177] Darum bezeichnet Dworkin die Sorge um zukünftige Generationen nicht nur hinsichtlich ihres biologischen Überlebens, sondern auch mit Blick auf ihr ökologisches und ökonomisches Überleben nicht als eine Frage der Gerechtigkeit, sondern sieht darin eine (allerdings meist intuitive und unreflektierte) Ahnung der *Heiligkeit menschlichen Lebens*, die von allen Menschen geteilt werde[178] und aufgrund derer menschliches Leben zu schützen sei.

Die Ahnung der *Heiligkeit* menschlichen Lebens manifestiert sich im Kontext der Religionen in der Konzeption der *Gottebenbildlichkeit*, kann aber im nicht-religiösen Kontext ebenso präsent sein und zeigt sich etwa daran, dass die Geburt eines Kindes auch von nichtreligiösen Menschen als „Wunder" bezeichnet wird,[179] welches seinerseits schon vorgeburtlich anhebe: „it begins in the genetic identity of an embryo."[180] An dieser Stelle zieht Dworkin aus der Beobachtung einer intuitiv empfundenen Heiligkeit des Lebens, die er phänomenologisch beschreibt, ethische Konsequenzen: Weil jedes heranwachsende menschliche Wesen eine komplexe Form von Kreativität repräsentiert, ist es, in welcher Gestalt auch immer, heilig und verlangt eine Form des Respekts und des Schutzes.[181] Die Heiligkeit dieses Lebens kann darum nicht gegen anderes Leben abgewogen werden; vielmehr zeigt sich in der Ahnung der Heiligkeit ein Respekt vor dem menschlichen Sein als solchem.

Die von fast allen Menschen sowohl im religiösen als auch im nichtreligiösen Kontext geteilte Empfindung von Heiligkeit hat dabei nach der Beobachtung von Dworkin zwei Quellen und für die Beurteilung einer Entität als *heilig* auch zwei Gesichtspunkte: *menschliche* und *natürliche* Kreativität, wobei letztere häufig mit einer transzendenten, *göttlichen* Kreativität assoziiert werde. Wenn sich ein Mensch eher an der Kreativität der *Natur* oder *Gottes* ausrichte, so folge daraus tendenziell ein konservativer Standpunkt etwa in

---

[177] Dworkin, ebd.

[178] „Our concern for future generations is not a matter of justice at all but of our instinctive sense that human flourishing as well as human survival is of sacred importance." (Dworkin, a.a.O., 166.)

[179] Dworkin, a.a.O., 170f.

[180] Dworkin, a.a.O., 171.

[181] Eine schwer zu beurteilende Grauzone bildet für Dworkin die Zeit des *frühen* Embryos vor der Nidation. In dieser Frage nimmt er an, dass die genetische Entwicklung des Embryos erst mit der Nidation abgeschlossen ist. „Fetal development is a continuing creative process, a process that has barely begun at the instant of conception. Indeed, since genetic individuation is not yet complete at that point, we might say that the development of a unique human being has not started until approximately fourteen days later, at implantation." (Dworkin, a.a.O., 176.)

der Frage nach der ethischen Beurteilung des Schwangerschaftsabbruchs, denn die Heiligkeit des Lebens beruhe auf der Kreativität der dem Menschen gegenüber größeren Natur oder einer höheren transzendenten Macht.[182] Liege der Schwerpunkt der Begründung von Heiligkeit demgegenüber eher auf der *menschlichen* Kreativität, so urteilten Menschen in dieser Frage eher so, dass es das kleinere Übel bedeuten könne, eine Schwangerschaft abzubrechen. Ähnliches kann auch für die Frage nach der ethischen Beurteilung der Embryonenforschung angenommen werden: vertreten Menschen die grundlegende Ansicht einer Heiligkeit der *Natur*, so werden sie verbrauchende Forschung an Embryonen eher ablehnen, als wenn sie den Schwerpunkt auf der Heiligkeit der *menschlichen* Schaffenskraft legen.

Mit dieser Unterscheidung einer Heiligkeit der natürlichen und der menschlichen Kreativität führt Dworkin einen neuen Gesichtspunkt in die Debatte ein: Seine grundlegende These lautet in diesem Zusammenhang, dass der Unterschied zwischen konservativen und liberalen Positionen hinsichtlich des Umgangs mit menschlichen Embryonen[183] weniger in der Frage besteht, ob der Embryo eine *Person* sei oder nicht. Denn diese Frage können auch konservative Vertreter in der Abtreibungsdebatte verneinen. Entscheidend sei, ob der Schwerpunkt eher bei *natürlicher* oder *menschlicher* Kreativität gelegt werde. Eine eher liberale Position, die eine prosperierende menschliche Kreativität intendiere, gehe deswegen ebenso wie eine konservative Position davon aus, dass Schwangerschaftsabbruch grundsätzlich moralisch bedenklich sei, halte ihn aber in bestimmten Fällen für das kleinere Übel, wenn etwa das ungeborene Kind schwer behindert sei und die Lebensqualität und die Kreativität der werdenden Eltern unzumutbar einschränke.[184]

---

[182] Dworkin, a.a.O., 178f.: „A strongly orthodox or fundamentalist person can insist that abortion is always morally wrong because the deliberate destruction of something created as sacred by God can never be redeemed by any human benefit."

[183] Die Frage nach der *Forschung* an Embryonen nimmt in den Überlegungen Dworkins keinen Raum ein; er beschäftigt sich vielmehr mit der Frage nach der ethischen Beurteilung des Schwangerschaftsabbruchs. Meines Erachtens spricht allerdings viel dafür, dass seine Aussagen zum Schwangerschaftsabbruch auch auf die Forschung an menschlichen Embryonen angewandt werden können. Diese beiden ethischen Probleme sind zwar durch schwerwiegende Unterschiede gekennzeichnet, die Konvergenz besteht aber in diesem Zusammenhang in der Differenz der Schwerpunktsetzung auf *menschlicher* und *natürlicher* Kreativität – auch wenn Dworkin selbst annimmt, dass die genetische Identität eines Embryos erst mit dem Abschluss der Nidation besteht.

[184] „Liberals think that abortion is permissible when the birth of a fetus would have a very bad effect on the qualities of lives. The exceptions liberals recognize on that ground fall into two main groups: those that seek to avoid frustration of the life of the child, and those that seek to prevent frustration of the life of the mother and other family members." (Dworkin, a.a.O., 183f.)

Seinen Beobachtungen folgend, benennt Dworkin darum die eigentliche Kontroverse nicht als eine philosophische, sondern als eine spirituelle, wobei die intuitiv empfundene Heiligkeit des Lebens für keine der Parteien außer Frage stehe.[185] Diese Intuition der Heiligkeit des Lebens bestimme die eigene Position zum Umgang mit ungeborenen Leben, aber etwa auch die Sicht auf den eigenen Tod und das Interesse, das Menschen in der Frage der aktiven Sterbehilfe daran haben zu sterben. Sie liegt darum auf einer anderen Ebene als eine argumentativ begründete Position.

Dworkins[186] Analyse lässt sich insofern der Mitgifttheorie in der Begründungsfrage für Menschenwürde zuordnen, als sie *Heiligkeit* (*sanctity*) als ein dem Individuum vorgängiges Gut versteht. Für die Begründung des Wertes (*value*) vor allem menschlichen Lebens wird ausdrücklich keine religiöse oder metaphysische Begründungsstruktur wie die menschliche Geschöpflichkeit oder die Gottebenbildlichkeit herangezogen, sondern phänomenologisch auf intuitiv empfundene Abneigung oder Zustimmung rekurriert. Dworkins Überlegungen haben daher auch eher einen deskriptiven als einen präskriptiv-normativen Impetus in der Frage nach dem Umgang mit menschlichen Embryonen. Vor allem die Begriffe des *Lebens* (*life*), der *Heiligkeit* (*sanctity*) und des *Wertes* (*value*) sind aber für theologische Überlegungen zur Gottebenbildlichkeit und zur Menschenwürde anschlussfähig. Nach Dworkins Dafürhalten und seiner Analyse folgend, können sie offenbar auch im nichtreligiösen liberalen Kontext verstanden und rezipiert werden.

Die von Dworkin entwickelte Phänomenologie hat den Vorzug, dass das Unbehagen, das Menschen angesichts bestimmter Vorgehensweisen und Sachverhalte empfinden, ohne es in Worte fassen zu können, ernst genommen wird. Der Rekurs auf dieses Unbehagen und auf eine instinktive, nicht immer reflektierte Ahnung, die Dworkin mit der Ahnung der „Heiligkeit" benennt, nimmt die Tatsache ernst, dass in jedem philosophischen, ethischen und/oder politischen Modell zugleich Motive wirksam sind, die es orientieren, sich aber dem unmittelbaren argumentativen Zugriff entziehen. Darüber hinaus liegt ein Vorteil darin, dass mit der Heiligkeit des Lebens aufgrund der Interpretationsoffenheit des Begriffs offenbar argumentiert werden kann, ohne eine theologische Begründungsstruktur wie die Gottebenbildlichkeit dafür in Anspruch zu nehmen, die in der Begründung von *Menschenwürde*, wie der vorangegangene Abschnitt gezeigt hat, nicht so „klassisch" und eindeutig ist wie möglicherweise vermutet.

---

[185] Dworkin, a.a.O., 187.

[186] Die vorangegangenen Überlegungen rezipieren vor allem den kurzen Text von Dworkin in dem von John Harris herausgegebenen Sammelband Bioethics. Vgl. aber außerdem die beiden einflussreichen Bücher Dworkin, Taking Rights seriously, 1996 und Dworkin, Life's Dominion. An Argument about Abortion, Euthanasia and Individual Freedom, 1994. Beide Bücher sind auch in deutscher Übersetzung erschienen.

Allerdings ergibt sich ein struktureller Unterschied beider Begründungsformen – der Gottebenbildlichkeit und der Heiligkeit – insofern, als die Konzeption der menschlichen Gottebenbildlichkeit eine explizit *anthropologische* Bestimmung darstellt, während die intuitiv empfundene „Heiligkeit des Lebens" mit ihrer Tendenz zum Pantheismus zwar anthropologische Bestimmungen einschließt, aber darüber hinausgeht.

Die aufgrund der Gottebenbildlichkeit dem Menschen zukommende *Würde* des Menschen verdankt sich nach theologischer Reflexion außerdem nicht dem menschlichen Zuschreiben und einer menschlichen Intuition, sondern ist als Ergebnis des schöpferischen Wirkens Gottes dem menschlichen Zugriff entzogen, also *unverfügbar.* Die auf Intuition beruhende Ahnung der Heiligkeit *kann* ihren Ursprung in einer über das Menschsein hinausgehenden Quelle haben, und auch wenn der Akzent auf der menschlichen Kreativität liegt, als unverfügbar verstanden, angenommen oder geglaubt werden. Eine Unverfügbarkeit liegt aber aufgrund ihrer Herleitung nicht in ihrem Begriff selbst, insofern sich die Heiligkeit aufgrund des Rekurses auf Intuition auch menschlicher Zuschreibung verdanken kann. Der Begriff der *Heiligkeit* ist auch aufgrund seines Verzichts auf Normativität darum noch offener als derjenige der *Menschenwürde.*

Die deskriptive Ausrichtung von Dworkins Ansatz verhilft insofern zu einer Präzisierung und Klärung, als sie die Tatsache verdeutlicht, dass ethische Konzeptionen auf individuellen Voraussetzungen aufruhen, die nicht nur argumentativen, sondern auch spirituellen und intuitiven Ursprungs sind. Dabei liegt im Zugang über Intuitionen eine gewisse Vagheit, die sich der argumentativen Auseinandersetzung entzieht. Auch wenn intuitive Eindrücke in Reflexionen einfließen, sind sie doch nicht immer so kommunikabel, dass sie sich auch Gesprächspartnern erschließen können. Insofern erscheint der Rekurs auf Intuitionen ergänzungsbedürftig.

Dworkin gehört zu den einflussreichsten Rechtsphilosophen im englischsprachigen Raum. Mit seinem Wirken sowohl in Großbritannien als auch in den Vereinigten Staaten erreicht er ein großes sowohl akademisches als auch akademisch interessiertes Publikum. Trotz der terminologischen Differenzen – wenn Dworkin weniger von *dignity* als vielmehr von *sanctity* und *value* spricht – ist die Tatsache an sich, dass im englischsprachigen Raum eine nichtreligiöse Konzeption ausgemacht werden kann, die sich, unter den eben gegebenen Einschränkungen, der Mitgifttheorie zuordnen lässt, bemerkenswert und für eine am Ende des Buches zu leistende abschließende Überlegung zu Menschenwürde und *human dignity* möglicherweise anschlussfähig.

Die Argumentation mit der „Heiligkeit" des Lebens stellt einen Versuch dar, neben dem Theologumenon der Gottebenbildlichkeit eine Struktur zu finden, die für die Diskussion um die Forschung an Embryonen kommunikabel ist und für eine Begründung von Menschenwürde herangezogen werden kann. Bevor ich hinsichtlich der Begründung von Menschenwürde, Gottebenbildlichkeit und Lebensschutz nach grundsätzlichen Argumentationstypologien innerhalb von katholischer und evangelischer Bioethik beim Umgang mit menschlichem Leben frage, stelle ich im folgenden Abschnitt eine vor allem in der *katholischen* Ethik, aber auch in der evangelischen und der philosophischen Ethik rezipierte Gruppe von Argumenten dar, die sich *für* den Schutz des frühen Embryos aussprechen. Aufgrund ihrer Annahme der Notwendigkeit eines absoluten Lebensschutzes für menschliche Wesen von Anfang an gehören sie zweifelsfrei in die Mitgifttheorie.

III. 2. 3 Argumente für den frühen Beginn des Embryonenschutzes: die SKIP-Gruppe

Wird dafür plädiert, menschlichen Embryonen von Beginn an Lebensschutz zuzugestehen, so wird dies häufig damit begründet, dass ihnen von Anfang an Menschenwürde und damit derselbe moralische Status wie geborenen Menschen zukommt. Meist wird dabei davon ausgegangen, dass Embryonen über dieselben, absoluten Lebensschutz gewährleistenden intrinsischen Wesenseigenschaften verfügen wie geborene Menschen.

In diesem Zusammenhang wird eine Gruppe von Argumenten immer wieder herangeführt, die nach ihren Anfangsbuchstaben als SKIP-Gruppe[187] zusammengefasst wird.[188] Diese gehen davon aus, dass menschliche Wesen vom Zeitpunkt der Kernverschmelzung an zu schützen sind, weil sie ab diesem Zeitpunkt über Würde und damit einen mit anderen Rechtsgütern unabwägbaren Wert verfügen. Die Argumente der SKIP-Gruppe stehen im größeren Zusammenhang der für die gesamte Debatte zentralen Frage nach dem *moralischen Status des Embryos*, die sich in allen maßgeblichen Dokumenten der öffentlichen politischen, rechtlichen und ethischen Diskussion um den Umgang mit menschlichem Leben am Lebensbeginn findet – sowohl in der

[187] Zur SKIP-Argumentation vgl. G. Damschen/D. Schönecker (Hrsg.), Der moralische Status menschlicher Embryonen. Pro und contra Spezies-, Kontinuums-, Identitäts- und Potentialitätsargument, Berlin/New York 2003.

[188] Die SKIP-Argumente sind keineswegs die einzigen möglichen Argumente, die den Embryo in den ersten Tagen nach der Befruchtung insofern unter einen unbedingten Schutz stellen, als sie ihm einen absoluten Wert – meist Menschenwürde oder Personalität – zusprechen. Eine andere mögliche Form der Argumentation liegt darin, dem extrakorporalen Embryo aufgrund seiner besonderen *Verletzlichkeit* einen besonderen Status zuzusprechen und die Spezieszugehörigkeit und die Potentialität, die der Embryo mitbringt, als Indikatoren für seine Schutzwürdigkeit anzuerkennen. Vgl. G. Maio (Hrsg.), Der Status des extrakorporalen Embryo. Perspektiven eines interdisziplinären Zugangs, Stuttgart 2007. Die Mitarbeiter an diesem Forschungsprojekt, in dessen Zusammenhang der Sammelband entstanden ist, grenzen sich in ihren Kriterien explizit gegen die SKIP-Argumentation ab.

deutschen als auch in der englischen Debatte.[189]

Mit kleineren Abweichungen lassen sich vier unterschiedliche Akzentuierungen von Argumenten innerhalb der SKIP-Gruppe ausmachen, die in unterschiedlichen Kombinationen verwendet werden:

- das **S**pezies-Argument,
- das **K**ontinuums-Argument,
- das **I**dentitätsargument sowie
- das **P**otentialitätsargument.[190]

Das Spezies-Argument

Das Spezies-Argument kann folgendermaßen wiedergegeben werden:[191]

- Jedes Mitglied der *Spezies* Mensch (*homo sapiens sapiens*) hat Würde aufgrund seiner natürlichen Artzugehörigkeit.
- Jeder menschliche Embryo ist von Anfang an Mitglied der Spezies Mensch.
- Also: Jeder Embryo hat Würde.

Das Argument geht von der spezifischen Verfasstheit des Menschen gegenüber allen anderen Spezies aus und leitet aus der Zugehörigkeit von Menschen zur Gattung *homo sapiens sapiens* deren moralischen Status ab. Dabei begründet es die menschliche Besonderheit gegenüber Angehörigen aller anderen Spezies in der Regel mit dem Vermögen zum sittlichen Subjekt-Sein, das darüber hinaus in Anlehnung an Kant häufig mit dem Personstatus des Menschen verbunden wird:[192] Weil alle Angehörigen der Spezies *homo sapiens sapiens* – egal in welchem Entwicklungsstadium sie sich befinden – zum sittlichen Subjekt-Sein befähigt seien, seien sie als würdebegabt und darum schutzwürdig anzusehen.

[189] Auch im Warnock-Report 1984: „It is obvious that the central objection to the use of human embryos as research subjects is a fundamental objection, based on moral principles. Put simply, the main argument is that the use of human embryos for research is morally wrong because of the very fact that they are human... The human embryo is seen as having the same status as a child or an adult, by virtue of its potential for human life." (61.)

[190] Vor allem die S-, I- und P-Argumente werden von katholischen Ethikern vertreten, wobei das Verständnis des Menschen als eines moralischen Subjekts eine besondere Rolle spielt. Das K-Argument fügt sich am besten in eine *relationale* Ontologie und Erkenntnistheorie und wird eher von der evangelischen Ethik gebraucht. Vgl. T. Latzel, Wann beginnt menschliches Leben? Der Beginn menschlichen Lebens aus ethischer Sicht: Kontinuum oder Zäsur? in: W. Härle (Hrsg.), Ethik im Kontinuum. Beiträge zur relationalen Erkenntnistheorie und Ontologie, Leipzig 2008, 143-154.

[191] E. Schockenhoff in der Argumentation für das Spezies-Argument, in: Damschen/Schönecker, Der moralische Status menschlicher Embryonen, 11.

[192] Vgl. Schockenhoff, a.a.O., 12.

Ideengeschichtlich kann sich die Vorstellung, dass alle Angehörigen der menschlichen Spezies an der menschlichen Vernunftnatur teilhaben, auf die Definition des Boethius zurückführen, nach der die *Person* als individuelle Substanz einer vernünftigen Natur verstanden wird,[193] auch wenn im 18. Jahrhundert mit den Konzeptionen von John Locke und Immanuel Kant neue Positionen zum Verständnis von Personalität hinzugetreten sind.[194] Die Auffassung, dass die spezifische *intrinsische* Besonderheit der menschlichen Spezies in der sittlichen Verfasstheit und der Fähigkeit zur Moral liege, verdankt sich in weiten Teilen der kantischen Philosophie.

Dabei wird von den Befürwortern des Spezies-Arguments vertreten, dass eine personale Identität des Individuums bereits vor der Feststellung seiner Interessen vorausgesetzt werden muss, dass also der empirische Personbegriff, der sich von der Tradition des Lockeschen Empirismus bis hin zum Präferenzutilitarismus entwickelt hat, nicht hinreichend sei.[195] Denn wenn die *Einheit der Person* nicht vorausgesetzt werde, sei es nicht möglich, für Schlafende, reversibel Bewusstlose oder emotional Verwirrte den Status einer Person anzunehmen, und es wäre möglich, sie in dieser nichtpersonalen Zwischenzeit, in der sie keine Interessen vertreten, zu töten.[196]

In diesem Zusammenhang geht eine Position, die das Spezies-Argument unterstützt, von der Auffassung aus, dass die *Fähigkeit zur Moral*, die als Minimalwürde allen Menschen in jedem Entwicklungsstand eigne, Menschenwürde konstituiere. Diese wird unterschieden von einem Verständnis von Würde, das sich etwa an dem attributiven Ausdruck der „menschenwürdigen Zustände“ festmacht und unterschiedlich verstanden und inhaltlich gefüllt wird. Die allen Menschen zukommende (basale) Menschenwürde, die sich nicht dem Einverständnis anderer verdanke, und die durch „würdiges“ Verhalten verwirklichte Menschenwürde etwa in der Achtung der Menschenrechte seien aber im Sinne der Unterscheidung von Fundament und Realisierungsgestalt voneinander zu differenzieren.[197]

---

[193] Von Boethius stammt die Definition der Person als „naturae rationabilis individua substantia“ im Anschluss an den griechischen Hypostasis-Begriff. Vgl. Anicius Manlius Severinus Boethius, Tracatus V. Contra Eutychen et Nestorium III, in: Boethius, Die Theologischen Traktate, zweisprachige Ausgabe, Hamburg 1988, 74-76.

[194] Zum kantischen und dem vor allem in der Ethik Peter Singers einflussreichen Lockeschen Begriff von Personalität s. unten, Abschnitt III.4, S. 138ff.

[195] Vgl. Schockenhoff, a.a.O., 18: „Die Einheit der Person muß als mit sich identische, die Zeit überdauernde Bezugsgröße bereits vorausgesetzt werden, damit die einzelnen Bewußtseinserlebnisse als ein einheitlicher Bewußtseinsstrom interpretiert und ihr zugeschrieben werden können.“

[196] Vgl. Schockenhoff, ebd.

[197] Zum „doppelten Begriff der Menschenwürde“ vgl. Schockenhoff, a.a.O., 19ff. Schokkenhoff versteht darin ausdrücklich den Menschenwürdebegriff als *normativen* Begriff

Auch wenn die terminologische Unterscheidung von Minimal- und Maximalwürde sich deswegen als missverständlich darstellt, weil sie ein abgestuftes Verständnis von Menschenwürde nahe legen könnte, das gerade nicht im Sinne der Vertreter einer *universalen* Menschenwürde-Konzeption liegt, bietet diese Unterscheidung der Sache nach den Vorteil, dass unterschiedliche Verständnismöglichkeiten von Menschenwürde differenziert werden können und so zu einer weiteren Präzisierungsstufe gelangt wird.[198]

Das basale, grundlegende Verständnis von Menschenwürde oder ihr normativer Kern, der eine Realisierung der Menschenwürde in der Achtung der Menschenrechte allererst ermöglicht, schließt nach dem S-Argument eine Begründung durch bestimmte *Eigenschaften* oder *Entwicklungsstufen* aus, indem es impliziert, dass Menschenwürde *allen* Angehörigen der Spezies Mensch zukommt, ohne dass sie ihnen von anderen erst zugeschrieben werden müsste.[199] Dabei wird die besondere Konstitution von Menschenwürde in der leibseelischen Verfasstheit des Menschen und seiner Fähigkeit zum moralischen Subjektsein begründet, in jedem Fall aber als ein dem Menschen aufgrund seiner naturalen Ausstattung zukommendes Attribut verstanden, das er sich nicht allererst erwerben müsste.

Das Kontinuumsargument

Das Kontinuumsargument lässt sich wie folgt zusammenfassen:[200]

· Jedes menschliche Wesen, das aktual φ ist, hat Würde.

---

im Sinne eines Minimalbegriffs. Eine etwas andere Unterscheidung ist von Leon Kass vorgeschlagen worden: danach könne unterschieden werden zwischen der „dignity of human *being*" und der „dignity of being *human*" (Kass, Defending Human Dignity, in: Human Dignity and Bioethics, 2008, 304f. und passim. Der Text ist ein Report des President's Council of Bioethics, s. http://www.bioethics.gov/reports/ human_dignity/index.html). Dabei wird die erste Form von Menschenwürde für alle menschlichen Wesen vertreten, um eine Würde des Menschseins an sich auszusagen, während die Würde des *erfüllten Menschseins* vor allem im Gegenüber zu Techniken verteidigt wird, bei denen man Menschlichkeit verletzt sieht. Die eigentlich ethisch zentrale und normative Form von Menschenwürde sieht Kass in der „dignity of human *being*".

[198] Ich folge darum im weiteren Verlauf des Buches terminologisch nicht der Unterscheidung von *Minimal-* und *Maximal*würde, behalte die Unterscheidung an sich aber bei und spreche eher von der grundlegenden Gestalt von Menschenwürde und ihrer attributiven Realisierungsgestalt oder -form.

[199] Vgl. Schockenhoff, a.a.O., 21: „Wenn wir kraft eigenen Rechts als Menschen existieren und nicht durch den Willen der anderen Mitglieder der menschlichen Gemeinschaft berufen werden, dann kann allein die naturale Zugehörigkeit zur biologischen Spezies, das Merkmal menschlicher Abstammung, den Ausschlag geben."

[200] Vgl. L. Honnefelder in der Argumentation für das Kontinuumsargument, in: Damschen/Schönecker, Moralischer Status, 62.

- Jeder menschliche Embryo ist aktual φ, weil er ein menschliches Lebewesen ist, das sich unter normalen Bedingungen kontinuierlich ohne moralrelevante Einschnitte zu einem geborenen menschlichen Wesen entwickelt, das unzweifelhaft aktual φ ist.
- Also: Jeder menschliche Embryo hat Würde.

Die Befürworter des Kontinuumsarguments weisen darauf hin, dass zunächst zu klären sei, welcher Status bereits *geborenen* Menschen zukomme, um anschließend zu prüfen, ob dieser Status auch für *ungeborene* Menschen gelte. Dass der geborene Mensch aufgrund seiner naturhaften Zugehörigkeit zur Spezies Mensch und aufgrund seines vernunftbegabten Seins sowie seiner darin wurzelnden Befähigung zum sittlichen Handeln einen bestimmten moralischen Status habe, wird angenommen.[201] Ebenso wird davon ausgegangen, dass der ungeborene Mensch in Kontinuität zum bereits geborenen stehe und keine echte moralrelevante Zäsur in der Entwicklung angenommen werden könne. Identitäts- und Kontinuitätsargument stehen darum in enger Nachbarschaft, werden häufig aber auch mit dem Speziesargument verknüpft.[202]

Darüber hinaus sei wegen der empfundenen kontinuierlichen Identität, in der wir uns erleben, eine *personale Kontinuität* des konkreten Menschen anzunehmen, die den „Lebewesen von dem Augenblick an eigen ist, in dem sie entstanden sind, und die dazu führt, daß sie – die üblichen Umstände vorausgesetzt – zu dem werden, was zu ihrer Art gehört."[203] Diese spezifische kontinuierliche Entwicklungsfähigkeit sei nicht dasselbe wie die Potentialität des Kronprinzen, eines Tages König zu werden, die auch uneingelöst bleiben könne und der darum keine wirkliche Kontinuität eigne. Die kontinuierliche Entwicklungsfähigkeit sei vielmehr dem sich entwickelnden Wesen – unter normalen Umständen – inhärent.[204] Während der Kronprinz aufgrund kontingenter Umstände nicht in jedem Fall automatisch König würde, sondern ein Leben lang Kronprinz bleiben und auf diese Entwicklung darüber hinaus Einfluss nehmen könne, entwickele sich der Embryo, normale Umstände und

[201] Vgl. Honnefelder, a.a.O., 65f.

[202] Honnefelder, a.a.O., 67: „Denn ohne Zweifel gehört der ungeborene Mensch nicht nur der gleichen Spezies an wie der geborene; es ist *ein und dasselbe* Lebewesen, das sich über die verschiedenen Phasen der Schwangerschaft hinweg zu dem geborenen Menschen entwickelt. Auch die Weise, in der wir uns rück- und vorblickend als mit uns identisch erfahren und uns eine unverwechselbare und in ununterbrochener Kontinuität sich durchhaltende Identität zuschreiben, ist unlöslich an die diachrone Identität des Lebewesens gebunden, das wir sind."

[203] Honnefelder, a.a.O., 68.

[204] Mit dem Verweis auf den Kronprinzen nimmt die Argumentation ein populäres Argument von Gegnern des Kontinuums- und – vor allem – des Potentialitätsarguments auf. Vgl. auch W. Wieland, in: Damschen/Schönecker, a.a.O., 152-154.

Wachstumsbedingungen vorausgesetzt, *automatisch* und *kontinuierlich* zu dem Wesen, das seiner Art entspreche.

Für Befürworter des Kontinuitätsarguments muss aufgrund des kontinuierlichen Entwicklungsprozesses ohne moralrelevante Einschnitte, der für menschliche Lebewesen angenommen wird, keine Bewusstheit in der Befolgung von Interessen vorliegen, damit ein Individuum schutzwürdig wird.[205] Darum ist es folgerichtig, auch eine ungeborene Entität so zu behandeln, wie sie es wünschte und wie es erforderlich wäre, wenn sie bereits geboren wäre.

Der Personbegriff wird in diesem Zusammenhang entweder analog zu seinem Gebrauch innerhalb des Spezies-Arguments oder gar nicht verwendet. Die demgegenüber vor allem von Vertretern des Präferenzutilitarismus eingezogene Unterscheidung von Menschen und Personen setzt in den Augen von Befürwortern des Kontinuumsarguments voraus, dass „Person" nicht als ein Substanz-Sortal und damit als ein für alle Angehörigen der menschlichen Gattung kontinuierlich geltender Begriff, sondern als Phasen-Sortal verstanden werde, weil der Terminus „Person" nur auf Menschen in bestimmten Phasen aufgrund bestimmter Kriterien zutreffe. Im Zusammenhang des Kontinuumsarguments wird dagegen eingewandt, dass ein Verständnis des Personbegriffs im Sinne eines Phasen-Sortals als kontraintuitiv anzusehen sei.[206] Denn für Angehörige sei etwa ein Sterbender im vegetativen Zustand immer noch die vertraute Person, und für die eigene Entwicklung würden die meisten Menschen keine Zäsur annehmen, aufgrund derer sie sich zu einer Person entwickelten,[207] sondern ihre personale Entwicklung von Beginn an als kontinuierlich verstehen.[208]

---

[205] Neben der Kontinuität eines menschlichen Lebens nach vorne hin, im Zusammenhang mit der davon ausgegangen werden muss, dass eine Kontinuität von sich entwikkelndem Embryo und geborenem Menschen besteht, muss auch eine Kontinuität nach hinten hin angenommen werden, in deren Zusammenhang auch der demente, komatöse und sterbende Mensch mit dem Menschen kontinuierlich identisch ist, aus dem er sich bis zu dem Zustand, in dem er sich jetzt befindet, entwickelt hat.

[206] Honnefelder, a.a.O., 70.

[207] Ähnlich argumentiert auch das Buch von Norman M. Ford, When did I begin? Conception of the human individual in history, philosophy and science, Cambridge 1988. Es ist allerdings vor der Stammzellkontroverse erschienen. Vgl. auch G. Meilaender, Bioethics. A Primer for Christians, Grand Rapids/Cambridge [2]2005, 32: „Each of our personal histories begins with very limited capacities and may end in the same way. Personhood is not a thing we possess only at some moments in that history; we are persons throughout it."

[208] Darüber hinaus berge die Annahme von Personalität als eines Phasen- und nicht als eines Substanz-Sortals alle Probleme, die utilitaristischer Ethik im allgemeinen inhärierten: die Schwierigkeit einer interpersonalen Interessenabwägung, das Fehlen des Gerechtigkeitsprinzips und schließlich die Möglichkeit eines Verstoßes gegen die

Bei der Überlegung hinsichtlich des moralischen Status von Embryonen *in vitro* seien über das Gesagte zum Embryo *in utero* hinaus weitere Anstrengungen zu unternehmen, weil die Kontinuität des befruchteten Embryos in der Petrischale mit einem geborenen Menschen nicht ohne weiteres gesehen und in bestimmten Fällen auch nicht gewährleistet werden könne. Von Gegnern des Kontinuumsarguments werde außerdem eine Kontinuität eines Embryos *in vitro* mit einem geborenen Menschen als hochgradig kontraintuitiv empfunden, so dass der Zeitpunkt, an dem die Kontinuität beginne, darum allererst bestimmt werden müsse.

Ausgehend vom Begriff des *Lebewesens* ist dieser Zeitpunkt nach dem Kontinuumsargument aber unstrittig, weil dieser als mit der Kernverschmelzung beginnend angesetzt werden müsse, wenn die selbstgesteuerte Entwicklung gemäß dem individuellen Genom angestoßen werde. Zu diesem Zeitpunkt sei zwar die Möglichkeit der Mehrlingsbildung noch nicht ausgeschlossen, was gegen die Annahme einer Kontinuität sprechen könnte. Eine spätere Teilung des Embryos in zwei Individuen mache aber lediglich aus bislang einem zwei Individuen, so dass die genetische Einzigartigkeit des Individuums zu keinem Zeitpunkt *nicht* mit Individualität verbunden sei. Daher kann für Befürworter des Kontinuumsarguments auch die frühe Phase der Embryonalentwicklung nicht als präindividuell und der Embryo nicht als „Prä-Embryo“ bezeichnet werden,[209] so dass die Kontinuität in der Embryonalentwicklung sowohl für den Embryo *in vitro* als auch für den Embryo *in utero* als mit der Kernverschmelzung beginnend angenommen werden müsse. Aus dieser Annahme einer kontinuierlichen Entwicklung ergibt sich für das K-Argument aber für Embryonen derselbe moralische Anspruch einer absoluten Schutzwürdigkeit, der auch geborenen Menschen zukommt.

Die sich gleichwohl ereignenden Zäsuren innerhalb der embryonalen Entwicklung werden insofern als nicht moralrelevant beurteilt, als sich bei ihnen für den Embryo keine Statusveränderung ereigne. Gegen gradualistische Positionen, die ebenfalls eine kontinuierliche Embryonalentwicklung, aber gleichzeitig einen graduell ansteigenden Lebensschutz annehmen,[210] spreche

Selbstzwecklichkeit des Menschen bei seiner Verwendung als Mittel zu einem anderen Zweck. Vgl. Honnefelder, a.a.O., 70.

[209] Honnefelder, a.a.O., 72: „Da in keiner Phase genetische Einzigartigkeit nicht mit Individualität verbunden ist, erlaubt es dieser Befund nicht, den Zustand bis zu diesem Zeitpunkt [sc. bis zum Ausschluss der Mehrlingsbildung] *prä*individuell zu nennen und dementsprechend von einem *Prä*embryonen zu sprechen; doch führt er die Sprache, in der wir über Individuation sprechen, an ihre Grenzen, jedenfalls, wenn wir im üblichen Sprachgebrauch unter Individualität nicht nur Un*geteiltheit*, sondern auch Un*teilbarkeit* verstehen.“

[210] Honnefelder, a.a.O., 73. Honnefelder nennt als Beispiel das Votum der Warnock-Kommission, das dem Embryo in jeder Phase zwar einen „special status“ zuspricht, aber von einer *abzustufenden* Schutzwürdigkeit des Embryos ausgeht. S. oben, S. 30ff.

auf diesem Hintergrund, dass innerhalb der kontinuierlichen Entwicklung keine moralrelevanten Zäsuren zu finden seien, die eine gradualistische Position rechtfertigten.[211] Darum sei das einen absoluten Schutz einfordernde Menschsein auch von keinen anderen Voraussetzungen[212] abhängig als allein vom *Beginn* des Menschseins. Dieses wird aber mit der Kernverschmelzung als dem absoluten Beginn datiert.[213]

An diesem Punkt konvergieren Spezies- und Kontinuums-Argument insofern, als beide aufgrund der Zugehörigkeit eines menschlichen Embryos zur Spezies *homo sapiens sapiens* vom Zeitpunkt der Kernverschmelzung an davon ausgehen, dass dieser aufgrund dieser Zugehörigkeit auch kontinuierlich schutzwürdig ist, weil – für das Kontinuumsargument – seine Entwicklung keine statusverändernden Zäsuren aufweist und er aufgrund seiner Menschheit – für das Spezies-Argument – als ein mit der Fähigkeit zur moralischen Entwicklung begabtes Wesen anzusehen ist. Auch das Identitätsargument hängt mit diesen beiden Aspekten eng zusammen.

Das Identitätsargument

Das Identitätsargument lässt sich wie folgt zusammenfassen:[214]

- Jedes Wesen, das aktual φ ist, hat Würde.
- Erwachsene, die aktual φ sind, sind mit Embryonen *in moralrelevanter Hinsicht* identisch.
- Also: Die Embryonen, mit denen sie genetisch identisch sind, haben Würde.

---

[211] Honnefelder, ebd.: „Daß wir in bezug auf Kontinuen quantitativer und qualitativer Art in anderen Zusammenhängen erfolgreich Unterscheidungen vornehmen, widerlegt dies nicht. Denn im Fall des Embryos handelt es sich um ein Kontinuum der organischen Entwicklung, die ein Lebewesen unter den üblichen Bedingungen von sich aus nimmt. Eine solche Entwicklung legt es nahe, bei der Frage nach dem Beginn auf den Zeitpunkt zu verweisen, in dem der Entstehungsprozeß den Charakter der Selbstentwicklung eines eigenen Lebewesens annimmt."

[212] Damit haben auch notwendige Stimuli für die weitere Entwicklung wie die Implantation des Embryos in den Uterus keine moralrelevante Bedeutung für den Status des Embryos als Menschen.

[213] Honnefelder, a.a.O., 76: „Wenn der Schutz der Menschenwürde dem Menschen *als Menschen* zukommt, kann sein Beginn nicht von anderen Voraussetzungen abhängig gemacht werden als dem Beginn des Menschseins selbst." Eine Grauzone bilden die Tage vor der Nidation, wie sich in den Debatten seit dem letzten Drittel des 20. Jahrhunderts zeigt. Wird aber der Beginn der kontinuierlichen menschlichen Entwicklung bei der Nidation und damit bei der Interaktion von Embryo und Mutter und dem Ausschluss der Mehrlingsbildung angesetzt, so wird damit von einer kontinuierlichen Entwicklung des *Menschseins* zugunsten einer Annäherung an eine gradualistische Position Abstand genommen. Damit wird das K-Argument aber nicht mehr konsequent vertreten.

[214] Vgl. Damschen/Schönecker, Moralischer Status, 4.

- Wenn irgendein Embryo Würde hat, dann alle.
- Also: Jeder Embryo hat Würde.

Nach dem Identitätsargument sind auch menschliche Embryonen jederzeit Menschen, weil sie genetisch mit dem Wesen identisch sind, zu dem sie sich entwickeln.[215] Nicht nur genetisch seien menschliche Embryonen aber mit Erwachsenen, zu denen sie sich – unter normalen Umständen – entwickeln, identisch, sondern auch insofern, als das Spezifikum des Menschen darin gesehen werden müsse, dass er Träger von Rechten und Adressat von Pflichten sei, was zugleich seine Würde ausmache. Aufgrund seiner biologischen Zugehörigkeit zur Spezies Mensch sei der menschliche Embryo ebenso wie jeder geborene Mensch Träger der moralisch relevanten Attribute der *Humanitas*. Weil ein Embryo Mensch sei und als solcher mit dem Menschen identisch, zu dem er sich entwickeln werde, habe er dieselben Rechte wie ein erwachsener Mensch.[216] Dieser Prozess beginne mit der Verschmelzung von Ei- und Samenzelle, mit der ein neues Genom entstehe, das die weitere Entwicklung des Embryos steuere. Damit gehen die drei bislang referierten Argumente von folgenden Voraussetzungen aus:

- Die genetische Zugehörigkeit zur menschlichen Spezies an sich ist hinreichend für eine Bestimmung des moralischen Status jedes ihrer Angehörigen.
- Die Entwicklung innerhalb der Spezies erfolgt ohne moralrelevante qualitative Einschnitte. Die einzige qualitative Statusveränderung liegt im Beginn des neuen Genoms zum Zeitpunkt der Kernverschmelzung.
- Daraus ergeben sich eine *genetische*, aber auch eine *moralische* Identität von ungeborenen und geborenen menschlichen Wesen und eine kontinuierliche Entwicklung derselben.
- Die Eigenart der menschlichen Spezies gegenüber den anderen Spezies wird als die in der Teilhaben an der *Vernunft* begründete *sittliche Verfasstheit* des Menschen verstanden und meist als *Personalität* bezeichnet.
- Weil diese Eigenart der menschlichen Spezies für alle Angehörigen der menschlichen Spezies gilt und nicht von ihrer konkreten Verwirklichung abhängt, also dem Menschen aufgrund seines *Menschseins* mitgegeben

[215] Vgl. R. Enskat in seiner Argumentation für das Identitätsargument, in: Damschen/Schönecker, a.a.O., 101-127.

[216] Die Wahrnehmung von menschlichen Pflichten kann vom Embryo natürlich noch nicht geleistet werden. „Vom moralischen Status des erwachsenen Menschen unterscheidet sich der des menschlichen Embryos zwar selbstverständlich dadurch, daß er noch nicht fähig ist, eine unbedingte Verpflichtung auch bloß zu vernehmen, geschweige denn danach zu trachten, ihr gerecht zu werden und das korrespondierende unbedingte Recht wahrzunehmen. Gleichwohl ist... der menschliche Embryo... nur dann Inhaber von Würde, wenn er sowohl Adressat einer unbedingten Verpflichtung wie Träger des korrespondierenden unbedingten Rechts ist.“ (Enskat, a.a.O., 107.)

und vorgegeben ist, ist die Gruppe der SKIP-Argumente eindeutig der Argumentation innerhalb der Mitgifttheorie zuzuordnen.

Das Potentialitätsargument fällt in diesem Zusammenhang insofern aus dem Rahmen der übrigen Argumente der Gruppe, als es auf zweierlei Weise gelesen werden kann: zum einen als mit den übrigen drei Argumenten der SKIP-Gruppe konsistent in dem Sinne, dass sich das bei Embryonen zu beobachtende Potential *automatisch* aktualisiert und darum aufgrund dieser Potentialität denselben moralischen Status bei Embryonen begründet wie bei geborenen Menschen. Zum anderen aber kann das Argument auch so gelesen werden, dass dem Potentialen ein geringerer moralischer Anspruch eignet als dem Aktualen. Dann spricht das Argument nicht für den Embryonenschutz von der Kernverschmelzung an und ist als solches das schwächste in der SKIP-Gruppe.

Das Potentialitätsargument
Das Potentialitätsargument lässt sich wie folgt zusammenfassen:[217]
· Jedes Wesen, das potentiell φ ist, hat Würde.
· Jeder menschliche Embryo ist ein Wesen, das potentiell φ ist.
· Also: Jeder menschliche Embryo hat Würde.

Das Potentialitätsargument spielt in der Diskussion über den moralischen Status des Embryo eine untergeordnete Rolle, weil der Begriff der *Potentialität* mehrdeutig ist. Das häufig gegen das Potentialitätsargument angeführte Kronprinzargument etwa führt eine eindeutige Differenz zwischen potentiellem und aktuellem Herrscher ein:[218] Dem potentiellen Monarchen kommen andere Rechte zu als dem aktuell herrschenden König – darum sei der moralische Status von mit Potentialität begabten Wesen augenscheinlich ein anderer als der von aktualen Wesen.

Ob dieses Argument auch im Bereich von Menschenwürde und Menschenrechten gilt, wird dann fraglich, wenn das Potentialitätsargument als Argument gelesen wird, das dem Embryo aufgrund von dessen Entwicklungspotential, welches sich *automatisch* – wenn die Umstände es erlauben – entfaltet, einen dem geborenen Menschen vergleichbaren moralischen Status zuerkennt.

Aus diesem Grunde muss in der Befürwortung des Potentialitätsarguments darauf hingewiesen werden, dass es unterschiedliche Begriffe von

---

[217] Vgl. W. Wieland in der Argumentation für das Potentialitätsargument, in: Damschen/Schönecker, Moralischer Status, 149-168, hier 149.

[218] Wieland, a.a.O., 153: „Es basiert auf dem kaum zu bestreitenden Gedanken, daß die verfassungsmäßigen Rechte des herrschenden Monarchen nicht zugleich auch dem Kronprinzen zukommen, den man, als dessen designierten Nachfolger, auch als den potentiellen Monarchen ansprechen kann."

Potentialität gibt, die miteinander konkurrieren, aber in ihrer Unterschiedlichkeit nicht immer klar zu Tage treten. Vertritt man das Kronprinzargument und bestreitet damit das P-Argument, so wird mit einem anderen Begriff von Potentialität operiert als bei einer Befürwortung des Potentialitätsarguments im Zusammenhang mit dem Umgang mit menschlichem Leben am Lebensbeginn. Potentialität kann auf der einen Seite bedeuten, dass eine Eigenschaft in einer Entität angelegt ist und sich die Entität unter normalen Umständen *automatisch* dahin entwickelt, die entsprechende Eigenschaft auch tatsächlich zu besitzen. Demgegenüber kann Potentialität aber auch so verstanden werden, dass damit eine Eigenschaft bezeichnet wird, die in einer Entität noch nicht vorhanden ist und bei der es von bestimmten *Voraussetzungen* abhängt, ob diese Eigenschaft auch zu einer aktuellen Eigenschaft wird.

Menschenwürde ist daher für die Vertreter der Ansicht, sie komme auch frühen Embryonen zu, nicht empirisch, sondern normativ zu bestimmen, und muss mit der Annahme begründet werden, dass der Mensch ein Wesen ist, das nicht in seinen physischen, psychischen und mentalen Eigenschaften aufgeht.[219]

Als moralisch relevante Eigenschaft des Menschen gilt in diesem Zusammenhang innerhalb des P-Arguments meist im Anschluss an Kant die moralische Begabung des Menschen,[220] die sich durch bloße Beobachtung nicht feststellen lasse und auch nicht lediglich gelte, wenn ein Mensch sich ethisch reflektiert verhalte.[221] Diese Moralfähigkeit komme nicht nur dem Erwachsenen zu, sondern auch dem sich entwickelnden Menschen, auch wenn und gerade weil ihre Ausübung sich lebenslang fortentwickele. Mit dem Rekurs auf die menschliche Fähigkeit zum sittlichen Subjektsein sei gewährleistet, dass Menschenwürde nicht von der kontingenten Entwicklung eines Menschen oder ihrer Zuschreibung durch andere abhänge. Denn ebenso wie die Menschenrechte beruhe sie nicht auf Entscheidungen, die Einzelne über Einzelne oder Gruppen zu treffen haben, sondern auf Einsichten, die sich als vorgegeben erschließen müssten.

Bei einem solchen Verständnis des Potentialitätsarguments stellt sich insofern wiederum eine enge Verbindung mit dem Speziesargument dar, als

---

[219] Vgl. Wieland, a.a.O., 161.

[220] Wieland, a.a.O., 161f.: „Sein Wesen ist nicht nur durch das bestimmt, was er in der Welt der Natur und in der sozialen Welt *ist*, sondern weit mehr noch durch das, was er *sein soll* und was von ihm gefordert wird."

[221] Wieland, a.a.O., 162: „Relevant ist nur, daß er als ein essentiell durch seine Moralfähigkeit bestimmtes Wesen daraufhin angelegt ist, diese Forderungen wahrzunehmen und sein Handeln und Verhalten durch sie motivieren zu können, auch wenn er von dieser Fähigkeit nicht in jedem Augenblick seiner physischen Existenz Gebrauch macht, ja noch nicht einmal immer Gebrauch machen kann."

beide von der dem Menschen innewohnenden *Potentialität zu moralischem Verhalten* ausgehen. Damit wird die Normativität der von Beginn an zu achtenden Menschenwürde nicht auf Kooptation oder arbiträre Entscheidungen gegründet, sondern auf die Ansicht, dass sie allen menschlichen Wesen, die in die Gruppe der Menschenwürdeträger eintreten, kraft der genetischen Zugehörigkeit in die menschliche Spezies von Anfang an zukomme und niemandem aufgrund von Entscheidungen anderer verliehen werde, dass also niemand für sie dankbar sein müsse.

Neben der meist vertretenen Begründung des Potentialitätsarguments und der anderen Argumente innerhalb der SKIP-Gruppe mit der menschlichen Anlage zum *moralischen Verhalten* besteht darüber hinaus die Möglichkeit, Menschsein als wesentlich *bezogenes* Sein anzusehen und menschliche *Relationalität* als moral- und lebensschutzbegründend zu verstehen. Dass ein Mensch aufgrund einer *Beziehung* ins Leben tritt und sich selbst in Beziehung sowohl zu sich selbst, als auch zu seiner Umwelt und seinem Ursprung oder seiner Abstammung erfährt und sich dieser Bezogenheit im Laufe seiner Entwicklung bewusst wird und sie in Beziehungen bewusst gestaltet, wäre dann das konstitutiv Unterscheidende, das ihn von anderen Spezies unterscheidet. Die Fähigkeit zu sittlichem Verhalten müsste dabei als ein Aspekt der menschlichen Relationalität und Sozialität angesehen werden.

In diesem Zusammenhang könnte ein menschliches Potential im Sinne der – vorgegebenen – *Bezogenheit*, in die sich ein Mensch hinein entwickelt, von aktuell *verwirklichten Beziehungen* differenziert werden. Mit einem Rekurs auf Relationalität wäre gewonnen, dass die Argumentation nicht auf menschliche Rationalität und Begabung zur Moral zurückgreifen müsste, sondern phänomenologisch auf menschliche Bezogenheit rekurrieren könnte, indem sie diese zunächst beschreibt und anschließend reflektiert.[222]

Für die Zeit *vor* dem Abschluss der Nidation stellt sich bei dieser Argumentation allerdings die Frage, ob auch schon der frühe Embryo unter diese Beschreibung von Bezogenheit fällt. Innerhalb der Debatte um die Forschung an Embryonen wird diese Phase aus zwei Gründen häufig als noch nicht in Beziehung stehendes und darum schutzwürdiges Sein verstanden: zum einen endet ein großer Anteil von Schwangerschaften in diesem Zeitraum unbemerkt, zum anderen kann vor dem Abschluss der Nidation noch keine Interaktion und Interdependenz des sich entwickelnden Embryos mit dem mütterlichen Organismus angenommen werden. Das Faktum, dass zahlreiche Schwangerschaften in den ersten Tagen bereits enden, ist allerdings nicht von selbst norm- und statusbegründend, weil es nicht von sich aus eine anthropologische Aussage macht. Wird menschliche Relationalität nach der

[222] Dieser Spur, die auf die menschliche Relationalität rekurriert, soll im abschließenden Kapitel nachgegangen werden. S. unten, S. 199ff.

Argumentationsstruktur des P-Arguments als menschliche Bezogenheit verstanden, in die der sich entwickelnde Mensch hinein tritt und die in ihm angelegt ist, so stellt außerdem nicht erst die *Verwirklichung* dieser Anlage Menschsein dar, insofern diese sich – günstige Umstände vorausgesetzt – *automatisch* zu einer Interaktion hin entfaltet.

Der Zusammenhang von Relationalität in ihrer doppelten Gestalt als *Bezogenheit* und aktualisierter *Beziehung* und dem Potentialitätsargument liegt nach diesen Überlegungen darin, dass die konstitutiv relationale Verfasstheit des Menschen menschliches Sein als zunächst *bezogenes* Sein verstehen lässt, das seine Bezogenheit in *Beziehungen* allererst allmählich realisiert. *Bezogensein* kann in diesem Zusammenhang als *potentielles* Stehen in Beziehung angesehen werden, das durch verwirklichte und bewusst gestaltete *Beziehungen* – zu sich selbst, zu seiner Umwelt und zu seiner Abstammung oder seinem Ursprung – aktualisiert wird. Der Potentialitätsbegriff in diesem Verständnis unterliegt nicht dem Dual von potentiell im Sinne von unwirklich und aktuell im Sinne von wirklich. Moralrelevant ist in dieser Hinsicht auch nicht der aktuell verwirklichte Beziehungsstatus, sondern die den gelebten Beziehungen vorgängige Bezogenheit in der relationalen Verfasstheit, die mit dem Menschsein an sich gegeben ist.[223]

Bei einer Zusammenfassung der Argumente innerhalb der SKIP-Gruppe lässt sich feststellen, dass die Befürworter des jeweiligen Arguments meist mit einem *intrinsischen* Wert von menschlichem Leben argumentieren, der im Rahmen der „Mitgifttheorie" zur Begründung von Menschenwürde eingezeichnet und als Grundprinzip für Ethik, Recht und Moral nicht gegen andere Werte und Interessen abgewogen werden kann. Dieser intrinsische Wert, der mit dem Menschsein an sich gegeben ist, kann nicht empirisch begründet werden, weswegen sich die meisten Ausführungen an kantischer Ethik oder theologischen Grundannahmen orientieren. Dabei wird mit den Argumenten der SKIP-Gruppe eine Stellungnahme zur gegenwärtigen bioethischen Debatte verbunden, ohne dass von der menschlichen Gottebenbildlichkeit immer explizit die Rede ist. Mit dem *Menschenwürde*-Begriff wird in diesem Zusammenhang gleichwohl operiert.

Diese intrinsische, nicht auf empirischem Wege zu findende Auszeichnung des Menschen in seinem Wesen und aufgrund seiner Menschheit *an sich*, die zugleich einen absoluten und unabwägbaren Lebensschutz begründet, kann in der bioethischen Debatte allerdings nicht als konsensbegründend angesehen werden. Während die deutsche Gesetzgebung mit ihr konform geht, kann eine solche Annahme in der britischen Gesetzgebung nicht ausgemacht wer-

---

[223] Zur Unterscheidung von Beziehung und der Beziehung vorgängiger Bezogenheit und zur sich dreifach gliedernden menschlichen Bezogenheit vgl. klar W. Härle, Systematische Philosophie. Eine Einführung für Theologiestudenten, München ^{2}1987, 211-216.

den. Die Gegenargumente gegen die SKIP-Gruppe sollen im folgenden kurz referiert werden.[224]

Gegenargumente gegen die SKIP-Gruppe

Gegen das *Spezies*argument wird vor allem eingewandt, dass es sich um einen Sein-Sollens-Fehlschluss[225] handele, wenn aus dem Sein des Embryos, also seiner Zugehörigkeit zur menschlichen Gattung, sein moralischer Status abgeleitet werde. Denn die Trägerschaft von Grundrechten werde auch bei geborenen Menschen nicht allein aus der biologischen Gattung, sondern mit bestimmten speziesspezifischen *Eigenschaften* begründet, die moralisch schutzwürdig und schutzbedürftig seien. Weil frühe Embryonen nicht über diese Eigenschaften verfügten, könne ihr Schutz lediglich über eine weitere Norm begründet werden, die generell einen solidarischen gesellschaftlichen Konsens erfordere. Dieser sei als objektive Norm zum Schutz des Embryos aber aufgrund der pluralistischen Verfassung der Gesellschaft nicht mehr einzufordern.[226] Subjektive moralische Recht könnten gegenüber den objektiven gesellschaftlich anerkannten solidarischen Rechten zwar deutlich weitergehen, hätten aber keinen gesellschaftlichen Konsens hinter sich und seien deswegen moralisch nicht universal und normativ bindend.

Aufgrund der fehlenden subjektiven Erlebensqualität beim frühen Embryo vor der Ausbildung des Nervensystems seien frühe Embryonen strukturell mit Hirntoten zu vergleichen, welche ebenfalls keine Möglichkeit zu subjektivem Erleben hätten und über die aufgrund des Votums ihrer Angehörigen auch verfügt werden dürfe.[227] In Anlehnung an diese Analogie

---

[224] Dabei haben die SKIP-Argumente eine deutlich größere Resonanz im deutschen Sprachraum; sie werden in der englischsprachigen Debatte allenfalls von katholischen Beiträgen rezipiert. Die Gegenargumente konzentrieren sich vor allem auf die Unterscheidung von Personen und Nicht-Personen und auf ein Verständnis von Autonomie und Moral nach empirischen Maßgaben. Beide Aspekte werden in den Abschnitten III.3 und III.4 eine Rolle spielen.

[225] Ein naturalistischer Sein-Sollens-Fehlschluss könnte allerdings mit dem gleichen Recht den *Kritikern* des Spezies-Arguments vorgeworfen werden, wenn diese bestimmte empirisch nachweisbare Voraussetzungen als moralbegründend verstehen. Deutlich wird in diesem Zusammenhang vor allem die Tatsache, dass ethische Urteile weltanschauungs- und interessegeleitet sind.

[226] Vgl. R. Merkel bei seiner Argumentation gegen das Speziesargument, in: Damschen/Schönecker, a.a.O., 35.

[227] Merkel räumt ein: „Freilich ist, was die Möglichkeit des subjektiven Erlebens angeht, auch der Unterschied zwischen Hirntotem und Embryo evident: Dieser kann sich, wenn man ihn läßt, zu einem erlebnisfähigen menschlichen Wesen entwickeln, jener hat ein solches Potential nicht mehr.“ (Merkel, a.a.O., 43.) Eine strukturelle Vergleichbarkeit von „verwaisten“ Embryonen und Hirntoten wird auch von P. Dabrock/L. Klinnert/S.

sei ein graduell ansteigender und gegen andere Werte abwägbarer[228] Schutz der Menschenwürde für den frühen Embryo anzunehmen, der auf der einen Seite die Intuition vieler Menschen berücksichtige, dass menschliche Embryonen einen besonderen Status innehaben,[229] zugleich aber eine Abstufung erlaube, die auch in anderen moralischen Urteilen als zulässig angesehen werde.[230]

Kritiker des *Kontinuums*arguments[231] weisen darauf hin, dass zum Erhalt und zur Ausübung von Rechten auch eine gewisse *Bewusstheit* dieser Rechte gehöre und dass es als kontraintuitiv angesehen werden müsse, wenn bereits frühen Embryonen derselbe Status und dieselben Rechte zugeschrieben würden wie geborenen Menschen, da ein großer Anteil von Schwangerschaften bereits in einem frühen Stadium ende und es kein Ritual und keine gesellschaftlich anerkannte Form gebe, diese Embryonen, die nach dem Kontinuumsargument bereits als Personen anzusehen wären, zu betrauern.

Schardien angenommen: Menschenwürde und Lebensschutz. Herausforderungen theologischer Bioethik, Gütersloh 2004, 193ff.

[228] „Da der frühe Embryo gänzlich erlebensunfähig und deshalb aktuell nicht verletzbar ist, und zwar auch durch seine Tötung nicht, da er aber andererseits (regelmäßig) das Potential der Entwicklung zur erlebensfähigen Person hat, obliegt uns ihm gegenüber eine prima facie-Schutzpflicht aus dem Prinzip der Solidarität. Diese Pflicht ist gegenüber anderen Belangen Einzelner und der Gemeinschaft abwägbar." (Merkel, a.a.O., 51.) Eine solche Abwägbarkeit ereigne sich zudem bereits in der Frage des Schwangerschaftsabbruchs, der in der westlichen Welt weitgehend legal sei. Dieses Argument übersieht allerdings, dass es sich bei den angeführten Beispielen um *Konfliktsituationen* handelt, in denen ein *Leben* gegen ein anderes *Leben* steht.

[229] In dieser Hinsicht steht die Bestreitung des Speziesarguments in der Nähe zum Votum der Warnock-Kommission.

[230] Ähnlich die Zentrale Ethikkommission der Bundesärztekammer, Stellungnahme der Zentralen Kommission zur Wahrung ethischer Grundsätze in der Medizin und ihren Grenzgebieten (Zentrale Ethikkommission) bei der Bundesärztekammer zum Forschungsklonen mit dem Ziel therapeutischer Anwendungen, 2006, 9: „Aber auch über diese Grundkonvergenz hinaus steht man hinsichtlich Art und Umfang des Schutzes frühesten menschlichen Lebens nach Auffassung der ZEKO nicht vor einer Alles-oder-Nichts-Alternative. Statt eines streng binären Denkens spricht viel für ein gradualistisches Denken, das die moralische Akzeptabilität des Umgangs mit frühestem menschlichen Leben nach bestimmten Kriterien abstuft. Auch in anderen Bereichen kennen Moral und Recht nicht nur Ja-Nein-Urteile, sondern verfügen über ein vielfach abgestuftes Spektrum normativer Beurteilungen von Handlungen im Umgang mit menschlichem Leben." (www.zentrale-ethikkommission.de/downloads/TherapKlonen.pdf.)

[231] Vgl. z.B. M. Kaufmann in der Argumentation gegen das Kontinuumsargument, in: Damschen/Schönecker, a.a.O., 83-98.

Die *Potentialität*, die Embryonen eigen sei,[232] müsse vielmehr dazu führen, sie moralisch anders zu behandeln als bereits geborene Menschen. Dieses Argument spielt ebenfalls in der englischsprachigen Debatte im Zusammenhang mit der Forschung an Embryonen eine Rolle: da zahlreiche Schwangerschaften vor der Nidation unbemerkt von der Mutter aus unterschiedlichsten Gründen enden, verstoße eine Forschung an Embryonen in diesem frühen Stadium nicht gegen ethische Grundsätze – denn ein „Verbrauch" von Embryonen finde auch in der Natur statt.[233]

In diesem Zusammenhang wird die Frage nach dem moralischen Status von Embryonen mit der Frage nach der Zulässigkeit einer gradualistischen Position hinsichtlich ihrer Schutzwürdigkeit eng verknüpft. Wie auch der Warnock-Report zeigt, kann eine gradualistische Position hinsichtlich der Schutzwürdigkeit von Embryonen eingenommen werden, wenn die Überzeugung vorliegt, dass Embryonen zwar von der Kernverschmelzung an einen besonderen Status innehaben, sich dieser Status aber im Laufe der weiteren Entwicklung aufgrund von moralisch relevanten qualitativen Einschnitten noch verändere und Auswirkungen auf die ebenfalls graduell ansteigende Schutzwürdigkeit habe. Nach dieser Ansicht entwickelt sich die personale Existenz gemeinsam mit der Ausbildung bestimmter *Eigenschaften*, weswegen eine Kontinuität ohne moralrelevante Einschnitte nicht besteht. In diesen Zusammenhang kann auch die terminologische Unterscheidung von „prä-individuellem" und „individuellen" Sein resp. „Prä-Embryo" und „Embryo" eingezeichnet werden.

Gegen das *Identitäts*argument wird eingewandt, dass eine Zygote, Morula oder Blastozyste phänomenologisch nicht mit dem Säugling oder dem Erwachsenen identisch seien,[234] zu dem sie sich entwickeln und man aus der

---

[232] Die von der Kritik am Kontinuumsargument angeführte *Potentialität* des Embryo hat in diesem Zusammenhang andere Konnotationen als der innerhalb des Potentialitätsargument verwendete Potentialitätsbegriff und schreibt potentiellem Sein einen geringeren Status zu als aktuellem Sein.

[233] Vgl. John Harris, The Ethical Use of Human Embryonic Stem Cells in Research and Therapy, in: J. Burley/J. Harris (Hrsg.), A Companion to Genethics, Oxford 2002, 158-174, 164: „We now know that for every successful pregnancy which results in a live birth, many, perhaps as many as five, early embryos will be lost or 'miscarry'... Many of these embryos will be lost because of genetic abnormalities , but some would have been viable... Thus the sacrifice of embryos seems to be an inescapable and inevitable part of the process of procreation."

[234] Angeführt wird damit die *phänomenologische Unähnlichkeit* von Embryonen und Geborenen, deren einzige Ähnlichkeitsbeziehung darin bestehe, dass sie dasselbe Genom haben. Genauso wenig wie Raupen und Puppen mit Schmetterlingen identisch seien, seien es aber geborene Menschen und Embryonen. Denn nur ein Teil der befruchteten Eizelle entwickele sich zum Kind, während ein anderer Teil des frühen Embryos sich zu Plazentagewebe entwickele, mit dem der spätere Mensch nicht identisch sei.

genetischen Identität keine Würde, also keinen moralischen Status ableiten könne.[235] Bei der Lesart, ein Embryo habe aktual die würdebegründende Eigenschaft φ und deswegen dieselbe Würde wie ein geborener Mensch, handele es sich um eine *Petitio principii.* Lese man das Argument aber so, als würden Embryonen irgendwann einmal die Eigenschaft φ bekommen, die ihre Würde konstituiere, seien sie also *potentiell* würdebegabt, so müsse das Argument als widerlegt gelten, denn in diesem Falle hätten sie die Eigenschaft als Embryonen noch nicht und seien in moralischer Hinsicht *nicht* mit Geborenen identisch.

Das dem Identitätsargument zugrunde liegende Verständnis von Identität muss nach Ansicht seiner Kritiker deswegen problematisiert werden, weil eine Identität von Embryo und Erwachsenem nicht angenommen werden könne, lege man die üblichen Beweggründe als Maßstab an, die uns normalerweise veranlassen, davon zu sprechen, dass zwei Entitäten identisch seien.[236] *Personale Identität* sei demgegenüber als Konstruktion zu verstehen, die sich aufgrund einer Kette von Ereignissen und Stadien auf dem individuellen Weg eines Menschen ergeben und die dieser für seine personale Identität halte. Identität stelle sich darum als eine Identität im Erleben, nicht als genetische Identität dar. Personalität könne in diesem Zusammenhang auch nicht als dem geborenen Menschen bereits vorgegeben verstanden werden, sondern beruhe auf dem Prozess einer Entwicklung von Eigenschaften.

Bei der Auseinandersetzung mit dem Identitätsargument operieren Befürworter und Kritiker des Identitätsbegriffs offenbar mit unterschiedlichen Konzeptionen von Identität: während Kritiker eine Identität wegen der phänomenologischen Unähnlichkeit von Embryo und geborenem Menschen ausschließen, nehmen Befürworter des I-Arguments eine sich im Rückblick erschließende Erlebens-Identität neben der von beiden Seiten unbestrittenen, aber normativ unterschiedlich bewerteten genetischen Identität an. Ob Identität in diesem Zusammenhang vorgegeben ist oder sich erst innerhalb der individuellen Entwicklung konstruiert, ist damit noch nicht entschieden und beruht auf impliziten anthropologischen Vorannahmen der jeweiligen Argumentation.

Kritiker des *Potentialitäts*arguments schließlich bestreiten den Zusammenhang von Potentialität und Menschenwürde und gehen davon aus, dass frühen Embryonen keine Menschenwürde zukommt. Embryonale Potentialität wird gleichwohl als moralisch normativ verstanden, weil ihr eine Notwendigkeit bei der Entwicklung des Embryos zum geborenen Kind zukommt. Aus diesem Potential leitet sich die grundsätzliche Forderung eines allerdings nicht als ab-

[235] So R. Stoecker bei der Auseinandersetzung mit dem Identitätsargument, in Damschen/Schönecker, a.a.O., 129-145.

[236] Stoecker geht so weit, eine kontinuierliche personale Identität abzulehnen und stattdessen eine „eng verzahnte Ahnenreihe momentaner Personenzustände" anzunehmen (Stoecker, a.a.O., 134).

solut verstandenen Lebensschutzes ab, weil moralische Rechte allererst beim Eintritt in die soziale Welt *geschuldet* werden. Das Potential, das Embryonen unzweifelhaft innewohnt, ist aus diesem Grund für Gegner des Potentialitätsarguments noch kein hinreichender Grund, Embryonen als moralisch gleichwertig gegenüber geborenen Menschen zu betrachten. Vielmehr könne der den Embryonen zu gewährende Lebensschutz gegen hochrangige Ziele wie die der medizinischen Forschung abgewogen werden.[237]

Bei einem Vergleich der Argumente und Gegenargumente der SKIP-Gruppe zeigt sich nach dieser Darstellung, dass zwei oder sogar drei offenbar miteinander unvereinbare vorausgesetzte Grundannahmen vorliegen:[238]

1. Die Grundannahme einer intrinsischen[239] und von der Zuschreibung durch andere unabhängigen Wesenseigenschaft von menschlichen Wesen, die einen absoluten Lebensschutz erfordert, der gegen kein anderes Gut wie etwa die Freiheit der Forschung oder die Hoffnung auf Therapie und damit einen gemeinschaftlichen Nutzen abgewogen werden kann,
2. die Grundannahme einer *graduell* ansteigenden und mit empirisch festzustellenden Eigenschaften zu begründenden Schutzwürdigkeit von menschlichen Wesen, die gegen hochrangige andere Güter abgewogen werden kann.
3. Darüber hinaus kann die Annahme vertreten werden, dass eine Schutzwürdigkeit menschlichen Lebens auf bestimmten Kriterien beruht, die empirisch festzustellen sind und sich erst an einem *bestimmten Zeitpunkt* einstellen.

Während die erste Grundannahme typologisch der Mitgifttheorie zuzuordnen ist, finden sich in der zweiten und dritten Grundannahme Elemente der Leistungstheorie und – wenn auch weniger ausgeprägt – der Kommunikationstheorie. Die erste Position spiegelt die Grundentscheidung der deutschen Gesetzgebung hinsichtlich des Embryonenschutzes, während die zweite dem Warnock-Report und der britischen Gesetzgebung ähnelt,[240] die dritte aber

[237] „Lebensschutz für menschliche Embryonen ist nur unter der Bedingung begründet zu fordern und zu praktizieren, *daß* sie ein Potential zur Kind-Entwicklung haben. Moralisch geschuldet werden ihnen Lebensschutzpflichten aber erst *aufgrund* ihres Eintritts in die Sphäre der moralischen Adressaten." (Schöne-Seifert bei der Auseinandersetzung mit dem Potentialitätsargument, in: Damschen/Schönecker, a.a.O., 182.)

[238] Nach der Typologie von Dworkin (s. oben, S. 81ff.) legt die erste Grundannahme den Schwerpunkt auf *natürliche*, die zweite und dritte akzentuieren eher *menschliche* Kreativität.

[239] Die Differenzierung einer als intrinsisch verstandenen und einer auf relationalen Überlegungen beruhenden Menschenwürde ist noch kenntlich zu machen.

[240] Die Stellungnahmen der Kirchen in England und Deutschland sind ebenfalls typologisch den ersten beiden Positionen zuzuordnen: während die römisch-katholische Kirche in Deutschland und England die erste Position vertritt und sowohl die *Church*

eine „Alles-oder-Nichts-Position“ darstellt, die am ehesten in gegenwärtigen utilitaristischen Konzeptionen zu finden ist.

Wenn Dworkin mit seiner Analyse Recht hat, so stellt zumindest für die ersten beiden Gruppen menschliches Leben an sich einen Wert dar, der aufgrund seiner intuitiv empfundenen Heiligkeit unbedingt zu schützen ist.[241] Für diese These spricht, dass auch die Vertreter einer gradualistischen Position einen grundsätzlichen Respekt gegenüber menschlichem Leben einfordern und etwa in der Frage nach der ethischen Zulässigkeit von Embryonenforschung auch frühen Embryonen einen „besonderen Status“ (*special status*) einräumen. Der fundamentale Dissens liegt darum weniger in der Frage, ob menschliche Wesen an sich einen Wert oder eine Würde haben oder nicht, sondern wie dieser Wert begründet wird, an welchen Eigenschaften oder Merkmalen er sich festmacht und in der Konsequenz dann auch, an welchem Zeitpunkt sein Beginn zu datieren ist bzw. ob er graduell wächst. Es handelt sich dabei um eine grundlegende anthropologische Fragestellung, die mit der eigenen *vision of life*[242] verbunden ist und hinter die offenbar nicht zurückgegangen werden kann, also mit derjenigen Lebensgewissheit, die als vorwissenschaftliche (damit aber nicht notwendig unwissenschaftliche oder gar unvernünftige), durch Überzeugungen und Prägungen allmählich geformte Einstellung unser ethisches Urteilen und Handeln orientiert.

Die Begründung der Menschenwürde im Sinne der Mitgifttheorie mit den Konzepten von Gottebenbildlichkeit und Heiligkeit habe ich in den vorangegangenen Abschnitten entfaltet. Bevor ich mit der kantischen Philosophie zu einer weiteren zentralen Begründungsstruktur von Menschenwürde komme (III.3), die – je nach interpretierendem Rahmen – auf der Grenze von Mitgift- und Leistungstheorie liegt, richte ich das Augenmerk im folgenden Abschnitt auf ein Detail, das sich aus der Darstellung der Argumentation der SKIP-Gruppe ergibt.

---

of England als auch die *Church of Scotland* weitgehend der zweiten Position zuneigen, tendiert die Evangelische Kirche in Deutschland zur ersten Ansicht.

[241] Bei Position 3., die menschlichem Leben nicht *per se* einen „besonderen Status“ zusprechen würde, stellt menschliches Leben an sich keinen unbedingt zu schützenden Wert dar. Hier wird etwa zwischen menschlichem und personalem Leben unterschieden und nicht von einer „Heiligkeit“ menschlichen Lebens ausgegangen.

[242] Ich verwende den Begriff als einen ethikbegründenden, selbst aber nicht ethischen, sondern weltanschaulich geprägten Begriff. Mit diesem Verständnis folge ich den Arbeiten von Eilert Herms und Wilfried Härle. Vgl. Herms, Grundlinien einer ethischen Theorie der Bildung von ethischen Vorzüglichkeitsurteilen, in: Ders., Gesellschaft gestalten. Beiträge zur evangelischen Sozialethik, Tübingen 1991, 44-55; Härle, Die weltanschaulichen Voraussetzungen jeder normativen Ethik, in: Ders., Christlicher Glaube in unserer Lebenswelt. Studien zur Ekklesiologie und Ethik, Leipzig 2007, 210-237.

III. 2.4 Intrinsischer Wert und relationale Begründung – eine sich fortsetzende kontroverstheologische Alternative?

Die Argumente der SKIP-Gruppe werden in der Debatte über den Lebensschutz für frühe Embryonen vor allem von Vertretern der christlichen Kirchen verwendet. Dabei zeigt sich eine Differenz vor allem zwischen römisch-katholischer Argumentation auf der einen und protestantischer Argumentation auf der anderen Seite, wobei die (anglikanische) *Church of England* in diesem Zusammenhang eher der protestantischen Seite zugehört.

Während katholische Stellungnahmen sowohl im deutschsprachigen als auch im englischsprachigen Raum die Position vertreten, eine Forschung an Embryonen, im Verlaufe derer der Embryo vernichtet wird, sei ethisch unvertretbar, weil sie die Rechte verletze, die der Embryo ab dem Zeitpunkt der Kernverschmelzung habe und die Heiligkeit und Selbstzwecklichkeit des Lebens nicht achte,[243] vertreten sowohl die (anglikanische) *Church of England* als auch die (reformierte) *Church of Scotland*, dass die ethische Beurteilung der Embryonenforschung auf der einen Seite ein komplexes Problem darstelle, auf der anderen Seite aber in bestimmten Situationen, unter bestimmten Bedingungen und mit klaren Grenzen ethisch zulässig sei.[244]

Die unterschiedlichen Stellungnahmen der Kirchen in Deutschland, wo die katholische Kirche ebenfalls eine Position *gegen* die verbrauchende Forschung an Embryonen einnimmt,[245] während die EKD zu keiner vollkommen einheitlichen Äußerung finden konnte,[246] sich aber Ende 2007/Anfang 2008 einer einmaligen Verschiebung des Stichtags im Stammzellgesetz öffnete, haben bereits Erwähnung gefunden.

---

[243] So etwa in den Texten des Linacre Centres for Health Care Ethics (www.linacre.org) oder im von der katholischen Bischofskonferenz von England und Wales verabschiedeten Text Cherishing Life von 2004 (vgl. www.catholic-ew.org.uk/ccb/content/download/956/9550/file/Cherishing_Life_2004.pdf). In den katholischen Texten wird explizit mit *dignity* argumentiert, die dem menschlichen Leben als personalem Leben zukomme. Forschung an Embryonen, im Verlaufe derer der Embryo zerstört werde, sei ein Handeln gegen die Würde, die schon Embryonen eigne.

[244] So in Dokumenten der *Church of England*, die eine eindeutige Stellungnahme vermeiden, etwa im Text der *Ethical Investment Advisory Group* unter dem Titel „Human Embryonic Stem Cell Research: on the Path to an Investment Framework" (2003). Die *Church of Scotland* betont das der Kirche aufgegebene Ethos des Heilens, das einen Verbrauch von frühen Embryonen zur Heilung von schweren Erkrankungen rechtfertige. Vgl. das Dokument des *Church of Scotland Church and Society Council, Report of the Working Group on Embryo Research, Human Stem Cells and Cloned Embryos*, 2006.

[245] So in verschiedenen Äußerungen der deutschen Bischofskonferenz zum Stammzellgesetz und einer eventuellen Lockerung. Vgl. die Darstellungen auf www.dbk.de.

[246] Im EKD-Dokument *Im Geist der Liebe mit dem Leben umgehen* (2002), in dem die Kammer für Öffentliche Verantwortung hinsichtlich des Embryos vor der Nidation zu keiner einheitlichen Stellungnahme finden konnte.

In diesen unterschiedlichen Positionen, bei denen römisch-katholische Stellungnahmen vertreten, eine Forschung an frühen Embryonen sei aufgrund der normativen *intrinsischen* Wesenseigenschaften von Menschen ethisch generell unzulässig, während evangelische Positionen – mit unterschiedlicher Gewichtung – aufgeschlossener gegenüber dieser Forschung sind, könnte sich eine grundsätzlich unterschiedliche ontologische Konzeption verbergen, ohne dass diese Beobachtung verabsolutiert werden darf.

Die katholische Tradition neigt in dieser Frage dazu, naturrechtlich und deontologisch im Rückgriff auf universale Regeln zu argumentieren und den Status des Embryos als eines (möglicherweise potentiellen) sittlichen Subjekts zu definieren.[247] Die Begründung von Menschenwürde wird im Rekurs auf menschliche Eigenschaften wie die Befähigung zur Moral geleistet, so dass sie als *eigenschaftsgestützt* bezeichnet werden kann.

Demgegenüber argumentieren evangelische Positionen eher situativ, relational und seltener naturrechtlich im Rekurs auf universale Pflichten und/oder menschliche Eigenschaften. Dies führt zum einen zu einer großen Bandbreite an ethischen Positionen im evangelischen Bereich, und zum anderen häufig dazu, dass Embryonenforschung als ganze nicht abgelehnt, sondern in engen Grenzen und unter bestimmten Auflagen zugelassen wird – im Kontext der britischen Diskussion häufiger und eindeutiger als im deutschsprachigen Bereich.[248] Die den „Status" des Embryos bestimmenden Argumente der SKIP-Gruppe,[249] die fast ausnahmslos von katholischen Forschern in Anspruch genommen werden, verstärken den Eindruck, dass konfessionelle Unterschiede in der Beurteilung der Probleme am menschlichen Lebensbeginn meinungsbildend sind, weil konfessionelle Prägungen offenbar mit unterschiedlichen ontologischen Grundannahmen verbunden sind.

---

[247] Ähnlich auch im jüngsten Dokument des kirchlichen Lehramts „Dignitas personae" vom September 2008. http://www.vatican.va/roman_curia/congregations/cfaith/documents/rc_con_cfaith_doc_20081208_dignitas-personae_ge.html.

[248] Neben den bereits genannten EKD-Texten vgl. R. Anselm/U.H.J. Körtner (Hrsg.), Streitfall Biomedizin. Urteilsfindung in christlicher Verantwortung, Göttingen 2003; P. Dabrock/L. Klinnert/S. Schardien, Menschenwürde und Lebensschutz. Herausforderungen theologischer Bioethik, Gütersloh 2004; U.H.J. Körtner, Unverfügbarkeit des Lebens? Grundfragen der Bioethik und der medizinischen Ethik, Neukirchen-Vluyn [2]2004. Eine Positionen *gegen* die Forschung an Embryonen vertritt z.B. W. Härle, Menschenwürde – konkret und grundsätzlich, in: Ders., Menschsein in Beziehungen. Studien zur Rechtfertigungslehre und Anthropologie, Tübingen 2005, 379-410.

[249] Innerhalb der SKIP-Gruppe ist vor allem das Kontinuums-Argument geeignet, einen relationalen Argumentationsansatz zu vertreten. Wenn menschliches Leben als ein solches Kontinuum verstanden wird, so kann es als Sein-in-Beziehung und Sein-in-Entwicklung wahrgenommen werden, dem Würde nicht aufgrund einer besonderen *Eigenschaft* oder eines besonderen *Status* zukommt, sondern dessen Würde sich auf dieses *Sein-in-Entwicklung* bezieht.

Dabei kann die Frage nach dem „Status“ des Embryos implizieren, dass ein bestimmter Status, der zu achten und zu schützen ist, aufgrund bestimmter *Eigenschaften* besteht. In diesem Zusammenhang tritt die Frage nach der aktuellen Situation und ihrer ethischen Beurteilung eher in den Hintergrund. Die Konzentration auf die universale Verpflichtung, die der natürliche Status mit sich bringt, neigt zu einem Denken vom Einzelnen her, dem aufgrund bestimmter Eigenschaften ein bestimmter Status eignet – im Falle der Forschung an frühen Embryonen wird dieser Status meist als sittliches Subjektsein von Anfang an verstanden.

In den dogmatischen Prolegomena in der theologischen Debatte seit den 60er Jahren des 20. Jahrhunderts haben deutsche evangelische Theologen wie etwa Gerhard Ebeling und Wilfried Joest für dieses Denken vom Einzelnen her, der *als Einzelner* Beziehungen eingeht, den Begriff der Substanzontologie geprägt.[250]

In der Zuerkennung einer Würde für das Sein-im-Werden und das Sein-in-Entwicklung firmiert demgegenüber, anders als in einem substanzontologischen Konzept, die Anerkennung des dem Erkenntnissubjekt vorgängigen und es affizierenden Seins-in-Beziehung. Ein solcher Zugang ist weniger eigenschaftsgestützt, weil als dasjenige menschliche Merkmal, das Menschsein konstituiert, das grundlegende menschliche Ausgreifen über sich in seinem konkreten Erleben hinaus angesehen wird. Diese Reflexion des konstitutiv menschlichen Seins-in-Beziehung unterscheidet sich insofern von der Feststellung einer *intrinsischen* Werthaftigkeit des Menschseins, als das Spezifikum menschlichen Lebens in diesem Zusammenhang nicht in einer im Menschsein als solchem liegenden *Eigenschaft*, sondern in seiner *Bezogenheit* auf ihm extrinsisch bleibende Instanzen wie seine Umwelt, seinen Ursprung oder seine Abstammung oder auch sich selbst über seine derzeitige konkrete Gestalt hinaus gesehen wird.

Zur Begründung von Menschenwürde innerhalb der Mitgifttheorie und im Anschluss an die theologische Figur der Gottebenbildlichkeit ist darum am Abschluss dieses Abschnitts differenzierend zu unterscheiden zwischen einer Bestimmung von einer Würde des menschlichen Lebens, die diesem als *intrinsischer Wert* universal aufgrund seines Menschseins, also der Zugehörigkeit zur Gattung *homo sapiens sapiens,* der genetischen Identität mit geborenen Angehörigen der Gattung und seiner Begabung zur Sittlichkeit eignet, und einer Bestimmung, die Menschsein *in Entwicklung* und *in Beziehung* verortet und als konstitutiv für das Menschsein das Bezogensein auf Andere versteht.

Mit der Begründungsfigur, die ich als zweite genannt habe, ist nicht notwendigerweise ein mit der Kernverschmelzung beginnender Lebensschutz

---

[250] Vgl. Ebeling, Dogmatik des christlichen Glaubens, Bd. 1, Tübingen [3]1987, 346ff. Außerdem Joest, Ontologie der Person bei Luther, Göttingen 1967.

impliziert, weil der Beginn von Bezogenheit auch am Zeitpunkt der Nidation (oder sogar noch später) datiert werden kann. Beide Zugangsweisen können aber aufgrund ihrer *Vorgegebenheit* und *Unverfügbarkeit*, die sich nicht an bestimmten Leistungsmerkmalen ausrichtet, der Mitgifttheorie zugeordnet werden und werden idealtypisch von den christlichen Kirchen vertreten, die mit dem Wert und der Würde des Embryos die Heiligkeit und Geschöpflichkeit des Lebens verbinden.

Während in diesem Zusammenhang römisch-katholische Argumentation einer eigenschaftsgestützten Begründung von Menschenwürde zuneigt, tendiert evangelisch-theologische Ethik zu einer relationalen Begründungsstruktur, die am ehesten mit dem Kontinuums-Argument konvergiert, aber auch das Potentialitätsargument rezipieren kann. Dabei darf diese Differenz nicht verabsolutiert werden, zumal auch eine relationale Konzeption insofern auf eine eigenschaftsgestützte Konzeption zurückgreift, als sie klären muss, warum die Bezogenheit auf sich selbst und über sich selbst hinaus als Spezifikum ausgerechnet für *Menschen* (und nicht auch für andere Lebewesen) gelten soll. Und eine Begründungsstruktur, die mit einer intrinsischen Begabung argumentiert, kann sehr wohl von menschlicher Relationalität ausgehen. Insofern sind die aufgezeigten Unterschiede idealtypisch zu nennen, geben aber gleichwohl eine in sich differenzierte Argumentationstypologie zu erkennen, die mit unterschiedlichen ontologischen Grundannahmen verbunden ist.

Menschenwürde wird innerhalb der „Mitgifttheorie" nicht ausschließlich mit Gottebenbildlichkeit konnotiert, sondern ebenso mit der menschlichen Vernunftnatur und der menschlichen Begabung zur Moralität, was sich bereits bei der Darstellung der SKIP-Argumente gezeigt hat. Vor allem in der Philosophie der Aufklärung spielt dieser Ansatz eine maßgebliche Rolle, und ihr prominentester Vertreter im deutschsprachigen Raum ist Immanuel Kant, mit dessen Würdeverständnis und seiner Rezeption vor allem im englischen Sprachraum sich der nun folgende Abschnitt beschäftigt. Ich gehe damit einen Schritt weiter, indem ich Begründungsmodelle, die der Theologie inhärent sind, verlasse und mich mit Kant (III.3) und dem Utilitarismus (III.4) einigen *philosophisch-ideengeschichtlichen Wurzeln* der bioethischen Debatte in Deutschland und England zuwende.

III. 3 Menschenwürde, Autonomie und Rationalität. Das Würdeverständnis von Kant und seine Interpretation in der Gegenwart

III. 3. 1 Das Verständnis von Menschenwürde bei Immanuel Kant

Die Würdekonzeption von Immanuel Kant (1724–1804) stellt neben der Begründung von Menschenwürde mit der *Gottebenbildlichkeit* die wichtigste Argumentationsfigur bereit, Menschenwürde als menschliche Wesenseigenschaft im Sinne der Mitgifttheorie zu begründen. Sie ist in der deutschen Philosophie und Gesetzgebung hinsichtlich der ethischen und rechtlichen Probleme am menschlichen Lebensbeginn[251] auch deswegen als einflussreich anzusehen, weil sie eine Interpretation von Menschenwürde bereitstellt, die nicht explizit auf den Begründungstypos der menschlichen Gottebenbildlichkeit rekurriert, sondern auf Rationalität oder Geistigkeit, und damit eine Begründungsform liefert, die auch außerhalb der Theologie in der deutschen Gesetzgebung und Rechtsprechung seit der Mitte des 20. Jahrhunderts immense Bedeutung erlangen konnte. Aber auch in der englischsprachigen Debatte wird die kantische Konzeption breit rezipiert.

Dabei hat Kant mit der Unterscheidung von Zweck und Mittel innerhalb der „praktischen Form" seines *Kategorischen* Imperativs[252] eine Unterscheidung geprägt, die in der 1958 verwendeten Formulierung der „Objektformel"[253] von Günter Dürig eine immense Breitenwirkung in der Auslegung von Artikel 1 I des Grundgesetzes bis in das letzte Drittel des 20. Jahrhunderts hinein gehabt hat.

Die von Kant in der *Kritik der reinen Vernunft* gegebene Verhältnissetzung von Freiheit und Kausalität[254] bildet den Verstehenshintergrund auch für die kantische Würdekonzeption. Während Freiheit das Vermögen meint, einen Zustand von selbst beginnen zu können,[255] steht diese doch nicht in Konkurrenz zur von Kant ebenfalls angenommenen Kausalität der Natur. Dem Subjekt muss vielmehr *innerhalb* der Bedingtheit durch Kausalität Freiheit zugestanden werden, die sich im Zusammenhang der Ethik als Hervorbringung einer *guten Willensgesinnung* äußert.

---

[251] Dass die folgenden Ausführungen Kant nicht gerecht werden können, erscheint mir mehr als deutlich. Aufgrund der Fragestellung konzentriere ich mich auf Kants Konzeption der *Menschenwürde*. Die in den Anmerkungen gebrauchten Abkürzungen für die Werke entsprechen den gängigen Abkürzungen in der Kant-Literatur.

[252] „Handle so, dass du die Menschheit, sowohl in deiner als in der Person eines jeden anderen, niemals nur als Mittel, sondern jederzeit zugleich als Zweck brauchest." Kant, Grundlegung zur Metaphysik der Sitten, BA 67, in der von Weischedel hrsg. Werkausgabe (Weischedel (Hrsg.), Immanuel Kant, Werke in sechs Bänden, Bd. IV, Schriften zur Ethik und Religionsphilosophie, Darmstadt [5]1998) S. 61. Ich verwende in den folgenden Ausführungen die von C. Horn, C. Mieth und N. Scarano hrsg. und kommentierte Ausgabe der Grundlegung (Frankfurt/Main 2007). Die praktische Form des Kategorischen Imperativs findet sich hier auf S. 62.

[253] So Günter Dürig in der Auslegung von Art. 1 I GG, 1958, Randnummer 28: „Die Menschenwürde ist getroffen, wenn der konkrete Mensch zum Objekt, zu einem bloßen Mittel, zur vertretbaren Größe herabgewürdigt wird."

[254] KrV, B 831.

[255] KrV, B 561

In dieser Dialektik von empirischer, kausal bedingter Welt auf der einen und transzendentaler, von Freiheit bestimmter Welt auf der anderen Seite erhebt Kant die Notwendigkeit des Glaubens an die unbedingte Freiheit des Subjekts. Damit ist Freiheit mit dem Glauben konnotiert; der Glaube wiederum ist der Selbstvollzug der freien Vernunft.[256] In diesem Zusammenhang sind die Ideen von *Gott*, *Freiheit* und *Unsterblichkeit der Seele* der Vernunft als notwendige Ideen im kantischen System vorgegeben.

Zur Begründung der *Würde* der menschlichen Natur unterscheidet Kant auf diesem Hintergrund zwischen Entitäten, die – als *freie* und *vernünftige* Wesen – einen *Zweck* an sich selbst oder einen *absoluten* Wert und eine Würde und denjenigen, die – als *bedingte* Wesen – einen nur *relativen* Wert oder einen Preis haben und bezeichnet den Menschen „und überhaupt jedes vernünftige Wesen“[257] als eine solche Entität, die als Zweck an sich selbst existiert und nicht bloß als Mittel zum Gebrauch für diesen oder jenen Willen zur Verfügung stehen kann. Aufgrund dieses absoluten Wertes oder seiner Würde muss der Mensch nach Ansicht von Kant jederzeit zugleich als Zweck behandelt werden und darf niemals ausschließlich ein Mittel für einen anderen Zweck sein.

Für diesen Dual von absolutem und relativem Wert wiederum ist Kants Unterscheidung zwischen empirischer, auf Kausalität beruhender, und transzendentaler, mit Freiheit konnotierter Welt als Hintergrundannahme anzusehen. Diese Unterscheidung nämlich ereignet sich insofern auch im Menschen selbst, als dieser als *homo phainomenon* und *homo noumenon* an beiden Welten partizipiert.

Die Selbstzwecklichkeit des Menschen, die es auch ermöglicht, vom Menschen als von einer *Person* zu sprechen, begründet Kant mit der menschlichen Vernunftnatur und der aus dieser folgenden Autonomie, wobei Autonomie im wörtlichen Sinne (*Auto-nomie*) als die Fähigkeit verstanden wird, sich sein eigenes moralisches Gesetz zu geben. „Das vernünftige Wesen muß sich jederzeit als gesetzgebend in einem durch Freiheit des Willens möglichen Reiche der Zwecke betrachten.“[258] Weil das menschliche Wesen *vernünftig* ist, hat es die Fähigkeit zur Selbstgesetzgebung, so dass es dem moralischen Gesetz nicht nur folgt, weil andere es von ihm verlangen, sondern selbst von dessen Notwendigkeit überzeugt ist und es sich aufgrund seiner Freiheit als Gesetz zu eigen macht.

---

[256] Zum ganzen s. J. Dierken, Freiheit als religiöse Leitkategorie. Protestantische Denkformen zwischen Luther und Kant, in: Ders. (Hrsg.), Freiheit und Menschenwürde. Studien zum Beitrag des Protestantismus, Tübingen 2005, 119-144.

[257] Grundlegung zur Metaphysik der Sitten, in der von C. Horn u. a. herausgegebenen und kommentierten Fassung, 61.

[258] Grundlegung, 68.

In der so verstandenen Moralität als Fähigkeit zur Selbstgesetzgebung (Autonomie) ruht für Kant die Würde der menschlichen Person. Der oben angedeutete Dual von Empirie und Transzendentalität, resp. *homo noumenon* und *homo phainomenon* kehrt darum in der Unterscheidung von Würde und Preis wieder, wenn Kant demjenigen Wesen Würde zuspricht, das „über allen Preis erhaben ist, mithin kein Äquivalent verstattet".[259] Denn in der allen vernünftigen Wesen möglichen freien Selbstgesetzgebung liegt für Kant ein unabwägbarer Achtung gebietender Wert, der die Würde des Menschen und jeder vernünftigen Natur ausmacht: Weil die vernünftige Natur dazu fähig ist, aus eigenem Willen sittlich zu handeln, muss sie in ihrer Würde sowohl durch sich selbst als auch durch andere geachtet werden. Nicht die Vernunftnatur *als solche* stellt darum für Kant die Begründung für die Notwendigkeit der Achtung der Würde dar, sondern die darin liegende Befähigung zur Sittlichkeit.[260] An dieser Stelle zeigt sich, dass ein großer Teil der SKIP-Argumente auf kantischen Voraussetzungen aufruht.

Nun könnte Kants Konzeption so interpretiert werden, als gelte die Achtung gebietende Eigenschaft des Menschen, die in seiner Vernunftnatur und der Hinordnung zur Moralität liegt, nur für Menschen, die ihre Autonomie auch aktiv ausüben und selbstgesetzgebend tätig sein können.[261] Die „praktische" Form, in der Kant die Selbstzwecklichkeit des Menschen mit dem Kategorischen Imperativ formuliert, gibt aber einen Hinweis darauf, dass Kant nicht an einer *empirischen* Begründung von Menschenwürde interessiert ist,

[259] Grundlegung, 69.

[260] Weil Kant die menschliche Befähigung zur Sittlichkeit als konstitutiv ansieht, besteht für ihn bei jedem Menschen auch eine grundsätzliche Befähigung, dem Sittengesetz zu folgen und das eigene Handeln im Sinne des Kategorischen Imperativs zu reflektieren und zu universalisieren. Die schon von Hegel monierte Schwäche des Kategorischen Imperativs, dass dieser eine rein formale Bestimmung sei und keine Handlungsvorgaben mache, löst sich bei Kant insofern, als er davon ausgeht, dass der Mensch als Vernunftwesen gleichsam automatisch dem *Guten* folgt, wenn er sich nur seiner Autonomie bedient. Kants formale Regel folgt damit einem bestimmten Rahmen und kann darum auch – entgegen seiner eigenen Ansicht – als nicht so universal und formal angesehen werden, wie er selbst es intendiert hatte. W. Härle hat meines Erachtens überzeugend gezeigt, dass Kants Konzeption – wie jede andere ethische Konzeption – auf weltanschaulichen Voraussetzungen basiert. Vgl. Härle, Die weltanschaulichen Voraussetzungen jeder normativen Ethik, in: Ders., Christlicher Glaube in unserer Lebenswelt. Studien zur Ekklesiologie und Ethik, Leipzig 2007, 210-237. Bei einer Übernahme dieser formalen Regel in die gegenwärtige Moralphilosophie muss, wenn der kantische Interpretationsrahmen mit seiner Transzendentalität strittig wird, ein anderer Rahmen gefunden werden, was etwa Alan Gewirth versucht. S. unten, S. 116ff.

[261] Tatsächlich scheint ein großer Teil der englischsprachigen Kant-Interpretation dieses Verständnis zu vertreten. Vgl. etwa das Votum von Raanan Gillon, s. oben, S. 60, Anm. 120.

wenn er schreibt: „Handle so, daß du die Menschheit sowohl in deiner Person, als in der Person eines jeden anderen, jederzeit zugleich als Zweck, niemals bloß als Mittel brauchest."[262]

Mit dem Begriff „Menschheit" geht Kant nicht vorrangig von der menschlichen Gattung oder Spezies aus, die jeder Mensch in sich selbst und in anderen zu achten hätte, sondern meint offenbar die *noumenale* Seite des Menschen als transzendentale Idee:[263] Aufgrund seiner Partizipation an der Menschheit wird auch der phänomenale Mensch von Kant als intrinsisch mit Würde begabt verstanden. Diese Interpretation nimmt allererst die grundlegende kantische Unterscheidung zwischen *homo phainomenon* und *homo noumenon* ernst, nach der ersterer den Menschen als Naturwesen bezeichnet, der an der Natur und der in ihr wirksamen Kausalität partizipiert und auch mit empirischen Mitteln beschrieben und untersucht werden kann. Der *homo noumenon* bezeichnet demgegenüber die mit Freiheit begabte und zur Selbstgesetzgebung befähigte Mensch*heit* und ist aufgrund dessen sowohl durch sich selbst als auch durch andere in seinem intrinsischen, absoluten Wert zu achten.

Von einer *empirischen* Begründung der Würde und Sittlichkeit der menschlichen Natur grenzt Kant sich aufgrund dieser Unterscheidung ab. Eine empirische Ableitung von Moralität würde vielmehr dazu führen, dass Menschen ihren Neigungen und Interessen folgen und nicht dem universalen Sittengesetz. Eine beobachtete Unsittlichkeit von Menschen oder ihre aktuelle, temporäre oder dauerhafte Unfähigkeit zur Befolgung des Sittengesetzes führt darum die sittliche Bestimmung und Begabung des Menschen und seine darin liegende Würde nicht *ad absurdum*.

Die menschliche Begabung mit Vernunft und Sittlichkeit und seine Fähigkeit zur Moralität durch Autonomie veranlassen Kant also dazu, *jedem* Menschen Würde zuzuerkennen, auch wenn (aus unterschiedlichen Gründen) die menschliche Vernunftnatur beim vorfindlichen Menschen nicht, noch nicht, nicht mehr oder nur teilweise empirisch ausgemacht werden kann.[264] Darum

---

[262] Grundlegung, 62, im Original kursiv. S. auch schon oben, S. 110f., Anm. 252.

[263] Vgl. Horn u. a., Kommentar zur Grundlegung der Metaphysik der Sitten, 247: „Was Kant hier mit der Menschheit meint, ist die intelligible oder noumenale Seite des Menschen... Wiederholt unterscheidet Kant zwischen der Menschheit (als dem *homo noumenon*) und dem Menschen (als dem *homo phaenomenon*); gemeint ist einerseits der Mensch als 'moralisches Wesen' und andererseits der Mensch als 'physisches Wesen'."

[264] Offenbar setzt Kant den Beginn der Partizipation des empirischen Menschen an der autonomen Menschheit mit der Zeugung an: „Wenn man aus der Natur des erwachsenen Menschen auf dessen ewige Dauer schließen kann, so muß auch der neugebohrne Mensch eben dieses hoffen lassen. Also auch der Embryo, das ovulum, das ovulum vom ovulo." (Kant, Akademie-Ausgabe XVII, 473, Nr. 4239.) Das „Erzeugte" sei „eine Person" (Metaphysik der Sitten, § 28, B112, in der von Weischedel hrsg. Ausgabe Bd. IV, S. 393), und Kant beurteilt die Idee als „richtig... und auch notwendig..., den Akt der Zeugung als einen solchen anzusehen, wodurch wir eine Person ohne ihre Einwilligung auf die

muss ein Begriff der *Freiheit* ebenso wie ein Begriff der *Autonomie* für die Beschreibung des Menschen nach Kant als konstitutiv angesehen werden. Diese bewegen sich aber im Bereich der transzendentalen Ideen,[265] sind also empirisch weder zu verifizieren noch zu falsifizieren. Aufgrund dieses transzendentalen Rahmens, der für die kantische Philosophie die entscheidende Grundannahme darstellt, kann Kants Konzeption der Menschenwürde der Mitgifttheorie zugerechnet werden. Sie traut dem Menschen viel zu und kann in ihrer Wertschätzung einer *intrinsischen* moralisch relevanten Begabung von Menschen als anthropozentrisch gekennzeichnet werden. Dabei geht sie von einer absolut und universal geltenden Werthaftigkeit menschlichen Lebens aus, die unter keinen Umständen gegen andere Werte abgewogen werden darf.

III. 3. 2 Interpretationen von Kants Konzeption im 20. Jahrhundert

In der deutschen Debatte hat die kantische Philosophie unter anderem in der Formulierung einer Begründung von *Menschenwürde* nachgewirkt, während für die britische Diskussion Kants *Autonomie*begriff in stärkerem Maße rezipiert worden ist. Beide Aspekte sind im folgenden darzustellen. An ihnen erhellt sich meines Erachtens ein wesentlicher Grund für die Differenzen bei der Beurteilung von menschlichem Leben am Lebensbeginn in der deutschen und britischen Gesetzgebung.

III. 3. 2. 1 Die Begründung von „Menschenwürde" in Dürigs Objektformel

In der deutschen Gesetzgebung und der Kommentierung des Grundgesetzes bei Art. 1 I durch Günter Dürig (1958) hat die Menschenwürde-Konzeption von Kant eine weit reichende Rolle vor allem in der Formulierung der so genannten Objektformel gespielt: „Die Menschenwürde ist getroffen, wenn der konkrete Mensch zum Objekt, zu einem bloßen Mittel, zur vertretbaren Größe herabgewürdigt wird."[266] Dürig schließt sich mit dieser Interpretation der nach 1945 in das Grundgesetz aufgenommenen Achtung der Menschenwürde offenbar an kantische Terminologie an. Vor allem in der Unterscheidung von Objekt/Mittel und Subjekt/Zweck nimmt er Kants Unterscheidung von Mittel und Zweck in der praktischen Form des Kategorischen Imperativs auf.

Trotzdem zeigen sich bei genauerer Betrachtung einige tief greifende Differenzen. Denn in der Interpretation von Dürig ist zunächst die Grundannahme der transzendentalen *Menschheit* nicht mehr wie bei Kant prägend,

---

Welt gesetzt, und eigenmächtig in sie herüber gebracht haben" (B 113, in der von Weischedel hrsg. Ausgabe S. 394).

[265] Der *homo noumenon* nimmt damit im Zusammenhang der anthropologischen Fundierung von Kants Ethik bezogen auf den Menschen die Stelle des *Dings an sich* ein.

[266] Dürig in der Auslegung von Art. 1 I GG (1958), Randnummer 28. S. auch schon oben, S. 110, Anm. 253.

sondern der Blick geht auf den *konkreten* Menschen, dessen Würde missachtet wird, wenn er zum Objekt herabgewürdigt wird. Mit der Konzentration auf den konkreten Menschen aber stellt sich die von Kant aufgrund von dessen Annahme einer grundsätzlichen Teilhabe *jedes* menschlichen Wesens an der *noumenalen* Menschheit noch nicht gestellte Frage nach der *Ausdehnung* von Menschsein: wann beginnt das Sein eines „konkreten Menschen", und wann endet es, und welche Kriterien müssen erfüllt sein, damit von Menschsein gesprochen werden kann, das unter dem Schutz der Rechtsgemeinschaft steht?

Auch wenn in der Kommentierung von Dürig diese Fragen noch nicht gestellt werden, spielen sie in der gegenwärtigen Debatte um die Auslegung von Art. 1 I GG eine enorme Rolle. Über diese Akzentverschiebung hinaus hat sich die von Kant vertretene transzendentale Idee der *Menschheit* in der Idee einer *Gattungswürde* fortgesetzt, die aber ebenfalls in der gegenwärtigen Auslegung von Art. 1 I GG meist nicht mehr vertreten wird.[267]

Weil die *Menschheit* in Kants Konzeption den noumenalen und transzendentalen Rahmen für das sittliche Handeln des Individuums bildet, das voraussetzende „Ding an sich", das allenfalls festgestellt, nicht aber bewiesen werden kann, und weil in der Menschheit als dem Ding an sich, an dem der phänomenale Mensch partizipiert, aufgrund deren Vernunftnatur die Begründung für Würde liegt, kann für Kant Würde nicht mit empirischen Mitteln festgestellt werden. Wird Kants Konzeption in der Würdebegründung demgegenüber in einen empirischen Interpretationsrahmen gestellt und auf den „konkreten Menschen" bezogen, so zeigen sich die Grenzen einer Begründung der Menschenwürde aufgrund von Autonomie und Rationalität. Empirisch gelesen, führt Kants Ansatz zu einer Position, die Autonomie als Selbstbestimmung versteht und Menschenwürde lediglich für diejenigen Menschen annimmt, die aktuell rational handeln können.[268] Eine solche Tendenz zeichnet sich ab, wenn in der „Objektformel" nicht vom „Menschen an sich" oder der *Menschheit*, sondern vom *konkreten* Menschen gesprochen wird, dessen Würde missachtet wird, wenn er zum Objekt degradiert wird. Es stellt sich dabei die Frage nach einer zeitlichen Ausdehnung des Seins von Menschen sowohl am Beginn als auch am Ende des Lebens, so dass die Anfragen an die

[267] Eine Nachwirkung hat die Annahme einer Gattungswürde beim S-Argument der SKIP-Gruppe, wenn davon ausgegangen wird, dass allein die Zugehörigkeit eines Individuums zur Spezies *homo sapiens sapiens* dafür ausreicht, dieses Individuum als mit Menschenwürde begabt zu verstehen.

[268] Innerhalb eines solchen Interpretationsrahmens wird die kantische Philosophie aber weitgehend modifiziert. Vgl. meine Versuche zu einer Gegenüberstellung von Kant und englischsprachiger Kant-Rezeption in den „Principles of biomedical ethics" (T. Beauchamp/J. Childress): S. Rolf, Respekt vor Patientenautonomie und Achtung der Menschenwürde. Beobachtungen zu anthropologischen Implikationen in deutscher und englischsprachiger Bioethik-Debatte, ZEE 52, 2008, 201-212.

rechtsbegründende Funktion eines universalen Menschenwürdebegriffs am Ende des 20. Jahrhunderts folgerichtig erscheinen.

Die Fassung des kantischen Duals von Mittel und Zweck in der Objektformel übersieht darüber hinaus, dass „Objekt" nicht der Gegenbegriff zu „Zweck" ist. Ein Objekt ist ein Gegenstand oder ein Ding, das für seinen Besitzer durchaus zu einem Zweck werden kann und nicht ein bloßes Mittel zu bleiben braucht. Die Objektformel von Dürig spricht sich gegen eine Pervertierung von Menschen zu Objekten, die man besitzen kann und deren Freiheit man raubt, aus, ist darum aber mit der Kantischen Formulierung der *Selbstzwecklichkeit* des Menschen nicht deckungsgleich. Sie vertritt dabei allerdings einen bescheideneren Anspruch als die Formulierung einer *absoluten* Selbstzwecklichkeit des Menschen bei Kant selbst.

In der neueren *englischsprachigen* Debatte wird innerhalb einer gleichwohl verbreiteten Kant-Rezeption der transzendentale Interpretationsrahmen meist nicht übernommen bzw. durch andere Bezugsrahmen ersetzt. Dabei wird die Relevanz der kantischen Konzeption durch die englischsprachige Philosophie und Ethik vor allem in zwei Aspekten gesehen:

- Der Idee der *Universalisierbarkeit* und *Gegenseitigkeit* von moralischem Handeln,
- Der Idee der menschlichen *Autonomie*.

Beide Aspekte sollen in den folgenden Abschnitten entfaltet werden, wobei Universalität und Gegenseitigkeit vor allem in der zuerst darzustellenden Konzeption des Neukantianers Alan Gewirth und ihrer Rezeption durch Deryck Beyleveld und Roger Brownsword von Bedeutung sind.

III. 3. 2. 2 Menschenwürde und Handlungsagenten – Kants Interpretation durch Alan Gewirth

Der nun folgende Abschnitt stellt mit der Arbeit des amerikanischen Philosophen Alan Gewirth[269] und der Vermittlung der Konzeption Gewirths nach Großbritannien durch Deryck Beyleveld und Roger Brownsword[270] einen englischsprachigen Versuch dar, kantische Ethik für die Gegenwart zu rezipieren und darin ohne das „Ding an sich" und die Unterscheidung von *noumenaler* und *phainomenaler* Welt auszukommen. Darin stellt er einen bedeutenden Entwurf innerhalb der englischsprachigen Kant-Rezeption dar. Für unseren Zusammenhang besonders relevant ist die Tatsache, dass Beyleveld/Brownsword eine Konzeption von *Menschenwürde* für den englischen Sprachraum entwickeln.

---

269 Vgl. vor allem Gewirth, Reason and Morality, Chicago/London 1978.

270 Deryck Beyleveld/Roger Bronsword, Human Dignity in Bioethics and Biolaw, Oxford 2001.

Alan Gewirth versucht die schon von Hegel angemerkten Schwierigkeiten eines Formalismus der kantischen Philosophie zu vermeiden und durch einen *konkreten* Zugang zu interpretieren. Die kantische Hochschätzung von menschlicher Moralität bleibt darin erhalten, nicht aber die Begründung von Menschenwürde mit *transzendentaler* Rationalität. Um kantische Ethik kommunikabel zu machen, stellt Alan Gewirth das „Prinzip der konstitutiven Konsistenz" (*Principle of Generic Consistency*, PGC)[271] auf, mit dem er versucht, das Begründungsproblem normativer Ethik nicht wie Kant mit einem *transzendentalen* Interpretationsrahmen, sondern mit einem *empirisch nachvollziehbaren* Modell menschlichen Handelns zu lösen. Von den britischen Juristen und Rechtsphilosophen Deryck Beyleveld und Roger Brownsword ist dieses Prinzip auf die Diskussion um die Menschenwürde appliziert worden.[272]

Die Konzeption von Gewirth und dieser folgend die Begründung der Menschenwürde durch Beyleveld/Brownsword gehen davon aus, dass jeder Handelnde bzw. Handlungsfähige in seinem Handeln immer schon eine Verbindung von Tatsachen- und Werturteilen knüpft. Er handelt, weil er zum einen eine Tatsache erkennt und zum anderen mit dieser Tatsache einen bestimmten Wert wie Ablehnung, Bejahung, Sehnsucht, Verlangen oder Furcht verbindet. *Handeln* wird in diesem Zusammenhang als freiwilliges und zweck- oder zielgerichtetes (intentionales) Tun und Lassen verstanden. Ich stelle zunächst den Handlungsbegriff von Alan Gewirth und das darin begründete „Principle of Generic Consistency" dar, um daran anschließend die Applikation dieses Modells auf die Begründung von Menschenwürde durch Beyleveld/Brownsword zu referieren.

Für Gewirth ergeben sich folgende Beobachtungen für menschliche Handlungen: Handlungen erfolgen zum einen *spontan*, sind zum anderen aber auch durch den Handelnden aufgrund seines Werturteils *final* bestimmt und darum Tätigkeiten, die sowohl ein Willens- als auch ein Wissensmoment enthalten. Sie sind dem Handelnden zurechenbar, der seinerseits rechenschaftsfähig und -pflichtig im Hinblick auf seine Handlungen ist, weil er selbst handelt und die Verantwortung sowohl für die Handlung als auch für die Handlungsfolgen trägt.

In der Intentionalität, der Spontaneität und der Zurechenbarkeit von Handlungen liegt dabei für Gewirth die Implikation von Werturteilen: wir tun etwas, weil wir es für richtig halten, so zu handeln. Wir handeln in einer bestimmten Art und Weise, weil wir ein bestimmtes Ziel erreichen wollen, das uns als begehrenswert und erstrebenswert erscheint. Aus diesem Grund sind Handlungen nicht „wertneutral", sondern implizieren Werte und Prioritäten des Handelnden, die das Handeln orientieren.

---

[271] Gewirth, Reason, 129ff.

[272] Vgl. Beyleveld/Brownsword, Human Dignity, 69ff.

Dass Menschen nicht immer und mit jeder ihrer Handlungen freiwillig und intentional handeln, muss dabei vorausgesetzt werden. Automatisierte, nicht reflektierte oder erzwungene Handlungen widersprechen aber dem Handlungskonzept von Gewirth nicht. Denn mit dem vorgestellten Handlungsbegriff, der *Handlungen im engeren Sinne* (zu denen auch Unterlassungen zählen) als freiwillig und intentional versteht, wird ein Nachdenken über Sittlichkeit und ethisches Verhalten allererst ermöglicht.

Dabei ist das intentionale und freiwillige Handeln dadurch ausgezeichnet, dass *jemand etwas um etwas willen* tut oder unterlässt. Es besteht für Gewirth sogar die *Notwendigkeit* der Formel „ich tue X wegen eines Z“, weil der Handelnde diese Formel nicht bestreiten kann, ohne in einen Selbstwiderspruch zu geraten. Denn in der Handlung des Handelnden wird deutlich, dass diese einer bestimmten Intention folgt und einen bestimmten Zweck hat,[273] also mit Wissens- und Werturteilen des Handelnden verknüpft ist. Wird dieser Zusammenhang von Intentionalität, Wert und Wissen durch den Handelnden bestritten, so untergräbt er seine eigene Handlungsintentionalität und widerspricht sich selbst.[274]

Gewirth zeigt im Anschluss an die Entwicklung dieses Handlungsbegriffs, dass, wer handelnd das Urteil „ich tue X wegen eines Z“[275] trifft, weitere Urteile trifft, die in diesem ersten Urteil impliziert sind, etwa dass Z ein erstrebenswertes Gut ist, um dessentwillen es sich zu handeln lohnt. Diese Implikation wird von Gewirth als „dialektische Notwendigkeit“ bezeichnet und beschreibt die implizite Werthaftigkeit von Handlungen und Handlungszielen für den Handelnden.

Wenn aber Handelnde mit ihrem Handeln ein Urteil fällen, das in ihrem Handeln impliziert ist, gehen sie zugleich von einem moralischen Prinzip aus, das ihrem Handeln innewohnt, auch wenn sie sich nicht immer über dieses Prinzip Rechenschaft geben. Wenn sie handelnd aussagen „ich tue X um eines Z willen“, bringen sie damit die Folgerung zum Ausdruck „Ich will Z“, was wiederum impliziert „Z ist gut“ und das damit äquivalente Urteil „Z ist ein Gut“. Mit ihrem Handeln fällen sie zwar kein assertorisches Urteil, nach dem Z ein objektives Gut für jeden und zu jeder Zeit wäre. Für sich selbst aber wählen sie Z, weil sie Z als gut erachten, und implizieren damit gleichzeitig, dass Z auch für andere ein Gut sein oder werden könnte. Die Beurteilung von

[273] Gewirth, Reason and Morality, 41: „In the broad sense... volutariness and purposiveness exhaust the generic features of action.“

[274] Vgl. Gewirth, a.a.O., 48: „The main thesis of this book is that every agent, by the fact of engaging in action, is logically committed to accept a supreme moral principle having a certain determinate normative content. Because any agent who denies or violates this principle contradicts himself, the principle stands unchallenged as the criterion of moral rightness, and conformity with its requirements is categorically obligatory.“

[275] Bei Gewirth: „I do X for purpose E“ (a.a.O., 49).

Z als einem erstrebenswerten Gut für sie selbst lässt die Erlangung dieses Guts zu einem potentiellen moralischen Handlungsprinzip auch für andere werden.

Neben dem mit dem Handeln erstrebten Gut stellen aber die *Grundlagen* des Handelns, die Handlungs*fähigkeit* und die Handlungs*freiheit* für das Handeln ebenfalls notwendige Güter dar, weil ohne diese eine Handlung nicht vollzogen werden kann: werden Menschen in ihrem Handeln entweder von außen gehindert durch Einschränkung ihrer Handlungs*freiheit*, oder von innen aufgrund einer noch nicht entwickelten oder nicht mehr vorhandenen Handlungs*fähigkeit* eingeschränkt, so können sie die Handlungen nicht vollziehen, die zur Erreichung des von ihnen erstrebten Gutes führen.

In dieser Überlegung liegt aber schließlich die Begründung der fundamentalen These Gewirths: wenn der Handelnde ohne die Möglichkeit zu handeln und ohne Handlungsfreiheit nicht handeln kann, so geht er implizit davon aus, dass die Gewährung seiner Handlungsfreiheit ein Rechtsgut zu seinen Gunsten darstellen muss. Von seinem Standpunkt aus ist der Handelnde also genötigt anzunehmen, dass er anderen gegenüber einen *Rechtsanspruch* auf die Gewährung der äußeren Bedingungen für seinen Handlungserfolg hat (auch wenn dieser Rechtsanspruch *de facto* nicht zu jeder Zeit eingelöst wird).[276] Vor allem seine Handlungsfreiheit sieht er als ein durch die Gemeinschaft, in der er lebt, zu gewährleistendes Gut an, das er – reziprok – auch den anderen Mitgliedern der Gemeinschaft zugesteht.

Damit verschränken sich in diesem von Gewirth entwickelten Handlungsbegriff eine faktische Bedürftigkeit von Handelnden und ein subjektiv empfundenes Wollen, mit dem Handelnde ihre eigene Bedürftigkeit von Freiheit und Wohlergehen für ihr Handeln empfinden und diese auch unkonditioniert verwirklicht sehen wollen. Der Rechtsanspruch richtet sich vornehmlich an andere, die ihre Freiheit und ihr Wohlergehen einschränken könnten. Mit diesem subjektiven Wollen ist noch keine *absolute* Begründung für den Rechtsanspruch auf die Gewährung von Freiheit geliefert, wohl aber der Aufweis, dass jeder Handlungsagent für das Gelingen *seiner* Handlungen die Gewährung von Freiheit als *conditio sine qua non* beanspruchen muss.

In dieser Perspektive des Wollens des Handlungsagenten bleibt der individuelle Rechtsanspruch noch subjektiver Natur und stellt kein oberstes moralisches Prinzip dar. Nach dem (kantischen) Prinzip der Universalisierung kommt der Handelnde nach Gewirth aber von dem Schluss, dass er selbst als Handelnder einen Rechtsanspruch auf Freiheit und Wohlergehen hat, ebenfalls zu dem Schluss, dass dieselben Rechtsansprüche für alle anderen

[276] „Since the agent regards as necessary goods the freedom and well-being that constitute the generic features of his successful action, he logically must also hold that he has rights to these generic features, and he implicitly makes a corresponding right-claim." (Gewirth, a.a.O., 63.)

Handlungsagenten ebenso gelten müssen wie für ihn. Jeder Handelnde, der freiwillig und intentional handelt bzw. die Fähigkeit hat, freiwillig und intentional zu handeln, muss darum dieselben Rechte haben wie er selbst. Mit dem Rechts*anspruch* korrespondiert daher die *Verpflichtung*, die Handlungsfähigkeit und Handlungsfreiheit keines anderen Handlungsfähigen einzuschränken. Eine Reziprozität der gegenseitigen Anerkennung der notwendigen Handlungsbedingungen ist darum nach Gewirth logisch gefordert.

Hieraus ergibt sich schließlich der Imperativ, dass jeder Handelnde stets in Übereinstimmung mit den konstitutiven Rechten der Empfänger seiner Handlung wie auch seiner selbst handeln soll. Damit wird das Prinzip der konstitutiven Konsistenz begründet („Principle of Generic Consistency")[277]: Der Handelnde handelt in Übereinstimmung mit seiner Freiheit und seinem Wohlergehen und achtet bei seinem Handeln darauf, dass diese notwendigen Bedingungen des Handelns auch für jeden von seinem Handeln unmittelbar und mittelbar betroffenen Handelnden erfüllt sind.

Damit läuft der Begründungsweg für moralische Prinzipien bei Gewirth nicht wie bei Kant über die Universalisierbarkeit des moralischen Sittengesetzes, sondern über die Universalisierbarkeit von Handlungsbedingungen, die gleichwohl mit der Konzeption der Werthaftigkeit von Handlungen zumindest die Möglichkeit der universalen Geltung eines Handlungsgutes für jeden Menschen zu jeder Zeit einschließt, auch wenn Gewirth von dem transzendentalen Interpretationsrahmen Kants in der Unterscheidung von *phainomenaler* und *noumenaler* Welt keinen Gebrauch macht. Ich wende mich im folgenden der Begründung einer Konzeption von *Menschenwürde* im Anschluss an den Handlungsbegriff von Gewirth zu.

Mit dem Prinzip der *Reziprozität* und dem Begründungsweg der dem Handeln impliziten *Werturteile* leiten Deryck Beyleveld und Roger Brownsword in Anlehnung an Gewirth eine Begründung der universalen Menschenrechte und der diese begründenden Menschenwürde ab: danach gehe jeder Handelnde in seinem Handeln davon aus, dass er einen *Rechtsanspruch* auf *Freiheitsrechte* habe, um sein Handeln so durchführen zu können, dass es erfolgreich sei, also seiner Freiwilligkeit und seiner Intention entspreche. Damit impliziere er nach dem (kantischen) Prinzip der Universalisierbarkeit aber, dass diese Freiheitsrechte für jeden Handelnden ebenso gelten wie für ihn. Weil Handelnde für sich selbst Rechte beanspruchen könnten, müssten sie

---

[277] Gewirth, a.a.O., 135: „The general principle of these obligations and rights [die ein Handelnder anderen gegenüber hat] may be expressed as the following precept addressed to every agent: *Act in accord with the generic rights of your recipients as well as of yourself.* I shall call this the *Principle of Generic Consistency (PGC)*, since it combines the formal consideration of consistency with the material consideration of rights to the generic features or goods of action." Dass die Formulierung des *Principle of Generic Consistency* dieselbe Struktur hat wie der Kategorische Imperativ, zeigt Gewirths Suche nach einem universalen moralischen Prinzip.

aufgrund des Prinzips der konstitutiven Konsistenz (PGC) diese Rechte auch allen anderen Handlungsagenten zugestehen.

Von dieser Begründung von universalen Rechten von Handlungsagenten aus schließen Beyleveld/Brownsword auf eine universale *Würde*, die die Grundlage der Rechte bilde und darin liege, dass Menschen zum einen handeln und sich zum anderen Rechenschaft über die Grenzen und Bedingungen ihres Handelns geben können. Menschenwürde bildet in dieser Konzeption ausdrücklich die Grundlage von Rechten und wird damit begründet, dass Menschen zu einem Handeln aus Intentionalität und Spontaneität zumindest potentiell befähigt seien:[278] wer Rechte habe, habe auch Würde, bzw. Würde komme denjenigen zu, die handeln könnten und denen ein Recht zu autonomen intentionalen Handlungen zugestanden werden müsse.

Damit rekurriert das von Beyleveld/Brownsword in Anlehnung an Gewirth konzipierte Modell von universaler Menschenwürde auf das Handeln von Handelnden und (auch potentiell) Handlungsfähigen und steht hinsichtlich der Wertschätzung der Handlungs*autonomie* in der Nachbarschaft zur Konzeption von Immanuel Kant.[279] Die Pflichten sich selbst und anderen gegenüber, in denen sich für Kant allererst die Autonomie der Handlung zeigt und die Kant beispielsweise dazu veranlassen, den Suizid strikt abzulehnen,[280] werden aber bei Gewirth und Beyleveld/Brownsword anders aufgefasst, weil etwa der Selbstmord einem autonomen Willen und der Freiwilligkeit entspringen könne und als solcher nicht moralisch zu verurteilen sei.

Während die Konzeption von Kant eher eine Theorie hinsichtlich von Pflichten ist, stellt die Theorie von Gewirth und Beyelveld/Brownsword primär eine Theorie zur Konsolidierung von Rechten dar.[281] Konstitutive Rechte beziehen sich nach diesem Verständnis auf den zweckgerichteten und sponta-

[278] Beyleveld/Brownsword, Human Dignity, 122ff. „Finally, it is worth noting that precautionary reasoning requires agents to grant some moral status to creatures that appear to be potential agents." (A.a.O., 125.)

[279] Eine Nähe von Kant und Gewirth und der eigenen Konzeption von universaler Würde sehen ebenfalls Beyleveld/Brownsword, a.a.O., 87: „Most importantly, Kant and Gewirth agree that (a) morality *purports* to impose categorically binding standards for action; (b) there is a supreme principle of morality, which *actually* is categorically binding; (c) a principle can be justified *as* categorically binding only by demonstrating that it is an absolutely unconditional requirement of reason."

[280] Kant, Grundlegung zur Metaphysik der Sitten, in der oben genannten von Horn u. a. hrsg. und kommentierten Ausgabe S. 63: „Der Mensch... ist keine Sache, mithin nicht etwas, das *bloß* als Mittel gebraucht werden kann, sondern muß bei allen seinen Handlungen jederzeit als Zweck an sich selbst betrachtet werden. Also kann ich über den Menschen in meiner Person nicht disponieren, ihn zu verstümmeln, zu verderben oder zu töten."

[281] So auch Beyleveld/Brownsword, a.a.O., 99.

nen Willen des Handelnden und weniger auf seine Pflicht, einem universalen Sittengesetz folgend, die „Menschheit“ in anderen und sich selbst nicht als Mittel zu einem Zweck zu benutzen. Eine Pflicht gegen sich selbst und gegen andere besteht bei Gewirth und Beyleveld/Brownsword vielmehr darin, das Prinzip der konstitutiven Konsistenz für sich selbst und andere anzuerkennen. Damit verbindet sich der kantische Universalisierungsanspruch mit einem grundsätzlich liberalistischen Impetus, der die Grenzen der eigenen Freiheit an den Grenzen der Freiheit des anderen verortet.

Nach der bisherigen Darstellung könnte sich der Eindruck eingestellt haben, als sei die Konzeption von Gewirth und Beyleveld/Brownsword eine empiristische Verschiebung der Konzeption Kants, insofern sie auf die Spontaneität und Zweckgerichtetheit von *aktuellen* Handlungsagenten bezogen ist. Gewirth und Beyleveld/Brownsword unterscheiden in diesem Zusammenhang aber zwischen dem gegenwärtigen und dem zukünftigen Selbst eines Handelnden, welchem gegenüber das gegenwärtige Selbst genauso Pflichten habe wie gegenüber anderen Handlungsagenten. Diese zeitliche Differenzierung im Rekurs auf gegenwärtiges und zukünftiges Selbst übernimmt bei Gewirth die Funktion, die bei Kant die Unterscheidung von vorfindlichem, *phainomenalen* und *noumenalem* Menschen innehat und ermöglicht es, auch von der Würde zukünftiger Handlungsagenten auszugehen, weil auch sie in der Zukunft Handlungsagenten sein und nach dem Prinzip der konstitutiven Konsistenz das Recht haben werden, ihre Handlungen so auszuführen, wie es ihrer Intention entspricht.

Was Gewirth intendiert hatte, nämlich die kantische Ethikkonzeption für die Gegenwart fruchtbar zu machen, ohne die Unterscheidung von Erscheinung und Ding an sich zu übernehmen, löst er – vergleichbar mit einigen Aspekten der Argumente innerhalb der SKIP-Gruppe – mit der Konzeption einer zeitlichen Kontinuität und der damit zusammenhängenden Potentialität von zukünftigen Handlungsagenten ein.

Dabei ist aber folgende Differenz zu Kant auszumachen: der *homo noumenon* bezeichnet bei Kant eine autonome Instanz, worin auch seine Würde besteht, weil seine Autonomie seine „Menschheit“ in dem Sinne konstituiert, dass sie ihn befähigt und sogar automatisch dazu hintreibt, dass er dem Kategorischen Imperativ folgt. Der *homo phainomenon* partizipiert an der „Menschheit“ und erhält vom *homo noumenon* den Imperativ mit der Aufforderung, sich (autonom) den Kategorischen Imperativ als Handlungsgesetz zu geben. Eine Teilhabe von Handlungsagenten an einem transzendentalen Handelnden nehmen Gewirth und Beyleveld/Brownsword demgegenüber nicht an: Die Würde des Menschen besteht in ihrer Konzeption in der Autonomie, die sich aus der Fähigkeit ergibt, dass dieser als ein bestimmter und konkreter Mensch handeln und zwischen Alternativen wählen, bzw. zu einem autonomen Handelnden *werden* kann. Damit wird aber ein von Kant unterschiedener Autonomiebegriff verwendet.

Mit der von Beyleveld/Brownsword in Anlehnung an Gewirth gegebenen Begründung von Menschenwürde aus dem Begriff des Handelns und der Handlungsautonomie ist insofern viel gewonnen, als sich über die Argumentation mit den notwendigen Bedingungen für Handlungen die Reziprozität von Rechten begründen lässt: wenn und weil ich handle, brauche ich bestimmte für mein Handeln notwendige Bedingungen, die dieses ermöglichen und auf die ich einen Rechtsanspruch habe, den ich umgekehrt auch allen anderen Handelnden einräumen muss. Damit wird die Konstitution von Rechten vertragstheoretisch einsichtig begründet und empirisch nachvollziehbar. Die Fundierung der Rechte in der *Würde*, die durch die Handlungs*fähigkeit* konstituiert wird, weist ihrerseits darauf hin, dass Rechte auf einer menschlichen Konstitution beruhen, die diese Rechte allererst begründet. Würde ist darum nicht das oberste Menschenrecht, sondern die Fundierung aller Rechte. Beyleveld drückt es kurz aus: Es gibt kein Recht auf Würde,[282] sondern allenfalls ein Recht auf Achtung der dem Recht vorhergehenden Würde.

Angreifbar wird die Konzeption bei der Frage, inwieweit Rechte und rechtsbegründende Würde auf diejenigen zu applizieren sind, die nicht, noch nicht oder nicht mehr über Handlungsfähigkeit verfügen und keine autonomen Handlungen vollziehen können. Mit der Unterscheidung von *homo noumenon* und *homo phainomenon* hatte Kant eine transzendentale Ebene eingeführt, die dieses Problem gelöst hatte. Bei Gewirth und Beyleveld/Brownsword, die den kantischen transzendentalen Interpretationsrahmen nicht nachvollziehen, bleibt dieses Problem als Frage bestehen und wird im ethischen Umgang etwa mit menschlichem Leben am Lebensbeginn virulent. Dieses Problem wird zum einen, wie bisher noch nicht erwähnt wurde, mit dem Verweis auf die *Verletzlichkeit* („vulnerability") von Handelnden und (auch zukünftig) Handlungsfähigen beantwortet, die diesen gegenüber eine besondere Achtsamkeit einfordert, und zum anderen, wie schon dargestellt, mit der *Potentialität* von Handelnden innerhalb eines zeitlichen Kontinuums.

Wenn aber die Konzeption eines zeitlichen Kontinuums nicht nachvollzogen und gleichzeitig verneint wird, dass eine *potentiell* handlungsfähige Person denselben moralischen Status hat wie eine *gegenwärtig* handlungsfähige, und ebenso verneint wird, dass aus der Verletzlichkeit von Handlungsfähigkeit eine moralische Normativität folgt, könnte auch konsistent verneint werden, dass dieses Wesen bestimmte Rechte hat, die für sein Handeln notwendig sind, werden oder gewesen sind.[283] Wie sich dann eine universale Menschenwürde für menschliche Wesen aussagen lässt, die etwa im Zusam-

[282] So Deryck Beyleveld im Gespräch mit mir im Dezember 2007. S. auch Human Dignity, 13: „because all humans have dignity, they hold these rights [human rights] *equally*. So understood, human dignity is the rock on which the superstructure of human rights is built."

[283] Vgl. Beyleveld/Brownsword a.a.O., 114ff.

menhang mit der Embryonenforschung nie geboren werden und insofern keine potentielle Handlungsfähigkeit haben, als sie zu keinem Zeitpunkt in der Lage sein werden, autonome und freiwillige Handlungen zu vollziehen,[284] wird vor allem mit dem Verweis auf ein zeitliches Kontinuum nicht deutlich.

Das Prinzip der Gegenseitigkeit kann zusammen mit dem Argument der *Verletzlichkeit* zu einem Schutz aus *Vorsichtsgründen* führen,[285] nach dem Kindern oder Ungeborenen gegenüber deswegen die Pflicht zur Gewährung bestimmter Lebensrechte besteht, weil sie besonders verletzliche Wesen sind und wir ihnen gegenüber mit Vorsicht („under precaution") zu agieren haben.[286] Auf Embryonen *in vitro* sind aufgrund des häufig nicht gegebenen Kontinuums von Embryo *in vitro* und *in vivo* diese Annahmen allerdings nicht ohne weiteres applizierbar.

Obwohl mit der an Gewirth angelehnten Konzeption von Beyleveld/Brownsword eine Begründung für Menschenwürde im englischen Sprachraum vorliegt, wird diese Konzeption im allgemeinen nicht zur Begründung eines Lebensschutzes für Embryonen herangezogen. Ein Grund für diese Vorsicht gegenüber dem *dignity*-Begriff in diesem Zusammenhang könnte in dem schon bei der Darstellung der SKIP-Gruppe als mehrdeutig gekennzeichneten Potentialitätsbegriff liegen. Wenn nämlich Kinder, Säuglinge und Embryonen *potentielle* Handlungsagenten sind, so kann ihnen konsistent auch eine potentielle Würde zuerkannt werden, die aber über den auch von der Warnock-Kommission festgestellten „special status" kaum hinausgeht und mit dem auch eine „verbrauchende" Forschung an Embryonen ethisch gerechtfertigt werden kann.

Die von Beyleveld/Brownsword im Anschluss an Gewirth gegebene Kombination aus Potentialitätsargument und einer Argumentation aus Vorsichts-

---

[284] Gewirth vollzieht den Schluss nicht, solchen menschlichen Wesen Menschenrechte und Menschenwürde abzusprechen, sondern argumentiert mit dem Potentialitätsargument, nach dem etwa Kinder potentielle Handelnde sind, was auch auf Ungeborene appliziert werden könne. Damit haben Kinder, Säuglinge und Embryonen noch nicht dieselben Rechte wie erwachsene Handlungsagenten, wohl aber das Recht, so zu handeln, dass sie ihre Freiheit in den Grenzen leben können, in denen sie niemanden in seiner Freiheit beeinträchtigen. Damit wird in diesem Zusammenhang eine Form des P-Arguments vertreten.

[285] Das Vorsichtsargument kann auch als *tutioristisches* Argument benannt werden. Dies besagt, dass in dem Fall, wenn nicht eindeutig ist, ob ein menschliches Wesen einen bestimmten Rechtsanspruch besitzt oder nicht, weil nicht eindeutig ist, ob es die für diesen Rechtsanspruch erforderlichen Kriterien erfüllt, es aus Vorsichtsgründen so behandelt werden soll, als *habe* es den Rechtsanspruch, damit der größere moralische Schaden vermieden wird, der entstünde, wenn man es als Wesen ohne Rechtsansprüche behandelt, es aber trotzdem Rechtsansprüche hat. Zu einer tutioristischen Argumentationsweise s. unten, Abschnitt III.6, S. 189ff.

[286] Vgl. Beyleveld/Brownsword, Human Dignity, 132.

gründen aufgrund von Vulnerabilität hat den Vorteil, dass sie gegenwärtig aufgrund ihrer geringeren Voraussetzungen vor allem im englischen Sprachraum breiter kommunikabel ist als der kantische Rekurs auf ein „Ding an sich“ oder der theologische Rekurs auf die *imago Dei*. Darüber hinaus hat eine Begründung von Menschenwürde über die menschliche Handlungsfähigkeit den Vorteil, dass sie die reine Vernunftorientierung zugunsten eines ganzheitlicheren Ansatzes überwindet und das Faktum ernst nehmen kann, dass unser Handeln nicht lediglich von Vernunftentschlüssen, sondern in hohem Maße von unser intentionalen Orientierung geleitet wird. Die noch nicht geschlossene Lücke sehe ich dabei für unseren Zusammenhang vor allem im Umgang mit zum Handeln nicht mehr oder noch nicht fähigen Wesen, so dass nach einer Begründung einer *intrinsischen* Wesenseigenschaft oder einer *relationalen* Struktur neben dem Handlungsbegriff noch gefragt werden könnte.

Ausgehend vom oben dargestellten Differenzierungsmodell von Deutungen der *Menschenwürde* favorisiert der Gewirth folgende Ansatz von Beyleveld/Brownsword jedenfalls nicht ausschließlich ein Verständnis von Menschenwürde im Rahmen der Mitgifttheorie, sondern enthält auch Elemente sowohl der Leistungs- als auch der Kommunikationstheorie.[287] Denn Würde in ihrer Begründung durch Handlungsautonomie wird zwar verstanden als rechtsbegründender und mit dem Menschsein gegebener Status, hängt gleichzeitig aber von der Zuschreibung und der Interpretation durch andere ab.

Die Konzeption, die Beyleveld/Brownsword im Anschluss an Gewirth ausarbeiten, ist insofern als wichtiger Beitrag in der englischsprachigen Kant-Rezeption und Bioethik-Debatte anzusehen, als sie am rechtsbegründenden Status von Würde festhält und unterschiedliche Interpretationen von Würdebegründung auffächert und durchspielt. *Dignity* ist also offenbar auch in Großbritannien ein konsensfähiger rechtsbegründender Begriff – allerdings nur in Grenzen für die Forschung an menschlichen Embryonen. Menschenwürde als menschliche Wesenseigenschaft von Anfang an, die einen Rechtsanspruch auf Lebensschutz begründet, wie es sich vor allem in der römisch-katholischen Rezeption der menschlichen Gottebenbildlichkeit darstellt und auch nach der kantischen Philosophie angenommen werden kann, kann unter diesen Umständen nicht ohne weiteres begründet werden. Diese Distanz dem Kantianismus gegenüber konvergiert mit der Tatsache, dass eine Würdebegabung von menschlichen Embryonen von der englischen Gesetzgebung offenbar nicht angenommen wird.

[287] Anders wäre es, wenn Würde nicht auf der aktuellen oder potentiellen Handlungs*fähigkeit*, sondern auf der im Menschsein schlechthin angelegten Handlungs*möglichkeit* gründen würde. Dann handelte man sich allerdings wieder das Problem des uneindeutigen Potentialitätsbegriffs ein, das der Konzeption von Beyleveld/ Brownsword ohnehin inhärent ist.

Nicht nur hinsichtlich von *Würde* und *Universalisierbarkeit* bestehen aber Referenzen der britischen Bioethik auf die kantische Konzeption, sondern auch der *Autonomie*-Begriff scheint zumindest terminologische Parallelen mit der kantischen Philosophie aufzuweisen. Mit diesem Aspekt beschäftigt sich der nun folgenden Abschnitt.

III. 3. 2. 3 Menschenwürde und Autonomie? Gegenwärtige Interpretationen von Autonomie im englischen Sprachraum und ihr Bezug zum kantischen Autonomiebegriff

Für Kant hat dasjenige vernunftbegabte Wesen Würde, das autonom ist, wobei Autonomie die Fähigkeit meint, sich selbst ein Handlungsgesetz zu geben und aus freiem Willen dem universalen Sittengesetz zu folgen. Autonomie im kantischen Sinne bedeutet aus diesem Grund noch nicht vor allem die Fähigkeit, eine eigenständige und selbstbestimmte Entscheidung zu treffen. Selbstbestimmte Entscheidungen – die gegenwärtig häufig als autonom bezeichnet werden – können für Kant heteronom sein, wenn sie eigenen Neigungen oder Interessen folgen oder sich an den Wünschen anderer (und nicht am universalen Sittengesetz) ausrichten. Auf diesem Hintergrund unterscheidet sich die kantische Konzeption von Autonomie aber von einem Begriff von Autonomie, wie er seit den 70er Jahren des 20. Jahrhunderts innerhalb der medizinethischen Diskussion vor allem im englischen, zunehmend aber auch im deutschen Sprachraum vorherrschend geworden ist.

Das Prinzip der Achtung vor Autonomie, das Mitte der 70er Jahre neben dem Prinzip des Patientennutzens, dem Prinzip nicht zu schaden und demjenigen der Gerechtigkeit in den „Principles of Biomedical Ethics" von Tom Beauchamp und James Childress[288] aufgestellt worden ist, bildet einen integralen Bestandteil dieses im englischen Sprachraum immer noch immens einflussreichen medizinethischen Ansatzes.

Beauchamp und Childress verstehen unter Autonomie die Fähigkeit, eigenständig Entscheidungen zu treffen und sich darin von niemandem beeinflussen zu lassen, so dass Autonomie zu einem anderen Wort für Selbstbe-

[288] Beauchamp/Childress, Principles of Biomedical Ethics, Oxford u. a. ⁵2001. Dieses Lehrbuch ist in der englischsprachigen biomedizinischen und bioethischen Debatte als wegweisend anzusehen. Es wurde Mitte der 70er Jahre zeitgleich mit dem US-amerikanischen *Belmont-Report* verfasst. Darin werden ebenfalls Prinzipien des bioethischen Handelns entwickelt: der Respekt vor der Person, der eine Richtlinie für den „informed consent" bilden soll, *Beneficence* als Richtlinie für risikovermeidende Handlungen und Gerechtigkeit als Kriterium für die Auswahl von Handlungsoptionen. Vgl. Tom L. Beauchamp, The Origins, Goals, and Core Commitments of The Belmont Report and Principles of Biomedical Ethics, in: Jennifer K. Walter / Eran P. Klein (Hrsg.), The Story of Bioethics. From seminal Works to contemporary Explorations, Washington D.C. 2003, 17-46. Der prinzipienbasierte Zugang innerhalb der Bioethik ist auch von anderen Lehrwerken übernommen worden. Vgl. als Beispiel nur das britische Lehrbuch von R. Ashcroft u. a. (Hrsg.), Principles of Health Care Ethics, Chichester ²2007.

stimmung wird, im Sinne von „self-rule that is free from both controlling interference by others and from limitations, such as inadequate understanding, that prevent meaningful choice".[289] Das *Gegenteil* von Autonomie ist darum bei Beauchamp/Childress nicht wie bei Kant Heteronomie im Sinne eines unvernünftigen, von Neigungen getriebenen und letztlich unsittlichen Verhaltens, sondern Paternalismus als Bevormundung durch andere. Darum gebietet das Prinzip der Achtung vor der Patientenautonomie die Achtung vor eigenen Entscheidungen des Patienten, auch wenn sie vom Arzt nicht gebilligt werden, weil dieser etwa die persönlichen und weltanschaulichen Voraussetzungen des Patienten nicht teilt.[290]

Ist ein Patient nach den Prinzipien von Beauchamp/Childress nicht zu Autonomie im Sinne von Selbstbestimmung[291] in der Lage, so greifen die anderen Prinzipien biomedizinischen Handelns. Autonomie ist aufgrund dieser Ergänzungsbedürftigkeit darum nicht diejenige Eigenschaft, die die *conditio humana* allererst ausmacht.[292] Dies wiederum steht im Gegensatz zur kantischen Kon-

[289] Beauchamp/Childress, Principles, 58.

[290] Beauchamp/Childress, a.a.O., 63: „To respect an autonomous agent is, at a minimum, to acknowledge that person's right to hold views, to make choices, and to take actions based on personal values and beliefs."

[291] Der Respekt vor der Patientenautonomie wird von James Childress präzisierend differenziert, indem er zwischen einer Autonomie ersten Grades und einer Autonomie zweiten Grades unterscheidet: Während Autonomie ersten Grades die aktuell ausgeübte Entscheidungsfreiheit meint, bezeichnet Autonomie zweiten Grades die Tatsache, dass ein Mensch Entscheidungen über sein Tun und Ergehen freiwillig in die Hände eines anderen gelegt hat, der für ihn entscheiden soll. Vgl. Childress, The Place of Autonomy in Bioethics, The Hastings Report 20, No. 1, 1990, 12-17.

[292] Vgl. Beauchamp/Childress, a.a.O., 113ff. Das Prinzip, *niemandem zu schaden* (*nonmaleficence*), findet sich schon in der hippokratischen Formulierung „primum non nocere". Aus diesem Prinzip ist auch das Verbot abzuleiten, Versuche an Nichteinwilligungsfähigen durchzuführen, die ihnen Schmerz oder Schaden zufügen. (Vgl. den Abschnitt „Protecting Incompetent Patients", Beauchamp/Childress, a.a.O., 152ff.) Das Prinzip des Nicht-Schadens ist innerhalb der prinzipienorientierten Systematik mit dem Prinzip des *Nutzens* (*beneficence*) abzuwägen (Beauchamp/Childress, a.a.O., 165ff). Mit diesem formalen Prinzip ist noch nicht gesagt, wie ein Verhalten im Einzelfall dem Patienten nützt, so dass in das Prinzip ein utilitaristisches Kalkül einfließen kann. Die Ausführungen von Beauchamp/Childress differenzieren das Prinzip des Nutzens in diesem Zusammenhang als seinerseits aus zwei Prinzipien bestehend: dem positiven Nutzen (*positive beneficence*) und der Nützlichkeit (*utility*). Vgl. Beauchamp/Childress, a.a.O., 165. Der Aspekt des Nutzens bezieht sich darüber hinaus sowohl auf den einzelnen Patienten als auch auf die gesamte Gesellschaft. Der im Auftrag der US-amerikanischen Regierung ungefähr zeitgleich mit den Prinzipien entstandene *Belmont-Report* verzichtet trotz des prinzipienorientierten Umgangs, den auch er vertritt, auf ein Prinzip des Nutzens, weil er vertritt, dass dieses in dem Prinzip, keinen Schaden zuzufügen, implizit enthalten sei. Dieser Vorschlag ist von Childress und Beauchamp aber zugunsten der vier Prinzipien abgelehnt worden. Vgl. Beauchamp, Origins, Goals, and Core Com-

zeption, nach der in der Autonomie die Auszeichnung der vernünftigen Natur besteht und diese würdekonstituierend wirkt. Wird demgegenüber Autonomie im Sinne der vier Prinzipien von Childress und Beauchamp verstanden, so beschränkte sich, insofern sie würdebegründend wäre, die Würde auf diejenige Gruppe von Menschen, die aktuell ihre Selbstbestimmung ausüben können.

Die „Principles of Biomedical Ethics“ sind in der englischsprachigen Medizinethik bis in die Gegenwart von immensem Einfluss. Die Debatte um den Umgang mit ungeborenem menschlichen Leben spielt darin deswegen keine Rolle, weil der Fokus dieses Standardwerkes auf der ethischen Reflexion des ärztlichen Handelns mit Patienten liegt. Dennoch lassen sich im Zusammenwirken der Prinzipien ethische Grundannahmen ausmachen, die von Beauchamp/Childress als „common morality“ benannt werden.[293] In diesem Zusammenhang werden normative Konzepte wie der Utilitarismus, der Kantianismus, der Liberalismus und der Kommunitarismus als gleichwertig beurteilt und eklektisch zusammengestellt. Das pragmatische Grundinteresse liegt in der Konstitution einer Anwendungsethik für ärztliches Handeln.[294]

Obwohl normative anthropologische Grundannahmen darin keine tragende Rolle spielen – was auch für den Begriff *dignity* gilt, der vor allem im Zusammenhang mit dem Lebensende („death with dignity“) gebraucht, aber auch mit dem Autonomie-Begriff assoziiert wird[295] –, können in den *Principles implizite* anthropologische Grundannahmen ausgemacht werden, die ihrerseits nicht weniger prägend und einflussreich sind.

Das Prinzip der Achtung vor der Patientenautonomie[296] hat eine terminologische Parallele zum kantischen Autonomiekonzept, mit dem Kant universale

---

mitments, 25f. Das letzte der vier Prinzipien beschäftigt sich mit der Verteilungsgerechtigkeit im Gesundheitswesen (*justice*), vgl. Beauchamp/Childress, a.a.O., 225ff. Gerecht ist danach, wenn ähnliche Fälle in ähnlichen Situationen auch ähnlich behandelt werden. Das von Beauchamp und Childress vertretene Prinzip der Gerechtigkeit geht fundamental von einem *distributiven* Prinzip von Gerechtigkeit aus, nach dem gleiches gleich behandelt wird, damit alle möglichst einen gleichen Anteil an den zur Verfügung stehenden Ressourcen und Mitteln erhalten. Eine weitere – von Beauchamp/Childress nicht verfolgte – Möglichkeit wäre, Gerechtigkeit in einem *kommutativen* Sinne zu verstehen, nach dem jeder das erhält, wessen er bedarf.

[293] Principles, 23 und passim.

[294] Vgl. Beauchamp/Childress, a.a.O., 377: „Reasons exist, then, for holding that moral theory is an important enterprise, but that distinctions among types of theory are not as significant for *practical* ethics as some proclaim.“

[295] „A person's dignity... comes from being morally autonomous.“ (A.a.O., 351.)

[296] Das Prinzip der Achtung vor der Patientenautonomie hat sich in den letzten Jahrzehnten zum am meisten geschätzten Handlungsprinzip der Bioethik entwickelt. „Today autonomy is generally the most heavily weighted principle in bioethics. When the autonomy of a competent adult comes into conflict with virtually any other principle in bioethics, particularly beneficence, autonomy virtually always takes priority.“ (S.B.

Menschenwürde begründet. Auch wenn Beauchamp/Childress Anleihen bei mehreren ethisch-philosophischen Konzeptionen machen und ihren prinzipienorientierten Entwurf in einer „common morality" gründen,[297] entstehen Prinzipien aber nicht im Vakuum, sondern sind vielmehr von grundlegenden Überzeugungen getragen.[298] Auch die „common morality", von der Beauchamp/Childress ausgehen, ist darum nicht voraussetzungsfrei. Die inhaltlichen Unterschiede aber, die sich im Verständnis von Autonomie bei Kant und Beauchamp/Childress ergeben, sind für die Entwicklung der Bioethik im englischen Sprachraum folgenreich.

Autonomie wird in den Prinzipien von Beauchamp/Childress anders als bei Kant nicht als menschliche Wesenseigenschaft verstanden,[299] sondern als Fähigkeit, die *einigen* Menschen zukommt, anderen aber nicht, weil sie sich vor allem auf autonomes *Handeln* bezieht: „We analyze autonomous action in terms of normal choosers who act (1) intentionally, (2) with understanding, and (3) without controlling influences that determine their action."[300] Bei denjenigen Menschen, die aus unterschiedlichen Gründen nicht autonom handeln können, ist darum im Ansatz von Beauchamp/Childress auch nicht das Prinzip des Respekts vor der Patientenautonomie zu befolgen, weil an dieser Stelle andere Prinzipien greifen, vor allem das Prinzip des Patientennutzens und das Prinzip, Schaden zu vermeiden. Dabei ist aber der Autonomiebegriff von der kantischen Konzeption eindeutig zu unterscheiden.[301]

Rae/ P.M. Cox, Bioethics. A Christian Approach in a Pluralistic Age, Grand Rapids/ Michigan/Cambridge 1999, 207f.)

[297] Vgl. vor allem Beauchamp/Childress, a.a.O., 401ff., aber auch schon 2-5. „We will refer to the set of norms that all morally serious persons share as the *common morality*. The common morality contains moral norms that bind all persons in all places; no norms are more basic in the moral life." (A.a.O., 3.)

[298] Vgl. Meilaender, Bioethics. A Primer for Christians, Grand Rapids/Cambridge, ²2005, 1: „How we understand such principles, and how we understand the situations we encounter, will depend on background beliefs that we bring to moral reflection – beliefs about the meaning of human life, the significance of suffering and dying, and the ultimate context in which to understand our being and doing."

[299] Dass Autonomie in der bioethischen Debatte dem prinzipienorientierten Zugang folgend meist als ein *empirischer* und nicht als *transzendentaler* Begriff verstanden wird, lässt sich an der Tatsache zeigen, dass unterschiedliche Prinzipien miteinander in Konflikt geraten können. Für Kant müssten etwa Autonomie und Benefizenz nicht kollidieren, insofern Benefizenz diejenige Handlung meint, die dem Patienten nützt und für jeden Menschen in einer ähnlichen Situation einen solchen Nutzen bedeuten würde, so dass der autonome Mensch diese Behandlung in jedem Falle wählen würde. Dabei wäre die Autonomie allerdings nicht phänomenologisch am Handeln festzumachen.

[300] Beauchamp/Childress, Principles 59.

[301] Beauchamp/Childress konzedieren selbst, dass sie von einem anderen Autonomie-Begriff ausgehen als Kant: „We saw... that the word *autonomy* typically refers to what

Darüber hinaus legt der prinzipienorientierte Zugang als solcher nahe, dass die Achtung vor Autonomie gegenüber weiteren gleichberechtigten Prinzipien abwäg- und ergänzbar ist. Für die Frage nach der Forschung an Nichteinwilligungsfähigen impliziert die Konzeption, dass auch das Prinzip nicht zu schaden und das Prinzip zu nützen abwägbar und nicht nur der einzelne Patient, an dem gehandelt wird, sondern auch die gesellschaftliche Situation und der Gesamtnutzen in Anschlag zu bringen sind. Diese Grundlegung ist, auch wenn keine Aussagen zur Forschung an Embryonen als solcher gemacht werden, dennoch für den Umgang mit Nichteinwilligungsfähigen und damit mit frühen Embryonen aufgrund der breiten Rezeption des Buches im englischen Sprachraum prägend. Strukturell legt die Möglichkeit einer Abwägbarkeit von ethischen Handlungsoptionen eine Nähe zum noch darzustellenden Utilitarismus nahe und erschwert die Annahme eines universal geltenden normativen Anthropologumenons.

Bei einem Vergleich unterschiedlicher Konzeptionen des Autonomiebegriffs ist darum auch bei ausdrücklichem begrifflichen Rekurs auf die Tradition nach Kant ein unterschiedlicher Interpretationsrahmen festzustellen. Dabei liegt im Begriff von *Handlungen* eine Überschneidung der Konzeptionen von Gewirth/Beyleveld/Brownsword mit den bioethischen Prinzipien von Beauchamp/Childress vor, denen gemeinsam ist, dass sie von einer moralbegründenden *Handlungsautonomie* des Individuums ausgehen.

Mit dem Fokus auf autonomen *Handlungen* und *Entscheidungen* wird von diesen Ansätzen aber eine implizite Anthropologie vertreten, die ein zu respektierendes autonomes Menschsein mit Handlungs- und Entscheidungsfähigkeit sowie Selbstbestimmtheit assoziiert. Während der Warnock-Report die Schutzwürdigkeit menschlichen Lebens an die Ausbildung von Individualität bindet und mit dieser pragmatisch orientierten Position die implizite anthropologische Aussage macht, dass schutzwürdiges Menschsein beginnt, wenn zweifelsfrei von einem *Individuum* zu sprechen ist, verknüpfen sowohl Gewirth/Beyleveld/Brownsword als auch Beauchamp/Childress Würde und Autonomie – wenn auch mit unterschiedlichen Stoßrichtungen – konstitutiv mit *Handlungs-* und *Entscheidungsfähigkeit*.[302]

Der maßgebliche Grund für die Unterschiede eines rationalistisch-transzendentalen Zugangs, wie ihn Kant vertritt, und eines empirisch-pragmatischen Zugangs muss dabei wahrscheinlich in der unterschiedlichen Ideenge-

---

makes judgement and actions one's own. This conception of autonomy is emphatically not Kant's." (A.a.O., 351.) Die kantische Ethik wird darum vor allem aufgrund der darin entwickelten *Universalisierbarkeit von Handlungsmaximen* rezipiert. Vgl. a.a.O., 355.

[302] Gleichwohl wird in beiden Konzeptionen auch die Schutzwürdigkeit menschlichen Lebens festgehalten: bei Gewirth/Beyleveld/Brownsword mit dem Rekurs auf Potentialität und einem grundsätzlich tutioristischen Argumentationsmuster, bei Beauchamp/Childress mit der Betonung der Ergänzungsbedürftigkeit des Prinzips der Achtung vor der Autonomie durch andere Prinzipien.

schichte gesucht werden, wenn derselbe Begriff „Autonomie" in unterschiedlichen Kontexten unterschiedliche Bedeutungsbestimmungen erfahren hat. Der Autonomiebegriff, wie ihn Childress und Beauchamp vertreten, ist auf diesem Hintergrund für die Debatte zum Lebensschutz am Lebensbeginn nur wenig hilfreich, weil er nicht würdebegründend für nicht-autonomes Leben wirkt und sich nicht auf menschliches Sein als solches bezieht. Die bei Beauchamp/Childress zu konstatierende Verknüpfung von *dignity* und *autonomy* ist aber im englischen Sprachraum weit verbreitet und findet allenfalls eine terminologische, keine semantische Parallele in der kantischen Philosophie.

Innerhalb der englischsprachigen bio- und medizinethischen Debatte bildet der Respekt vor der Autonomie des Individuum häufig im Zusammenhang mit seiner Würde nicht nur in dem klassischen Werk von Beauchamp/Childress ein unhintergehbares Prinzip. Aus diesem Grund lohnt es sich, über das bisher Dargestellte hinaus grundsätzlich nach der Verwendung von *dignity* und ihrem Verhältnis zu *autonomy* im englischen Kulturraum[303] zu fragen. Denn dies erhellt, warum *dignity* als Wesensmerkmal von Embryonen in der Debatte um die Forschung an Stammzellen offenbar keine oder zumindest keine weit reichend normbegründende Rolle spielt.

Dignity spielt im britischen Kontext seit den 70er Jahren des 20. Jahrhunderts meist im Zusammenhang mit den Problemen und Herausforderungen am menschlichen Lebensende eine Rolle[304] und wird im Zusammenhang mit

[303] Die folgenden Beobachtungen beziehen sich auf den britischen Kontext. In Nordamerika wird gegenüber der britischen Debatte häufiger von „Human Dignity" gesprochen, sowohl im Zusammenhang mit einem „menschenwürdigen Sterben", als auch im Zusammenhang mit den Problemen am Lebensbeginn. Vgl. z.B. den von George W. Bush in Auftrag gegebenen Bericht *Human Cloning and human dignity: An ethical inquiry*, The President's Council on Bioethics, Washington DC 2002. Seit 1993 existiert in den USA das interdisziplinär arbeitende „Center for Bioethics and Human Dignity" (http://www.cbhd.org/index.html). Das *President's Council of Bioethics* hat im Frühjahr 2008 einen über 500 Seiten starken Report zu aktuellen bioethischen Fragestellungen vorgelegt unter dem Titel *Human Dignity and Bioethics* (http://www.bioethics.gov/reports/human_dignity/index.html). Darin heißt es präzisierend in einem Artikel des früheren Chairmans des Komitees, Leon Kass, der eine Anzahl von Werken verfasst hat, die sich mit *human dignity* beschäftigen: „In contrast to continental Europe and even Canada, human dignity has not been a powerful idea in American public discourse, devoted as we are instead to the language of rights and the pursuit of equality. Among us, the very idea of 'dignity' smacks too much of aristocracy for egalitarians and too much of religion for secularists and libertarians. Moreover, it seems to be too private and vague a matter to be the basis for legislation or public policy." (Human Dignity and Bioethics, 298.) Vgl. auch Leon Kass, Life, Liberty, and the Defense of Dignity: the Challenge for Bioethics, San Francisco 2002. Offenbar wird der Begriff *dignity* in den USA aber dennoch häufiger gebraucht als in Großbritannien.

[304] Vgl. exemplarisch R. Deech/A. Smajdor, From IVF to Immortality, (s.o., S. 52, Anm. 97), 108: „Dignity is a concept which is notoriously hard to pin down. However, it is

den Problemen am Lebensbeginn weniger gebraucht. Die innerhalb dieses Sprachgebrauchs von *dignity* eine zentrale Rolle spielende Autonomie wird dabei häufig als Fähigkeit verstanden, informiert und bewusst individuelle Entscheidungen zu treffen. Die darauf aufbauende Wortverbindung „death/dying with dignity",[305] „Sterben in Würde", meint ein autonomes Sterben und kann auch ein Sterben implizieren, dessen Zeitpunkt die Entscheidung des Sterbenden selbst setzt, auch wenn aktive Sterbehilfe nach britischem Recht gegenwärtig verboten ist.[306] Dieser Begriff von *dignity* ist offenbar ein anderer als eine anthropologische Wesenseigenschaft und meint eine phänomenologisch erkennbare Eigenschaft, die menschliches Verhalten – ähnlich dem klassischen Verständnis einer Tugend – orientiert und disponiert. In deutscher Übersetzung würde ein solcher Würdebegriff in diesem Zusammenhang insofern wahrscheinlich eher attributiv gebraucht, als von einem „würdigen Sterben" gesprochen würde.[307]

Die Wortverbindung „death/dying with dignity" spielte ursprünglich in der von England Ende der 60er Jahre des 20. Jahrhunderts ausgegangenen Hospizbewegung[308] eine wesentliche Rolle, hat sich aber im Zusammenhang mit der Konzeption von Autonomie im Sinne von Selbstbestimmung inzwischen so verselbständigt, dass sie auch Euthanasie und assistierten Suizid einschließen kann: „Dying with dignity" meint inzwischen häufig ein Sterben ohne lebensverlängernde Maßnahmen und das Recht auf eine informierte Zustimmung oder Ablehnung bestimmter medizinischer Therapien.

Als würdebegründend wird in diesem Zusammenhang vor allem Selbstbestimmung angesehen und das „würdige" Verhalten, das durch bestimmte Rahmenbedingungen ermöglicht wird. Dass im Zusammenhang mit den Problemen am menschlichen Lebens*beginn* von *dignity* auffallend selten die Rede ist, ist mit dieser Beobachtung konsistent. Denn Autonomie spielt hier, wie schon in der Darstellung der Konzepte von Gewirth/Beyleveld/Brownsword

often associated with respect for autonomy and with integrity, both physical and moral. Patients whose ability to make their own decisions, or to control their bodily functions, is impaired may feel this acutely as a loss of dignity. Patients who have lost all or most of their faculties may be too ill to experience their loss of dignity as such."

[305] Vgl. auch Beauchamp/Childress, Principles, 127.

[306] Anders wird es durch die seit 1997 in Geltung stehende *Death with Dignity Act* in Oregon, USA, geregelt, aufgrund derer Ärzte tödliche Medikamente an Patienten verschreiben können, die älter sind als 18 Jahre. S. www.oregon.gov.

[307] Die Unterscheidung zwischen einem attributiven Würdeverständnis und einem Verständnis von Würde als intrinsischer Wesenseigenschaft werde ich noch aufgreifen.

[308] Begonnen hat die Hospizbewegung 1967 in der Nähe von London mit der Gründung des St. Christopher's Hospice durch Cicely Saunders. Für die deutsche Hospizbewegung vgl. vor allem die Bücher von Christoph Student. S. etwa J. C. Student/T. Klie, Sterben in Würde. Auswege aus dem Dilemma Sterbehilfe, Freiburg i.Br. 2007.

deutlich wurde, allenfalls als *potentielle* Autonomie eine Rolle.[309] An dieser Stelle deutet sich ein zweifaches mögliches Verständnis von *dignity* resp. *Menschenwürde* an: während die kantische und theologische Interpretation eine *Wesenseigenschaft* nahe legen, die sie mit Würde assoziieren und die universal statusbegründend wirkt, nimmt die englischsprachige Diskussion eine sich eher im *Verhalten* zeigende attributiv verstandene Würde an, die auf konkretem Handeln beruht.

Wird *dignity* im Sinne von Autonomie bzw. die Achtung der Würde als Achtung vor der Entscheidungsfreiheit des Patienten verstanden, so ergibt sich aber fast zwangsläufig eine im englischen Sprachraum relativ verbreitete Kritik, dass *dignity* der in der medizinethischen Debatte ohnehin schon verankerten Achtung vor *Personen* nichts entscheidendes hinzufüge. Werde die Achtung vor der Würde als Achtung vor der Selbstbestimmung verstanden,[310] so sei sie nichts anderes als die Achtung des individuellen Patienten.[311] In diesem Zusammenhang ist Menschenwürde sogar als nutzloses Konzept (*useless concept*) beurteilt worden.[312]

Diese Kritik versteht *dignity* als religiösen Begriff, der vor allem im römischen Katholizismus, aber auch in der kontinentalen Tradition der Aufklärungsphilosophie eine maßgebliche Rolle gespielt habe und in begründender Funktion in internationale Dokumente zu den Menschenrechten aufgenom-

---

[309] In diesem Zusammenhang wird zu Recht angemerkt, dass das (so verstandene) Autonomie-Konzept für die Begründung einer universalen Menschenwürde nur begrenzt hilfreich ist. So etwa die Juristin Dr. Mary Ford in der Diskussion nach einem Vortrag auf einer Tageskonferenz des *Scottisch Council for Human Bioethics* über *Human Dignity* am 19. Januar 2008 in Edinburgh.

[310] Bei der Rezeption von *Dignity* im englischen Sprachraum unterscheidet Richard Ashcroft vier unterschiedliche Zugänge zur Interpretation von *Dignity*, vgl. Ashcroft, Making sense of dignity, Journal for Medical Ethics 2005, 31, 679-682:

- *Dignity* ist ein nicht hilfreicher, im schlimmsten Fall irreführender Begriff, der in der medizinethischen Diskussion nichts zu suchen hat. Diese Position werde von der Mehrzahl der englischsprachigen Forscher vertreten.
- *Dignity* kann in der Debatte eine Rolle spielen und hilfreich wirken, allerdings nur interpretiert als Autonomie.
- *Dignity* sollte als Konzept eine Rolle spielen und interpretiert werden im Zusammenhang mit sozialer Interaktion und der Fähigkeit des sozialen Miteinanders von Menschen.
- *Dignity* ist eine metaphysische Charaktereigenschaft von Menschen und begründet ethische Philosophie sowie die Menschenrechte. Diese Konzeption werde von einer Mehrzahl kontinentaleuropäischer Forscher vertreten und bilde den Hintergrund von zahlreichen theologischen Veröffentlichungen.

[311] So die Professorin für Medizinethik Ruth Macklin, Dignity is a useless concept, British Medical Journal 2003, 327, 1419f.

[312] Macklin, Dignity, 1420: „Dignity is a useless concept in medical ethics and can be eliminated without any loss of content.“

men worden sei. Als zentraler Begriff in diesen beiden Interpretationszusammenhängen habe er Eingang auch in die medizinethische Debatte gefunden, könne aber hier keine zentrale Rolle spielen, weil das, was er aussage, nämlich die Notwendigkeit der Achtung vor Patienten, bereits in den medizinethischen Curricula verankert sei. Diese Beobachtung erhellt wiederum, warum *dignity* in der Debatte im englischen Sprachraum über die Forschung an menschlichen Embryonen so selten verwendet wird und der Begriff, wenn er gebraucht wird, auf wenig Verständnis und Konsens stößt.

Soll trotzdem am Menschenwürdebegriff festgehalten und soll die Beurteilung, *dignity* sei ein „useless concept" nicht nachvollzogen werden, lässt sich argumentativ auf zweierlei Weise vorgehen:

- Durch die Fundierung von *Menschenwürde/dignity* in einem anderen anthropologischen Konzept als der menschlichen Autonomie,
- oder durch ein Verständnis von Autonomie, das über aktuelle *Selbstbestimmung* hinausgeht.[313]

Wird *dignity* mit *autonomy* assoziiert und diese als die *aktuelle* Befähigung eines Menschen zur Selbstbestimmung verstanden, so ergibt sich zwar eine terminologische Parallele von kantischer Ethik und gegenwärtiger bioethischer Debatte, die ihrerseits aber, wie deutlich geworden sein sollte, eine weit reichende semantische Differenz aufweist. Soll *dignity* ein auch für die Forschung an menschlichen Embryonen sinnvoller Begriff sein, so schließen diese inhaltlichen Differenzen die zu enge Assoziation von *dignity* und *autonomy* offenbar aus.

Die Begriffe allein sind darum nicht tragfähig für einen internationalen Konsens, weil sie je nach Herkunft und Deutungskontext unterschiedliche Grundannahmen aufweisen. Der Autonomie-Begriff legt nicht von sich aus eine Beschreibung jedes Menschen als mit Autonomie im Sinne einer intrinsischen Wesenseigenschaft begabten Wesens nahe. Soll an der Autonomie als einer *würdebegründenden* Eigenschaft für jedes menschliche Wesen festgehalten werden, muss nach einem Konzept gesucht werden, dass diese als mit dem Menschsein gegeben versteht – zumindest wenn Würde auf jedes menschliche Wesen appliziert werden soll.

III. 3. 2. 4 Auf dem Weg zur Leistungstheorie? Schwierigkeiten eines autonomieorientierten Konzepts von Menschenwürde

Ich fasse die bisherigen Überlegungen zusammen, indem ich aus meiner Sicht auf die Grenzen eines autonomiebasierten Zugangs für die gegenwärtige Bioethik und den Zusammenhang mit Menschenwürde vor allem hinsichtlich der strittigen Frage der Forschung an menschlichen Embryonen eingehe.

---

[313] Darüber hinaus muss in diesem Fall von einem Würdebegriff ausgegangen werden, der Würde im *Sein*, nicht im *Verhalten* verortet.

- Bei der Interpretation von *Autonomie* im Zusammenhang mit *Würde* oder *Wert* des menschlichen Lebens stellt sich die Frage, wie mit denjenigen Menschen und menschlichen Wesen umzugehen ist, die nicht, nicht mehr, noch nicht oder nie autonom zu sein befähigt sind. Bildet eine empirisch nachweisbare Form von Autonomie die Begründung von Menschenwürde, so haben diejenigen keine Menschenwürde, die nicht autonom sind. Die Frage stellt sich bereits bei Schlafenden und verschärft sich bei Bewusstlosen, Komatösen und Nichteinwilligungsfähigen.
- Wird dieses Problem zu lösen versucht, so kann entweder mit einer Unterscheidung von *phainomenaler* und *noumenaler* Welt (Kant) oder mit *Potentialität* (Gewirth/Beyleveld/Brownsword) argumentiert werden, um auch für dasjenige Menschsein Menschenwürde festzuhalten, das nicht aktuell autonom ist. Während die Lösung von Kant spekulativ erscheint, hat die Lösung der vulnerablen Potentialität von Beyleveld/Brownsword den Vorzug, dass sie nachvollziehbarer zu sein scheint. Zugleich haftet ihr eine gewisse Willkürlichkeit an. Die Schwierigkeit verkompliziert sich durch die Uneindeutigkeit des Potentialitäts-Begriffs.
- Wird zur Begründung von Würde auch bei Nicht-Autonomen auf Zusatzannahmen verzichtet, so kann, wenn für alle Angehörigen der Spezies Mensch eine Würdebegabung zumindest nicht ausgeschlossen werden soll, tutioristisch argumentiert werden, indem davon ausgegangen wird, dass der moralische Status von nicht-autonomen menschlichen Wesen nicht klar erwiesen werden kann, der Schaden, der entstünde, wenn diese als würdelos behandelt würden, aber größer wäre als der Nutzen, der sich aus ihrem Gebrauch ergäbe, und man deswegen im Umgang mit ihnen Vorsicht walten lassen müsse. Es stellt sich in diesem Zusammenhang die Frage, ob dieses eher formale Prinzip durch eine inhaltliche Bestimmung von Menschsein und Menschenwürde, die von der Theologie zu leisten ist, eingeholt werden kann.
- Wird auf Zusatzannahmen wie die Unterscheidung von *phainomenaler* und *noumenaler* Welt oder *Potentialität* verzichtet und auch eine tutioristische Argumentation nicht in Anspruch genommen, so ergibt sich ein Hang zur Leistungstheorie, insofern *konkrete* Autonomie als dasjenige Kriterium verstanden wird, das den Menschen als Menschen bestimmt und auszeichnet und seine Schutzwürdigkeit begründet.[314] Mit einem solchen Zugang ist eine gradualistische Position vereinbar, nicht aber ein Lebensschutz von menschlichen Embryonen von Anfang an.

---

[314] Ohne den transzendentalen Interpretationsrahmen muss die kantische Konzeption der Leistungstheorie zugerechnet werden. Mein Eindruck ist, dass die englischsprachige Kant-Auslegung zu einer solchen empirischen Kant-Interpretation tendiert. Vgl. etwa A. Sutton, Christian Bioethics. A Guide for the Perplexed, London/New York 2008, wo S. 24f. Kant in einem Atemzug mit Locke und Descartes bei einer rationalistischen Begründung des Personbegriffs genannt wird.

Über diese vier Anfragen hinaus, die einen direkten Bezug zum Umgang mit menschlichen Embryonen haben, nenne ich folgende grundlegende Aspekte:

- Wird Autonomie zu einem insgesamt begründenden Konzept innerhalb der Bioethik, so wird damit ein Individualismus befördert, der vor allem auf die Bedürfnisse und die Selbstbestimmung *des Einzelnen* fokussiert und weniger das Individuum in seiner *relationalen* Verfasstheit und seinen *Gewordenheiten* ernst nimmt.[315]

---

[315] Auch der Impetus, eine *intrinsische* Wesenseigenschaft des Menschen als rechtsbegründend zu verstehen, hat einen solchen Hang zum Individualismus und darüber hinaus, was sich etwa an der von Kant geprägten Formel der Selbstzwecklichkeit des Menschen feststellen lässt, zu einem Anthropozentrismus, der in seiner Absolutheit die menschliche Bezogenheit auf seine menschliche und nichtmenschliche Umwelt nicht ernst nimmt.
Gegenüber der Hochschätzung von individueller Autonomie innerhalb eines prinzipienbasierten Zugangs zur Bioethik sind in der neueren englischsprachigen ethischen Debatte Überlegungen vorgenommen worden, die weniger die Selbstbestimmung des Individuums, als vielmehr seine konstitutiv *relationale* Verfasstheit in den Mittelpunkt stellen. Der Patient kommt in diesem Zusammenhang weniger als autonomer Mensch in den Fokus, als vielmehr als in *Beziehungen* stehendes Wesen. Beispiele solcher eher relational orientierten Positionen innerhalb der englischsprachigen Bioethik finden sich etwa bei Robert Veatch oder Paul Ramsey. Robert Veatch (*1939) ist Philosoph, Pharmazeut und Pharmakologe und Professor für Medizinethik an der Universität von Georgetown; Paul Ramsey (1913-1988, Theologe in Princeton) war einer der ersten Bioethiker im englischen Sprachraum überhaupt. Veatch (vgl. A Theory of Medical Ethics, 1981, oder auch seinen Text in J. Walter/ E. Klein (Hrsg.), The story of bioethics. From seminal Works to contemporary Explorations, Washington 2003, 68-89) sucht in Anschluss an die Rawlsche Theorie der Gerechtigkeit nach Alternativen zu einer hippokratischen Orientierung der Medizin. „The first breakthrough in my own mind was the eventual realization that the old Hippocratic oath was a terribly implausible, indeed immoral basis for practicing almost any kind of medicine that people in any culture of the world would accept. Its core principle, that the physician should work always to benefit the patient and to protect the patient from harm, offends any believer in the Universal Declaration of Human Rights because it recognizes no such rights." (Veatch, in Walter/ Klein, a.a.O., 70.) Veatch begründet in Aufnahme der Konzeption von John Rawls eine dreistufige Vertragstheorie: der erste Teil des Vertrags besteht darin, dass Menschen sich in einer Gesellschaft zusammenfinden, um gemeinsam einen hypothetischen Vertrag schließen. Der zweite Vertrag wird zwischen medizinischem Personal und medizinischen Laien geschlossen. Er ermächtigt etwa Ärzte grundsätzlich dazu, Menschen zu behandeln, auch wenn mit der Behandlung Eingriffe in die Privatsphäre verbunden sind. Während dieser zweite Vertrag innerhalb einer Gesellschaft grundsätzlich gilt, ist im Einzelfall darüber hinaus ein dritter Vertrag zwischen dem einzelnen Kranken und dem ihn behandelnden Arzt abzuschließen. Eine wesentliche Erkenntnis Veatchs besteht in seiner Einsicht, dass bei aller Hochschätzung von Autonomie der einzelne (autonome oder selbstbestimmte) Mensch mit seinen Vertragspartnern in einem Geflecht von *Beziehungen* steht.
Eine stark der Theologie von Karl Barth verpflichtete theologische Bioethik wird – im englischen Sprachraum ausgesprochen einflussreich und als eines der ersten theologi-

- Wird Autonomie, wie es die Tradition seit Kant vorgibt, mit der *Vernunftnatur* des Menschen begründet, so kann sich ein reduktionistisches Menschenbild ergeben, das den Menschen vor allem als Vernunftwesen beurteilt und die Bedeutung etwa der Affekte und der Intentionalität sowie die individuelle Genese der Vernunft und ihre Einbettung beim Einzelnen in bestimmte Lebenserfahrungen und Bezogenheiten nicht ernst nimmt.
- Aus der Perspektive evangelischer Theologie stellt sich schließlich die Frage, ob eine Betonung menschlicher Autonomie die vor allem von den Reformatoren theologisch begründete menschliche Begrenztheit und Unfreiheit[316] der Vernunft, aber auch ihre geschichtliche Bedingtheit ernst genug nimmt und ob nicht vielmehr mit einer Beschreibung christlicher Freiheit in *Bindung* an den dreieinigen Gott eine qualifizierte Bestimmung auch der Vernunft und so letztlich des Menschen an sich und seiner Freiheit allererst adäquat zu leisten ist.

Ein Autonomieverständnis, das diese im Sinne einer *empirischen* Wesenseigenschaft des Menschen versteht und im Rahmen dieses Verständnisses auf

schen Konzepte zur Bio- und Medizinethik – in der zweiten Hälfte des 20. Jahrhunderts von *Paul Ramsey* vertreten, der auf die föderale Bundestheologie der reformierten Theologie und vor allem bei Karl Barth rekurriert. Vgl. P. Ramsey, Basic Christian Ethics, Westminster, Neue Ausgabe 1993. Ramsey fundiert seine bioethische Position in der Liebe, wie sie sich im Leben, in der Lehre und im Sterben und Auferstehen Jesu Christi zeigt, und wie sie im *Bund* von Menschen mit Gott speziell im Verhältnis von Israel und Gott miteinander gelebt wird. Von dieser christozentrisch und föderaltheologisch begründeten Liebe könne das biblische Prinzip der Gerechtigkeit abgeleitet werden, das das Maß dessen angebe, wozu Menschen verpflichtet seien: So wie Gott jedem gebe, was er brauche, sollen auch Menschen ihrem Nächsten geben, was notwendig sei. „The Christian understanding of righteousness... means ready obedience to the *present* reign of God, the alignment of the human will with the divine will that men should live together in covenant-love no matter what the morrow brings, even if it brings nothing.“ (Ramsey, Deeds and Rules in Christian Ethics, New York 1967, 109.) Den Modellen von R. Veatch und P. Ramsey ist ein Vorbehalt gegenüber Positionen gemeinsam, die Menschsein vor allem als *individuiertes autonomes* Sein verstehen. Beide Konzeptionen sind bioethische Konzeptionen nicht explizit zur Forschung an Embryonen zur Stammzellgewinnung. Beide machen aber mit der grundlegenden Aussage menschlicher Relationalität anthropologische Aussagen zum Menschsein an sich und sind damit dem Paradigma von Autonomie gegenüber kritisch eingestellt.

[316] Evangelische Theologie fügt darum der grundsätzlichen Hochschätzung menschlicher Selbstbestimmung und Verantwortlichkeit phänomenologisch die Erkenntnis des Menschen als eines sich und seine Selbstbestimmung immer auch verfehlenden Wesens hinzu, die sich in der theologischen Lehre der *Sünde* ausdrückt. Das Festhalten an der *Bestimmung* des Menschen und ihrer gleichzeitigen *Verfehlung* kann als das Proprium von Theologie festgehalten werden. Diese Einsicht wird im abschließenden Kapitel noch einmal eine Rolle spielen.

Autonomie zur Begründung von Menschenwürde rekurriert, kann auf dem Hintergrund der dargestellten Überlegungen nicht konsensbildend wirken.[317] Werden aber keine anderen Verständnismodelle für die Interpretation für *dignity* bereitgestellt, so stellt *dignity* keinen belastbaren Begriff für die bioethische Debatte zumindest im Umgang mit Nichteinwilligungsfähigen dar.

Zum einen muss also der Grund für den britischen Vorbehalt gegenüber dem *dignity*-Begriff darin gesehen werden, dass offenbar das im englischen Sprachraum einflussreichste Konzept von Autonomie mit der Idee der Menschenwürde als einer menschlichen *Wesenseigenschaft*, mit der im Zusammenhang mit der Forschung an menschlichen Embryonen für die Begründung des Lebensschutzes argumentiert werden müsste, nicht kompatibel ist, weil sich *dignity* eher auf das selbstbestimmte „würdevolle" *Verhalten* von (autonomen) Individuen bezieht. Zum anderen spiegeln sich in der Differenz unterschiedliche ideengeschichtliche Voraussetzungen, aufgrund derer die englische Diskussion in ihrer Begründung von Autonomie eher empirisch operiert.

In diesem Zusammenhang spielt die in Großbritannien immer noch prägende Konzeption des Utilitarismus mit seiner Folgenorientierung eine wichtige Rolle, die im Mittelpunkt des folgenden Abschnitts steht. Dabei wird sich zeigen, dass dieser Konzeption die grundlegende Wertschätzung einer *Abwägung* unterschiedlicher Güter inhäriert, die im Gegensatz zum kantischen Universalanspruch steht. Nach einer knappen Rekapitulation des klassischen Utilitarismus wende ich mich der im gegenwärtigen Utilitarismus einflussreichen Differenzierung von Menschsein und Personsein zu.

III. 4 Menschenwürde als Personwürde? Zur Frage nach der Konstitution von personaler Identität

Die britische bioethische Diskussion ist ebenso wie die Gesetzgebung ideengeschichtlich in starkem Maße vom Utilitarismus nach Jeremy Bentham und vor allem John Stuart Mill in Verbindung mit der Tradition des Liberalismus geprägt. Der nun folgende Abschnitt rekapituliert die klassische Konzeption des Utilitarismus und wendet sich daran anschließend neueren utilitaristischen Konzeptionen zu. Ein besonderer Schwerpunkt der Darstellung liegt dabei auf der Frage, warum das Konzept *dignity* im Kontext der britischen Ideengeschichte nicht konsensual moralbegründend wirken konnte und in-

[317] Vgl. exemplarisch die Diskussion nach dem Votum von Callum McKellar, dem Forschungs-Direktor des *Scottish Council for Human Bioethics*, in dem vom *House of Commons, Science and Technology Committee* hrsg. Text *Government proposals for the regulation of hybrid and chimera embryos*, 2007, Ev 22ff. Der *dignity*-Begriff konnte in diesem Zusammenhang nicht überzeugend wirken.

wiefern der Utilitarismus als einflussreich für die Gesetzgebung hinsichtlich des Umgangs mit menschlichen Embryonen anzusehen ist.

III. 4. 1 Der klassische Utilitarismus: Jeremy Bentham und John Stuart Mill – eine Erinnerung

Jeremy Bentham (1748-1832), ein Freund des Vaters von John Stuart Mill, gilt als der Begründer des klassischen Utilitarismus. Schon vor ihm hatte David Hume (1711-1776) vom „größten Glück" aller gesprochen und die Nützlichkeit (*utility*) in die Ethik eingeführt. Erst von Bentham aber wird das Prinzip der Nützlichkeit (*principle of utility*) als Grundlage von Ethik verstanden. Dabei versteht Bentham unter dem Prinzip der Nützlichkeit dasjenige Prinzip, „which approves or disapproves of every action whatsoever, according to the tendency which it appears to have to augment or diminish the happiness of the party whose interest is in question: or, what is the same thing in other words, to promote or to oppose that happiness."[318] Die Vorzüglichkeit einer Handlung bemisst sich für Bentham an ihrer Nützlichkeit, indem sie Glück vermehrt und Leiden vermindert.

Dasjenige, was getan werden muss und darum ethisch empfehlenswert ist, ist deswegen das, was nützlich ist für die Vermehrung des eigenen und des gemeinschaftlichen Glücks, nicht dasjenige, was *intrinsisch* gut oder richtig ist. Aufgrund dieser Voraussetzungen sind alle anderen Prinzipien, die nicht das Prinzip der Nützlichkeit umfassen und nach dem größtmöglichen Nutzen einer Handlung fragen, für Bentham falsche Prinzipien.[319] Das Prinzip der Nützlichkeit erfordert keine weiteren Prinzipien, die es einschränken, erklären oder präzisieren, sondern ist in sich ausreichend für das Leben der Gesellschaft,[320] so dass sich die staatliche Gesetzgebung aus diesem Grund vor allem darauf konzentrieren muss, für die Mitglieder der Gesellschaft Leiden zu vermeiden und Glück oder Vergnügen zu vermehren.

Der grundlegende Impetus der zuerst von Bentham geprägten utilitaristischen Ethik geht darum von den Handlungs*folgen* aus, die sich mit dem Prinzip des größtmöglichen Nutzens und Glücks für die größtmögliche Anzahl von Menschen zusammenfassen lassen.[321] In der Verfolgung des Glücks

---

[318] Bentham, An Introduction to the Principles of Morals and Legislation, in: J. S. Mill/ J. Bentham, Utilitarianism and other Essays, hrsg. von A. Ryan, Harmondsworth/Middlesex u. a. 1987, 65.

[319] Vgl. auch den Sammelband von O. Höffe (Hrsg.), Einführung in die utilitaristische Ethik. Klassische und zeitgenössische Texte, Tübingen/Basel ³2003.

[320] Diesen Grundgedanken fügt Bentham eine breit ausgearbeitete Kasuistik bei, was genau Schmerz und Vergnügen meine, in welchen Fällen Menschen wie zu bestrafen seien usw.

[321] Die Klassifizierung, nach der die Ethik Kants als deontologisch, der Utilitarismus als teleologisch zu charakterisieren ist, ist grundsätzlich zutreffend. In diesem Zusammen-

gibt es dabei für Bentham keine qualitativen Unterschiede bei Handlungen, die Glück versprechen. Bentham hat dafür den häufig zitierten Satz geprägt: „Push-pin is as good as poetry",[322] wonach intellektuelles Glück nicht höher zu schätzen ist als Glück im Spiel. Diese von Bentham explizit nicht getroffene qualitative Unterscheidung unterschiedlicher Glückszustände ist von John Stuart Mill modifiziert worden.

Der Essay „Utilitarismus" (Utilitarianism, 1863) von J. S. Mill[323] (1806-1873), einer der meistgelesenen philosophischen englischen Texte, stellt einen bedeutenden Beitrag innerhalb der britischen Ideengeschichte dar. Bei der Begründung einer Ethik nach dem Prinzip der Nützlichkeit, in der Mill sich an Bentham anschließt, spielt die Frage nach dem *erstrebenswerten Gut* für Mill die zentrale Rolle einer Begründung von moralischem Handeln. Der von Mill geprägte Utilitarismus kann darum ebenfalls als konsequentialistisch gekennzeichnet werden.

De facto sieht Mill jede Handlung als von einer bestimmten Vorstellung nach ihrem Zweck bestimmt an,[324] den der Handelnde verfolgt. Mill macht zwei unterschiedliche Formen von moralischen Handlungsbegründungen geltend: entweder werden moralische Prinzipien als Sätze *a priori* verstanden, die von den Handelnden entdeckt und begriffen werden müssen, oder es werden moralische Prinzipien wie wahr und falsch oder gut und böse aufgrund von Beobachtung und Erfahrung gewonnen. Beiden Konzeptionen ist gemeinsam, dass sie suggerieren, Moral sei von Prinzipien zu deduzieren und es gebe so etwas wie eine „Wissenschaft der Moral". Dabei vernachlässigen beide Modelle von Moralbegründung nach Ansicht von Mill aber die Beobachtung, dass Handlungen immer auch zur Vermehrung von individuellem und sozialem *Glück* führen sollen. Mill präferiert darum ein Modell, das auf *empirischem* Wege das Gute und Richtige für *konkrete Situationen* findet und

---

hang muss darüber hinaus daran festgehalten werden, dass der mit dem Utilitarismus eng verbundene *Liberalismus* einen starken sozialethischen Impuls hat, der vor allem in seiner Entstehungszeit, dem Beginn der Industrialisierung, für die Freiheitsrechte jedes Bürgers eingetreten ist. Die mit dem Utilitarismus entstehende Wohlfahrtsökonomie hat die Lebensqualität für eine große Anzahl britischer Bürger verbessert.

[322] So in der Darstellung von Mill: „quantity of pleasure being equal, push-pin is as good as poetry" (zitiert bei Höffe, Einführung, S. 22. Bei Bentham selbst heißt es: „Prejudice apart, the game of push-pin is of equal value with the arts and sciences of music and poetry. If the game of push-pin furnishes more pleasure, it is more valuable than either." (Works, hrsg. von J. Bowring, Edinburgh 1843, Bd. II, S. 253f.)

[323] Im Sammelband von Höffe auf den Seiten 84ff., in einer zweisprachigen Ausgabe Utilitarianism, Der Utilitarismus, Ditzingen 2006. Auch in dem oben, Anm. 318 angegebenen Sammelband.

[324] „All action is for the sake of some end, and rules of action, it seems natural to suppose, must take their whole character and colour from the end to which they are subservient." (Mill, Utilitarianism, in: Bentham/Mill, Utilitarianism, 273.)

lehnt einen prinzipienorientierten Zugang mit der Deduktion von Handlungsregeln aus vorgängigen überempirischen Prinzipien ab.[325]

Auf dieser Grundlegung aufbauend, arbeitet Mill wie auch schon Bentham das Handlungsziel des größten Glücks für die größtmögliche Anzahl von Menschen (*greatest happiness of the greatest number*) heraus, modifiziert aber die Theorie, die er von Epikur[326] und Bentham rezipiert, insofern, als er nicht von einer qualitativen Gleichheit aller Glück schaffenden Aktionen ausgeht, sondern intellektuelle Befriedigung als höherwertig ansieht als leibliche.[327]

Der mit dem Prinzip der Nützlichkeit verbundene höchste Endzweck allen Handelns ist für Mill eine Existenz so weit entfernt vom Schmerz wie irgend möglich, ein Leben in Genuss und Erfüllung in größtmöglichem Maße, sowohl hinsichtlich der *Quantität* des Glücks als auch seiner *Qualität*. Mill konzediert, dass es für keinen Menschen ein Leben in kontinuierlichem Glückszustand und kontinuierlicher Erfüllung seiner Bedürfnisse gibt und stellt daher für das Individuum die Forderung auf, sich so zu verhalten, dass für möglichst viele Mitglieder der Gesellschaft das individuelle und das gesellschaftliche Glück erhöht wird.[328] In diesem Sinne versteht Mill auch die klassischen Tugenden nicht als einen Zweck an sich, sondern als ein Mittel, das einem Menschen dazu verhilft, sein Glück zu finden.

Dabei geht der von Mill geprägte Utilitarismus mit einem sozialethischen Liberalismus einher,[329] nach dem das Prinzip der individuellen *Freiheit* handlungsleitend innerhalb von Gesellschaft und Politik ist. Zum Menschsein gehört konstitutiv die Freiheit in der Gestaltung der eigenen Möglichkeiten und das Recht auf eine freiheitlich selbst gewählte Lebensführung. Diese Freiheit ist durch die Grenze der Freiheit anderer begrenzt, kann aber auch durch ihre Selbstentäußerung nicht aufgehoben werden. Wie Kant operiert Mill explizit mit dem Freiheitsbegriff, versteht ihn aber nicht als eine transzendentale

[325] Dabei entwickelt und begründet Mill lediglich das Prinzip, dass der Mensch ein nach Glück strebendes Wesen ist und dass darum das größte Bestreben einer Gemeinschaft dahin gehen muss, das Glück des Einzelnen zu befördern. Vgl. Mill im Sammelband von Höffe, S. 97.

[326] Der griechische Philosoph Epikur (341-270 v.Chr.) gilt als der Begründer des Hedonismus, weil er als ethisches Prinzip ansieht, diejenige Handlung zu vermehren, die dem Handelnden Lust (*hedone*) bringt. Im Gegensatz zu einem gegenwärtigen Lustgewinn-Hedonismus kann für Epikur aber auch die geistige Lust unter den Lustbegriff subsumiert werden.

[327] Vgl. das berühmte Zitat: „It is better to be a human dissatisfied than a pig satisfied; better to be Socrates dissatisfied than a fool satisfied. And if the fool, or the pig, is of a different opinion, it is because they only know their own side of the question. The other party to the comparison knows both sides." (Mill, Utilitarianism, 281.)

[328] Mill, a.a.O., 307: „The utilitarian doctrine is that happiness is desirable, and the only thing desirable, as an end; all other things being only desirable as means to that end."

[329] Vgl. Mills Essay *On Liberty* (1859).

Entität, sondern sieht Freiheit verwirklicht in der freien Lebensführung des Individuums innerhalb der Gesellschaft, mit der dieses dazu befähigt ist, an der Verwirklichung seines eigenen und des gesellschaftlichen Nutzens und Glücks zu arbeiten.[330]

Mit dem Ziel des größtmöglichen Glücks einer größtmöglichen Anzahl von Menschen ist eine häufig angemerkte Schwierigkeit des Utilitarismus verbunden: Mit dem Prinzip der Nützlichkeit[331] kann der Gedanke der *Gerechtigkeit* kollidieren.[332] Während deontologische Konzeptionen davon ausgehen, dass Gerechtigkeit als ein absolutes handlungsleitendes Prinzip besteht, ist für Mill der Sinn von Gerechtigkeit ein Gefühl, das von der persönlichen Prägung und den Interessen des Individuums abhängt, auch wenn jeder Mensch von der objektiven Gültigkeit seines eigenen Gerechtigkeitsempfindens überzeugt ist. Gerechtigkeit ist kein höchstes Gut, das absolut zu erstreben ist, sondern ein Nebenprodukt des wichtigeren handlungsleitenden Prinzips der Nützlichkeit. In diesem Verständnis der Gerechtigkeit wird deutlich, dass es für den Utilitarismus keine absolute Pflicht gibt. Pflichten (oder Tugenden) werden vielmehr deswegen als verpflichtend angesehen, weil sie dem persönlichen oder allgemeinen Nutzen dienen, Glück vermehren und Schmerz vermeiden.[333]

Die von Mill im Anschluss an Bentham ausgearbeitete Theorie des Utilitarismus ist eine vor allem in Großbritannien immer noch einflussreiche pragmatische Gesellschaftstheorie, nach der das Wohlergehen aller konzeptionell entscheidend ist.[334] Insofern das Wohlergehen aller dabei gegen das Wohlerge-

---

[330] In der weiteren Entwicklung des Utilitarismus ist zwischen zwei Formen der Glücksvermehrung unterschieden worden: Zum einen kann die Priorität bei der insgesamt gegebenen *Summe* des Glücks innerhalb einer Gemeinschaft gelegt werden, so dass es nichts ausmacht, ob einige viel und andere weniger Glück haben. Zum anderen kann das *durchschnittliche* Glück als entscheidend angesehen werden, so dass es wichtiger ist, dass alle Mitglieder einer Gemeinschaft durchschnittlich über möglichst viel Glück verfügen, als dass einige Mitglieder besonders glücklich sind.

[331] Das Prinzip der Nützlichkeit bildet das oberste Prinzip, in dem weitere Teilkriterien zusammenfinden: das Folgen- (Konsequenzen-), das Nutzen- (Utilitäts-), sowie das hedonistische und das universalistische Prinzip. Vgl. Höffe, Einführung, 11.

[332] Diese Kritik am Utilitarismus ist vor allem von John Rawls geübt worden: Rawls, Eine Theorie der Gerechtigkeit, Frankfurt/Main [15]2006.

[333] Mill, Utilitarianism, 336: „But this great moral duty rests upon a still deeper foundation, being a direct emanation from the first principle of morals, and not a mere logical corollary from secondary or derivative doctrines. It is involved in the very meaning of Utility, or the Greatest Happiness Principle. That principle is a mere form of words without rational signification, unless one person's happiness, supposed equal in degree... is counted for exactly as much as another's."

[334] So auch der utilitaristische kategorische Imperativ: „Handle so, daß die Folgen deiner Handlung bzw. Handlungsregel für das Wohlergehen aller Betroffenen optimal sind." (Höffe, Einführung, 11.)

hen Einzelner stehen kann und keine absoluten Vorgaben dafür gegeben werden, was grundsätzlich ethisch akzeptabel ist, können etwa Todesstrafe oder Folter nicht *per se* als moralisch verwerflich verstanden werden, wenn damit dem Wohlergehen einer möglichst großen Anzahl gedient werden kann.[335]

Die Forschung an menschlichen Embryonen zur Erzeugung von embryonalen Stammzellen kann mit dem Instrumentarium des Utilitarismus deutlich einfacher ethisch legitimiert werden als mit einem deontologischen Konzept. Denn schon die Hoffnung auf die Entwicklung von Therapien gegen degenerative Erkrankungen rechtfertigt die Forschung, weil mit ihr dem Nutzen und dem Glück vieler potentiell gedient wird. Kann darüber hinaus davon ausgegangen werden, dass eine Forschung an Embryonen für diese nicht zu einem *schmerzvollen* Tod führt, weil die entsprechenden neuronalen Voraussetzungen bei frühen Embryonen noch nicht vorliegen, so gibt es im Rahmen des klassischen Utilitarismus, soweit ich sehe, kein Argument, das grundsätzlich gegen eine Forschung an Embryonen spricht, im Verlaufe derer diese vernichtet werden und die ihnen nicht selbst zugute kommt.

Die Stärke des Utilitarismus liegt darin, dass er flexibel auf Anforderungen der jeweiligen Situation und der gesellschaftlichen und politischen Debatten reagieren kann und keine moralischen Normen im Sinne von zeitlosen Prinzipien bei der Urteilsfindung zu berücksichtigen hat. Eine schnelle und flexible Entscheidung in ethisch komplizierten Fragen ist deswegen leichter möglich als bei deontologisch orientierten Konzeptionen.

Die Frage nach dem den Utilitarismus prägenden Menschenbild im Zusammenhang mit der Frage nach dem Spezifikum des Menschen und seiner Würde resp. *dignity* erlangt in besonderer Weise Bedeutung im Hinblick auf die Forschung an menschlichen Embryonen. Auch wenn Mill bei der Begründung des Utilitarismus keine *explizite* Anthropologie ausarbeitet, wird der Mensch als grundsätzlich bestimmt von seinem Streben nach Glück und der Suche, Leid und Schmerz zu vermeiden, beschrieben. Darüber hinaus bildet dasjenige, was den Menschen auszeichnet, für Mill offenbar die Freiheit, die sich in der Freiheit zur individuellen Lebensführung oder der Freiheit zur eigenen Glücksmaximierung manifestiert.

Dabei macht Mill aber seine anthropologischen Grundannahmen, anders als Vertreter eines gegenwärtigen Utilitarismus, insofern nicht normativ explizit, als er daraus Richtlinien für den Umgang mit menschlichen Wesen ableitete und etwa eine Gruppe von menschlichen Wesen aufgrund bestimm-

[335] Dabei ist das Beispiel der *Todesstrafe* insofern noch nicht ausreichend, als auch Kant um des Sühneaspekts willen die Todesstrafe für moralisch akzeptabel gehalten hat. Als problematisch und als Verstoß gegen die Menschenwürde werden von Kant allererst Handlungen verstanden, die gegen die Selbstzwecklichkeit des Menschen verstoßen. Zum ethischen Problem der *Folterandrohung* bei unterschiedlichen ethischen Konzeptionen vgl. W. Härle, Kann die Anwendung von Folter in Extremsituationen aus der Sicht christlicher Ethik gerechtfertigt werden?, ZEE 49, 2005, 198-212.

ter Kriterien als „Personen" verstünde, die einen anderen moralischen Status innehätten als die Gruppe von menschlichen Wesen, die nicht als Personen zu kennzeichnen wären. Der klassische Utilitarismus vertritt keine universale normative anthropologische Grundkonzeption, die für alle Mitglieder einer Gesellschaft moralbegründend sein könnte.

Auch die Frage, ob es ein *Recht auf Glück* oder *Gesundheit* gibt, die zumindest implizit in der ethischen Debatte um die Forschung an Embryonen gegenwärtig eine wichtige Rolle spielt, bleibt im 18. Jahrhundert offen. Neuere utilitaristische Konzeptionen können dagegen argumentieren, dass es ethisch geboten sei, das technisch Mögliche zur Vermeidung und Linderung von Leid auch zu tun, dass also eine moralische *Pflicht* dazu bestehe, alle Möglichkeiten zum Gemeinwohl und der individuellen Gesundheit auszuschöpfen.[336]

Eine solche Position soll im folgenden Abschnitt mit der Konzeption des englischen Juristen und Ethikers John Harris dargestellt werden. Daran anschließend wende ich mich der in Deutschland bereits breiter bekannten und teilweise rezipierten Konzeption von Peter Singer unter der speziellen Fragestellung zu, welche Anthropologie ihr implizit ist, um daran anschließend die vor allem vom englischen Liberalismus und Utilitarismus geprägte Unterscheidung von menschlichem und personalem Leben zu entfalten.

III. 4. 2 Enhancement und das Bild vom Menschen. Neuere Formen utilitaristischer Konzeptionen bei John Harris und Peter Singer

In der gegenwärtigen englischsprachigen Bioethikdebatte spielt der Utilitarismus eine prägende Rolle, wobei die utilitaristischen Prinzipien aufgenommen und insofern teilweise modifiziert werden, als sie mit einer expliziten Anthropologie verbunden werden. Einer der in der britischen Öffentlichkeit einflussreichsten Vertreter einer neueren utilitaristischen Konzeption ist der englische Ethiker und Jurist John Harris.[337] In zahlreichen Veröffentlichungen hat Harris – den Grundsätzen des klassischen Utilitarismus folgend – die Position vertreten, dass *Enhancement* (Steigerung) der menschlichen Konsti-

[336] Eine ähnliche Argumentation war strukturell schon bei der Auffassung begegnet, eine Forschung an menschlichen Embryonen verstoße nicht gegen die Menschenwürde, weil sie dazu beitrage, dass Therapien für bisher unheilbar erkrankte Menschen gefunden werden könnten. Wenn eine solche Forschung nicht unternommen werde, sei in diesem *Unterlassen* vielmehr ein Verstoß gegen die Achtung der Menschenwürde zu sehen. Vgl. oben, S. 60f., Anm. 120.

[337] Harris bekleidet gegenwärtig einen Lehrstuhl für Bioethik an der Universität Manchester und ist als Berater in zahlreichen bioethischen Kommissionen in Großbritannien tätig. Bekannte Veröffentlichungen sind etwa die Monographien Enhancing Evolution. The Ethical Case for Making Better People, 2007; On Cloning, 2004; The Value of Life: An Introduction to medical Ethics, 1985; Wonderwoman and Superman: The Ethics of Human Biotechnology, 1992. Erwähnenswert ist auch das von ihm herausgegebene Kompendium Bioethics, Oxford 2001.

tution sowohl beim Individuum als Gentherapie, als auch für zukünftige Generationen als Keimbahntherapie moralisch geboten sei, wenn es technisch möglich sei, und dass es eine moralische *Pflicht* darstelle, die Möglichkeiten der Embryonenforschung, die sich seit den späten 90er Jahren aufgetan haben, auch zur Therapie von Krankheiten zu nutzen, wenn diese zahlreichen an degenerativen Erkrankungen leidenden Menschen zugute komme. Der grundsätzliche utilitaristische Impetus der Glücksmaximierung und der Leidvermeidung wird von Harris damit auf die gegenwärtige biomedizinische Forschung übertragen.

Dabei dient Harris der Terminus *Enhancement* als Schlüssel für seine ethische Konzeption. Die von Kritikern gezogene Grenze zwischen – ethisch erlaubter – *Therapie* zur Heilung und Linderung von Krankheitszuständen und – ethisch verwerflichem, weil in die menschliche Natur etwa auf dem Wege der Gentherapie eingreifenden – *Enhancement* zur Steigerung und Verbesserung der menschlichen Konstitution bei der Vermeidung von Krankheiten und der Linderung ihres Verlaufs lehnt Harris mit der Begründung ab, dass alles, was bei Menschen Leid vermindert oder vermeidet und Glück steigert, ethisch legitim und sogar ethisch geboten sei.[338] *Enhancement* meint nach Meinung von Harris eine *Verbesserung* eines vorherigen „natürlichen" Zustandes mit dem Ziel, Wohlergehen zu steigern. Darum seien auch Impfungen als *Enhancement* anzusehen, weil sie die menschliche Konstitution so verändern, dass bestimmte Krankheiten nicht mehr auftreten können.[339]

Weil die oberste Priorität im Zusammenhang mit Medizin und Therapie die Gewährleistung desjenigen ist, was für möglichst viele Menschen Schaden vermeidet und Nutzen schafft,[340] ist *Enhancement* für Harris ethisch verpflichtend. Weil es Leben rettet und Leiden mindert, zählt *Enhancement* darum zu den durch die Medizin erstrebenswerten Gütern.[341] Die einzige Frage, die sich in diesem Zusammenhang stellt, ist darum diejenige, ob das *Risiko* einer Therapie den zu erwartenden Nutzen aufwiegt.[342] Die ethisch gebotene

---

[338] „Most of what passes for therapy is an enhancement for the individual relative to her state prior to the therapy." (Harris, Enhancing, 44.)

[339] Andere, für Harris ebenfalls legitime Beispiele für *Enhancements* sind Hormone und Steroide im Zusammenhang mit Leistungssport.

[340] Enhancing, 58: „The overwhelming moral imperative for both therapy and enhancement is to prevent harm and confer benefit."

[341] Enhancing Evolution, 54: „Saving lives or – what is the same thing – postponing death, removing or preventing disability or disease, or enhancing human functionings are examples of these goods."

[342] Dieses Argument ist bei der Debatte um die Forschung an embryonalen Stammzellen insofern wichtig, als eine Therapie mit menschlichen embryonalen Stammzellen derzeit noch zu riskant ist, weil zum einen Abstoßungsreaktionen beobachtet werden und die Zellen zum anderen aufgrund ihrer Plastizität canzerogen wirken können.

Folgerung aus dieser Frage ist der Versuch einer Verringerung des Risikos, um nicht zu unnötigem Leid beizutragen, nicht aber ein Einstellen der entsprechenden Forschung aus ethischen Gesichtspunkten, weil etwa universale Prinzipien damit verletzt würden.

Mit der Priorität der Glücksvermehrung und der Leidvermeidung vertritt Harris eine utilitaristische Position in Verbindung mit einem ausgeprägten Forschungsoptimismus. Dabei postuliert er eine moralische *Pflicht*, Therapien für degenerative Erkrankungen zu entwickeln.[343] Implizit nimmt diese Konzeption aber auch alle geborenen Menschen in die Pflicht, *Enhancement* an sich selbst geschehen zu lassen, für sich selbst zu suchen und andere bei ihrer Suche nach *Enhancement* zu unterstützen.

Bei der Frage nach den Anthropologumena der Konzeption von Harris ist zu konstatieren, dass Harris sich strukturell eng an den klassischen Utilitarismus nach Bentham/Mill anlehnt. Das von diesen konstitutiv gesetzte menschliche Streben nach Glück wird von ihm im Zusammenhang der Medizin- und Bioethik, in dem sich seine Beiträge vor allem bewegen, als ein Streben nach Gesundheit, Heilung und *Enhancement* verstanden, das ethisch nicht nur akzeptabel, sondern vorzugswürdig und in dieser Hinsicht sogar verpflichtend sei. Gegenüber einer von deontologischen Positionen vertretenen intrinsischen Schutzwürdigkeit von Menschen vertritt er eine grundsätzliche Verbesserungswürdigkeit und Verbesserungsnotwendigkeit menschlicher Konstitution auf dem Wege der Steigerung. Personalität und Lebensrecht sind für Harris nicht an sich gegeben, sondern werden aufgrund empirischer Beobachtung zugeschrieben. Dabei gibt es einen Ausgleich von konkurrierenden Glücksbestrebungen nur unter denjenigen, die (als Personen) aktiv an der Steigerung ihrer Konstitution mitwirken können.

Ein Abwägen von unterschiedlichen Glücksbestrebungen schließt nur *personales* Leben ein. Um *Enhancement* zu erwirken, dürfen darum für Harris auch Mittel gebraucht werden, die die Vernichtung menschlichen nichtpersonalen Lebens einschließen, solange dies nicht mit einer Zufügung von Schmerz verbunden ist. Denn bis zu dem Zeitpunkt, an dem sich Personalität einstellt, hat menschliches Leben einen anderen moralischen Status als per-

[343] Vgl. auch Harris, The Ethical Use of Human Embryonic Stem Cells in Research and Therapy, in: J. Burley/J. Harris (Hrsg.), A Companion to Genethics, Oxford 2002, 158-174. Darin argumentiert Harris vor allem damit, dass zahlreiche Embryonen ohnehin aufgrund von Spontanaborten in den ersten Wochen zerstört werden und dass eine Ablehnung von embryonaler Stammzellforschung mit dieser Tatsache inkonsistent sei. Darüber hinaus seien die Embryonen nicht einfach zu verwerfen, wenn sie einem anderen Zweck dienen könnten: „Surely no one could believe that it could be better (more ethical) to allow the fetal material to go to waste than to use it for some good purpose?" (A.a.O., 169.)

sonales Leben.[344] Die noch näher zu untersuchende Frage, wie Personalität in der Abgrenzung zu Nicht-Personalität verstanden wird, die im klassischen Utilitarismus noch keine ethisch relevante Rolle spielt, deutet sich an dieser Stelle an. Anders als der Warnock-Report und die britische Gesetzgebung vertritt Harris damit keine gradualistische Position.

Die von dem australischen Ethiker *Peter Singer*[345] vertrete Form des Utilitarismus[346] orientiert sich weniger ausdrücklich an den Maximen der Schadensvermeidung und der Glücksmaximierung, als vielmehr an den Präferenzen (Interessen), die ein Individuum oder eine Gruppe vertreten. Der grundsätzliche Imperativ in dieser Konzeption sieht vor, dass jedes Individuum das Recht haben soll, seine eigenen Präferenzen zu verfolgen und in der Verfolgung der jeweils eigenen Interessen glücklich zu werden, wobei die Erfüllung von personalen Präferenzen ein Mittel zum Zweck der individuellen und gesellschaftlichen Glücksmaximierung bildet.

Ethik richtet sich dabei auch bei Singer an den Handlungs*folgen*, nicht an den Handlungs*motiven* aus, so dass seine Konzeption dem Konsequenz-Prinzip folgt.[347] Singer nimmt für sich in Anspruch, eine ethische Konzeption zu vertreten, die der Realität gerecht wird und mit der es möglich ist, das

---

[344] In seinem Buch The Value of Life, London 1985, S. 18f., macht Harris die Unterscheidung von Menschen und Personen explizit: „On this concept of the person, the moral difference between persons and non-persons lies in the value that people give to their own lives. The reason it is wrong to kill a person is that to do so robs that individual of something they value, and of the very thing that makes possible valuing anything at all. To kill a person not only frustrates their wishes for their own futures, but frustrates every wish a person has. Creatures that cannot value their own existence cannot be wronged in that way, for their death deprives them of nothing they can value." Wird der Wert einer Person damit an die Wertschätzung gebunden, die diese ihrem eigenen Dasein gegenüber empfindet und vertritt, so ist damit die Befürwortung der aktiven Sterbehilfe ebenso kohärent wie der Schwangerschaftsabbruch, die Forschung an menschlichen Embryonen und die Tötung Bewusstloser, Komatöser und Dementer. Wichtig in diesem Zusammenhang ist, dass eine solche Tötung keine unnötigen Schmerzen verursacht. „Of course non-persons can be harmed in other ways, by being subjected to pain for example, and there are good reasons for avoiding any sentient creatures to pain if this can be avoided." (Harris, a.a.O., 19.)

[345] Singer bekleidet seit 1999 eine Position an der Universität in Princeton am Center for Human Values, nachdem er zuvor in Oxford, New York und Melbourne gelehrt hatte.

[346] In der deutschen Diskussion vertritt eine ähnliche Position wie Singer etwa Norbert Hoerster, vgl. Hoerster, Ethik und Interesse, 2003; Ethik des Embryonenschutzes. Ein rechtsphilosophischer Essay, 2002.

[347] Auch die anderen oben in Anm. 331 genannten Prinzipien des Utilitarismus (Utilität, Hedonismus und Universalität) finden sich in Singers Konzeption wieder, wobei ein besonderer Schwerpunkt auf der Verfolgung von *Präferenzen* liegt, weswegen Singer seine ethische Position als „Präferenz-Utilitarismus" bezeichnet.

praktische Handeln an den Erfordernissen der jeweils konkreten Situation auszurichten und zu bewerten.[348] Eine solche von ihm selbst als vernünftig[349] verstandene Ethik der Folgenorientierung wird in einer Zeit vertreten, in der seiner Ansicht nach traditionelle Ethik-Konzeptionen gescheitert sind,[350] was etwa an der Diskussion über aktive Sterbehilfe und Schwangerschaftsabbruch zu erkennen sei.

An diesem Punkt des Scheiterns traditioneller Ethik-Entwürfe sei eine universale Ethik notwendig, die nicht nur jedem Individuum die Verfolgung seiner eigenen Interessen gestatte, um glücklich zu werden. Vielmehr müsse im gesellschaftlichen Ganzen nach der *Universalisierbarkeit* von Interessen gefragt werden.[351] Diese Einsicht in die Notwendigkeit einer grundlegenden Universalisierbarkeit von utilitaristisch beeinflusster Interesseverfolgung impliziert bei Singer eine anthropologische Orientierung, insofern der Adressat ethischen Handelns ebenso wie ethischer Reflexion nicht *jeder* Mensch ist, sondern derjenige Mensch, der Interessen verfolgen und artikulieren kann. Diejenigen Menschen, die ein Bewusstsein ihrer eigenen Interessen haben

---

[348] Singer, Praktische Ethik, 17f.: „Die Konsequenzen einer Handlung variieren, je nach den Umständen, unter denen sie vollzogen wird. Daher kann ein Utilitarist eigentlich nie eines Mangels an Realitätssinn oder einer rigiden Befolgung von Idealen unter Mißachtung praktischer Erfahrung bezichtigt werden. Ein Utilitarist wird Lügen unter gewissen Umständen als gut, unter anderen als schlecht beurteilen, je nach den Folgen." Eine entschiedene Ablehnung der Lüge (auch für „gute Zwecke") vertritt demgegenüber Kant, da diese die eigene Menschenwürde und die anderer antaste. In der Grundlegung zur Metaphysik der Sitten: „*Zweitens*, was die notwendige oder schuldige Pflicht gegen andere betrifft, so wird der, so ein lügenhaftes Versprechen gegen andere zu tun im Sinne hat, sofort einsehen, daß er sich eines anderen Menschen *bloß als Mittels* bedienen will, ohne daß dieser zugleich den Zweck in sich enthalte." (In der von Horn hrsg. Ausgabe auf S. 63.) Ausführlich auch in der kurzen Schrift „Über ein vermeintliches Recht aus Menschenliebe zu lügen", die Kant 1797 im Alter von 73 Jahren veröffentlicht hat.

[349] Singer, Praktische Ethik, 24: „Das Folgende ist die Skizze einer Auffassung von Ethik, die der Vernunft eine wichtige Rolle in moralischen Entscheidungen zugesteht. Es ist nicht die einzig mögliche Auffassung von Ethik, aber es ist eine, die plausibel ist."

[350] Singer, Rethinking Life and Death. The Collapse of Our Traditional Ethics, Oxford 1995, 1: „After ruling our thoughts and our decisions about life and death for nearly two thousand years, the traditional western ethic has collapsed."

[351] Mit dem Anspruch der Universalisierbarkeit von Interessen vertritt Singer eine utilitaristische Position „im weiteren Sinne". (Praktische Ethik, 29.) Etwas später heißt es: „Indem ich akzeptiere, daß moralische Urteile von einem universalen Standpunkt aus getroffen werden müssen, akzeptiere ich, daß meine eigenen Interessen nicht einfach deshalb, weil sie meine Interessen sind, mehr zählen als die Interessen von jemand anderem. Daher muß, wenn ich moralisch denke, mein ganz natürliches Bestreben, daß für meine Interessen gesorgt wird, ausgedehnt werden auf die Interessen anderer." (Ebd.)

können, haben darum einen anderen moralischen Status als Menschen, die ein solches Bewusstsein nicht haben.

Der Definition von John Locke folgend,[352] unterscheidet Singer ähnlich wie Harris in diesem Zusammenhang zwischen Menschen und Personen: während erstere alle Angehörigen der Spezies *homo sapiens sapiens* sind, folgt aus der bloßen Spezieszugehörigkeit Singer zufolge noch kein moralischer Imperativ. Ein Mensch ist aufgrund seiner *Spezieszugehörigkeit* nicht mehr zu schützen als ein Tier; beiden ist, weil sie mit Empfindungsfähigkeit ausgestattet sind, nicht willentlich Schmerz zuzufügen. Allein aufgrund seines Menschseins aber steht ein Mensch hinsichtlich seines moralischen Status nicht über dem Tier.

Ein ethischer Imperativ folgt dagegen aus dem *Personstatus* eines Menschen, aufgrund dessen dieser sich selbst als zeitliches Wesen mit Interessen in einem Kontinuum von Vergangenheit und Zukunft verstehen kann. Die Interessenverfolgung von Personen muss nach Annahme Singers insofern universalisiert werden, als es moralisch denkenden und handelnden Menschen nicht nur darum gehen kann, eigene Interessen zu verfolgen, sondern auch die Interessen anderer rationaler und selbstbewusster Menschen zu achten: Wer selbst Interessen habe, werde daran interessiert sein, die Interessen von anderen zu schützen, um auch den Schutz für seine eigenen Interessen zu gewährleisten.[353] Singer hält es in diesem Zusammenhang für möglich, Präferenzen miteinander abzuwägen und so zu einem ähnlichen Nutzenkalkül zu gelangen wie der klassische Utilitarismus, wobei aber nicht nur die Handlungs*folgen*, sondern auch die eine Handlung motivierenden und die von einer Handlung betroffenen *Interessen* miteinander abgewogen werden müssen. Andere *Personen* zu töten, wird darum von Singer als in der Regel falsch beurteilt, „weil Personen in ihren Präferenzen sehr zukunftsorientiert sind. Eine Person zu töten bedeutet darum normalerweise nicht nur eine, sondern eine Vielzahl der zentralsten und bedeutendsten Präferenzen, die ein Wesen haben kann, zu verletzen.“[354]

In der Frage des Schwangerschaftsabbruchs argumentiert Singer nach der Unterscheidung von Menschen und Personen[355] folgerichtig nicht mit *Po-*

---

[352] Eine Person wird von Locke definiert als ein „denkendes und intelligentes Wesen, das Vernunft und Reflexion besitzt und sich als sich selbst denken kann, als dasselbe denkende Etwas in verschiedenen Zeiten und an verschiedenen Orten.“ (Singer, Praktische Ethik, 120.)

[353] Praktische Ethik, 128: „Nach dem Präferenz-Utilitarismus ist eine Handlung, die der Präferenz irgendeines Wesens entgegensteht, ohne daß diese Präferenz durch entgegengesetzte Präferenzen ausgeglichen wird, moralisch falsch.“

[354] Praktische Ethik, 129.

[355] Als Personen können darum auch hoch entwickelte Säugetiere angesehen werden. Vgl. Singer, a.a.O., 147ff. „Einige nichtmenschliche Tiere sind... nach unserer Definition

tentialität oder einem *intrinsischen Wert*, die einem Embryo zugestanden werden müssten, weil er sich zu einem rationalen Lebewesen entwickelt, sondern ausschließlich mit dem Blick auf Interessen: hat eine Person an dem Leben eines Embryos ein Interesse, so ist eine Schwangerschaft aufrecht zu erhalten; eine Schutzwürdigkeit kann für Embryonen selbst, weil sie sich nicht als zeitliche Wesen mit Interessen begreifen können und darum keine Personen sind, nicht angenommen werden.[356]

Singer hält darum auch die Forschung an menschlichen Embryonen für moralisch legitim, solange an der sich entwickelnden befruchteten menschlichen Eizelle keine Eigenschaften ausgemacht werden könnten, die anzeigen, dass diese sich als Mensch entwickele, solange Plazenta- und embryonales Gewebe nicht wirklich voneinander unterschieden werden könnten und die Möglichkeit der Mehrlingsbildung nicht ausgeschlossen sei. Vielmehr habe der Embryo, weil er keine Person, sondern allenfalls ein empfindungsfähiges Lebewesen sei, nicht die Rechte einer Person, sondern lediglich das Recht, im Zweifelsfall so schmerzfrei wie möglich getötet zu werden.[357]

Personen.“ (A.a.O., 155.) Etwas später heißt es: „Bei den großen Menschenaffen – Schimpansen, Gorillas und Orang-Utans – ist es wohl am deutlichsten, daß sie nichtmenschliche Personen sind, aber es gibt sicher auch andere. Systematische Beobachtungen von Walen und Delphinen stecken demgegenüber aus offensichtlichen Gründen noch in den Anfängen, aber es ist gut möglich, daß sich diese Säugetiere mit ihren großen Gehirnen als vernunftbegabt und selbstbewußt herausstellen.“ (A.a.O., 157.)

[356] Singer argumentiert in diesem Zusammenhang: „Abtreibung und Experimente, die zur Vernichtung von Embryonen führen, werfen schwierige ethische Fragen auf; denn die Entwicklung eines menschlichen Wesens ist ein stufenweiser Prozeß. Wenn wir das befruchtete Ei unmittelbar nach der Empfängnis entfernen, ist es schwer, sich über seinen Tod zu beunruhigen. Das befruchtete Ei ist eine einzelne Zelle. Nach einigen Tagen ist es immer noch lediglich ein kleiner Zellklumpen, ohne daß auch nur ein einziges anatomisches Detail des späteren Wesens erkennbar würde.“ (Praktische Ethik, 179.)

[357] Praktische Ethik, 213f.: „Im Zweifelsfall wäre es vernünftig, den frühestmöglichen Zeitpunkt der Empfindungsfähigkeit als die Grenze anzusetzen, jenseits derer der Fötus Schutz genießen sollte. Deshalb sollten wir das unsichere Anzeichen des Wachseins außer acht lassen und als definitivere zeitliche Trennlinie die physische Fähigkeit des Gehirns wählen, die für das Bewußtsein notwendigen Signale zu empfangen: also etwa ab der 18. Schwangerschaftswoche. Vor dieser Zeit gibt es kaum einen vernünftigen Grund für die Annahme, daß ein Fötus vor schädigenden Eingriffen der Forschung zu schützen sei; denn dem Fötus kann kein Schaden zugefügt werden.“ Norbert Hoerster geht in seiner Einschätzung zum Embryonenschutz noch weiter, indem er diesen als frühestens mit der Geburt beginnend versteht. Vgl. etwa Hoerster, Ethik des Embryonenschutzes. Ein rechtsphilosophischer Essay, Stuttgart 2002, 92: „Die Grenze der Geburt ist nicht nur für jedermann auf den ersten Blick ungleich leichter feststellbar als jede andere zur Sicherung des Überlebensinteresses überhaupt in Frage kommende Grenze. Sie hat vor allem auch den folgenden ganz entscheidenden Vorzug im Hinblick auf das aus dem Lebensrecht ableitbare strikte Verbot des Tötens: Sie verbietet weder zu viel noch zu wenig.“ Hoerster vertritt im Gegensatz zu Singer den grundlegenden Be-

Die Frage, ob aus der Zugehörigkeit eines Menschen zur Spezies *homo sapiens sapiens* ein moralischer Anspruch, eine Schutzwürdigkeit und bestimmte Rechte folgen, wird von Singer darum verneint, indem er eine solche Haltung, die die Zugehörigkeit des Menschen zur Spezies als statusbegründend ansieht, als Speziesismus bezeichnet und strukturell mit Rassismus vergleicht.[358] Der moralische Status eines Wesens wird von Singer nicht mit seiner Spezieszugehörigkeit oder der Potentialität seiner Rationalität begründet, sondern mit der Zielgerichtetheit seiner Interessen.

Vor allem die aufgrund empirischer Kriteriologie erfolgende Unterscheidung zwischen Menschen und Personen bzw. Nicht-Personen und Personen zieht in den Ansatz von Singer und Harris eine explizite Anthropologie ein, die für die Frage nach der verbrauchenden Forschung an Embryonen insofern folgenreich ist, als Embryonen aufgrund ihrer fehlenden Orientierung in einem zeitlichen Kontinuum und aufgrund ihrer nicht vorhandenen Verfolgung und Artikulation von Interessen nicht als Personen gelten können, so dass über ihren Status die Interessen derjenigen entscheiden, die mit ihnen – als Eltern, als Forscher oder als Patienten – umgehen.

Diese Unterscheidung von Menschen und Personen steht in einer breiten Tradition der britischen Ideengeschichte seit John Locke und fügt dem Konzept des Utilitarismus einen normativen Aspekt hinzu, den dieser nicht von sich aus gehabt hat. Dabei ist die Unterscheidung nicht auf den Präferenzutilitarismus beschränkt. Sie wird allerdings in der britischen Gesetzgebung und im Warnock-Report ausdrücklich nicht verfolgt, wenn dem menschlichen Embryo dort „some protection in law" zugebilligt wird. Singer und Harris vertreten keine gradualistisch-pragmatische, sondern vielmehr eine Position, die ich als „Alles-oder-Nichts-Position" gekennzeichnet habe.[359] Weil die Frage nach der Personalität in der Debatte so zentral ist, soll sie im folgenden Abschnitt noch einmal gesondert Beachtung finden.

III. 4. 3 Sind Embryonen Personen? Personalität und Menschenwürde

Die Frage danach, welchen *moralischen Status* Embryonen haben, hat sich sowohl in Deutschland – hier unter anderem als Frage nach der Menschen-

griff des „Überlebensinteresses", nicht die Relevanz von weiter gefassten Präferenzen. Darüber hinaus spielt der als vage empfundene Personbegriff für Hoerster keine Rolle (vgl. etwa Hoerster, a.a.O., 108).

[358] Die Einführung des Speziesmus-Arguments hat bei Singer zunächst eine positive Form: „Ich schlage... vor, daß wir, wenn wir das Prinzip der Gleichheit als eine vernünftige moralische Basis für unsere Beziehungen zu den Mitgliedern unserer Gattung akzeptiert haben, auch verpflichtet sind, es als eine vernünftige moralische Basis für unsere Beziehungen zu denen außerhalb unserer Gattung anzuerkennen – den nichtmenschlichen Lebewesen." (Praktische Ethik, 82.)

[359] S. oben, S. 66, 105.

würde –, als auch in England – unter anderem als Frage nach dem Wert (*value* oder *worth*) oder der Würde (*dignity*) menschlichen Lebens und seiner Personalität – als entscheidende Frage in der ethischen Debatte zur Embryonenforschung entwickelt. Die Debatte um den moralischen Status des Embryos lässt sich auch als Debatte um die moralrelevanten Wesensmerkmale des Embryos und die aus diesen Wesensmerkmalen folgende Annahme seiner Schutzwürdigkeit, also den aus den Wesensmerkmalen folgenden ethisch normativen Kriterien verstehen. An der Diskussion über den moralischen Status von Embryonen zeigt sich zugleich, dass *jede* Stellungnahme hinsichtlich des Umgangs mit menschlichem Leben eine anthropologische Aussage macht, auch wenn diese nicht immer explizit gemacht wird.[360]

Die Notwendigkeit einer anthropologischen Explizierung des grundlegenden Status des Embryos spielt in der Frage nach einer inhaltlichen Bestimmung der häufig gebrauchten Formel des *Respekts vor dem Wesen des Embryos* eine Rolle.[361] Das Verständnis des Respekts vor dem besonderen Status des Embryos und seine Folgerungen daraus haben entscheidend damit zu tun, als was der Embryo verstanden und angesehen wird. Warum Respekt vor menschlichen Wesen überhaupt angemessen ist, wird in der gegenwärtigen Bioethik vor allem mit zwei Denkfiguren beantwortet, die miteinander verbunden sein, aber auch unabhängig voneinander stehen können und ihrerseits eine Fülle von inhaltlichen Bestimmungen und Interpretationen auf sich vereinen:

- Schutzwürdigkeit und Respekt kommt menschlichen Wesen zu, weil sie *Menschenwürde* haben,[362]

---

[360] So auch P. Gelhaus, Gentherapie und Weltanschauung. Ein Überblick über die genethische Diskussion, Darmstadt 2006, 33: „Der Hauptstreitpunkt bei der Beurteilung der Embryonenforschung ist der Status des Embryos. Wird er als vollgültiger Mensch anerkannt, so müssten für ihn auch alle Rücksichten gelten, die erwachsenen Menschen zugestanden werden, wenn in einem Forschungsprojekt an ihnen experimentiert wird. So müsste bei Organentnahme nach dem Tod die Einverständniserklärung vorgelegen haben – was bei Embryos natürlich nicht möglich ist. Außerdem dürfte man beim lebenden Embryo keine Versuche unternehmen, die sein Leben gefährden – beim jetzigen Stand der Forschung eine lächerliche Vorstellung. Wird der Embryo jedoch als Konglomerat von Zellen betrachtet, die günstigerweise menschliches Genom enthalten und somit für viele Zwecke zum Wohle ausgereifter Menschen zu verwenden wären, so ergibt sich eine moralische Pflicht zur Forschung an ihm. Zwischen diesen beiden Extremen gibt es viele Zwischenstufen, welche die Einstellung zu Versuchen an Embryonen beeinflussen."

[361] F. Baylis, Human Embryonic Stem Cell Research: Comments on the NBAC Report, in: Suzanne Holland/Karen Lebacqz/Laurie Zoloth (Hrsg.), The Human Embryonic Stem Cell Research, Cambridge/Massachusetts/London 2001, 51-60, 53: „But in the debate about moral status, respect is not simply about esteem or etiquette; rather it has to do with dignity independent of rank and merit. To respect something is to regard it as valuable in itself, to cherish it because of what it is."

[362] So bei den Vertretern einer Mitgifttheorie, die Menschenwürde als menschliche Wesenseigenschaft verstehen, etwa in den Argumenten der SKIP-Gruppe. Vgl. aber

· Schutzwürdigkeit und Respekt kommt menschlichen Wesen zu, weil sie als vernünftige Wesen mit *Personalität* anzusehen sind.[363]

Während etwa Immanuel Kant Menschenwürde und Personalität miteinander assoziiert,[364] hat sich in der englischsprachigen Ideengeschichte das Anthropologumenon der Personalität nicht mit *dignity* verbunden, sondern wird nach der Definition von John Locke kriteriologisch an bestimmte empirisch nachweisbare Fähigkeiten – etwa das Bewusstsein seiner selbst im Zeitkontinuum oder die Verfolgung von Präferenzen – geknüpft. Dabei wird meist das *Potential* für diese Fähigkeiten als für die Zuerkennung von Personalität nicht ausreichend angesehen, sondern das Kriterium des Selbstbewusstseins muss, damit von Personalität gesprochen werden kann, auch tatsächlich verwirklicht werden.[365] In diesem Zusammenhang hat sich in der Entwicklung der Bioethik bis ins 21. Jahrhundert hinein vor allem im Umgang mit menschlichem Leben am Lebensbeginn die Frage nach der *Personalität* als entscheidend entwickelt.[366] Aufgrund der zentralen Bedeutung, die dem Personbegriff

auch T. Peters, Embryonic Stem Cells and the Theology of Dignity, in: Suzanne Holland u. a. (Hrsg.), The Human Embryonic Stem Cell Debate, 127-139, 127: „It is my opinion that this strong commitment is to human dignity, and that the orientating question is whether dignity applies to the blastocyst that is destroyed when obtaining pluripotent cells." Peters argumentiert mit Kant und der Selbstzwecklichkeit des Menschen, nach der jeder Mensch niemals ausschließlich als Mittel zu gebrauchen ist. Er versteht dabei Menschenwürde zum einen als einem menschlichen Wesen „intrinsic", zum anderen aber auch als zuzuschreibende Realität, die zunächst von Gott einem Menschen zugeschrieben wird, woraufhin auch Menschen anderen Menschen Würde zuschreiben.

[363] Dabei ist die Verwendung des Personbegriffs mehrdeutig, was sich an der Unvereinbarkeit der Positionen etwa von Singer und Kant oder Vertretern der christlichen Theologie zeigt.

[364] Für Kant bezeichnet die Person sowohl das Subjekt, als auch das Objekt des Sittengesetzes, so dass er sagen kann: „Alle Achtung für eine Person ist eigentlich nur Achtung fürs Gesetz..., wovon jene uns das Beispiel gibt." (Grundlegung, 28.) Als Teil der vernünftigen Menschheit hat jede Person nicht nur einen äußeren Wert, sondern einen „inneren Wert, d.i. *Würde*" (Grundlegung, 69), was sich in der *praktischen Form* des Kategorischen Imperativs deutlich macht. S. oben, S. 113.

[365] Vgl. den von J. Harris hrsg. Sammelband Bioethics, Oxford/New York 2001. Darin etwa J. J. Thomson, A Defence of Abortion, 25-41: „A newly fertilized ovum, a newly implanted clump of cells, is no more a person than an acorn is an oak tree." (Zitat auf S. 26.)

[366] Vgl. Nuffield Council on Bioethics, Stem cell therapy: the ethical issues. A discussion paper, London, 2000, 6: „The debate about the moral status of the embryo has focused on the question of whether the embryo should be treated as a person, or, at least, a potential person. If the embryo is so considered, then it will be morally impermissible to use it merely as a means to an end, rather than as an end in itself. This would preclude both embryo research and any other procedure not directed to the benefit of that actual em-

in der Debatte zukommt, soll ein knapper Abriss Bedeutung und Deutungsgeschichte dieses Konzepts klären.

Ursprünglich kein theologischer Begriff, sondern als Bezeichnung „persona" (Rolle) im Bereich des Theaters, der Rechtsprechung, der Grammatik und der Rhetorik verwendet, erlangt der Terminus „Person" vor allem im Zusammenhang mit der Ausformulierung der christlichen Trinitätslehre Bekanntheit.[367] In diesem Zusammenhang spielt die von Tertullian um 200 n. Chr. geprägte Formulierung der „tres personae – una substantia" eine bedeutende Rolle. Im Laufe der Zeit wird die Dignität der Person von Gott und Engeln auch auf vernunftbegabte Wesen übertragen, was etwa in der Formel des Boethius (ca. 480-524) von der Person als „naturae rationabilis individua substantia"[368] seinen Ausdruck findet.[369]

Während sich die mittelalterliche Theologie mit ihrer der aristotelischen Philosophie entlehnten Bestimmung des Menschen als eines *animal rationale* an diese Konzeption von Personalität anschließt und auch Kant aufgrund der unterscheidenden Zuordnung von *homo noumenon* und *homo phainomenon* und der personalen Wesensbestimmung aufgrund der menschlichen *Vernunft* eine verwandte Auffassung vertritt, indem beide Personalität als gleichbedeutend mit dem rationalen Aspekt des Menschseins als solchen verstehen, tritt im englischen Empirismus die Zuordnung von Personalität und menschlichem Dasein *als solchem* insofern auseinander, als Personalität als kongruent und koextensional mit *aktuellem* Reflexionsvermögen und Selbstbewusstsein verstanden wird.[370]

---

bryo. The removal of cells from an embryo would therefore not be morally permissible, regardless of whether these cells were to be used for the benefit of some other person."

[367] Zu einer systematischen Entfaltung des Personbegriffs auch im Hinblick auf die Verbundenheit der Personalität Gottes und des Menschen vgl. den Aufsatz von E. Herms, Zur Systematik des Personbegriffs in reformatorischer Tradition, NZSTh 50, 2007, 377-413.

[368] S. oben, S. 89, Anm. 193.

[369] Zur geschichtlichen Entwicklung des Personbegriffs vgl. Heinz Husslik, Art. Person, EKL 3/9, 1131-1134.

[370] Vgl. Dieter Sturma, Art. Person, Enzyklopädie Philosophie, Hamburg 2001, 995: „Das systematische Zentrum von Lockes Ansatz ist die Theorie personaler Identität, die bis heute nur wenig von ihrer Virulenz eingebüßt hat. Weil er den Sachverhalt, daß Personen ihr Leben in der Zeit zu führen haben, in den Mittelpunkt seiner Argumentation stellt, kommt der Bestimmung des Identitätssinns über die Zeit hinweg entscheidende Bedeutung zu. Begründungstheoretisch entscheidend ist die Koextensionalitätsthese von Personalität und Bewußtsein, der zufolge die Identität einer P. so weit reiche wie das ihr zugängliche Bewußtsein von eigenen Gedanken und Handlungen. Sein Ansatz wird denn auch als ›memory theory‹ bezeichnet."

Die in der Folgezeit etwa von Joseph Butler[371] kritisch beurteilte Konzeption einer Koextensionalität von personaler Identität und *Bewusstseinszuständen* im Anschluss an John Locke bereitet gleichwohl die gegenwärtig etwa bei Michael Tooley, Peter Singer oder John Harris[372] einflussreiche Konzeption vor, nach der zwischen *personalem*, selbstbewussten und in der Zeit orientierten, und *nicht-personalem* Leben zu unterscheiden sei.

Im 20. und 21. Jahrhundert verbindet sich mit dem Personbegriff vor allem die Frage, ob und wie Personen auch vor dem Hintergrund ihrer offenkundigen physischen und psychischen Veränderungen an einem durchgehenden Identitätsbegriff festhalten können. Bei dieser Frage stehen im wesentlichen zwei Auffassungen einander gegenüber: während eine Position an einem eher substanzhaft orientierten Verständnis von Person festhält, das Personalität als basalen Sachverhalt begreift, der sich nicht aus empirisch nachweisbaren Eigenschaften speist, sondern dem Empfinden von Identität vorhergeht, geht eine andere Position davon aus, dass personale Identität anhand physischer und psychischer Veränderungsprozesse als sich entwickelnd zu verstehen sei.[373] Während die zuerst genannte Position Menschsein und Personsein als koextensional versteht,[374] unterscheidet die zweite Position Menschsein und Personsein, indem sie „Personalität" als Phasensortal verwendet.

Wird Personalität als Phasensortal verstanden, so ergibt sich zwangsläufig die Folgerung, dass Menschsein und Personsein nicht koextensional sind und – bei einer normativen Konsequenzziehung – Personen ein anderer moralischer Status zukommt als Menschen im allgemeinen bzw. Nicht-Personen, insofern ein absoluter Lebensschutz für Personen, nicht aber für Nicht-Personen vertreten wird. Eine verbrauchende Forschung und eine Erzeugung von menschlichen Embryonen zu Forschungszwecken impliziert dann keinen respektlosen Umgang mit dem Embryo, selbst wenn dieser als Mittel zu einem anderen Zweck verwendet wird, weil sich das Verbot der Verzwecklichung zumindest in seinem absoluten Anspruch lediglich auf personales Leben bezieht. Auf diesem Hintergrund kann die Forschung an menschlichen

[371] Vgl. vor allem Butler, The Analogy of Religion (1875), New York 2005.

[372] Zu den Publikationen von Singer und Harris s. oben, Abschnitt III.4.2, S. 144ff. Für den Standpunkt von M. Tooley vgl. etwa Tooley, Personhood, in: H. Kuhse/P. Singer (Hrsg.), A Companion to Bioethics, Oxford 1998, 117-126.

[373] In der Theorie wird die zuerst genannte Position als „simple view", die zweite Position als „complex view" gekennzeichnet. Vgl. Sturma, Art. Person, 995f.

[374] Diese Position wird meist von Repräsentanten der Kirchen vertreten, so in den bereits genannten Schriften „Gott ist ein Freund des Lebens" oder „Im Geist der Liebe mit dem Leben umgehen", aber auch im Zusammenhang der SKIP-Argumente oder etwa von Robert Spaemann in seinem Buch Personen. Versuche über den Unterschied zwischen etwas und jemand, Stuttgart ³2007.

Embryonen, sobald sie *Personen* zugute kommt, sogar als moralische Pflicht verstanden werden.

Wird demgegenüber davon ausgegangen, dass Personalität nicht an bestimmte allererst noch zu erfüllende Kriterien zu knüpfen, sondern mit dem Menschsein gegeben ist oder man zumindest nicht sicher sein kann, ob nicht Personstatus schon für frühe Embryonen angenommen werden muss,[375] ist eine Forschung an menschlichen Embryonen, im Verlaufe derer Embryonen getötet werden und die ihnen nicht direkt zugute kommt, ethisch nicht akzeptabel oder stellt zumindest ein ethisches Grundsatzproblem dar.

Bei der Annahme einer Koextensionalität von Menschsein und Personsein gründet menschliche Personalität beispielsweise in der intrinsischen Vernunftbegabung als solcher, die bei bestimmten Angehörigen der menschlichen Gattung auch als *potentielle* Vernunftbegabung vorliegen kann, oder in einem extrinsischen, menschlichen Wesen *von außen her* zukommenden Annerkennungsverhältnis.[376]

Der Person-Begriff hat sich in der neueren Bioethik vor allem in der englischsprachigen, aber auch in der deutschen Diskussion zu einem zentralen Topos entwickelt. „Person" bezieht sich in dieser Verwendung häufig nicht auf alle Angehörigen der Spezies Mensch, sondern bildet das verbindende Element von Entitäten, die über bestimmte Eigenschaften wie Vernunftgebrauch und Orientiertheit in Zeit und Raum sowie die Verfolgung von Interessen verfügen.[377] Dabei erlangt der Person-Begriff insofern Normativität, als Personen ausdrücklich nicht getötet werden dürfen, sondern einen absoluten Lebensschutz genießen.

Die Differenzierung von Menschen und Personen im eigentlichen Sinne beschränkt sich aber nicht auf einen bioethischen Utilitarismus. Die Tatsa-

---

[375] Dieses (tutioristische) Argument vertritt Robert Song in seinem Artikel "To be willing to kill what for all one knows is a person is to be willing to kill a person", in: B. Waters/R. Cole-Turner (Hrsg.), God and the embryo. Religious voices on stem cells and cloning, Washington 2003, 98-107.

[376] Damit kehrt die oben schon beobachtete Differenz von eigenschaftsgestützter und relationaler Begründung von Menschenwürde auch bei den Überlegungen zur Personalität wieder. Vgl. in der von der EKD verabschiedeten Stellungnahme „Im Geist der Liebe mit dem Leben umgehen", 2002: „Nach christlichem Verständnis gründet... das Personsein nicht in Eigenschaften und Fähigkeiten, sondern in einem Anerkennungsverhältnis." (S. 17f.)

[377] Die Unterscheidung von Menschen und Personen beschränkt sich nicht auf den Utilitarismus, ist in diesem Zusammenhang aber besonders verbreitet. Vgl. M. Tooley, Personhood, 117: „The term 'person' is... being used in a very different way - namely to refer, not to individuals belonging to a certain species, but instead to individuals who enjoy something comparable, in relevant respects, to the type of mental life that characterizes normal adult human beings." Vgl. auch J. Harris, Beings, human beings and persons, in: Ders., The value of life, London 1985, 7-27.

che, dass die Frage nach Personalität auch außerhalb von utilitaristisch geprägten bioethischen Konzeptionen eine Rolle spielt, belegt ihre Häufigkeit und breite Verwendung innerhalb des englischen Sprachraums. Ich stelle im folgenden einen weiteren Entwurf knapp dar.

Der amerikanische Theologe H. Tristam Engelhardt Junior vertritt ausdrücklich keinen utilitaristischen Standpunkt, sucht aber nach Alternativen zu dem in der englischsprachigen Bioethik[378] verbreiteten prinzipienorientierten Ansatz. Er versucht, Ethik innerhalb eines säkularen pluralistischen Umfeldes zu fundieren und eine Begründung für Bioethik in einem Kontext zu finden, in dem eine religiös fundierte, belastbare und konsensfähige Begründung aufgrund der Pluralität von Meinungen und Weltanschauungen praktisch nicht mehr existieren kann.[379]

Dabei geht Engelhardt von drei voraussetzenden Unterscheidungen aus:[380]

- Zwischen einer voll zustimmungsfähigen universalen Moral und einer prozeduralen Moral,
- zwischen „moralischen Freunden", die dieselbe Moral wie man selbst vertreten, und „moralischen Fremden", die einen anderen moralischen Hintergrund haben,
- zwischen Gemeinschaft und Gesellschaft: Während eine Gemeinschaft durch gemeinsame Grundsätze und eine gemeinsame Moral aneinander gebunden ist, leben wir gegenwärtig in einer Gesellschaft, die unterschiedliche moralische Hintergründe hat, was Überzeugungen und moralische Werte angeht, in der es also dementsprechend für jeden von uns moralische Freunde *und* moralische Fremde gibt. Innerhalb der Gesellschaft bestehen moralische Gemeinschaften für sich.

Auf dem Hintergrund dieser Unterscheidungen können für Engelhardt ethische Kontroversen, die in einer Gesellschaft aufgrund von unterschiedlichen moralischen Konzeptionen auftreten, nur auf folgende Weise gelöst werden: durch Gewalt (1), durch Bekehrung der einen Partei zum Standpunkt der anderen (2), durch vernünftige Auseinandersetzung (3) oder durch Übereinstimmung (4).[381]

[378] H. T. Engelhardt, Jr., The Foundations of Bioethics, 1996; Ders., The Foundations of Christian Bioethics, 2000. Die Konversion, die Engelhardt zur orthodoxen Kirche durchlaufen hat und die sich in seinem Buch zur christlichen Bioethik (The Foundations of Christian Bioethics) niederschlägt, widerspricht seiner eigenen Aussage zufolge nicht seinem grundsätzlich pluralismus-freundlichen früheren Zugang.

[379] „Engelhardt is attempting to construct a basis for bioethics in the midst of a postmodern culture and world." (Rae/Cox, Bioethics, 62.)

[380] Vgl. Rae/Cox, a.a.O., 63.

[381] Vgl. Rae/Cox, a.a.O., 64.

Engelhardt hält die Optionen der vernünftigen Auseinandersetzung und der Bekehrung für nicht realistisch, weil sie nicht in der Lage seien, die Lükke zu überbrücken, die sich zwischen unterschiedlichen Positionen unterschiedlicher Gemeinschaften innerhalb einer Gesellschaft auftue. Während er Gewalt nicht kategorisch ausschließt, stellt er doch fest, dass diese keine wirklich vernünftige und aufgeklärte Lösung für ein Problem sei und konstatiert als einzige wirklich realistische Lösung für eine ethische Kontroverse in einer Gesellschaft den Weg der gegenseitigen Übereinstimmung.[382] Eine solche gegenseitige Übereinstimmung muss nicht bedeuten, dass *inhaltliche Einigkeit* erzielt wird; Engelhardt zielt lediglich auf gegenseitige Anerkennung und Toleranz.[383]

Aufgrund seiner Hochschätzung der Toleranz hält Engelhardt seinen eigenen ethischen Entwurf, den er nach seiner Konversion zur orthodoxen Kirche verfasst hat und in dem er etwa in der Frage der Empfängnisverhütung oder des Schwangerschaftsabbruchs dezidiert orthodoxe Positionen vertritt, darum auch für konsistent mit der liberalen Position, die er vor seiner Konversion vertreten hatte.[384]

In der gegenseitigen Toleranz und Anerkennung liegt für Engelhardt der Schlüssel zu einem friedlichen Miteinander in einer extrem pluralistischen Gesellschaft. Konsensfähigkeit wird dabei in der Rationalität und Kommunikabilität einzelner Handlungen, nicht in einer normativ wirksamen Moral einer der Gemeinschaften innerhalb einer Gesellschaft gesucht. Darum ist die Basis, auf der moralische Handlungen, aber auch Zustimmung und Konsens gesellschaftlich möglich werden, der gegenseitige Respekt, mit dem die Mitglieder einer Gesellschaft miteinander umgehen. Dieser Respekt ermöglicht als grundlegende Basis menschlichen Zusammenlebens eine dem Rawlschen *overlapping consensus* strukturell entsprechende gesellschaftliche ethische Grundvereinbarung.

Gegenseitiger Respekt gründet für Engelhardt seinerseits in der persönlichen Autonomie des Individuums,[385] mit der dieses anderen Individuen Re-

---

[382] „If one cannot establish by sound rational argument a particular concrete moral viewpoint as canonically decisive..., then the only source of general secular authority for moral content and moral direction is agreement." (Engelhardt, The Foundations of Bioethics, New York ²1996, 68.)

[383] „This methodology provides a means for moral strangers to live together in a postmodern world without ever trying to resolve their ultimate moral commitments." (Rae/Cox, a.a.O., 65.)

[384] Engelhardt, Foundations of Christian Bioethics, 2000.

[385] Engelhardt geht im Gegensatz zu Beauchamp und Childress davon aus, dass *jede* Handlung, die autonom begründet wird, moralisch akzeptabel sei. Autonomie verleiht Individuen für Engelhardt das Recht, auch falsche Dinge zu tun. Wirklich unmoralisch, dann aber auch nicht-autonom werden Handlungen darum erst, wenn sie die Autonomie von anderen Menschen antasten. Vgl. Engelhardt, Foundations of Christian Ethics, 364:

spekt entgegenbringt und die die Kohärenz einer Partikularmoral auch im Rahmen des radikalen Pluralismus erweist.[386] Akte persönlicher Autonomie wiederum können lediglich von Handlungsagenten ausgeführt werden, die dazu auch befähigt sind, was für Engelhardt die *Personalität* von Handlungsagenten konstituiert: wer autonom ist, ist Person. Mit seinem Verständnis von Autonomie verbindet Engelhardt darum ein anthropologisches Konzept, nach dem *Personen im strengen Sinne* autonom sind.[387] Engelhardt unterscheidet in diesem Zusammenhang anders als der gegenwärtige Utilitarismus nicht Personen und Nicht-Personen voneinander, führt aber eine Unterscheidung von Personen im *strengen* und Personen im *sozialen* Sinne ein,[388] welche letzteren durch folgende Merkmale charakterisiert werden:[389]

- Menschen, die in der Vergangenheit Personen im strengen Sinn gewesen sind (und es jetzt, etwa aufgrund von Demenz oder anderen Erkrankungen, nicht mehr sind),
- Menschen, die wahrscheinlich einmal Personen werden und die in einer Umgebung leben, die ihnen einen gewissen gesellschaftlichen Status verleiht (etwa Kinder),
- Menschen, die niemals Personen waren und es auch niemals sein werden (etwa geistig retardierte Menschen).

„To summarize, true autonomy is not capricious choice, but rightly directed choice free of passions. It is a false autonomy to choose as one will, moved by powerful urges.“ Mit diesem Verständnis von Autonomie steht Engelhardt in der Nähe der kantischen Konzeption von Autonomie, insofern auch für Engelhardt autonome Akte an sich ethisch akzeptabel sind. Engelhardt unterscheidet sich allerdings insofern von Kant, als er wahre autonome Akte als Handlungen versteht, die zur Einigkeit mit Gott führen. Vgl. Engelhardt, a.a.O., 364: „Autonomy in its fullest sense is not just choice uninfluenced by the passions, but choice that unites to God“. Darüber hinaus reklamiert Engelhardt nicht für *jeden* Menschen Autonomie, sondern lediglich für Personen im eigentlichen Sinne.

[386] Rae/Scott, Bioethics, 67: „All conduct is to be evaluated in light of the principle of autonomy, and autonomy can override all other factors.“

[387] „It is persons who are the constituents of the secular moral community. Only persons are concerned about moral arguments and be convinced by them. Only persons can make agreements and convey authority to common projects through their concurrence. To choose, to make an agreement, is to be conscious of what one is doing.“ (Engelhardt, Foundations of Bioethics, 136.)

[388] Die Unterscheidung von Personen im eigentlichen und Personen im sozialen Sinn findet sich in Engelhardt, Foundations of Bioethics, 136ff. In seinem späteren Buch „The Foundations of Christian Bioethics“, das Engelhardt nach seiner Konversion zur orthodoxen Kirche verfasst hat, rekurriert er nicht mehr auf diese Unterscheidung, grenzt sich aber auch nicht von ihr ab.

[389] Vgl. Rae/Cox, a.a.O., 72.

Gegenüber den durch diese Merkmale ausgezeichneten *Personen im sozialen Sinne* sind den *Personen im eigentlichen Sinne*, weil sie autonome Handlungsagenten sind, auch die Rechte von Handlungsagenten zuzuschreiben, zu denen genuin der Schutz des Lebens gehört.

Die auf Autonomie beruhende Unterscheidung von Personen im strengen und Personen im sozialen Sinne hat im Zusammenhang mit der Unterscheidung von Gemeinschaft und Gesellschaft[390] und darin lebenden moralischen Freunden und moralischen Fremden Konsequenzen für bioethische Entscheidungen und Handlungen: wenn eine Gemeinschaft innerhalb der Gesellschaft für sich und ihre Mitglieder entscheidet, dass Embryonen *schutzwürdige* Personen (im sozialen Sinne) sind und deshalb etwa Schwangerschaftsabbruch oder die Forschung an Embryonen für moralisch verwerflich erklärt, so ermöglicht die Pluralität der Gesellschaft diesen Standpunkt. Allerdings kann daraus kein normativer Anspruch für die gesamte Gesellschaft abgeleitet werden, so dass Mitgliedern einer anderen Gemeinschaft innerhalb der Ge-

[390] Mit der Unterscheidung von Gemeinschaft und Gesellschaft vertritt Engelhardt die Plausibilität und Legitimität unterschiedlicher moralischer Entscheidungen von moralischen Gemeinschaften innerhalb des radikalen gesellschaftlichen Pluralismus. Rae/Cox, a.a.O., 73: „The principle of permission makes morality possible between moral strangers. Moreover, it is autonomous persons that constitute the moral sphere and its conditions. Indeed, all other principles of bioethics are ultimately grounded in the principle of permission, and in fact are justified and qualified by the principle of permission.“ Seine später entwickelte christlich-orthodoxe ethische Konzeption in den „Foundations of Christian Bioethics“ steht – auch wenn sie ausdrücklich nicht naturrechtlich argumentiert – in einer gewissen Nähe zur römisch-katholischen Position und unterscheidet sich von deutlich liberaleren Positionen der pluralistischen Gesellschaft, wird von Engelhardt aber als kohärent mit dem pluralistischen Gesellschaftsprinzip und der Unterscheidung von Gemeinschaften mit moralischen Freunden und Gesellschaften mit moralischen Fremden angesehen. Vgl. Engelhardt, Foundations of Christian Bioethics, 135: „The procedural framework allows individuals with diverse moral commitments in their own communities to act with common moral authority and live peaceably within a larger secular society“. Er beansprucht für seine ethische Konzeption folgerichtig keine absolute Geltung, sondern deren Gültigkeit lediglich innerhalb der Gemeinschaft, der er angehört. Der Vorteil einer solchen Konzeption liegt strukturell darin, dass klare Richtlinien für die eigene Gemeinschaft gefunden werden können, mit der diese sich auch von anderen Gemeinschaften der Gesellschaft deutlich unterscheiden kann. Dabei erscheint es als problematisch, dass diese Struktur zahlreiche Gemeinschaften unterstützt, die lediglich einen ethischen Minimalkonsens finden und bei der letztlich in der Rechtsprechung und Gesetzgebung wahrscheinlich eine Gemeinschaft die anderen nicht wegen rationaler Argumente, sondern aufgrund anderer Faktoren dominieren wird. In der Auseinandersetzung mit Engelhardts Position ist angemerkt worden, dass Mitglieder einer Gesellschaft im radikalen Pluralismus wahrscheinlich weniger miteinander verhandeln als vielmehr versuchen werden, den jeweils eigenen Standpunkt notfalls auch gewaltsam durchzusetzen. Vgl. Rae/Cox, a.a.O., 81. „In other words, postmodernity does not lead to negotiation, it inevitably leads to deception through language and imposed values through the use of power.“

sellschaft, für die Embryonen zwar Personen im sozialen Sinne, aber nicht absolut schutzwürdig sind, legitimerweise der Schwangerschaftsabbruch und die verbrauchende Forschung an Embryonen erlaubt werden muss.

Die zunächst an die Konzeption Kants oder den Neukantianismus von Gewirth erinnernde Verbindung von Autonomie und dem Personstatus eines Menschen gründet sich darum auch bei Engelhardt auf eine empirische Definition von Personalität, die strukturell zu einer ähnlichen Unterscheidung von Personen im *strengen* und Personen im *sozialen* Sinne gelangt wie die Konzeptionen des neueren Utilitarismus, auch wenn nicht mit Selbstbewusstsein, Interessensbewusstheit oder Selbstwertschätzung, sondern mit Handlungsautonomie operiert wird. Ein für eine gesamte Gesellschaft moralisch verbindlicher *intrinsischer* Wert wird von Engelhardt lediglich für autonome Personen im eigentlichen Sinne angenommen, während der Umgang mit Personen im sozialen Sinne gesellschaftlich verhandelbar ist, von Gemeinschaften unterschiedlich vertreten werden kann, aber keinen allgemeinen Geltungsanspruch für sich beanspruchen darf. Während für Personen im strengen Sinne ihre Handlungsautonomie moralisch statusbegründend wirkt, hängt der Status von Personen im sozialen Sinne von der Statuszuschreibung durch andere und damit von der Gemeinschaft ab, die mit ihnen umgeht.[391]

Nach der oben gegebenen Typologisierung der Interpretation von Menschenwürde vertritt Engelhardt – auch wenn er nicht explizit auf *Menschenwürde* rekurriert – damit eine modifizierte Leistungstheorie, die er mit Elementen einer Kommunikationstheorie insofern verbindet, als die jeweilige Gemeinschaft über den Umgang mit Personen im sozialen Sinne zu entscheiden hat. Moralische Verbindlichkeit besteht hinsichtlich des Umgangs mit Personen im eigentlichen Sinne in der gesamten *Gesellschaft*, hinsichtlich des Umgangs mit Personen im sozialen Sinne in der moralischen *Gemeinschaft*.

Engelhardt rekurriert anders als gegenwärtige Konzeptionen des Utilitarismus weder auf den Lockeschen Personbegriff, noch auf ein grundsätzliches menschliches Streben nach Glück und Vermeidung von Schmerz. Insofern unterscheidet sich sein Verständnis von menschlicher Personalität von den zuvor in diesem Abschnitt dargestellten Modellen. Dabei zeigt sich aber, dass die Begründung von Personalität sich vor allem an der Frage abarbeitet, ob Personalität *empirisch* aufgrund des Rekurses auf Selbstbewusstsein oder aktueller Handlungsautonomie oder *überempirisch* aufgrund eines anschließend noch näher zu bestimmenden transzendentalen oder transzendenten Rahmens begründet werden soll. Diese grundsätzliche Frage hat Auswirkungen auf bioethische Entscheidungen bis in die konkreten Empfehlungen der Gesetzgebung hinein. Den Abschnitt abschließend, gebe ich eine typo-

[391] Vgl. Engelhardt, Foundations of Bioethics, 150: „There is unavoidably a major distinction to be drawn between persons who are moral agents and persons to whom the rights of moral agents are imputed."

logische Zusammenfassung der Lexeme *Personalität*, *Menschsein* und *Menschenwürde*.

- Menschsein, Menschenwürde und Personalität sind koextensional.[392] Wer Mensch ist, ist auch Person oder muss zumindest als Person behandelt werden,[393] und wer Person ist, hat Menschenwürde. Menschenwürde kann darum auch als Personwürde bezeichnet werden.[394] Mit dieser Variante ist noch nicht beantwortet, welche Ausdehnung Menschsein hat, wann es also beginnt und wann es endet. Darum können für dieses Modell wiederum zwei Untermodelle[395] angenommen werden:
  - Menschsein beginnt mit der Kernverschmelzung, also dem Beginn des eigenständigen Genoms und endet mit dem Tod, also dem Verlust der Vitalität. Die Kriterien für Menschsein und Personsein sind Lebendigkeit *und* genetische Einzigartigkeit.

[392] Um von einer Kontinuität der Personalität auszugehen, nach der Embryonen ab dem Zeitpunkt der Kernverschmelzung zumindest wie Personen anzusehen und entsprechend zu schützen sind, ist mit dem Argument der Unterscheidung von Substanz und Akzidenz operiert worden, nach der Personalität diejenige Substanz ist, die innerhalb der Entwicklung eines Menschen ab dem Zeitpunkt der Kernverschmelzung kontinuierlich bleibt (Rae/Cox, Bioethics, 132 und passim). Damit wird gegen ein Verständnis von Personalität argumentiert, nach dem Personalität auf bestimmten Leistungen wie etwa dem Selbstbewusstsein beruht. Vgl. Rae/Cox, a.a.O., 168: „The inadequacies of functional criteria for personhood are clearly evident if we try to practice them consistently. Consider the person under general anesthesia. That person is clearly not conscious, has no expressed capacity for reason, is incapable of self-motivated activity, cannot possibly communicate, has no concept of himself or herself, and cannot remember the past or aspire fort he future."

[393] Ähnlich vorsichtig urteilt der päpstliche Text *Dignitas Personae* (2008), S. 4f., wenn er formuliert, dass der Embryo nicht unbedingt als Person bezeichnet werden sollte, weil mit dieser Bezeichnung eine Fülle von ungeklärten philosophischen Problemen entstehen, dass ihm aber, weil er ganz Mensch ist, die Würde einer Person zukommt.

[394] Vgl. z.B. N. M. Ford, The Prenatal Person. Ethics from Conception to Birth, Oxford 2002, 16: „Fetuses and infants gradually realize their own inherent natural active potential to become more fully what they already are – persons with potential, not potential persons. They remain persons even if they subsequently develop congenital defects which may permanently inhibit the expression of rational acts."

[395] Ein drittes Modell könnte folgendes vertreten: Menschsein, Personsein und Menschenwürde beginnen mit der Entwicklung eines neuen und eigenständigen Genoms und enden an einem Punkt der Zersetzung des Leichnams, gehen also über den Tod hinaus. Das Kriterium für Personalität liegt dann in der genetischen Einzigartigkeit, nicht nur in der Lebendigkeit. Für eine solche Position sind auch Leichname Menschen, denen dieselbe Würde und Personalität zuerkannt werden muss wie lebendigen Menschen. Wenn ich recht sehe, wird diese Position nicht ausdrücklich vertreten. Die *particula veri* liegt allerdings darin, dass das Sterben ebenso wie die pränatale Entwicklung ein kontinuierlicher Prozess ist und Würde als postmortale Würde über den Zeitpunkt des Todes noch weiterwirkt.

  - Menschsein und Personalität beginnen, wenn bestimmte Qualitäten wie Rationalität oder Selbstbewusstsein erfüllt sind, und enden, wenn diese nicht mehr erfüllt werden. Menschliche Wesen vor und nach der Erfüllung dieser Kriterien sind dann noch keine Menschen und keine Personen mehr, sondern etwa „Prä-Embryonen“ oder Wesen im vegetativen Status.
- Menschsein und Personalität sind nicht gleich extensional, die Klasse der Menschen ist größer als die Klasse der Personen. Personalität liegt dann vor, wenn Menschen bestimmte Merkmale aufweisen und bestimmte Kriterien erfüllen. Hier sind hinsichtlich der Ausdehnung von Menschenwürde wiederum zwei Untergruppen denkbar:
  - Menschenwürde und Personalität sind gleich extensional: wer Person ist, hat Menschenwürde, die nicht allen Menschen zukommt. Menschenwürde sollte dann allerdings genauer als Personwürde bezeichnet werden.
  - Menschenwürde und Personalität sind nicht gleich extensional. Dann ist die Gruppe der Personen kleiner als die Gruppe der Würdeträger. Wenn Personalität aufgrund von Leistungen zuerkannt wird, also die Gruppe von Personen kleiner ist als die Gruppe der Menschen, die Angehörigen der Gruppe der Menschen aber auch Würde haben, so unterscheidet sich die Würde von Personen von der basalen Würde aller Menschen. Die normativen Folgen müssen dann noch bestimmt werden.

Die unterschiedliche Interpretation vor allem der Begriffe *Autonomie* und *Personalität* und das damit assoziierte unterschiedliche Verständnis von *Menschenwürde* und *human dignity* zeigen deutlich, dass implizite anthropologische Grundannahmen zu unterschiedlichen Schlussfolgerungen führen. Dabei kann es sein, dass Anthropologumena, die traditionell Geltung hatten, aufgrund biomedizinischer Forschung eine Veränderung erfahren und klassische Begriffe eine neue Bedeutung erhalten.[396] Eine terminologische Konvergenz bedeutet keine inhaltliche Einigkeit, wie bei den dargestellten Problemen am Person- und Autonomiebegriff ebenso wie am *Menschenwürde*- resp. *dignity*-Begriff deutlich geworden ist. Vielmehr bilden die Grundannahmen das fundierende Konzept, das allererst offenzulegen ist.

Im Anschluss an die Darstellung utilitaristischer Grundmodelle und Anthropologumena zum menschlichen Personsein gebe ich im nun folgenden Abschnitt eine kritische Zusammenfassung.

396 Vgl. M. Junker-Kenny, Genes and the Self. Anthropological Questions to the Human Genome Project, in: C. Deane-Drummond (Hrsg.), Brave New World. Theology, Ethics and the Human Genome, London/New York 2003, 116-140.

III. 4. 4 Enhancement um jeden Preis? Grenzen des gegenwärtigen Utilitarismus und die menschliche Leiblichkeit

Mit der Unterscheidung von Menschen und Personen greifen der gegenwärtige Utilitarismus und weite Teile der bioethischen Debatte auf eine empirische Kriteriologie zur Begründung des Lebensschutzes für menschliche Wesen zurück. Der Rekurs auf empirische *versus* überempirische Begründungsmuster stellt dabei eine Differenz dar, die allenfalls festgestellt, nicht aber überwunden werden kann. Nicht jede Unstimmigkeit innerhalb der gegenwärtigen bioethischen Debatte kann auf diese Grunddifferenz zurückgeführt werden, aber sie gibt einen typologischen Verständnisrahmen vor, in den einzelne Positionen eingezeichnet werden können.

Während die anthropologische Grundunterscheidung zwischen Menschen und Personen im vorangegangenen Abschnitt aufgezeigt worden ist, stellen sich mir aus der Sicht evangelischer Theologie folgende weitere Aspekte bei einer Rezeption des Utilitarismus innerhalb der bioethischen Debatte als problematisch dar, bei denen teilweise ein direkter Bezug zur Forschung an Embryonen auszumachen ist, die teilweise aber auch darüber hinausgehen:

- die Tendenz zum Individualismus, der aufgrund seiner Orientierung am *individuellen* Glück und den Präferenzen innerhalb einer konkreten Situation die menschliche Sozialität und Relationalität und damit die Prägung und Gewordenheit von Interessen nicht ernst nimmt,
- die Orientierung am *Nutzen*, die über den Wert des Einzelnen gestellt wird,
- die sich mit dem *Enhancement* verbindende Vorstellung, das Leben sei kontrollierbar und/oder verbesserbar,
- das implizierte *Recht* auf Heilung und Gesundheit, das eine *Pflicht* zur Forschung begründet,
- der grundsätzliche *Forschungspositivismus* und *Forschungsoptimismus*, die möglicherweise eine nur unzureichende Technikfolgenabschätzung vornehmen, sowie schließlich
- die Tatsache, dass die menschliche *Verletzlichkeit* und die Endlichkeit der leiblichen Existenz nicht ernst genommen wird.

Die Tendenz zum *Individualismus* wird in dem grundsätzlichen Impetus greifbar, die Verbesserung der individuellen Konstitution als moralisch verpflichtend anzusehen. Diese Orientierung am gegenwärtigen Individuum zeigt sich außerdem bei der Verwendung des Autonomie- und des Personbegriffs, wenn diese die *aktuelle* Handlungsautonomie einer *aktuell* selbstbewussten Person normativ setzen.[397]

---

[397] Eine ähnliche Orientierung am Individuum verbunden mit einer anthropozentrischen Absolutierung lässt sich auch bei Kant konzedieren.

Hinzu kommt ein Weiteres: Die Orientierung von Handlungsmaßstäben an personalen *Interessen* richtet sich ebenfalls am (personalen) Individuum in seiner gegenwärtigen Situation aus. Die *Vernetzung* von Individuen tritt hierbei aber ebenso in den Hintergrund wie ein *Gewordensein* von Interessen und Präferenzen innerhalb von Beziehungen. Die von Singer für Personalität als maßgeblich angesehene Orientiertheit innerhalb von Vergangenheit und Zukunft nimmt das vergangene und zukünftige Beziehungsnetz eines Individuums, das sein Werden beeinflusst hat und in denen es keine Interessen verfolgt hat, sondern von der Zuwendung anderer abhängig war, nicht wahr. Erfahrungen, in denen ein Mensch keine Interessen artikulieren konnte, in denen aber seine gegenwärtigen Interessen prägend vorbereitet worden sind, sind mit dieser Konzeption nur schwer vermittelbar.

Damit bekommt die Orientierung an den Präferenzen von „gegenwärtigen Personen" und ihrem Glückszustand sowohl eine abstrakte Schlagseite, weil sie die affektive Prägung eines Menschen beim Werden seiner aktuellen Interessen nicht achtet, als auch einen Hang zum Kontingenten, insofern Präferenzen und Begründungen von Glückszuständen von momentanen Empfindungen abhängig gemacht werden und zukünftige Interessen nur dann berücksichtigt werden können, wenn sie artikulierte Interessen sind. Die Kehrseite dieser Orientierung an gegenwärtigen Präferenzen ist die damit zusammenhängende größere Achtung der Interessen einer *Gemeinschaft* über den Interessen eines Einzelnen, wenn die Interessen der Gemeinschaft schwerer wiegen als die Interessen des Individuums bzw. das Individuum als interesselos und damit als Nicht-Person angesehen wird.

Mit der vor allem von Harris vertretenen *Pflicht* zum *Enhancement* hängt darüber hinaus eine Geringschätzung der vorfindlichen Welt zusammen, die einen nicht zu unterschätzenden Druck ausüben kann. Wenn der Leib grundsätzlich verbessert und gesteigert werden muss, so wird damit an die Kräfte des Einzelnen appelliert und dieser dazu angehalten, sich selbst zu verbessern, was ihn in einer konkreten Situation wie Krankheit auch überfordern kann. Darüber hinaus geht mit diesem Appell eine Unzufriedenheit an der Gegenwart einher, als biete die menschliche Verfasstheit gleichsam das Rohmaterial, um so weit wie möglich an ein noch zu erreichendes Ideal angenähert zu werden.[398]

Das dabei implizierte *Recht* auf Therapie und die *Pflicht* zum *Enhancement* werfen die Frage auf, ob die an sich positiven Güter Heilung und Lebensverlängerung um jeden Preis verfolgt und zugebilligt werden sollten, oder ob nicht vielmehr gewichtige Gründe gegen eine Nutzung *aller* Mittel für Ge-

[398] Dass Impfungen, die von Harris schon als *Enhancement* verstanden werden, einen immensen Fortschritt der medizinischen Forschung darstellen, kann nicht bestritten werden. Als problematisch erscheint mir allerdings die ethische Folgerung, die Harris generalisierend aus dieser Tatsache zieht.

sundheit und Therapie bestehen. In der Konstituierung eines *Rechts* auf Gesundheit und Leidfreiheit stellen sich aus theologischer Sicht Zweifel darüber ein, ob ein solches Recht als menschliches Grundrecht anzusehen ist.

Hinzu kommt die vom Impetus des *Enhancement* implizit vorausgesetzte Vorstellung, die Welt sei kontrollierbar und durch technisches Handeln grundsätzlich beherrschbar, wobei nicht in Anschlag gebracht wird, dass häufig nicht alle Handlungsfolgen kontrolliert oder auch nur erwartungssicher abgeschätzt werden können. Multifaktorielle Entwicklungen und Kontingenzen können dabei nur schwer berücksichtigt bzw. erst *a posteriori* reguliert werden. Ob beispielsweise die Forschung an Embryonen tatsächlich das gewünschte Ergebnis liefert, oder ob nicht die technischen und medizinischen Risiken zu groß sind, um Anwendung zu finden, kann ebenso wenig ausgeschlossen werden wie die Möglichkeit des Missbrauchs der Technik etwa zum reproduktiven Klonen oder zur Eugenik.

Eine Tendenz der *nachträglichen* Regulierung von Handlungsfolgen, um unerwünschte Ergebnisse zu verhindern, sehe ich strukturell ebenfalls in der Einsetzung der britischen *Human Fertilisation and Embryology Authority* (HFEA), die *nachlaufend* Forschungsanwendungen reguliert, auch wenn die britische Gesetzgebung im allgemeinen nicht alle Folgerungen des utilitaristischen Zugangs nachvollzieht und sich vor allem bei der normativen Unterscheidung von Personen und Nicht-Personen kritisch zeigt. Ein mit dem *Menschsein* an sich gegebener absoluter Wert ist aber in der britischen Gesetzgebung nicht vorgesehen, und die dem Utilitarismus inhärente Abwägbarkeit unterschiedlicher Güter mit dem Ziel, das Glück und Wohlergehen möglichst vieler zu vermehren, ist mit dem Warnock-Report konsistent.

Mit der Postulierung eines Rechts auf Gesundheit und einer Pflicht zum *Enhancement* wird schließlich die konstitutive menschliche *Verletzlichkeit* unterboten, aufgrund derer Menschen nicht immer in der Lage sind, sich selbst aus eigenen Kräften zu verbessern und zu steigern, insofern sie auch als auf Andere angewiesene, in Entwicklung begriffene Wesen zu kennzeichnen sind – nicht nur, aber auch am Beginn und am Ende des Lebens.

Im Anschluss an die aufgezeigten Schwierigkeiten lässt sich darum die Frage stellen, ob nicht der gegenwärtig breit unterstützten Forschung an menschlichem Leben eine *grundlegende* Problematik eignet, und ob sich darüber hinaus eine Entwicklung greifen lässt, die dazu geführt hat, *Enhancement* als Pflicht und Gesundheit als Recht zu verstehen. Diese Frage ist nicht erschöpfend zu beantworten; ich gebe mit den folgenden Ausführungen lediglich einige knappe Überlegungen zu bedenken.

Auch innerhalb der britischen theologischen Ethik-Debatte wird die gegenwärtige Entwicklung einer vom Utilitarismus geprägten Bioethik mit ihrer beschriebenen Problematik kritisch beobachtet, wobei aus unterschiedlichen

Perspektiven nach Alternativen gesucht wird.[399] Die Konzeption, die ich im folgenden knapp referiere, setzt sich mit fundamentalen Grundannahmen der biomedizinischen Entwicklung der Gegenwart und deren ethischem Konzept auseinander.

Gerald P. McKenny[400] führt die gegenwärtige Entwicklung der Bio- und Medizinethik mit ihrem Rekurs auf den Utilitarismus und dessen Folgeproblemen vor allem auf die Rezeption der Philosophie von René Descartes und Francis Bacon im englischen Sprachraum, aber auch in der übrigen westlichen Welt zurück, nach denen die westliche Kultur Gesundheit als ein eindeutig positives und erstrebenswertes Gut und Menscherecht betrachte, gesteigerten Wert auf technologische Medizin lege und den Leib als etwas ansehe, das man zu behandeln habe, in diesem Zusammenhang aber instrumentalisieren könne.

Die Folge einer Behandlung des Leibes als eines *Dings* hat nach der Analyse von McKenny dazu geführt, dass es der Medizin vor allem darum gegangen sei, Leid zu vermeiden, medizinische Therapie zu verbessern und Leben zu verlängern.[401]

Werde der Leib aber mit Distanz als ein zu behandelndes Ding wahrgenommen, so würden Krankheit und Leid als *Störungen* verstanden, die es zu beheben gelte. Aus dieser Wahrnehmung leite sich ein tief empfundenes *Recht* auf Gesundheit und Heilung ab, das als menschliches Grundrecht angesehen werde und medizinische Forschung rechtfertige, die diesem Recht dienen solle. Bioethik, die auf dieser Tradition aufbaue, könne darum nur schwer die Endlichkeit des Lebens akzeptieren und die Begrenztheiten der Medizin annehmen. Diese Unfähigkeit liege in einer Instrumentalisierung der Natur und verbinde sich mit der Sicht, dass Gott[402] – wenn von Gott überhaupt noch

---

[399] Neben Alternativen innerhalb philosophischer Ethik, die John Rawls mit dem Prinzip der Gerechtigkeit gesucht hat, sind, ebenso wie die schon erwähnten Konzeption von R. Veatch und P. Ramsey (S. oben, S. 136f., Anm. 315), etwa die Vertreter einer neuen Tugendethik im englischen Sprachraum wie A. MacIntyre und S. Hauerwas zu nennen, aber auch die – vor allem römisch-katholischen – Vertreter eines Naturrechts. Die zuletzt genannten Entwicklungen werden in Abschnitt III. 5.2 noch einmal eine Rolle spielen (S. unten, S. 182ff).

[400] Vgl. McKenny, Bioethics, the Body, and the Legacy of Bacon, in: S. Lammers/A. Verhey (Hrsg.), On Moral Medicine. Theological Perspectives in Medical Ethics, Grand Rapids/Cambridge ²1998, 308-323. Auch McKenny, To Relieve the Human Condition. Bioethics, Technology, and the Body, New York 1997.

[401] Vgl. McKenny, Bioethics, 314: „Indeed, one of the most characteristic features of technological medicine is the confidence among its practitioners that the elimination of suffering and the expansion of human choice, in short, the relief of human subjection to fate or necessity, are... unambigious goods whose fulfillment is made possible by technology".

[402] Mit diesen grundlegenden Annahmen korrespondiert nach Ansicht von McKenny ein deistisches Gottesbild, nach dem Gott zwar einmal die Welt geschaffen, sich an-

gesprochen werde – die Natur auch in Form der Naturwissenschaft und der medizinischen Forschung geschaffen habe, um menschliches Leben zu bewahren und zu steigern (*to enhance*).[403]

Auf diesem Hintergrund nimmt McKenny in der bioethischen Debatte der Gegenwart ein *anthropologisches* Defizit wahr, nach dem eine Selbstdistanzierung von der leiblichen Existenz und der Sterblichkeit vollzogen werde.[404] McKenny rekurriert darum auf Konzeptionen, die diese Selbstdistanzierung nicht nachvollziehen, sondern einen kritischen Gegenentwurf hinsichtlich der leiblichen Existenz des Menschen liefern: Vor allem die französische Phänomenologie bei Maurice Merleau-Ponty (1908-1961),[405] aber auch das paulinische Leibverständnis und seine Interpretation durch die Theologie in der zweiten Hälfte des 20. Jahrhunderts spielen dabei eine Rolle.[406]

Menschen *haben* danach nicht einen Leib, von dem sie sich distanzieren könnten, sondern *sind* Leib und nehmen die Welt, wie sie sie umgibt, leiblich als Welt wahr. Sie erleben nicht erst „etwas", um es anschließend bewusst zu reflektieren, sondern erfahren sich selbst ganzheitlich leiblich als einen Teil der wahrgenommenen Welt. Wenn der Leib demgegenüber als Instrument oder Maschine angesehen wird, die es bei Störung oder Ausfall zu reparieren gilt, so tritt eine Selbstdistanzierung vom Leib ein, in der dieser als fremdes Gegenüber angesehen und wahrgenommen wird, aber keine integrale Kraft hat, die Existenz als ganze zu bestimmen.

Das (als problematisch beurteilte) Erbe von Francis Bacon besteht nach der Analyse von McKenny darum darin, dass der menschliche Umgang mit Endlichkeit und Leiblichkeit innerhalb der medizinischen Therapie defizitär sei und die gegenwärtige Bioethik es nicht schaffe, angemessen mit der *Be-*

---

schließend aber zurückgezogen und den Lauf der Welt sich selbst überlassen habe. Der theologische Topos der *providentia Dei* werde verneint. Ebenso wenig würden die Inkarnation Christi und die *theologia crucis* wahrgenommen.

[403] Wird Gott als Ermöglichungsgrund für Naturwissenschaft und Technik in Anspruch genommen, so ergibt sich eine Ansicht, die Dworkin (s. oben, S. 81ff.) als Akzentlegung auf *menschliche* Kreativität bezeichnet hatte. Im Anschluss an die von McKenny gestellten Anfragen kann der deskriptiv orientierte Ansatz von Dworkin im Nachhinein der Kritik unterzogen werden, dass die Wertschätzung menschlicher Kreativität die *Begrenzung* menschlicher Möglichkeiten nicht genug in Anschlag bringt.

[404] „From this perspective Descartes's effort to separate himself as a subject from his body prone to disease, decay, and death, or more generally, the quest to make the body perfect and perfectly subject to our choices, can only be understood as a denial of the moral and spiritual significance of the body." (McKenny, Bioethics, 320.)

[405] M. Merleau-Ponty, Phänomenologie der Wahrnehmung, Berlin/New York [6]1976. Im deutschen Sprachraum ist die Phänomenologie der Leiblichkeit vor allem von Bernhard Waldenfels kommuniziert worden. Vgl. B. Waldenfels, Das leibliche Selbst. Vorlesungen zur Phänomenologie des Leibes, Frankfurt/Main [3]2000.

[406] Bei McKenny, To Relieve the Human Condition, 184ff.

grenzung von Leben und Therapien und mit der eigenen Endlichkeit umzugehen, weil in der Selbstwahrnehmung der Leib nicht mehr als Teil der eigenen Existenz und der Lebenswelt gelte.[407]

In Anknüpfung an diese Anfragen an die bioethische Entwicklung der vergangenen Jahrzehnte gewinnt die menschliche *Leiblichkeit,* ihre Verletzlichkeit und ihre Endlichkeit im ethischen und therapeutischen Umgang mit Nichteinwilligungsfähigen zu Beginn und am Ende des Lebens eine zentrale Bedeutung. Im Umgang mit menschlichen Embryonen und in der Frage, welche Status- und Wesensbestimmung Embryonen zukommt, ist die Frage nach der Bedeutung der Leiblichkeit letzthin entscheidend, weil in diesem Zusammenhang personale Selbstbestimmung und Autonomie ebenso wenig aktuell vorhanden sind wie zeitlich orientierte Interessen, sondern die konkrete, verletzliche Leiblichkeit die gegenwärtige Form der Existenz darstellt – auch wenn sich die embryonale Leiblichkeit vor allem zu Beginn des Lebens von der Leiblichkeit geborener Menschen phänomenologisch klar unterscheidet.

Wenn McKenny recht hat, dann ist die Selbstdistanzierung von der eigenen Leiblichkeit, ihrer Verletzlichkeit, ihrer Begrenztheit und ihrer Sterblichkeit ein gewichtiger Grund dafür, dass medizinisches Handeln sich seit dem 18. Jahrhundert allmählich signifikant gewandelt hat. Für diese Annahme spricht der utilitaristische Imperativ von John Harris, *Enhancement* sei ethisch geboten und der gegenwärtige Zustand der individuellen Gesundheit sei kontrollierbar, es bestehe sogar eine Pflicht dazu, biomedizinische Forschung so weit wie möglich voranzutreiben, um bei möglichst

---

[407] Mehr als 50 Jahre vor der Publikation der Thesen von McKenny hat schon der englische Literaturwissenschaftler *C. S. Lewis* in einer Vortragsreihe an der Universität Durham (1943), die unter dem Titel „Die Abschaffung des Menschen" (The Abolition of Man) veröffentlich worden ist, auf die Gefahren einer Verdinglichung menschlichen Lebens und einer Selbstdistanzierung von der eigenen Wirklichkeit hingewiesen. (Lewis, Die Abschaffung des Menschen, Einsiedeln [6]2007.) Lewis, a.a.O., 70: „Der Sieg des Menschen über die Natur erweist sich im Augenblick seines scheinbaren Gelingens als Sieg der Natur über den Menschen." Etwas später heißt es (a.a.O., 74): „Der eigentliche Einwand liegt darin, daß der Mensch, der sich selbst als Rohmaterial verstehen will, auch Rohmaterial wird; nicht, wie er sich gutgläubig einbildet, Rohmaterial, das er selber manipulieren wird, sondern das manipuliert wird durch den bloßen Trieb, das heißt durch die bloße Natur in Gestalt seiner ent-menschlichten Konditionierer." Bezogen auf das Problem der In-Vitro-Fertilisation sieht der anglikanische Theologe *Oliver O'Donovan* ähnliche Probleme einer Verdinglichung menschlichen Lebens wie C. S. Lewis. Vgl. O'Donovan, Begotten or Made? Human Procreation or Medical Technique? Oxford 1984: „The practice of producing embryos by IVF with the intention of exploiting their special status for use in research is the clearest possible demonstration that when we start making human beings we necessarily stop loving them; that that which is made rather than begotten becomes something that we have at our disposal, not someone with whom we can engage in brotherly fellowship" (a.a.O., 65).

vielen Menschen Leiden zu vermindern und zu vermeiden. Auch die Möglichkeit, um hochrangiger Forschungsziele willen menschliches Leben einer Abwägung zu unterziehen, wie es der Warnock-Report impliziert, könnte ebenfalls ein Indiz für diese Selbstdistanzierung der eigenen Endlichkeit gegenüber sein.[408]

Mit dem nun folgenden Abschnitt gebe ich einen letzten Aspekt im Zusammenhang mit dem Verständnis von *Menschenwürde* und Embryonenforschung zu bedenken, der in der oben[409] gegebenen Typologisierung das vierte Modell darstellte. Um utilitaristisches Nutzenkalkül von seiner Willkürlichkeit zu befreien, wird der Utilitarismus häufig mit einer Orientierung an Grund- oder Menschenrechten verbunden, weil die Problematik dem Utilitarismus inhäriert, dass das Wohl einiger dem Glück anderer geopfert werden kann. Werden utilitaristische Grundannahmen hingegen mit einer Orientierung an universalen Menschenrechten verbunden, so kann das Problem der Infragestellung von Gerechtigkeitsprinzipien vermieden werden.

Grundrechte werden dabei im internationalen Kontext als Menschenrechte meist mit *Menschenwürde* begründet. Im Zusammenhang mit dieser rechtsbegründenden Funktion von Menschenwürde stellt sich die Frage, ob die Sprache der *Menschenrechte* für die ethische Auseinandersetzung zum Umgang mit menschlichem Leben am Lebensbeginn hilfreich ist oder werden könnte. Immerhin werden die Menschenrechte im Zusammenhang internationaler Völkerrechtsdokumente mit einer universalen, jedem Menschen zukommenden Menschenwürde begründet, und in der englischen Gesetzgebung ist seit dem Jahr 2000 die in ihrer Bedeutung kaum zu überschätzende *Human Rights Act* in Kraft. Ob Menschenrechte auch auf Embryonen zu applizieren sind, beantwortet sich dabei noch nicht von selbst.

Darüber hinaus ist in den letzten beiden Jahrzehnten eine allmähliche internationale Akzentverschiebung von Menschen*rechten* hin zum verstärkten Rekurs auf Menschen*würde* bzw. *human dignity* zu beobachten, was etwa an der Verabschiedung der „Bioethik-Konvention" von Oviedo schon deutlich geworden ist. Hierin manifestiert sich eine offenbar gewachsene Unsicherheit im ethischen und rechtlichen Umgang mit menschlichem Leben an den Grenzen des Lebens vor allem mit Nichteinwilligungsfähigen, bei der mit der Konzeption der Menschenrechte noch nicht befriedigend argumentiert

[408] Dabei ist festzuhalten, dass sich die Distanzierung von der eigenen Endlichkeit und der Begrenzung medizinischer Möglichkeiten nicht auf den britischen Kontext beschränken lässt, sondern nach der Analyse von McKenny im gesamten westlichen Kulturraum zu greifen ist. Allein die britische Gesetzgebung hinsichtlich der Forschung an menschlichen Embryonen zeigt diese Tendenz deutlicher als die deutsche Gesetzgebung, was wiederum historische und ideengeschichtliche Gründe hat.

[409] S. oben, S. 71f.

werden kann, sondern nach einer diese begründenden anthropologischen Bestimmung wie der Menschenwürde gesucht wird. Auch wenn in den bisherigen Überlegungen ein deutlich unterschiedliches Verständnis von *Menschenwürde* im deutschen und englischen Kontext festgestellt wurde, könnte der Zusammenhang von Menschenwürde und Menschenrechten grenzüberschreitend kommunikabel sein – es sei denn, auch in der Frage nach dem Verständnis der Menschenrechte bestehen wiederum tief greifende Unterschiede zwischen britischer und kontinentaler Interpretation. Der folgende Abschnitt hat dies zu klären.

Bereits die neukantianische Konzeption von Alan Gewirth und ihre Rezeption bei Beyleveld/Brownsword hatten ein Begründungsraster für die Formulierung universaler Menschenrechte mit der Menschenwürde bereit gestellt. Darum werden einige Aspekte erneut aufgegriffen, die schon einmal eine Rolle gespielt hatten. Damit schließt sich der Kreis der Darstellung.

III. 5 Forschung an menschlichen Embryonen als Verstoss gegen die Menschenrechte? Zum Verhältnis von Menschenwürde und Menschenrechten

Menschenwürde als menschliche Wesenseigenschaft im Sinne der Mitgifttheorie, aber auch im Anschluss an empirische Kriterien im Sinne der Leistungs- und der Kommunikationstheorie kann als Grundlegung der unveräußerlichen Menschen*rechte* begriffen werden: wer Würde hat, hat darum auch Rechte.[410] In diesem Zusammenhang gehen vor allem internationale Menschenrechtsdokumente von *Menschenwürde* aus und verstehen diese als für die universal geltenden Menschenrechte als rechtsbegründend. Zwei Aspekte indizieren, dass Menschenwürde in diesem Zusammenhang auch im englischsprachigen Kontext eine zentrale Bedeutung hat: zum einen die internationale Menschenrechtsgeschichte nach 1945, die im Kontext der britischen Gesetzgebung zur Verabschiedung der *Human Rights Act* geführt hat, zum anderen der Rekurs auf Menschenwürde in internationalen bioethischen und biopolitischen Texten seit dem letzten Viertel des 20. Jahrhunderts. Insbesondere das im englischen Sprachraum prägende *naturrechtliche* Verständnis von Menschenrechten könnte in diesem Zusammenhang auch für die gegenwärtige bioethische Debatte von Bedeutung sein.

---

[410] Diese grundlegende Zuordnung hatten auch Beyleveld/Brownsword vertreten. S. oben, S. 120ff.

III. 5. 1 Zum Verhältnis von Menschenwürde und Menschenrechten und der zunehmenden Relevanz von Menschenwürde in Bioethik und Biopolitik

Nach den Erfahrungen mit dem nationalsozialistischen Deutschland und mit offensichtlichen Verletzungen der Achtung der Menschenwürde[411] in Menschenversuchen durch deutsche Ärzte oder rassistischen Klassifizierungen von Menschen in erste und zweite Klasse ist auf internationaler Ebene das Bedürfnis entstanden, Menschenrechte zu schützen und die Unantastbarkeit der Menschenwürde zu wahren. Ein maßgeblicher Text ist in diesem Zusammenhang – ebenso wie das deutsche Grundgesetz – die Menschenrechtserklärung der Vereinten Nationen von 1948. Darin wird die Würde des Menschen als rechtsbegründendes Prinzip angenommen[412] und auf internationaler Ebene kommuniziert, was für zahlreiche Einzelstaaten Anlass war, Menschenwürde auch als nationales Verfassungsprinzip aufzunehmen.[413]

Bereits die Charta der Vereinten Nationen (1945) bekennt sich zu den fundamentalen Menschenrechten, zu Würde und Wert der menschlichen Person und zu gleichen Rechten für Frauen und Männer.[414] In der Menschenrechtserklärung von 1948 ist drei Jahre später von der allen Menschen inhärenten (*inherent*) Würde[415] und ihren unveräußerlichen Rechten die

---

[411] Menschenwürde als *Rechts*begriff und Menschenwürde als *ethischer* Begriff müssen gleichwohl voneinander unterschieden werden. Das Bundesverfassungsgericht hat dieser Einsicht Rechnung getragen, indem es in Fragen nach dem Schutz der Menschenwürde immer wieder vorsichtig geurteilt hat.

[412] Neben der Möglichkeit, Menschenwürde als Begründung der Menschenrechte im Sinne eines intrinsischen, unveräußerlichen Wertes anzuerkennen, der den Menschenrechten zugrunde liegt, gibt es die Möglichkeit, Menschenwürde als gesellschaftliches Gut zu verstehen, das den Einzelnen in die Pflicht nimmt, für das Allgemeinwohl und die Wahrung der Menschenrechte zu sorgen. Während das erstgenannte Verständnis von Menschenwürde diese als *empowerment* versteht, kann der zweite Aspekt als *constraint* bezeichnet werden. Vgl. Beyleveld/Brownsword, Human dignity, 46 u.ö.

[413] Schon 1937 ist *dignity* in die irische Verfassung in der Präambel aufgenommen worden. Vgl. http://www.taoiseach.gov.ie/index.asp?docID=243.

[414] So in der Präambel der Charta (1945): „We the peoples of the United Nations determined... to reaffirm faith in fundamental human rights, in the dignity and worth of the human person, in the equal rights of men and women and of nations large and small".

[415] Schon im 18. Jahrhundert wird in den USA von den strukturell der Menschenwürde vergleichbaren „inherent rights" gesprochen. So etwa in der Virginia Declaration of Rights (1776): „That all men are *by nature* equally free and independent and have certain *inherent rights*, of which, when they enter into a state of society, they cannot, by any compact, deprive or divest their posterity". (Hervorhebung S.R.) In den letzten Jahren scheint der Bezug auf *human dignity* in den USA an Bedeutung zu gewinnen. Ein Beispiel liefert ein offizielles Dokument der Bush-Regierung nach dem 11. September 2001 (The National Security Strategy of the United States of America, http://www.whitehouse.gov./nsc/nss.html). „References to 'human rights' can be found sparsely

Rede.[416] Würde und Rechte werden in diesem Dokument[417] als allen Menschen gleichermaßen zukommend angesehen,[418] wobei die Würde die Fundierung und Grundlage der Rechte darstellt und die Menschenrechte wiederum der Garant dafür sind, dass Menschen ein Leben in Würde führen können.[419]

Human Dignity und die Bewahrung ihrer Achtung sind in der Interpretation der UN-Charta[420] und der UN-Menschenrechtsdeklaration darum als

---

strung about the document, but even more apparent were references to 'human dignity', a notion that seems to be replacing the language of human rights in American foreign policy." (David P. Forsythe, Human Rights in International Relations, Cambridge ²2006, 166.) Dieser Befund scheint der Feststellung von Leon Kass zu widersprechen, dass *human dignity* in den USA eine weniger zentrale Bedeutung hat als im kontinentalen Europa (s. oben, S. 131, Anm. 303). Wahrscheinlich hat Kass aber insofern Recht, als die Tradition der Aufklärung, die im deutschen Sprachraum zu einer breiten Rezeption von *Menschenwürde* geführt hat, in den USA weniger rezipiert worden ist. Aufgrund der einflussreichen *naturrechtlichen* Tradition, die in den USA stärker nachgewirkt hat als der Utilitarismus, wird auf *human dignity* aber in Nordamerika deutlich häufiger zurückgegriffen als im britischen Kontext.

[416] Auch die am 7. Dezember 2000 feierlich proklamierte Charta der Grundrechte der Europäischen Union stellt die Würde des Menschen als rechtsbegründendes Prinzip in Artikel 1 fest: „Die Würde des Menschen ist unantastbar. Sie ist zu achten und zu schützen."

[417] „Whereas recognition of the inherent dignity and of the equal and inalienable rights of all members of the human family is the foundation of freedom, justice and peace in the world..., now therefore, The General Assembly proclaims This Universal Declaration of Human Rights as a common standard of achievement for all peoples and all nations, to the end that every individual and every organ of society, keeping this Declaration constantly in mind, shall strive by teaching and education to promote respect for these rights and freedoms".

[418] Beyleveld/Brownsword, Human dignity, 13: „These provisions are firmly tied to an important cluster of preambular ideas: namely, that each and every human being has inherent *dignity*; that it is this *inherent* dignity that grounds (or accounts for) the possession of human rights (it is from such inherent dignity that such rights are *derived*); that these are *inalienable* rights; and that, because all humans have dignity, they hold these rights *equally*."

[419] Vgl. Forsythe, Human rights, 3: „Human rights are widely considered to be those fundamental moral rights of the person that are necessary for a life with human dignity. Human rights are thus means to a greater social end, and it is the legal system that tells us at any given point in time which rights are considered most fundamental in society."

[420] Die sich darin ausdrückende begründende Funktion, die der Menschenwürde im Zusammenhang mit den Menschenrechten zukommt, ist auch für andere UN-Dokumente als fundmental anzusehen. Ein neueres Beispiel bildet die Deklaration der UNESCO zum menschlichen Genom (1997). Vgl. auch R. Andorno, Human Dignity and the UNESCO Declaration on the Human Genome, Ethics, Law and Society Bd. 1, hrsg. von J. Gunning und S. Holm, Aldershot, Ashgate 2005, 73-84.

Zweck formuliert worden, dessen Mittel die *Human Rights* sind.[421] Die Menschenrechte bilden in diesem Verständnis den sanktionsbewehrten Schutzraum für die Menschenwürde, deren Achtung sich wiederum in der Wahrung der Menschenrechte manifestiert. Es gibt in diesem Interpretationszusammenhang kein „Recht auf Würde", weil die Würde den Rechten als ihnen vorlaufendes und sie begründendes Gut vorausgesetzt werden muss. Wohl aber gibt es ein unveräußerliches Recht auf *Wahrung* und *Achtung* der jedem Menschen inhärierenden Würde. In diesem Verständnis sind Menschenwürde und Menschenrechte aufeinander verwiesen und stehen in einem gleichwohl asymmetrischen, aber korrelativen Verhältnis zueinander.

Die im Anschluss an die UN-Deklaration verfasste *Europäische* Menschenrechtskonvention[422] von 1950 gibt den Bürgern der Europäischen Gemeinschaft zum einen ein Mittel an die Hand, gegen Menschenrechtsverletzungen durch ihre Regierung zu klagen und hat zum anderen internationale Geltung im Verhältnis der Staaten untereinander. Die Erklärung der Menschenrechte durch die UNO wird darin so für die einzelnen Mitglieder der europäischen Rechtsgemeinschaft operationalisiert, dass nach ihrem Wortlaut jeder Mensch das Recht darauf hat, ein Leben in den Umständen zu führen, die ihm eine ungestörte Lebensweise ermöglichen.

Die anthropologische Grundlage bildet in der Europäischen Menschenrechtskonvention das auf der natürlichen Gleichheit aller Menschen beruhende natürliche Recht, nach dem kein Individuum mehr Rechte auf Leben, persönlichen Wohlstand und Freiheit hat als ein anderes.[423] In diesem Zusammenhang wird allerdings – auch in der Präambel – anders als in der UN-Menschenrechtsdeklaration *nicht* explizit auf die Tradition der Menschenwürde rekurriert. Die begründende philosophische Tradition der Europäischen Menschenrechtskonvention bildet demgegenüber eher der Liberalismus in der Prägung durch John Locke[424]: es ist wohl von Grundfrei-

[421] „*Human dignity itself, and human rights as a means to that end,* are contested constructs whose meaning must be established in a neverceasing process of moral, political, and legal debate and review." (Forsythe, a.a.O., 253.)

[422] Der Text der Europäischen Menschenrechtskonvention findet sich in deutscher Sprache etwa bei https://www.uni-potsdam.de/u/mrz/coe/emrk/emrk-de.htm.

[423] Vgl. S. Greer, The European Convention on Human Rights. Achievements, Problems and Prospects, Studies in European Law and Policy, Cambridge 2006, 3: „According to this view, the political state and civil society can be conceived as a contract between rational, self-interested, formally equal individuals to secure their fundamental natural rights, with the social and political order this suggests retaining its legitimacy only in so far as these contractual commitments continue to be fulfilled."

[424] Für Locke war um der Sicherstellung der gleichen Rechte aller Individuen in einem Staat willen die konstitutionelle Verankerung dieser Rechte von zentraler Bedeutung. Damit geht bei Locke ein Verständnis des Naturrechts einher, nach dem allen Individuen aufgrund ihrer *Natur* gleiche Freiheitsrechte zukommen. Naturrechtliche Kon-

heiten, nicht aber von „inhärenten Rechten" oder einer „inhärenten Würde" die Rede.

Für die Entwicklung der Menschenrechtsdokumente innerhalb der Vereinten Nationen und der Europäischen Gemeinschaft müssen darum offenbar unterschiedliche begründende Voraussetzungen angenommen werden, die auch unterschiedliche anthropologische Grundannahmen implizieren. Vergleichbare Differenzen bei der Interpretation der universalen Menschenrechte lassen sich aber auch innerhalb des europäischen Kontextes im Ländervergleich von Deutschland und England beobachten: Während mit der Verabschiedung des deutschen Grundgesetzes sowohl die Unantastbarkeit der *Menschenwürde* in Art. 1 I aufgenommen, als auch ein Grundrechtekatalog der Formulierung der Achtung vor der Menschenwürde beigelegt wurde, hat die Positivierung der Menschenrechte und die Übernahme der Europäischen Menschenrechtskonvention in England eine längere Geschichte und setzt andere Akzente. *Menschenwürde* erhält darin anders als in Deutschland, aber ähnlich wie in der Europäischen Deklaration keinen rechtsbegründenden Status.

In Großbritannien ist die der Europäischen Menschenrechtsvereinbarung folgende *Human Rights Act* seit dem Jahr 2000 in Geltung.[425] Sie rezipiert die Europäische Menschenrechtskonvention und appliziert sie auf die britische Gesetzgebung. Ebenso wie in der Europäischen Konvention und anders als in der Erklärung der Menschenrechte durch die Vereinten Nationen werden darin die Menschenrechte aber nicht explizit mit *human dignity* begründet, sondern vielmehr als Freiheitsrechte[426] des Individuums verstanden.[427]

In diesem Zusammenhang spricht das englische Gesetz anders als US-amerikanische Dokumente nicht von „inherent rights", so dass auch nicht von einer *Implikation* einer universalen *Menschenwürde* im britischen Doku-

---

zeptionen sind in der Auseinandersetzung mit Locke von Edmund Burke oder Jeremy Bentham kritisch beurteilt worden. Erst mit der Modifikation des Utilitarismus durch John Stuart Mill, der dem Nutzenkalkül den (naturrechtlichen) Gedanken der gleichen Freiheit aller Individuen hinzufügte, hat sich die Verbindung von Utilitarismus und Naturrecht in England als dominante Theorie für etwa 100 Jahre entwickelt. In der weiteren Entwicklung internationaler Menschenrechtstexte spielt der explizite Naturrechtsgedanke allerdings keine tragende Rolle mehr. Vgl. zum ganzen Greer, a.a.O., 5f.

[425] S. http://www.opsi.gov.uk/acts/acts1998/ukpga_19980042_en_1.

[426] „In this Act 'the Convention rights' mean the rights and fundamental freedoms", die in der Europäischen Menschenrechtskonvention niedergeschrieben sind. (Human Rights Act Art. I 1.)

[427] David Hoffman/John Rowe, Human Rights in the UK. A general Introduction to the Human Rights Act 1998, Harlow 2003, 1: „Human rights are those fundamental freedoms and entitlements that each person possesses by virtue of nothing more than their status as a human being."

ment ausgegangen werden kann. Als ein eigenes Statut ist die *Human Rights Act* gleichwohl zu einem zentralen Teil der britischen Gesetzgebung geworden.[428] Da sie die Menschenrechte jedes Menschen gegenüber dem Parlament rechtlich absichert, hat sie insofern einen immensen Geltungsumfang, als sie sich auch auf bereits verabschiedete Gesetze und noch zukünftige Gesetze in Großbritannien bezieht.[429]

Dabei war in Großbritannien über lange Zeit die Idee maßgeblich, dass kein Gesetz notwendig sei, das die Rechte des Einzelnen explizit festschreibe, sondern der Verweis auf die *Magna Charta* (1215) als Festsetzung der Rechte des Individuums gegenüber dem Staat ausreiche.[430] Auch Mitte des 20. Jahrhunderts, als von England aus vehement die Notwendigkeit eines *internationalen* Dokuments vertreten wurde, in dem die Menschenrechte abgesichert werden – Großbritannien drängte als Vorreiternation auf eine internationale Erklärung der Menschenrechte, die in der UN-Deklaration ihre Gestalt gefunden hat –, erscheint den Briten eine Menschenrechtsgesetzgebung für das eigene Land nicht notwendig. Obwohl Großbritannien als erster Staat am 8. Mai 1951 auch die Europäische Menschenrechtskonventi-

[428] Obwohl sie im Rahmen eines Gesetzes erst im Jahr 2000 in Kraft traten, blicken die Menschenrechte als Freiheitsrechte auf eine lange Tradition in England zurück, die mit der *Magna Charta Libertatum* im Jahr 1215 beginnt, in der den englischen Ständen Freiheitsrechte verbürgt werden. Diese Freiheitsrechte gelten freilich nicht für alle Individuen. Vgl. Hoffman/Rowe, a.a.O., 17: „On the contrary, it was meant to protect the interests of the barons who had revolted against King John and forced him to grant the Charter, and only incidentally benefited everyone else. Nonetheless, the theme of Magna Carta is that of limiting the power of the King, which is an important statement of the idea behind the rule of the law, that is, that there should be government according to the law and not according to the arbitrary wishes of the ruler." Die Begrenzung monarchischer Regierungsgewalt ist auch die Intention der *Bill of Rights* (1688), mit der die Rechte des Parlaments gegenüber der Krone abgesichert, noch nicht aber die individuellen Freiheitsrechte gewährt werden. Die Idee der Gleichheit der Individuen und der daraus resultierenden Freiheit des Einzelnen stammt vornehmlich von John Locke, der die Ansicht vertritt, dass das Eigentum eines Bürgers vom Staat nicht ohne weiteres beschlagnahmt werden kann. Diese Entwicklung hat einen enormen Einfluss auf die Entwicklung der Freiheitsrechte in Nordamerika gehabt, die schließlich 1776 in die amerikanische Unabhängigkeitserklärung mündete, aufgrund derer die amerikanischen Siedler sich unter anderem deswegen von ihrem Mutterland distanziert haben, weil sie sich in ihren Freiheitsrechten nicht geachtet fühlten. Anders als in Großbritannien ist aber in den USA das naturrechtliche Denken einflussreich geblieben, während im englischen Mutterland ein stärkerer Säkularisierungsschub eingesetzt hat.

[429] Hoffman/Rowe, a.a.O., 2: „So for the first time in the United Kingdom there is one standard for the protection of rights by which all laws are considered."

[430] Nach diesem Verständnis sichert das englische *Common Law* die Rechte des Einzelnen anderen Einzelnen und der Gesamtgemeinschaft gegenüber insofern ab, als dieser tun darf, was nicht verboten ist, solange er die Rechte des Anderen nicht antastet.

on ratifiziert hat,[431] hat man lange Zeit keine Notwendigkeit gesehen, einen Schutz der Menschenrechte in der britischen Gesetzgebung zu verankern, weil man die Menschenrechte im eigenen Land durch das *Common Law* und die Geschichte der Freiheitsrechte als ausreichend geschützt ansah.[432]

Erst in den 80er und 90er Jahren des 20. Jahrhunderts änderte sich das Bewusstsein der britischen Öffentlichkeit und Politik dahingehend, dass die Menschenrechte Bestandteil der britischen Gesetzgebung und ein Regulativ für bereits verabschiedete und noch zu verabschiedende Gesetze werden sollten. Der Grund für diesen Wandel lag vor allem darin, dass zunehmend Fälle aufgetreten waren, in denen britische Bürger an den Europäischen Gerichtshof für Menschenrechte appellierten, weil sie ihre Rechte als durch ihre Regierung eingeschränkt empfanden.[433] Eine Gesetzgebung, die Menschenrechtsfälle auch in Großbritannien zu verhandeln erlaubte, würde Kosten sparen und Verzögerungen vermeiden. Nach dem Wahlsieg der Labour Party unter Tony Blair im Jahr 1997 hat die damalige neue Regierung in einem *White Paper* eine Aufnahme der Menschenrechtskonvention in die britische Gesetzgebung zunächst in Parlamentsdebatten eingebracht, bis 1998 die *Human Rights Act* beschlossen wurde und im Jahr 2000 in Kraft trat.

Die *Human Rights Act* spielt als Gesetz innerhalb der britischen Gesetzgebung seitdem eine Sonderrolle, weil sie es erlaubt, dass alle übrigen Gesetze an ihr gemessen werden und durch ihren Maßstab Korrektur finden.[434] Das *Common Law* wird auf diese Weise präzisiert, indem ausdrücklich die Rechte des Einzelnen gegenüber der Gemeinschaft und dem Staat rechtlich geschützt werden, was gegenüber der bisherigen Gesetzgebung einen Perspektiven-

---

431 Vgl. Hoffman/Rowe, a.a.O., 26.

432 Hoffman/Rowe, a.a.O., 27: „Indeed, the British involvement in the drafting of the Convention supported the government´s view that the European Convention itself reflected the standards of protection provided by the tradition of English common law."

433 Die Europäische Menschenrechts-Deklaration ist zwar von der Ratifizierung an als auch für Großbritannien bindend verstanden worden. Ähnlich wie andere internationale Verträge regelte die Europäische Konvention aber das Verhältnis von Großbritannien zu anderen *Staaten*, nicht notwendigerweise die Menschenrechte *innerhalb* von Großbritannien selbst. Daher konnte ein solcher internationaler Vertrag auch nicht zur Kritik der nationalen Gesetzgebung verwendet werden. „However, just because the United Kingdom has signed up to a treaty, this does not mean that the treaty can be used to challenge the law which is laid down in an Act of Parliament. Under our constitutional law, treaties entered into with other countries have no effect in our national law unless and until they are passed as a law by Parliament." (Hoffman/Rowe, a.a.O., 43.)

434 Verbunden mit der Tatsache, dass es in Großbritannien keinen zusammenhängenden Verfassungstext gibt, sondern nur einzelne Verfassungsdokumente, die gleichwohl einen zentralen Rang für die Gesetzgebung und das öffentliche Bewusstsein innehaben, kommt der *Human Rights Act* aufgrund ihrer interpretierenden Funktion den übrigen Rechten gegenüber ein verfassungsrechtlicher Rang zu.

wechsel zugunsten des Einzelnen mit sich bringt:[435] Menschenrechte sind im Verständnis der *Human Rights Act* Rechte gegenüber kollektiven Interessen. Sie beziehen sich als fundamentale Rechte auf jeden Menschen zu allen Zeiten, sind darum unabhängig von kulturellen Voraussetzungen und situativen Umständen[436] und erfordern einen gleich bleibend großen Respekt für jedes menschliche Mitglied der Gesellschaft.[437]

Eine legitime *Begrenzung* der Menschenrechte ergibt sich nach britischem Verständnis allerdings dann, wenn individuelle Rechte mit Rechten einer größeren Gruppe von Individuen konfligieren, was etwa im Fall der nationalen Sicherheit greift. Allerdings ist das kollektive Interesse noch kein Grund in sich selbst und muss sich in jeder Situation rechtfertigen, in der mit ihm gegenüber den Rechten des Individuums argumentiert wird.[438] „An interference with rights *always* needs to be justified."[439]

Auch wenn die *Human Rights Act* in Großbritannien als ein Text von hoher Relevanz angesehen werden muss, ist darin eine Fundierung der Menschenrechte in einer Präambel mit anthropologischer Grundaussage nicht vorgesehen. Anders als in der Deklaration der Menschenrechte durch die UN und im deutschen Grundgesetz wird keine Aussage über eine die Menschenrechte begründende menschliche Wesenseigenschaft getroffen. Da es sich bei der *Human Rights Act* um ein rechtliches Dokument handelt, das keine grundlegenden anthropologischen Aussagen macht und sich auf die Gemeinschaft von *geborenen* Menschen und deren Freiheitsrechte bezieht, kann sie *per se* keine Aussagen zum ungeborenen Leben machen; *de jure* sind darum der Schwangerschaftsabbruch oder die verbrauchende Embryonenforschung mit der *Human Rights Act* ebenso wie mit der Europäischen Konvention für

[435] Vgl. Hoffman/Rowe, a.a.O., 2: „Thus, our law will inevitably be more focused on the perspective of individual rights than it has been previously – and this has the potential to lead to a major shift in how we see each other as citizens of our country."

[436] In diesem Zusammenhang kann gefragt werden, ob die Forschung an Embryonen gegen die *Human Rights Act* verstößt, oder ob die Freiheit und der Nutzen der Forschung höher zu werten sind. Da für die *Human Fertilisation and Embryology Act* nach den Vorgaben des Warnock-Reports menschliche Embryonen zwar einen besonderen Status haben, aber nicht als Menschen absolut zu schützen sind, greift die *Human Rights Act* in diesem Fall nicht, weil sie ausschließlich auf (geborene) Menschen bezogen ist.

[437] Hoffman/Rowe, a.a.O., 9: „because all human beings are equal and therefore have equal human rights, there is no legitimate basis for distinguishing between persons in respect of their basic entitlements."

[438] Vgl. Hoffman/Rowe, a.a.O., 10: „But this collective interest has to justify itself in the face of any other individual right it wishes to over-rule. The very need for this justification reminds us that we should not ignore the interests of people whose rights conflict with a course of action, even though we may think that this course of action is in the best interests of the whole community."

[439] Hoffman/Rowe, a.a.O., 10.

Menschenrechte kompatibel,[440] weil das Recht auf Leben, das dem Fötus zukommt, nicht ohne das Lebensrecht der Mutter und der Patienten, denen eine Forschung potentiell nützt, betrachtet werden kann.[441] Die gesetzlich geschützten Menschenrechte beziehen sich nach dem Verständnis der meisten britischen Rechtsausleger darum auf *geborene* Menschen.

Auch in dieser Hinsicht ist die Entwicklung in England mit der deutschen Entwicklung nur wenig vergleichbar. Ähnlich wie in Großbritannien hat sich in Deutschland nach 1945 bald das Bewusstsein durchgesetzt, dass zum Schutz vor nochmaligen Missachtungen der Menschenrechte ein gesetzliches Dokument notwendig sei, um Menschenrechte und die Achtung der Menschenwürde zu schützen. Anders als in Großbritannien hat sich aber in Deutschland nach Kriegsende die Gesetzgebung mit der Verabschiedung des deutschen Grundgesetzes (1949) so entwickelt, dass zum einen ein nationales Verfassungsdokument zur Wahrung der Menschenrechte, die im nationalen Kontext als „Grundrechte" bezeichnet werden, geschaffen wurde und diese Wahrung der Menschenrechte zum anderen auf eine anthropologische Grundlegung in Art. 1 I zurückverweist: „Die Würde des Menschen ist unantastbar." Durch die „Ewigkeitsklausel" (Art. 79 III) wird die so konstituierte Achtung der Menschenwürde vor der Aufhebung durch die gesetzgebende Gewalt geschützt. Während in Großbritannien der Fokus der verfassungsrechtlichen Texte auf der Wahrung der *Menschenrechte* als der individuellen *Freiheitsrechte* liegt, deren höchstes Recht das Recht auf Leben ist, macht das deutsche Grundgesetz in Art. 1 I eine explizite (allerdings nicht definierte) Aussage zur *Wesenseigenschaft* des Menschen, aufgrund derer diesem Grundrechte zukommen. Die unterschiedliche ideengeschichtliche Tradition beider Länder hat auch in diesem Zusammenhang ganz offenbar grundlegend gewirkt.

Die Begründung der Grundrechte durch die Feststellung einer anthropologischen Wesenseigenschaft hat innerhalb der deutschen Gesetzgebung dazu geführt, dass zumindest die Frage aufkommen konnte, ob Menschenwürde und darauf aufbauend Grundrechte auch für *ungeborene* Menschen

---

[440] In der Verabschiedung der *Human Fertilisation and Embryology Act* wird keine Missachtung der Menschenrechte gesehen, auch wenn als ein möglicher Einwand gegen die Erzeugung von cytoplasmischen Hybrid-Embryonen ein Verstoß gegen die Menschenrechte genannt wird, wie das oben (S. 55, Anm. 106) bereits aufgenommene Zitat zeigt: House of Commons, Science and Technology Committee, Government proposals for the regulation of hybrid and chimera embryos 2007, 24: „In very broad terms, the main arguments for and against the creation of human and human-animal embryos can be divided into three categories: arguments which take into account potential violation of human rights; arguments which centre on the value of the research; and arguments which consider the impact of such research on human dignity." Da die entstehenden Embryonen aber keine *Menschen* seien, bestehe auch kein Verstoß gegen die *Menschenrechte*.

[441] Vgl. Hoffman/Rowe, a.a.O., 103.

– Nasciturі – angenommen werden müssten. Auch wenn innerhalb der deutschen Debatte diese Frage für menschliches Leben in den ersten 14 Tagen keinesfalls als konsensual entschieden angesehen werden kann, so wird sie doch aufgrund des verfassungsmäßigen Rekurses auf die Menschenwürde allererst erlaubt, weil das Grundgesetz weder die Extension noch die inhaltliche Bedeutung von Menschenwürde und Grundrechten explizit bestimmt und auch eine Applikation auf Ungeborene mit dem Grundgesetz konform zu gehen scheint.

Weil das Grundgesetz eine Aussage zur *Wesenseigenschaft* des Menschen macht, wird mit dem Rekurs auf Art. 1 I in der deutschen Gesetzgebung etwa durch das Stammzellgesetz begründet, dass verbrauchende Embryonenforschung mit der Achtung der Menschenwürde nicht zu vereinbaren ist: das Stammzellgesetz bezieht sich explizit auf die staatliche Verpflichtung zum Schutz der Menschenwürde, die eine Tötung von Embryonen zu Forschungszwecken ausschließt.[442]

Während in der britischen Rechtsentwicklung mit der Verabschiedung der *Human Rights Act* ein Gesetzestext in Kraft getreten ist, der die individuellen Menschenrechte als Freiheitsrechte schützt, macht das deutsche Grundgesetz – ähnlich wie die Menschenrechtsdeklaration der Vereinten Nationen – eine die Menschen- bzw. Grundrechte begründende Aussage zum *Wesen* des Menschen, aus der auch im weiteren Verlauf hinsichtlich des Embryonenschutzes sowohl in der Gesetzgebung als auch in der Rechtsprechung Konsequenzen gezogen worden sind. Auch in diesem Zusammenhang zeigt sich damit die im Ländervergleich bereits hinreichend deutlich gewordene Differenz von deut-

[442] 1975 hat das Bundesverfassungsgericht im Zusammenhang mit der Diskussion über den Schwangerschaftsabbruch nach §218 StGB geurteilt, dass „Leben im Sinne der geschichtlichen Existenz eines menschlichen Individuums... nach gesicherter biologisch-physiologischer Erkenntnis *jedenfalls vom 14. Tage nach der Empfängnis (Nidation, Individuation) an* [besteht]... Der damit begonnene Entwicklungsprozeß ist ein kontinuierlicher Vorgang, der keine scharfen Einschnitte aufweist und eine genaue Abgrenzung der verschiedenen Entwicklungsstufen des menschlichen Lebens nicht zuläßt. Er ist auch nicht mit der Geburt beendet; die für die menschliche Persönlichkeit spezifischen Bewußtseinsphänomene z.B. treten erst längere Zeit nach der Geburt auf. Deshalb kann der Schutz des Art. 2 Abs. 2 Satz 1 GG weder auf den ‚fertigen' Menschen nach der Geburt noch auf den selbständig lebensfähigen Nasciturus beschränkt werden. Das Recht auf Leben wird jedem gewährleistet, der ‚lebt'; zwischen einzelnen Abschnitten des sich entwickelnden Lebens vor der Geburt oder zwischen ungeborenem und geborenem Leben kann hier kein Unterschied gemacht werden. ‚Jeder' im Sinne des Art. 2 Abs. 2 Satz 1 GG ist ‚jeder Lebende', anders ausgedrückt: jedes Leben besitzende menschliche Individuum; ‚jeder' ist daher auch das noch ungeborene menschliche Wesen." (Abs. 133.) „*Wo menschliches Leben existiert, kommt ihm Menschenwürde zu*; es ist nicht entscheidend, ob der Träger sich dieser Würde bewußt ist und sie selbst zu wahren weiß. Die von Anfang an im menschlichen Sein angelegten potentiellen Fähigkeiten genügen, um die Menschenwürde zu begründen." (Abs. 148.) (BVerfGE 39, alle Hervorhebungen sind von mir.)

scher und englischsprachiger Tradition. Die Menschenrechtstradition bietet also insofern keine Hilfe hinsichtlich einer ethischen Beurteilung der Forschung an menschlichen Embryonen, als diese im britischen Zusammenhang auf Nascituri nicht applizierbar ist.

Neben der Relevanz, die dem Begriff *human dignity* innerhalb internationaler und nationaler *Menschenrechtsdokumente* zukommt, liegt seine Bedeutung seit dem letzten Drittel oder Viertel des 20. Jahrhunderts aber zunehmend im Bereich der *Bioethik* und *Biopolitik*. Die sich immens weiterentwickelnde biomedizinische Forschung, das weitgehende Wissen um das menschliche Genom und die Entwicklung der Forschung an humanen embryonalen Stammzellen haben in den letzten Jahren zunehmend die Frage aufkommen lassen, in welchem Verhältnis die biomedizinische Forschung, die nationale und internationale Rechtsprechung und eine anthropologische Konzeption wie die Menschenwürde stehen.[443] Auch die bereits erwähnte Europäische Bioethikkonvention[444] argumentiert in diesem Zusammenhang explizit mit *Menschenwürde*.[445] Dass *Menschenwürde*, die seit der Mitte des 20. Jahrhunderts den politisch-rechtlichen Hintergrund und das Fundament der *Menschenrechte* bildet, im Zusammenhang mit der Entwicklung der Biomedizin in den Vordergrund getreten ist, ist auffallend[446] und zeigt eine zunehmende Besorgnis angesichts des biomedizinischen Fortschritts und einen ethischen Orientierungsbedarf sowohl auf nationaler als auch auf internationaler Ebene.

Offenbar verbindet sich innerhalb der Bioethik mit dem Gebrauch des Terms „Menschenwürde" die Einsicht, dass in Fragen hinsichtlich der Forschung an ungeborenen menschlichen Wesen noch nicht konsistent mit Menschenrechten argumentiert werden kann, zumal die Tradition der Menschenrechte in sich nicht einheitlich ist, wie es der Vergleich von britischer und deutscher Menschenrechtsgesetzgebung zeigt, sondern es einer anthropolo-

---

[443] Vgl. Beyleveld/Brownsword, Human dignity, 9. „What is surprising, perhaps, is that the bioscientific revolution has provoked a parallel demand for human dignity to be respected."

[444] Ein ähnliches Dokument ist im selben Jahr von der UNESCO verabschiedet worden: „Universal Declaration on the Human Genome and Human Rights".

[445] So schon im Titel: „Convention for the Protection of Human Rights and Dignity of the Human Being with Regard to the Application of Biology and Medicine". Auch in Art. 1 („Parties to this Convention shall protect the dignity and identity of all human beings and guarantee everyone, without discrimination, respect for their integrity and other rights and fundamental freedoms with regard to the application of biology and medicine").

[446] Beyleveld/Brownsword, a.a.O., 10: „Our puzzle, then, is to understand what the idea of human dignity – which tends to lie in the background of (secularized) human rights instruments *in general* – is now being thrust into the foreground of instruments dealing *specifically with biomedicine*."

gischen Grundlegung bedarf, um zu klären, ob diese Forschung gegen den Grundzug einer menschlichen Wesenseigenschaft verstößt.

Darum ist die weit verbreitete Argumentation mit *Menschenwürde* im ausgehenden 20. und beginnenden 21. Jahrhundert nicht ausschließlich als inflationär anzusehen, insofern sich hierin ein ethisch-anthropologischer Orientierungsbedarf manifestiert,[447] aufgrund dessen sich die Mitte des 20. Jahrhunderts noch verbreitete Konzentration auf die *Menschenrechte* in den letzten Jahrzehnten zu einer Akzentuierung der *Menschenwürde* vor allem in Hinblick auf die Probleme am Lebensbeginn und Lebensende verschoben hat.[448] Diese Wendung allerdings vollzieht sich in Großbritannien, wie konzediert werden muss, allenfalls zögerlich. In ihr liegt aber unter Umständen die Möglichkeit, über den international im Zusammenhang der Bioethik an Bedeutung gewinnenden Begriff *human dignity* zu einer Neubewertung seiner Relevanz für die englische Debatte im Umgang mit Nichteinwilligungsfähigen zu gelangen.

III. 5. 2 Menschenwürde als universales Rechtsgut? Naturrechtliche Aufbrüche

Die Beobachtung einer zunehmenden Relevanz des Menschenwürde-Begriffs im Kontext einer zunehmenden Unsicherheit und eines gesteigerten

---

[447] Auch eine vermehrte Verwendung von „Menschenwürde“ löst nicht das Problem, dass *Menschenwürde* ein inhaltlich mehrdeutiger Begriff ist. Das Problem einer Begründung der Menschenrechte mit der nicht näher definierten Menschenwürde ist von Beyleveld/Brownsword so umschrieben worden: „it is that we are right to think of human dignity as empowerment only so long as we think it right to so think.“ (Beyleveld/ Brownsword, a.a.O., 25.) Dem Begriff *Menschenwürde* eignet *per se* eine Zirkularität, weil er nicht aus sich selbst heraus verständlich ist, sondern unterschiedliche Auslegungs- und Verständnistraditionen vereint.

[448] Auch die von der UNO verabschiedete „International convention against the reproductive cloning of human beings“ (2005), in der sich die Vereinten Nationen gegen das reproduktive Klonen aussprechen, begründet die Stellungnahme gegen reproduktives Klonen mit dem Schutz der Menschenwürde und des menschlichen Lebens. Bei der Konvention unter (b): „Member States are called upon to prohibit all forms of human cloning inasmuch as they are incompatible with human dignity and the protection of human life.“ Während Deutschland für die Konvention als Ganze gestimmt hat, hat Großbritannien die Konvention als Ganze abgelehnt. Die britische *Human Reproductive Cloning Act* (2001) verbietet ausdrücklich reproduktives Klonen in England, argumentiert aber nicht mit einer menschlichen Wesenseigenschaft. Im November 2007 hat das United Nations University Institute for Advanced Studies unter Rückbezug auf *Menschenwürde* eine generelle Einschränkung des Klonens von menschlichen Embryonen empfohlen mit dem Ziel, reproduktives Klonen grundsätzlich auszuschließen: „Is Human Reproductive Cloning Inevitable: Future Options for UN Governance“. Darin wird die Dringlichkeit einer weltweit einheitlichen Gesetzgebung zum Klonen angemahnt und das Menschenwürdeprinzip als Grundprinzip innerhalb bioethischer Urteilsbildung festgehalten. Im Bericht auf den Seiten 9ff.

ethischen Orientierungsbedarfs, dem mit dem Rekurs auf ein als universalen Wert verstandenes Anthropologumenon offenbar Rechnung getragen werden soll, koinzidiert mit der Tatsache, dass die Idee eines universalen, für alle Zeiten und alle Orte geltenden Rechtsfundaments für die Entwicklung der Menschenrechte prägend gewesen ist, die sich auch schon vor dem Aufkommen der neuzeitlichen Menschenrechte – gleichwohl in vielfältigen Ausformungen – als *lex naturalis*[449] darstellt und auf die das häufig zitierte Diktum von Ernst-Wolfgang Böckenförde anspielt,[450] dass auch die moderne freiheitliche Demokratie auf Wurzeln beruhe, die sie selbst nicht schaffen könne: Menschenwürde und Menschenrechte haben eine immense Affinität zum *Naturrecht*.

Im englischen Sprachraum[451] wird gegenwärtig von der Rechtsphilosophie und der Theologie nach der Möglichkeit einer Neufassung des traditionellen Naturrechts gesucht.[452] Neben der klassischen, auch gegenwärtig noch inner-

[449] Vertreter von naturrechtlichen Konzeptionen sind neben Aristoteles und Thomas von Aquin in Antike und Mittelalter vor allem Samuel Pufendorf und Hugo Grotius in der frühen Neuzeit, aber auch Thomas Hobbes und John Locke innerhalb der englischen Philosophie. Maßgeblich geprägt wurde das Naturrecht aber schon innerhalb der Stoa vor allem bei Cicero, der auch explizit von „Menschenwürde" spricht (*dignitas humana*): Cicero, De officiis I, 106f. (deutsch: Vom rechten Handeln, hrsg. und übersetzt von Karl Büchner, lateinisch-deutsche Ausgabe, München/Zürich [4]1994.)

[450] „Der freiheitliche, säkularisierte Staat lebt von Voraussetzungen, die er selbst nicht garantieren kann. Das ist das große Wagnis, das er, um der Freiheit willen, eingegangen ist. Als freiheitlicher Staat kann er einerseits nur bestehen, wenn sich die Freiheit, die er seinen Bürgern gewährt, von innen her, aus der moralischen Substanz des einzelnen und der Homogenität der Gesellschaft, reguliert. Anderseits kann er diese inneren Regulierungskräfte nicht von sich aus, das heißt, mit den Mitteln des Rechtszwanges und autoritativen Gebots zu garantieren versuchen, ohne seine Freiheitlichkeit aufzugeben und - auf säkularisierter Ebene - in jenen Totalitätsanspruch zurückzufallen, aus dem er in den konfessionellen Bürgerkriegen herausgeführt hat." (Staat, Gesellschaft, Freiheit. Studien zur Staatstheorie und zum Verfassungsrecht, Frankfurt/Main 1976, S. 60)

[451] Vgl. für die deutschsprachige Rechtsphilosophie und Ethik auch W. Härle/B. Vogel (Hrsg.), „Vom Rechte, das mit uns geboren ist". Aktuelle Probleme des Naturrechts, Freiburg/Breisgau 2007; W. Härle/B. Vogel (Hrsg.), Begründung von Menschenwürde und Menschenrechten, Freiburg/Breisgau 2008; F. Lohmann, Zwischen Naturrecht und Partikularismus. Grundlegung christlicher Ethik mit Blick auf die Debatte um eine universale Begründbarkeit der Menschenrechte, TBT 116, Berlin/New York 2002; E. Schockenhoff, Naturrecht und Menschenwürde. Universale Ethik in einer geschichtlichen Welt, Ostfildern 1996.

[452] Vgl. etwa Jean Porter, Natural and Divine Law. Reclaiming the Tradition for Christian Ethics, Ottawa 1999; Dies., Nature as Reason. A Thomistic Theory of the Natural Law, Grand Rapids 2005. Während J. Porter die katholische Tradition vertritt, vgl. für die reformierte Tradition S. J. Grabill, Rediscovering the Natural Law in Reformed Theological Ethics, Grand Rapids 2006. Für die im englischen Sprachraum vertretene „New Natural

halb der katholischen Theologie[453] vertretenen Konzeption des Naturrechts haben sich in den letzten Jahrzehnten des 20. Jahrhunderts weitere Positionen in diesem Zusammenhang entwickelt, die nicht vorrangig auf die Theologie rekurrieren. Das gesteigerte Interesse am Naturrecht indiziert, dass die Frage danach, was dem *Wesen* bzw. der *Natur* des Menschen angemessen ist und positiven Rechtsbestimmungen vorausgehen soll, im 21. Jahrhundert angesichts neuer Herausforderungen auch durch den biotechnologischen Fortschritt im englischen Sprachraum an Bedeutung gewonnen hat.

Im Zusammenhang mit diesem gesteigerten Interesse am „Naturrecht" hat sich die konzeptionelle Bandbreite stark aufgefächert:[454] Während die klassische Theorie des Naturrechts mit der Frage danach, was der geschöpflichen *Natur* gemäß ist, der katholischen Moralphilosophie zuzuordnen ist,[455] sind im englischen Sprachraum in den vergangenen Jahrzehnten Konzeptio-

---

Law Theory" vgl. J. Finnis, Natural law and natural rights, Oxford 1980; G. Grisez, The Way of the Lord Jesus, 3 Bände, Chicago 1983ff.; N. Biggar/R. Black (Hrsg.), The Revival of Natural Law. Philosophical, theological and ethical responses to the Finnis-Grisez School, Aldershot 2002. Zur Kritik am Naturrecht vgl. schon S. Hauerwas, The peaceable Kingdom. A Primer in Christian Ethics, Notre Dame/ London 1983.

[453] Mitte des 20. Jahrhunderts war es vor allem die katholische Theologie, die in ethischen Fragen naturrechtlich argumentierte. Vgl. auch noch den Sammelband C. E. Curran / R. McCormick (Hrsg.), Natural law and theology, New York 1991. Nach dem Zweiten Vatikanischen Konzil wird dezidiert nach einer Universalisierbarkeit des Naturrechts und seinen spezifischen christlichen Implikationen für die Ethik gesucht. Einer der einflussreichsten englischsprachigen katholischen Moraltheologen der zweiten Hälfte des 20. Jahrhunderts ist der in bioethischen Fragen ausdrücklich eine thomistische Position des Naturrechts vertretende amerikanische Theologe Richard McCormick, vgl. McCormick, How brave a new world. Dilemmas in Bioethics, Washington 1981.

[454] Dabei ist der Begriff „Naturrecht" vor allem deswegen uneindeutig, weil er zu behaupten scheint, dass es eine klare Definition dessen gibt, was „Natur" meint. Auch bei einem Verweis auf ein Naturrecht, das dem positiven Recht vorhergeht und das etwa Menschenwürde und Menschenrechte in sich enthält, die universal und kulturell unabhängig für alle Menschen und alle Kulturen gelten und insofern als rechtsbegründend angesehen werden müssten, löst sich das Problem einer Offenheit des Naturbegriffs nicht, sondern verschiebt sich. Der Begriff *Natur* leitet sich etymologisch von lat. *nasci* (geboren werden) ab, wobei aber die Bedeutung dieses *Ursprungs*, der mit *nasci* ausgesagt wird, umstritten ist. Vgl. Schockenhoff, Naturrecht, 31: „Sowohl die ökumenischen als auch die innerkatholischen Differenzen über das Naturrecht erklären sich letztlich aus der Schwierigkeit, die Frage nach der Natur des Menschen im Fadenkreuz anderer theologischer Grundfragen richtig zu verorten."

[455] In der sich unabhängig von der Theologie entwickelnden *Rechts*philosophie ist das Naturrecht vor allem mit den Freiheitsrechten konnotiert worden. Naturrecht wird von positivem Recht als eine überpositive Norm unterschieden, die dem positiven Recht vorausgeht. Während die *ethische* Theorie des Naturrechts meist nicht zwischen Recht und Moral unterscheidet, zieht die *rechtstheoretische* Konzeption des Naturrechts diese Differenz ein.

nen entstanden, die in der Ausrichtung auf die Begründung allgemeiner *Menschenrechte* eher in die Rechtsphilosophie gehören. Hier ist seit Beginn der 80er Jahre eine „New Natural Law Theory" entwickelt worden, die zwar auf die Tradition des Naturrechts in der Philosophie von Thomas von Aquin und Hugo Grotius aufbaut, aber – meist in der Rezeption des Kantianismus – im Gegenüber zu römisch-katholischen Konzeptionen eigene Akzente setzt.

Gegen die Grundannahme eines ethischen Relativismus, nach der ethische Überzeugungen aufgrund unterschiedlicher kultureller Voraussetzungen nicht allgemein kommunikabel sind, stellt John Finnis, neben Germain Grisez einer der Hauptvertreter der „New Natural Law Theory", fest, dass es in allen Gesellschaften universale Kontinuen gebe, nach denen übereinstimmend bestimmte Verhaltensweisen erwünscht oder verboten seien. Alle Gesellschaften betrachteten etwa menschliches Leben als einen Wert, erlaubten das Töten eines anderen Menschen nur unter bestimmten genau definierten Umständen, sähen Selbstschutz als ein legitimes Motiv für Handlungen an und verböten Inzest.[456] In dieser Universalität von Werten unterscheiden sich nach Annahme von Finnis zwar die Prioritäten, die Menschen einzelnen Werten beilegen, je nach Kultur und Geschichte, Neigungen und Bedürfnissen,[457] ein gesellschaftlich geltendes Grundgerüst von Werten könne aber ausgemacht werden. In ihrer unterschiedlichen Ausprägung sei darum jedem Wert Respekt zu erweisen:[458] Vernünftige Moralität achtet die Werte anderer und partizipiert an der Gemeinschaft derer, die Werte haben.

Wenn es aber für das Individuum Werte gibt, die von allen Mitgliedern der Gemeinschaft geachtet werden, so gibt es nach Ansicht von Finnis auch für die Gemeinschaft als Ganze ein gemeinsames Gut (*common good*), das von allen Mitgliedern zu achten ist, auf dem die Gesetzgebung dieser Gemeinschaft aufbaut[459] und in dem sich die praktische universale Vernunft ausdrückt. Die

---

[456] Finnis, Natural law and natural rights, 83.

[457] Finnis, a.a.O., 84: „The universality of a few basic values in a vast diversity of realizations emphasizes *both* the connection between a basic human urge / drive / inclination / tendency and the corresponding basic form of human good, *and* at the same time the great difference between following an urge and intellegently pursuing a particular realization of a form of human good that is never completely realized and exhausted by any one action, or lifetime, or institution, or culture (nor by any finite number of them)".

[458] Finnis, a.a.O., 120: „Reason requires that every basic value be at least respected in each and every action."

[459] Finnis, a.a.O., 155: „Yet there is a common good of the political community, and it is definite enough to exclude a considerable number of types of political arrangement, laws, etc... For there is a 'common good' for human beings, inasmuch as life, knowledge, play, aesthetic experience, friendship, religion, and freedom in practical reasonableness are good for any and every person. And each of these human values is itself a 'common good' inasmuch as it can be participated in by an inexhaustible number of persons in an inexhaustible variety of ways or on an inexhaustable variety of occasions."

Befolgung der praktischen Vernunft in der Achtung allgemeiner Werte und des gemeinsamen moralischen Guts ist darum zugleich die Gewährleistung von natürlichen Rechten für alle Mitglieder der Gemeinschaft. Mit dieser Argumentation, die zum einen auf praktische Vernunft zurückgreift und zum anderen eine Universalisierung von Werten für zentral hält, rezipiert Finnis Grundzüge kantischer Ethik und bietet zugleich eine Begründungsstrategie für die universalen Menschenrechte. Denn schon das Faktum, *dass* eine Gesellschaft sich universale Menschenrechte als rechtliche Grundlage des Zusammenlebens gebe, zeige, dass es eine gesellschaftlich akzeptierte Form des moralischen Guts gebe, das individuell zwar unterschiedlich verstanden werde, grundsätzlich aber für die Gesellschaft als Ganze tragfähig sei.[460]

Mit seiner Begründung von Menschenrechten auf dem Weg der Argumentation über das in einer Gesellschaft geltende gemeinsame Gut intendiert Finnis, die Allgemeingültigkeit von Rechten innerhalb eines universal geltenden *Naturrechts* zu begründen. Der Argumentationsweg beginnt beim Individuum, das bestimmte Bedürfnisse hat, damit sein Wohlergehen gesichert ist, und diese Bedürfnisse auch bei anderen respektiert. In dieser Hinsicht erinnert die Konzeption der *New Natural Law Theory* an die Begründung von Menschenrechten bei Alan Gewirth und die von Beyleveld/Brownsword in deren Anschluss gegebene Begründung der Menschenwürde von handelnden Subjekten her, die für ihre Handlungen auf bestimmte Voraussetzungen angewiesen sind.

Die Argumentation von Finnis läuft zwar nicht über den Handlungsbegriff, sondern zum einen über die Konzeption des „common good", zum anderen über den Begriff der „praktischen Vernunft". Gewirth und Finnis weisen insofern aber strukturelle Argumentationsparallelen auf, als beide im Anschluss an Kant von einer Universalisierbarkeit von ethischen Imperativen ausgehen.[461]

---

[460] Finnis stellt fest, „that it is always unreasonable to choose directly against any basic value, whether in oneself or in one's fellow human beings. And the basic values are not mere abstractions; they are aspects of the real well-being of flesh-and-blood-individuals." (Finnis, a.a.O., 225.) Zu den absoluten, universalen Rechten gehören für Finnis das Recht auf Leben und das Recht, dass das eigene Leben nicht als Mittel zu einem anderen Zweck genommen wird. Diese Rechte bei sich selbst zu erkennen und anderen zuzuerkennen, konsolidiert die Konzeption von absoluten Menschenrechten, die in diesem Zusammenhang keine abstrakte Forderung bilden und auch nicht zukünftige Konsequenzen des Handelns in den Blick nehmen. Vielmehr richtet sich diese Konzeption an die konkreten Bedürfnisse des Individuums, die für eine naturrechtliche Konzeption universalisiert werden.

[461] Dabei spielt der Begriff der „Gerechtigkeit" eine zentrale Rolle, wonach Menschen das bekommen und ihnen diejenigen Lebensumstände als Rechte zustehen müssen, in denen es ihnen wohl ergeht, sie diese Umstände und Rahmenbedingungen aber auch denjenigen zugestehen müssen, die sie nötig haben. Finnis rezipiert dabei sowohl eine Konzeption der distributiven als auch der kommutativen Gerechtigkeit. Distributive

Damit schließt sich am Ende dieses Kapitels der mit der englischsprachigen Kant-Auslegung begonnene Kreis. Vom Handlungsbegriff und dem Begriff eines allgemeinen moralischen Konsenses her ist eine Begründung von Menschenrechten auch im Sinne eines überpositiven Naturrechts im englischen Sprachraum und auf dem Hintergrund der englischen Ideengeschichte offenbar möglich und kommunikabel. Für diejenige Extension von Menschenrechten, über die keine gesellschaftliche Übereinkunft besteht, stellt diese Konzeption aber das schon im Anschluss an Gewirth/Beyleveld/Brownsword festgestellte Problem dar, dass der Umgang mit verletzlichen menschlichen Wesen an den Grenzen des Daseins, am Lebensanfang und am Lebensende nicht zweifelsfrei geklärt werden kann. Im Umgang mit „Personen im sozialen Sinne" hatte sich dieses Problem auch bei der von Engelhardt geprägten Unterscheidung von moralischen Freunden und moralischen Fremden ergeben.

Dass seit dem Ende des 20. Jahrhunderts verstärkt nach der Begründung eines universal geltenden Naturrechts gefragt wird, das sich vor allem in der Gewährung der Menschenrechte äußert, zeigt ein vermehrtes Interesse an international verbrieften Menschenrechten, aber auch einen verstärkten ethischen Orientierungsbedarf, der sich in der Suche nach überpositiven und allgemein geltenden Normen äußert.[462] Solche Normen sind international im Umgang mit

---

Gerechtigkeit rekurriert auf das Kriterium der Gleichheit: „In particular, *all* members of a community *equally* have the right to respectful consideration when the problem of distribution arises". (Finnis, a.a.O., 173.) Dieses Verständnis der Gerechtigkeit wird auch von Childress und Beauchamp in ihren Principles of biomedical ethics ([5]2001) vertreten. Es baut auf dem Verständnis auf, dass ähnliches ähnlich behandelt werden muss: „Treat like cases alike." (Finnis, a.a.O., 173.) Das Wohlergehen aller ist aber nicht automatisch mit einer Gleichbehandlung aller zu erreichen. Finnis verbindet darum mit distributiver Gerechtigkeit ein Verständnis von kommutativer Gerechtigkeit, nach dem das Individuum das erhält, was es braucht, was für jeden Einzelfall immens variieren kann. Vgl. Finnis, a.a.O., 165-184.

[462] Innerhalb der protestantischen Theologie wird der Naturrechtsgedanke nicht einmütig rezipiert. Die Problematik naturrechtlicher Konzeptionen wird von Kritikern in mehreren Aspekten gesehen:
- Gesetzlichkeit,
- zu geringe Beachtung der individuellen *Situation* aufgrund des Anspruchs, *universal* gültig zu sein,
- zu starker Akzent auf *Handlung* und *Entscheidung* bei zu geringer Beachtung der handelnden *Person*,
- logischer Fehler im Sein-Sollens-Fehlschluss,
- der Gedanke, Normen aus der Natur – wie auch immer sie verstanden wird – abzuleiten, entspreche menschlicher Hybris.

Vertreter einer Kritik am Naturrecht sind – neben Konzeptionen der von Karl Barth und seinen Nachfolgern geprägten Theologie – unter anderem Vertreter einer theologischen Tugendethik, die im letzten Drittel des 20. Jahrhunderts vor allem im englischsprachigen Bereich entwickelt worden ist. Eine Notwendigkeit zur Entwicklung einer

menschlichem Leben spätestens ab der Geburt, wahrscheinlich auch schon ab dem Zeitpunkt nach der Nidation bzw. dem Auftreten des Primitovstreifens weitgehend konsensfähig. Aufgrund der Uneindeutigkeit des Naturbegriffs und der Unklarheit dessen, wo der ethisch relevante Beginn des Menschseins anzusetzen ist, scheinen sie für den *Beginn* des menschlichen Lebens in den ersten 14 Tagen nach der Kernverschmelzung aber in der internationalen Debatte nicht belastbar zu sein, insofern in dieser Zeit weder der Handlungsbegriff, noch eine konsensuale gesellschaftliche Übereinkunft greifen.

Es zeigt sich damit nach der Darstellung des gesamten Abschnittes, dass die Konzeption der die Menschenrechte begründenden *Menschenwürde*, die in internationalen Völkerrechtstexten und biopolitischen Konventionen zentral und auch im deutschen Grundgesetz verfassungsrechtlich grundlegend ist, für die englische Interpretation von Menschenrechten keine zentrale Rolle gespielt hat. Im Zusammenhang der englischen Menschenrechtsentwicklung sind die Menschenrechte als *Freiheitsrechte* von größerer Bedeutung als die Fundierung der Menschenrechte in einer grundlegenden anthropologischen Bestimmung.

Auch der im englischen Sprachraum in den letzten Jahrzehnten zunehmend bedeutende Rekurs auf das Naturrecht und damit ein universales vorpositives und überpositives Begründungsmodell des positiven Rechts bietet im Zusammenhang mit der Frage nach der Zulässigkeit der Forschung an menschlichen Embryonen insofern keine Hilfe, als damit ein absoluter Lebensschutz für Nasciturі allenfalls ab der Nidation bzw. Individuation, womöglich auch erst für Geborene ausgesagt werden kann: Eine Forschung an menschlichen Embryonen verstößt nicht gegen die Menschenrechte. Anders wäre dies, wenn für die Begründung der universalen Menschenrechte eine überempirische Entität in Anspruch genommen würde und auch Embryonen

---

theologisch qualifizierten Güterlehre, zu der die Tugendlehre gerechnet werden kann, wird gleichwohl auch schon von Friedrich Schleiermacher vertreten. Für die neuere englischsprachige Tugendethik: Nach dem einflussreichen Buch von A. McIntyre, After Virtue. A study in moral theology, London/Notre Dame 1981 (32007) vgl. etwa S. Hauerwas, Christians among the virtues. Theological conversations with ancient and modern ethics, Notre Dame 1997; Ders., The peaceable Kingdom. A Primer in Christian Ethics, Notre Dame/ London 1983. Dabei sind die drei zentralen Aspekte, die von einer neueren Tugendethik vor allem im englischen Sprachraum vertreten werden, der Gottesdienst (worship), die Nachfolge Jesu Christi (discipleship) und die Gemeinschaft der Kirche (community). Erneuertes Handeln folgt nach der Tugendethik nicht zeitlosen Regeln, sondern einer erneuerten Selbstgewissheit und einem durch den Glauben erneuerten Sein. Hauerwas, der sich mit dieser Position gegen eine Rezeption naturrechtlicher Konzeptionen abgrenzt, unterscheidet damit zwischen natürlich-menschlicher und spezifisch christlicher Weltsicht und vertritt, dass das christliche Wirklichkeitsverständnis ein Handeln freisetze, mit dem sich Christen von Nicht-Christen unterscheiden. Ethik ist darum für Hauerwas nicht von den übrigen theologischen Disziplinen zu trennen, sondern wurzelt genuin im *Glauben*. Hauerwas, Kingdom, 60: „By virtue of the distinctive narrative that forms their community, Christians are distinct from the world."

als Menschen verstanden würden, so dass eine Forschung an ihnen gegen die menschliche „Natur“ verstieße. Hierüber ist aber offenbar kein Konsens zu erzielen, weil die Annahme des „prä-Status“ von frühen Embryonen deren Menschsein allenfalls als potentielles Menschsein feststellen kann.

Für die deutsche Gesetzgebung kollidiert die Forschung an menschlichen Embryonen zwar mit der gebotenen Achtung der Menschenwürde.[463] Im Zusammenhang mit der britischen Menschenrechtslegislatur aber wird Menschenwürde nicht als rechtsbegründende anthropologische Grundvoraussetzung angenommen. Auch die „Sprache der Menschenrechte“ ist darum von ihrem Vorverständnis abhängig – sie kann in der deutschen Debatte und bei einigen Vertretern im englischen Sprachraum durchaus für einen starken Embryonenschutz in Anspruch genommen werden, ist aber keine überall gleichermaßen verständliche Sprache und setzt unterschiedliche Folgerungen aus sich heraus. *Menschenwürde*, wie sie im internationalen Zusammenhang eine Rolle bei der Begründung der *Menschenrechte* spielt und wie sie in der aktuellen Bioethik-Debatte gebraucht wird, ist ein voraussetzungsreicher, interpretationsoffener Begriff und erfordert weitere klärende Denkanstrengungen – auch von Seiten der evangelischen Theologie: *Die* Menschenwürde gibt es ebenso wenig wie *die* Menschenrechte.

Damit zeigt sich noch einmal deutlich die Unvereinbarkeit von Grundannahmen, hinter die nicht zurückgegangen werden kann. Diese können lediglich offen gelegt und innerhalb des gesellschaftlichen Pluralismus als unvereinbare Grundannahmen ausgehalten werden. Diese schlichte Folgerung führt zu einem bescheidenen abschließenden Aspekt (III.6) und zu einer Zusammenfassung (III.7), bevor das Schlusskapitel einen eigenen Versuch zur Formulierung dessen bietet, wie Menschenwürde verstanden werden könnte und welche Extension sie in diesem Verständnis hinsichtlich der Forschung an menschlichen Embryonen hat.

III. 6 In dubio pro embryone – tutioristischer Umgang mit menschlichen Embryonen?

Nach den dargestellten Konzeptionen zu Menschenwürde, Autonomie und Personalität ausgehend von der Frage nach den Gründen für die unterschiedliche Embryonenschutzgesetzgebung in England und Deutschland stellt sich

[463] Diese Tatsache zeigt sich zum einen an der Aufnahme von Art. 1 I GG im deutschen Stammzellgesetz, wird zum anderen aber auch von Verfassungsrechtlern etwa mit der These vertreten, dass Forschung an menschlichen Embryonen und schon die Einfuhr und Verwendung von im Ausland hergestellten embryonalen Stammzellen gegen das deutsche Grundgesetz verstoße. Vgl. C. Hillgruber, Die Forschung an embryonalen Stammzellen, HFR 10/2008, 111-118. Gleichwohl besteht in dieser Frage kein Verfassungsauslegungskonsens.

möglicherweise eine sowohl nüchterne als auch enttäuschte Einsicht ein: einen Konsens hinsichtlich des moralischen Status von frühen Embryonen zu finden, ist angesichts unterschiedlicher Denkvoraussetzungen, unterschiedlicher kultureller und ideengeschichtlicher Hintergründe und innerhalb des radikalen gesellschaftlichen Pluralismus im deutsch-britischen Kontext offenbar unmöglich. Was im Rahmen einer nationalen Gesetzgebung schon schwierig erscheint und mit immensen Kompromissleistungen verbunden ist, wird im internationalen Kontext noch ungleich schwieriger, weil in diesem Zusammenhang nicht nur unterschiedliche Interessen, sondern auch unterschiedliche kulturelle Prägungen eine Rolle spielen. Es muss wohl dabei bleiben: England und Deutschland nehmen innerhalb der Debatte um die Forschung an menschlichen Embryonen einander entgegengesetzte Positionen ein. Immerhin konnten einige hinter diesen Positionen stehende prägende Grundannahmen offen gelegt werden.

Angesichts der Umstrittenheit innerhalb der Diskussion und des hohen emotionalen Engagements, mit dem in dieser Debatte gestritten wird, sowie der letztlich ungeklärten Statusbestimmung von menschlichem Leben vor dem 14. Tag bietet sich für die Begründung eines starken Embryonenschutzes, der sowohl in der deutschen als auch in der britischen Diskussion kommuniziert werden kann, als Ausweg an, in dieser Frage *tutioristisch* zu argumentieren und die Forschung an menschlichen Embryonen deswegen auszuschließen, weil der moralische Status des Embryos nicht klar und übereinstimmend benannt werden kann: Im Zweifel ist aus Vorsichtsgründen, wenn mehrere Handlungsoptionen offen stehen, danach eher *für* den Embryo zu entscheiden.[464] Denn nach dem Tutiorismus sollte in Situationen, in denen Zweifel darüber besteht, ob ein Wesen in einen bestimmten ethischen Anwendungsbereich fällt, es hinreichend starke Argumente *für* diese Annahme gibt, zugleich aber die mit der *gegenteiligen* Annahme sich ergebenden positiven Auswirkungen in einem negativen Verhältnis zum entstehenden moralischen Schaden stehen, aus Vorsichtsgründen für diejenige Position votiert werden, die den kleineren moralischen Schaden aus sich heraussetzt.

Im Zusammenhang des Umgangs mit menschlichen Embryonen erscheint eine tutioristische Argumentationsweise vor allem deswegen sinnvoll, weil über den Status von Embryonen kein letztgültiges und breit zustimmungsfähiges Urteil gefällt werden kann. Ob Embryonen Personen sind oder zumindest Personen moralisch gleichgestellt werden müssen, ob ihnen Menschenwürde eignet und ob sie unter absolutem Lebensschutz stehen müssen, wird,

[464] Eine solche Position vertritt auch Robert Song, To Be Willing to Kill What for All One Knows Is A Person Is to Be Willing to Kill a Person. In: Waters/Brent/Cole-Turner (Hrsg.), God and the Embryo. Religious Voices on Stem Cells and Cloning, Washington D.C. 2003, 98-107. Ähnlich Damschen/Schönecker, Moralischer Status, 187-267, die auch die Formulierung geprägt haben: „in dubio pro embryone".

wie deutlich wurde, unterschiedlich gesehen und begründet. Auch wenn viel *gegen* ihren Personstatus spricht, ist einer tutioristischen Argumentation zufolge der moralische Schaden, der entsteht, wenn man sie als Nicht-Personen behandelt, größer als der Nutzen, der sich aus ihrer Verzwecklichung – selbst im Zusammenhang mit hochrangiger Forschung – ergibt. Aus diesem Grund aber sollten sie so behandelt werden, als ob sie Personen wären und ihnen daher absolute Schutzwürdigkeit zukäme. Denn unter der Voraussetzung, *dass* menschlichen Embryonen Würde und Personstatus eignet, ist ihre Tötung moralisch ebenso verwerflich, wie es die Tötung von allen würdetragenden Lebewesen, also Personen, ist, so dass auch der Nutzen einer breiten Therapie für eine große Anzahl von Patienten den entstehenden Schaden nicht aufwiegen kann. Im Zusammenhang mit der Forschung an menschlichen Embryonen wird diese Vorsicht von der Annahme gestützt, dass es sich beim Embryo und dem späteren Erwachsenen, der sich aus dem Embryo entwikkelt, zumindest um eine numerische genetische Identität handelt, dass also die Würde, die der Erwachsene innehat, auch dem numerisch identischen Embryo nicht ohne weiteres abgesprochen werden kann.

Ein weiteres den tutioristischen Zugang stützendes Argument liegt in der Tatsache, dass es mit der Forschung an adulten Stammzellen ernstzunehmende Alternativen zur Forschung an humanen embryonalen Stammzellen zu geben scheint,[465] also eine absolute Notwendigkeit für die Forschung nicht gegeben ist. Verbunden mit einem tutioristischen Zugang greift dabei das so genannte *slippery slope*-Argument, nach dem sich bei Erlaubnis einer bestimmten Technik weitere Techniken als wünschenswert ergeben könnten, die jetzt noch verboten sind. Um unerwünschte Folgerungen zu vermeiden, so kann eine tutioristische Argumentation vertreten, sollte eine schiefe Ebene gar nicht erst betreten werden.[466]

---

[465] In diesem Zusammenhang ergibt sich allerdings die Schwierigkeit, dass *für* die Forschung an menschlichen Embryonen zur Gewinnung von menschlichen embryonalen Stammzellen vor allem zwei Argumente gebraucht werden: das Argument einer aus humanen embryonalen Stammzellen zu gewinnenden *Therapie* von degenerativen Erkrankungen zum einen, und das Argument der Notwendigkeit von humanen embryonalen Stammzellen als *Vergleichsmaterial* für die Forschung an adulten Stammzellen zum anderen. Lediglich für das erste Argument können adulte Stammzellen als Alternative für embryonale Stammzellen geltend gemacht werden. Das zweite Argument behandelt embryonale Stammzellen im Rahmen einer Grundlagenforschung, die (noch) keine Therapieziele hat. Für die inhaltliche Auseinandersetzung mit diesem Argument, das vor allem in Deutschland bei der Debatte um die Verschiebung der Stichtagsregelung eine wesentliche Rolle spielte, fehlt mir die naturwissenschaftliche Expertise. Mit den jetzt bestehenden Stammzelllinien aus embryonalen Stammzellen liegt aber ein relativ breites Forschungsmaterial vor, das für Vergleichsforschungen an adulten Stammzellen eingesetzt werden kann, so dass der „Verbrauch“ von weiteren Embryonen damit zu vermeiden wäre.

[466] Vor kurzem ist das Argument der schiefen Ebene erneut in Deutschland in der Auseinandersetzung um die Verschiebung des Stichtags im Stammzellgesetz vertreten

Über das bei moralischen Zweifelsfällen greifende Argument aus Vorsichtsgründen hinaus hat eine tutioristische Argumentation eine weitere Stoßrichtung: sie legt Interessen und Hintergründe offen, die für ethische Positionen bestimmend sind.[467] Interessegeleitete Entscheidungen sind einerseits grundsätzlich als legitim zu beurteilen, unterliegen anderseits aber der Fragestellung, ob es hinreichende Zweifel an ihrer ethischen Zulässigkeit gibt, die dazu nötigen, in der entsprechenden Frage vorsichtig zu urteilen. Rein wirtschaftliche Interessen oder das Verfolgen von Forschungsprestige ist in diesem Zusammenhang als ethisch fragwürdig zu beurteilen, und die erklärte Suche nach Therapien für degenerative Erkrankungen hat sich möglicherweise die Frage nach dem Umgang mit der eigenen Endlichkeit und den Grenzen der Medizin stellen zu lassen, die im Anschluss an Abschnitt III.4.4 aufgeworfen worden war.[468]

Eine tutioristische Argumentation im Zusammenhang mit der Forschung an Embryonen hat darum zwei miteinander verbundene Akzentuierungen: sie fragt zum einen nach den impliziten anthropologischen und weltanschaulichen Grundannahmen, die hinter einer Position stehen und wägt Schaden und Nutzen ab, die sich aus einem Vergleich unterschiedlicher Vorgangsweisen ergeben. Zum anderen urteilt sie prinzipiell vorsichtig, führt ihre Argumentation aber weniger an inhaltlichen Aspekten als vielmehr auf einer metaethischen Formalebene durch. Dabei kann sie für sich beanspruchen, innerhalb einer säkularen und weltanschaulich pluralen Gesellschaft aus unterschiedlichen „Lagern" Unterstützung zu erhalten. Mit einer solchen Offenheit führt sie unter Umständen weiter als die Argumentation mit substantiellen Argumenten. Möglicherweise ist eine tutioristische Argumentation im Zusammenhang mit der Forschung an menschlichen Embryonen diejenige Argumentation, die am ehesten einen gesellschaftlich auch international tragfähigen Konsens finden kann. Darum ist theologische Ethik dieser Argumentationsweise gegenüber grundsätzlich aufgeschlossen. Darauf wird im Abschlusskapitel noch einmal zurückzukommen sein.

---

worden. Das Argument lautete, dass nicht sicher ausgemacht werden könne, ob mit einer einmaligen Verschiebung des Stichtags nicht weiteren Verschiebungen und schließlich einer Aufhebung des Stammzellgesetzes die Türen geöffnet werden könnten. Ähnlich wird auch in der Frage der Hybrid-Embryonen geurteilt.

[467] Damschen/Schönecker, a.a.O., 255: „Was den Zweifel am Würdestatus menschlicher Embryonen nährt oder vielleicht sogar überhaupt erst in Gang bringt, ist unbestreitbar das Interesse, das mit einem solchen Zweifel verbunden ist (sei es das medizinische und damit verbundene ökonomische Interesse an der Stammzellforschung, sei es das persönliche Interesse an der Abtreibung)."

[468] S. oben, S. 166ff.

III. 7 Menschenwürde und *human dignity*. Der Status des menschlichen Embryos im deutsch-englischen Ländervergleich

Hinsichtlich der Regelungen des Schutzes von menschlichen Embryonen in den ersten 14 Tagen nach der Kernverschmelzung stehen die deutsche und die britische Gesetzgebung im Ländervergleich an entgegengesetzten Polen. Während in Großbritannien eine verbrauchende Forschung an Embryonen, die Erzeugung von Embryonen zu Forschungszwecken, die Klonierung von Embryonen und die Erzeugung von cytoplasmischen Hybrid-Embryonen sowie von „echten Hybriden" (*true hybrids*) zu Forschungszwecken unter Aufsicht der Regulierungsbehörde HFEA gesetzlich gestattet ist, ist nach dem deutschen Stammzellgesetz der Novellierung von 2008 folgend lediglich ein Import von im Ausland erzeugten embryonalen Stammzelllinien erlaubt, die vor dem 1. Mai 2007 hergestellt worden sind. Die deutsche Gesetzgebung argumentiert dabei mit der Menschenwürde, deren Achtung mit dem Recht auf Forschungsfreiheit (Art. 5 III GG) so kollidiert, dass ein Kompromiss gefunden werden musste; die britische Gesetzgebung billigt dem Embryo demgegenüber einen „special status" und eine darin begründete Schutzwürdigkeit („some protection in law") zu, wägt diese aber gegen hochrangige medizinische Forschungsziele ab.

Dieser unterschiedliche rechtliche Umgang mit dem Lebensschutz hat mehrere Gründe. Ein gewichtiger Grund für die strikte deutsche Gesetzgebung liegt im Verstoß gegen die Achtung der Menschenwürde durch den Nationalsozialismus, der Menschenversuche erlaubt und durchgeführt und zur rechtlichen Begründung dieser Experimente eine Unterscheidung von wertem und unwertem Leben eingeführt hat. Eine Nachwirkung dieser Geschichte ist die Menschenwürde-Formulierung innerhalb des deutschen Grundgesetzes und in internationalen Menschenrechts-Dokumenten, mit denen eine Wiederholung dieses menschenverachtenden Umgangs mit Menschen für die Zukunft verhindert werden soll.

Ein weiterer Grund für die deutsche gesetzgebende und öffentliche Zurückhaltung gegenüber der Forschung an menschlichen Embryonen liegt aber in der unterschiedlichen ideengeschichtlichen Entwicklung in Deutschland und England: Während die deutsche philosophische Ethik in starkem Maße von der Aufklärungsphilosophie nach Immanuel Kant geprägt ist, der Würde als ein integrales Merkmal von Menschsein in jedem Entwicklungsstadium versteht, ist in England der von Jeremy Bentham und vor allem John Stuart Mill formulierte Utilitarismus verbunden mit einem liberalistischen und pragmatischen Impetus enorm einflussreich, und auch wenn, wie bereits einleitend gesagt, die unterschiedliche Gesetzgebung nicht auf diese Grunddifferenz reduziert werden darf, so erklärt diese doch typologisch unterschiedliche ethische Begründungsstrategien.

Diese unterschiedliche ideengeschichtliche Prägung erklärt zumindest die stärkere Affinität der *deutschen* Debatte zum Konzept der „Menschenwürde" und dessen Verständnis bis zum letzten Drittel des 20. Jahrhunderts im Sinne der Mitgifttheorie und einer rechtsbegründenden Funktion von Menschenwürde im Zusammenhang der Menschenrechte-Diskussion, aber auch die stärkere Affinität der *englischen* Debatte zum Konzept der Notwendigkeit von Selbstbestimmung und Forschungsfreiheit, sowie zur Orientierung am Nutzen für eine größtmögliche Anzahl von Menschen.

Diese Beobachtungen korrespondieren mit der Tatsache, dass *human dignity* in der britischen Debatte deutlich seltener verwendet wird als *Menschenwürde* in der deutschen bioethischen Diskussion. Obwohl auch in Deutschland gelegentlich ein inflationärer Gebrauch des Begriffs beklagt wird, ist er in der englischen Medizinethik als „useless concept" bezeichnet worden und spielt insgesamt eine deutlich geringere Rolle als in der deutschsprachigen Diskussion. *Dignity* wird im Sinne eines „würdigen Verhaltens" vor allem mit Selbstbestimmung konnotiert und im Zusammenhang mit einer Würde am Lebensende gebraucht (*dying with dignity*). Mit einer *dignity* von Embryonen wird in der englischsprachigen bioethischen Debatte demgegenüber nur selten operiert, und wenn, dann entweder durch römisch-katholische Ethik oder mit einer gewissen begrifflichen Unschärfe und Vagheit, meist mit Bezug auf *human rights*. Dabei ist aber in der britischen *Human Rights Act* anders als in der UN-Deklaration der Menschenrechte und im deutschen Grundgesetz keine anthropologische Bestimmung wie *dignity* zu finden, die Menschenrechte begründete.

Neben der Differenzierung in Mitgift-, Leistungs- und Kommunikationsmodell und der Verhältnissetzung von Menschenwürde und Menschenrechten zeigt sich auf diesem Hintergrund nochmals eine doppelte Bedeutungsnuance von *Würde* resp. *dignity*:

- Würde bezeichnet eine verhaltensunabhängige menschliche *Wesenseigenschaft* und wird als *Menschenwürde* bezeichnet.
- Würde konstituiert sich durch „würdevolles" *Verhalten* (*dignified behaviour*), wird attributiv verstanden und Menschen von anderen Menschen zuerkannt.

Während beide Formen des Würdeverständnisses in der deutschen Debatte kommunikabel sind, herrscht in der englischen Diskussion offenbar das zweite Modell vor.[469]

Für das deutsch-englische Gespräch ist der Würde-Begriff darum im Zusammenhang mit der verbrauchenden Forschung an menschlichen Em-

---

[469] Diese Unterscheidung im Verständnis von Würde hat eine Nähe zur Unterscheidung einer basalen Minimalwürde und einer im Rechtsvollzug verwirklichten Maximalwürde, die ich aber terminologisch aufgrund der begrifflichen Abstufung nicht nachvollzogen habe. S. oben, S. 89f.

bryonen nicht hilfreich, weil er aufgrund der unterschiedlichen ideengeschichtlichen Prägungen nicht wechselseitig kommuniziert und verstanden werden kann. In der englischsprachigen Debatte spielt demgegenüber zur Frage nach dem Umgang mit menschlichem Leben am Lebensbeginn eine Gruppe von Begriffen wie *worth*, *value* oder *status* (als *moral status* oder *special status*) eine Rolle, wobei vor allem die beiden zuerst genannten Begriffe ähnlich positiv konnotiert sind wie *Würde*, sich aber der interpretationsoffene *Status*-Begriff zunehmend auch in der deutschen Bioethik-Debatte findet.[470]

Die entscheidende Frage für die theologische Ethik in diesem Zusammenhang ist darum aber nicht diejenige nach einer *begrifflichen* Übereinstimmung oder Nicht-Übereinstimmung hinsichtlich des Lebensschutzes, sondern vielmehr die Frage nach den anthropologischen Grundannahmen, die sowohl von der Gesetzgebung, als auch von der öffentlichen politischen und ethischen Diskussion über den Umgang mit menschlichem Leben am Lebensbeginn transportiert werden. Weder der Menschenwürde-Begriff als solcher noch Begriffe wie *value*, *worth* oder *status* leisten eine solche Offenlegung, weil sie keine eindeutigen Begriffe sind, sondern vielmehr eine Vielzahl von Interpretationsmöglichkeiten auf sich vereinen. Beim Beispiel der Menschenwürde wurde diese Deutungspluralität mit Hilfe der Unterscheidung von Mitgift-, Leistungs- und Kommunikationsmodell sowie der Zuordnung von Menschenrechten und Menschenwürde deutlich.

Bei der Frage nach der ethischen Beurteilung der fremdnützigen Forschung an menschlichen Embryonen, die Anlass des Buches gewesen ist, ist *Menschenwürde per se* darum noch nicht als Begründung für oder gegen die Forschung an menschlichen Embryonen in Anspruch zu nehmen: *Menschenwürde* kann sowohl als ein Argument *gegen* die fremdnützige Forschung an menschlichen Embryonen verwendet werden, als auch als ein Argument *für* die Forschung, wenn die Hoffnung auf medizinischen Fortschritt motivierend wirkt. Insofern scheint die von Ronald Dworkin eingeführte Unterscheidung zwischen der Achtung einer *natürlichen* und einer *menschlichen* Kreativität auch auf einen unterschiedlichen Umgang mit menschlichen Embryonen im Ländervergleich anwendbar zu sein.

Für die Begründung eines frühen *Embryonenschutzes* kann *Menschenwürde* dabei nur verwendet werden, wenn sie im Rahmen der Mitgifttheorie als *intrinsische* oder von Anfang an *zugeeignete* menschliche Wesenseigenschaft verstanden wird bzw. mit der Kommunikationstheorie mit dem Beginn des neuen Genoms bei der Kernverschmelzung beginnt. Alle gradualistischen oder Alles-oder-Nichts-Positionen, die vor allem der Leistungs- oder der Kom-

[470] So etwa bei den häufiger herangezogenen Sammelbänden G. Damschen/D. Schönekker (Hrsg.), Der moralische Status menschlicher Embryonen, Berlin/New York 2002; G. Maio (Hrsg.), Der Status des extrakorporalen Embryo, Stuttgart 2007.

munikationstheorie[471] zugerechnet werden können, scheiden für die Begründung des Lebensschutzes für frühe Embryonen aus.

Die eine bioethische Position begründenden Vorannahmen liegen darum in den vorausgesetzten moralrelevanten menschlichen Eigenschaften, die als solche den moralischen Status menschlicher Wesen begründen. Beim exemplarischen Durchgang durch klassische prägende philosophische und theologische Ethik-Konzeptionen im deutschen und englischen Sprachraum haben sich als kriteriologische Aspekte für die Bestimmung von Menschsein vor allem drei Zugänge erwiesen:

- Menschsein wird ausgezeichnet durch *Autonomie*. Dieser Gruppe kann sowohl die Konzeption von Immanuel Kant, als auch die neuere vor allem englischsprachige Medizinethik-Debatte zugerechnet werden. Die Bestimmung von Autonomie hat darum noch einmal mehrere Untergruppen:
  - Autonomie als Selbstgesetzgebung des sittlichen Subjekts, an der jeder Mensch partizipiert (Kant),
  - Autonomie als Fähigkeit zum sittlichen Subjektsein, die in jedem Menschen als angelegt vorhanden anzusehen ist (Kant und SKIP-Argumente),
  - Autonomie als Selbstbestimmung des konkreten Patienten (prinzipienbasierte Medizinethik bei Beauchamp/Childress),
  - Autonomie als Fähigkeit zu selbstbestimmtem Handeln bei menschlichen Handlungsagenten, die konstituierend für Menschenrechte wirkt (Gewirth/Beyleveld/Brownsword und Aspekte der *New Natural Law Theory*).
- Menschsein wird zu *Personsein* in ein Verhältnis gesetzt. Dabei gibt es wiederum unterschiedliche Verständnismöglichkeiten:
  - Menschsein und Personsein werden unterschieden, und Personalität wird durch eine bestimmte Kriteriologie festgestellt (Singer, Harris, Tooley, Engelhardt),
  - Menschsein und Personsein werden als gleich extensional verstanden (Kant, Vertreter theologischer Ethik und SKIP-Argumente).
- Menschsein wird konstitutiv *relational* verstanden und ereignet sich in Beziehung. Das *specificum humanum* besteht darin, auf Andere und sich selbst bezogen zu sein. Auch hier können Unterscheidungen getroffen werden:
  - Menschen treten schon vorgeburtlich in Beziehungen hinein, entweder schon bei der Entstehung ihres Genoms im Zusammenhang mit der

[471] Dabei ist auch der Zugang der Mitgifttheorie mit einer gradualistischen Position vereinbar, dann nämlich, wenn der Beginn einer moralbegründenden menschlichen Wesenseigenschaft mit dem Abschluss der Nidation verbunden wird.

Kernverschmelzung, oder wenn sich ihre Implantation in den mütterlichen Organismus ereignet.[472]

- Sein-in-Beziehung spielt für das Menschsein mit dem Eintritt in die Welt, also mit der Geburt eine entscheidende und prägende Rolle, wie es etwa die Diskurs-Ethik (Habermas) vertritt.

Alle Aspekte haben bei der Darstellung des Buches eine Rolle gespielt. Sie sind mit den Interpretationsmodellen von Menschenwürde[473] vergleichbar, an dieser Stelle aber insofern weiter formuliert, als es hier um die Bestimmung von *Menschsein* als solchem geht und damit um eine breitere Bestimmung als eine inhaltliche Übereinkunft über das Konzept *Menschenwürde*, das terminologisch für den englischen Sprachraum offenbar nicht leicht vermittelbar ist. An dieser Stelle muss allerdings sofort hinzugefügt werden, dass eine interpretierende Bestimmung dessen, was „Menschenwürde" ist, dasjenige bestimmt, was das Achtenswerte am *Menschsein* als solchem ausmacht.[474]

Bei einer Fokussierung auf die Fragestellung nach dem Achtenswerten des Menschseins als solchen lassen sich in das damit gegebene Raster auch die Überlegungen zu den Menschenrechten mit ihren unterschiedlichen Akzentuierungen und zum Naturrecht einzeichnen. Danach entscheidet das zugrunde liegende Verständnis des Menschseins darüber, ob Menschenrechte auch auf Nascituri oder Hybride appliziert werden sollten (was von einem Großteil der Rechtsausleger bestritten wird[475]), und welche vom freiheitlichen säkularen Staat nicht zu schaffenden Voraussetzungen das Recht orientierend in Geltung sind und sein sollten.

Bei der ethischen Beurteilung der strittigen Forschung an menschlichen Embryonen steht nach diesen Überlegungen vor allem die Frage nach dem

[472] Die zuletzt genannte Möglichkeit spielt auch bei Erfahrungsberichten von Frauen eine Rolle, die sich einer IVF-Behandlung unterzogen haben. Teilweise handelt es sich auch um Frauen, die „überzählige Embryonen" zu Forschungszwecken zur Verfügung stellen. Zu diesem Aspekt vgl. die Studie von E. Haimes/R. Porz/J. Sculler/C. Rehmann-Sutter, „So what is an embryo?" A comparative study of the views of those asked to donate embryos for hESC research, New Genetics and Society 27, 2008, 113-126.

[473] S. oben, S. 69f.

[474] So auch W. Härle, Menschenwürde – konkret und grundsätzlich, in: Ders., Menschsein in Beziehungen, Tübingen 2005, 379ff, 389: „Menschenwürde ist... nichts anderes als *das Menschsein selbst*, das Achtung gebietet bzw. fordert."

[475] So etwa das Statement von Alan Johnson innerhalb der Debatte um die *Human Fertilisation and Embryology Bill* im Hinblick auf die Europäische Menschenrechtskonvention: „In my view the provisions of the Human Fertilisation and Embryology Bill [HL] are compatible with the Convention rights." (In der 2007 veröffentlichten Debatte, die – wie alle *Bills* und *Acts* der britischen Gesetzgebung – im Internet auf den Seiten des Parlaments zu finden ist: http://www.publications.parliament.uk/pa/cm200708/cmbills/120/08120.i-iv.html.)

Verständnis von Menschsein überhaupt und speziell nach dem Verständnis des menschlichen Embryos auf dem Plan: „So what ist an embryo?" Jede ethische Position wird diese Frage für sich selbst zu klären haben. Dabei stellt sich diese Frage nicht nur bei rein menschlichen Embryonen, sondern auch bei den jüngst in England rechtlich erlaubten „Misch-Embryonen", die zum allergrößten Teil aus menschlichem Gen-Material bestehen,[476] und kann als Frage nach der zeitlichen Ausdehnung (wann beginnt Menschsein?), der semantischen Bestimmung (was ist Menschsein?) und den normativen Konsequenzen zusammengefasst werden (welche ethischen Notwendigkeiten ergeben sich aus welcher Bestimmung des Menschseins?).

Es kann auf dem Hintergrund dieser zusammenfassenden Überlegungen für theologische Ethik darum vor allem um zweierlei gehen: zum einen hat eine Analyse zu zeigen, was Menschsein für eine bioethische Konzeption bedeutet, welche Implikationen und Grundannahmen sich also mit ethischen Standpunkten verbinden, und diese offenzulegen. Eine solche Analyse habe ich an verschiedenen Beispielen in der vorangegangenen Darstellung zu leisten versucht. Zum anderen ist eine eigene Grundlagenklärung erforderlich, die theologisch verantwortet und begründet werden muss. Eine solche Grundlagenklärung versucht das folgende abschließende Kapitel zu geben und operiert dabei ausdrücklich mit dem Menschenwürde-Begriff, auch wenn dieser international keinen Begriffskonsens auf sich vereinigen kann. *Menschenwürde* wird in diesem Zusammenhang aber in enger Verbindung mit *Menschsein* als solchem verstanden und vor allem deswegen verwendet, weil der Begriff in der deutschen Debatte immer noch in hohem Maße positiv konnotiert ist.

Bei einer inhaltlichen Bestimmung des Verständnisses von Menschsein und „Menschenwürde" könnten anschließend weitere auch im englischen Sprachraum positiv konnotierte Begriffe wie *value*, *worth* oder *sanctity* aufgenommen und eingefügt werden. Es geht also, anders als im Eingangskapitel dieses Buches, in diesen abschließenden Überlegungen weniger um den Vergleich des Begriffsgebrauchs von *Menschenwürde* in England und Deutschland, sondern vielmehr grundsätzlicher um anthropologische Überlegungen danach, wie theologisch Menschsein zu bestimmen ist, um von hier her ethische Folgerungen auch für eine Forschung an menschlichen Embryonen zu ziehen.

---

[476] Sie stellt sich aber auch bei Klonen, die zu Forschungszwecken erzeugt worden sind.

IV. WAS IST DER MENSCH? (Ps 8,5)

In den Darstellungen der vorangegangenen Kapitel hat sich immer wieder gezeigt, dass das Verständnis vom Menschen und von der Notwendigkeit des Lebensschutzes für menschliche Wesen von den kulturellen, philosophischen, anthropologischen und damit ideengeschichtlichen und weltanschaulichen Vorerfahrungen geprägt und bestimmt wird, die in einer Gesellschaft vorherrschen. Eine weltanschauungs- und voraussetzungslose Bioethik gibt es nicht. Über diese Prägung hinaus spielten in der Gesetzesentwicklung sowohl in Deutschland als auch in Großbritannien kontingente Faktoren wie Mehrheitsbildungen, ökonomische Interessen und Lobbygruppen eine Rolle. Beide Aspekte – die kulturelle Prägung und die Einflussnahme anderer Faktoren – haben dazu geführt, dass die Gesetzgebung hinsichtlich der Forschung an menschlichen Embryonen bei nahezu gleicher Ausgangslage in England und Deutschland zu einander entgegengesetzten Bestimmungen geführt hat.

Sowohl politische und gesetzgebende Entscheidungen als auch ethische Positionen gehen von Anthropologumena aus, die sie nicht immer offen legen, die aber ihre Argumentation maßgeblich bestimmen. Die Frage, ab wann und bis zu welchem Zeitpunkt menschliches Leben aus welchem Grund zu schützen ist, ob und aufgrund welcher Kriterien ihm Personalität eignet und wie der moralische Status ungeborenen menschlichen Lebens anzusehen ist, wird deswegen je nach der impliziten oder expliziten anthropologischen Konzeption, die dabei vertreten wird, und je nach den die Entscheidung orientierenden Interessen unterschiedlich beantwortet.

Über diese Einsicht hinaus ist festgestellt worden, dass die Argumentation mit dem Menschenwürdebegriff im englischen Sprachraum aufgrund der ideengeschichtlichen Differenzen nicht so kommunikabel ist wie in der deutschsprachigen Debatte. Die mit dem deutschen Begriff transportierte Realität kann gleichwohl mit der Terminologie des „moral status of the embryo" ausgedrückt werden, wobei diese interpretationsoffener ist als der positiv konnotierte Begriff der *Menschenwürde*. Zusätzlich wird mit Begriffen wie *worth*, *value* oder *sanctity* operiert, die eine starke identifikatorische Kraft haben.

Im nun abschließenden Teil des Buches soll eine theologische Bestimmung dessen versucht werden, wie Menschenwürde als ein *universales* Anthropologumenon verstanden werden könnte, wie sie theologisch begründet werden kann und welche Folgen für die bioethische Debatte sich aus diesem Verständnis ergeben. Diese Reflexion erhebt einen grundlegenden normativen Anspruch, nach dem die Bestimmung von Menschenwürde und ihre rechtlichen und politischen Folgen nicht ausschließlich für den kirchlichen Binnenbereich zu gelten haben.[477] Dabei versteht sie das Begründungsmodell, auf das sie rekurriert, gleichwohl als ein explizit theologisches, das seine Prägung der biblisch-reformatorischen Theologie verdankt. Als solches wendet sie sich zunächst der theologischen Konzeption der Gottebenbildlichkeit des Menschen zu und zieht daran anschließend Folgerungen für ein theologisch verantwortetes Verständnis von Menschenwürde und deren ethischen Konsequenzen. Dies schließt auch eine Stellungnahme *gegen* eine liberale Embryonenschutzgesetzgebung ein, wie sie in Großbritannien durchgeführt und in Deutschland diskutiert wird, und begründet diese mit dem zuvor entwickelten theologischen Verständnis des Menschseins.

Wie der Abschnitt III.2.1 gezeigt hat, ist die theologiegeschichtliche Verknüpfung von Menschenwürde und Gottebenbildlichkeit als eher locker anzusehen. Dieser Tatsache tragen die folgenden Ausführungen Rechnung, indem in direktem Anschluss an biblisch-reformatorische Theologie ein Verständnis von Gottebenbildlichkeit zu entwickeln versucht wird, das nicht *historisch*, sondern *systematisch* mit Menschsein und Menschenwürde verbunden wird. Dabei gebe ich ein dogmatisches Fundament für ethische Folgeentscheidungen, was sich aus der Einsicht ergibt, dass eine weltanschauungslose ethische Position nicht vertreten werden kann, weltanschauliche Gebundenheit vielmehr transparent zu machen ist.[478]

Christliche Theologie versteht den Menschen als *Geschöpf* Gottes. Die menschliche Geschöpflichkeit trägt zu einer Bestimmung des Menschen sowohl ein unterscheidendes, als auch eine verbindendes Moment im Zusammenhang mit der nichtmenschlichen Schöpfung ein.[479] Denn der Mensch wird

---

[477] Dieser universale Anspruch, der dem Menschenwürde-Begriff inhärent ist, unterscheidet meine Konzeption ausdrücklich von der in den letzten Jahrzehnten im englischen Sprachraum vertretenen neueren Form der Tugendethik, die mit ihrer Akzentuierung auf Gottesdienst und Nachfolge nach einer spezifisch *christlichen* Ethik für den Raum der Kirche sucht. Der universale Anspruch des Menschenwürde-Begriffs geht demgegenüber davon aus, dass seine Normativität nicht nur für eine (christliche) Gemeinschaft innerhalb der pluralistischen Gesellschaft gilt, sondern für die Gesellschaft als ganze. Andernfalls machte er keine Aussage zum Menschsein *im allgemeinen*, sondern nur zum Menschsein von Angehörigen der eigenen Gemeinschaft.

[478] Dieser Zugang nimmt auch die Tatsache ernst, dass in englischsprachiger Theologie in Auseinandersetzung mit der Forschung an Embryonen häufig mit dem *imago Dei*-Begriff *ohne* Verbindung mit *human dignity* argumentiert wird. Vgl. R. Page, The Human Genome and the Image of God, in: C. Deane-Drummond (Hrsg.), Brave New World? Theology, Ethics and the Human Genome, London 2003, 68-85.

[479] In ähnlicher Weise kommt die klassische Bestimmung des Menschen als eines *animal rationale* zu der Formulierung, der Mensch sei - wie die Tiere - ein Lebewesen, von diesen aber durch seine *ratio* unterschieden.

gemeinsam mit der übrigen geschöpflichen Welt als Geschöpf Gottes verstanden und auf diese Weise in den Zusammenhang mit der nichtmenschlichen Schöpfung eingeordnet. Zugleich tritt er aber, wie die christliche Theologie klassisch im Anschluss an die Schöpfungsberichte, vor allem an Gen 1,26f. vertritt, als Gottes *Ebenbild* aus der nichtmenschlichen Schöpfung heraus.[480]

Das Gemeinsame von menschlicher und nichtmenschlicher Schöpfung liegt darin, dass das Geschöpf sein Leben nicht sich selbst und seiner eigenen Schaffenskraft verdankt, sondern dem Schöpfer, der es ins Leben gerufen hat und für es sorgt (im Sinne einer *creatio originans* und *continua*). Als Reflex seiner Geschöpflichkeit staunt aber, zumindest soweit wir es wissen, nur der Mensch darüber, dass Gott ihn geschaffen hat und erhält: „Was ist der Mensch, dass du seiner gedenkest?“ (Ps 8,5) Offenbar eröffnet sich nur dem Menschen eine Ahnung dessen, dass seine Geschöpflichkeit ihm Anlass zur Freude und zur Dankbarkeit werden kann, die ihren Ausdruck im Gebet finden, in dem er sich auf seinen Schöpfer zurück bezieht.

Diese grundlegende responsorische Struktur wiederum eröffnet eine Interpretationsmöglichkeit für das Theologumenon der menschlichen Gottebenbildlichkeit. Denn die darin ausgedrückte Ähnlichkeits- und Entsprechungsbeziehung von Gott und Mensch gründet offenbar im gegenseitigen Bezogensein von Mensch und Gott.

Danach wird der Mensch theologisch adäquat nicht nur als Geschöpf und Ebenbild Gottes verstanden, sondern als zur *Gemeinschaft mit Gott* bestimmtes Geschöpf, dessen Gott gedenkt und das umgekehrt seinerseits Vertrauen und Liebe zu Gott fassen kann, darf und soll. Dabei beginnt das Gedenken Gottes nach der Erfahrung der biblischen Autoren schon vorgeburtlich (Ps 139,16: „deine Augen sahen mich, als ich noch nicht bereitet war“) und geht über den Tod hinaus (Ps 139,8: „bettete ich mich bei den Toten, siehe, so bist du auch da“). Die Propheten erfahren und bekennen sich in diesem Zusammenhang als schon vor ihrer Geburt von Gott berufen und beauftragt (Jer 1,5: „ich kannte dich, ehe ich dich im Mutterleib bereitete“).[481]

---

[480] Zur menschlichen Gottebenbildlichkeit in exegetischer Hinsicht vgl. den Aufsatz von B. Janowski, Die lebendige Statue Gottes. Zur Anthropologie der priesterlichen Urgeschichte, in: M. Witte (Hrsg.), Gott und Mensch im Dialog, FS O. Kaiser zum 80. Geburtstag, BZAW, Berlin/New York 2004, 183-214.

[481] Von einer rückblickenden Einsicht in ihre Bezogenheit auf Gott schon vor dem Zeitpunkt der Geburt sprechen außer Ps 139,13-16 und Jer 1,5 auch Jes 49,1 und Hi 10,8-12. Aus diesen Stellen kann keine biblische Aussage zur Personalität und damit dem „Status“ des Embryos abgeleitet werden, insofern sie die Erfahrung, dass Gott im Leben schon vorgeburtlich wirksam war, erst *im Nachhinein* reflektieren. Vgl. J.C. Peterson, Is the Human Embryo a Human Being?, in: B. Waters/R. Cole-Turner (Hrsg.), God and the Embryo. Religious Voices on Stem Cells and Cloning, Washington 2003, 77-87. „Embryos are in God's presence, as is all the rest of life. We are responsible for how we treat them, but when precisely they become persons is not taught in these texts.“ (A.a.O., 79.)

Die Beziehung, die der Schöpfer zu seinem Geschöpf hat, beginnt nach biblischer Theologie also nicht mit dem Zeitpunkt, an dem das Geschöpf antworten kann, und endet nicht, wenn die menschlichen Antwortmöglichkeiten erschöpft sind. Vielmehr überschreitet sie die Grenzen der vom Geschöpf bewusst erlebten und gestalteten Zeit. Nach biblischer Anthropologie ist der Mensch darum nicht nur *creatura Dei*, wie es auch eine deistische Konzeption für sich reklamieren könnte. Vielmehr akzentuiert biblische Theologie, dass der Schöpfer sein Geschöpf liebt, seiner gedenkt, es beruft und für es sorgt, ohne dass das Geschöpf diese Sorge für sich verdienen könnte oder auch nur selbst damit begönne. Das Geschöpf wiederum, das sich in diesem Zusammenhang von Liebe und Gedenken erfährt, ist seinerseits dazu bestimmt, sich auf die ihm zuvorkommende Liebe zurückzubeziehen.

Die Sorge Gottes um sein Geschöpf, die um eine Antwort wirbt, kann auch mit dem Begriff der *Beziehung* bezeichnet werden, die Gott mit einem Menschen eingeht, oder mit der *Bezogenheit*, aufgrund derer der Mensch auf Gott bezogen ist. Dabei ist die menschliche Bezogenheit auf Gott keine zusätzlich zum Menschsein hinzutretende Eigenschaft, sondern aufgrund seiner Geschöpflichkeit mit dem Menschsein konstitutiv gegeben.[482] Mit der Bezogenheit des Menschen auf Gott realisiert sich aber insofern seine Gottebenbildlichkeit, als es ihm die Bezogenheit auf Gott ermöglicht, Gott antwortend „zu entsprechen" und sich auf ihn zurück zu beziehen, also in demjenigen Verhältnis zu Gott zu leben, das ihm als Bestimmung aufgegeben und vorgegeben ist.

In diesem Aspekt liegt ein Unterschied reformatorisch-theologischer Anthropologie zu einem Ansatz, der die menschliche Gottebenbildlichkeit als *intrinsische* Wesenseigenschaft des Menschen formuliert und etwa mit der menschlichen Vernunft- und Willensbegabung begründet. Mit der *relationalen* Akzentuierung kann vor allem die *Unverfügbarkeit* der Gottebenbildlichkeit gewährleistet werden, insofern die menschliche Bezogenheit auf Gott vom Menschen nicht „besessen" oder über sie verfügt werden kann.

Die Begabung mit Gottebenbildlichkeit[483] bestimmt den Menschen zu ei-

---

[482] Diese Einsicht der menschlichen Bezogenheit steht im Hintergrund, wenn vor allem von systematischer Theologie der Begriff „relationale Ontologie" gebraucht wird. Der Begriff einer „relationalen Ontologie" verdankt sich in der deutschsprachigen Theologie in starkem Maße den Arbeiten von Wilfried Joest und Gerhard Ebeling. Vgl. Joest, Ontologie der Person bei Luther, Göttingen 1967, und Ebeling, Dogmatik des christlichen Glaubens, 3 Bände, Tübingen ³1987/³1989/³1993. Für die englische Theologie vgl. z.B. P.R. Sponheim, Relational Theology, Chalice Press 2006; M.S. Medley, Imago Trinitatis: Towards a Relational Understanding of Becoming Human, University Press of America 2002; J.A. Bracken, Trinity in Process: A Relational Theology of God, New York 1997.

[483] Die biblischen Belegstellen, in denen neben Gen 1,26f. noch Gen 5,1 und Gen 9,6 von der Gottebenbildlichkeit des Menschen gesprochen und diese Figur im Neuen Testament (1 Kor 11,7; Kol 3,10; Jak 3,9) aufgenommen wird, geben keine definitorische Antwort auf die Frage, wie Gottebenbildlichkeit genau zu verstehen ist. Den Status

nem Leben, das Gott entspricht[484] und diejenige Liebe und Sorge spiegelt, die Gott um seine Schöpfung hegt. Die Rede von der Gottebenbildlichkeit reflektiert darum die *Bestimmung* des Menschen, Gott entsprechend zu leben und die Beziehung, in der er von Gott her geborgen ist, sein Leben durchdringen zu lassen.

Gleichwohl weiß die Theologie auch um das Scheitern des Menschen, diese Bestimmung zu erfüllen und kennt seine Verkrümmung in sich selbst, die ihn am Antworten auf Gottes Zuspruch und an der Entsprechung zu Gottes Liebe und Sorge hindert. Sie spricht dem Menschen in diesem Zusammenhang weder seine Geschöpflichkeit noch seine Bestimmung zur Gottebenbildlichkeit ab, versteht seine Gottebenbildlichkeit aber als durch seine Selbstverkrümmung korrumpiert.[485]

Die Dialektik von Bestimmung und Verfehlung im Zusammenhang mit der Gottebenbildlichkeit wird im Neuen Testament in den Kontext gestellt, dass Jesus Christus das *wahre* Ebenbild Gottes sei (2 Kor 4,4; Kol 1,15; Hebr 1,3). Christus steht nach dieser Einsicht nicht in dem alle Menschen verbindenden Zusammenhang der Reflexion auf sich selbst, sondern lebt die menschliche Bestimmung zur Bezogenheit auf Gott und damit die Bestimmung zur Ebenbildlichkeit, zur Entsprechung und Ähnlichkeit im Gegenüber zu Gott auf vollkommene Weise. Die Gottebenbildlichkeit Jesu Christi ist von Martin Luther mit dem Bild ausgedrückt worden, Christus sei der „Spiegel des väterlichen Herzens“:[486] Darin, wie Christus gelebt hat, gestorben und auferstanden ist, können wir darum Gott in seinem Wesen wahrnehmen, wie er für uns ist und wie er sich uns zeigen will – in seinem Ebenbild Jesus Christus, in dem aber zugleich auch die menschliche Bestimmung zur Gottebenbildlichkeit so

des Menschen als *imago Dei* verstehen sie aber, auch wenn er nicht definiert wird, als Begabung, Auszeichnung und Aufgabe, die sich etwa im Herrschaftsauftrag in der Paradieserzählung (Gen 1,28) äußert und im Neuen Testament im Umgang von Menschen miteinander handlungsbegründend verwendet werden kann (1 Kor 11,7).

[484] Vgl. E. Jüngel, Der Gott entsprechende Mensch. Bemerkungen zur Gottebenbildlichkeit als Grundfigur theologischer Anthropologie, in: Ders., Entsprechungen: Gott – Wahrheit – Mensch. Theologische Erörterungen II, Tübingen ³2002, 243-260.

[485] So auch Luther in der Disputatio de homine, Thesen 21-24, LDStA 1, 666,9-18:* „Homo est creatura Dei carne et anima spirante constans, ab initio ad imaginem Dei facta sine peccato... Post lapsum vero Adae subiecta potestati Diaboli, peccato et morti... Quibus stantibus pulcherrima illa et excellentissima res rerum, quanta est ratio post peccatum, relicta sub potestate Diaboli tamen esse concluditur.“ – Der Mensch ist Gottes Geschöpf, das aus Fleisch und einer lebendigen Seele besteht, vom Anfang an zum Bilde Gottes geschaffen ohne Sünde... Aber nach dem Fall Adams der Macht des Teufels unterworfen, der Sünde und dem Tod... Unter diesen Umständen ist jene allerschönste und ausgezeichnetste Hauptsache, als die die Vernunft nach dem Sündenfall geblieben ist, dennoch, so muss gefolgert werden, unter der Macht des Teufels.

[486] Im Großen Katechismus, BSLK 660,42.

verwirklicht ist, wie ein Mensch auf Gott bezogen sein und sich auf ihn verlassen kann.

Die Tatsache, dass *Christus* im Neuen Testament als wahres Ebenbild Gottes verstanden und beschrieben wird, indiziert auch vom Christusgeschehen her ein relationales Verständnismodell von Gottebenbildlichkeit. Im von Paulus zitierten Philipperhymnus (Phil 2,6-11) drückt sich die besondere Weise aus, wie Christus in seinem Leben und Sterben, seiner Auferstehung und Erhöhung von der Alten Kirche geglaubt und bekannt wurde. Nach diesem Text hat Christus seine Ebenbildlichkeit und Wesensgleichheit mit Gott nicht für sich selbst behalten und eingesetzt, sondern sich erniedrigt zugunsten der Menschen, indem er bis zur letzten Konsequenz des Todes am Kreuz Gott gegenüber Gehorsam erwiesen und die Menschen in seine Geschichte so hineingenommen hat, dass diese zur Antwort gegenüber Gott von neuem befähigt und befreit werden können: Die Bezogenheit auf Gott, die Christus gelebt hat, öffnet auch für den in sich selbst verkrümmten Sünder einen Raum, diese Bezogenheit zu leben.

Dieser *partizipatorische* Aspekt, nach dem Christus dem Glaubenden im Glauben und durch den Glauben seine Gottebenbildlichkeit mitteilt und es in dieser Partizipation dem Glaubenden ermöglicht, in Beziehung zu Gott zu leben, was aber seinerseits auch auf seine Beziehungen zu sich selbst und seine Umwelt ausstrahlt, ist theologiegeschichtlich etwa von Martin Luther vertreten worden.[487] Die Lutherforschung in der 2. Hälfte des 20. Jahrhunderts hat, Luthers Ontologie weiter entwickelnd, vom exzentrischen, responsorischen und eschatologischen Charakter des Person-Seins bei Luther gesprochen.[488]

Gottebenbildlichkeit ist nach diesen Überlegungen darum sowohl schöpfungstheologisch als auch – mit Blick auf die menschliche Sünde und die Gerechtigkeit in Christus durch den Glauben – christologisch-soteriologisch zu bestimmen. Dabei ist sie als Bestimmung[489] des Menschen diesem zwar

[487] Dieses Verständnis der menschlichen Gottebenbildlichkeit steht als explizit theologisches Verständnis in enger Nähe zu einem reformatorischen Verständnis der Rechtfertigung und Gerechtigkeit. Zum partizipatorischen Aspekt und dem christologischen Fokus in Luthers Rechtfertigungslehre vgl. mein Buch Zum Herzen sprechen. Eine Studie zum imputativen Aspekt in Martin Luthers Rechtfertigungslehre und zu seinen Konsequenzen für die Predigt des Evangeliums, ASTh 1, Leipzig 2008, v.a. S.180ff.

[488] Vgl. vor allem W. Joest, Ontologie der Person bei Luther, Göttingen 1967. Fruchtbare Schlüsse aus Luthers Theologie für die theologische und ethische Diskussion der Gegenwart zieht in der gegenwärtigen deutschen evangelischen Theologie etwa Wilfried Härle. Vgl. Härle, Menschsein in Beziehungen. Studien zur Rechtfertigungslehre und Anthropologie, Tübingen 2005. Den eben angeklungenen Personbegriff nehme ich weiter unten noch einmal auf.

[489] Der treffende Begriff der „Bestimmung des Menschen" ist wahrscheinlich von Johann J. Spalding geprägt worden, vgl. Spalding, Die Bestimmung des Menschen, hrsg. von W. E. Müller, Waltrop 1997.

mitgegeben, vorgegeben und aufgegeben, zugleich aber ein sich erst am Ende der Zeit eschatisch vollends verwirklichendes Gut, das in Christus in der Zeit aufscheint und dem Menschen partizpatorisch zugeeignet wird, zugleich aber aufgrund der Sünde bis ans Ende der Zeit als angefochtenes und nur unter der Bedingung seiner Zueignung *durch Christus* als verwirklichtes Gut anzusehen ist. Luther hat die Angefochtenheit der menschlichen Bestimmung, die fragmentarische Zueignung der Gottebenbildlichkeit in Christus und die gleichzeitige Verdrehung des Menschen in sich selbst, seine Unfähigkeit und Unwilligkeit zur Beziehung mit Gott und seine gleichzeitige Partizipation an der Gottebenbildlichkeit Christi mit der Formel „simul iustus et peccator" begrifflich gefasst.

Wird im Rahmen von biblisch-reformatorischer Theologie ein christologisch-soteriologisches Verständnis der menschlichen Gottebenbildlichkeit wie eben angedeutet entwickelt, so liegt dieses Verständnis in großer Nähe zu einem Verständnis von christlicher *Gerechtigkeit*, die ihrerseits als Gemeinschaftstreue und Liebe zu Gott einem Menschen als Bestimmung so aufgegeben ist, dass er, lebt er im Vertrauen und in der Liebe zu Gott, seiner Bestimmung gemäß „gerecht" lebt, was aber unter den Bedingungen dieses Lebens aufgrund der immer gegenwärtigen Selbstsucht und Selbstliebe nur angefochten möglich ist und der steten „Zurechnung" der Gemeinschaftstreue durch Gott (*imputatio*) in der Partizipation an der von Christus gelebten und mitgeteilten Gemeinschaftstreue bedarf.[490]

„Gerechtigkeit" ist ebenso wie Gottebenbildlichkeit dem Menschen also insofern entzogen und *unverfügbar*, als er sie nicht selbst herstellen, ja, noch nicht einmal aus eigenen Kräften vollkommen leben und verwirklichen kann. Vielmehr wird sie ihm zugeeignet in der Beziehung zu Gott, als im Glauben, in dem er so mit Christus vereint wird, dass sich ihm Christi Gemeinschaftstreue mitteilt und er selbst in der Partizipation an Christus zu einem „Gott entsprechenden Menschen" (Eberhard Jüngel) wird. Darum liegt seine Gottebenbildlichkeit strukturell auf einer anderen Ebene als seine vernünftige Weltgestaltung. Denn sie wird ihm verliehen, von ihm aber nicht besessen. Sie ereignet sich im Glauben und zwar gerade so, dass ein Mensch am meisten seine Gottebenbildlichkeit lebt, wenn er am wenigsten auf sich selbst reflektiert.[491] Sie gilt aber in ihrer Eigenschaft als *Bestimmung* nicht nur für den Glaubenden, sondern für jeden Menschen, weil sie sich aufgrund der Bezogenheit jedes Menschen auf Gott nicht auf diejenigen Menschen beschränken lässt, an denen „Glauben" wahrnehmbar wäre. Vielmehr verkennt ein menschliches Gradmessen des Glaubens, das sich dieser als schöpferisches

---

[490] Vgl. dazu nochmals mein Buch Zum Herzen sprechen, v.a. S. 376ff.

[491] Die beste knappe Beschreibung dessen, was Gottebenbildlichkeit meint, finde ich immer noch in Luthers Zitat: „Wir sollen menschen und nicht Gott sein. Das ist die summa." (Luther an Spalatin von der Veste Coburg 1530, WA.B 5, 415,45 f.)

Geschenk von Gott her ereignet. Darum ist die für den Menschen unverfügbare Gottebenbildlichkeit im Umgang mit anderen Menschen und mit sich selbst zugleich als *unantastbar* zu kennzeichnen.

Nach dem eben entwickelten Verständnis von Gottebenbildlichkeit im Anschluss an biblisch-reformatorische Theologie liegt die besondere Auszeichnung, das „Menschliche" am Menschsein, das klassischerweise mit dem Würdebegriff assoziiert wird, in der menschlichen Geschöpflichkeit, mehr noch aber in der Bestimmung dazu, diese Geschöpflichkeit als antwortende, reflektierende und auf den Schöpfer bezogene Geschöpflichkeit zu leben. Die Fähigkeit und die Anlage, sich als Geschöpf auf seinen Schöpfer zu beziehen, weil der Schöpfer sich auf das Geschöpf bezogen hat, macht seine Würde und damit dasjenige aus, was unbedingte Achtung gebietet,[492] weil es ihn als Menschen auszeichnet.[493]

Es ist diesen Überlegungen folgend weniger die menschliche Geschöpflichkeit oder „Gottebenbildlichkeit" an sich als *Eigenschaft*, die – naturrechtlich oder substanzontologisch – eine intrinsische *Menschenwürde* begründet, sondern die mit der Geschöpflichkeit gegebene Bezogenheit des Menschen auf den Schöpfer, die sich von Gottes Seite her als gnädiges Gedenken (Ps 8,5) äußert und von der Seite des Menschen als Wahrnehmung des Gedenkens Gottes. Soll in diesem Zusammenhang naturrechtlich argumentiert und damit dasjenige festgehalten werden, das einer positiv-rechtlichen Sicherung des Schutzes der Achtung der Menschenwürde vorausgeht, so ist als das Achtung Gebietende am Menschen noch nicht ausschließlich seine „Natur", sondern vielmehr die Tatsache anzusehen, dass diese Natur über sich selbst hinaus verweist auf Gott, der seines Geschöpfes gedenkt. Darum ist die Rede von der Menschenwürde als einer intrinsischen *Eigenschaft* des Menschen[494]

---

[492] Die Würde als dasjenige am Menschen, das Achtung gebietet, geht auf eine Formulierung von Wilfried Härle zurück. Vgl. B. Vogel (Hrsg.), Im Zentrum: Menschenwürde. Politisches Handeln aus christlicher Verantwortung. Christliche Ethik als Orientierungshilfe, Konrad-Adenauer-Stiftung Berlin 2006.

[493] Im Anschluss an H. Thielicke hat Karen Lebacqz sich mit dem Konzept einer „alien dignity" beschäftigt, die auf der menschlichen Gottebenbildlichkeit beruht. Vgl. Lebacqz, Alien Dignity: The Legacy of Helmut Thielicke for Bioethics, in: S. Lammers u. a. (Hrsg.), On Moral Medicine: Theological Perspectives in Medical Ethics, Grand Rapids/ Cambridge ²1998, 184-192. Dieser Text ist einer der wenigen im englischen Sprachraum, die *human dignity* aus der *imago Dei* ableiten. Lebacqz zieht aus der Entzogenheit (*alien dignity*) der Würde die Konsequenz, Würde sei unantastbar (*inalienable/inviolable*, S. 186f.) und begründe daher einen unbedingten Schutzanspruch.

[494] Gleichwohl liegt die *particula veri* einer eigenschaftsgestützten Begründung von Menschenwürde darin, dass offenbar die *Wahrnehmung* der göttlichen Sorge um sein Geschöpf und die *Reaktion* darauf ein Spezifikum für den *Menschen* ist. Würde daran nicht festgehalten, so könnte ein besonderer Status auch für Delphine, Menschenaffen oder Marienkäfer angenommen werden.

auf diesem Hintergrund nur dann angemessen, wenn zugleich von einer *Unverfügbarkeit* der Würde aufgrund der Konzeption der Gottebenbildlichkeit als der antwortenden Entsprechung zu Gott die Rede ist. Eine verabsolutierte Mitgifttheorie kann demgegenüber zu einer Verabsolutierung des Menschseins im Gegenüber zu Gott führen. „Alien dignity requires a relational view of human beings.“[495]

Nach der Unterscheidung der Verständnisformen von Menschenwürde im Sinne eines grundlegenden Begriffs und im Sinne einer durch Verhalten konstituierten Gestalt wäre ein solches Verständnis von Menschenwürde eine Interpretation im Sinne einer *grundlegenden Würde*, die allen Angehörigen der menschlichen Spezies zukommt, ohne dass sie sie verdienen müssten. Denn das Gedenken Gottes und die Bezogenheit auf Gott gelten für jeden Menschen, auch wenn sie sich nicht jedem erschließen. Vielmehr liegt diese grundlegende Würde darin, dass ein Mensch als Geschöpf Gottes dazu geschaffen, berufen und bestimmt ist, mit Gott in Beziehung zu treten, ihm zu glauben und zu vertrauen, also Gottes Schöpfung und Sorge um sein Geschöpf wahrzunehmen und anzunehmen: Allein die *Anlage* zu dieser Beziehung aber, die Bezogenheit des Menschen auf Gott, auch wenn sie nicht von jedem Menschen zu jeder Zeit in gleicher Weise verwirklicht wird, macht die grundlegende Würde des Menschen aus, weil sie in derjenigen Beziehung, die Gott zu seinem Geschöpf hat, schon verwirklicht ist.

Erfülltes, blühendes Menschsein, das seiner Bestimmung entspricht und auf vollkommene Weise von Christus gelebt wurde, ist das eschatische Ziel des Menschen (die vollkommen realisierte Würde),[496] auf das dieser zugeht und das unter den Bedingungen der Sünde in seinem Leben allenfalls fragmentarisch und angefochten verwirklicht ist. In theologischer Terminologie lässt sich auch in diesem Zusammenhang von Gerechtigkeit, Gemeinschaftstreue oder Heiligkeit sprechen. Hierin liegt die Bestimmung, die Aufgabe und das Ziel des Menschseins. Diese vollständig realisierte Würde ist aber nicht diejenige Würde, die gemeint ist, wenn von einer *allen* Menschen zukommenden und bei allen menschlichen Wesen zu achtenden Menschenwürde gesprochen wird. Vielmehr liegt darin das Bild desjenigen Seins, in das die Beziehung zu Gott einen Menschen verwandeln will.

Auf diesem Hintergrund aber kann *Menschenwürde* nicht verdient und nicht von anderen Menschen verliehen und zuerkannt, sondern nur als schon

[495] Lebacqz, a.a.O., 191.

[496] Damit wohnt einer solchen Bestimmung von Menschenwürde zugleich insofern eine Teleologie inne, als die in Christus verwirklichte Gottebenbildlichkeit das Ziel markiert, auf das Menschen zugehen und das am Ende der Zeit eschatisch in vollkommener Weise verwirklicht sein wird. Darin, dass die Welt auf dieses Ziel wartet und ihm entgegenstrebt, offenbart sich in letztem Ernst die Unverfügbarkeit der Menschenwürde, die sich schon innerhalb der schöpfungstheologischen und soteriologischen Argumentation angedeutet hatte.

bestehender Zustand anerkannt und geachtet werden, und es kann, wenn sie in der Bestimmung des Menschen zum Leben seiner Geschöpflichkeit liegt, meines Erachtens auch kein Zeitpunkt ausgemacht werden, an dem sie bei einem sich entwickelnden menschlichen Wesen noch nicht begonnen hat. Auch wenn über eine Beziehung Gottes zum frühen menschlichen Embryo keine abschließende Aussage gemacht werden kann, so kann doch auf der anderen Seite theologisch nicht konsistent verneint werden, dass eine solche Bezogenheit auch des frühen Embryos bereits angelegt ist und dass von Seiten Gottes eine Beziehung zum sich entwickelnden Embryo theologisch als möglich erscheint.[497] Immerhin erstreckt sich die göttliche Schöpfertätigkeit auf menschliches Leben von Beginn an. Sie erstreckt sich auch auf Klone und Hybride.[498]

Diesen Überlegungen folgend, ist „Menschenwürde" als ein dem Menschen aufgrund seines Menschseins zukommender Wert zu verstehen, aufgrund dessen sein Menschsein Achtung gebietet und Lebensschutz und Anerkennung verlangt. Der Begriff „Menschenwürde" zeigt sich als fast entbehrlich oder zumindest durch die oben gegebene Interpretation deutbar und durch den Begriff des „Menschseins" ersetzbar, wobei dann ein theologisch gefüllter Begriff von Menschsein vorausgesetzt wird. Darüber hinaus versteht eine Interpretation wie die eben gegebene „Menschenwürde" nur teilweise als eine intrinsische menschliche Wesenseigenschaft. Vielmehr besteht sie darauf, dass das Wesen des Menschseins dem Menschen als Unverfügbares und Unantastbares entzogen ist, er in dieses vielmehr hinein tritt und es sich als sein eigenes Wesen aneignet, ohne dass es ihm aber vollkommen verfügbar wird. Die im englischen Sprachraum gebrauchten Begriffe *value, worth* oder *sanctity* sind mit dieser Interpretation selbstverständlich vereinbar.

Innerhalb der bioethischen Argumentation zur Menschenwürde am Beginn des menschlichen Lebens ist in den letzten Jahren von allen christlichen Konfessionen, vermehrt allerdings von der evangelischen Kirche, ein relationaler Ansatz vertreten worden. Im Laufe der Debatte hat sich die Argumentationslage in den letzten Jahren insofern leicht verschoben, als römisch-katholische Theologie (auch in Großbritannien) gegenwärtig davon ausgeht, dass eine fremdnützige Forschung an menschlichen Embryonen ethisch nicht akzeptabel ist, weil

[497] Das Argument, dass 50-75 % aller Embryonen noch vor ihrer Implantation – von der Mutter unbemerkt – abgehen, scheint mir kein Gegenargument zu sein. Zumindest setzt der Selektionsprozess der *Natur* nicht notwendigerweise ein Argument für eine Forschung an Embryonen durch *Menschen* frei. „Der Herr tötet und macht lebendig" (1 Sam 2,6) ist nur unter Billigung eines darwinistischen Zugangs direkt auf menschliches Handeln übertragbar.

[498] Ob „Menschenwürde" auch für Klone und Hybride gilt, kann ich nur so beantworten, dass sie unzweifelhaft Klonen zukommt und aufgrund des fast vollkommenen menschlichen Genoms auch für „Cybrids" angenommen werden muss. Bei „true hybrids" besteht allerdings eine Unsicherheit, wobei sich grundlegend die Frage nach der ethischen Legitimität von speziesübergreifender Forschung an sich stellt.

sie gegen die Unantastbarkeit der Menschenwürde verstößt, und in diesem Zusammenhang vor allem naturrechtlich argumentiert. Demgegenüber argumentiert eine große Anzahl von evangelischen Ethikern, dass – einem relationalen Ansatz entsprechend – in dieser Frage nicht deontologisch, sondern situativ zu urteilen sei, was unter Umständen auch die ethische Erlaubnis von verbrauchender Embryonenforschung – in strengen Grenzen – rechtfertigen könne.[499]

Wird Menschenwürde im Sinne von Menschsein aber als ein dem Menschen entzogenes, unantastbares und unverfügbares *Sein in Beziehung* verstanden, das in diesem *Bezogensein* seine besondere Würde und seinen besonderen Status hat, so ist aus meiner Sicht eine Forschung, bei der menschliche Wesen getötet und zu anderen Zwecken als dem ihrer Heilung gebraucht werden, kritisch zu beurteilen. Auch das an sich wertvolle Motiv einer medizinischen Forschung zur Heilung und Linderung von Krankheiten anderer kann nicht legitimieren, dass menschliche Wesen „verbraucht" werden. Dabei ist keine wirklich plausible Zäsur innerhalb der kontinuierlichen Entwicklung eines Menschen anzunehmen, die die Annahme eines sich graduell entwikkelnden Menschseins rechtfertigen könnte.

Wenn nämlich die geschöpfliche Bezogenheit eines menschlichen Wesens Menschsein als solches auszeichnet, so muss diese ihren Beginn am Beginn des Lebens haben;[500] sie geriete andernfalls zu einer willkürlichen Setzung und einer Zuschreibung durch Menschen, was ihre theologische Qualifikation der Unverfügbarkeit unterböte. Daher halte ich in diesem Zusammenhang die Position der Befürwortung eines strengen Lebensschutzes für mit theologischer Anthropologie konsistent und damit letztlich für konsequent. Auch das Auftreten des Primitivstreifens mit dem damit einhergehenden Ausschluss der Mehrlingsbildung stellt meines Erachtens keine moralrelevante Zäsur dar, insofern zwar damit die weitere „numerische" individuelle Entwicklung bestätigt wird, aber der Embryo, der bis zu diesem Zeitpunkt potentiell teilbar gewesen ist, nicht als „Nicht-Individuum" verstanden werden kann.[501]

---

[499] So in dem bereits zitierten Sammelband von Anselm/Körtner (Hrsg.), Streitfall Biomedizin, Göttingen 2003; vgl. auch Dabrock/Schardien/Klinnert, Menschenwürde und Lebensschutz, Gütersloh 2004. So aber auch in den Äußerungen der *Church of Scotland* in ihrem Summary Report from the Church and Society Council to the 2006 Church of Scotland General Assembly: Embryo Research, Human Stem Cells and Cloned Embryos (s. oben, S. 58, Anm. 117) und der *Church of England* im „Human Embryonic Stem Cell Research: on the Path to an Investment Framework" (2003), s. oben, S. 58, Anm. 116.

[500] Auch die Annahme einer Sukzessiv-Beseelung, die von Aristoteles und ihm folgend einem Großteil der scholastischen Theologie vertreten worden ist, nach dem der Embryo erst nach einer gewissen Zeit (40 Tage bei männlichen, 80 Tage bei weiblichen Embryonen) von Gott eine Seele erhält, die ihm Schutzwürdigkeit verleiht, scheidet damit aus.

[501] Mit diesem Argument gehe ich davon aus, dass die *Möglichkeit* einer Teilbarkeit der *Wirklichkeit* von Individualität nicht widerspricht, was allerdings wiederum einen bestimmten Begriff von Potentialität impliziert.

Nach diesen theologischen Überlegungen verstehe ich Menschenwürde ähnlich wie die kantische Philosophie als unabhängig von Leistung jedem Menschen zukommende *Mitgift*, begründe diese aber nicht mit der (auch potentiellen) menschlichen Rationalität und Sittlichkeit oder der Unterscheidung von Wesen und Ding an sich, sondern der konstitutiven menschlichen Relationalität.[502] Der kantische Anthropozentrismus, der in der Formulierung der *Selbstzwecklichkeit* des Menschen liegt, könnte so vermieden werden. Dass der Mensch ein *Beziehungs*wesen ist und sich von dieser Einsicht her auch seine spezifische Würde erschließt, wird meines Erachtens von Kant im Zusammenhang der Aufklärung und des Rationalismus zu wenig gesehen. Diese *relationale* Kapazität macht aber nach biblischer Theologie das *Specificum Humanum* aus und ist deswegen sowohl in der eigenen Person als auch in der Person eines jeden anderen zu achten. In der konstitutiven menschlichen Relationalität liegt der Grund, dass Menschenwürde nicht nur eine intrinsische Wesenseigenschaft des Menschen, sondern zugleich eine fremde, unverfügbare, unantastbare, aber zugeeignete Realität darstellt. Möglicherweise ist dabei auch die Einsicht noch gar nicht ausgeschöpft, dass sich die Missachtung der Menschenwürde nicht nur auf die Würde anderer bezieht, sondern auch auf die eigene Würde.

Aus der Einsicht der grundlegenden *Bezogenheit* des Menschen ergibt sich eine weitere Folgerung, insofern diese seinem eigenen Handeln vorhergeht und nicht von ihrer Realisierungsgestalt abhängt: Wenn nach theologischer Anthropologie nicht dasjenige den Menschen gegenüber der nicht-menschlichen Kreatur auszeichnet, was er selbst schafft, sondern dasjenige, was an ihm – aufgrund seiner Bezogenheit – getan wird, während er passiv ist und es an sich geschehen lässt, so haben menschliche Wesen, die diese Passivität symbolisieren, eine besondere Anschauungskraft. Zu diesen Passiven gehören schon Schlafende, aber auch Bewusstlose, Neugeborene und Ungeborene, Sterbende und Schwerstbehinderte. Weil sie in besonderem Maße darauf angewiesen

---

[502] Für Luther besteht in seiner Disputation über den Menschen (1536) das Wesen *jedes* Menschen darin, dass er ein von Gott zu Rechtfertigender ist (*hominem iustificari fide*), also ein Wesen, das aufgrund seiner Verfehlung der ihm aufgegeben Beziehung zu Gott des erneuten Zuspruchs der Beziehung bedarf, oder kurz, ein Wesen, an dem Gott handelt. Die Bestimmung, dass ein Mensch von Gott in der Gottesbeziehung zurecht gebracht werden muss, wird von Luther ausdrücklich nicht auf Christenmenschen beschränkt, sondern als für *jeden Menschen* geltend festgestellt. „Et hominem indefinite, id est, universaliter accipit, ut concludat totum mundum, seu *quidquid vocatur homo, sub peccato*." Thesen 34 und 35 (LDStA 1, 668,6f:) Und „Mensch" nimmt er [hierbei] unbegrenzt, das heißt, ganz umfassend, um die ganze Welt oder was auch immer „Mensch" genannt wird, unter der Sünde zusammenzuschließen. (Übersetzung von W. Härle, LDStA 1, 669,8-10.) Im US-amerikanischen Kontext versucht vor allem das Buch von Douglas John Hall, Imaging God: Dominion as Stewardship (1986) in Auseinandersetzung mit lutherischer Theologie einen relationalen Verständnishorizont für die Konzeption der Gottebenbildlichkeit zu gewinnen.

sind, dass an ihnen gehandelt wird, stellen sie in besonderem Maße dar, was geschöpfliches Menschsein ausmacht. In ihrer Verletzlichkeit sind sie darum auch in besonderem Maße zu schützen und zu achten, und zwar zum einen wegen ihrer Verletzlichkeit,[503] zum anderen aber auch, weil ihr Sein ein Bild vom Menschsein vor Gott im allgemeinen besonders anschaulich ausdrückt.

Diese Überlegungen stellen insofern einen Bezug zu den in Abschnitt III. 4.4 ausgeführten Gedanken zur menschlichen Leiblichkeit dar, als bei einem Verständnis des Menschseins als bezogen auf eine ihm externe Instanz das Leben und der Leib nicht als kontrollierbar erscheinen und eine Selbstdistanzierung von der eigenen Leiblichkeit zusammen mit einer Technisierung von Medizin und Therapie auch von hierher als fragwürdig erscheinen müssen. Menschen tragen zwar eine Verantwortung für ihren Leib und seine Gesundheit, besitzen ihn aber nicht. Auch ein *Recht* auf Gesundheit oder eine *Pflicht* zur Therapie und zum *Enhancement* können auf diesem Hintergrund nicht zugestanden werden, wohl aber ein Recht auf Achtung der leib-seelischen Integrität.

Ich schließe diesen Abschnitt mit einigen knappen Überlegungen zum menschlichen Person-Sein. Die Kontinuität von Personalität wird von Vertretern neuerer bioethischer Ansätze in Frage gestellt, indem sie Person-Sein als auf bestimmten nachweisbaren Kriterien beruhend verstehen. Wird Personalität mit Selbstbewusstsein und aktuellem Vernunftvollzug assoziiert, so kann sie für Ungeborene, Bewusstlose und Säuglinge nicht ausgesagt werden, und schon bei Schlafenden müssen Hilfskonstrukte gefunden werden.

Wird Person-Sein aber im Anschluss an die oben angestellten Überlegungen als nicht in sich selbst gründend, sondern durch ein von außen her geschehendes Anerkennungsverhältnis konstituiert verstanden,[504] so treten andere Nuancen in den Fokus, die Wilfried Joest im Anschluss an Luther als responsorisch, exzentrisch und eschatologisch bestimmt hat.[505] Person-Sein impliziert danach ein Sein-in-Beziehung, das nicht durch sich selbst zu sich selbst kommen kann und zugleich als noch unabgeschlossen zu gelten hat. Damit ist ein so verstandenes theologisches Person-Verständnis grundsätzlich kritisch gegenüber einem rationalistischen, empiristischen und individualistischen Menschenbild.

---

[503] Die Verletzlichkeit dieser menschlicher Wesen korrespondiert mit ihrer Leiblichkeit. Dazu sind die Beiträge von G. McKenny hilfreich, die oben (S. 167ff.) schon eine Rolle gespielt haben.

[504] Dabei muss theologisch ernst genommen werden, dass nicht nur Menschen Personen sind, sondern dass der Personbegriff sich auch – als konstitutiv relationaler Begriff – auf das Personsein *Gottes* bezieht, von wo aus er auch allererst angemessen zu verstehen ist. Vgl. dazu den instruktiven Artikel von E. Herms, Zur Systematik des Personbegriffs in reformatorischer Tradition, NZSTh 50, 2007, 377-413, v.a. 392-399.

[505] Vgl. Joest, Ontologie der Person, 232ff.

Wird Personsein als in einem externen Anerkennungsverhältnis gründend verstanden, so kann es sich nicht ausschließlich auf bestimmte Phasen des Menschseins beziehen, sondern muss dem Menschsein in jedem Stadium zukommen. „The human person is identified as such because of his or her human, and thus personal, nature and his or her familial relationship with other persons."[506]

Fraglich erscheint allerdings auch in diesem Zusammenhang noch die Bewertung der ersten 14 Tage des menschlichen Lebens, zumal für Embryonen *in vitro*: in dieser Zeit steht der sich entwickelnde Embryo zum einen noch in keiner Beziehung zur ihn umgebenden Umwelt, zum anderen ist eine Teilung in zwei sich entwickelnde Embryonen bis zu diesem Zeitpunkt möglich. Embryonen *in vitro* entwickeln sich darüber hinaus nicht automatisch als Menschen, sondern nur, wenn sie an den Ort versetzt werden, der für ihre weitere Entwicklung notwendig ist. Diese Unsicherheit hat innerhalb der Kammer für Öffentliche Verantwortung der Evangelischen Kirche in Deutschland (EKD) einen nicht unerheblichen Teil der Mitglieder dazu bewogen, das genuin Menschliche in der *Entwicklungsmöglichkeit* des Embryo zu sehen, die auf äußere Rahmenbedingungen angewiesen ist, und im Blick auf Embryonen, die sich nicht in den Uterus einnisten, nicht von sich entwickelnden Menschen zu sprechen.[507]

Wird Person-Sein aber genuin als exzentrisch, responsorisch und eschatologisch verstanden, so ist es in *jedem* Stadium seines Seins auf die Bereitstellung der notwendigen äußeren Rahmenbedingungen angewiesen und in jedem Stadium konstitutiv ein sich entwickelndes Sein. Der Abschluss der Nidation oder der Implantation nach IVF stellen in dieser Hinsicht keine kategorialen Zäsuren dar, sie benennen zwar – ebenso wie die Geburt – einen Ortswechsel, konstituieren den sich entwickelnden Embryo aber nicht neu. Der Ausschluss der Mehrlingsbildung macht in diesem Zusammenhang eine numerische, nicht eine Identitäts-Aussage. Mit einer konsequent relationalen Anthropologie ergibt sich darum in meinen Augen, auch dem Kontinuitätsargument folgend, die Konsequenz, von menschlichem Leben als personalem Leben ab dem Zeitpunkt der Kernverschmelzung zu sprechen und ab diesem Zeitpunkt auch eine absolute Schutzwürdigkeit zu garantieren. Dass der sich entwickelnde Embryo seinerseits erst mit dem Abschluss der Nidation in Beziehung zu seiner Umwelt tritt, widerspricht dieser Folgerung nicht, weil seine genuine *Orientierung auf Beziehung hin* schon vor diesem Zeitpunkt besteht und kontinuierlich sein Leben bestimmen wird.

Diese Überlegungen erhellen abschließend das Verhältnis von Menschenwürde und Menschenrechten. Da sich Rechte in der klassischen Auslegung

---

[506] A. Sutton, Christian Bioethics, 32.

[507] Vgl. die schon häufiger zitierte Schrift *Im Geist der Liebe mit dem Leben umgehen*, 22.

auf diejenigen Menschen beziehen, die *geboren* sind, haben ungeborene Menschen noch keine Menschenrechte. Für den Zusammenhang der Forschung an menschlichen Embryonen muss wahrscheinlich gesagt werden, dass die Sprache der „Menschenrechte“ für die Debatte zum menschlichen Lebensbeginn zumindest nicht hilfreich ist. Es kann aber dennoch konstatiert werden, dass, wenn Menschenwürde als verdankte, unverfügbare und unantastbare Realität verstanden wird, diese die Grundlage der Menschenrechte bildet: Menschenrechte und Grundrechte hat ein Mensch, weil er Mensch ist. Die nationalen und internationalen Dokumente, die Menschenrechte mit der Menschenwürde begründen, auch wenn sie keine inhaltliche Bestimmung von Menschenwürde geben, transportieren darum eine wichtige Einsicht.

Zugleich ist festzuhalten, dass die Verwirklichung der Menschenrechte und ihre rechtliche Positivierung die Realisierungsgestalt der Menschenwürde bildet: werden die Menschenrechte rechtlich gesichert, so wird die Würde des Menschen anerkannt und geachtet.

Mit dieser Überlegung lässt sich aber eine weitere Folgerung ziehen. Wird in der bioethischen Debatte der Akzent auf die Menschen*würde* gelegt, so ist es wahrscheinlicher, dass von einer absoluten Schutzwürdigkeit auch des ungeborenen Menschen ausgegangen wird. In einem Rechtssystem, das eine explizite Aussage zur Wesensbestimmung des Menschen macht und diese mit dem Menschenwürdebegriff verknüpft, wird die Forschung an menschlichen Wesen wahrscheinlich eher verboten werden als in Rechtssystemen, die eine solche verfassungsmäßige Wesensbestimmung von Menschen vermeiden. In Rechtssystemen dagegen, die eher von den Menschen*rechten* als Freiheitsrechten geprägt sind, wird wahrscheinlich eher mit der Freiheit von Forschern und dem (potentiellen) Nutzen gegenwärtiger und zukünftiger Patienten argumentiert, weil der potentielle Nutzen der Forschung die ethische Problematik überwiegt.

In der Pluralität der kulturellen und ideengeschichtlichen Prägungen besteht der Beitrag evangelischer Theologie zur bioethischen Debatte meines Erachtens darin, ausgehend von der biblisch-reformatorischen Anthropologie eine theologische Wesensbestimmung des Menschen zu entwickeln und von hierher in das Gespräch mit anderen Anthropologumena einzutreten. Eine solche theologische Wesensbestimmung habe ich auf den vorhergehenden Seiten zu geben versucht. Wenn diese mit anderen Anthropologumena in das Gespräch eintritt, so heißt dies zunächst, Menschenbilder offenzulegen, die nicht explizit gemacht worden sind, und aus der Sicht theologischer Anthropologie deren Stärken und Schwächen zu benennen. Auch dies habe ich zu leisten versucht. Dabei kann es nicht darum gehen, die eigene Position als moralisch höherwertig anzusehen und anderen Konzeptionen mangelnde Sensibilität oder Reflexion vorzuwerfen. Es kann lediglich darum gehen, einen eigenen Standpunkt zu vertreten (der auch seine blinden Flecken hat) und die Voraussetzungen des eigenen und anderer Standpunkte zu benennen.

Es kann in der sensiblen Frage der Forschung an menschlichen Embryonen auch nicht darum gehen, Patienten, die an einer bislang unheilbaren degenerativen Krankheit erkrankt sind, die Hoffnung auf Linderung und Therapie zu nehmen. Dabei aber kann von christlicher Theologie her allerdings kein Recht auf Leidensfreiheit und keine Pflicht zur Leidvermeidung festgestellt werden.[508]

Eine theologische Anthropologie versteht sich nicht von selbst. Sie beruht auf dem Glauben daran, dass der dreieinige Gott sich in der Geschichte offenbart hat, seine Liebe, Gnade und Vergebung Menschen geschenkt hat und sich selbst in das Geschick von Menschen hat verwickeln lassen. Diese Anthropologie muss sich so erschließen, wie sich einem Menschen eine Liebesbotschaft erschließt – indem sie sein Herz berührt und damit den Kern seiner Existenz affiziert. Wenn von einer solchen existenzverändernden Erfahrung her argumentiert wird, so ist die damit verbundene Haltung nicht Selbstgerechtigkeit, sondern vielmehr Hoffnung auf die „gewinnende Kraft des Guten".[509]

Die meiner Argumentation inhärente Anthropologie ist darum nicht pragmatisch, sondern erschließt sich aufgrund einer Lebens- und Selbstgewissheit, deren Ursprung in einer personalen existentiellen Neuausrichtung liegt. Kann diese Argumentation aber aus den unterschiedlichsten Gründen nicht nachvollzogen werden, so erschließt sich möglicherweise eine Ahnung dessen, dass der Grund von Menschsein nicht in dem liegt, was Menschen tun und leisten. In diesem Zusammenhang wäre eine Ablehnung von verbrauchender Forschung an menschlichen Embryonen und von Erzeugung von Embryonen zu Forschungszwecken, sowohl *in vitro* als auch durch Klonierung und in der Erzeugung von Hybriden, aus *Vorsichtsgründen*, wie sie tutioristische Argumentationswege vorsehen, mit theologischer Ethik konsistent und für die Gesetzgebung wünschenswert – sowohl in Deutschland als auch im internationalen Kontext.

Kann also der theologische Verständnisrahmen nicht nachvollzogen werden, ist meines Erachtens der Rekurs auf das Kontinuumsargument in Verbindung mit einer grundsätzlichen ethischen Vorsicht hinsichtlich der Forschung an menschlichem Leben am überzeugendsten. Die Menschlichkeit einer Gesellschaft bemisst sich daran, wie sie mit ihren verletzlichsten Mitgliedern umgeht. Wer diese sind, sollte nicht durch einen Mehrheitsentscheid bestimmt werden.

---

[508] Vielmehr kann von christlicher Theologie darauf hingewiesen werden, dass Gott selbst sich auch ins Leiden hat verwickeln lassen. Vgl. dazu meinen Aufsatz Crux sola est nostra theologia. Die Bedeutung der Kreuzestheologie für die Theodizeefrage, NZSTh 49, 2007, 223-240.

[509] Vgl. W. Härle, Die gewinnende Kraft des Guten, in: Ders., Menschsein in Beziehungen, 347ff.

Register

Literaturverzeichnis

Monographien, Artikel und Aufsätze

Ammicht-Quinn, Regina u. a. (Hrsg.), The discourse of human dignity, Concilium 2003/2.

Dies., Würde als Verletzbarkeit. Eine theologisch-ethische Grundkategorie im Kontext zeitgenössischer Kultur, Theologische Quartalschrift 184, 2004, 37-48.

Anselm, Rainer/Körtner, Ulrich H. J. (Hrsg.), Streitfall Biomedizin. Urteilsfindung in christlicher Verantwortung, Göttingen: Vandenhoeck & Ruprecht 2003.

Ashcroft, Richard E., Making sense of dignity, Journal for Medical Ethics 2005, 31, 679-682.

Baylis, Francoise, Human Embryonic Stem Cell Research: Comments on the NBAC Report, in: Suzanne Holland/Karen Lebacqz/Laurie Zoloth (Hrsg.), The Human Embryonic Stem Cell Debate, Cambridge/Massachusetts und London: MIT Press 2001, 51-60.

Beauchamp, T. L./Childress, J. F., Principles of Biomedical Ethics, Oxford: Oxford University Press [5]2001.

Bedford-Strohm, Heinrich, Sacred body? Stem cell research and human cloning, Ecumenical Review 54, 2002, 240-250.

Beyleveld, Deryck/Bronsword, Roger, Human Dignity in Bioethics and Biolaw, Oxford: Oxford University Press 2001.

Böckenförde, Ernst-Wolfgang/Spaemann, Robert (Hrsg.), Menschenrechte und Menschenwürde. Historische Voraussetzungen – säkulare Gestalt – christliches Verständnis, Stuttgart: Klett Cotta 1987.

Bucar, Elizabeth M./Barnett, Barbra (Hrsg.), Does Human Rights need God? Grand Rapids/Cambridge: Eerdmans Pub. 2005.

Charnovitz, Steve u. a. (Hrsg.), Law in the Service of Human Dignity: Essays in Honour of Florentino Feliciano, Melbourne: Cambridge University Press 2005.

Church of Scotland, Church and Society Council, Report of the Working Group on Embryo Research, Human Stem Cells and Cloned Embryos, 2006.

Collste, Göran, Is Human Life Special? Religious and Philosophical Perspectives on the Principle of Human Dignity, Bern u. a.: Peter Lang 2002.

Colson, Charles W./Cameron, Nigel M. de S. (Hrsg.), Human Dignity in the Biotech Century. A Christian Vision for public Policy, Downers Grove: InterVarsity Press 2004.

Dabrock, Peter/Kinnert, Lars / Schardien, Stefanie, Menschenwürde und Lebensschutz. Herausforderungen theologischer Bioethik, Gütersloh: Gütersloher Verlagshaus 2004.

Damschen, G. / Schönecker, D. (Hrsg.), Der moralische Status menschlicher Embryonen. Pro und contra Spezies-, Kontinuums-, Identitäts- und Potentialitätsargument, Berlin/New York: de Gruyter 2003.

Deech, Ruth/Smajdor, Anna, From IVF to Immortality. Controversy in the Era of Reproductive Technology, Oxford: Oxford University Press 2007.

Dean-Drummond, Celia (Hrsg.), Brave new World? Theology, Ethics and the Human Genome, London/New York: t & t clark 2003.

Dierken, Jörg/von Scheliha, Arnulf (Hrsg.), Freiheit und Menschenwürde. Studien zum Beitrag des Protestantismus, Tübingen: Mohr Siebeck 2005.

Dreier, Horst, Menschenwürde aus verfassungsrechtlicher Sicht, in: Härle/Preul (Hrsg.), Menschenwürde, MJTh XVII, MThS 89, Marburg 2005, 167-210.

Duffy, Regis (Hrsg.), Made in God's Image: The Catholic Vision of Human Dignity, Mahwah, USA: Paulist Press International 1999.

Dworkin, Ronald, Die Grenzen des Lebens. Abtreibung, Euthanasie und persönliche Freiheit, übersetzt von S. Höbel u. a., Reinbek: Rowohlt 1994.

Ders., Bürgerrechte ernstgenommen, übersetzt von Ursula Wolf, Frankfurt/Main: Suhrkamp 1984.

Ders., What is sacred?, in: Harris (Hrsg.), Bioethics, Oxford/New York: Oxford University Press 2001, 157-204.

Eide, Asbjørn u. a. (Hrsg.), The Universal Declaration of Human Rights: A Commentary, Oxford: Aschehoug 1992.

European Neonatal Research. Consent, ethics, committees and law, hrsg. von Su Mason und Chris Megone, Aldershot u. a.: Ashgate 2001.

Feldman, David (Hrsg.), English Public Law, Oxford: Oxford University Press 2004.

Finnis, John, Natural Law and Natural Rights, Oxford: Clarendon Press 1980.

Ford, Norman M., The Prenatal Person. Ethics from Conception to Birth, Oxford: Blackwell 2002.

Forsythe, David P., Human Rights in International Relations, Cambridge: Cambridge University Press 22006.

Foster, Claire, Bentham on the slippery slope? Discussing embryo research in Britain's Parliament and Churches, ZEE 46, 2002, 61-65.

Friele, M. B., Rechtsethik der Embryonenforschung. Rechtsharmonisierung in moralisch umstrittenen Bereichen, Paderborn: mentis 2008.

Gandhi, P. R. (Hrsg.), International Human Rights Documents, Oxford: Oxford University Press ^{5}2006.

Gelhaus, Petra, Gentherapie und Weltanschauung. Ein Überblick über die gen-ethische Diskussion, Darmstadt: Wissenschaftliche Buchgesellschaft 2006.

Gewirth, Alan, Reason and Morality, Chicago/London: University of Chicago Press 1978.

Goodhart, Michael, Origins and Universality in the Human Rights Debate: Cultural Essentialism and the Challenge of Globalization, Human Rights Quarterly 25, 2003, 935-964 .

Greer, Steven, The European Convention on Human Rights. Achievements, Problems and Prospects, Studies in European Law and Policy, Cambridge: Cambridge University Press 2006.

Grisez, Germain, The Way of the Lord Jesus, 3 Bände, Chicago: Franciscan Herald Press 1983ff.

Habermas, Jürgen, Die Zukunft der menschlichen Natur. Auf dem Weg zu einer liberalen Eugenik? Frankfurt/Main: Suhrkamp 2005.

Hansen, Hendrik, Menschenwürde und Individualismus. Westliche Werte in Europa und Amerika, Veröffentlichung des Goethe-Instituts Chicago, http://www.goethe.de/ins/us/chi/ acv/ztg/de1714381.htm.

Härle, Wilfried (Hrsg.), Ethik im Kontinuum. Beiträge zur relationalen Erkenntnistheorie und Ontologie, Leipzig: Evangelische Verlagsanstalt 2008.

Ders., Menschsein in Beziehungen. Studien zur Anthropologie und Rechtfertigungslehre, Tübingen: Mohr Siebeck 2005.

Ders./Vogel, Bernhard (Hrsg.), Vom Recht, das mit uns geboren ist. Aktuelle Probleme des Naturrechts, Freiburg/Breisgau: Herder 2007.

Ders./Vogel, Bernhard (Hrsg.), Begründung von Menschenwürde und Menschenrechten, Freiburg/Breisgau: Herder 2008

Harris, John (Hrsg.), Bioethics, Oxford: Oxford University Press 2001.

Ders., Cloning and Human Dignity, in: M.Ruse/A. Sheppard (Hrsg.), Cloning: Responsible Science or Technomadness? Amherst/New York: Prometheus Books 2001, 172-178.

Ders., Enhancing Evolution. The Ethical Case for Making Better People, Princeton/Oxford: Princeton University Press 2007.

Ders., The Ethical Use of Human Embyonic Stem Cells in Research and Therapy, in: J. Bulrely/J. Harris (Hrsg.), A Companion to Genethics, Oxford: WileyBlackwell 2002, 158-174.

Hauerwas, Stanley, The peaceable Kingdom. A Primer in Christian Ethics, Notre Dame/London: SCM 1983.

Haßmann, H., Embryonenschutz im Spannungsfeld internationaler Menschenrechte, staatlicher Grundrechte und nationaler Regelungsmodelle zur Embryonenforschung, Heidelberg/Berlin: Springer 2003.

Herms, Eilert, Zur Systematik des Personbegriffs in reformatorischer Tradition, NZSTh 50, 2007, 377-413.

Heyer, M., Präimplantationsdiagnostik, Embryonenforschung, Klonen. Ein vergleichender Überblick zur Rechtslage in ausgewählten Ländern, Freiburg/München: Alber 2007.

Hill, Thomas E. Jr., Dignity and Practical Reason in Kant's Moral Theory, New York: Cornell University Press 1992.

Hoerster, Norbert, Ethik des Embryonenschutzes. Ein rechtsphilosophischer Essay, Stuttgart: Reclam 2002.

Hoffman, David/Rowe, John, Human Rights in the UK. A general Introduction to the Human Rights Act 1998, Harlow: Longman 2003.

Hollenbach, David, The Global Face of Public Faith. Politics, Human Rights, and Christian Ethics, Washington DC: Georgetown University Press 2003.

Horton, Richard, Rediscovering Human Dignity, Lancet 2004, 364, 1081-1085.

Human Fertilisation and Embryology Authority, Hybrids and Chimeras. A consultation on the ethical and social implications of creating human/animal embryos in research, 2007.

Jeffreys, D. S., Defending Human Dignity. John Paul II and Political Realism, Michigan: Brazos Press 2004.

Ders., The influence of Kant on Christian Theology: A Debate About Human Dignity and Christian Personalism, Journal of Markets and Morality 7, Nr. 2 (Herbst 2004), 507-516.

Junker-Kenny, Maureen, Genes and the Self. Anthropological Questions to the Human Genome Project, in: C. Deane-Drummond (Hrsg.), Brave New World. Theology, Ethics and the Human Genome, London/New York: t & t clark 2003, 116-140.

Kaczor, Christopher, The Edge of Life. Human Dignity and contemporary Bioethics, Dordrecht: Springer 2005.

Kant, Immanuel, Grundlegung zur Metaphysik der Sitten, hrsg. mit Kommentar von Christoph Horn, Corinna Mieth und Nico Scarano, Frankfurt/Main: Suhrkamp 2007.

Ders., Werke in sechs Bänden, hrsg. von Wilheim Weischedel, Wiesbaden: Insel 1960, Nachdruck Darmstadt: Wissenschaftliche Buchgesellschaft 1998.

Kass, Leon R., Life, Liberty and the Defense of Dignity. The Challenge for Bioethics, San Francisco: Encounter Books 2002.

Kilner, John F., Art. Human Dignity, Encyclopedia of Bioethics [3]2003, 1193-1200.

Knoepffler, Nikolaus, Menschenwürde in der Bioethik, Berlin/Heidelberg: Springer 2004.

Körtner, Ulrich H. J., Geburtlichkeit. Theologische Gesichtspunkte einer anthropologischen Grundbestimmung im Kontext medizinethischer Fragestellungen, ZEE 52, 2008, 9-22.

Kranjc, Janez, The right to human dignity, in: Bostjan Zalar (Hrsg.), Five Challenges for European Courts: The Experiences of German and Slovenian Courts, Ljubljana: 2004, 457-473.

Krantz, Susan F., Refuting Peter Singer's Ethical Theory. The Importance of Human Dignity, Westport/Connecticut/London: Greenwood Press 2002.

Kraynak, Robert P./Tinder, Glenn (Hrsg.), In Defense of Human Dignity. Essays for our Times, Notre Dame/Indiana: University of Notre Dame Press 2003.

Kretzmer, David/Klein, Eckart (Hrsg.), The Concept of Human Dignity in Human Rights Discourse, The Hague/London/New York: Brill 2002.

Kuhse, H./Singer, P. (Hrsg.), A Companion to Bioethics, Oxford: WileyBlackwell 1998.

Luban, David, Legal Ethics and Human Dignity, Cambridge: Cambridge University Press 2007.

Macklin, Ruth, Dignity is a useless concept, British Medical Journal 2003, 327, 1419-1420.

Maio, G. (Hrsg.), Der Status des extrakorporalen Embryo. Perspektiven eines interdisziplinären Zugangs, Stuttgart: Frommann-Holzboog 2007.

Mason, Ian (Hrsg.), The Right to Human Dignity and other lectures, Sir Thomas More Lecture 2003, London: Simmonds & Hill Pub. 2005.

McKenny, Gerald, Bioethics, the Body, and the Legacy of Bacon, in: S. Lammers / A. Verhey (Hrsg.), On Moral Medicine. Theological Perspectives in Medical Ethics, Grand Rapids/Cambridge: Eerdmans Pub. [2]1998, 308-323.

Ders., To Relieve the Human Condition. Bioethics, Technology, and the Body, New York: State University of New York Press 1997.

Meilaender, Gilbert, Bioethics. A Primer for Christians, Grand Rapids/Cambridge: Eerdmans Pub. [2]2005.

Mill, John Stewart/Bentham, Jeremy, Utilitarianism and other Essays, hrsg. von A. Ryan, Harmondsworth/Middlesex u. a.: Penguin Books 1987.

Mulkay, Michael, The embryo research debate. Science and the politics of reproduction, Cambridge: Cambridge University Press 1997.

Nuffield Council on Bioethics, Stem cell therapy: the ethical issues. A discussion paper, London 2000.

Ovey, Clare/White, Robin, Jacobs and White, The European Convention of Human Rights, Oxford: Oxford University Press [3]2002.

Peters, Ted, Embryonic Stem Cells and the Theology of Dignity, in: Suzanne Holland/Karen Lebacqz/Laurie Zoloth (Hrsg.), The Human Embryonic Stem Cell Research, Cambridge/Massachusetts und London: Eerdmans Pub. 2001, 127-139.

Porter, Jean, Natural and Divine Law. Reclaiming the Tradition for Christian Ethics, Grand Rapids/Cambridge: Eerdmans Pub. 1999.

Pullman, Daryl, Universalism, Particularism and the Ethics of Dignity, Christian Bioethics 7, 2001, 333-358.

Rae, Scott B./Cox, Paul M., Bioethics. A Christian Approach in a Pluralistic Age, Grand Rapids/Michigan / Cambridge: Eerdmans Pub. 1999.

Report of the committee of inquiry into human fertilisation and embryology (Warnock-Report) by Command of Her Majesty, London 1984.

Richardt, Nicole, A Comparative Analysis of the Embryological Research Debate in Great Britain and Germany, Social Politics: International Studies in Gender, State and Society 10.1 (2003) 86-128.

Rolf, Sibylle, Menschenwürde – Grund oder Spitze der Menschenrechte?, in: F. M. Brunn u. a. (Hrsg.), Menschenbild und Theologie. Beiträge zum interdisziplinären Gespräch, Festgabe für Wilfried Härle, MThS 100, Leipzig: Evangelische Verlagsanstalt 2007, 141-160.

Rousseau, Richard W., Human Dignity and the Common Good. The Great Papal Social Encyclicals from Leo XII. to John Paul II., Oxford: Greenwood Press 2001.

Runzo, Joseph u. a. (Hrsg.), Human Rights and Responsibilities in the World Religions, Oxford: Oneworld Publications 2003.

Ruston, Roger, Human Rights and the Image of God, London: SCM Press 2004.

Schmidt-Jortzig, Edzard, „Menschenwürde“ als Zauberwort der öffentlichen Debatte. Demokratische Meinungsbildung in hoch komplexen Problemfeldern, ZEE 52, 2008, 50-56.

Schockenhoff, Eberhard, Naturrecht und Menschenwürde. Universale Ethik in einer geschichtlichen Welt, Mainz: Matthias-Grünewald-Verlag 1996.

Schweiker, William (Hrsg.), The Blackwell Companion to Religious Ethics, Malden (USA)/ Oxford/Victoria (Australia): WileyBlackwell 2005.

Singer, Peter, Praktische Ethik (engl. Practical ethics, Cambridge 1979), Stuttgart : Reclam 1999.

Ders., Rethinking Life and Death. The Collapse of Our Traditional Ethics, Oxford: Oxford Paperbacks 1995.

Smith, Janet E., I Knit You in Your Mother's Womb, Christian Bioethics 8, 2002, 125-146.

Soulen, R. K. / Woodhead, L. (Hrsg.), God and Human Dignity, Michigan/Cambridge: Georgetown University Press 2006.

Spaemann, Robert, Personen. Versuche über den Unterschied zwischen etwas und jemand, Stuttgart: Klett-Cotta 32007.

Stellungnahme der Zentralen Kommission zur Wahrung ethischer Grundsätze in der Medizin und ihren Grenzgebieten (Zentrale Ethikkommission) bei der Bundesärztekammer zum Forschungsklonen mit dem Ziel therapeutischer Anwendungen, 2006, www.zentrale-ethikkommission.de/downloads/TherapKlonen.pdf.

Sutton, Agneta, Christian Bioethics. A Guide for the Perplexed, London: t & t clark 2008.

Tauer, Carol A., Art. Embryo and Fetus II., Embryo Research, Encyclopedia of Bioethics, 32003, 712-722.

Taupitz, J., Rechtliche Regelung der Embryonenforschung im internationalen Vergleich, Berlin/Heidelberg: Springer 2003.

Uertz, Rudolf, Vom Gottesrecht zum Menschenrecht. Das katholische Staatsdenken in Deutschland von der Französischen Revolution bis zum II. Vatikanischen Konzil (1789-1965), Politik- und Kommunikationswissenschaftliche Veröffentlichungen der Görres-Gesellschaft 25, Paderborn u. a.: Schöningh 2005.

Van Ness, Peter (Hrsg.), Debating Human Rights. Critical essays from the United States and Asia, London/New York: Routledge 1999.

Verspieren, Patrick, Dignity in Political and Bioethical Debates, in: Regina Ammicht-Quinn u. a. (Hrsg.), The discourse of human dignity, Concilium 2003/2, 13-22.

Vögele, Wolfgang, Menschenwürde zwischen Recht und Theologie. Begründungen von Menschenrechten in der Perspektive öffentlicher Theologie, Öffentliche Theologie 14, Gütersloh: Gütersloher Verlagshaus 2000.

Vogel, Bernhard (Hrsg.), Im Zentrum: Menschenwürde. Politisches Handeln aus christlicher Verantwortung. Christliche Ethik als Orientierungshilfe, eine Veröffentlichung der Konrad-Adenauer-Stiftung e.V., Berlin 2006

Walter, Jennifer K./Klein, Eran P. (Hrsg.), The Story of Bioethics. From seminal Works to contemporary Explorations, Washington D.C.: Georgetown University Press 2003.

Waters, Brent/Cole-Turner, Ronald (Hrsg.), God and the Embryo. Religious Voices on Stem Cells and Cloning, Washington D.C.: Georgetown University Press 2003.

Weltärztebund, Deklaration des Weltärztebundes von Helsinki, Ethische Grundsätze für die medizinische Forschung am Menschen, Helsinki 1964 (erneuert 1975, 1983, 1989, 1996, 2000, 2002, 2004), www.arzt.de/page.asp?his=2.49.1761.

Zimmerman, Anthony, Zygotes and embryos are people, Homiletic and pastoral review 100, 2000, 16-22.

Gesetzestexte, Konventionen und Parlamentarische Texte

Charta der Grundrechte der Europäischen Union, 2000, www.europarl.europa.eu/charter/pdf/text_de.pdf.

Council of Europe, Convention for the protection of human rights and dignity of the human being with regard to the application of biology and medicine: Convention on human rights and biomedicine, Oviedo, 4.4.1997, European Treaty Series No. 164, http://conventions.coe.int/treaty/EN/Treaties/Html/164.htm.

The European Convention for the Protection of Human Rights and Fundamental Freedoms, 1948, http://conventions.coe.int/treaty/EN/Treaties/html/005.htm.

Gesetz zum Schutz von Embryonen (13. Dezember 1990), http://www.gesetze-im-internet.de/eschg/BJNR027460990.html.

Gesetz zur Sicherstellung des Embryonenschutzes im Zusammenhang mit Einfuhr und Verwendung menschlicher embryonaler Stammzellen (Stammzellgesetz - StZG), 28. Juni 2002, www.bmbf.de/pub/stammzellgesetz.pdf.

Grundgesetz der Bundesrepublik Deutschland, 1949, www.gesetze-im-internet.de/bundesrecht/gg/gesamt.pdf.

House of Commons, Science and Technology Committee, Government proposals for the regulation of hybrid and chimera embryos, Fifth Report of Session 2006/2007, www.parliament.the-stationery-office.com/pa/cm200607/cmselect/cmsctech/272/272i.pdf.

House of Lords/House of Commons, Joint Committee on the Human Tissues and Embryo (Draft) Bill, reports, August 2007, http://www.parliament.the-stationery-office.com/pa/jt/jtembryos.htm.

Human Cloning and human dignity: An ethical inquiry, The President's Council on Bioethics, Washington DC 2002, http://www.bioethics.gov/reports/cloningreport/index.html.

Human Fertilisation and Embryology Act, 1990, www.opsi.gov.uk/Acts/acts1990/Ukpga_19900037_en_1.htm.

Human Fertilisation and Embryology Bill, 2007, http://services.parliament.uk/bills/2007-08/humanfertilisationandembryology.html.

Human Reproductive Cloning Act, 2001, www.opsi.gov.uk/ACTS/acts2001/ukpga_20010023_en_1.

Human Rights Act, 1998, www.opsi.gov.uk/ACTS/acts1998/ukpga_19980042_en_1.

Human Tissue Act, 2004, www.opsi.gov.uk/ACTS/acts2004/ukpga_20040030_en_1.

Parliamentary Office of Science and Technology, Postnote Nr. 141, June 2000: Stem Cell Research, www.parliament.uk/parliamentary_offices/post/pubs2000.cfm.

Parliamentary Office of Science and Technology, Postnote Nr. 174, March 2002: Stem Cell Research, www.parliament.uk/post/pn174.pdf.

Parliamentary Office of Science and Technology, Postnote Nr. 221, June 2004: Regulating Stem Cell Therapy, www.parliament.uk/documents/upload/postpn221.pdf.

The Universal Declaration of Human Rights, 1948, www.un.org/Overview/rights.html.

RELEVANTE INTERNETSEITEN (NACH WEBSITES GEORDNET)

UK Stem Cell Initiative: http://www.advisorybodies.doh.gov.uk/uksci/

US- amerikanischer Bericht zu Bioethik und Menschenwürde: http://www.bioethics.gov/reports/human_dignity/index.html

Protestseite zur europäischen Bioethik-Konvention: http://www.bioethik-konvention.de

Stammzellgesetz: www.bmbf.de/pub/stammzellgesetz.pdf

Berliner Rede von Johannes Rau (2001): http://www.bundespraesident.de/Reden-und-Interviews/Berliner-Reden-,12091/Berliner-Rede-2001.htm

Cherishing Life, Text der englisch/walisischen römisch-katholischen Bischofskonferenz: www.catholic-ew.org.uk/ccb/content/download/956/9550/file/Cherishing_Life_2004.pdf

Katholische Bischofskonferenz von England und Wales: http://www.catholicchurch.org.uk/ccb/catholic_church

US-amerikanisches Center for Bioethics and Human Dignity: http://www.cbhd.org/index.html

Stellungnahmen der Church of Scotland zur Forschung an menschlichen Embryonen: http://www.churchofscotland.org.uk/councils/churchsociety/cssrtp.htm

Seite der Church of England: http://www.cofe.anglican.org

Stellungnahmen der Deutschen Bischofskonferenz zur Stammzelldebatte: http://www.dbk.de/aktuell/meldungen/2920/index.html

Informationsseite der Deutschen Forschungsgemeinschaft zu Stammzellen: http://www.dfg.de/aktuelles_presse/themen_dokumentationen/stammzellen/was_sind_stammzellen.html

EKD-Text „Im Geist der Liebe mit dem Leben umgehen" (2002): http://www.ekd.de/EKD-Texte/30655.html

Stellungnahme des Deutschen Ethikrats zur Stammzellforschung: http://www.ethikrat.org/stellungnahmen/stellungnahmen.html

Bericht der HFEA zur Produktion von Hybriden: http://www.hfea.gov.uk/en/1517.html#report

Protestseite gegen die HFE Bill: http://hfebill.org

Katholisches Linacre Centre for Health Care Ethics (England): www.linacre.org

Britische Gesetze: http://www.opsi.gov.uk/acts.htm

Britisches Parlament: www.parliament.uk

UN-Deklaration zum menschlichen Genom und den Menschenrechten (1997): http://portal.unesco.org/shs/en/ev.php-URL_ID=1881&URL_DO=DO_TOPIC&URL_SECTION=201.html

HFE Bill: http://www.publications.parliament.uk/pa/cm200708/cmbills/120/08120.i-iv.html

Seite der Church of Scotland zu Klonierung und Stammzellforschung: http://www.srtp.org.uk/cloning.shtml

Allgemeine Menschenrechtserklärung der UNO (deutsch): http://www.unhchr.ch/udhr/lang/ger.htm

Dignitas Persona, Veröffentlichung des Vatikan zu bioethischen Fragen (2008): http://www.vatican.va/roman_curia/congregations/cfaith/documents/rc_con_cfaith_doc_20081208_dignitas-personae_ge.html

Evangelium Vitae zu Reproduktionsmedizin: http://www.vatican.va/holy_father/john_paul_ii/encyclicals/documents/hf_jp-ii_enc_25031995_evangelium-vitae_ge.html